THE 200mph STEAMROLLER!

BOOK ONE: RED REIGN

FEBRUARY - MAY 1962

THE 200mph STEAMROLLER!
BOOK ONE: RED REIGN
FEBRUARY - MAY 1962

BY
BS LEVY

THE FIFTH NOVEL IN *THE LAST OPEN ROAD* SERIES

THE FIRST NOVEL IN *THE 200MPH STEAMROLLER!* SERIES

COVER GRAPHICS & ART DIRECTION BY
ART EASTMAN - REBECCA STARR

EDITING, RESEARCH, FACT CHECKING & ASSORTED BS REMOVAL BY
BILL SIEGFRIEDT

MIKE ARGETSINGER, DAVID BOOKER, JOHN GARDNER, BILL GEHRING, DAN GURNEY,

ADAM LEVY, BILL LYMAN, DENISE MCCLUGGAGE, SHARON O'BRIEN & SAM SMITH

MORE THAN YOU'LL EVER KNOW FROM
CAROL LEVY & KAREN MILLER

THINK FAST INK L.L.C.
OAK PARK, ILLINOIS
WWW.LASTOPENROAD.COM
2010

COPYRIGHT 2010 BY BS LEVY

PUBLISHED BY:

THINK FAST INK

1010 LAKE STREET

OAK PARK, ILLINOIS 60301

WRITTEN AND MANUFACTURED IN THE UNITED STATES OF AMERICA

FIRST EDITION

OCTOBER 2010

OTHER TITLES BY BS LEVY

THE LAST OPEN ROAD 1994

MONTEZUMA'S FERRARI 1999

A POTSIDE COMPANION 2001

THE FABULOUS TRASHWAGON 2002

TOLY'S GHOST 2006

LIBRARY OF CONGRESS CATALOGING IN PUBLICATION DATA:

LEVY, BURT S., 1945 -

THE 200MPH STEAMROLLER!

BOOK ONE: RED REIGN

1. AUTOMOBILE RACING   2. THE 1960S

LIBRARY OF CONGRESS CONTROL NUMBER:

2010930698

ISBN: 978-0-9642107-7-6

FOR MY VALUED AND TRUSTED FRIEND, GO-TO GRAPHICS GUY,
OCCASIONAL TRAVELING COMPANION, RESPECTED
COLLEAGUE AND FELLOW SICK PETROLHEAD

ART EASTMAN

THIS IS YOUR GET WELL CARD, BUDDY!

AUTHOR'S NOTE: I'D LIKE TO MAKE IT PARTICULARLY CLEAR THAT THE TOTALLY FICTICIOUS AMERICAN CAR COMPANY IN THIS BOOK IS DEFINITELY NOT A SPECIFIC PARODY OF THE FORD MOTOR COMPANY BUT RATHER (HOPEFULLY) A PARODY ON LARGE, 2ND- AND 3RD- GENERATION FAMILY-CONTROLLED CORPORATIONS IN GENERAL. I SADLY DID NOT KNOW ANY OF THE TALENTED, DRIVEN AND DEDICATED PEOPLE WORKING AT AND WITH FORD AT THE TIME IN QUESTION, AND I WAS ABSOLUTELY THRILLED AND DELIGHTED, LIKE ALL AMERICAN ENTHUSIASTS, WHEN THE FORD MOTOR COMPANY TOOK ON AND BEAT EUROPE'S BEST IN THEIR OWN BACK YARD. I ALSO HAVE PERSONALLY BOUGHT, OWNED, DRIVEN AND ENJOYED MANY FORD PRODUCTS OVER THE YEARS (INCLUDING THE ONE I CURRENTLY USE TO HAUL BOOKS ALL OVER THE COUNTRY) AND I EVEN OWN SOME FORD STOCK THAT I'M HOPEFUL WILL SOMEDAY BE WORTH FAR MORE THAN WHAT I PAID FOR IT.
SO DON'T GO CALLING YOUR EFFING LAWYERS, OK?

Chapter 1: The Finger

I'd never been there before, but finding my way from the Detroit Metro airport to the huge Fairway Motor Company world headquarters, Michigan casting foundry and final assembly line complex on the outskirts of town was no big problem. Getting inside, however, was another matter entirely? It was your typically dreary, gloomy, rainy midwestern Thursday morning in the middle of February—halfway to sleet, actually—but I was snug and toasty warm inside the brand-spanking new, lipstick-red Fairway Flyer "Fiesta Flair Coupé" Special Edition that had been waiting for me, as promised, curbside at the airport. I could tell it was fresh off the assembly line, and its shiny red paint glistened through a layer of raindrop beads as I headed towards it in the rain. A brand-new car was quite an upgrade from the squeaks, rattles, rust, rheumatism and occasional outright refusal to start of the aging Fiat 600 Multipla that was sitting at that very moment on at least one dangerously low tire in the alley behind my crappy little flat above a commercial bakery about 10 miles southwest of central London. I'd bought the Fiat off one of the Scuderia Serenissima race mechanics at Monza because it looked like it'd be cheap to run and easy to maneuver and yet was roomy and clever enough on the inside that I could fold the seats down and sleep in it if I had to. I'd paid less than a hundred dollars American for it, but soon came to suspect I'd been over-charged because its *"just a-rebuilt"* engine used half a quart of oil every other tank of gas and left little bluish-white puff-clouds of smoke in its wake on every upshift. Not that I used it all that much. It generally sat parked and lonely next to the trash cans in the alley behind my apartment because I was usually either out of town or across an ocean covering races for *Car and Track* magazine or driving around in some brilliant new example of British Automotive Artistry that the company PR flacks hoped I'd write nice things about. Although I knew they all worried like hell because of that damn Vauxhall Victor (you remember: GM Great Britain's tinny, cartoonish attempt at a shrunken-down Pontiac Star Chief?) that wound up axle-deep in the shallow end of a pond in Regent's Park late one Saturday night between Christmas and New Years after a typically over-the-top off-season racing awards banquet. It was actually more like Sunday morning, come to think of it, and I can assure you someone else was at the wheel because I was fast asleep in the back seat. You might even say passed out, as it really was a good party. To this day I'm not exactly sure who was driving, but since we were apparently doing handbrake-turn figure-8s on the ice, I've always more-or-less suspected it was Cal Carrington. Although he denies it, of course. In any case, the water was only up to the hubcaps and not much slush got into the interior at all. But even so, I was the one who'd picked up the keys and signed the release paperwork, so the resulting cloud of mistrust and lingering stench of past malfeasance followed me around pretty much forever with the press-fleet managers of most of the popular British and European automakers.

Given the cold, ugly weather, I was genuinely happy to be driving around in a brand-new Fairway Flyer with the expected American-car virtues of a cushy ride, a smooth-shifting automatic transmission, decent windshield wipers and an absolutely phenomenal heating and defrosting system. But the quality was what you'd come to expect from middle-price-and-lower American sedans: the key was a rough, jangly fit in the locks, the door opened with a tight, tinny squeak and the interior reeked of cheap, plasticky New Car Smell—as if the carpets had been drenched in liquefied polymers and Air Wick. It damn near made your eyes water. I found an easy-to-follow direction sheet tucked inside the full-color, *"ALL NEW FOR '62 FAIRWAY FLYER!"* sales brochure that someone had thoughtfully left over the driver's-side sun visor.

Only now that I'd finally arrived at the huge, sprawling and foreboding Fairway Motors plant complex, I couldn't find my way inside! I must've spent the better part of half an hour driving around a seemingly endless perimeter of cinder-block and corrugated metal walls, gates I couldn't enter without the proper vehicle pass and runs of double-row, 12-foot chain-link fencing with coils of razor-edged concertina wire along the top. No question the people in charge were pretty damn serious about separating the Fairway Motor Company's enormous world headquarters, Michigan casting foundry and final assembly line plant from the rest of the civilized world. And right in the middle of all of it stood the unmistakable silhouette of Fairway Tower, sticking up through the earth's crust like a dull black railroad spike driven up into the sky. And that's precisely where I was heading.

If I could just find my fucking way inside, anyway.

It didn't help that I was exhausted from the flights over from Europe and nervous as hell that I'd be late for my meeting. Not that I had the slightest idea what these people wanted from me. But they clearly wanted to see me, and the travel connections Bob Wright's secretary had arranged for me ran dead on schedule and right on time from the moment I left the sad little Maserati press conference in Modena two days before. It was more like a wake or a funeral as a near-broke and on-the-ropes Maserati introduced their ungainly-looking "new" Tipo 64 sports/prototype for the '62 season. In spite of ongoing financial problems and no money available to run a true factory team, Maserati had enjoyed a pretty amazing run of success with their low, lithe and lovely Tipo 60 and 61 "Birdcage" models. They were deliciously attractive and effective little racecars, and earned the nickname "Birdcage" because of the way their frames were welded up in a fiendishly intricate, ingenious and complex structure of little tubular-steel boxes, triangles and pyramids. Literally hundreds of them! And even if Maserati couldn't afford a factory team, privateer Tipo 61s had stood tall and actually won races against the fearsome might of Scuderia Ferrari. Particularly the ones fielded by fast-talking American hustler Lucky Casner's **CAMORADI USA** team. **CAMORADI,** by the way, stood for CAsner MOtor RAcing Division (although it was never entirely clear what sort of larger enterprise CAMORADI USA might have been a division of) but Lucky was an absolute genius when it came to painting rosy pictures, making deals and raising sponsorship money. A CAMORADI Birdcage led the 1960 12 Hours of Sebring by miles until the rear end broke. But of course Lucky had money then (although not his own, of course) and had signed on the consensus two best road racers on the planet to drive for him in Stirling Moss and Dan Gurney. Those two ultimately delivered a breakthrough, outright win for the team—and for Maserati's Birdcage—later in the season at the damp and foggy 1000 Kilometers of the Nurburgring. That was a hell of an accomplishment for a dark-horse car fielded by a fly-by-night American privateer. A CAMORADI Birdcage led Sebring again in 1961—this time with Masten Gregory sharing the car with Moss after Dan Gurney moved on to a full-time deal with Porsche—but the engine went sour. Somewhat surprisingly, Gregory and bossman Casner himself teamed up to take a lucky but still damn worthy second straight CAMORADI victory at the Nurburgring later in the season.

Impressive stuff, no doubt about it.

Sadly, both the hot air and the sponsorship money were starting to leak out of Casner's team by then. But it was frankly amazing that they'd gotten as far and accomplished as much as they did with nothing but ambition, determination and a truly amazing line of bullshit for resources. And a lot of American race fans—me included—figured we owed Lucky one hell of a debt of gratitude along with the knowing nods, winks and snickers that followed in the team's wake.

In any case, the move to rear engines had caught Maserati pretty much flatfooted, and they responded by hastily rushing a new, mid-engined version of their Birdcage design into production to keep up with the upstart English *"garagistes"* and the omnipresent threat and usual domination of cross-town nemesis Ferrari. Old Enzo had taken a good, long look at the new, mid-engined "Monaco" and "Monte Carlo" sports/racers from Cooper and Lotus and then had his own engineers whip up a terrifically quick and moreover rock-solid little mid-engined sports/racer of their own, the Dino 246SP. Maserati's hastily-contrived response was dubbed the Tipo 63, and although it looked promising on paper, it appeared awkward and uncoordinated in the actual steel and alloy. And it ran about the same. Oh, it was plenty fast, but drivers didn't much like the handling. Or the iffy high-speed aerodynamics. And it was sheer hell to work on. Briggs Cunningham bought a couple of them, and his drivers Augie Pabst and Dr. Dick Thompson might well have won The 24 Hours of Le Mans in 1961 if it hadn't taken Alf Momo's mechanics damn near 20 minutes to change the fucking spark plugs. But you flat couldn't get at them. The Tipo 63's engine was a massive, gnarly monster of a 3-liter V12, and you had to snake your fingers and ratchet extensions in between all these spider-webbed frame tubes and oil lines and plumbing hoses and wiring looms and scalding-hot exhaust headers to get at them. And Momo's guys had to do it three different times! "We'd change 'em and the thing would run like an absolute bear for awhile," Augie told me after the race, "but then it'd start spitting and missing and losing power and we'd have to come in and change the plugs again. And it had dual ignition, so there were 24 of them to change each time...."

They wound up 4th overall at the checker, which was still pretty good, but you'd have to say it was also awfully damn disappointing.

Maserati of course decided that they had to re-engineer the car for the '62 season—paying particular attention to the spooky high-speed aerodynamics, compromised service access and wonky rear suspension—and unveiled their "new and improved" Tipo 64 at their annual race-shop model introduction in Modena. But the car still didn't look right to me. It reminded me of some strange, prehistoric crustacean with four odd, blunt fart megaphones sticking out the back end. Everybody knew Maserati was desperate to sell a few copies in order to keep their race shop afloat and their people employed. Which made things a little uncomfortable when the factory press relations guy—whom I liked very much—put on a big, confident smile and talked the Tipo 64 up like it was the grandest Maserati racing car ever. Which anyone with eyes could see it clearly wasn't. He also took pains to whisper privately to each and every motoring scribe on hand—in strictest confidence and completely on the hush-hush, of course—that Maserati had something really special in the pipeline for Le Mans. *"Tipo Wunna-Fifty-Wun"* he whispered behind his hand while his eyes darted around the room like someone from arch-rival Ferrari might be listening. And then he'd shoot his hand off in the general direction of Maranello to illustrate how incredibly fast this new *"Tipo Wunna-Fifty-Wun"* was going to be. But of course it wasn't done yet, so all he had to show the press was his "brilliantly new and improved" Tipo 64. Which looked like kind of a pig to me, if you want the truth of it. And an ugly pig, at that. And that of course reminded me of what my old ace race-mechanic pal Buddy Palumbo used to say: "If a racecar *looks* right, it may actually *be* right. But if it looks wrong...well, it probably is."

And now here I was, 4,325 air miles and just shy of two essentially sleepless days later, lost in a gloomy, icy drizzle as I circled my now mud- and slush-splattered Fairway Flyer Fiesta Flair Coupé around the endless, seemingly impenetrable outer perimeter of the Fairway Motor Company's massive Detroit complex. I was worried I'd be late for my meeting (even if I had no idea what it might be about) and also wondering just how the hell I was going to get some sleep, get properly cleaned up and make the connections I needed to make in order to get down to Jacksonville in time to catch that free luxury yacht cruise down the Florida coastline on the polished ebony decks of Count Giovanni Volpi's magnificent new 164-foot Benetti. And then it would be back to Italy again for Ferrari's famous annual motorsports press conference on February 24th. If you were lucky enough to get an invite, you didn't even think about not attending. After that I'd be heading back to London for a quick visit to my crappy little flat over a commercial bakery in a singularly dreary and uninspiring industrial section of town. But only just long enough to leave my bulging laundry bag for the flinty-but-kindly old Irish woman who looked after the place for me and grab a fresh supply of socks, shirts and underwear to take back to Florida for the 12 Hours of Sebring....

But all of that seemed worlds away as I drove through the rain puddles looking for an opening in the dark, gloomy outer walls of the Fairway plant complex and listening involuntarily to the impatient, incessant *whap-whap-whap-whap-whap* of the Fairway Flyer Fiesta Flair's windshield wipers. Now you should probably know that the Fiesta Flair Coupé paint-and-trim package was an attempt to add a little sizzle to the earnest but somewhat drab and uninspired Fairway Flyer "economy compact" that Fairway Motors introduced in 1960 "to take on the imports!" And, more importantly, all the other new "import-fighting compacts" from cross-town rivals Chrysler and GM. So they'd dressed the standard Flyer up with flashy "sport-spinner wheel covers," an extra splash of "stylish chrome sports trim" and a pair of glistening, "leather look, electronically pleated Vinylite sport bucket seats" that smelled a little like model airplane glue. Sitting between those "sport bucket seats" was the waffle-weave, cast aluminum-look plastic lid of the "security lockable center convenience console" (or at least that's how the ad copy in the sales brochure described it, anyway) which seemed to be a nice, practical touch. Even if the damn thing rattled like crazy and sat a good four inches too low to serve as a useful arm rest when you were actually driving.

As I said, this particular Fairway Flyer was a corporate courtesy car with less than 100 miles on the odometer—fresh off the assembly line!—and painted in a not very deep but terrifically shiny topcoat of "Matador Red" with a "Polar White" hardtop and matching "Polar White with Matador Red trim accents" Vinylite bucket seats. It fired up with a faint, metallic scraping noise from the ring gear followed by a fuzzy, 6-cylinder wheeze out the "dual chrome sports tip" exhausts, and I was frankly amazed by the noise the wipers made when I switched them on. Like two arthritic dwarfs were screwing somewhere behind the dashboard, their rickety little metal-framed bed repeatedly *whap-whap-whap-whapping* against the firewall. Then again, it was part of automobile manufacturing protocol everywhere—not just in Detroit—that you had to make cheap cars feel cheap if you wanted expensive cars to feel expensive by comparison. And there was a certain grand, elliptical logic to that. Even so, I had a hard time getting comfortable in those "leather look, electronically pleated Vinylite sport bucket seats" because they were cold and slippery under my butt and the padding in the center somehow seemed higher than the bolsters on either side... in direct opposition to the contours of your average human backside. Worse yet, in an effort to make the Fairway Flyer feel stable on the Interstate, comfortable around town and moreover familiar to would-be buyers used to big, soft American sedans like Fairway Motors' own, second-best-selling-automobile-on-the-face-of-the-earth Fairway Freeway, the engineers had made the power steering fingertip light but totally devoid of feel. I figured it at about six or seven turns lock to lock with two full inches of limp, queasy free play right in the middle. And the suspension bushings, shocks and springs were so soggy that my Fiesta Flair Flyer wallowed its way around corners like a baby hippopotamus attempting to heave itself out of a mud hole. But the heater and defroster were absolutely first-rate, and I suspected the air conditioning probably was, too. That's one thing you couldn't beat about American cars: the heating and air conditioning systems. And the automatic transmissions. And the power windows. When it came to those things, American car companies made the best in the whole fucking world. Hands down.

Like everyone else on the *Car and Track* staff, I was glad to see Detroit finally starting to build smaller, lighter, handier and more sensible cars (and, to be fair, they weren't any worse than a lot of the go-to-market crapwagons being built overseas) but it was hard to believe that the designers and engineers who worked on cars like my Fiesta Flair Flyer actually spent much time behind the wheel. Most of my colleagues in the sporty-car press sneered down their noses at the big American car companies. Said their top brass didn't really *like* cars. Or didn't enjoy driving them, anyway. And it was a hard point to argue when you found yourself behind the wheel of something like my Fairway Flyer Fiesta Flair Coupé.

When I finally located the proper entrance for the Fairway Tower executive building, the square-jawed guard at the security gate made it clear he was in no particular hurry to let me in. He stood a blunt-and-brooding six-and-a-half feet tall and a yard wide at the shoulders, and cold rain dripped off the brim of his cap and onto my sleeve as he stared at the few short, direct lines of type on the sheet of Fairway Motors' letterhead I'd handed him through the window.

"You Henry M. Lyons?" he growled without looking up from the sheet of paper in his hand.

I told him I was.

"What's the 'M' stand for?"

I wanted to ask him what the hell difference it made? Or maybe tell him it stood for "Merlin," "Macbeth," "Mencken," "Machiavelli," "Mussolini," "Marlowe," "Thomas Mann," "Marcus Aurelius" or "Mephistopheles," just to see if he got the reference. But I thought better of it. If you've lived long enough to understand the rent-a-cop mentality, you know that the easy way is inevitably the straight, respectful, deferential way. So you bite your tongue. "Michael," I told him.

"You got any identification?"

I showed him my California driver's license.

He looked at it and scowled. "This here license has expired."

So I showed him the British tourist license I used when I worked in Europe. Which was really most of the time by then, except for occasional trips back to the states to cover races like Sebring, the Daytona Continental and the U.S. Grand Prix at Watkins Glen. He stared at the British tourist license like it had to be a fake. "This isn't from America, is it?" he observed.

"No, it isn't. It's English."

He gave me the stink eye. "This thing for real?"

I assured him it was. And then he locked eyeballs with me for what seemed like ten or fifteen seconds. Like he didn't really believe me, you know, but couldn't decide exactly what to do about it. Run me in, maybe, for impersonating an Englishman. Then again, I probably looked a little rough around the edges to be calling on the world-wide executive headquarters of Fairway Motors. After all, I'd come straight from the airport (and that after a long, generally sleepless set of flights in from Milan by way of Paris and New York), I surely needed a shave and I wasn't dressed like the sort of smart-looking, suit-and-tie gent you might expect to find seeking entrance to Fairway Tower. My shirt was rumpled, my corduroy jacket was frayed at the cuffs and my only silk tie was loose around my neck and showed a big coffee stain off to one side and an older, somewhat less conspicuous wine stain a little lower and to the left. But it was a maroon tie and I'd been drinking Lambrusco at the time, so you could hardly see it. And meanwhile the rain was dripping off the brim of his cap and causing the deep blue fountain-pen ink of Fairway Motors' President/Chief Executive Officer Robert "Bob" Wright's signature to start drooling its way down the page.

"Look," I finally told him, "if you want to call Bob Wright's office..." Mind you, I'd never actually met Bob Wright at that point—not even once—and I had no idea if he'd appreciate me calling him by his first name. But it sure seemed to work. The guard gave me a disgusted snort, glared at me a little more, handed back my sheet of letterhead, made a face like he'd eaten something that didn't agree with him, opened the gate with a dismissive grunt and waved me on through.

The Fairway Motors world headquarters, Michigan casting foundry and final assembly plant complex was a cacophonous, confusing, intimidating and bewildering place to an outsider. Dark, narrow, concrete alleyways spider-webbed between huge, windowless factory buildings surrounded by fenced lots, equipment garages, small, mysterious metal sheds, vast parts-storage warehouses and all sorts of assorted outbuildings with not much at all in the way of signs or directions to help the uninitiated find their way around. Then again, the people who worked there and belonged there seemed to know where the hell they were going, and if you didn't work there or belong there, then what the hell were you doing there in the first place?

Now everybody and his brother knows that Fairway Motors is a genuine colossus in the automotive world—or any other sort of world you'd care to mention—and their huge, city-unto-itself Detroit plant was merely one of over a hundred-and-fifty-five various and sundry manufacturing facilities, sub-assembly plants, foundries, forges, textile mills, transport depots, warehouses, logistics centers, procurement offices, import/export offices, legal and financial divisions, branch outposts, dealer liaison networks and associated subsidiaries that Fairway Motors owned and operated all over the world. Or all over what the *Detroit Free Press, Chicago Tribune, Wall Street Journal* and *New York Times* somewhat euphemistically referred to as "the free world," even if that description could get a little sketchy in certain areas of Central America, South America, Africa, Asia, the Middle East, the Far East and random tropical islands where Fairway Motors did business. It made your head spin just thinking about the stupefying overall scope and crushing, maddening tiny details that went into it.

All I could do was keep blundering my way along through the teeming, noisy, soot-blackened maze of cinder-block and correguated-metal walls, yawning overhead doorways and scurrying fork lift trucks that seemed in a terrible hurry and left oily tracks through the frost-edged rain puddles. Everything on all sides had been slathered in thick, drooling coats of the same identical dove gray with navy blue trim that looked so clean and smart on the company letterhead and at the bottom of their Sunday-supplement newspaper advertising. But of course you couldn't keep anything looking clean and fresh for long in an industrial environment. The soot, smoke, dust, grease and chemical fumes saw to that....

I was trying to find my way to the Fairway Tower executive building, of course, but I wasn't having much luck. Hell, I'd been able to see from the damn exit ramp at the airport. But now, inside the rat's maze of high, dark walls and rain-slicked alleyways, I couldn't seem to find my way to it. I was sure I'd gotten off course somehow when I passed by the drop-forge building for the second or third time. It was a huge, barn-like thing—big as a downtown sports arena!—with the roof opened up like a tackle box on top to let the heat, fumes and smoke out. I could hear and even feel the clanging, banging and pounding of the massive 50,000- and 100,000-pound steam hammers inside. Sizzling-hot gurgling-and-hissing noises came from the next big building along with the smell of molten-hot metal pouring cherry-red into the casting molds. Two buildings further down it was the dull, plaintive bleat of sheet steel being forced, yanked, punched, drawn and bent into the shape of roofs, hoods, doors, trunk lids and fender panels in the stamping presses. And the entire facility smelled something awful. Steam reeking with sulfur fumes billowed up from the forge and foundry buildings. Thick, powder-black smoke belched from at least a dozen smokestacks. And all of it mingled together in the huge, dirty gray cloud that hung over the entire plant—except for occasional Sundays and legal holidays—before settling back down to earth like a carpet of powdery ash. And then you had the additional, ground-level stink from the acid dip baths and chemical solvents in the paint shops and the smell of shaved metal and hot cutting oil from the machine shops. And right in the middle of it all you had the relentless, 24-hours-a-day/7-days-a-week (at least when business was good) grind, chatter, clatter, hum, clank, bump, bang, crunch and relentless air-ratchet sputter from the four-block long, eight-lane wide Final Assembly Line, where the company's bread-and-butter Fairway Freeway and upscale Fairway Freeway Frigate models came together from literally thousands upon thousands of individual parts and sub-assemblies.

Now and then I'd pass small, meandering squadrons of union workers—most of them in standard-issue yellow rain slickers and rubberized boots—who all seemed to know where they were going but appeared in no particular hurry to get there. I pressed the button that made the window suck down into the driver's door. "Excuse me," I asked as the rain pelted in at me, "I'm trying to get to Fairway Tower."

A grease-stained face that looked like it'd been through the landing at Normandy stared back at me suspiciously, then nodded back in the direction I'd come from. "Y'need t'turn aroun' an' take the next two lefs, then a right," he said like it made perfect sense. But of course the alleyway was far too narrow to turn around in, so I had to either try backing up or head on to the next alley where I could turn. I thought I saw the guy snickering to one of his union buddies as they disappeared around a corner.

But he'd given me the right directions, and a few moments later I came around the far side of the massive Final Assembly Line building and found myself in the towering shadow of the Fairway Finger. Or at least that's what everybody in Detroit called it, anyway. Particularly the rank-and-file union types in steel-toed boots, coveralls and plaid lumberjack shirts who streamed in from the far parking lots like a tide of lunch pail-carrying lemmings three times a day. Famous American industrial icon Harold Richard Fairway himself had made the decision to put his corporate headquarters right smack-dab in the middle of his fast-growing Detroit manufacturing facility. He made that decision back in the early twenties when the American stock market was booming, cars were selling like hotcakes and business was better than good. Oh, he could have easily put his corporate nerve center in a ritzy downtown office building like General Motors or out in the far more serene and agreeable farmland meadows of the outlying suburbs. His executive staff would have loved that. And the local politicians and chamber-of-commerce types would have surely cut him one hell of a deal on the real estate and kicked him back plenty on tax breaks, zoning, benefits and extras.

But Harold Richard Fairway liked to keep an eye on things....

Fairway Motors could sell everything it could build back then, and old Harold Richard or "H.R." as he was respectfully called to his face and within earshot behind his back made it his personal mission to build as many damn cars as he could and make money on every single one. *"The fat part of the market,"* he famously remarked, *"is right in the middle of the bell-shaped curve."* And he repeated that line often to his ne'er-do-well son, Harold Richard Fairway Junior, as the young man was growing up and attempting to learn the family business. The accuracy of H.R. Senior's assessment was borne out by the company's success and the way its Detroit manufacturing plant kept expanding across the surrounding Michigan farmland like the fuzzy, greenish-brown mold in the star Petri dish of some high school sophomore's B-minus science project.

Old H.R. Senior had decided that he needed someplace way up high, above all the stench and bustle and clamor, where he could marshal his subordinates, have closed-door meetings with his department heads, plan his moves, consider his options and strategies, keep private counsel with his team of lawyers and financial bean-counters and entertain selected government officials and occasional union stoolies. Yet he always wanted to keep an eye on in his massive manufacturing and assembly plant below. The end result was The Finger. But of course that wasn't the tower's official name. The lettering carved into the veined marble mantle between the more-or-less Corinthian columns of the grand entranceway read "Fairway Tower." But even the architects and construction crews had begun calling it "The Finger" before it grew more than a story or two out of its deep-rooted concrete foundations. Harold Richard Fairway Senior seemed to get a perverse kick out of that nickname, even though he'd snort and glare at anyone he overheard using it in his presence. But it kind of fit, since H.R. Senior was famous for the way he used his long and gnarly but amazingly articulated index finger to point out the errors in other people's ways, shake under the noses of underlings during snarling fits of rage, poke hard into his managers' chests when he was trying to make a point, prod ample young secretaries from the typing pool in their fleshy bosoms and backsides and, in moments of solitude behind the polished mahogany doors of his private executive office, pick at the hairs in his nose and ears. At least when he wasn't working bits of tender veal, prime tenderloin or chicken cordon bleu from between his teeth with the engraved, silver-inlaid ivory toothpick that he carried in a little cylindrical silver case at the end of his watch chain. "Dat looks like a leetle mezuzah," a grey-bearded, thickly accented upholstery-and-trim supplier from Brooklyn once joked mere moments before losing the Fairway account.

Fairway Tower was clad in somber black stone and stood a full thirteen stories high, and the top floor was all double thickness, amber-tinted plate glass from floor to ceiling. The east and west walls were angled in towards the top like the business end of a blacksmith's chisel, and Fairway Tower was justly famous for the way its top floor caught the early morning and late evening sunlight or the cold, icy-blue glow of a full moon. You'd see it in all its light-reflecting glory on heavily retouched postcards offered for sale on all the newsstand kiosks at the Detroit airport, its long, dark shaft and glinting, golden tip usually superimposed over a stunning, most un-Detroitlike yellow-to-orange-to-rose-to-mauve-to-violet-to-purple sunset that was probably lifted from a Caribbean travel brochure. And just about everyone in Detroit (along with virtually all the working scribes from the motoring press) knew the story of how, after perhaps a few too many celebratory glasses of champagne at Fairway Tower's formal dedication in June of 1923, old **H.R.** Senior himself famously intoned: "Ladies and gentlemen, it is with great pride and a grand sense of occasion that I give you...*The Finger."*

Even though he'd long since passed on to his eternal reward, the presence, will, can-do spirit and plain old flinty cussedness of **H.R.** Senior still pervaded and energized the hallways, offices and meeting rooms of Fairway Tower. Right down to the tiniest nook and cranny. And it hit you right between the eyes the moment you walked up those marble steps, passed between those stately, near-Corinthian columns and entered the lobby. Because there he was, old **H.R.** Senior himself, staring down balefully from an eight-foot-high, six-foot-wide bas-relief bronze wall plaque directly across from the main entrance. Even immortalized in bronze, old Harold Richard Senior had darty little weasel eyes and the suspicious, up-from-under-his-eyelids glare of Lionel Barrymore as mean old skinflint Mr. Potter in *It's a Wonderful Life.* Below his jutting lower jaw and heavily starched collar were several etched-in-bronze paragraphs explaining the many impressive innovations, honors and accomplishments Harold Richard Fairway Senior had amassed during his 86 years on this planet. Although anybody who read the funny papers knew the part about "loving husband, father and family man" was a bit of a stretch.

Fellow motoring scribes had warned me that the buttons in the main bank of elevators only went up to the 12th floor, and sure enough it was true. There was no number or even button for the thirteenth and uppermost floor. It turned out there was another, rather special elevator leading up to the executive level. One with polished brass-and-nickel, art-deco doors and a permanent, uniformed security guard standing in front of it connecting the 12th and 13th floors. Only those who belonged or were summoned ever made it to the uppermost floor of Fairway Tower.

And that's precisely where I was heading.

It wasn't the sort of thing I could easily wrap my brain around.

But the security guard didn't even bat an eye. He just looked at my pass and nodded me on through. Like I was expected, you know? A moment later, those gleaming, polished brass-and-nickel doors slid silently open and I stepped gingerly inside. As they closed behind me, I couldn't help remembering that other elevator story that orbited around old **H.R.** Senior. The one that dated back to the dark, uncertain days of the Great Depression, when sales were down, factories had to be closed and shuttered, employees were laid off and weary, threadbare men with sad, lost eyes and rough, calloused hands formed long lines in front of charity soup kitchens. It was also the time when shaggy, bearded Bolsheviks with urgent voices and mad-bomber eyes preached openly in the streets about the rights of ordinary workers and against the righteousness of capitalism and the ordained divinity of inherited wealth. Those were deeply troubled times. Or at least they were until the war came along, enlistment and the draft skimmed off the over-supply of available workers and the factories started humming like crazy again—24 hours a day, 6 and even 7 days a week!—making all the tanks, guns, ammunition, knapsacks, boots, convoy trucks, dive bombers, stew pots, gauze bandages, P.T. boats and hospital beds it took to fight and win a world war.

It was magnificent.

But before that there was much worry and uncertainty. And that's when old H.R. Senior allegedly built himself a small, secret elevator hidden away behind a false wall in a bathroom service closet on the 13th floor. An elevator that only responded to a tiny brass key that forever dangled at the end of old Harold Richard Fairway Senior's personal watch chain, right next to his silver-inlaid ivory toothpick in its mezuzah-like little silver case. The story went that a sworn-to-secrecy electrician from Eugene, Oregon—who'd been smuggled in secretly at night to work on the project—spilled the beans to a scandal-hungry tabloid reporter many years later in exchange for forty dollars in cash and some un-retouched cheesecake photographs of Veronica Lake. According to him (if he ever really existed) that hidden elevator sat parked and waiting at the top of its shaft at all hours of the day and night, ready to whoosh its occupant(s) directly from the 13th and uppermost floor of Fairway Tower to a secret, subterranean tunnel deep beneath the basement floor. There, a small, motorized handcar sat on a set of electrified railway tracks (although there was a backup battery in case of a power outage), ready to whisk whomever might know of it and need it to an equally secret, Pinkerton-guarded landing dock on the Detroit River where a custom-built Hacker-Craft dual-cockpit speedboat with a 2540 cubic-inch Packard V12 aero engine nestled inside its long, daggerlike hull sat idling at dockside with a full tank of avgas, bulletproof windscreens, a tommy gun, sawed-off 12-gauge and two .38 caliber police pistols clipped under the seats, a steamer trunk full of clothes, wigs, false mustaches, fake identification and assorted disguises packed below decks and some three million dollars in unmarked cash, precious gems and antique gold coins stuffed inside the life preservers.

Just in case, you know?

After all, labor negotiations could get a little sticky now and then. Especially during the Great Depression. And you always had to worry about the leftist egghead agitators (mostly Jews, of course!), street-preaching Bolsheviks, fellow-traveler academics, do-gooder priests and the spawn-of-hell, share-the-wealth communists who were running the damn labor unions....

The elevator came to a soft, cushioned stop, the doors slid silently open, and I could instantly appreciate why old Harold Richard Fairway Senior loved the all-glass top floor of his tower so much. The elevator landing faced east, overlooking a few low parts warehouse and supply buildings surrounded by a huge expanse of employee parking lots and storage yards full-to-the-fences with newly-minted Fairway Freeways and Fairway Freeway Frigates awaiting shipment to dealerships all across America. But from the opposite side, where H.R. Senior's office filled the entire northwest corner of the executive corridor, the floor-to-ceiling, amber-tinted glass offered a commanding view of almost the entire working facility. It allowed H.R. Senior to keep a keen eye on everything even well on into his later years thanks to the pair of crinkle-finish, Luftwaffe-issue Zeiss binoculars he kept locked away in a felt-lined, stainless steel box in the credenza behind his desk. Rumor had it that they'd once belonged to Hermann Goering. Even though he'd made much of his fortune building arms and military vehicles to defeat the Germans—it saved his company, when you got right down to it!—old H.R. Senior had a bit of a soft spot for the Nazis. They knew how to organize things, understood the importance of discipline and quality workmanship, demanded and expected excellence in all things and had come up with, at least in H.R. Senior's opinion, by far the most practical approach for dealing with Jews, gypsies, communists, anarchists and homosexuals. They also produced some really well-engineered and beautifully manufactured mechanical things. Like his crinkle-finished, Luftwaffe-issue Zeiss binoculars, for example. He spent hour after satisfying hour with them, looking out his floor-to-ceiling, amber plate-glass windows while spying on his workers below. And he was always quick to invite his honored Fairway Tower guests to do the same. Only not through his beloved Zeiss binoculars, of course. He made a point of never, ever passing them around.

For everyone else, H.R. Senior had put up a row of permanently mounted, coin-operated swivel binoculars on evenly spaced nickel-steel posts the kind you might see along the Scenic Vista railings at major tourist attractions like Niagara Falls, Mount Rushmore and the Grand Canyon. He got a heck of a deal on them after purchasing a small and apparently worthless little strip of real estate directly across the highway from a quaint little mom-and-pop tourist stop/burger stand/gift shop overlooking Badwater Basin in Death Valley. Now Badwater Basin was an altogether unattractive and inhospitable scrap of land, but it was nonetheless—at 282 feet below sea level—the lowest point in the continental United States and something of a tourist attraction. So the little mom-and-pop tourist stop did a nice little business eight or nine months out of the year. Or at least they did until old H.R. Senior erected a Fairway Motors billboard and completely blocked the view of Badwater Basin from the little mom-and-pop tourist stop. The coin-operated swivel binoculars became available shortly thereafter at a very attractive price. Along with the little mom-and-pop tourist stop/burger stand/gift shop, although he didn't bother to buy that. Who wanted to see a Godforsaken place like Badwater Basin anyway?

Rumor also had it that H.R. Senior kept a small canvas bag full of pinball-game slugs in the top drawer of his desk to hand out to favored guests. Everybody else had to use their own damn nickels. Especially union representatives, tax people, government people and vendors or suppliers who'd somehow managed to weasel their way up to the 13th floor of Fairway Tower.

To tell the truth, old H.R. Senior had a bit of a reputation as a skinflint. A lot of people said he actually prided himself on it. But he never seemed to mind spending money on his tower. Or at least not on the top floor, anyway. It was air conditioned back when *nobody* had air conditioning, and he had the architects and "interior desecrators" (as he inevitably referred to interior decorators with a deprecating cackle) tilt the floor ever-so-slightly so as to put his desk on a mild, barely percep-tible uphill slant. He likewise made sure that the legs on his chair were precisely three-quarters of an inch taller than the legs on the ostensibly identical chairs across from him. H.R. Senior was sure it gave him both a psychological and physiological edge in negotiations.

And no doubt it did.

Besides, he liked looking down on people.

H.R. Senior bragged loudly and often about how he'd had the entire tower sound-proofed for the comfort of his staff. But he made certain that the engineers and con-struction crews didn't do too elaborate a job of it on the lower floors where all the clerks and middle-management types worked. After all (as he often said), your staff had to keep their collective ear to the ground (as well as their collective eye on the ball and collective nose to the grindstone) in order to stay one jump ahead of the competition. And the damn government. And the damn unions. Besides, he'd always believed that the muffled clanging, banging, grinding, chattering and clattering of cars being built helped keep his lower-level executive staff on edge. H.R. Senior main-tained it was vital to keep his non-union, white-collar, managerial, clerical, financial, legal and logistical employees on edge. *"A nervous worker is a busy worker,"* old Harold Richard Senior used to say, *"and busy workers get things done!"*

If not, they were fired.

You could do that with non-union workers.

Just like that.

Any time you pleased.

It was wonderful....

But of course old Harold Richard Fairway Senior was long gone by the time I arrived on the top floor of Fairway Tower on a rainy Thursday morning in February of 1962. He'd fallen victim to death's inevitable scythe almost a decade before, at the tender age of 86, mostly thanks to the rigors, trials and challenges of his incredibly industrious lifestyle. And maybe a bad piece of fish. But even on his deathbed, he whispered hoarsely that he was damn *proud* of the way he'd worked every single day of his life Sundays and holidays included and he clearly muttered out loud, even as his final moments on this earth approached and with his family gathered close around him, asking the Lord on High why the hell couldn't he get the same kind of service and dedication out of his fucking employees.

Harold Richard Fairway Senior left behind an iconic cultural and industrial legacy along with what was, by any measure you'd care to employ, the biggest and most powerful family-controlled (even if ostensibly publicly held) business empire on the face of God's green earth. Left it to a family that didn't have the slightest idea what to do with it and a less-than-beloved only son, Harold Richard Fairway Junior who, at least according to the general consensus of my friends in the Detroit-area automotive press, had cat food between his ears and not one single clue as to how to run the fucking thing.

Even so, it was pretty damn exciting—not to mention intimidating—to find myself walking through those polished brass-and-nickel doors onto the gleaming, ivory-colored marble flooring of the 13th floor of Fairway Tower. There I was, at the very heart, soul and nerve center of the famous and far-flung Fairway Motors empire! I felt my knees go all weak and queasy under me as I looked out through those amber-tinted, floor-to-ceiling windows at all the grit, bustle, stench, hustle, muffled noise and staggering expanse of Fairway Motors' first-ever and still biggest production facility. To tell the truth, I kind of wondered just what the hell I was doing there. Why, I was just a scruffy, underpaid, 29-year-old European-scene motorsports correspondent for *Car and Track* magazine who rarely had twenty bucks cash in his pocket, drove a clapped-out Fiat and lived over a damn commercial bakery 10 miles southwest of central London.

What the hell could they possibly want with me?

Chapter 2: A Traveling Companion

The whole thing really started for me down in Florida, barely two weeks before. I always made the trip over from my cold, crappy apartment on the southwestern edge of London to cover the big 12-Hour race at Sebring for the magazine, and it was always nice to get a little dose of Florida sunshine around that time of year. Not that there was any real question who would win it in March of 1962. It was going to be Ferrari, and the only thing to be settled was which one. Only this time I found myself on my way to Florida over a month early to take in the first-ever "Daytona Continental" sports car race at Big Bill France's impressive new Daytona International Speedway. And then I had to hightail it right back to Europe to cover the Maserati press introduction in Modena early the next week. Although a few days in Italy is hardly ever a bad thing. Even if you're doing it on the cheap. But with almost six weeks in hand between the Daytona and Sebring dates and nothing much going on back in England except cold, gloomy weather, between-season down time and new car press introductions from the British *"garagiste"* constructors and moreover plenty of sun, surf and skimpy bathing suits on offer down in Florida, I figured it wouldn't be such a bad idea to head back across the Atlantic to sit on a beach, soak up a little beer and sunshine and maybe do a little key-beating on the forever unfinished racing novel I kept promising myself to actually finish one day. There was even the possibility of cadging a free place to stay if I could find some sponsor, dilettante driver or rich team owner with a spare room available between races. That actually happened from time to time if you wrote nice things about people. Hell, I could write the stuff on the Lotus, BRM and Cooper press launches from the dark side of the moon if I had to. I knew a lot of the mechanics and where they hung out after work, so I already had the inside dope on most of the technical tidbits (although I generally got the scoop on the new stuff at Lotus from the BRM and Cooper guys and the new BRM stuff from the Lotus and Cooper guys and so forth), so all I really needed was the final word on the driver lineups and a picture or two to go along with it. And I could easily get those from fellow motoring scribes like my friend Bob Storck or that prince of jerks Eric Gibbon (although Eric would surely make me buy him drinks or writhe on my belly like a reptile in order to get what I needed).

I even entertained daydreams about doing a little free-form traveling between races. There were always a lot of private planes around any race weekend, and I might be able to hitch a ride back home to Southern California to drop in on my mom and the jerk she'd married after she blew off my dad and the two jerks who came after him. I could also stop by to see Warren and Isabelle Bertrand at the *Car and Track* offices in Orange County. I hadn't seen either one of them for more than a year. Sure, I wrote for them in every issue, but I was stationed in Europe and they were in California and so most of our contact was by phone or through the mail or by occasional and hideously expensive emergency telegram. That's just the way things are when you're an overseas correspondent for a stateside magazine.

Or maybe I could catch a New York connection and visit my old ace race-me-chanic pal Buddy Palumbo and his family up in New Jersey. I hadn't seen Buddy in years, and I really, truly missed him. Even if his wife Julie didn't have much use for me. She always looked at me like I might try to swipe the silverware or some-thing when her back was turned. But Buddy and I had shared a lot of grand ad-ventures together—racing and otherwise—and he was the guy I always thought about calling whenever I had some new, hush-hush, top-secret, don't-tell-anybody racing gossip that was just screaming to be repeated. I could trust him with stuff like that. He was also the guy I felt like calling when anything was eating at me. Even personal stuff. Oh, he wasn't much of a talker—never was—but it was nice just knowing there was someone who understood and commiserated at the other end of the line.

I rarely got to see him, though, since I was over covering the motorsports scene in Europe (and Florida every March, and sometimes even in South America, Mex-ico, South Africa, Australia and New Zealand) and Buddy was pretty much nailed to the floor with his family and his race shop/car restoration business in New Jersey. He and Julie had four kids by then and a really nice house with a big back yard up near Englewood Cliffs, and he'd even mentioned in one of his short, crappy letters that he'd been thinking about packing up everything—shop, family, the whole works—and moving it all up to Connecticut. That should give you some idea how well he was doing. But of course he'd really made out when he and Big Ed Baum-stein sold their VW dealership lock, stock and barrel to that Harry Metropolis character of the shimmering silk shirts, shifty eyes and white leather shoes. Buddy never told me what he'd made on that deal and I never asked him, but you can bet it was one *very* considerable pile of currency. But Buddy was never the type to do anything big or flashy with money, not even now that he had it. He was a quiet, earnest, hard-working, nose-to-the-grindstone blue-collar type through and through, and he figured you had to keep working—even after you'd made yourself a nice chunk of change—because that's what human beings were put on this earth to do. I think he caught that particular character flaw from old Butch Bohunk back in the Finzio's Sinclair days, and he never got shrewd, spoiled, lazy, sneaky or jaded enough to shake it.

Good for him.

Anyhow, it was nice to know that things were going well for him. According to the grapevine, he had more work than he could handle, and even more lined up trying to get in. That's what generally happens when a shop gets a reputation for knowing what to do, doing good work, being honest and reliable, getting things done (if not always on time), telling people the truth in all except the most extreme circumstances and not screwing people over. Or at least not on purpose, anyway....

Every now and then I'd write Buddy these long, involved letters about what was going on with his driver friends Cal Carrington and Tommy Edwards, and after every fourth or fifth one, he'd send me an awkward, hand-scrawled note on two or three sheets of loose-leaf notebook paper that looked like some struggling fifth grader's book report. To tell the truth, Buddy wasn't much of a writer. Why, he couldn't write a simple, declarative sentence to save his life. All he ever knew how to do was digress. And then he'd digress from his digressions. Which made his letters damn hard to follow. Plus any self-respecting grade-school English teacher would've put him in irons for what he did with modifiers and verb tenses. And don't even get me started about run-on sentences. Then again, I couldn't fix a sick Jaguar, restore a Duesenberg SJ or race-prepare an Alfa Giulietta, so I guess we were about even. But I sure missed him. We'd shared an awful lot of miles and smiles together. And some dark times, too. The kind that really make you close. But there's a curious thing about great racing friends. You run into them again— even after years apart—and it's like you can pick up the conversation right where you left off. Without even skipping a beat! I don't know how or why that's true, but I know for sure that it is.

I first met Buddy when we shared a plane ride together on our way to *La Carrera Panamericana* together back in the fall of 1952. He was wrenching on cars for Big Ed Baumstein and Cal Carrington and Tommy Edwards and some other guys out of Old Man Finzio's Sinclair station in Passaic, New Jersey and I was trying to make a living—albeit not much of a living—writing race reports for magazines and newspapers. It was obvious right away that we had a lot in common. Then we met up at Sebring a couple times and Watkins Glen and Elkhart Lake and even wound up standing pretty much side-by-side that terrible June afternoon in 1955 when Pierre Levegh's Mercedes SLR launched itself off the back of Lance Macklin's Austin Healey 100, smashed into a concrete stanchion and exploded into the start-finish line crowd like a meteor shower.

It was the worst thing either one of us had ever seen.

But there were good times, too—lots of them—and Buddy and I always got along because we saw and understood a lot of the same things about both racing and people. Only now Buddy was pretty much anchored at home and my late teenage/early twenties apprenticeship as a motorsports scribe had evolved into a genuine, full-time occupation. Even if it didn't pay particularly well. But I'd have to say I was happy with it anyway. Although writing race reports can get a little stale now and then since you're essentially writing the same damn story over and over and over again. But I suppose it's the same for any sports reporter. Imagine trying to keep nine long, boring innings of baseball fresh and exciting from the first pitch of spring training clear through the last fucking out of the World Series! Besides, not many people get to live out their fantasies. It was what I'd always wanted to do, and writing about motorsports is pretty interesting once you get past the loneliness and the travel and the living on the cheap all the time and seeing drivers you know as friends losing their rides or nerve or desire or, worse yet, getting themselves hurt or killed every now and then. Not to mention that cloistered monks have better sex lives than your average motoring journalist. But no life is all sweet cream custard with a cherry on top, is it?

I'd never been to Big Bill France's immense new Daytona International Speedway before (although, like everybody else, I'd read all the breathless press releases and seen plenty of pictures) and I'd have to say I was genuinely curious you could even say a bit skeptical about the notion of running an international-grade, World Manufacturers' Championship sports car race on a steeply banked, 2.5-mile stock car oval. Sure, I'd seen the diagram of how they'd added a "road course" infield section, but it all looked kind of flat, forced and artificial to me. Plus the race was only going to run three hours, which was more than a flat-out sprint but way too short to qualify as a genuine endurance grind like Sebring or Le Mans. A lot of drivers were even planning to do it solo.

But you couldn't argue with the success and notoriety Daytona International Speedway had achieved in an astoundingly short period of time. Gas station mechanic-cum-house painter-cum-repair shop owner-cum-racecar driver-cum-race promoter-cum-NASCAR founder Big Bill France had been running races on the beach at Daytona since before the war. But although they'd attracted quite a following of both fans and racers, the sand got carved up pretty badly with ruts and soft spots and collecting admissions was hit-or-miss since people could just wander in around the haphazard security. So Bill France fronted up his idea for a purpose-built speedway back in the early 1950s to mostly yawns, raised eyebrows and catcalls and he and son Bill Jr. persevered through tough times, cash binds, construction delays and several near-bankruptcies to present the first-ever Daytona 500 stock car race in February of 1959. He and Bill Jr. had to do everything from driving the bulldozers to riding herd on the construction crews to making presentations to likely investors, local politicians and chamber-of-commerce types, and an awful lot of newspaper editors, "concerned local citizens," meddlesome do-gooders and self-styled "experts" expressed the opinion that the new track would never be finished. And, if it was, it would amount to nothing more than a white-elephant eyesore and an enormous financial boondoggle.

That didn't stop old Bill Sr. He kept pushing and hustling, and surely must have been gratified when that first Daytona 500 not only drew a decent crowd but came down to a dramatic, side-by-side, too-close-to-call/dead-heat photo finish between Lee Petty's Oldsmobile and Johnny Beauchamp's Thunderbird after 500 long, hard miles of racing. Pit stops included! After a lot of shouting, arm waving, bared teeth, brandished fists and spirited arguments between the drivers, crews and the

NASCAR officials, Johnny Beauchamp's Thunderbird was declared the winner and ushered into victory lane. Which of course led to even more arguing, arm waving, bared teeth, brandished fists, etc., etc. on the part of Lee Petty's supporters. Which included not only fans and the race team, but also several "concerned bystanders" who worked for Oldsmobile's engineering and marketing departments up in Lansing, Michigan, and just happened to be "down in Florida on vacation," since all the Detroit manufacturers were still paying at least lip service to the stupid Automobile Manufacturers Association racing ban they'd all signed back in 1957. Thanks to that dumbass agreement, nobody from Detroit's Big Three (or Studebaker down in South Bend or American Motors up in Kenosha, Wisconsin) could have anything to do with any sort of motorsports activity. Or any other kind of performance-oriented engineering, advertising or promotional efforts, come to that.

Right.

In any case, the finish of that first Daytona 500 was so close that they couldn't really certify the results until the track officials found some still photos and a grainy strip of newsreel footage that actually captured the cars flashing side-by-side under the checkered flag. In the end, some two-and-a-half days later, the NASCAR officials reversed themselves and declared Lee Petty's Olds the winner. Which naturally set off another round of arguing, shouting, arm waving, bared teeth, brandished fists, etc. etc. that is probably still going on today in small-town southern bars and around after-race beer kegs on Friday and Saturday nights. But that was just fine with Big Bill France. He understood the value of publicity, and knew that nothing generates publicity like controversy. Better yet, he'd provided a genuinely exciting show with a thrilling, dramatic finish, and the majority of fans were frankly amazed that anybody would build a facility this immense, grand and modern dedicated to stock car racing. And so they brought their cousins, in-laws, friends and neighbors along the following year to show it off to them. Plus Big Bill knew how to take care of the press, and invited everybody from the New York Times clear down to hack sports writers from every small-town paper in the south, and made sure they got free coffee and breakfast on race morning, sandwiches and cold beer or soft drinks at lunchtime and special, reserved seats up at the very top of the main straight grandstand. He also provided them with plenty of press releases to help them write their stories. Including the one that pegged the total number of spectators at a highly optimistic 40,000 souls.

Big Bill France knew how to run a sanctioning body, too. He understood the politics of power, knew how to make decisions and stick to them, had a knack for handling people and moreover was blessed with an intuitive, seat-of-the-pants feel for what to do next. Like the famous story from the early days of NASCAR when some of his drivers started thinking about forming a drivers' union to protect their collective interests and get a little more say in how the money was doled out. That didn't sit real well with Big Bill France. The way he saw it, you needed both a father figure and an absolute dictator to run a successful business—racing or otherwise—and a quick glance at how the officious, self-important envoys, delegates and committees at the F.I.A. in Paris managed to muck up European racing on a regular basis made you wonder if he might not be right. In any case, Big Bill always kept his ear to the ground and heard rumblings about the union plans before much of anything happened. So he showed up at the next drivers' meeting with a large-caliber pistol strapped to his hip, and that was essentially the end of any drivers' union talk in NASCAR....

Big Bill was also a natural-born promoter and entrepreneur, and always seemed to have more dreams and ideas in the pipeline. Among them was a plan to bring international-grade sports car racing to his new speedway. He'd seen the crowds at The 12 Hours of Sebring, and there was no question in his mind that his immense, clean and modern new speedway was one hell of a lot more hospitable than the middle-of-nowhere cracked concrete, rusted-out hangars, smelly, primitive johns and fire ant colonies at Sebring. Not to mention that it was easier to get to and just a few miles inland from a whole Atlantic oceanfront full of hotels, motels, tourist rooms, bars, boardwalk attractions and eateries that would be only too happy to accommodate his fans. And he was probably right about all of that. But the 12 Hours of Sebring had been around for a dozen years and had developed both international stature and a loyal following of fans. Not to mention a style, tradition and ambience all its own. Like a lot of memorable places, the quirkiness, inconvenience, discomfort and even occasional pure agony of Sebring were precisely what made it so captivating. It wasn't the sort of thing you could duplicate in an antiseptic stadium oval, no matter how big or grand. And there were politics to consider, too. The organizers at Sebring weren't exactly thrilled with the notion of a second big, international-grade sports car race just five weeks before and 125 miles away. In fact, the powers-that-be at Sebring refused Big Bill's request for credentials when he casually asked if he could bring some of his people down to check things out back when plans for his own sports car race were no more than whispered rumors. But Big Bill France wasn't the kind of guy to take "no" for an answer. And no question he had a flair for showmanship. So he flew himself and his guys down to Sebring in a private plane, landed on the runway right behind the back straight—neatly side-stepping the credential office at the front gate—and proceeded to glad-hand his way through the paddock like a visiting dignitary, smiling, shaking hands, telling stories, chatting people up and generally acting like an honored guest and V.I.P. celebrity. There wasn't much of anything the Sebring brass could do about it, either. And you can bet Big Bill made sure he had full F.I.A. sanction (along with those all-important F.I.A. World Manufacturers' Championship points on offer) before he announced his race or started soliciting entries. You had to be impressed by the way Big Bill France did business.

All that said, a lot of sportycar types had reservations about how a World Manufacturers' Championship race would play on a big, steeply-banked stadium oval. And also whether the fans would come to see it. Stock car racing and sports car racing were two entirely different genres—like different religions, almost—and nobody knew that better than a seasoned motorsports journalist like myself. The way I saw it, there were basically four major divisions in American motorsports, and they really didn't mix or cross-pollinate much in the way of participants, machinery, style or fan base. That was something people outside the racing world rarely grasped, and I always used a simple, easy-to-understand music analogy when trying to explain it to a casual new acquaintance or some far-flung family relation who didn't have a clue. Like the pleasant but bored-looking young English woman who wound up occupying the seat next to mine on the connecting flight from Atlanta three days before the race. She looked about my age, wore glasses and not much makeup and had her hair drawn up in a tight, tidy little bun behind her head. On first glance she was either plain in a pretty sort of way or pretty in a plain sort of way—take your pick—and I'd actually noticed her a few rows ahead of me on the long flight over from Heathrow. She was seated next to a huge, fat American woman in a polka dot dress who ordered herself a fresh brandy cocktail every time the stewardess passed by, ate buttered popcorn from an enormous, grease-stained paper bag and talked incessantly the entire trip. She obviously found herself terribly amusing, and had one of those high, screechy, irritating laughs that send electric shocks through your eardrums. Even from several rows back. In any case, the pretty/plain young English woman and I wound up, as she put it, "waiting in line for the loo together," and in the process shared one of those silent, funny, fellow-traveler Eye Locks of Helpless Commiseration about her seat-mate in the polka-dot dress.

I noticed her again at the gate for the flight to Daytona, trying to grab a few impossible minutes of sleep sitting sideways across two chairs while I thumbed aimlessly through a day-old *Florida News-Sun* that somebody had left on one of the seats. There wasn't much on the front page except rumblings about our ever-worsening relations with Castro's Cuba—President Kennedy had just ordered a total ban on Cuban imports—along with a Pentagon story about why it was absolutely necessary to have American "military advisors" over in Viet Nam to help them fight the good fight against godless communism. And two pages further back was a three-column/four-alarm exposé—complete with pictures of skyrocketing pop star Chubby Checker and a frowning, dour-looking medical doctor in a white lab coat—about the alarming increase in slipped discs, wonky knees, wrenched backs and sacroiliac disorders attributed to the dangerous new "Twist" dance craze that had been sweeping the country since before the first of the year. To be honest, the "Twist" fad had pretty much run its course by the middle of February and nobody was really paying much attention to it any more. Except the newspapers, of course.

Right around dawn they led us across the flight apron to a waiting Convair 580 turboprop, and I was more than pleasantly surprised to find the pretty/plain young English woman assigned to the seat next to me. Now to be brutally honest, motorsports scribes have never been especially renowned for their success, talent, conquests, prowess or even pure, dumb luck where the female of the species is concerned. I know that's probably hard for you to believe. But it's sort of an occupational hazard, since racing writers spend most of their time hanging out on corners shooting pictures or cruising through the pits looking for stories or snooping around race-shop garages or sitting on their asses shooting the breeze with other motoring scribes in racetrack press rooms or trying to cadge drinks at racetrack-convenient watering holes or pounding out copy in cheap apartments or even cheaper motel rooms well into the wee hours of the morning. None of which places are frequented by available or even semi-available members of the opposite sex. Except the bars, of course. And in the bars you're forever fourth or fifth in line behind dashing, aggressive hero drivers, rich team owners, fast-talking sponsor-and-marketing types, the rowdy, raunchy and more-than-occasionally randy traveling mechanics and even some of the busboys and kitchen help when it comes to competing for female attention. Plus I can tell you, from extensive personal experience, that even if you do somehow manage to make feminine contact, you don't generally find yourself sharing a conversation about Shakespeare sonnets, Renaissance painting, Hemingway prose, current events, braking points, the Bay of Pigs fiasco, Baroque music, the disappearance of the dinosaurs, Ferrari cylinder head technology or Beat Generation poets with the kind of females you come across in places like that. And that's assuming you can get them to talk to you in the first place.

To be honest, adventures with women haven't exactly amounted to the thickest chapter in my life story. There was Louise Pangborn, whose blond pigtails sat directly, tantalizingly in front of me all through the sixth grade and the back of whose neck I will remember longingly and adoringly until I take my last breath. After that came a few fitful, painfully awkward movie-and-burgers dates during high school—usually girls with coarse hair and iffy complexions from the editorial staff of the student paper—followed by a memorable if crudely consummated semi-romance with a gawky but spirited and unrepentantly adventurous girl named Jillian Greene the summer after my senior year in high school. I was already starting to cover a few of the local races for Warren and Isabelle Bertrand at *Car and Track,* and Jillian and I plotted to borrow my then-stepfather's lethargic old '46 Nash Ambassador (under the thoroughly transparent pretext of "helping a friend move," of course) so the two of us could sneak off to the races at Pebble Beach together. We'd planned the trip for weeks (she'd told her mother she was "staying over with a girlfriend"), and both of us knew without ever saying it out loud what we both had in mind.

It was my bright idea to take the much longer but far more scenic Coast Highway up through Santa Barbara, San Luis Obispo, Morro Bay and Big Sur with the ocean, rocks and beaches on one side and sheer, dramatic cliffs and dense, forested hills on the other. But the damn Nash broke down before we got much north of Oxnard, so we spent the entire weekend—along with all the money we had between us—camped out at a damn gas station trying to get the car fixed so I could bring it and us home by Sunday night without anybody being the wiser. Not that Jillian much cared what anybody thought. Particularly her parents. Or that's what she said, anyway. With a bottle of cheap rum for both fuel and inspiration, we explored what certainly has to be one of the shortest, clumsiest, most uncomfortable and least satisfying examples of unbridled teenage passion in recorded human history. There we were, twisted up all arms, legs, thighs, necks, lips, tongues, fingers, zippers, bra straps, window-crank handle hooked on underwear elastic, buttocks, flailing belt buckles and sweaty, naked bellies on top of each other in the folded-down seat of that broken-down Nash sitting behind a gas station somewhere north of Oxnard at something like two-thirty in the morning. And then, as I will forever recall, I got sick all over both of us. An inexperienced 19-year-old should really know better than to consume by far the larger portion of a full bottle of rum on top of nothing all day but half a hot dog, a few sticks of Juicy Fruit and some potato chips. But of course you don't.

Jillian and I saw each other on and off for the balance of the summer, but I think it was more convenience and curiosity than anything else. You could say we were each other's extra-credit study class in procreation mechanics. But we were careful—oh, my, we were careful!—since neither one of us were sure what we wanted or where, if anywhere, we wanted to go with the relationship. Then late August rolled around and she left for some artsy girls' school out East where the teachers wore black leotards as both underwear and outerwear, not much in the way of makeup or lipstick and big, clunky, anthropologically-oriented Mexican, American Indian and Sub-Saharan African jewelry like turquoise belts, bleached bone or leopard claw necklaces and dangly, scorpion-motif silver earrings that weighed in at a quarter-pound each. Jillian wrote me all about it in a pair of tightly spaced, multi-page letters that she mailed on successive days that very first week she was away.

After that, I never heard from her again.

C'est la vie.

But I didn't really care. Or at least not much after the usual, requisite, post-adolescent two or three months of near-suicidal longing, languishing and loneliness passed by. Naturally I tried to lose myself in my work (and that was fairly easy, since I was pretty much lost in it already) and that's when my budding career as a motorsports journalist really started gaining traction. To be honest, I found it easy, occupying and consuming—not to mention exciting—and I was more than willing to let it suck me along into its slipstream. Which ultimately meant east to Elkhart Lake and Watkins Glen and southeast to Sebring and then even further east—*much further east!*—to England and Europe. And I have to admit I pretty much loved it. But that sort of life can be absolutely ruinous to your social career vis-à-vis members of the opposite sex.

People think about women in the context of motor racing and they inevitably visualize all those glamorous, gorgeous, sexy, slinky-or-voluptuous girls who are inevitably found at the elbows of or whispering into the ears of or leaning their tanned or porcelain cheeks against the shoulders of all the handsome, devil-may-care young racing drivers. Or their fat and graying (but exceedingly well-fixed) sponsors and team owners. And those girls do indeed exist. I've seen them. In fact, I've stared at them. Stared at them slack-jawed, goggle-eyed, weak-kneed and wobbly to the point of needing something to lean on for support. I have no idea where women like that come from, how they find their way onto the racing scene or where they go after they're done with it. Or after it's done with them, as is more often the case. But there's a seemingly endless supply of them, and I know from my own dearth of hands-on, personal experience that they're not for me and I am, most certainly, not for them. There are beautiful people in this world and there are not-so-beautiful people in this world, and it's been my observation that the beautiful types tend to stick together and keep to themselves. Although it's also been my observation that not-so-beautiful people or even downright ugly and/or unpleasant people with either family money, social position or some sort of flash-in-the-pan notoriety can make the cut as well. But not, as a rule, motorsports journalists. Besides, what could your average, scruffy motoring scribe possibly have to say to a woman like that? And what could she possibly say back to you? To be honest, I have no idea. And the fates have surely conspired to keep it that way.

Aside from that, the motorsports world is generally ruled, run and populated almost exclusively by men. Or given to moods, fits and tantrums little schoolboys dressed up as men, anyway. And so there isn't much opportunity for a person such as myself, immersed as I am in the forever fascinating, ever-evolving and yet singularly cloistered motorsport scene, to meet anyone or make a worthwhile connection. Many of my automotive writer and photographer friends are already married—Lord only knows how once you've witnessed their eating, drinking and personal hygiene habits and know what they earn—and I'm certain that their long periods away from home must surely aid in maintaining their marital status. Mind you, there's an awful lot of fooling around that goes on in the racing world. In fact, it's famous for it: wives (yours or someone else's), girlfriends, secretaries, "special assistants," weekend dates, whirlwind affairs, one-night stands, three-month fiancées, trophy girls, bored socialites, fashion models, piano bar singers, stewardesses, drum majorettes, corner workers, upscale or down-and-dirty cocktail waitresses, rental car company desk clerks, occasional threesomes or foursomes and creatures of the same biological gender included. But not much of that ever filters down to the motoring scribe level. Or maybe it's we scruffy motoring scribes who don't filter up to it? But the end result is that a person like myself rarely gets an opportunity to meet anyone worthwhile of the female persuasion. Oh, there are always those other kinds of girls you can find in most any town—pay-by-the-job or the loose and easy freelancers—but I never got much satisfaction along with the perfunctory ten or fifteen seconds of mind-blanking escape, and I always felt un-fulfilled, uncomfortable and somehow shameful both before and after. But that's just me, and I've observed that many men (and particularly the team mechanics) don't seem to share my sensibilities.

Not that it's really any of your business.

In any case, I've always believed that anyone the fates and the airlines put in the seat next to yours is fair game. Not to mention a captive audience. And this young woman seemed particularly neat, well-groomed, self-possessed and pleasant. Not to mention approachable. I have to admit to being shy by nature but, following a long, sleepless flight in from London and more than a few airline cocktails along the way, I figured: *why the hell not?* I saw she had her head leaned back against the seat with her eyes half-closed, just waiting for the plane to start rolling. "You heading for Daytona?" I asked her.

"If I'm not," she answered without opening her eyes, "I'm on the wrong bloody airplane." She had a lovely English accent. Not stiff upper crust, but not working class, either. To my ear she sounded educated, professional and, most of all, open to a little aimless small talk.

I rolled on through the usual stupid pleasantries about the weather and such as the plane taxied towards the runway, and made sure to slip in right at the beginning that I was a magazine writer who covered motor racing for a living and that I was moreover working on an as-yet unfinished novel on the same topic and also by the way heading for a major and important (not to mention inaugural) World Manufacturers' Championship race meeting at Daytona's amazing and astounding new International Speedway. And that was all in the first breath. The news made her left eyebrow appear to arch up by a millimeter or two. Or I thought it did, anyway. By then the pilot had our Convair lined up at the end of the runway, and a moment later he opened up the throttles and cut it loose. The Allison gas tur-bines whirled up to speed, the props spun into a blur and I could feel my shoulder blades pressing back into the seat cushion as the engines desperately shrieked and whined us towards the end of the runway. I always close my eyes to savor that nervous little tingle you get when the plane you're riding in separates itself from the earth. But first I glanced over and saw that she was doing the exact same thing: eyes pressed gently shut, fingers wrapped firmly but not desperately around the end of the armrests and a tight, anticipatory little smile drawn out across her face. It struck me again that it looked to be a very nice face, and that's what I was thinking as I closed my eyes again and felt the wheels thump off the far end of the runway as the plane began clawing its way up into the sky....

When I opened my eyes, I saw she was leaned against the window watching the still-shadowy city of Atlanta dropping away below us. I craned my neck over her shoulder to watch it, too. She had a nice smell on her. Or at least as nice a smell as you could expect after twenty-some hours of plane rides with nothing but public washrooms along the way. We leveled off at cruising altitude with harsh shafts of early sunlight cutting through the cabin, and the young English woman pulled her shade down to shield us. I thanked her. And immediately started trying to figure out how I could gracefully segue back into our earlier conversation. Right where I left off, in fact. But she beat me to it. "Tell me," she asked like she was actually somewhat interested. "How does one become a motorsports writer?"

"One starts by being unfit for any sort of honest work," I replied with what I hoped was a pretty fair fake British accent.

The ends of her mouth crinkled up. "No, honestly," she insisted. "I'm curious."

So I told her all about it. After all, I'd been with *Car and Track* since almost the beginning. I'd originally met the magazine's serious-looking founder/editor/publisher Warren Bertrand and his wife, Isabelle, at a Cal Club race at Palm Springs in the spring of 1951. I was going to community college at the time—supposedly studying journalism, history and photography, but mostly just marking time and screwing off—and doing race reports for the Cal Club newsletter in return for bum-a-ride travel and the occasional free bed or meal. By the end of the weekend, Warren and Isabelle had offered me thirty dollars a race *plus* a small travel allowance to write essentially the same stories for *Car and Track* that I was doing for the Cal Club newsletter. Plus an additional five bucks for any photos I took that wound up in the magazine. Sure, that didn't sound like much by 1962 standards, but to an 18-year-old would-be-writer in 1951, it was like winning a damn Pulitzer Prize! And I have to admit to being awed, gob-smacked and thunderstruck the first time I saw my work and byline laid out in neat, perfectly justified columns on the pages of a real, ink-on-glossy-paper magazine that you could find on damn near any street-corner newsstand in America. My community college journalism teacher who loved big words called it "an epiphany," and no question he had it right. Plus I really liked working for Warren and Isabelle. Especially her. Warren was always kind of cold, detached and stand-offish—that's just the way he was—but Isabelle was like another mom to me. Maybe even better than the one I came with as original equipment. The two of them ran the magazine as a more-or-less mom-and-pop operation and did almost everything themselves. Warren was one of those reserved, furrowed-brow, pipe-smoker types who came from a little quiet family money and considered everything—including what to order off the lunch menu at a roadside truck stop—

like it was a weighty and momentous decision. Isabelle was a lot warmer and friendlier, and as I got to know them better, I came to realize that she was the one who really got most things done around the *Car and Track* offices. Of course she was working in her husband's shadow most of the time, but she was one of those earnest, loyal, capable, do-anything sort of frontier wives who I imagine got the pioneers across the great plains and mountain ranges and out to California in the first place.

"That's a very nice thing for you to say," the young English woman said.

"Well, it's true," I shrugged. "If it's true, then that's the way you've got to tell it."

She gave me a wry little smile. "I'm afraid not all writers share your sensibilities."

I thought about that little weasel Eric Gibbon and quickly agreed with her. And then I heaved right back into my life story. After all, I didn't get to tell it very often.

"Back in the early fifties," I continued, "the imported sports car boom and the stateside road racing scene were just coming into their own. And nowhere more so than where I lived out in Southern California. And *Car and Track* was growing bigger, thicker and more popular right along with it. I guess you'd say I happened along in the right place at the right time, because it was beginning to dawn on Warren and Isabelle that they couldn't be everywhere they needed to be or cover all the events they needed to cover or wear all the hats they had to wear in order to produce a magazine. You know: reporter, editor, layout artist, proofreader, publisher, printing contractor, distributor and—most important of all for any magazine's survival—advertising salesman, accountant and collection agent."

She nodded like she understood exactly what I meant. So I went on:

"Hell, I was just an overgrown high-school kid with a portable typewriter and a second-hand camera. But I knew the cars and I knew the people and I knew the local scene with its import dealers and race shops pretty well. Besides," I added with a wink, "I'd work cheap."

"That's generally a major consideration for any position, isn't it?"

"Indeed it is."

"And you liked working for them?"

"Oh, yeah," I nodded. "And I still do. Even if Warren always keeps me at kind of a distance. But that's just the way he is, you know? I always tell myself it's a sign of professionalism and respect. And maybe it is. But he's never been the kind of guy you could warm up to. Some people are just like that."

"Yes they are," she agreed.

"Personally, I always liked Isabelle a lot better. But she usually had to stay in the office so I didn't get to see her much. Still, she always made all the travel and credential arrangements and did all the proofreading and editing when my stories came in." I looked out the little bottom sliver of window at the clouds below us. "It was really special to show up at events and have press credentials and parking passes waiting for me. And it always made me feel pretty damn proud when I saw my stories in print in the magazine. Hell, I would've done it for free! So it was like frosting on the cake whenever I got a check in the mail—even if it wasn't much of a check!—four or five weeks later. Or seven or eight weeks if advertiser collections were running a little slow..."

She gave me a polite little flutter of a laugh to let me know she was paying attention.

"...But the best part was that I loved doing it. And I had a near-endless supply of things to write about. There always seemed to be another big race coming up or some hot new car being flown in from England or Italy or wherever or some promising new special taking shape in one of the garage shops or dealership service departments around Los Angeles. And writing for the magazine made me a genuine insider. Or at least it did once people got used to seeing my byline."

"You make it sound exciting."

"Yeah," I allowed like it was only the axis the earth turned on, "I suppose you could say it is."

"And you do this full time now?"

"Pretty much," I told her with what I hoped sounded like magnanimous humility. "My name's right up at the top of the masthead these days. Right below Warren's and Isabelle's."

She looked mildly impressed. "And what is your name?"

"Henry Lyons," I more or less bragged. Then clawed my hand over the armrest for an awkward shake. "But my friends call me 'Hank.'"

"Nice to meet you, Henry," she teased.

I ignored that. "I'm pretty much stationed over in London now," I continued expansively, "covering the European scene."

"Oh really? London?"

I nodded.

"Whereabouts in London?"

To tell the truth, I didn't want to go into much detail about my crappy second-floor apartment over a commercial bakery in a semi-seedy industrial section southwest of central London. "I'm not too far from Surbiton," I told her obliquely. "John and Charlie Cooper's race shop isn't far away, and that makes it convenient when it comes to rumors and scuttlebutt. But I spend most of my time traveling once the season starts. And I get back to the states now and then to cover some of the big races over here."

"Like that famous one in Indianapolis?"

And that was a perfect opening for the Standard Music Analogy I always use to try and explain the different types of racing to the uninitiated. Or uncaring and disinterested, as is more often the case. "Automobile racing is a lot like music," I told her grandly. "There are different styles, schools and disciplines to it. And they're produced by different sorts of people and appeal to completely different groups of fans."

"Oh, really?"

I nodded emphatically. "And, just as in music, you don't have a lot of cross-pollination from one style, school or discipline to another."

"You don't say?"

She looked mildly interested. Or maybe she was just being polite. But I was just getting warmed up.

"Here in the states we have Drag Racing," I explained like some sort of college professor, "and it's a lot like our Rock and Roll. It's loud and explosive and easy to grasp and over in a hurry. You don't need much of an attention span to appreciate Drag Racing. And, just like rock and roll, it appeals mostly to the young."

"I think I've heard of it," she said like we were discussing the weather. But that wasn't about to stop me. Hell, I had enough enthusiasm for both of us.

"Drag racing is a genuine, home-grown, all-American form of motorsport. Hell, we probably had the first street-corner drag race here in America about five minutes after the first set of traffic lights went up."

She nodded for me to go on.

"Drag strips are a quarter-mile long, two lanes wide and straight as an arrow. The light turns green, the cars leap off the line and it's all about who gets to the finish line first. It's over in a handful of seconds, and the guy who crosses the finish line first goes on to the next round and the guy who loses puts his car back in the trailer and heads for home. He's done for the weekend."

Her brow knitted into a frown. "It doesn't sound particularly complicated, does it?"

That's when I tossed in my standard Western Movie Analogy. Hell, everybody likes a good western. "You know," I told her like I was just thinking it up for the very first time, "Drag Racing always reminds me of those classic old Hollywood western where two gunslingers face off on a dusty frontier Main Street..."

I could see she was visualizing it.

"...and when the light goes green, they both go for their guns. *BAM!* A heartbeat later, one of them is walking away with a tight-lipped smile and the other one is face-down in the dirt with a big, ugly hole through his chest..."

"You paint quite a picture!" she laughed.

I felt my cheeks heating up.

"But it honestly doesn't sound like there's much to it."

"Oh, there's more than you'd think," I tried to explain. "You wouldn't believe the time, money, effort and ingenuity that goes into every hundredth—or even thousandth—of a second. There's a real science to it. Really there is. And the strip is always changing, even from one run to the next. You've got to be willing to try things and experiment around with new tricks and ideas. Plus sometimes you've got to rebuild a blown-up motor between runs. That's a pretty damn impressive thing to see."

"But what about driving skill? It sounds awfully simple, doesn't it? I mean, you just put your foot down and *go!*"

"Believe me," I told her, "the drivers at the top of the game are *really* good at what they do. They can get a supercharged, nitromethane-spiked dragster launched and away before the average Joe can even get his wheels spinning."

"I'm sure it's fascinating," she allowed politely, "but I don't think it sounds like my cup of tea." She gave me a quizzical look. "Tell me about Indianapolis. That's your most famous race, isn't it?"

"We've had open-wheel oval track racing here in the states ever since the early 1900s. It's another homegrown, all-American form of the sport. And the real heart and soul of it—the Mecca, the top of the mountain, the holiest of holies—has always been the Indianapolis 500. Every guy running on a dusty dirt oval from Long Island to Long Beach dreams of running in the Indy 500 one day." I segued back to my music analogy. "You could say that kind of racing is like traditional, mainstream American music. You know, the stuff everybody used to listen to before rock-and-roll came along: Tommy Dorsey, Guy Lombardo, Glen Miller, 4th of July marches, The Andrews Sisters, Frank Sinatra...that sort of thing."

She looked only halfway interested, so I added darkly:

"It's a dangerous place, too."

"Indianapolis?"

I nodded. "The speeds are unbelievably high, and there's nothing but concrete walls all around you if things go wrong." I shook my head solemnly. "A lot of brave men have died at Indianapolis."

"You make it sound awful."

"Not really," I shrugged. "It's just part of the deal. In fact, in some ways it's what sets Indy apart."

"The danger?"

"No, the challenge. And the risk. And the reward. It's the richest race on earth, plain and simple. And you can make your entire career—as a driver, a team owner, a crew chief or a car builder—by winning the Indianapolis 500 on Memorial Day."

She looked impressed. So it was time to move on.

"And then you've got stock car racing, which is also run on ovals. But it grew up in the southeast and it's more like country music. Stock Car Racing started from the same roots as country music, with rural southern hog farmers and bootleggers and gas station pump jockeys running their beat-up jalopies on broken-down little backwoods ovals scattered across the south."

"Aren't the tracks all the same?"

"Well, they're all ovals. But no two are alike. Some are paved, some are dirt, some are clay, some are loose, some are hard-packed, some are asphalt and a few are even concrete. And no matter what they are, they change as the race wears on. Plus some are pancake flat while others are banked so high and steep you can't even walk up the bankings. And they come in all sorts of different shapes and sizes, from tight little 1/4- and 3/8-mile bullrings to huge, wide-open superspeedways like the one I'm headed for at Daytona this weekend. No two ovals are ever the same. Hell, no two corners on the same oval are ever the same."

"And you can run the same car on all those different tracks?" It was actually a pretty sophisticated question, but I didn't pick up on it at the time.

"Well, stock cars may all *look* the same, but you need different tires and different gears and different suspension setups and different weight distribution and even different driving styles and strategies for each track. Stock car racing looks simple and obvious from the outside, but it's really quite subtle and technical once you start digging into it." I gave her a knowing smile. "There's a backwoods, backwards, aw-shucks, cracker-barrel sort of surface veneer on stock car racing, but don't let it fool you. Those guys know what the hell they're doing—know all the tricks, tweaks and angles—but they're not the kind to spell it out for you in so many words. Not those guys. You've got to learn and earn your way in with the stock car crowd."

"I'll remember that."

"It's a good thing to know."

She thought it over for a moment. "But none of that is the kind of racing you're involved with, is it?"

"No, it isn't." I admitted with poorly concealed pride. "I cover road racing. Mostly over in England and Europe where it came from, but over here in the states, too."

"And that's your favorite, isn't it?"

I felt a proud sort of grin spreading its way across my face. "Yeah, I suppose it is. I've always thought road racing is more like, you know, like *classical* music..." I tried not to make it sound too much more stylish, elegant, elevated, cerebral, fascinating, noble, worthy or refined than the other three, but of course it just did. Or it did to me, anyway. "Road racing tracks go left and right and up and down hill, through deep valleys and across sunlit meadows and even right up the sides of mountains sometimes, with every possible kind of bend, corner, contour, climb, dip, crown, camber and pavement variety. Like a favorite section of country road, you know?"

She nodded like she was getting it all.

"In fact, our type of racing actually started out on country roads, and some of our circuits are still made up of country roads even today. Like Spa Francorchamps over in Belgium and Le Mans in France, for instance."

"I've heard of Le Mans, of course."

"Sure you have," I nodded. "Everybody has. Especially in England. In fact, one of my scribe friends always calls it 'a French race run for Englishmen....'"

I waited for a laugh, but none came.

"...Anyhow, it's an absolutely magnificent event and an enormous occasion. Without a doubt it's the biggest, most important sports car race in the world. And I guess I'd have to say it's my favorite, too."

"Oh?" she asked, her eyebrows arching again. "And why is that?"

"Oh, you have to see it for yourself!" I fairly gushed. "It runs twice around the clock—twenty-four hours straight!—through rain and fog and darkness and dawn and...." I took a deep breath while a whole montage of Le Mans memories swirled behind my eyes. Including the one I could never get rid of. "I had probably the worst day of my life at Le Mans in 1955," I admitted without looking at her. "I saw the worst racing accident I'd ever seen. Hell, the worst racing accident anybody has ever seen." I looked her right in the eyes. "Pierre Levegh's Mercedes got launched off the back of Lance Macklin's Austin-Healey, hit a concrete stanchion at the tunnel underpass and exploded into the start/finish line crowd. The body-work was made out of magnesium, so it was like an incendiary bomb."

"Oh, how horrible!"

I nodded as my mind's eye relived it, sweeping helplessly around the scattered, still-smoldering debris and the bodies like rumpled piles of discarded clothing in quietly growing pools of blood. And then the rising chorus of cries and screams of horror, moans and whimpers from the injured and dying while the racecars continued to howl past in the background and the clanging warble of ambulances grew louder as they streaked towards the scene....

I shook my head to get rid of it.

"Are you all right?"

"Yeah," I nodded, "I'm OK." And then I gave off an odd, high-pitched little laugh that I didn't really understand. "It's just a hard thing to get out of your brain. Like something that happened in the war."

She was staring into my eyes like she was looking for something. "But you still love it anyway, don't you?"

"Yeah," I admitted as the images slowly faded. "I really do."

A faraway look came into her eyes. "People get addicted to war, you know. I think it has something to do with the urgency and immediacy of it."

What she'd said went right through me. "I've always thought racing's a lot like war," I told her. "Especially endurance racing. It's the only place left in life where you can give every ounce of strength and effort and planning and cunning and genius and teamwork and not hold anything back. And everyone involved knows that the checkered flag will come down at a certain, predetermined time and that everyone will know who won and who lost." I shook my head again. "There's nothing like that in the rest of life. It's just slop."

"You make it sound almost romantic..."

"Oh, it *is!*" I assured her. "Sure, we have flat-out Grand Prix races for Formula One cars that decide the World Driving Championship, and a lot of people—drivers, fans and writers—think that's the absolute pinnacle...."

"But you don't?"

I shook my head. "I suppose it is when it works the way it's supposed to. But more often than not, one team has the best car—it was Ferrari in a landslide last year—and everybody else is fighting it out for the scraps and leftovers."

"So it's mostly the car in Formula One?"

I pretended to think it over. "Almost all the drivers are good once you get up to Formula One And when all the drivers are good, there's a natural compression of talent and so the car becomes a more and more important part of the equation."

"So in other words, the higher up you go the better the drivers are, and the better the drivers are, the more everything depends on the car?"

"That's about it," I told her. "A star driver can really stand out against a field of duffers and amateurs. But it gets tougher and tougher up near the top. Oh, like any other sport, you've always got those one or two special cases who just seem to have that little something extra. Fangio had it. He won five World Championships driving for four different teams. That's pretty damn impressive."

"What happened to him?"

"Oh, he faded towards the end like everyone ultimately does. Your heart goes out of it eventually, no matter who you are."

"Was he killed?"

"No, he retired. He's got a string of Mercedes dealerships in South America. But he was the best there was for quite awhile."

"Was anyone else that good?"

"It's hard to compare drivers from different eras. But of course we do it all the time. No question Nuvolari had it all before the war. He was incredibly tough, brave and determined. But of course he's dead now."

"Did he die racing?"

"No," I almost laughed. "And that's the irony of it. He died in bed, of all things. Sick and hobbled after two debilitating strokes. It was very sad."

"Not what you'd expect."

"No, it's not. But life never gives you what you expect, does it?"

"Or deserve," she added with an odd look in her eye. But then they brightened again like she'd thrown a little switch somewhere inside. "So tell me," she wanted to know: "who has it now?"

"Has what?"

"That 'something extra.'"

"Oh, Stirling Moss," I answered without hesitation. "No question about it. He's the best driver in the world right now. And by a fairly consistent margin."

"He's English, isn't he?" she said with an ill-concealed swirl of national pride.

"Yeah, he's a Brit," I admitted. "But there are always plenty of guys knocking on the door. Mike Hawthorn, Archie Scott-Brown and Jean Behra proved they could run even-up with him on their day. But of course they're all gone now..."

"Did they die racing?"

"They all died in wrecks, if that's what you mean. Archie at Spa and Behra at Avus. But Hawthorn was killed in a stupid road accident on the Guildford by-pass. After he'd already won the World Championship and retired."

"I remember reading about it."

"He was trying to prove he could beat Rob Walker's 300SL with a Jaguar sedan in the rain." I gave off a weak little shrug. "Racing's full of dark ironies. It's a real gold mine for a writer if you don't let it get to you."

That's about when the stewardess came around to collect our cups and papers for the descent into Daytona. The Convair banked into its landing pattern and we could see a low, dark cloud cover clinging to the Florida coastline like the frayed sleeve of a second-hand coat. The back of her head was only inches from my nostrils and I caught her smell again. For some reason it reminded me of jade, even though jade doesn't smell like anything. And then, as we came in on our approach and descended through the cloud bank, I got my first-ever glimpse of the immense Daytona speed oval spread out on the rain-slicked grassland next to the airport. You couldn't miss the narrow, oddly and perfectly rectangular lake nestled in alongside the backstretch. It didn't look like any kind of lake I'd ever seen before. Or any kind of racetrack I'd ever seen before, either. Not even Indianapolis.

"It looks awfully big," she said under her breath.

"Empty, too," I nodded as the landing gear thumped down. "But maybe it'll fill up on race day."

"It'll take an awfully large number of people," she observed as we taxied towards the terminal. You could see it had rained hard overnight, but only a few scattered drops were still pinging into the puddles on the runway. "So," I finally asked her as we approached our gate, "you know just about everything there is to know about me. Who I am. What I do. Where I'm going. But I don't know one single thing about you."

"Well, let's see, Henry," she allowed through a sly little smile. "My name is Audrey Denbeigh, I live with my father on the southeast side of London, near Bromley..." she was looking right at me, watching for my reaction "...his name is Walter Denbeigh, and he worked as a fabricating engineer for de Havilland Aircraft during the war when I was little..."

"Really?"

She nodded, starting to blush a little "He was a section chief on the Mosquito bomber project. Do you know the Mosquito?"

"That's the one made out of plywood, isn't it? Like a model airplane...."

"That's it exactly!" she nodded excitedly. "Good for you!"

I could feel the heat coming up in my cheeks again.

"He's retired from that now, of course..." she continued with a strange, mischievous glint in her eyes. "...and these days he does a bit of freelance fabricating work for Eric Broadley over at the Lola shops in Bromley..."

She might as well have hit me with a brick.

"...and helps out with the preparation work on Clive Stanley's Imperial Crown Tea team. They rent space in Broadley's shop, you know..."

Make that two bricks.

"...so I'm coincidentally also on my way to the Speedway to take care of the timing and scoring charts for Mr. Stanley's team..." she was watching me to see how I was taking it. "We've got an Aston Martin DB4GT Zagato running in the 4-liter GT class with Ian Snell and Tommy Edwards signed on to drive. But you probably knew that already, didn't you?"

I opened my mouth to try and say something, but no words came out. So she continued:

"...Although I'm afraid we don't stand much of a chance against the Ferrari Berlinettas for overall GT honors. Especially that new, experimental one they rolled out at Le Mans last year. Tommy and my father say it's nothing but a bloody Testa Rossa wrapped up in GT bodywork." She leaned in close and almost whispered: "We've heard they've got Stirling Moss signed on to drive it this weekend..."

It took me a few seconds to collect myself. "So," I finally fumbled out, "you've been having me on a bit, haven't you?"

"Yes, I suppose I have," she laughed. "But you were having such fun and doing such a marvelous job. I hated to stop you."

I was still pretty stunned, but then she gave me the nicest smile and it all turned funny for me, too. "I'll get even, you know," I growled playfully as we headed for the exit.

I'm very much looking forward to it," she assured me, still laughing. "But I warn you," she wagged a finger under my nose, "I won't make it easy for you."

Chapter 3: New Rules, New Track, New Faces

I wound up giving Audrey a ride over to the racetrack in my rental car—a base, stripper Fairway Freeway 4-door the color of Boston coffee with "houndstooth embossed" Vinylite bench seats, 2600 miles on the clock and a faint but annoying rotational click coming from somewhere under the transmission tunnel. But it had a huge trunk—even with the stupid spare tire sitting smack-dab in the middle of it!—and plenty of shoulder, gut and leg room front and rear. Plus a smooth-shifting automatic that whisked us away from the curb like a cabin cruiser easing out to sea.

"You Americans drive such enormous cars," Audrey observed from the far side of the front seat.

"Yeah," I had to agree as I stared at the expanse of houndstooth embossed Vinylite between us. "But they're starting to build some smaller ones in Detroit these days. More like what you have over in England." And naturally that swirled up a little patriotic guilt twinge in my gut, so I quickly added: "But we've got a lot of space over here and lots of stuff to carry around and great, long distances to cover..." I could feel the all-American jingoism welling up inside me "...and this Fairway Freeway will still be wheezing along on four bald tires with a family of hillbillies or Puerto Ricans inside of it when most of your Austins, Hillmans and Vauxhalls will be rusting away in junkyards...."

"You don't have to get defensive about it, Henry," she said in a sort of scolding schoolteacher voice that really made my hackles come up for an instant.

And then we both broke out laughing.

The overnight rain had left wide, shallow puddles on the pavement and the cloud cover clinging along the Florida coastline made the day look dull, drab and lifeless. But the sun broke through just as we were driving through the deep, corrugated metal tunnel leading into the infield, so we were greeted with a burst of brilliant Florida sunshine when we emerged on the other side. And what a scene! I'd never seen anything like the Daytona infield. Turn Four's 31-degree banking towered over us like a great, gray tidal wave, and I frankly couldn't believe how tall or steep it was. Or how huge, vast and empty the infield seemed. You could barely make out the Turn Two banking way off in the distance, and there was nothing in between but flat, open grass with just a few narrow access roads, some power poles and porta-johns scattered here and there and a run of chainlink fencing along the back of the main straightaway to cordon off the paddock from the spectator areas. The rest was just open, empty atmosphere with a flock of squawking seagulls circling around in it over the long, strangely and perfectly rectangular lake next to the back straight. It looked like the world's biggest swimming pool. I learned later that the construction crews needed tons and tons of dirt to fill in behind the speedway's bankings, so rather than buy it on the open market, Big Bill France had them bulldoze a monstrous, rectangular hole in the infield—29 acres worth!—and simply filled the hole up with water when they were done. They named it Lake Lloyd, and Big Bill ran powerboat races and water skiing exhibitions there from time to time as an added attraction.

"What do you think of it?" I asked as we made our way towards the paddock.

Audrey's eyes swept slowly around us. "It's awfully *big,* isn't it?" she mumbled as her eyes came full circle.

"Yes it is," I mumbled back, still more than a little awestruck. And yet something didn't feel right about it. Big Bill France's incredible, immense and amazing new speedway felt more like a gigantic, oversized sports stadium than any kind of road racing track I'd ever known. And I remember silently hoping that I wasn't looking at the future of our sport laid out before me. Oh, the size, scale and presentation of it were absolutely stunning. But it didn't strike me as particularly welcoming or attractive. Just big. And a little bit sterile, too. To be honest, I much preferred the hills, valleys, trees and greenery of natural road courses like Watkins Glen, Lime Rock and Elkhart Lake. Or Spa, Le Mans and the Nurburgring over in Europe. Or even the jagged concrete and old, rusting hangers at Sebring. At least they had a little character. And history. And tradition. But no question Daytona was here to stay, and no doubt it would start building its own character, history and tradition as a road-racing circuit that very weekend. And all the scribes, fans and racers were simply going to have to get used to it. Plus, like all the *real* racers always say about any new racetrack: *"Hey, it's the same for everybody...."*

It was late morning by the time we got past the wizened and leathery old security guard and into the paddock, but first practice hadn't started yet because of some sort of glitch with the communications network. While the track crews worked to sort it out, white-suited corner workers were doing their best to clear the worst of the standing water off pit lane and the infield road course sections using squeegees and push brooms. The bankings, of course, drained fine all by themselves. So everything was strangely quiet for a first morning of practice on the very first weekend of the World Manufacturers' Championship season, with just the squish and scrape of brooms and squeegees pushing water across the pavement and the soft, low rumble of panel vans shuttling the communications crews around. And then, from the far end of the paddock, we heard the unmistakable, metallic howl of a Porsche 4-cam four firing up and revving, revving, revving like Porsche mechanics seem to love to make them do. Followed almost immediately by the spluttering bark of an unhappy Jag or Aston straight six with a flat miss in it echoing through the empty grandstands.

"That sounds like my boys," Audrey said through a bit of a grimace. "They were chasing some sort of fuel system gremlins before we left, but it doesn't sound like they've gotten it sorted out yet."

I headed towards the sound.

As we trundled through the busy, bustling paddock, I came to realize that Daytona was really Audrey's first-ever full-on World Manufacturers' Championship race. Oh, she'd done the late-season Tourist Trophy event at Goodwood, the Coppa Inter-Europa at Monza and the Paris 1000 Ks at Montlhéry with Clive Stanley's team the previous season (along with a few second- and third-tier club events in the U.K.), but they were all GT-only races, and so she'd never seen the top-level factory teams like Ferrari or Porsche before. "It's pretty neat, isn't it?" I asked rhetorically.

"Definitely," she readily agreed.

I really liked the way it made her eyes light up.

We found Clive Stanley's pale green Aston Zagato sitting next to its transporter near the far west end of the paddock, and sure enough the hood was up and two weary-looking mechanics in pea-soup green coveralls were hard at work dismantling the Weber carburetors for maybe the fourth or fifth time. Audrey quickly introduced me around, and I already knew the younger one pretty well because I'd enjoyed drinks with him a time or two at the races. His name was Peter Bryant, and he was a short, blunt little fireplug of a man with a sharp wit, a quick, cutting laugh and a generally devilish glint in his eye. Peter figured he knew hell's own amount about damn near everything in racing (and he did) and loved telling stories on his peers. It got him into trouble now and then. His older and obviously senior partner was a fleshy, beleaguered-looking lifer mechanic named Georgie Smales. I'd seen him around, too. Georgie was one of those dull, plodding mechanics who always look like they've been rolling around on the shop floor, constantly complain about things that have broken or gone wrong and regularly struggle to get anything fixed properly. Georgie had a broad, glistening forehead that usually had a streak of grease across it, wild clumps of unruly, reddish-brown hair on either side, a matching, scraggly mustache and a nasty little snort of a laugh that rarely had any fun in it. You could see that he was both disgusted and preoccupied with a flat engine miss that stubbornly defied solution, and you could sense that Peter Bryant was just waiting for him to give up and get the hell out of the way so he could have a try at it. I knew the best thing to do under those circumstances was leave them both the hell alone.

I'd really hoped to run into my old friend Tommy Edwards while I was there, but he and co-driver Ian Snell were behind closed doors having a "private strategy meeting" with team manager Geoff Britten and car owner Clive Stanley. Audrey explained that Clive was rightfully famous for both an occasionally short fuse and long, belabored team meetings that rambled on and on and on while getting essentially nowhere, and so she doubted I'd be seeing Tommy any time soon.

"Look, I really need to be heading up to the press room to find out about the delay and pick up a copy of the final entry list."

"Everybody's got to earn a living," she smiled at me. It was a hell of a nice smile. "And thanks so much for the lift in."

"My pleasure."

"Mine, too."

I turned to go, but stopped myself. "I sure hope we run into each other again."

She turned her smile up another couple watts. "You know where to find me."

After that there wasn't much to do but say goodbye and wander off towards the press room. If I'm not mistaken, I was whistling. *Blue Skies,* I think.

The main press room at Daytona was a prefabricated metal building mounted up on a skeletal, stilt-like superstructure behind the very top row of the pit-straight grandstand. It had a long row of windows that offered a commanding view of the pits and the sweeping, steeply-banked start/finish straightaway all the way down to where the cars had to brake hard for the tight, flat, double-apex buttonhook left into the infield. It was a pretty good climb to get up to the press room, but inside it was neat and well-lit with plenty of chairs, counter space, typewriters and phone lines, air conditioning for hot Florida racedays and a nice buffet breakfast every morning for the working press. Plus freshly-brewed coffee and finger snacks at all hours and a media information desk where a pleasant, smiling young college girl with a friendly southern accent would be only too happy to hand you copies of the latest entry list and track-supplied pit notes and information sheets. She was also quick to bring you up to date on the communications delay: *"The storm did something to one of the power lines last night, and we just cain't run out there without race control bein' able to talk t'all the corners. But they've about got it fixed now an' we should be up and running in another fifteen minutes or so."* That was pretty damn good service for a racetrack press room! Some tracks treat writers and photographers like nuisances (or worse!), but Big Bill France always made a point of taking good care of the press. In fact, he'd hosted a big, blowout party at the ultra-posh 21 Club in New York just a few days before to publicize his first big international road race and introduce some of the European drivers to the famously jaded and sophisticated New York press corps. It's been my observation over the years that many New Yorkers believe they live at the center of the whole damn universe (and maybe, just maybe, they do) but Big Bill knew they wielded the pens, typewriters and influence he needed to spread the word about what he was doing at Daytona. And he was shrewd enough to know that they didn't like leaving their home turf—particularly for some low-brow, Neanderthal car race someplace nobody ever heard of down in Florida—and moreover that they were absolute suckers for big money, glamour and foreign accents. So that's what he provided. Right in their own back yard. Big Bill also made sure to invite all the grunt-level motorsports scribes who regularly covered the World Manufacturers' Championship, since they tended to say nicer things about you, your track and your car race if you included them in on a fancy party.

"You really should have been there, Lyons," an all-too-familiar voice admonished me from behind. Sure enough, it was motorsports writer, authority and raconteur par excellence (just ask him!) and fulltime pompous asshole Eric Gibbon. Eric had the enviable position of field correspondent for the oldest, most respected and arguably most literate motor racing magazine in the English language, *Motoring Sport,* but he was well known around the press room for double-dipping some of his race reports to lesser magazines under a collection of assumed names borrowed from little-known Elizabethan poets. He thought it was hilariously ironic that they'd all died in obscurity and penniless while he was, as he put it, '*putting a few extra bob in my pocket on their behalf.*'

"It was a marvelous party in New York," Eric continued grandly. "Top class all the way." He looked down his nose at me and repeated: "You really should have been there, Lyons."

As was typical for a race-weekend morning, Eric smelled a bit of stale liquor and was shoving as much of the free press breakfast as he could into his face while looking down disdainfully at the pit lane, the stadium-style grandstands and the immense, banked tri-oval laid out in front of us. "This is so bloody American," he proclaimed to no one in particular as he gnawed on a sausage link. "A monument to excess as only the Americans could do it." Eric had a high, loud, irritating sort of voice that made me cringe even more than usual since the track's press relations guy, the pleasant young girl at the media desk and several local Florida newspaper scribes were all well within earshot.

"You don't think much of it, do you?" one of them asked icily.

"I don't think anything of it at all," Eric allowed between smacks of sausage. "It's big and it's dumb and it's bloody interesting as a linoleum floor..."

You could see the press officer stiffen.

"...Mind you, they've put a lot of bloody money and effort in—you can see that on the face of it—but why bother? Why put a bloody road racing circuit inside an overblown football stadium. It makes no sense." He took a swig of tea to wash down his sausage and picked up a forkful of pancakes laden with syrup. "In point of fact," he continued as he chewed, smacked and swallowed, "it's gaudy, it's artificial and it offends the senses."

I generally tried to avoid Eric Gibbon, but running into him at races was more or less an occupational hazard. And I did need favors from him now and then (although he always made me pay for them, if not in cash then in kind). But you had to give the arrogant little bastard his due: he was damn good at what he did and really knew his stuff. Boy, did he *ever* know his stuff! Even so, listening to him expound, expand, elucidate, illuminate, prophesy, proselytize, prattle and pontificate on the world of motor racing (or any other topic) was to fervently desire to punch him in the fucking nose. Or at least that's what it made me want to do, anyway. Although I grudgingly had to agree with his assessment of Big Bill France's monumental new racetrack. But no matter what you thought of it, it was pretty damn rude to talk about it like that in the neat, well-equipped, air-conditioned press room the track had kindly provided and moreover while filling your face with the free breakfast they'd put out for you as well. God knows most of the press facilities in Europe weren't nearly so accommodating. But Eric got an obvious charge out of making people around him uncomfortable. He was pretty damn good at it, too.

Of course the hottest topic of conversation in the Daytona press room was the F.I.A.'s unfathomable and most likely asinine decision to base the 1962 World Manufacturers' Championship on points earned in the GT classes rather than those scored by the all-out sports/prototypes that would actually win all the races. To be honest, it was hard to understand why they'd done it, since the sports/prototypes were the cars that the fans really came out to see. Then again, the F.I.A. seemed to enjoy changing up the rules every now and then just to show everybody they could, and they seemed particularly pleased when it pissed everyone off completely. Particularly the British, Germans and Italians! Eric opined that it was a form of typically Gallic retribution for the way the rest of Europe had essentially mopped the floor with France in two successive world wars. Not to mention that the French hadn't had a serious, world-class racing team in years—not in sports cars *or* Formula One—so the only pride they could puff up or power they could wield was by flexing their political muscle at the F.I.A. headquarters in Paris.

To be honest, the F.I.A.'s new rules didn't sit well with a lot of people, and you could hear the wailing and gnashing of teeth from teams, fans, writers and race promoters almost as soon as they were announced. Not that the F.I.A. in Paris gave a shit. Or at least not until the organizers at Le Mans, *L' Automobile Club de l'Ouest,* announced that they were having none of it and were going with their own rules, classes and scoring at what was surely the most prestigious and important race on the calendar. Not to mention damn near a national holiday in France. And, just to rub a little salt in, *L' Automobile Club de l'Ouest* included a special, Le Mans-only "Experimental" class for sports/prototypes up to 4 liters, even though the F.I.A.'s own limit for sports/racers was capped at 3000cc. Which meant a car that didn't even fit in any recognized F.I.A. class would most likely win the most important race of the year! This set off a terrific row between the F.I.A. in Paris and the organizers at Le Mans just 200 kilometers up the road, and Eric and I agreed that there's nothing quite so entertaining as one group of stubborn, outraged, opinionated and indignant Frenchmen having an extended difference of opinion with another group of stubborn, outraged, opinionated and indignant Frenchmen. "It's great political theatre," Eric snickered, "and absolutely guaranteed never to arrive at any sort of amicable solution."

"Much the opposite," I had to agree, and we both laughed.

Eric polished off his last gnaw of sausage. "You know," he sighed philosophically, "No Englishman ever really understands the French. History proves it. Oh, one comes to appreciate their charm, wit and style, but one also learns to steer well clear of their petty prides, politics and posturing."

I seemed to recall him using the exact same alliteration about the Italians a year before at Monza.

Speaking of Italians, who should wander in next but charming, diminutive and generally delightful little Italian motorsports journo Vincenzo Pittacora. Or "Vinci," as everybody called him. He was a stylish, nattily dressed little guy from Milan with neatly slicked-back hair, an Adolphe Menjou mustache and terribly sad eyes that women found irresistible. Although he didn't have much English, Vinci had a way of making himself understood through a combination of sighs, winks and hand gestures, and he always seemed to have the inside dope on what was going on at Ferrari. Then again, he wrote wonderful things about Ferrari every time he sat down at his Olivetti portable and did more than a little surreptitious snooping, spying and stooging for Ferrari whenever he was around the British teams or nuzzling up to any F.I.A. officials. It was an open secret that Ferrari's race shop had been hard at work all winter on a new model aimed at maximizing their World Manufacturers' Championship chances under the new rules along with a rumored "something special" for the new 4-liter "Experimental Prototype" class at Le Mans. Old Enzo would be officially unveiling his new GTO at his annual press conference in Maranello on February 24th (even though his existing Short Wheelbase Berlinettas were already the class of the Grand Touring field) and his race shop was already well along on a special, 4-liter version of its well-proven Testa Rossa sports/racer aimed at another overall victory at Le Mans. Although how Enzo got advance notice about the new rules at Le Mans was something of a mystery. Oh, I knew that Ferrari kept a powerful and influential French industrialist on his so-called "board of directors" (not that Ferrari took much in the way of direction from anybody!) and it was generally suspected that this particular, well-connected gentleman had a way of eavesdropping and intervening on Ferrari's behalf with the F.I.A. bigwigs in Paris and the *L'Automobile Club de l'Ouest* officials down the road at Le Mans. In return, Ferrari allowed him the opportunity to buy specially tweaked, custom-coachwork Ferraris that just weren't available to the average customer. Vinci Pittacora answered with a knowing shrug when I asked him about it, but of course Eric Gibbon said he'd known all about it for quite some time. "Ferrari doesn't like to lose," Eric explained like he was bored with it, "and Enzo knows how to play the insider political game better than anybody."

Vinci shot me a snide little wink to show we shared a common opinion of Eric Gibbon, and then wandered over to have a few choice words—in halting, uncertain English liberally oiled with florid, mellifluous Italian—with the pretty young college girl at the media counter. He even turned up the pain in his eyes a little for the occasion.

Eric looked up at me from the remains of his breakfast. *"So!"* he exclaimed with a vicious little flourish, "I understand your magazine's on the block."

I blinked a couple times. "I beg your pardon."

"Oh. Sorry," he apologized, not meaning a word of it. "Didn't know you were still in the dark...."

I could feel my eyes narrowing. I hadn't heard a thing. "Oh, really?" I said like it was no big thing to me. "Do you mind telling me what you've heard?"

"Oh, it might be just a loose rumor, of course..." he continued airily as he picked up another syrupy sausage link between his thumb and forefinger, inspected it in front of his nose, bit off half of it and made a dramatic little circle in the air with remaining end "...you know how those things go 'round and 'round."

He was stringing me along and I knew it. And I could tell the little weasel was loving it, too. "So," I prodded again. "What have you heard?"

"Oh, this and that," he continued in cat-and-mouse fashion. "Just the stuff that's out there...."

"Out *where?*" I could feel the heat coming up around my ears.

"You know..." he shoved the remaining bit of sausage his mouth and started chewing "...out there in the ozone."

I was getting well past impatient, and I'm sure Eric noticed my hands clenching and unclenching. But he just sat there and gloated at me with his eyes. And that's when I grabbed him by the fucking shirt collar and yanked him up to where the tip of my nose was damn near poking him in the eye. *"DAMMIT, ERIC!"* I snarled. *"Spill it. What the fuck do you know??!!"* To be honest, I surprised myself a little. I'm generally more on the receiving end of threats and bullying rather than dishing them out. But don't press me too far.

In any case, it sure startled the hell out of Eric Gibbon. He tried to pull back from me—eyes wide as fried eggs—but I had a good, solid grip on him and he wasn't going anywhere. *"You know,"* he squeaked helplessly, like everybody and his brother already knew all about it: *"the rumor about Pletsch and Deering buying up Car and Track..."*

A sinking feeling went through me. *"WHO??!!"*

"Pletsch and Deering. The big New York publishing house. Bloody colossal, in fact." I let go of his shirt and he shook himself upright. Eric was always quick to get his composure back. His arrogance, too. He leaned his head back so he could stare down his nose at me again. "You've heard of them, I'm sure...."

I was sure I had, too. Only I couldn't remember when, where or in what context. The names sure sounded familiar, though.

"...Talk of a wholesale buyout is what I've heard," Eric explained as he dabbed at the corners of his mouth with a napkin. There were still bits of sausage and pancake stuck in his beard when he was done. "But of course there may be nothing to it at all." And with that he gave me a maddeningly indifferent smile, rose up on his stubby little legs and waddled importantly out of the press room. He left his breakfast mess behind for someone else to clean up, too....

I was still trying to make sense of it when my old race-photographer friend Hal Crockett came banging through the press room door with cameras, lenses and camera bags hanging all over him. He was a big, tall guy with a bushy beard and a game leg from getting hit hard by an errant club racer at Savannah many years before, and you could see he'd had a tough time climbing the steps to the press room. "You ought to take up another line of work," I snickered at him.

"I'm not good at anything else," he snorted right back, and set to work changing lenses and loading film into his collection of Nikons. He had pet names for each one of them. He always carried the fast black-and-white film in "Speedy Gonzales," the really slow Kodachrome 25 in "Randy Rembrandt," the medium-speed black-and-white in "Henry the Handyman" and the faster color stock in "Sunset Lil." He was a hell of a shooter, and if you listened close, you could hear him kind of muttering to his cameras—talking to them—while he was working. He talked to his decrepit and decaying old bullet-nose Studebaker Land Cruiser the same way, and had me halfway convinced that was the only way to keep the damn thing running. We'd worked on quite a few race reports and magazine projects together, and I was always impressed with his lens work. Oh, I kidded myself that I was something of a shooter in my own right and I could usually manage to come up with a few decent images if I shot enough film. The problem was coming out on the plus side after I paid for the damn processing. You're supposed to be able to bill the magazine for that (in fact, some shooters just send in their rolls of film and let the art directors take it from there) but I was always kind of embarrassed to let Warren and Isabelle know how many rolls of film it took to fudge my way to a few useable images. Hal called that "the rule of big numbers," and he didn't have much use for it. He'd had a promising career coming up as an advertising/fashion-magazine shooter before he got sucked into the world of automobile racing. Like a lot of other writers and photographers—me included—it wound up drawing him in like a moth to a flame. And that's what put him in what he figured was a reasonably secure position not too far from Savannah's Turn One when two cars got tangled up in the braking zone and one of them bounced off at a screwy angle, took a weird, gyrating leap off the edge of the grass and pretty much mowed him down. "I saw it coming and did everything just the way I should to get my ass out of the way," he'd tell you, the irony hardly lost on him, "but that damn car was *after* me...."

The accident put Hal in the hospital for quite a long, painful spell, but he was back at it again once he got well enough—game leg and all—and you'd still see him shooting from places where a lot of other photographers simply wouldn't go. And the pictures he took spoke for themselves. But there wasn't a lot of money in it if you were just out free-lancing for the newspapers and magazines. So Hal worked hard at getting shooting assignments from teams and sponsors, which were steadier and paid better. His big break came when Lucky Casner hired him on as "official photographer" for his CAMORADI USA racing team. Of course that was back at the beginning when Casner had promised, hustled and sweet-talked his way into a truly amazing pile of cash—a lot of it from Goodyear Tire—and he was buying cars, signing name drivers and generally spreading it around just as fast as he could bring it in. Sometimes even faster. And Hal did a good job for Lucky Casner's team. Right up until the sponsors started asking questions and the money started running out.

Hal and I had shared a few cheap hotel rooms together as a way to cut down on expenses during race weekends, and he was always a good kind of roommate to have because we appreciated a lot of the same things—like the slinky, sultry women some of the playboy drivers and rich team owners had at their elbows and seedy little small-town restaurants where the waitresses were missing a few teeth and you could get a genuine southern breakfast with eggs, ham, grits, biscuits and gravy for less than a buck. Hal moreover knew how to keep his mouth shut when I was trying to write. Even when it was two or three in the morning and I'd locked myself in the bathroom with my trusty Olivetti portable on my knees so as not to wake him up (although at that time of night, my supposedly "silent" Olivetti Lettera 22 sounded like a small-caliber machine gun). But he never even brought it up. Oh, Hal was a little bit of a rough character and he could have a short fuse and an unforgiving attitude at times, but he was maybe the only person I'd ever known who could transform being irritable, irascible and taciturn into engaging personality traits.

"You going to Sebring?" he grunted without looking up from his cameras.

"Sure. Wouldn't miss it."

He twisted his eyes up at me. "You been there before?"

"You know I have."

"And you still wouldn't miss it?"

We had a pretty good laugh off of that. And then we talked a bit about this new track at Daytona—he obviously shared a lot of the same aesthetic misgivings I had—and also about maybe sharing a room again in the cheap, hidden-away little motel nobody else knew about that he'd found between a defunct used car lot and a building materials yard no too far south of Sebring. It generally catered to migrant fruit-pickers, but cheap rooms were hard to come by near Sebring on the 12 Hour weekend.

"Sure," I told him. "We could split a room."

"You're shitty company."

"So are you."

"Good. It's a date." He stuck his hand out, but quickly thumbed it over his shoulder hitchhiker-style when I put mine out to shake it.

We had a good laugh off of that, too. And then I asked him if he'd heard any-thing about *Car and Track* being sold.

"Nah," he said as he fussed with his Nikons. "But don't go by me. I never hear anything until after it's already ancient history. And even then I don't generally lis-ten. Hell, I don't even know if the Spanish Civil War's been settled yet!"

I have to admit Eric's news about the magazine possibly being sold had shaken me a little. Hell, I'd been with *Car and Track* since almost the very beginning. But I also knew Warren and Isabelle, and I didn't think they'd do anything like that without talking to me about it first. After all, they'd always been straight and honest with me. And I knew they appreciated my work. But you never really know about people, do you? Especially when money's involved. And it crossed my mind more than once that, should *Car and Track* be sold, that weasel Eric Gibbon would be in there angling for my job before the ink was even dry on the contracts. And I had to grudgingly admit that it made a lot of sense. Race reporting doesn't exactly pay very well, and there are always travel expenses to consider. Plus Eric already had a track record when it came to covering the same events for multiple magazines (under assumed *noms de plume,* of course), and there were obvious economies of scale involved and financial benefits on both sides. I decided I'd better give Is-abelle a call to check things out. And also to find out whatever I could about this Pletsch and Deering outfit. But there was no point going off in a mad panic and calling the magazine office 8am California time. And then I wondered if that might not be exactly what Eric wanted me to do. I wouldn't put it past him. No, probably best to go at this quietly and carefully. Besides, I had a race report to do. So I stuffed one last chunk of blueberry muffin into my face, drained the last of my cof-fee, grabbed my copy of the entry list and headed off into the paddock to check out the cars and teams.

If you love racing, you can't help but enjoy wandering through the first Thursday morning paddock of a new season. You can feel the buzz of anticipation and the giddy, cautious optimism—hey, nobody's lost anything yet!—percolating in the air. And it's invigorating, no matter how many times you've done it or how clearly you can already see who'll be going home with the shiny trophies and prize money and who'll just be going home.

Of course my first stop had to be the Ferrari garages. Only they weren't really garages at Daytona, just a bunch of evenly-spaced wooden posts with corrugated metal roofing nailed on top. But the weather was generally pretty friendly at Day-tona, and so the open-air "garages" were plenty good enough to keep the sun and rain off the cars and crews. Even when the rain came down in gushing torrents, as it tends to do now and then down in Florida. The only real garage at Daytona was at the far east end of the paddock by the gas pumps, and one of the teams—none of the English or European regulars seemed sure which one—had somehow managed to commandeer it for the weekend. But they had it buttoned up like a drum with the overhead doors down and the windows covered over with newspaper. I made a mental note to cruise by later on and see what I could find out.

No question Ferrari was the odds-on favorite in both the Sports/Prototype and GT classes at Daytona, even though the official Scuderia Ferrari factory team hadn't bothered to make the trip. But they'd sent a couple obviously factory cars for North American distributor Carlo Sebastian to enter, along with a set of animated, gesticulating Italian mechanics with thick Modenese accents. Not to mention a full compliment of top factory drivers like Phil Hill, Cal Carrington, teenage Mexican phenom Ricardo Rodriguez and none other than Stirling Moss wheeling the odd-looking, softly rounded, ice blue-with-white-stripes Berlinetta Le Mans Speciale Aerodinamico Audrey had mentioned on the plane. Plus Carlo Sebastian almost always had a few seats available (most often in good but somewhat second-tier cars) for dilettante drivers with acceptable experience and a fat checkbook or up-and-coming hopefuls with a sugar daddy or sponsor eager to advance their careers. Beyond that, you had the usual collection of "customer" Ferraris of varying types, class and speed potential in the hands of privateer teams. Ferrari was just a tiny, autocratic little fiefdom in the worldwide automobile business, but they'd come to dominate the motorsports scene in almost every category they'd attempted. That's because, beyond all the talent, effort and experience, Ferrari was a *racer,* and totally committed to winning at all costs. So when flash-in-the-pan successes like Maserati's Tipo 61 Birdcage or the threatening new crop of mid-engined, Formula One-based sports/racers from British constructors like the Cooper and Lotus threatened to put old Enzo and his team on their collective back foot, they'd double-down and work even harder to claw their way back to the top again. You had to respect that kind of passion, desire and dedication, no matter what you thought about the Machiavellian politics and fulminating polemics at Ferrari.

I found most of the top Ferraris clustered under in a set of open-air garages near the far west end of the paddock, and the car closest to me as I approached was the nicely prepared 250 Short Wheelbase Berlinetta that suave, aristocratic Belgian ace Olivier Gendebien was going to drive for enthusiastic young Italian Count Giovanni Volpi di Misurata's Scuderia Serenissima team. And that was a story all by itself:

Young Count Giovanni was born into impossibly well-to-do circumstances. His family had been among the very top tier of Venetian wealth, privilege and nobility for generations, and his well-connected father Giuseppe served as a governor and then finance minister under Benito Mussolini. But son Giovanni had no such aspirations, and was smitten by the glamour and challenge of motor racing from a very early age. So when he finally came into his inheritance in 1960 at the age of 24, he immediately formed his own racing team, Scuderia Serenissima, and started buying up the very latest and best of whatever Ferrari or Maserati (or anyone else) had on offer. Young Count Giovanni approached his racing seriously as well as impetuously, and he got a lot of good advice and signed good talent—both behind the wheel and in the pits—and Scuderia Serenissima quickly emerged as one of the more formidable, well-financed, well-prepared and successful privateer teams. The factories all loved the young count because his money was good and he liked to field the best cars he could find in both the sports/prototype and GT classes. Which meant he bought a *lot* of cars. And paid out even more to the factory customer race shops for the latest updates and modifications, between-race engine, transmission and rear-end rebuilds and the usual and unavoidable crash damage and mechanical repairs. Better yet, his checks always cleared...unlike a lot of other team owners who came and went from time to time.

But the young count had fallen out of favor with Ferrari ever since he'd helped bankroll a group of renegade Ferrari employees—including competition director Carlo Chiti, racing team manager Romolo Tavoni and talented, hands-on Short Wheelbase Berlinetta and GTO development engineer Giotto Bizzarrini—who'd walked out *en masse* (or been fired *en masse,* depending on whose version of the story you chose to believe) in November of 1961. The defectors must have felt pretty sure of themselves at the time. The shark-nosed sports cars and open-wheelers they'd designed, built and campaigned for Ferrari had essentially steamrollered the opposition in both Formula One *and* the World Manufacturers' Championship throughout the '61 season. Flushed with that success and figuring they'd had about enough of the politics and swirling intrigues at Ferrari—especially Enzo's prickly and meddlesome wife Laura, who'd taken to traveling with the race team as her husband's spy and was forever sticking her nose in where it wasn't wanted—they decided to confront *Il Commendatore* with their grievances. They were fed up with Ferrari's autocratic, manipulative management style and the way he pitted them one against the other to keep them down and in line and hogged all the limelight for himself. I suppose it was a battle of egos as much as anything, and the story I heard from Vinci Pittacora was that the disgruntled lieutenants confronted Ferrari face-to-face after at the end of the '61 season. But instead of listening and negotiating or softening his position, old Enzo acted hurt, martyred and betrayed and dug his heels in even deeper. So they all quit (or were fired?) and quickly formed their own company on the other side of Modena under the A.T.S. *(Automobili Turismo e Sport)* banner, and prepared to design and build their own high-end GT and racing cars with an eye towards beating Ferrari at his own game. And it was the rich and perhaps somewhat naive young Count Giovanni who became one of their chief financial benefactors. Naturally Ferrari was furious about this "defection of the brains" (as my friend Vinci Pittacora quickly dubbed it), and even less enamored of the young

Venetian count who'd helped the mutineers with their financing. As a result, it didn't look like Scuderia Serenissima would be getting any of the latest and best out of Ferrari any more. Or much of anything else, for that matter.

Ba Fangu!

The irony at Daytona was that the paddock stewards had inadvertently stuck Count Giovanni's Scuderia Serenissima Short Wheelbase Berlinetta under the same corrugated tin roof with Carlo Sebastian's more or less factory works team Ferraris, and you could feel a little bit of tension in the air, even though all the drivers and mechanics knew each other and had worked side-by-side over the years. That sort of camaraderie just doesn't evaporate with changing team allegiances or signatures on paychecks, and Count Giovanni went even further to ease the situation by inviting everybody—and I mean *everybody!*—in the Ferrari garages to a big, blowout party Friday evening aboard his newly launched and utterly spectacular Benetti motor yacht, *L'Albatro d'Oro,* which he had moored conveniently at dockside just a few minutes down the road in Daytona Beach. That's the kind of thing you can do if you have style, breeding, a large helping of noblesse oblige and a truly obscene old family bankroll to back it all up.

Like all the other scribes, I wanted to get a closer look at Carlo Sebastian's ice-blue-with-white-racing-stripes Berlinetta Le Mans Speciale Aerodinamico that Stirling Moss was slated to drive. It was unusual and even a little scary to see Moss in a quasi-factory Ferrari, and Vinci Pittacora told me in a combination of words and gestures that Moss had actually done some of the initial testing on the car at Monza with none other than old Enzo himself in attendance. And that was surprising news since everyone knew Stirling had avoided driving Ferraris ever since that fateful September day in 1951 when he showed up at Bari for what was supposed to be his first-ever drive for the team and found that "his" car had been given away to Italian champion Piero Taruffi. And that's a story worth repeating:

By 1951, just about everyone recognized what a special sort of talent young Stirling Moss was, and what followed was your typical, intrigue-laden Ferrari soap opera. It started with a note from Enzo himself—delivered through a respected member of the British Racing Drivers' Club—inviting young Stirling to drive for Scuderia Ferrari at Rouen in France and the British Grand Prix at Silverstone. But Moss had already agreed to drive for the game-but-hopeless little HWM team in the French race, and Stirling was simply not the sort to go back on his word. But Ferrari would have none of it. It was both races or nothing! So Stirling found himself stuck in the HWM in France (which retired with a broken gearbox) while Scuderia Ferrari cruised to yet another crushing victory.

At that point, Stirling must have thought his chance with Ferrari had passed him by. But another communication arrived from Italy less than a week later. Enzo wanted Stirling to come down to the factory for a face-to-face meeting. So 21-year-old Stirling, accompanied by his father, traveled down to Maranello and sat across the desk from old man Ferrari in his famous private office. And there, in an awkward combination of poor French and almost non-existent English and Italian, they hammered out a deal. Stirling would be given a car for the non-championship Bari Grand Prix on September 2nd and, if all went well, he would join the team for the South American Temporada races over the winter and, if that also went well, a full factory drive was in the offing for the '52 season.

Only when Stirling arrived at the pits in Bari and tried to lower himself into what he assumed was "his" car to try it on for size, the Ferrari mechanics shooed him away. That was Piero Taruffi's car, and there was no Ferrari at Bari for any green but promising young Englishman named Stirling Moss....

In Ferrari's defense, he'd come under intense pressure from the race promoter to put Taruffi in the car in front of the highly partisan Italian crowd. Not to mention that Ferrari always liked to keep his drivers (and the rest of his staff) off balance, on the defensive and in their place. And his favored method was to keep them endlessly guessing and worrying about their position on the team. No question Enzo believed it made them try harder and risk more. Sometimes even more than they were willing to give. But it was a rude awakening for young Stirling about the way old man Ferrari did business. And he never forgot it.

As a result, Moss spent most of his brilliant career racing *against* the Ferraris. He preferred driving for British teams anyway (his stint as Number Two to Fangio on the Mercedes team notwithstanding) and he proved to be quite a major thorn in Ferrari's side, playing a key role in Vanwall's Grand Prix Constructor's Championship in 1958, Aston Martin's Le Mans victory and World Manufacturers' Championship in 1959 and single-handedly beating the powerful and dominant shark-nose Ferraris with Rob Walker's Lotus at the grands prix of Monaco and the Nurburgring in 1961.

But the results were almost a foregone conclusion whenever Moss did climb behind the wheel of a Ferrari. Like at the Nassau Speed Week in December of '57, when Moss lent his works Aston DBR2 to an attractive young driver from California for the Ladies' Race. She somehow managed to roll it into a ball while dicing for the lead with Denise McCluggage's Porsche, and the car was battered beyond immediate repair. That's when another car owner offered Stirling his somewhat shopworn Farrari for the balance of the week, and Moss won both feature races with it. And Stirling utterly decimated the field two years in a row at the GT-only Tourist Trophy at Goodwood driving a Scottish-blue-with-white-stripe-around-its-nose Short Wheelbase Berlinetta for his friend and oftentimes car entrant Rob Walker of the Johnny Walker whiskey family. There were even rumors going around about a secret deal to sell Rob a brand new Ferrari 156 Formula One car for Moss to drive—in Walker colors, of course—during the upcoming '62 Grand

Prix season. And that had all the other teams very nervous indeed. Especially since Stirling's regular mechanic, Alf Francis, had shown more than once that he could tweak and tune a racecar better than the factory who built it! A Scottish-blue-with-white-stripe-'round-its-nose Rob Walker Cooper with Alf Francis spinning the wrenches and Stirling at the wheel had scored Cooper's first-ever Formula One victory in Argentina in 1958, and the team did the same for Lotus when they won with their Lotus 18 at Monaco in 1960. You put the best driver in the quickest car, throw in a decisive team owner and a sharp, clever mechanic with a free hand to try his own ideas (while neatly side-stepping the usual pecking order, politics, divisiveness and infighting of your usual factory team) and, if you have luck and things break right, you can leave everybody else pretty much scrambling for leftovers.

In any case, it was apparent that Stirling's position regarding driving Ferraris had softened a bit. He remained rightfully wary of the factory team, but with Carlo Sebastian running the show (and moreover eager to win those all-important World Manufacturers' Championship points for Ferrari in the GT class) plus a fat wad of starting money on offer, he'd agreed to drive the GTO-prototype Berlinetta Le Mans Speciale Aerodinamico at Daytona. Although he wasn't entirely happy about it, and had some typically direct, Moss-like comments about the F.I.A.'s new rules: *"It's a shame that the winning car that will actually receive the Manufacturers' Championship points cannot possibly finish first overall against the pure racing sports cars."* You could always count on Moss to speak his mind. And he echoed what a lot of us in the press corps were already thinking.

There's no question that all the in-the-know types in the press room—myself, Vinci Pittacora and Eric Gibbon included—reckoned Stirling and his Berlinetta Le Mans Speciale Aerodinamico as the car to beat in the GT ranks. Even so, the Short Wheelbase Berlinetta that was getting the lion's share of the attention from all the homegrown sports writers and local newspaper scribes—far more than Stirling's entry—was the much more standard-issue, deep red entry out of Carlo Sebastian's stable wearing #22—the one with southern stock car hero and iconic Daytona fan favorite Freddie Fritter at the wheel.

Now Freddie Fritter was something of an institution on the southern stock car circuit. I'd never met him, but I'd seen his big, genial mug smiling out at me from literally hundreds of newspaper articles, magazine spreads and victory lane photographs. Freddie was a big, beefy guy with curly black hair, winking, mischievous eyes and a billboard-sized *"glad t'meet ch'all"* smile, and you couldn't find a hog farmer, gas station pump jockey, short order cook or parts store counterman from the Mason-Dixon Line clear down to the southern tip of Florida who didn't absolutely adore him. He was their kind of guy. And the record books left no doubt that Freddie was one hell of a race driver, too. Or at least he was in stock cars, anyway.

Legend had it that Freddie's daddy was founder and proprietor of the best damn moonshine still in all of Franklin County. And Franklin County, Virginia, was widely and rightfully acknowledged as the de facto capital of the un-taxed, non-regulated American distillery business. His operation was tucked quietly away in the woodsy foothills of the Blue Ridge Mountains in the irregular triangle between Charity, Ferrum and Figsboro, and not far at all from the popular little oval track at Martinsville. Most of the locals claimed that Freddie's daddy produced the best damn hooch in all of Franklin County—which, by extension, made it the best damn 'shine on the planet—and testimonials abounded that it was clear as rainwater, went down easy (at least after the first few pulls, anyway) and burned with a pure, silent, near-invisible flame. The story went that young Freddie took time off from school now and then (but never from church!) to help his daddy out in the moonshine business. By the time he was thirteen, Freddie was making middle-of-the-night delivery runs across county lines and into the adjoining states of Kentucky, West Virginia, Tennessee and North Carolina as well. He drove stripped-down, hopped-up Hudsons and Mercurys mostly, with the back seats pulled out and wooden crates bolted to the floorboards to hold the Mason jars full of 'shine that was clear as rainwater and potent as copperhead venom. Freddie and his daddy wrapped those jars in flannel rags and old newspapers to cushion them against the jolts and jostling if the cops gave chase and the run got a little rough. In the beginning, Freddie had to sit on a stack of bed pillows or old Sears Roebuck catalogs just to see over the steering wheel. But that didn't last very long.

Freddie Fritter grew up big, wide, tall and fast, and he took his daddy's line of work seriously. He committed all the twisting mountain two-lanes and dusty gravel back roads to memory—hell, he could drive most of them with the lights turned off at night, even under a new moon—and it became apparent pretty quickly that young Freddie had a genuine knack for fast driving. He also had a hands-on gift for fixing, figuring out and modifying the cars. Like he learned it was better to use a truck rear-axle ratio for acceleration up the hills rather than worrying about top speed that you couldn't use anyway. And you wanted to keep the weight of the 'shine down as low as possible and between the axle centers for better balance. It helped to add a couple leaves to the rear springs and to use two shock absorbers on each end of the axle—one in front and one behind—to make a loaded-down 'shine hauler handle a little sweeter through the curves.

Behind the wheel, Freddie developed an uncanny instinct for knowing when to run like hell and when to simply play possum, switching off the lights and ducking in behind some thicket, tree line, hog pen or farmer's barn until the coast was clear. The law chased him often, but they never got close enough to bring him down. Not even when they had multiple cars and 2-way radios. And things might have continued on like that forever except for a faulty, military-surplus relief valve on a ¾-inch gas line that caused his daddy's still to blow sky-high in spectacular fashion just as he was stocking up merchandise for the 4th of July weekend. The blast set the whole damn mountainside on fire (which burned, according to local legend, with a pure, silent, near-invisible flame) and everyone knows the story of how Freddie heard the explosion and saw the flash in his rearview mirror, did an immediate handbrake turn, charged back up Possum Hill Road without ever touching the brakes, drove right into the flames, grabbed his daddy by the straps of his bib overalls and took him all the way up to the big new hospital in Roanoke with the gas pedal mashed to the firewall and triple digits showing on the speedometer the whole way.

Freddie's daddy was in the hospital the better part of three months while his broken pelvis, fractured skull and burns healed up, and that was followed by a three-and-a-half-year stretch (counting time off for good behavior) as one of Uncle Sam's guests at the federal penitentiary over in Jonesville. Meanwhile, young Freddie was pretty much on his own. And with his daddy's family to take care of, too. All he'd ever known was moonshining, hopping-up cars and fast driving, so Freddie took a job as a wrench-twister at nearby truck stop/farm implement garage over by Boone's Mill, and it's well known everywhere that he owns that same exact place today, and that it's generally regarded as the best damn truck stop in the south. And maybe in the whole cotton-picking country, come to that. Truckers bring their rigs in from all over just to have Freddie and his guys work on them, and the 24-hour restaurant up front has the freshest coffee, tastiest sausage gravy, best grits and fluffiest damn buttermilk pancakes you ever tasted. Best of all, you can still find Freddie himself working there between races, always with that big 'ol *"glad t'meet ch'all"* smile plastered across his face, his coveralls on and most usually either scratching behind the ears of his favorite black-and-tan coon hound, Beauregard, or with a wrench, pliers, screwdriver or prybar in his hand and at least half of his ample torso buried under the hood or up inside the fenderwell of a White, Diamond T, Reo, Kenworth or Peterbilt.

But of course it took a lot of time and even more hard work to build all that up, and Freddie readily admits it was tough going at first. He'd come up in racing the hard way, through two-bit jalopies and gas-station hot rods running at scruffy dirt tracks and poorly paved asphalt ovals all over western Virginia and the surrounding states. And while Freddie could be as fast as anybody when he needed to be and won his share of races—more than his share, in fact—what the fans loved most was the way he kept on smiling, shaking hands, chatting, signing autographs, scratching behind Beauregard's ears and taking it all in stride, win *or* lose. And car owners sure appreciated the way he looked after the equipment and brought their cars home in the points and in the money when they didn't have the steam to win outright. Lots of eager young drivers would just run them into the wall or blow them up trying. Freddie Fritter became justly famous for driving smart, keeping his head, staying out of trouble and saving the car and the tires for the end of the race when it really counted. He'd already won himself two NASCAR championships by the spring of 1962, and he was probably the most recognized face and best-known personality in the game.

Even so, I wondered how he'd get along with a road course and a GT Ferrari. Or how he'd measure up against that good ole English boy Stirling Moss in Carlo Sebastian's *other* 250 Short Wheelbase Berlinetta. The ice-blue one with the funny, sloped-back roof, rounded rump and razor-edged exhaust note. I was also a little curious about how the hell he'd manage to fit in one, since Short Wheelbase Berlinettas weren't exactly built for a guy his size.

I eventually found the dark red #22 over at the far end of the line in the garage area, and I could see the crew had already pulled most of the stuffing out of the seat cushions and one of the Modenese mechanics was in the process of removing the interior door panel to give Freddie a little more elbow room. *"Y'all better butter me up on both sides t'stick me in there,"* Freddie grinned as he strapped on his helmet and got ready to slide behind the wheel. *"And don't be botherin' with no co-driver. Once I'm in that there thing, the only thing's gonna get me out is a checkered flag or a gas fire."* He saw me pointing my camera lens at him as he struggled his way behind the wheel and shot me a half-hearted thumbs-up and a big, friendly smile. *"Hell, three hours ain't much a'anything 'round this here place anyway."*

It was hard not to like this guy.

I saw my old friend Cal Carrington standing in a corner cleaning his goggles and walked up to him. "Good to see you," I told him. And it was.

"It's good to be seen," he grinned back.

"Another season beckons, eh?"

"That it does."

"You looking forward to it?"

"If you're not looking forward to it, you shouldn't be doing it."

"Glad to be back in the States?"

His eyes swept around the garage area and the surrounding paddock like he was seeing it for the very first time. "Hell, Hank, I'm glad to be anywhere."

There were only a handful of sports/prototypes on hand with a realistic shot at winning the race outright, and I was happy to see that Cal was in one of them. But not the one he wanted, and I could tell that was bugging him. Carlo Sebastian had entered two of the factory's latest and quickest mid-engined V6 Dinos but, typical of Ferrari, they were hedging their bets with one of the proven and reliable (if older, heavier and more cumbersome) front-engined Testa Rossa V12s. Newly crowned World Champ Phil Hill and scary-fast young Mexican Ricardo Rodriguez were slated to share one of the new 246SP Dino models, while Cal and promising young

Canadian Peter Ryan were assigned to the front-engined Testa Rossa. To be honest, I thought the older car was better looking than the stubby little 246. It had a certain stature, grace and nobility to it. And the V12 made a far grander noise than the raspy Dino V6. But mid-engined racecars were the wave of the future, and there was no avoiding it. "So," I needled, "they gave you the old nail, didn't they?"

"It's a good car," Cal argued lamely. "It's got more power and top end than the Dino, and Testa Rossas are damn near bulletproof if you take it easy on their clutches and rear ends."

"So you're happy with it?"

The corners of Cal's mouth bent down. "Like I said," he answered evenly, "I'm happy just to be here."

"You're happy to be anywhere, right?"

The old Cal Carrington smile flashed back across his face again. "That's what I said, isn't it?"

We talked a little more about the cars, and you couldn't miss that he was disappointed about not drawing the Dino for the race. Then again, Phil Hill *was* the reigning World Champ—first-ever for an American—and Ricardo Rodriguez was unquestionably blindingly fast and almost desperately brave. Ferrari had a penchant for drivers like that. Plus Ricardo's father habitually brought a fat wallet along, so there was really no question who should have first pick of the cars. That's just the way things were. I didn't say anything, but we both knew how easy it was for a driver to wind up on the outs at Ferrari. Or any other team, for that matter. But especially at Ferrari.

About then one of the mechanics squirted some gas down the intake trumpets of the Testa Rossa's carburetors while another whirred the starter and a third sat inside working the throttle linkage, and a heartbeat later the 3-liter V12 erupted into life. What a sound! There's no finer mechanical aria on earth than the snarl, whirr and howl of a Ferrari V12. It makes the hairs inside your ears tingle. Two of the mechanics moved over to start the smaller V6 in the Dino parked next to it while the third kept blipping the Testa Rossa's throttles to warm up the engine. You could see people stopping in their tracks and peering in to see where that marvelous sound was coming from.

"I'll come by after practice to see how you like the track," I hollered over the din.

"I'll like it fine," Cal hollered back as he strapped on his helmet.

I have to admit I was a little curious about how Cal's older but more powerful Testa Rossa would compare with the lighter and far handier 246SP Dino of Hill and Rodriguez at Daytona. And also how Freddie Fritter's #22 GT Ferrari would fare against Stirling Moss in the crisp-sounding, GTO-prototype Berlinetta Le Mans Speciale Aerodinamico. Not to mention Clive Stanley's pale green Aston Zagato with young hotshoe Ian Snell and my old friend Tommy Edwards sharing the driving and my intriguing new acquaintance Audrey Denbeigh handling the timing and scoring! Not that the Aston was anything more than a longshot when it came to overall Category 1 (over 2-liter) GT honors and the World Manufacturers' Championship points that went along with it. Or at least not without a lot of bad luck for a very large number of GT Ferraris! But I hadn't seen my ex-fighter-pilot chum Tommy Edwards in quite a long time, so I wandered down to Clive Stanley's pit box as the cars began queuing up for first practice. Besides, Audrey would probably be there. Not to mention that I'd always been a big Aston fan, and was really thrilled for them when they surprised old man Ferrari by winning both the 24 Hours of Le Mans *and* the World Manufacturers' Championship in 1959. But after that they more or less folded up their tent and went home. Mission accomplished, don't you know? Oh, their cars soldiered on with a few privateer teams, and their DB4GTs acquitted themselves fairly well in the GT class. But they were clumsy and heavyish compared to the best of the Ferrari Berlinettas, so Aston commissioned highly regarded but regularly outlandish Italian coachbuilder Zagato to build them a lighter, aerodynamically sleeker version specifically for GT racing. The resulting car was stunningly handsome from any angle, and looked like it actually might be able to challenge the Short Wheelbase Berlinettas for overall GT honors. But even though it had a bigger engine and ran a higher displacement class than the Short Wheelbase Berlinettas, the DB4GT Zagato was never quite light, poised or refined enough to beat the best of the Ferraris. Even back home in England, where Rob Walker's familiar, Scottish blue Ferrari Berlinetta with the white stripe around its nose (and Stirling Moss behind the wheel, of course!) was always the car to beat. Not to mention that there were always a lot of Ferraris running around in the GT category—including occasional factory and quasi-factory entries—against never more than one or two privateer Astons. And Ferrari's favored "concessionaire" teams always had the latest development tweaks (assuming someone had come up with the right-sized bag of lira) not to mention excellent spares support and experienced, race-savvy team managers and mechanics. And that made them even harder to beat. Especially in the longer races like Sebring and Le Mans.

Even so, there always seemed to be a supply of wealthy, patriotic, stiff-upper-lip Englishmen eager to "show the flag" and take on the Italians with an all-British team. And Clive Stanley was most assuredly one of them. Clive's family owned the Imperial Crown Tea brand along with some large, valuable chunks of English, Canadian and Bahamian real estate, a share of an auction house and a thoroughbred horse farm in Kentucky and a significant stake in a Midlands trunk railway, a South African diamond mine and a commercial shipping yard. Among other holdings. All of which made Clive what you might well call "a wealthy sportsman." He was also what you also might well call "a twit."

Clive originally got involved with racing while idling away the late fall and early winter of 1955 at his family's posh holiday estate on Nassau Island in the Bahamas. And that just happened to be the November when rogue race chairman and promoter extraordinaire Red Crise produced the first-ever Nassau Speed Weeks. Clive saw the entire thing from a front-row seat since his family was close with island enthusiasts Sir Harry and Lady Greta Oakes—they traveled in the same circles, don't you know?—who served as de facto host, hostess and all-purpose social directors for the entire, week-long party. They even arranged a borrowed XK120 for Clive to drive in the "all islanders" race, but he managed to spin it into the underbrush at the very first corner and never completed a lap. Even so, Clive Stanley was smitten. Although he never drove again himself—*"I leave that to my stalwart lads,"* he'd say with a soft, buttery lilt to his voice—he was enraptured and infatuated by the excitement, noise, speed, challenge, drama, style and glamour of motor racing. Clive Stanley absolutely adored drama, style and glamour. Not to mention his appreciation for all the daring, devil-may-care and occasionally desperate young racing drivers out looking for rides. Clive Stanley was rumored to be much enamored of them as well.

Although initially opposed to it, Clive's family eventually came around and agreed to let him pursue his interest in motor sport (as a team owner, anyway) since it got him rather conveniently out of the way. And most of them considered that a good thing, as Clive could be something of an embarrassment in certain social and business situations. Their only stipulations were that he should never actually race the cars himself not that he wanted to and that he must only campaign British cars and that they must furthermore always be painted in the rather unfortunate sickly pale green with antique gold accents of the Imperial Crown Tea tins and boxes. And also—please God!—that he should keep his name out of the bloody papers except for occasional, discreet mentions in the sports sections.

Clive Stanley was a slender, agitated little wisp of a man with thin lips, sad, eternally dissatisfied eyes and a flop of fine, white hair that he was forever brushing out of his eyes with pale, delicate hands ending in perfectly manicured fingernails. Clive was terribly careful about his appearance, and you never saw him anywhere without the appropriate tie and jacket: light pastel or brass-buttoned, Navy blue blazers for the late spring and summer and proper paddock tweeds with occasional leather shooting patches for the fall and winter months. He fancied hats, too, but they absolutely *had* to match the rest of his outfit. And he was equally obsessive about his watches, belts and shoes. For Thursday morning's practice session at Daytona, he'd fettled himself out in crisply creased, grayish-blue dress pants, a matching shirt, an off-white linen jacket plus a matching, off-white bow tie, off-white under grayish-blue saddle shoes (I figured he had to have those custom made) and topped it all off with a graceful, off-white Borsalino fedora with a matching, grayish-blue silk band above the brim. He looked like he'd stepped out of a toney magazine ad for expensive, single-malt scotch.

I'd met Clive a few times at race meetings and club events in England, and I always thought he was an okay sort of guy. A little urgent, fussy and whiny for my tastes, but no question he loved his racing and desperately wanted to do well at it. To be honest, I think he wanted to be taken seriously as much as anything. Clive knew quite a bit about cars and racing (or what you could pick up from books and magazines, anyway) but he was thoroughly hopeless when it came to any kind of hands-on mechanical work. Plus he tended to get flustered, anguished and dramatic over any little thing that went wrong. Any little thing at all. Which, to be honest, is not really what you want from a team owner involved in endurance racing. Oh, he was good enough at organizing menu, cold drink and snack details and absolutely meticulous when it came to getting the tires, fuel and oil, signaling equipment, tools and likely spares neatly organized in the team's pit stall. But he was a disaster under fire when the chips were down. A successful team manager needs to be calm, keen, decisive, strategically oriented, brutally realistic, ruthlessly opportunistic and always ready and willing to improvise, and not one of those things came naturally to Clive Stanley. Which tended to make his Imperial Crown Tea team a bit of a shambles now and then during races.

Ultimately Clive bit the bullet and hired on the highly regarded and experienced Geoff Britten as team manager during the 1960 season, and everyone on the scene—myself included—was waiting to see how that would work out. The two were as different as chalk and cheese, and their squabbles and differences of opinion were already legendary on the British club racing scene. Geoff was a shrewd, severe and terribly serious racing man who was well respected almost everywhere. He hadn't come from money or privilege, but as a young apprentice he swapped tires and sparkplugs for Woolf Barnato and the Bentley Boys, and learned and earned his way up while they were winning the 24 Hours of Le Mans four times in a row and five years out of seven between 1924 and 1930. During the war years, he served as a sapper and maintenance engineer for Montgomery's armored divisions as they fought claw-and-nail against Rommel in North Africa. That victory won, Geoff's mechanical and organizational skills helped push Hitler's panzers the rest of the way across Europe to the outskirts of Berlin. The war years tempered Geoff Britten into a tough, resourceful, disciplined and tight-lipped sort with a genuine gift for assessing situations, prioritizing needs, making decisions, taking responsibility and getting things done. And it was that experience and those exact qualities that made him such a brilliant team manager. Geoff Britten rarely ever shouted, but he could achieve much the same effect by simply lowering his voice to a cold, terse whisper under a fierce, withering glare. Tommy Edwards said he learned that trick as right-hand man to John "Death Ray" Wyer at Aston Martin during the late 1950s.

But Aston cut back their racing program some said wisely after their long-sought Le Mans victory and almost afterthought World Manufacturers' Championship in 1959, and Geoff more or less "came with the car" when Clive Stanley bought an ex-works Aston DBR1 sports/racer to replace his ageing Jaguar D-Type in the early spring of 1960. Geoff brought Georgie Smales along with him. They'd known each other since the fighting against Rommel in North Africa, when Georgie was a tank, truck and armored car wrench and Geoff was his superior officer. Geoff had had helped Georgie hire on at Aston after the war and then brought him along to Clive Stanley's team. Not that Georgie Smales was a particularly gifted mechanic. But he was married to Geoff's sister and reasonably honest and loyal, and that made up for a lot of incompetence, indolence and sloth.

It was a difficult proposition trying to put together a serious privateer team, assemble the right sort of personnel with the right kind of chemistry and deal with Clive Stanley's oft-unpredictable whims and fancies. And nowhere were their ideas more at odds than when it came to picking drivers. Clive tended to prefer young, daring, on-their-way-up (or out) hard-charger types, while Geoff favored smooth, steady, experienced and mechanically sympathetic journeymen who could be counted on to take care of the equipment and bring the damn thing home. Chargers were fine in a sprint race, but you needed a thoughtful, steady hand to get to the end of 1000 twisting kilometers at the Nurburgring, 12 hard, pounding hours at Sebring or twice around the clock at Le Mans. Initially Clive won out because he controlled those two most vital pieces of racing equipment on any motorsports team the pen and the checkbook! but a series of broken cars and not much to show for it eventually brought him closer to Geoff Britten's line of thinking. In fact, it was Geoff who recommended signing Tommy Edwards so he could serve as a steadying influence on Clive's seemingly endless string of aggressive young hot-shoes. And Tommy was thankful for the opportunity. Hell, at that stage of his career, he was happy for *any* opportunity.

I knew Tommy well because he was a great friend of my ace race mechanic pal Buddy Palumbo, and the three of us had shared a lot of adventures and excitement together. Tommy was a Brit, of course, and came from an upper-crust family that had pretty much run out of money (if not name or lingering social standing) during the tough depression years between the wars. He'd served as an R.A.F. pilot, squadron leader and flight instructor during the war years, and met and married a well-to-do American USO volunteer named Ronnie who came from an old-money New York banking family with an estate up in Westchester County. She brought Tommy back to the states with her after the armistice, but peacetime, domestic tranquility and the family banking business bored him to distraction. He flat couldn't stand it, and seemed to miss the danger and desperate circumstances he'd experienced during the war. Not to mention the excitement and camaraderie that went along with them. Tommy finally bought himself an Allard J2X with a Cadillac V8 stuffed inside (on her family's money, of course) and went racing. It turned out he was pretty good at it, and Tommy won several important stateside races—including Watkins Glen—and even co-drove with Sydney Allard himself at Le Mans. A lot of us ranked him as one of the best drivers around in the early 1950s. Me included. But then he got blamed for an accident that wasn't really his fault at Watkins Glen in 1952—his Allard got forced off-line and sideswiped the crowd at the south end of Franklin Street, killing a 7-year-old boy and injuring dozens more—and the SCMA pulled his license for a year in the aftermath. He and Ronnie were divorced not long after that, and Buddy told me he started drinking too much as everything seemed to be falling apart around him. But eventually he went back to England, got a British license and tried hard to make a career for himself out of racing. Only without the requisite fat wad of cash in his back pocket. Very few drivers make it on talent and determination alone.

Ask anyone.

But Tommy pressed on, and eventually landed a spot as sort of a bring-it-home journeyman for John Wyer's factory Aston Martin team in the mid-1950s. He worked hard at it, and learned enough technically to be useful as a test driver. But it was tough duty as the team struggled to develop the cars, and it got even tougher when Stirling Moss was hired on as the team's star driver in 1958. Aston already had Carroll Shelby and Roy Salvadori, and they were both formidable teammates. Comparisons with Moss made things even more difficult. Although his star never really rose at Aston (nor was it expected to), Tommy took care of the cars, didn't make silly mistakes and held his own in that company more often than not, and I was not alone in considering him an excellent choice for any long-distance racing team. He was never going to be the fastest driver around any more. Not at his age (he never mentioned it, but I reckoned him to be in his early fifties by then) and moreover burdened by the knowledge that he didn't have the money to buy other rides. As he put it: *"If I crash the car and wind up walking back to the pits with the bloody steering wheel in my hand, I might just as well keep walking...."*

And then there was the other driver on Clive Stanley's team: Ian Snell. Ian was a slight, edgy, spoiled and insouciant English kid who looked about half Tommy's age—if that—with vacant blue eyes and longish brown hair that he was forever spiraling around his forefinger whenever he wasn't wearing his helmet or busy chewing on his fingernails. You could sense the bundle of raw, jangled nerves running right beneath his detached, ostensibly disinterested exterior. Ian had made quite a name for himself qualifying on front rows, setting lap records and winning the occasional race or two for a variety of race shops and car owners on the British club scene.

He was also well known for sudden, impromptu explorations of the trackside scenery and knocking front and rear corners off assorted Coopers, Lolas and Elvas. He obviously came from some family money (you could tell that just by the way he walked, talked and held himself and the feel of his hand when you shook it) and I always suspected he decided to go racing out of lack of anything better to do. There was a lethargic tingle of ambition about him, and you got the sense that motor racing was the first thing he'd ever tried that he did well at. But it made you nervous to watch him—right on the wild, ragged edge, lap after lap and more than once I'd seen him use his undeniable bravery as a weapon against other drivers.

They were just fastening Ian into the car when I arrived at Clive Stanley's pit stall, and Clive had his Borsalino hat pressed deep into the Aston's off-side window, giving Ian instructions that I doubt he could even hear over the crackle and burble of the Aston's exhaust. At least they'd gotten the damn miss out of it. Geoff Britten was on the other side, double-checking starting tire pressures and looking generally disgusted. I saw my friend Tommy standing on the pit wall and climbed up next to him. *"Hey!"* I yelled over the engine noise.

"Hey, yourself, Sport."

I pointed to the brilliant sky above us. *"Welcome to sunny Florida."*

Tommy smiled at me from under a salt-and-pepper mustache that was more salt than pepper these days. *"Are you keeping well?"*

"Well enough."

A track official pulled the orange safety pylon out of the way at the end of pit lane and Ian Snell immediately revved the engine, popped the clutch and squirted the Imperial Crown Tea Aston Martin down pit lane and out towards the racetrack as Ian made sure he was first man out on the circuit. Tommy and I looked at the juddering black rubber streaks he'd left on the pavement and the long, long line of cars accelerating modestly out of pits behind him. We watched until the very last of them curled into the busy, buttonhook funnel of Turn One and disappeared into the infield. At least we didn't have to shout any more.

"Ian's a bit eager, isn't he?"

"No comment," Tommy answered dryly. Then added with a wink: "And you can quote me on that if you like."

"I'm not exactly here in my official capacity."

"Not snooping and scooping any more?"

"Sure. But Clive Stanley's pit isn't exactly where you'd find the latest hot racing news at Daytona this weekend, is it?"

Tommy's smile tightened. "You don't have to be bloody rude about it."

I felt sorry I'd said it—even in fun—and gave Tommy an apologetic half-shrug. "I gotta call 'em as I see 'em, Tommy," I told him. Then added lamely: "That's what motoring scribes are supposed to do." I pulled out my copy of the entry list and pretended to look it over. "How do *you* like your chances?"

Tommy stared at the empty track in front of us. "With a nice glass of scotch, most probably."

"It's not exactly the most promising ride, is it?"

"It's a decent car," he argued. "Even if it's not up to the best of the Ferraris."

"So you're happy driving it?"

"It beats driving a nail into a slab of shit."

We laughed and clinked a pair of imaginary glasses together.

"So how is it? I mean really."

"Oh, it's not so bad," he allowed. "Geoff is a capable man and Peter's good with the wrenches and Ian's bullet fast for as long as he can keep himself together"

"I bet you're just as fast if you want to be."

Tommy looked down at his driving shoes. "I'm not really, you know," he said softly. "Maybe I once was, but not any more." A wry little smile blossomed across his face. "It seems these days I've got to think about doing things I used to do without thinking..." his voice trailed off. But then he straightened himself up and added: "But it's not all about going fast as blazes every time you get in the bloody car. There's a lot more to it than that."

And that was true enough. But you had to be *fast,* too. There was no getting around that part. "So you like it here?" I asked to change the subject.

"It's a good enough opportunity. Clive's honest and he pays his bills and payroll on time, and that's more than you can say for a lot of team owners." Tommy sighed and stared out again at the banked tri-oval in front of us. "The Ferraris are all in the 3-liter class anyway. The only other cars in our class are a couple of those new Jaguar E-Types. They're not really sorted out yet, but Briggs Cunningham's got one with Walt Hansgen up—he's always quick—and there's another one from England with that ambitious young David Hobbs character in it."

"He's been making quite a name for himself back there, hasn't he?"

Tommy rubbed his chin. "I reckon you can count on hearing more from him in the future. He's bloody quick."

"But that's it in the 4-liter class? Just you and the two E-types?"

"That's about it," Tommy nodded. "And the two Pontiac Tempests, of course."

"Pontiac Tempests?" I echoed with some surprise.

"Didn't you see them on the entry list? I thought you were the great bloody insider racing scribe with your finger on the pulse of what's happening."

I pulled my entry list out and, sure enough, there they were. Way at the very bottom of the second page like they'd been added at the last minute. Four Pontiac Tempests, two in the 4-liter GT class running against Clive Stanley's Aston and the pair of E-types and two more in the over 5-liter GT class squared off against no less than eight Chevrolet Corvettes. "Have you seen them?" I asked.

Tommy shook his head. "No one has. They're the ones hidden away in that big permanent garage down at the far end of pit lane. But they've been keeping the bloody doors down and windows taped over. I don't think their transporter has even arrived yet."

"Are they *serious?*"

"Well, someone's apparently spent a piss-pot full of money to prove that they are. And just look who they've signed on to drive the bloody things."

I ran my eyes down the list again, and they got bigger as I read the names of the Pontiac drivers. Whoever was behind this thing had hired on some of the top Indy 500 and stock car drivers in America, including Rodger Ward, Paul Goldsmith, Junior Johnson and T.J. Huston. It made you wonder, that's for sure.

Ian Snell and the Imperial Crown Tea Aston Martin flew past all on their own at the end of lap one, and you couldn't miss how he held the throttle down longer and later than anyone before hammering on the brakes for the dive into Turn One.

"Everybody else is out there heating up the tires, bedding in brakes, looking for the last of the puddles and trying to make bloody sense of the circuit," Tommy grumbled. "But not our boy Ian. No, indeed. He's out there to win the first bloody lap of practice."

"Maybe Clive'll have a word with him?"

"Bloody hell he will," Tommy snorted, and nodded over to where Clive Stanley was standing on the pit apron, beaming from ear to ear. Geoff Britten was a few feet behind, scowling down angrily at the stopwatch in his hand.

"Hey," I said, "you can't blame the kid for wanting to go fast..."

"Like hell I can't!" Tommy snarled. "There's nothing to prove here. Nothing to be gained. You want to save the bloody car for the race, when it bloody well counts." He shook his head. "He'll be in soon enough. You'll see...."

Sure enough, Ian was late coming around two laps later. And then he came limping in with a bright orange safety pylon wedged under the front end. It made an ugly, grating noise against the pavement as Ian pulled the car to a halt in front of us. The track used the cones to mark where the "road course" veered off the tri-oval and into the infield, and no question Ian had managed to out-brake himself there. Geoff Britten stalked over, got down on his knees and peered under the car. There was no apparent damage, so he grabbed the cone and tried to pull it out from under the car. But it wouldn't budge. So he took it in both hands and gave another hefty yank. And then he stood up a bit so he could get his back into it and tried again. On the fourth try, the cone finally popped free, and the momentum was enough to deposit Geoff squarely on his backside in the middle of pit lane. It wasn't a particularly stylish or graceful maneuver, and neither was there any dignified way to recover from it. I felt Tommy choking back a laugh as he watched his team manager struggle to his feet, brush himself off and head over to the car on long, deliberate strides to have a bit of a chat with young Ian Snell. He rammed his head deep into the Aston's off-side window and you could see Geoff's mouth working angrily. But Ian Snell kept his helmet facing forward and his eyes focused on the end of pit lane the entire time. When Geoff finally pulled out and stalked away, a somewhat chastened Ian Snell eased the clutch out and motored gently towards the end of pit lane. But he had the throttle buried to the stops again by the time he got there....

"He'll never learn," Tommy muttered to no one in particular.

We watched Freddie Fritter howl past in the #22 Ferrari Berlinetta and Tommy fumbled for his stopwatch. A few moments later Moss came wailing by in Carlo Sebastian's Berlinetta Le Mans Speciale Aerodinamico and Tommy clicked the button.

"I thought you had somebody taking times?" I asked nonchalantly.

Tommy gave me the fish-eye. "Don't fool with me, Hank. Audrey already told us she met you on the bloody airplane."

I could feel my cheeks heating up. "Uh, yeah, we kind of ran into each other...."

"Ran into each other?" he needled. "I heard you gave her quite the bloody dissertation on motor racing."

Now they were burning.

Tommy's eyes widened. "My, my, look at this. You're actually blushing." He looked in even closer. "You don't have a bloody case for her, do you?"

"N-No. Of course not," I told him, looking at my shoes. "She just seemed, you know, *nice* is all."

"She *is* nice!" Tommy agreed with surprising ferocity. But then he looked me in the eyes and added: "Hard as it may be to believe, she didn't find you entirely awful, either."

"Really?"

"No accounting for taste, is there?" Tommy grinned.

"None whatsoever."

Tommy's smile faded and I could feel his eyes surveying mine, inspecting them for my intentions.

"She's had a bit of a rough go of it," he continued in a cool, detached voice. "Her father's not the easiest man in the world." He looked me straight in the eye. "She's given up quite a lot for him, you know."

"I really don't know anything about her."

So Tommy filled me in. She'd been a teacher somewhere near Cambridge—"a private tutor for upper-crust brats" was the way he put it—but came back home when her mother was diagnosed with cancer four years before. "She stayed on right through and past the end," he said grimly, "and wound up more or less taking care of her father and the house after she was gone. Then Walter had his stroke, of course," Tommy clicked his watch as Moss went by and frowned at the time on the dial. "It seemed to take all the air out of him when his wife fell ill." He looked me in the eye. "They'd been married fifty years..."

The two white Grady Davis Corvettes thundered past on the tri-oval, making some impressive top speed. But they both lifted off early for the braking zone into Turn One.

"Walter's come around quite a bit since the stroke," Tommy continued as the two Corvettes disappeared into the infield, "but he's..." I could feel him searching for words "...*difficult.*" Tommy looked me in the eye again. "Walter Denbeigh was never the easiest bloody man in the world."

"Oh? How so?"

Tommy gave me a "you'll find out" smile and didn't say anything.

"But how bad is he? I mean physically."

"Oh, he still comes in to do fabricating work at Eric Broadley's shop. First man there most mornings when he doesn't have his therapy. And he can still make you bloody anything you'd ever want out of a piece of metal. Steel, aluminum, welding, shaping, machine work...amazing talent for it, really." He punctuated with an appreciative nod. "But he's a crusty, independent old bloke who doesn't much like having people do anything for him. Not even Audrey. And he doesn't get on very well with the way his left side is still weak or how he gets tired now and then in the afternoon." Tommy leaned in and whispered: "I've seen him clamp his belt in the bloody bench vise to help keep him upright while he's working." He shook his head. "Amazing bloke, really...."

But Walter wasn't the Denbeigh I wanted to know about. "So," I asked like I was just making conversation, "how did Audrey ever get hooked up with the team?"

A smile crinkled across Tommy's face. "Well, it seems she's a bloody first-rate whiz at math. Absolutely brilliant when it comes to timing and lap charts. Speaks French, German, Spanish and Italian like she's a bloody native, too. Even has a little Portuguese and Dutch on tap if she needs it."

"Smart girl."

"That she is," Tommy nodded. "Bloody independent, too. Like her father." He gave me the hairy eyeball. "But also a bit shy..." you couldn't miss the shadow of a warning creeping into his voice, "...and perhaps a little naive about men."

"You know that from experience?"

Tommy's face turned to stone. "Let's just say I know it."

I looked at him sideways. "What are you trying to say?"

"I'm not saying anything," he insisted. "I just wanted you to know." His eyes took another quick inventory of mine. "Some of us on the team think a lot of her."

"Like you, for instance?"

Tommy cleared his throat and looked out at the racetrack. "Um...In a fatherly sort of way."

Now it was my turn to take inventory. "You're sure it's a fatherly way?"

Tommy glared at me. "If it wasn't, I would have bloody well told you so!"

We watched Cal howl past in the 3-liter Testa Rossa. And what a sound it made when he lifted off and heel-and-toe/double-clutch downshifted through the gears for Turn One. You could hear all twelve carburetor throats gargling fuel on the over-run and then spitting it out with a crackle and a belch of flame on every downchange. "So," I asked as the Testa Rossa disappeared around Turn One, "where is she now?"

"Oh, Geoff has her over at the bloody horseshoe in the infield. He thinks you can split the laps from there."

"Split the laps?"

Tommy nodded. "Break each lap into two segments: the twisty bits through the infield and the flat-out stuff around the bankings. Find out who's doing what where and which is more important to a decent time."

It was a good idea, but I wasn't convinced it had much practical application for Clive Stanley's Aston Zagato. I mean, there wasn't much they could change on the car, even if they wanted to. And I told Tommy as much.

"True enough," he agreed. "But Geoff Britten didn't get to be Geoff Britten without looking ahead a bit. He's always trying to figure things out about a new racetrack. Any new racetrack. You never know when it may come in handy."

We watched the rest of the session from the pit wall, and the thing that struck both of us was the disparity in speed and ability between the professional-grade drivers in the factory-effort Category 1 GTs and sports/prototypes and the dilettante privateers and club racers of widely varying skill, desire and equipment potential that made up the rest of the field. Sure, they all had their own class trophies and small bags of prize money to worry about (and no question they were thrilled to be running in the Big Time with their heroes) but it created a *lot* of traffic problems. Particularly up on the bankings, where the speed differentials could be downright terrifying. And also funneling into Turn One and the tight infield horseshoe where the line turned single-file here and there. Add in that some of the pros could be less than cordial while overtaking slower traffic and that some of the backmarkers were less than diligent about watching their mirrors and you had the makings of a few very ugly incidents.

In response, the chief steward called all the drivers together for a little Come to Jesus meeting after the end of first practice, and he made it clear in no uncertain terms that he wanted the slower cars to stay down low on the banked tri-oval and "leave the upper two grooves for the faster cars." That came as something of a shock to many of the drivers—pro and amateur alike—who simply couldn't believe that you could go three-wide up on the bankings. Even after they'd seen pictures of the stock car guys doing it in full-sized Pontiacs, Plymouths and Oldsmobiles...

Between sessions I wandered over to the big permanent garage at the east end of pit lane to check out the Tempests, but the overhead doors were still down and the side door was still locked, and there was no big car transporter parked outside, either. Just a plain, white panel van and a rental car. I saw that one of the overhead doors was up a few inches to let a little air in, so I got down on my hands and knees (like all good reporters need to when the situation demands) and pressed my cheek against the concrete so I could peer inside. It was dark and pretty much empty in there, with just three crew guys in white team coveralls gathered around a stack of tires playing liars' poker with rumpled dollar bills. They looked weary and disinterested and weren't talking very much. I yelled under the door to ask them when the cars would be coming, but they ignored me. But I kept at it like a good reporter is supposed to, and finally one of them turned halfway around, gave me a silent, exaggerated shrug and went back to his game.

With nothing much better to do, I wandered across the infield to watch second practice from the rickety little metal grandstand overlooking Daytona's enthusiastically named "International Horseshoe" hairpin. I was hoping I'd run into Audrey there, but it transpired that Geoff Britten had moved her over to the big, banked turns at the far east end of the speedway, where the fast guys were already learning that they could keep the loud pedal flat to the floor and just hang on. Even if it felt a little scary.

It didn't take more than a few laps to realize that Daytona's "International Horseshoe" was a frustrating turn for the drivers. It was basically just a flat, slow U-turn—2nd gear for just about everybody—and the fact that they'd used crushed-up seashells in the pavement mix made it slicker than eel snot. Even in the dry! Oh, you could go into the horseshoe two-wide for overtaking, but then it funneled down to pretty much single-file through the middle of the corner. But the real key was how fast you came out and how much momentum you carried onto the following straightaway. And that took patience. If you went in too deep or got impatient in the middle, the car would start pushing wide or step out sideways. And then the driver had no choice but to lift off just when he needed to be squeezing on the power for a good, solid exit.

It was maddening.

You could also tell a lot about the way the different cars handled through there. To my eyes, the mid-engined Cooper Monaco of promising young Pennsylvanian Roger Penske and the similar but arguably lighter and better Lotus 19s of Dan Gurney and Pedro Rodriguez looked particularly quick and impressive. Like all American enthusiasts (and particularly those of us from Southern California!) I was a huge Dan Gurney fan, and it was no real surprise to see him going so well. No question Dan was one of the quickest drivers on the planet and one of the few ever mentioned in the same breath with Stirling Moss. Even that asshole Eric Gibbon had to admit—grudgingly, of course, since Dan was an American—that he was a special sort of talent. But Dan hadn't always found his way into the best situations or most promising rides. His speed earned him a chance with Ferrari in 1959, but by then the mid-engined Cooper Formula One cars were the class of the field—even though the Ferraris were more powerful—and Dan found himself wheeling a bit of a dinosaur. He switched to BRM for 1960, but the cars kept letting him down. No question BRMs were beautifully made and adventurously designed, but they weren't always well thought out or properly developed at that stage. Dan had a miserable season and didn't score a single championship point, and the low point had to be when one of BRM's radical, single-disc rear brakes exploded while Dan was braking for the hairpin at Zandvoort. He went flying off—totally brakeless—and a spectator who had sneaked into a restricted area was sadly killed in the incident. It must have been a relief when he signed with Porsche for 1961. Sure, their cars were no match for the shark-nosed Ferraris or the best of the new British chassis, but they were solidly built and dead reliable and Dan took many top finishes and a well-deserved 3rd in the Championship standings at the end of the year. He also drove Porsche sports/racers in the World Manufacturers' Championship, but his contract allowed him to take other rides when Porsche didn't have an assignment for him. Which is how he wound up in California wine merchant Ernesto Julio's quick but potentially fragile Lotus 19 "Monte Carlo" at Daytona. It was a well-known laugh around the garages that Colin Chapman had christened his new 19 the "Monte Carlo" as a not-so-subtle dig at Cooper's toney "Monaco" name for their own mid-engined sports/racer. Strip all the bullshit away and they were both just widened-up 2.5-liter Formula One cars with full, 2-seater bodywork thrown on top. It was clear to most of the wags in the press room that Gurney's Lotus 19 and Roger Penske's Cooper Monaco (which was rumored to have the super-strong, 2.7-liter Climax FPF from Cooper's Indianapolis effort under its rear deck) were the quickest, best-handling and best-balanced cars at Daytona. But they were built awfully light, and their Formula One-spec engines and drivelines were perhaps a bit tightly wound for endurance racing. No question they'd never make the distance at a race like Sebring or Le Mans. But, at just 3 hours in length and with a new, ultra-smooth racing surface to play on, Daytona might be a race where they could shine.

There were a couple good Porsches on hand in the smallbore sports/racing classes including four of the latest-spec RS61s but they were all American privateers and the only genuine factory entry was one of Porsche's German/Italian Abarth Carrera coupes running in the 1600cc Grand Touring class and assigned to dapper Swedish ace/Porsche factory driver Jo Bonnier backed up (if necessary) by Porsche motorsports boss Huschke von Hanstein himself. The Abarth Carreras were the product of a somewhat unlikely but highly successful collaboration between the Porsche factory in Stuttgart and Carlo Abarth's Turin-based automotive accessory company/hop-up emporium in Turin. Abarth's company had become justly famous for its handsome, crinkle-finish, "free flow" (translation: "outrageously noisy") exhaust systems for sports cars, and they'd also had a lot of success building quick, light, low-volume GT racers based on mostly Fiat components. Even so, it came as a bit of a shock when Porsche sub-contracted the development of their new GT contender to the Italian firm in 1960. But Porsche's own, in-house racing department was spread paper thin with their evolving sports/racer program and fledgling Formula One team. Not to mention that "Italian" Carlo Abarth was actually born Karl Abarth in Vienna, Austria, had worked alongside Dr. Porsche on the brilliantly conceived but ultimately disappointing Cisitalia Grand Prix project after the war and was moreover married to the secretary of Porsche director (and Ferdinand Porsche's son-in-law) Anton Piech!

Abarth Carreras were essentially tweaked 356B chassis platforms with racing-spec, 4-cam Carrera engines shoved in back topped with lightweight and more aerodynamic all-alloy coupe bodywork that Abarth subcontracted out to small-volume, specialist Italian *carrozzeria* familiar with that type of work. The finished product was spectacularly good, and Abarth Carreras picked up dominating class wins along with frankly amazing top-10 overall finishes at the Targa Florio, Nurburgring and Le Mans in both 1960 and 1961! They were also quite a bit sleeker and more stylish than what you normally came to expect from Porsche, but (and this would be fairly typical of small, specialist Italian *carrozzerria)* no two Carrera Abarths were ever exactly alike. In fact, the left-hand side might not match the right-hand side on the same blessed car! And right there you had the basic difference between the Germans and the Italians. Or the scientific and artistic temperaments, if you will. But the cars were all Porsche underneath, and ran like you expected Porsches to run. Which is to say, until you switched them off with the damn key....

Although there were six different GT displacement classes at Daytona (1300, 1600, 2000, 3000, 4000 and over-5000cc), World Manufacturers' Championship points were only awarded on an Over 2-liter (Category 1) and Under 2-liter (Category 2) basis, and no question the factory-entered Carrera Abarth had been sent specifically to win Category 2 and bring those all-important World Manufacturers' Championship points home to Stuttgart. Over in Category 1, the 3-liter GT Ferraris were overwhelming favorites (particularly the Stirling Moss car) in spite of giving away a lot in the way of displacement to the 6-cylinder Jaguar E-Types and Clive Stanley's Aston Martin in the 4-liter class and no less than eight lumbering Chevrolet Corvettes in the over-5-liter class. The best of them surely had to be the pair of not-so-surreptitiously factory-assisted Corvettes entered by Gulf Oil vice president Grady Davis for Dr. Dick Thompson and Don Yenko, but while they figured to have loads of grunt out of the corners and plenty of top speed around the bankings, most press-room insiders figured they were too heavy, under-braked and cumbersome to be much of a threat for anything more than a bottom-of-the-top-ten finish and a shoo-in, uncontested class win. But that's probably all they were looking for anyway.

Far more intriguing to me were the Chevy-powered Chaparrals running in the over-5000cc "Experimental" class that Big Bill France had thrown in to give the local fans something to cheer for and the American scribes something to write about. I'd looked them over pretty carefully in the paddock, and came away highly impressed. The Chaparrals were simple, svelte, low-slung, straightforward and tidy, and you could see they were very well built. They were the handiwork of Dick Troutman and Tom Barnes, who'd done the construction work on the original, all-conquering Scarab sports cars for Hollywood rich kid Lance Reventlow. But after that project ran its course and Lance sold the cars off so he could go tilting at windmills in Formula One, Troutman and Barnes designed a sort of second-generation Scarab aimed at American privateers. They called it the "Riverside Racer" and, like the Scarab, it was a front-engined, Chevy-powered sports/racer. But it was lower and lighter than the Scarab, and featured 4-wheel disc brakes and fully-independent rear suspension. The bodywork reminded me of a sort of muscled-up, Americanized version of a Birdcage Maserati, and that was always one of my favorite cars. But Troutman and Barnes didn't have the cash to take the project much further than a stack of drawings and a few sales brochures.

Or at least not until Jim Hall came along.

Now Jim Hall was a lanky, soft-spoken, methodical and highly motivated young racing driver/engineer out of Midland, Texas, and although he never made a big show out of it, he had *very* deep pockets thanks to a family oil business. He also had an engineer's fascination, understanding and curiosity about the nuts-and-bolts mechanical details of racing cars. Jim had always favored big, powerful cars (he'd raced everything from a hogged-out, 5.7-liter Maserati 450S to a supercharged Lister-Chev!) and he'd always done pretty well with them. At least until they broke or ran out of brakes, anyway. In any case, Jim saw a lot he liked in Troutman and Barnes' new design. So he opened up his checkbook and became the project's angel. And test driver. And development engineer. And team leader. And along the way he changed that California-esque "Riverside Racer" name to "Chaparral" after the scrawny, bullet-fast road runner birds that streaked across the landscape down in his part of Texas.

I thought the Chaparral was a hell of a neat car—not to mention all-American—and with reasonably light weight, low frontal area, a straightforward but sophisticated chassis and plenty of V8 grunt under the hood, you had to figure it would be one of the fastest cars at Daytona. And you also had to be impressed with Jim Hall's driving. He never looked wild, flashy or flamboyant, but he put the car in the same place every lap, showed a lot of feel and patience, got on the power early and judged his overtaking moves beautifully through traffic. And sure enough, the stopwatch showed that his refrigerator-white #66 was one of the quickest cars out there. And not too far behind was Indianapolis star Dick Rathmann in the metallic-blue-and-white "customer" Chaparral fielded by Harry Heuer's "Meister-Brauser" team out of Chicago. And that was a story in itself:

Harry Heuer was the black-sheep heir-apparent to the Peter Hand Brewery business out of Chicago ("Meister Brau" was their most popular brand) and it was a well-known laugh in racing circles that Harry'd essentially blackmailed his strait-laced board of directors into approving an "advertising budget" for his racing activities by threatening to sell his company stock to the NAACP for fifty cents a share! They knew he'd do it, too.

I always thought Harry was a fun guy to be around (if he liked you, anyway...if he didn't, you might wind up with a split lip) and he always laughed at himself when he told the story of how he got started in racing with one of Bob Carnes' desperately beautiful but even more desperately godawful Bocars. Bob Carnes was a determined kitchen remodeler-cum-automotive tinkerer type out of Denver who figured he was going to build the fastest damn all-American sports cars that anybody had ever seen. The resulting Bocars were brutally handsome and powerful but somewhat crude in execution, and featured big, honking Chevy or Pontiac V8s under the hood, kit car-level trim and finish and VW-based front suspension. They were indeed fast (at least in a straight line, anyway) and looked absolutely fabulous (at least if you didn't look too close) and all the nutball American car magazines went into adverb- and adjective-laden rapture over them. So Harry bought one. And went racing. And eventually came to the realization that Bocars really weren't well sorted out and didn't actually brake or handle too well. Which represented a bit of a challenge for a raw, inexperienced rookie like Harry Heuer. But whatever else you could say about Harry, he never lacked for self-confidence. Or stubbornness. Or balls. He struggled with the Bocar but refused to give up, and I well remember a race at the brand-new Meadowdale track northwest of Chicago where the Bocar's fuel tank split wide open. I asked him afterwards what he was going to do with it (by then he'd bought one of the three ex-Lance Reventlow Scarabs for hired-gun teammate Augie Pabst to drive and was in the process of buying another for himself) and he gave me a typical, straight-from-the-hip Harry Heuer response: "I'm gonna park the damn thing in a bar and let anybody who drinks Meister Brau piss on it!"

Speaking of Meister Brau, it turned into a very sore subject around the Peter Hand boardroom in Chicago when Harry picked longtime pal Augie Pabst to be his number one driver. Augie was a talented, bright-eyed, fresh-faced Wisconsin kid who habitually wore a big, let's-give-it-a-try smile and a mischievous glint in his eye. Like Cal Carrington, he'd come from a well-to-do family that was none too thrilled with his racing ambitions. But there was no way he could give it up. He started out in his own TR3 and followed that up with a used 4-cylinder Ferrari, and it turned out that he was a pretty damned good racing driver. Maybe even better than pretty damned good. So there was nothing wrong with Augie's talent or driving skills as far as the Peter Hand hierarchy was concerned. But it seems Augie's last name was printed on every single bottle, can, case and carton of beer rolling out of arch-rival Pabst Brewing Company up in Milwaukee, Wisconsin. Although Augie didn't have any direct involvement with his family's brewery business at the time, having a "Pabst" driving for "Meister Brau" sparked a lot of snickers, raised eyebrows and sudsy remarks on both sides of the spectator fences. Not to mention in the executive offices of the Peter Hand Brewing Company back in Chicago. But you got the feeling Harry kind of enjoyed sticking the old needle in.

No question Augie's Meister Brauser drive turned out to be that elusive, right-place-at-the-right-time Big Break that every racer needs to move their career along. Augie had quite a run of wins and top finishes in the Meister Brauser Scarabs, and proved beyond question that he was in that small, upper echelon of drivers who could win if you gave them the best car. Augie parlayed his success with the Meister Brauser Scarabs into drives for Briggs Cunningham's team on the full international level, and was driving for Briggs' team at Daytona. Although he might have been better off driving that new Meister Brauser Chaparral for his old team, since he'd drawn the wrong straw at Cunningham and wound up with Briggs' ageing, underpowered and ill-suited-to-the-racetrack Maserati Birdcage. The Tipo 61 had been a brilliant car in 1960 and '61, but it never had an oversupply of horsepower and the new mid-engined cars were undeniably quicker through the twisty stuff by the beginning of 1962. Augie was clearly struggling trying to find competitive speed with it.

In any case, I was thrilled to see both Chaparrals up near the top of the time sheets after practice. Even if the general consensus in the press room—and particularly from his majesty Eric Gibbon—had it that front-engined racecars were going the way of the dinosaurs. And, like the dinosaurs, they were destined to be overrun and replaced by smaller, quicker, cleverer and more nimble little mechanical beasts that, at least as far as I was concerned, were far less entertaining to watch and failed to make the earth tremble when they thundered past. Like Phil Hill's 246SP Dino, for example, which looked terrifically quick, solid and tidy through the hairpin. And Roger Penske's Cooper Monaco and Gurney's Lotus 19 looked even better. It made me wonder how Cal and co-driver Peter Ryan would fare in that older, front-engined Testa Rossa. Sure enough, you could see Peter was having a hell of a time trying to find a graceful way through the International Horseshoe. If he braked too late or pushed too hard, the car would just roll over onto its outside-front tire and understeer like a pig. He almost plowed clear off the road once or twice during the early laps. But he quickly got the hang of it and his lap times started coming down accordingly. Peter wound up a half-second quicker than Cal by the time the second session was over (although track conditions had unquestionably improved with all of the moisture gone and some rubber laid down on the racing surface). Even so, I knew Peter's times wouldn't sit too well with Cal. But that's the way it always is with teammates. And particularly teammates at Ferrari.

The light little Porsche RSKs looked simply terrific through the hairpin, and the best of them—Bob Holbert in particular—knew how to use their low polar moment of inertia and rearward weight bias to rotate them into the corner, balance them on the throttle and then rocket out under full, howling power at the exit. But the RSKs just didn't have enough power to be a genuine threat at a track like Daytona. Not to mention that a short, 3-hour race on a high-speed track with a smooth, new surface worked against the RSK's usual advantages in terms of handling, durability, fuel economy and tire wear. But they'd likely be around at the finish, and that was more than you could say for some of their competition.

In the bigbore GT category, Stirling Moss quickly separated himself from the rest of the field in Carlo Sebastian's Berlinetta Le Mans Speciale Aerodinamico, and it was quite a shock the first few times he hit the button for the shatteringly loud air horn that Carlo's mechanics had installed to warn slower traffic out of the way. The sound was absolutely piercing, and it damn near put a few backmarkers off the road the first time they heard it! But Moss pulled in and parked it after just a handful of laps in the second session. Then again, he was already well clear of everyone else on the time sheets, so why take more out of the car?

I had to admit that Freddie Fritter looked surprisingly smooth, calm and unruffled in Carlo Sebastian's other Ferrari Berlinetta. Even though he filled the cockpit until you could barely see light coming through from the other side! According to the few laps I clicked off, his times were very much on par with 1958 Le Mans and 1959 Sebring winner Olivier Gendebien in Count Giovanni Volpi's Scuderia Serenissima Short Wheelbase Berlinetta. That was pretty damn impressive for a big, beefy stock car driver who'd never driven a Ferrari or been out on a road course before. I caught myself smiling as I stared down at my stopwatch. I was really starting to like that guy!

My friend Tommy Edwards seemed to be struggling a bit with Clive Stanley's Aston Martin. Like a lot of drivers, he was finding either terrible front-end plow or lifting off and getting it all stupid sideways in the hairpin, and it took him several laps to, as he put it later, "dial it back to 'fast.'" But he finally got the hang of it after a few lurid slides.

You can bet I razzed the hell out of him afterwards.

"You can't gain much time through that bloody corner and it's not really that important to a decent lap time," he said by way of explanation, "but you can sure as hell *lose* a lot of time through there if you're not bloody careful." That was a perfect driver quote for my race report, so I pulled my pen and notebook and jotted it down. And then I asked him about the rest of the track. "It's a mixed bag," he said carefully, his eyes trained on the pen in my hand. "Traffic can really make a mess of things at the hairpin. Faster *or* slower." He curled his lip under, trying to think it through. "It's like one of our English roundabouts. Everybody really needs to cooperate with one another through there."

"And do they?"

"Some do, some don't," he answered with a laugh. "Like always."

"And how about the bankings?"

"Well, I'll tell you this," he allowed, eyeballing my pen and notebook again, "you can't see much except what's right in front of your nose. Not in a bloody coupe, anyway."

I didn't get it at first, but then Tommy sat me down in the Aston and showed me how the leading edge of the roof chopped off most of the view when you were up in the hollowed-out bowl of the bankings. Why, you couldn't see more than a few hundred feet ahead! If that! And that's while traveling flat-out at 160-plus! "We've moved the seat as far forward as I can stand it and Geoff had the mechanics take about half the stuffing out of the cushion, but I still have to crane my neck like a bloody goose to see ahead. And even then I can't see much of anything."

I asked him if Ian was having the same problem.

"Well, he's a bit shorter than I on both ends, isn't he? So it's not quite so desperate for him."

About then Audrey came up with the latest timing sheets and handed us each a copy. Tommy looked down at his and frowned. "Besides," he muttered under his breath, "Ian doesn't much care if he hits anything...."

Audrey gave him a sad little grimace over her clipboard. You could tell she thought a lot of Tommy. But Ian Snell had gone over a full second quicker during the first session, damp racetrack and all. And that kind of thing eats away at a driver. Especially when it's staring back at him in black and white. Sure, Ian had been trying a lot harder—stupidly hard, in my opinion—and we all knew there was no point beating the crap out of the car just to show your teammate up during a meaningless Thursday practice session. Still, the time sheets are the time sheets, and they nail every driver to the cross whenever they come out. There's just no place to hide.

"So," I asked, trying to move us on to a new subject, "is there anything else the sporting public needs to know about Daytona?"

"Well," Tommy exhaled, "I have a whole new respect for those stock car blokes. I was coming up to pass young Jimmy Clark in his bloody Lotus Elite my first time up on the bankings—doing maybe a hundred-fifty-five and closing at a fairly good clip—and I swear, the gap between his Lotus and the outside wall looked about as wide as a bloody broom closet!" He held his hands about eighteen inches apart to illustrate. "It's different here at Daytona, all right. It takes some getting used to..."

And Daytona *was* different. I asked around the paddock, and while some drivers thought it was "rather simple" and some even called it "boring," others figured it was "dangerous as hell." No question it was different things to different people, and Big Bill France's new speedway was going to take a little getting used to for everybody.

I grabbed a dried-out sandwich from the press room and wandered over to the empty grandstand by Turn One to watch the last session of the afternoon. The light was getting low and I was hoping to get some decent, deep-shadow shots of the cars braking down from top speed with their noses all hunkered down and their rear ends all skatey up on tiptoes. But the session was red-flagged before I could even frame up a promising angle. I couldn't really tell what had happened, but all of a sudden the corner workers were brandishing red flags, the noise level dropped markedly and racecars started trundling slowly into pit lane and switching off, one-by-one. Everybody knew that Something Bad had happened. Pretty soon the entire track was dead silent, and silence is the most frightening sound there is at any racetrack. But there's nothing you can do except wonder who it is and how bad it might be.

I headed back into pit lane to find out what had happened, and it didn't take long for the whispers to find me. My grinning Wisconsin pal Augie Pabst had been hoofing it around the bankings in Briggs Cunningham's Maserati Birdcage—flat-out at something like 165 or so!—when the crankshaft snapped like a damn match-stick. There was speculation that the centrifugal force had pushed all the oil away from the pickup, but whatever happened, the engine seized with a horrendous *"CLANK!"* and the rear wheels locked up solid before Augie had a chance to react. Worse yet, the exploding bottom end dumped an entire sump-load of hot oil right under the Maserati's rear tires.

At that point, Augie was merely along for the ride....

Eyewitnesses told me it was a stupefying wreck: the car slewed wildly on the oil, scythed down the banking, bounced *HARD* off the sharp, unforgiving angle where the banking meets the apron, ricocheted back upwards again—showering sparks, parts, smoke and flames all the way!—banged off the top retaining wall and cata-pulted into a gut-wrenching series of end-for-end somersaults. The seat belt mounts broke and Augie was catapulted out of the car and went sliding, skittering and tum-bling along the banking like a rag doll shot out of a cannon. It was utterly horrifying, and when the track went quiet and stayed quiet, everybody at the speedway knew how bad it probably had to be.

I wandered through the paddock avoiding people's eyes while the medics got Augie loaded up in an ambulance and carted off to the hospital, but then I saw Cal standing over by the Ferrari garages with his helmet under his arm and a time sheet in his hand. He was staring more through it than at it, and I could see the sweat beads on his forehead and the grim expression on his face as I drew closer.

"Did you see the wreck?" I asked softly.

"I saw enough."

"How'd it look?"

His eyes swiveled up to mine. "It didn't look good."

"You know him very well?"

Cal nodded.

"He had a hell of a run for Cunningham at Le Mans last year," I said aimlessly, just trying to make conversation. "4th overall with Dick Thompson in the Cunningham Tipo 63...They might have even won the damn thing if the engine hadn't been burning up its sparkplugs...It'd run great for awhile and then the power would start to fade...Then they'd have to stop and change the plugs...All 24 of them...12 cylinders, two plugs per cylinder...And with the frame tubes and a bundle of hot exhaust pipes in the way...It took damn near 20 minutes each time, and they had to do it three different times...Momo's mechanics had to wear wet gloves and wrap wet rags around their arms to keep from getting burned. But they got burned anyway... I was there...I took pictures...."

Cal shook his head. "Well, he won't be driving anything but a hospital bed for awhile. And that's if he's lucky."

There wasn't anything you could say after that. There never is. But then you sigh and set it all aside and move on. Get back to the business at hand. The time sheets and the tactics and the teammates and the tire pressures and all the rest of it. I know that may sound callous to people on the outside, but I've learned better than to try and make excuses for it. Those of us on the inside of the sport are here by choice, and I'm pretty sure most of us would make the same choice again. People get hurt and killed in racing and people get hurt and killed in everyday life—nobody gets out of this life alive—and to be involved with something that actually seems to matter is worth the price. And maybe even the pain. Or that's how the people on the inside feel, anyway.

Chapter 4: Strange Endings and Stranger Beginnings

The news from the hospital was grim but not hopeless, and towards the end of the afternoon word came filtering through the paddock that Augie was out of surgery and that his condition was listed as "stable but guarded." He'd suffered a severe concussion, broken bones and some ghastly friction burns sliding along the pavement at around 100 miles an hour. One of the safety workers said his helmet was worn almost through on one side! But at least he was alive, and by nightfall the paddock rumor mill had it that he was awake and halfway alert and that his prospects for recovery were far better than anybody imagined just a few hours earlier. Still, it was a scary, haunting sort of wreck, and reminded everybody what could happen if things went wrong up on the high banks at Daytona. Especially in a fragile little sports car.

Thursday night is inevitably "where do we go for dinner?" night on any race weekend, and it gets a little confusing whenever the circus lands at a new venue where nobody really knows their way around. Daytona Beach being a resort town, there was no shortage of places to try, but it always takes a little something extra for a bar or restaurant (or, better yet, a bar *and* restaurant) to establish itself as a racers' hangout. It's got to have the right ambience and acoustics, it's got to be just a little bit out of the way and out of the ordinary and it can't be a tacky, tourist-trap joint with no character or local flavor. But of course you don't know any of that when you arrive at a new track in a previously uncharted and undiscovered part of the racing world.

Tommy Edwards invited me to tag along with the Imperial Crown Tea bunch to some out-of-the-way seafood joint called "Epifiano's Crab Shack" that one of the locals told Peter Bryant about. It was supposedly "just a few miles down the beach from the boardwalk," but the local also mentioned that Epifiano's might be a wee bit hard to find. So I left my rental car in the paddock and hitched a ride with Tommy, Geoff Britten, Audrey, Peter Bryant and Georgie Smales. We were jammed shoulder-to-shoulder and ribs-into-elbows in the sure-to-be-sorely-abused team rental car, which was one of Fairway Motors' upscale (but not quite so upscale as a Caddy Fleetwood or Chrysler Imperial) Fairway Freeway Frigate four-door "Filigree Festoon" luxury sedans, which included a "sumptuous Carpathian leather-look" interior, a phony wood-grain strip across the dash and little plastic-oval opera windows with fake etching on them that was really just a decal. Ian Snell and Clive Stanley of course went by themselves in the road-going Aston Martin DB4 that Clive had air-freighted over for runaround duty at Daytona. Although he whimpered a bit about right-hand drive being "such a frightful nuisance" in wrong-side-of-the-road American traffic. If you're just an average, lunchbucket Joe, you tend to wonder what it must be like to have that kind of money. But of course the people who have it (and especially those who have had it in their families for generations) don't even feel it. It's just there.

Naturally I got stuck in the usual scribe/hanger-on position, crammed between the two mechanics in the back seat with the driveshaft hump jamming my knees up into my chin. Audrey was up front between Tommy and Geoff Britten, so I didn't get to do much except stare at the back of her neck and try to catch her eyes in the bottom corner of the rearview mirror on our way to the restaurant. And meanwhile Tommy and Geoff and the mechanics were bantering back and forth about the car and the track surface and the tire pressures and so forth—punctuated by an occasional wink, grimace or eye roll whenever Clive or Ian's name came up—and I meanwhile concentrated on the soft, pale skin on the back of Audrey's neck and the lucky little wisps of hair clinging to it. Tommy drove like you come to expect racing drivers to drive in a turn-it-in-when-you're-through-with-it rental car. Which is to say flat out. To be fair, racing drivers generally glide along at what feels, at least to them, like a gentle, smooth, relaxed and socially responsible sort of pace. But it nonetheless tends to startle, amaze and infuriate drivers of other cars, and regularly causes everyone inside the vehicle to clench their teeth, clutch for something solid to hang onto and recall prayers learned in childhood. Rapidly closing, motorbike-sized holes in traffic look like wide-open freeway ramps to your average racing driver, and riding with them takes a little getting used to. In the end, all you can really do is trust the fact that they've somehow gotten to this point in their lives and hope that their apparent run of uncommon good fortune continues.

We crossed the big, wide bridge over the inland waterway at something around twice the posted limit—weaving in and out of astonished local citizens and startled retirees like a world cup skier on a slalom run—but Tommy had to lean hard on the brakes when a red light loomed and traffic suddenly and abruptly accordioned back to us. In fact, Tommy had to lock everything up to avoid running smack into the tailgate of some local shrimp fisherman's ancient pickup. We came close enough to read the "SUNSHINE STATE" lettering across the bottom of the license plate like it was the banner headline on a Sunday newspaper, and you could smell the tangled, rats' nest collection of nets, floats, coolers and galvanized tin buckets in the pickup bed.

"You damn near tagged him," Georgie Smales whined.

"But I didn't, did I?"

"What's that awful smell?"

"It's shrimp. I thought we might pick up a bit of appetizer."

We turned right on A1A and headed south through Daytona Beach, marveling at the garish, neon-incandescent business strip of sunset pink, peach, mauve, aqua green and robin's-egg blue tourist-trap arcades, restaurants, bars, swimsuit emporiums, beach-oriented straw hat, suntan lotion and sunglasses stores and big, swanky-looking ocean-front hotels with grand stucco arches, illuminated palm trees and circular drives. And scattered in between were what seemed like dozens upon dozens of smaller, faded little cheap-room motels for the motorcycle types and college kids. It went on for miles. But eventually the buildings, lights and neon signs got fewer and further between and you could see the dark, endless void of the ocean off to our left between the silhouettes of low, flat-roof cinder block buildings and scraggly palm trees.

"You sure we didn't pass it?" Georgie finally asked.

"The bloke told us it was well south of town," Peter answered.

"It doesn't look like there's bloody anything out here," Georgie groused.

"I think we must have passed it."

"Bloody hell we have."

"Maybe we should turn around?"

"Just cock the wheel and yank the bloody handbrake!" Peter suggested, trying to be of assistance.

"It's a stupid little pedal hidden under the dashboard," Tommy answered like he'd already been considering it. "And once you put the bloody thing down, it bloody well *stays* down!"

"Why on earth would anyone build it that way?"

"You know the Americans."

"I've met them, but I can't say as I *know* them..."

"THERE IT IS!" Audrey yelped, and pointed to a poorly lit, half-knocked-down wooden sign with a faded red crab, some slightly pinker shrimps and the name "EPIFIANO'S" in orange with a big, black arrow painted under it.

"GOT IT!" Tommy nodded as he dabbed the brakes, spun the wheel and sent our softly sprung and seriously overloaded Fairway Freeway Frigate "Filigree Festoon" luxury edition into a monstrous, sidewall-shuddering slide that bottomed out several times and threw off a truly magnificent roostertail of gravel as we dirt-tracked onto a humpbacked little side road that looked like some farmer's driveway. The sudden change of direction threw everyone inside all over each other like an amusement park ride. "Everyone OK back there?" Tommy asked apologetically while keeping his right foot planted to finish out the slide.

I pulled my nose out of Georgie Smale's armpit while Peter Bryant struggled to get his eyebrows disengaged from the zipper on my jacket. *"I feel like the pimento getting squeezed out of an olive!"* I hollered from the middle of the back seat, and everybody laughed. And meanwhile our Fairway Freeway Frigate was bouncing, leaping and fishtailing its way down this pitch-dark little side road at what felt like a hundred miles an hour. God only knows what would have happened if we'd met someone coming the other way! But we ultimately exploded over a final jump and burst out into a narrow, dimly-lit gravel parking lot packed chock-full of dusty rental cars. Apparently the word was already out on Epifiano's Crab Shack. The full parking lot caught Tommy by surprise, and he hit the brakes hard and skidded towards what looked like a sure-thing, brakes-locked impact with the rear quarter of a white Dodge Polara. But Tommy's racer instincts took over. He eased off the brakes off so he could steer again and, in a sudden, mad, desperate rush of bravado, cut the wheel hard left and slammed his foot down on the parking brake pedal. That sent our badly overloaded Freeway Frigate into a groaning, wallowing, gravel-grinding attempt at a bootleg spin. Only we weren't going fast enough to bring the car all the way around, so we slid to a dumb, ignominious halt cocked about three-quarters sideways between the parked cars and the bushes. To make matters worse, the engine died in the process so all the little dash warning lights came on. There was a moment of stunned silence followed by the soft, dusty, hail-like patter of a million tiny stones descending from the sky and landing on the roof, hood and rear deck of our Freeway Frigate and all around us in the parking lot.

Geoff Britten pretended to glare at Tommy: "You can't even do the bloody little simple things right, can you?"

Tommy looked back at him sheepishly, and we all laughed like hell. Especially the two mechanics. That was as much humor you usually got out of Geoff Britten in an entire season.

Epifiano's Crab Shack was an informal, thatched roof/island hut looking joint with indoor and outdoor tables and a yard strung with yellow-orange lights, neon beer signs and colored paper lanterns. There was a big, kind of open-air pavilion in the middle with stand-in-line food and beverage counters and plenty of well-used wooden picnic tables with yard torches scattered around them. The place was already packed with racing people. It never takes very long for the word to get around at any new racetrack. Especially when the food is good, the beer is cold, the pitchers and platters run big and the prices are reasonable. What more could you ask?

Clive was paying, so I ordered the top-of-the-line shrimp and rock lobster combo with corn on the cob, cole slaw and homemade cornbread and Audrey had a nice, fresh piece of snapper that I'm sure was swimming merrily away in the Atlantic not too many hours before. Table space was at a premium, and it didn't look like there was enough room for Audrey and me at the little round cocktail table Peter and Georgie had managed to commandeer in the bar. But it was louder than hell in there.

"Do you think we might find someplace a bit quieter?" Audrey shouted into my ear. "I've had racing engines in my ears all day long."

"Sounds good to me," I shouted back.

So I led her out past all the bustling, noisy lawn tables and we found our way down to a small wooden bench on a darkened boat dock jutting out into the Intracoastal waterway. We could still hear the noise from the bar in the background, but it had faded into kind of a distant, anonymous hum behind the quiet, intimate sound of water lapping around the dock pilings. It was dark there, too, with just the occasional running lights of a speedboat or cabin cruiser burbling past and a few steady dock lights twinkling at us from the opposite side. It wasn't like we'd planned it or anything, but there we were.

The awkward part was, I couldn't think of anything to say. And I don't think Audrey could, either. So we just started eating in silence, with just the sound of the water and the echoing yelps and hollers from the tables behind us for accompaniment. And then we heard something new. A kind of a soft, wet, slashing noise in the water right next to us. We looked at each other.

"What do you think it is?"

I gave her half a shrug. And right on cue we heard it again.

It didn't take long to discover that the local fish population knew all about Epifiano's Crab Shack, and if you threw a little piece of cornbread (or fish, or a shrimp tail, or just about anything else) into the water, there'd be an instantaneous splash and swirl accompanied by a flash of large, dull silver scales and it would be gone. Just like that. "That looks like a pretty big fish," I observed, just making conversation.

Audrey peered into the water. "What kind do you think it is?"

"Hungry," I told her, and we both laughed.

The food was pretty good—seafood is always better when it's fresh out of the ocean and served up at a place like Epifiano's—and it felt amazingly easy and comfortable to just sit there next to Audrey and enjoy our dinners without saying much of anything. I really didn't want it to end. So when I finished with my food, I decided the easiest thing would be to simply ask her just how she wound up handling the timing and scoring for Clive Stanley's team.

"I'm a teacher, actually," she laughed. "Or I suppose 'tutor' might be more appropriate."

"Tommy mentioned something about that."

"To be honest about it, I take care of rich, spoiled brats for stuck-up wealthy people who simply can't be bothered."

"Sounds like loads of fun."

"Oh, my life is an endless cornucopia of joy," she assured me with an unmistakable hint of bitterness. A heavy pause followed, and I scrambled to think of something else to say.

"So," I finally asked, "what subjects do you teach?"

"Oh, it depends on the age of the children and the circumstances. Whatever needs to be taught, really. That's the way it has to be in a service business."

"But what's your specialty?"

"Languages, mostly. I don't precisely know why, but I seem to have a knack for them."

I shook my head. "I've always been terrible at foreign languages."

"That's probably because you try to translate everything back-and-forth into English."

"That's what my French teacher said. Right before she flunked me. And my Spanish teacher, too. Right before she gave me a 'D.'"

"At least you made progress."

"Not so's you'd notice."

"And you're a writer. That probably has something to do with it."

"That must be it. I have a hell of a hard time making myself understood in English, and adding another layer of language just seems to complicate things."

That earned me a nice little laugh.

"So tell me," I prodded. "What else do you teach?"

"I suppose I'm weak in letters, history and philosophy, but I'm known as a bit of a whiz in math, geography and science."

I shook my head. "Well, if opposites attract, we're going to get on famously."

"I'm rather hoping we will," she said like there was no deeper meaning in it. But it sent a little charge through me anyway.

I fumbled for something else to ask. "So how did you get started?"

Audrey leaned her head back against the bench and looked up at the nighttime sky. "A lot of bloody school," she said dreamily. "Too much, probably." Her eyes swiveled over towards me. "I always did well at school," she said like it was something to be ashamed of. "I think I liked the order of it: knowing what you had to do and where you had to be every day." She let out a slow, sad sigh. "I never had the rogue imagination to be any other way."

"So how did you wind up on the racing team?"

"Oh, it's not nearly so unusual as it sounds. My father Walter does a bit of fabricating work for Eric Broadley's Lola shop in Bromley. I stopped in to see him one day and they needed some travel arrangements made for Montlhéry in France and everyone was scrambling like mad to get cars ready for Silverstone that weekend. I more or less volunteered, I suppose. And since I had the French to do it properly, it just seemed like a good fit for everyone concerned. I'd been to a few races when I was younger and so the next weekend I started doing a bit of charts and timing—it's really not that difficult once you learn to keep it all organized." She rolled her eyes back up to the sky again. "It helped immeasurably that I could deal with registrars and race officials and waiters and hotel keepers and such in their own language. In fact, it made me more-or-less indispensable." She snorted out a short, self-deprecating laugh. "It's really underrated how important that sort of thing can be."

"You don't have to tell me. You're looking at a guy with a stack of French, German, Spanish and Italian phrase books gathering dust on his desk."

"Oh? Do they help?"

"I suppose they would if I ever studied them or took them with me. I always seem to leave them behind."

"You never pack them?"

I looked at her sheepishly. "I got them all for a pound when a book shop next to a pub I know was going out of business. It seemed like an incredibly good deal: mastery of all the languages of Europe for a single pound."

"But you never used them?"

"To be honest, I don't think I've so much as opened a page on any of them." I offered up half a shrug. "The proper moment just never seemed to arrive...you know how it is with good intentions."

"Indeed I do," she laughed. "Indeed I do."

We sat in silence then, but it didn't seem awkward at all.

"Don't you ever miss them when you're traveling?" she started in again.

"Only in dire emergencies."

"Such as?"

"Such as when a toilet is overflowing and I don't know the local expressions for mop, plunger or terrible, stinking mess."

"I could see where that might be a problem."

"Oh, I can usually get by on pointing and sign language. And if that fails, I can always resort to the Old American Standard."

"What's the Old American Standard?"

"Repeating yourself over and over in English, only louder and slower each time."

"Oh? Does that work?"

"I assume it does if you do it slowly and loudly enough."

She favored me with a smile and tossed another chunk of cornbread into the water. There was an instantaneous flash of silver, a quick splash and then everything went quiet again. "So tell me," she asked absently, "what's it like to be a motorsports journalist?"

I thought about it for a moment. "It's like being everybody's favorite pariah," I finally answered.

"But don't you get invited absolutely everywhere?"

"Sometimes. On race weekends. Like tonight. Plus you get the launch parties for the teams and the new-car press junkets and things like that. But in between there are an awful lot of lonely nights and cheap motel rooms..."

"I can imagine."

"...And then there's the writing itself. People never think about it, but it takes a lot of time to put things properly into words. At least if you want to take pride in what you wind up with at the end."

"You make it sound noble and romantic."

"Oh, it is," I assured her. "Except when you're actually doing it. It's a long, lonely slog to get it done sometimes."

"If it were easy, then anyone could do it."

"I suppose. But it's aggravating and it's messy and it's frustrating as hell when you can't get it to come out right."

"I'm sure it is."

"Sometimes you have to fight and claw for every word and punctuation mark. And other times it comes out of you like...like vomit."

"Oh," she made a face. "How brilliantly colorful."

"No, really." I went on, searching for the exact, right words. "I don't know exactly how to explain it, but when it's coming like that, you couldn't stop it if you wanted to. It's like you're just the tube it flows through." I looked over and was pleased to see that she appeared to understand.

"So when do you write? Do you have a specific routine?"

"Some writers can do it anytime—even late at night—but it usually has to be early in the morning for me. Before my head gets filled up with the slop of everyday life."

"It sounds a bit fascinating."

"That's what writers want you to think," I assured her. "But you never want to be around a writer when he's wrapped up in something. Particularly if it's on deadline." I looked her in the eye. "Take my word for it. We're horrible company."

"Oh, you're just saying that."

"Trust me," I only half-laughed.

"But you must like doing it, mustn't you?"

"The truth is," I told her as I rolled it through my brain, "I feel lucky as hell to be doing what I'm doing." I threw off a guilty little smile. "Or at least I do most of the time, anyway...."

"You're lucky to feel that way."

"Yeah, I guess I am." I looked over at her again. "And how about you? How do you like traveling with a racing team?"

She dabbed at the corners of her mouth with her napkin. "I like it well enough."

"That doesn't exactly sound like a stirring endorsement."

"It has its awkward moments," she started in, but just as quickly stopped herself. "Look. Don't get me wrong. I do love the getting away. There's always such a sense of purpose and adventure to it."

"I know exactly what you mean."

"But, like you, I don't much enjoy the empty hotel rooms...."

"We could fix that for each other," I said without thinking. It was just one of those knee-jerk, smartass remarks guys make sometimes when they're trying to act cute or cool, and I felt the heat coming up in my cheeks as soon as I'd said it.

But Audrey just gave me an exasperated-schoolteacher glare and continued: "The fact is I always feel guilty about leaving my father. I worry about him now when he's on his own."

"Doesn't he ever come with?"

"Oh, he does sometimes when we're racing back in England. If it's nearby. But he doesn't travel so well any more. Not that he'd admit it." She looked out at the lights twinkling at us from the other side of the channel. "He's very independent, but he's also very much set in his ways these days. He likes his routine. And he doesn't really like to travel that much. Not really. Not any more."

"Not any more?"

"Oh, when he was fit and my mum was alive he couldn't wait to get away. Duty calls, you know. He was gone quite a bit when I was growing up, first with De Havilland and then with Aston and the rest after the war. But the magic of getting away has worn off for him since my mum passed. And of course it became more difficult after his stroke."

"Oh? How bad was it?"

She gave me a perfunctory shrug. "Oh, I suppose it wasn't too terrible as those things go. But he seems to like it better now staying close to home."

"Is he OK now physically?"

"Oh, he has a bit of trouble walking or standing for long periods of time. He uses a cane when he has to, but he hates it. He had to be in a wheelchair for a bit right after he got out of hospital, and he was thoroughly miserable about it." She shook her head and laughed: "Absolutely, thoroughly miserable about it the entire time."

"But he's better now?"

She nodded hesitantly. "He's made a rather miraculous recovery. Really he has. But then he's terrifically stubborn. Although I suppose 'determined' is a more flattering way to put it." She flashed me an apologetic smile. "People say I'm just like him."

"I'm sure you are."

She leaned back against the slats of the bench and stretched. "The rest of it is just old age and loneliness. I suppose we all get that eventually...."

Her words faded out over the water and all we could hear was the faint lapping of the waves against the pilings and the soft echo of the racing crews jabbering and laughing with each other back on the lawn. I had the sudden urge to kiss her—just to reach over and put my arms around her and pull her gently but inexorably towards me like you see leading men do in the movies. But we both had plates of food in our laps and, even if we didn't, it wasn't the sort of thing I imagined I had the style or self-confidence to pull off. So I tossed another shrimp tail in the water instead and watched the dull flash of silver break the surface again as the huge fish gobbled it up.

I was desperate for something to say.

"Tommy says your dad's the first one at the shop every morning," was the first thing that popped into my head.

"He's there when they unlock the door most days," she said proudly. "Except when he has his therapy." She fluttered out a weak laugh. "He hates that, too, of course."

I took a long, thoughtful sip of my beer. "The two of you live together?"

Audrey nodded as she threw another scrap of fish in the water. We saw a new, even larger silver flash appear and vanish below the surface. It made both of us blink. "I wonder if that's a shark?"

"Might be."

Audrey peered over the edge to get a closer look, but you couldn't see anything in the darkness. So she leaned her head back and stared up again at the bottomless pit of the sky. "This *is* a lovely night, isn't it?" she said dreamily.

"It surely seems to be."

She eased her eyes over to me. "Oh? Are things usually as they seem?"

"I suppose they are," I said like it actually meant something. And then quickly added: "Except when they're not, of course."

Audrey wrinkled her nose at me. "You know, Henry, you have a rare gift for inane conversation."

"Oh, I'm famous for it," I assured her. "In fact, I come from a long, distinguished line of inane conversationalists."

"I'm sure you do."

And then we just sat there, looking at each other, and I felt another sudden impulse to kiss her welling up inside of me. But how would I manage it? Should I gracefully excuse myself, lift the dinner plates smoothly and elegantly off our laps, set them gallantly on the dock, ease over closer to her, look back longingly into her eyes and hope that the moment hadn't passed? Or should I just take her in my arms and let them all tumble—let the soiled plates and spent, buttery corn cobs and uneaten remnants of shrimp tails and fish bones and the little styrofoam cups full of melted butter and tartar and cocktail sauce and creamy coleslaw spill all over us while we clenched in a desperate, steaming embrace like Burt Lancaster and Deborah Kerr in their famous, foam- and kelp-wrapped beach scene in *From Here to Eternity....*

"*Are you two about ready to go?*" Tommy's voice interrupted from behind us. The crew had finished their desserts and Geoff had already stopped Georgie and Peter from ordering another pitcher of beer.

"This has been a very pleasant dinner, Hank," Audrey said approvingly as I gathered up our plates and headed for one of the trash barrels on the lawn.

"Maybe we can do it again some time?" It made some strange little bundle of nerves tingle inside me when I said it.

"That would be nice," she agreed pleasantly. And I suppose that should have made me feel pretty good. But it just made that strange little bundle of nerves tingle even more.

Of course the bulk of the paddock chatter come Friday was about Augie Pabst's condition in the hospital—he was awake and alert and pretty much out of danger, but looking forward to a long, arduous and painful recovery—and the big, blowout Ferrari party on Count Giovanni Volpi's fabulous Benetti yacht scheduled for that evening. I really wanted to go, even though I didn't have an actual invitation or much of anything appropriate to wear. But Cal was going and I knew Cal (and he was moreover an official Ferrari factory driver) and I figured that amounted to at least half an invitation. And half an invitation is generally more than most motoring scribes usually require). On the other hand, I was kind of hoping that I could catch up with Clive Stanley's team again and maybe get a little more time in with Audrey Denbeigh. So I headed over to their paddock area after Friday's practice sessions were over. Only it turned out that Clive, as a fellow financial aristocrat, car owner and entrant, had been given an invite to Count Giovanni's yacht party, and he, Ian, Audrey and Tommy had already left to get cleaned up. "They hoped you might catch up with them at the party," Peter Bryant explained from inside the Aston's wheel well. He and Georgie had a lot of work to do mounting and balancing a set of fresh tires for qualifying, going through Geoff Britten's usual check list and sorting out a weepy front brake fitting, a lightly leaking left-side axle seal and an odd, unidentified clunk coming from somewhere under the Aston's rear end.

So I hurried back to my shitty motel room and got myself as presentable as possible, including a shower, a shave, washing my best and only white shirt in the bathroom sink and doing my best to dry and press it with a crappy steam iron I had to borrow from the front desk in my skivvies. And that's about when I realized that my camera bag was missing. I scrambled to get my clothes on and rushed back to the racetrack to see if I could find it, and naturally registration was long closed and the old geezer security guard at the front gate gave me a hell of a hard time about getting in without my pass. Which was neatly zipped into the side pocket of my camera bag, of course! And the more I argued and the more exasperated I got, the more the old guy seemed to enjoy getting ornery and officious right back at me. Most of the race-weekend security guards at Daytona are local retirees, and it's really a perfect job for them if they don't mind standing around out in the sun all day. It gives them a puffed-up sense of usefulness, authority and respect (along with a little much-appreciated spending money!) along with the chance to smile and wave at more people than they probably see the whole rest of the year. And every great once in awhile, it affords them a rare and delicious opportunity to get self-righteous and throw their weight around.

And I suppose you can't really blame them for that.

But it can sure piss you off when you're on the receiving end....

I'd been stranded at the tunnel entrance arguing with the guard for the better part of half an hour when the track press relations guy happened through. He sized everything up in an instant, had some whispered words with the guard and suddenly a big, false-teeth smile flashed across the old guy's face and he waved me on through. In the rearview mirror, I could see the press relations guy patting the old guy on the shoulder and complimenting him the fine job he'd done.

Naturally I found my camera bag right where I'd left it, sitting on a stack of freshly mounted Dunlops in Clive Stanley's garage area. "You left in quite a rush," Peter called out from under the car.

"We rather thought you'd be back for it," Georgie chimed in from beneath the left-front fenderwell. "Otherwise we were going to take it into town and see if we could locate ourselves a bloody pawn shop."

"And a bloody pub after that."

"And a proper girlie show, if we could find one."

"Some of the Jaguar lads found one last night. Said it was on a side street just a few blocks up from the boardwalk."

"I wonder what time it closes...."

Speaking of time, by the time I got down to the docks, Count Giovanni's gorgeous, 164-foot *L'Albatro d'Oro* had already cast off and was gliding gracefully out into the Atlantic. It was close enough that I could hear the sounds of a Brubeck-style jazz combo playing on deck, popping champagne corks, clinking glasses, shouts and laughter echoing across the water. I even saw Audrey standing at the railing surrounded by Tommy, Cal, Phil Hill, Ricardo Rodriguez and Olivier Gendebien. I called out to her and waved, but she couldn't hear me over the party noise and the low, confident exhaust burble from the big, twin diesels. "*You just missed her!*" a toothless old dock hand said like there was some kind of prize for it. And all I could do was just stand there and watch the glistening yacht slide gently away, with all my friends and all of that fun and music and laughter on board. And Audrey, too, of course....

With nothing much else to do, I wandered up the beach for awhile, just filling time and stupidly trying keep myself more or less parallel with the ever-diminishing silhouette of Count Giovanni's fabulous new yacht. There are only two ways you can go on the beach at Daytona—north or south—and my meandering eventually led me back to the boardwalk, where a small crowd of vacationing tourists, uniformed servicemen, a few other non-invitees from the racetrack and the usual smattering of stumbling, slobbering or slumbering Daytona Beach drunks loitered around the open-air bars, food stalls, carnival attractions and pinball arcades with rows of noisy Skee Ball machines out front. I tried my hand at a few Gottlieb pinballs inside one of them—I must've put a couple bucks-worth of change in one called "Dancing Dolls"—but it was awfully loud and jangly in there and the damn ball kept either falling into a gobble hole or draining right down the middle between the flippers where you couldn't do much of anything about it. I didn't win one free game. Or even an extra ball. I eventually wandered back out on the boardwalk and wasted another couple dollars throwing baseballs at a pyramid of silver-painted milk bottles that I can only assume were glued together and had several pounds of lead in the bottom. After that I bought myself a beer and a cardboard bowl of peppery fish chowder from one of the boardwalk vendors and then, with nothing much better to do, headed out towards the end of the fishing pier. There was a cool, crisp breeze fluttering in off the ocean and an endless series of low, slow breakers rolling in, and as the sounds of the boardwalk slowly faded behind me, I became aware of the loud, lonely clacking of my own footsteps on the wooden pier. You do it long enough and you get used to being on your own and living inside your own skin, and there's a certain comfort and familiarity to it. But it does tend to get a little lonely and melancholy now and then.

I was surprised to find a couple half-drunk shark fishermen huddled around a glowing Coleman lantern out at the far end of the pier. They were sitting on a pair of old, folding lawn chairs with a big, battered cooler, a backup case of beer and a large, shopworn tackle box between them. They had at least a half-dozen lines cast out on stout, deep-sea poles spaced out at regular intervals along the railing, and the remains of two crudely butchered amberjacks were strewn on the deck around them. The local tourist bureau offered a 25-dollar cash bounty on sharks caught anywhere near the beach, and they told me they came out every night the weather was halfway decent, hacked up some fresh mackerel or wahoo or pompano or whatever ("Y'gotta make sure it's good and bloody," one of them explained, holding up a severed fish head the size of a dinner platter so I could see), jammed big chunks of it onto hardened-steel shark hooks, threw their lines out, strapped their leather fighting harnesses around their waists and sat down to drink beer and wait for something to happen. Or not.

"Sometimes we're here all night," the first shark hunter said proudly.

"How often do you catch one?" I had to ask.

"Oh, that varies. Sometimes we get two or even three in a night. But they gotta be a'least three feet long or the bastids don't pay."

"We use them kind fer bait," the other one snorted.

The first one put a wavering hand on my forearm and pulled me in a little closer. He smelled of fish, beer and cheap cigars. "Oh, but lemme tell you," he hissed longingly. "Y'git you a *BIG* one on..." his hand tightened on my arm as his eyes rolled in an extended, euphoric swoon.

"Yessir," the other one nodded. "It don't git no better'n nat."

"An' in between," the first one added with a craggy, mischievous wink, "we just sit ourselves down an' drink ourselves some beer."

"It don't git no better'n nat, either!" the other one grinned. "Y'all wanna beer? We gots plenny." He pulled a bottle of beer out of his cooler, levered off the cap and handed it over.

"Thanks."

"Don'menshin it."

"But there's other times, too," the first one continued wistfully.

"Oh?"

"Why, we can go a week 'r more an' not git nothin'...'"

"Nuthin'!" The other one repeated disgustedly.

"But that's what makes it s'good, see," the first one corrected him. "The whole idea is to git a good'un 'fore we run outta beer money." His voice went down to a low, conspiratorial whisper: "We git a good'un, see, and we collects the bounty. We collects the bounty, see, and we buy us s'more beer." He gazed at me like he'd just shared one of the great secrets of the universe. "It always seems t'work out, see?"

"Yeah," the other one agreed grandly. "Have we got it knocked or what?"

"Sure looks like you do," I told him, and took another sip of my beer. To be honest, it felt a little chilly to be out at the end of a pier in the middle of a February evening drinking beer.

"You ready fr' a'nother 'un?"

"I've still got plenty left here."

"Y'gotta drink faster n'that around guys like us," he grinned proudly.

I'd somehow lost track of Count Giovanni's yacht out on the horizon. There was nothing but darkness along the horizon as far as I could see. I took another sip of beer and felt a cold, involuntary little shiver run up my spine. "Look, I really ought to be heading back now. I have to be over at the track early tomorrow morning...."

"Oh?" The first one asked. "Y'all over by the speedway?"

I nodded.

"You a *driver?*"

I shook my head. "Nah. I just kind of write about it."

He looked at me with renewed curiosity. "You do that for a *living?*"

I nodded, and he exchanged sets of faintly raised eyebrows with his partner.

"That must be real tough work," the second shark hunter observed. "I mean, tryin' t'make it sound interesting, all them cars just goin' 'round and 'round and 'round..." His eyes made slow, exaggerated loops like he was watching them go around. You could see it was making him a little dizzy.

"Well, good luck with your fishing," I told them. "And thanks for the beer."

"No problem," the second one grinned. "That's what the hell it's for!"

"You said it!" the first one agreed.

The second one beamed grandly at me and repeated: "Have we got it knocked or *what??!!"*

"It sure as heck looks that way."

"Y'all be sure an' stop back agin' if you're ever down this way," the first one yelled after me.

"I'll be sure and do that," I called back to him.

"We could prob'ly even find y'all a pole an' a harness if y'd want," the second one offered. "Me an' him's right here 'most ever' night...."

Saturday morning dawned bright and postcard-perfect at the speedway, and of course the hottest topic in the paddock was the big, blowout party on Count Giovanni's yacht the previous evening. "It was really rather special," Tommy allowed through a self-satisfied grin. "Although they had a little problem with the electrics and all the lights went out for awhile."

"The lights went out?"

"We had to make do with candles and lanterns until they got it sorted out. There were even suspicions it might have been done on purpose. Just for effect, you know."

So that's why I lost sight of the yacht when I was standing at the end of the pier with the shark fishermen.

"You should ask your friend Cal Carrington about it."

"Oh really? Why?"

Tommy flashed me a tight, narrow smile. "I believe he might have been with Audrey when it happened."

I felt a chill go through me. "Oh?"

Tommy nodded. So I excused myself and headed over to the Ferrari bivouac to have a word or two with Cal Carrington. And I didn't particularly like the things I was feeling inside. I hadn't felt anything like that for a long, long time, and I remembered all too well that it generally ended in misery.

I found Cal over by Carlo Sebastian's transporter drinking a morning cup of coffee. "So," I asked like it was no big thing, "how was the boat party last night?"

"You'd have to call it more than 'a boat.'"

"Okay, so how was the yacht party?"

The corners of his mouth curled up in a smile. "It was something else, Hank. It was really something else."

I waited for more, but nothing was coming. "So you had a good time?" I prodded.

"Hell, *everybody* had a good time!" He shot me a wink. "They had a great jazz combo and the lights went out for awhile. But they had all sorts of candles and Japanese lanterns. I think it may have even been planned." He shook his head. "It was really something, Hank. You should've been there."

"I tried, but I had to come back to the track for my credentials and camera bag. I got there too late. I just missed it."

"I know," he laughed. "We saw you on the dock." He took a sip of his coffee. "You looked so sad. Audrey said you looked like a lost puppy."

That went right through me. And it must have showed, because Cal's expression softened and he clapped his arm around my shoulder. "Hey, we missed you, pal," he assured me. "Really we did."

"You did?"

"Sure we did." He gave me an ambiguous wink. "Especially Audrey."

"She *did?*"

Cal looked me over like he wasn't exactly sure what sort of creature he had in front of him. "You're not very good at this, are you?"

"Good at what?"

Cal just smiled. "Look," he asked out of nowhere, "what're you doing between races?"

"What?"

"What're you doing between races," he repeated. "You know: between Daytona and Sebring."

"I dunno, Haven't really thought about it. I've got to fly back to Italy for the Maserati press briefing in Modena right after Daytona...."

"They're really up shit's creek, aren't they?"

"It doesn't look too good for them."

"I know we race against those guys, but it's a damn shame anyway."

"Yes it is," I agreed. "They've got a hell of a history."

"Yeah," Cal nodded. "And they've built some really great cars."

"They should've won the Grand Prix title *and* the World Manufacturers' Championship with Fangio and Moss in '57. But then it all went to shit in Caracas."

Cal looked into his coffee cup and sighed. "You need luck along with all the rest of it, don't you?"

"Yep," I agreed. "That you do."

Every racing driver knows about luck. When you have it, you have it. And when you don't, well....

"So what are you doing after the Maserati thing?" Cal started in again.

"Well, I've got the Ferrari press introduction in Maranello at the end of the month."

"Yeah," Cal nodded. "I've gotta be at that one, too."

"Be happy you're on the invite list," I reminded him.

"I'm *not* on the list," he corrected me. "I'm just the hired help."

"Be glad you're the hired help."

"I am," he said. "But the question is, for how long?"

"Why? Is something up?"

"Something's always up at Ferrari. The problem is no one ever knows what it is." He drained the last of his coffee and added: "Except the old man, of course. But he never shares his moves with anyone. Or not until they happen, anyway."

"That's always been his style."

"He's a great man, of course. A true colossus!" Cal looked down at the grounds in the bottom of his cup. "But you eventually come to realize that he's not a particularly nice person."

"If he were a nice person, he never would have achieved what he has. That's the way it is with a lot of great men."

We shared a moment of silent understanding.

"But how about after the Maserati thing?" Cal started in again. "You've got more than two weeks before the Ferrari press thing in Maranello?"

"I dunno," I shrugged. "I'd thought about going back to my place in London to pick up some fresh socks and underwear. Go through the bills I can't pay. See if my check's arrived yet from the magazine...."

"You sure know how to have a good time."

"I'd like to come back to Florida and sit on my ass on the beach for awhile, but I don't think I can scrape up the airfare to go back and forth to Italy twice."

"The magazine won't cover it?"

"Not hardly. I've only got one return ticket, and that's going to get me back for Sebring."

"That's too bad."

"Yeah, it is. I'd love to come back here instead of going back to London in fucking February."

"What would you do if you could come back?"

"I'd see if I could find a nice stretch of beach with a cheap room and somebody-or-other to share it with attached." I looked over at Cal. "Free would be even better."

"Free's always better," he agreed with a wink. "It costs less."

"That it does," I nodded. "I might even put in some work on that novel I'm never going to finish."

"I like a man with a positive attitude."

"Thanks."

Cal looked into his empty coffee cup. "How'dja like to go on an ocean cruise?" he asked out of nowhere.

"A *what?*"

"A sea cruise. On Count Giovanni's new yacht." He could see I wasn't connecting the dots. "You know," he moved his hand through the air like waves, "out on the ocean...."

It seems that Count Giovanni's *L'Albatro d'Oro* was heading up to a shipyard in Jacksonville to have a few new-yacht glitches ironed out and the electrical system checked over, and after that it was going on a little shakedown cruise up and down the Florida coastline. During the course of his party the previous evening, Count

Giovanni had quietly invited all the Ferrari drivers and thirty or forty of his close personal friends (some of whom he'd only met a few hours before) to come along for the ride.

"I think the timing might work out where we could just get back in time to fly over for the Ferrari thing in Maranello," Cal nodded.

"Boy, that would be great, wouldn't it? But I don't really think I can afford the extra airfare. Besides, I didn't really get an invitation."

"Hey, you're with *me!*" he said like that would take care of everything. "Besides, I don't think the Count will likely remember who-all he invited by the end of last night."

That's the way it goes sometimes in the world of international racing. You don't necessarily need to be rich to enjoy a bucks-up lifestyle, just in the right place at the right time. "It sounds like a hell of an opportunity," I had to admit.

"I don't think we should miss it," Cal grinned, and I had to agree. Only I couldn't really see how I could make it happen....

And that's about when a big, white transporter with Indiana plates on the back rolled into the paddock and headed for the permanent garage at the far end. No question the mysterious Pontiac Tempests were packed inside, so I took off for the far end of the pit lane to watch them unload. There was a white panel van and a new Pontiac station wagon parked next to the garage, and you could see by the zombie look in all the white-clad crew members' eyes that they'd driven straight-through from wherever the hell they'd come from and that they'd been up for who-knew-how-many days getting the cars finished. Or mostly finished, anyway. There were four Tempests in the transporter, and although they all looked freshly painted and nicely turned out, you could tell from the look of hopeless, worn-down panic on the crewmen's faces that they weren't really ready. But they hustled like hell anyway getting the cars unloaded, fluids and tire pressures checked, fired up and through tech inspection in time for the final practice session before qualifying.

I was standing on the pit wall next to Tommy Edwards when the four refrigerator-white Pontiac Tempests came chuffing down pit lane and headed out for their very first taste of a racetrack. "Whaddaya think?" I asked Tommy.

"I don't know what to think," he shrugged. "They look a bit large for it, don't they?"

Sure enough, the Tempests looked more like 7/8-scale stock cars than anything you might find on a road circuit. The two running in the 4.0-liter class had reasonably healthy exhaust notes—one was certainly a four and the other had to be a small V8—but you could feel the thunder off the other two right up through the soles of your shoes when they went by. There were obviously some *very* serious motors in those cars, and I made a mental note to head over and check them out as soon as the practice session was over.

Tommy and I wandered down to Turn One to get a better look, and along the way I tried to explain what the four oversized Pontiacs might be doing at Daytona. Pontiac's head of engineering was an ambitious, promotionally-oriented man-on-the-corporate-rise kind of guy named John Z. DeLorean, and no question he was on a mission to make Pontiac's Tempest stand out from the crowd. And that included its near-identical Buick Skylark and Oldsmobile F-85 corporate siblings at GM as much as the imports from overseas. So Pontiac's new Tempest was unique in offering a rear-mounted transaxle and a flexible-steel driveshaft that that provided better weight distribution and allowed for a lower driveline tunnel in the interior. Although some of the marketing guys from the other Detroit manufacturers (including some of GM's own divisions!) were derisively referring to it as "rope drive." John Z. also had the bright idea of essentially sawing one of Pontiac's 389 cubic-inch V8s in half to turn the right-hand cylinder bank into the base "Trophy 4" powerplant for the new Tempest, which surely cut down on tooling costs. Delorean was also a firm believer in the value of motorsports as an image-builder for his division. In fact, he was the one urging the rest of the Pontiac brass—right up to division chief Bunkie Knudsen and square in the face of the stupid AMA racing ban that GM and the rest of the American manufacturers had signed in June of 1957—to jump into racing and performance-oriented marketing campaigns with both feet. Now Pontiac was hardly the only American manufacturer doing a little back-door funding, encouraging, finagling and "special duty" parts development by February of 1962, and everybody from the drag strips in Podunk, Pomona and Englishtown to the Bonneville Salt Flats to the big NASCAR superspeedways knew all about it. But, except for a few fitful efforts with the 2-seater Thunderbird before the AMA ban came down and Chevy's proud but too often stifled, ignored or misunderstood Corvette program, none of the Detroit manufacturers had really fronted up much of a presence in road racing.

Or at least not until now....

It was obvious that someone had ponied up a large pile of cash to bring the four Pontiac Tempests to Daytona. And I must admit I wished them well. But the cars looked bulky, clumsy and uncoordinated trying to fumble their way through Daytona's Turn One buttonhook. They were just too damn big and heavy. Sure, their stock car-inspired suspensions worked great up on the bankings, but they handled pretty much like tug boats through the infield. But you could sure feel the throb when the two big-inch Tempests running in the over-5000cc GT class thundered down the straightaways. Especially Indianapolis 500 ace T.J. Huston's bellowing #53....

"Think they'll be able to keep brakes in them?" I asked Tommy.

"Not bloody likely," he allowed. "But you really need to know what they weigh. Size doesn't matter nearly as much as weight."

And that of course was true.

During lunch break I headed over to check out the Pontiacs, but they had the overhead doors down again and the side door locked. But I managed a peek through the window you could see exhausted crewmen flailing away like mad on all four of them. That's the way it always goes when you show up late with barely finished cars. And it surely didn't help at all that all four cars were running different engine and driveline combinations. One had a mildly hot-rodded "Trophy 4" under the hood and another had a warmed-over version of GM's new aluminum V8. But the two big-inch cars were stuffed chock-full of the same 4-bolt-main/NASCAR-head "Super Duty" 421 that had turned Pontiac into a big winner at drag strips and stock-car ovals just about everywhere. It was the biggest engine in racing when it was first introduced towards the end of the '61 season, and it was for sure the biggest engine at the Daytona Continental. They'd moreover put the two big-inch Tempests in the hands of tough-as-nails Indianapolis star T.J. Huston and front-running Pontiac stock car regular Paul Goldsmith, and no question both of those guys knew how to drive a damn racecar.

The Tempests had been race-prepped and entered by Ray and Frank Nichels of Nichels Engineering in Highland, Indiana, who had pretty much become Pontiac's back-door racing skunkworks and built most of the winning cars and motors for Pontiac's favored stock-car teams. Pontiac was doing an awful lot of winning at the time—particularly on the big tri-oval at Daytona—so they obviously knew what the hell they were doing. But stock cars on the tri-oval and sports cars on the road-racing layout were vastly different propositions, and I frankly wondered how Pontiac had managed (or even bothered?) to get the big-motor Tempests homologated for the over-5000cc GT class, since there was no such thing as a big-inch, V8-powered Tempest in Pontiac's model lineup. Or at least there wasn't in February of 1962, anyway....

General consensus in the press room was that the Tempests didn't stand a chance at Daytona. Or even lasting the distance, come to that. Not in this kind of race on this type of track against this kind of opposition. But somebody at some hidden desk deep inside the corporate bowels of Pontiac had made sure they had plenty to work with in terms of funding, parts and talent behind the wheel. The only thing they didn't have nearly enough of was time.

But even if I couldn't take the Tempests seriously as genuine contenders, I made a point of getting up early the next morning to get a closer look at the cars before the race. I arrived at the track just after sunup, and this time the overhead doors were wide open and crewmen were hustling like mad getting tires and pit equipment ready while others were still flailing away on the cars. So I just kind of waltzed right in. I even picked up a cup of coffee and a doughnut off a workbench and nobody said a thing.

Sure enough, at close range the Pontiacs looked every bit as tall, wide and bulky as they did out on the racetrack. But you had to admit they were well turned out. Pontiacs had been pretty much dominating the NASCAR stock car circuit (they'd won no less than 30 of the 52 Grand National stock car races during the '61 season—including the Daytona 500 with Marvin Panch—and Fireball Roberts would win the '62 edition of that race a few weeks later with one of Pontiac's new-for-'62 "Grand Prix" models) and you could see the guys in the Pontiac garage were seasoned racers who knew the ropes. It was also apparent that they were getting more than mere encouragement from the corporate types at Pontiac. In fact, it was impossible to miss the mixture of deep southern twangs and plain old Midwestern English as the guys in the team uniforms and the guys in golf shirts and sunglasses with "guest" passes clipped to their belts whispered back-and-forth to each other. But they all seemed pretty tight-lipped when it came to talking to the press. Then again, I don't think I was really supposed to be there.

I was looking with ill-disguised amazement at the monstrous, cast-iron 421 V8 under the hood of the #53 Tempest when I felt a pair of eyes boring two small, cold holes into my back. So I turned around and found myself face-to-face with none other than T.J. Huston himself! I'd seen his face a thousand times in magazines and race programs and newspaper stories, and he had eyes that could just about stare right through you. They were sharp hazel-grey with gunfighter crinkles at the corners, and even when they were looking straight at you, they seemed to be focused someplace further and deeper. T.J. had the build of a football linebacker—only maybe half-a-head shorter—wore his hair in a crew cut and carried himself like a cocked pistol. I'd actually met him once or twice before—not that he'd remember—and by February of 1962 he'd already won the Indy 500 and the USAC driving title and was clearly on every car owner's short list of guys you wanted driving for you rather than against you. T.J. came up the hard way from the little bullring ovals in Texas, and he'd climbed up through the midget and sprint car ranks banging tires off walls and other cars three and even four times a week at county fairs and little dirt and asphalt ovals all over the country. His toughness and determination were already legendary, and T.J. had a reputation as a guy you didn't want to mess with. And here I was more-or-less smirking at the huge, cast-iron V8 under the hood of his car.

"Y'all don't think too much of my racecar, do ya, Lyons?" he drawled around a fat wad of chewing gum.

I couldn't believe he knew who I was. "I-I was just kind of looking at it," I more-or-less stammered. It sounded pretty lame, even to my own ears.

"Naw," he said like he was genuinely thinking it over, "I believe what you was doin' was *laughin'* at my car."

I didn't know whether to duck, apologize or try to come up with some sort of snappy response. But I never got the chance.

"Tell you what," he continued, gum smacking but eyes never blinking, "I got ten bucks says I lead the first lap." He stopped chewing and I watched the corners of his mouth curl up into a rattlesnake smile. "You got ten bucks on you?"

"S-sure," I answered while mentally totaling up the loose change in my pockets. "Sure I've got ten bucks."

"Well then, why don't let's bet on it?"

"B-bet on it?"

"*Sure!*" he grinned, and started in on the gum again. "My ten bucks says I lead the first lap of this here race today, and your ten bucks says I don't..."

My mouth opened and closed a few times, but nothing of any consequence came out.

"Look," he shrugged. "You got all your Fee-rah-rees and Jag-wires an' crap out there, an' all I've got is this little ol' Tempest that ain't hardly born yet..." he stared me right in the eyes. "Seems like easy money to me..."

I didn't say a thing.

He looked me up and down. Real slow, you know, like he was taking inventory. "...Or are you one of these typical writer guys who's all mouth and opinions but not much on backbone?"

I felt a cool breeze of panic go through my gut as he extended his hand. "C'mon," he urged through a Cheshire Cat smile, "Put'cher money where your mouth is."

God help me, I took his hand and shook it....

Of course, what T.J. knew and I didn't at the time was that the Daytona organizers, in an effort to provide a better show for the fans and avoid the likely carnage when the 53-car field exploded away from a Le Mans-style start along pit lane and attempted to bang, barge and jostle their way through the narrow, doubles-back-on-itself confines of Turn One, decided to run the first lap around the NASCAR tri-oval and only then, after the field had sorted itself out a bit, peel off into the infield at the beginning of Lap Two. The organizers had furthermore decided to grid the cars by displacement rather than qualifying times, and that put T.J. Huston and Paul Goldsmith and their two hulking Pontiacs up at the front of the field. Followed by all eight Corvettes, two aging Lister-Chevys and the two Chevy-powered Chaparrals, Clive Stanley's Aston and the two Jaguar E-Types before you got down to the 3-liter-and-under Ferrari sports/racers and GTs that were actually likely to be on top at the end of three hours. You got the feeling that some of the speedway's friends up in Michigan might have wanted a nice publicity shot of their oh-so-practical-and-affordable Pontiac Tempests leading a field that included some of the best, most famous and most expensive sports cars on the planet.

Like they say, a picture is worth 1000 words.

Although, as my motorsports photographer pal Hal Crockett constantly reminded me, it doesn't pay as well.

Big Bill France was well known for his promotional prowess, and he'd brought in a bunch of celebrities and dignitaries for his first-ever international road race and made sure they got paraded around in front of the grandstands in open convertibles.

Including the reigning Miss Universe, Marlene Schmidt, who was Official Race Queen for the Daytona Continental and managed to snap necks, slacken jaws and leave trails of drool behind her wherever she went all day. And then Bill's old friend John Holman did a demonstration run in the quietly whooshing, turbine-powered Thunderbird 2-seater he'd built as kind of a engineering exercise back in 1956. Although that was a little underwhelming since it didn't make much noise (although you had to be impressed with how quickly it gained speed and the billowing curtain of heat waves it left in its wake).

But eventually all the hoopla, high school bands and pre-race presentations came to an end, the National Anthem played and everyone's gaze focused down on the racecars lined up at a slant against the low concrete wall along pit lane and the drivers standing nervously across from them. And I suppose it really shouldn't have come as any great surprise when T.J. Huston borrowed a page from Stirling Moss' playbook and anticipated the flag drop by at least a step or two. Or maybe three or four. In any case, he was in his car and away quicker than anybody. Not to mention that he was starting from the very front of the field and had the other big-inch Tempest and all the Corvettes right behind, clogging up any possible passing lanes until the cars got well out on the banking. And it didn't help that poor Dick Rathmann hit the primer knob for the Hilborn fuel injection instead of the starter button on the unfamiliar dash of his Meister Brauser Chaparral (which was of course gridded well up towards the front) and flooded the engine. And that necked down the available maneuvering room even more. By that time T.J. was up on the banking with his right foot all the way to the throttle stops, and I felt a cold, sinking feeling coming from the general area of my wallet. There was no way in hell anybody was going to catch him before the cars swept past the start/finish line on the tri-oval and peeled off into the infield. The sight of T.J. Houston's Tempest leading the all those fancy-pants European cars and famous European drivers set off a round of whoops and cheers from the local newspaper scribes and syndicated stick-and-ball writers up in the press box. Many of whom, at least at that particular moment, had no idea what they were watching.

"Y'all oughta come down here fr' the 500..." the one on the stool next to me hollered. *"...See you some REAL racin'! Not this fiddly-ass shit through the infield!"*

But of course his enthusiasm was destined to be short-lived. T.J.'s Tempest thundered past us in the lead and damn near stood on its nose as he braked it hard and early for Turn 1. The accordion closed in quickly behind him, and he got passed in a hurry once the cars funneled down towards the hairpin—first by Roger Penske's Cooper and then by Phil Hill's Ferrari Dino—and the Pontiac's engine blew up in an enormous cloud of smoke before T.J. even got it back up on the banking. And Paul Goldsmith didn't fare much better, pulling in with terminal grinding noises coming from the rear end at the end of Lap 2. But even if the big-inch Pontiacs turned out to be nickel rockets—comically so, in fact—I was surely ten dollars poorer and T.J. Huston was just as surely ten dollars richer. To be honest, I kind of hoped I could avoid him for the rest of the day (or, better yet, that he'd take off rather than hanging around after his car broke). Not that I was trying to stiff him, you understand. I'd lost the bet fair and square and I had every intention of paying off fair and square. Every intention in the world. But there were six weeks between the two Florida races with two press conferences in Italy and a possible yacht cruise down the Florida coast in between, and money was sure to be tight. I figured it would be ever so much more convenient if we could settle up later....

In the meantime, The Meister Brauser mechanics had rushed out to pit lane, yanked the hood off the Chaparral and flailed away desperately at the Hilborn-injected Chevy underneath. But the engine was badly flooded and it took several long, agonizing laps to change all the plugs and get it running again. Rathmann drove like absolute stink after that, and set some of the fastest laps of the race on his way to a remarkable but generally unnoticed 6th place finish.

All in all, the inaugural Daytona Continental turned out to be a pretty interesting race. Especially towards the end. Phil Hill in the mid-engined Ferrari Dino managed to wrest the lead away from Roger Penske's prudently driven Cooper Monaco and immediately began pulling away. It looked to me like Roger had wisely set his sights on the end of the race three hours hence rather than the dubious honor of leading the early laps. Phil and the 246 Dino looked like they had the legs on everybody. But Dan Gurney in Ernesto Julio's Lotus 19 was hanging in there, driving at a smooth, conservative pace yet keeping the leaders comfortably in sight. You got the idea he had a little something in hand for later when it counted. But of course the big question marks on a Lotus are always sturdiness and reliability, not speed. Pedro Rodriguez underlined that fact when the rear suspension on his 19 collapsed barely an hour into the race. It made you realize all over again how important preparation is on a car like that, and to appreciate what a meticulous job ace California wrench Jerry Eisert had done on the 19 Gurney was driving.

I was pleased to see my friend Cal Carrington doing a better than decent job in Carlo Sebastian's Testa Rossa, powering up through the field and really howling around the bankings. No question it was one of the fastest of all—along with the two Chaparrals—when it came to sheer, flat-out top speed. Cal managed to catch and pass Gurney's carefully driven Lotus 19 and Penske's ditto Cooper Monaco up on the bankings, and a lot of us in the press room were getting lulled into the inevitability of another boring Ferrari 1-2. Or at least we were until poor Phil Hill had an absolutely horrible pit stop where everything went wrong. And then he had to come in a second time because they didn't get the damn gas cap closed and fuel was sloshing out all over the place! So Hill and Rodriguez were relegated to playing catch-up the whole rest of the race. And then Cal's Testa Rossa inhaled a damn seagull down the backstraight at something like 175 or so—no, really!—and a few laps later it blew a front tire (on the same side) while running around the Turn 4 banking. It was a spooky moment and Cal had to do a bit of wheel-wrestling to get everything back under control. He was past any hope of making the pit entry, so he had to limp around for an entire lap with the tire carcass flailing before he could get to the pits to have it replaced. So he dropped well back, too. And then the Climax engine in Roger Penske's Cooper started losing oil pressure (again, maybe from the centrifugal force on the bankings forcing oil away from the pickup?) and he had to pull it in and retire at about two-thirds distance. All of which left Dan Gurney's presumably fragile Lotus 19 with a secure-looking lead over Jim Hall's Chaparral while young Ricardo Rodriguez was driving the Dino like a madman, trying to catch up.

The Ferrari Berlinettas were, as expected, totally dominating the bigbore GT category and running well up in the overall standings. Stirling Moss was taking full advantage of his ride in Carlo Sebastian's Le Mans Speciale Aerodinamico, tootling its klaxon horn to warn backmarkers out of the way and pretty much running away from everybody. Which came as a bit of a shock to the local newspaper types who were counting on Freddie Fritter to put all those sit-down-to-pee foreign drivers in their place. Although, to be honest, Freddie was doing a pretty amazing job in his first-ever sports car race. He'd gotten a more than respectable Le Mans start for a guy who didn't look at all like a sprinter and could barely fit in the damn car. And after that he put in a hell of a drive, picking his way quickly but carefully through the Corvette and Jaguar traffic and putting some really solid laps in when he was on his own. Of course, he couldn't do much of anything about Moss (then again, neither could anybody else) as Stirling motored serenely off into the distance. You could've fit a whole Indian River grapefruit into the wide-open mouth of the local scribe sitting next to me as Moss pulled inexorably away from Freddie in the early going. And I'd be lying if I didn't admit I got a little charge off of it.

"He's just savin' his car fer the end," the guy next to me said hopefully. But you couldn't miss the hollow little waver in his voice.

"I got ten bucks that says Moss beats him by over a lap at the end," I sneered at him. Truth is, I was just trying to get the money back that I'd already lost to T.J. Huston and his damn Pontiac. And I knew you've got to challenge a guy's manhood a little if you want him to take a sucker bet.

But the local scribe knew better and backed up in a hurry. "Uh, I'm not much of a bettin' man," he mumbled lamely. "My church don't allow it."

Damn.

But as the race wore on, I had to give Freddie Fritter his due. He was doing one hell of a fine job! Towards the middle of the first stint he found himself battling Clive Stanley's Aston Zagato for 2nd in the bigbore GT category. Ian Snell had made his usual berserker start in the Aston and managed to split a pair of side-by-side Corvettes as they braked hard for Turn 1 at the start of the second lap. He just about had to suck in the door handles to get it done, and it looked like a pretty damn impressive move until you stepped back and realized there were another two hours and fifty-eight minutes to go. But that was Ian's style: flat-out and then some. You could see he was all flailing arms and elbows trying to stay ahead of Freddie Fritter and not lose sight of Stirling Moss (who was nonetheless motoring nonchalantly off into the distance at something like a second per lap). And Freddie seemed perfectly content to just sit there on the Aston's rear deck and enjoy the show rather than risking anything reckless at that stage of the race. Smart. And it surely must have been an entertaining show, since Ian was kicking up dust at the apexes and corner exits everywhere, bulling his way through slower traffic and doing some highly ambitious motoring in the process. Freddie finally got by when Ian guessed wrong in traffic and had to go onto the grass at the International Horseshoe to avoid collecting some guy in an Alfa SZ who was minding his own business. After that Freddie just motored gently away, even though Ian was driving at about eleven-tenths to claw back up to him. Freddie was also easing away from all the other Ferarri Berlinettas (except Moss, of course), and some of them were in the hands of highly regarded and far more experienced road racers.

I stopped by Clive Stanley's pit several times during the three hours—mostly to chat up Audrey, if you want the truth of it—and I was there towards the end of the first stint when Ian was having his epic battle with Freddie Fritter's Ferrari Berlinetta. It was keeping Audrey pretty busy since there were still a lot of cars running, and it got even worse when cars started peeling off into pit lane for their first round of fuel stops. And that's about when it all started going to shit for Clive Stanley's team. At around the fifty-minute mark, Ian got himself chopped and then collected when he tried passing a backmarker heading through the little dogleg kink at the end of Turn 1. It was dumb, ill-considered and avoidable as far as Hal Crockett could see (and he was right there taking pictures and saw the whole thing) and the impact crumpled the fender down on the left-front tire. Which of course blew with an enormous *"BANG!"* as Ian hammered back up onto the banking. So he had to limp the rest of the way around on the bottom apron (on three good tires and a naked, pretzelized wheel rim) before he could bring it in for repairs. Then Georgie Smales had a hell of a time getting the bent wheel off and the rumpled sheet metal pulled and pounded away. Peter Bryant kept trying to get in there to help, but Georgie kept pushing him away even while Geoff Britten was yelling for him to move aside. As you can imagine, Clive Stanley was going absolutely berserk on the pit wall, wringing his hands and shouting contradictory instructions in a high, frantic little voice while his face turned an entire tropical-sunset range of colors under his stylish Borsalino hat. Peter Bryant finally got in there with a big pair of shears and cut some ragged slits in the sheet metal so they could bend, fold and pound it out of the way, and then he and Georgie slathered about five pounds of duct tape over everything, filled it up with fuel and sent Tommy on his way. Tommy gave a half-hearted thumbs-up as he droned past at the end of his first lap, but you could see he was eyeballing that raggedy left-front fender and the way it was bulging and flapping at 150-plus on the tri-oval.

I clambered up onto the rickety little timing stand next to Audrey. She had her nose buried in her lap chart and a bank of four stopwatches running in front of her—it's not easy keeping track of all five Ferraris GTs, the Cunningham E-Type and the lone, 4-cylinder Pontiac Tempest that was still running plus all eight Corvettes—and she was still hard at it even though Ian's ill-advised crash and the long pit stop that followed had all but taken them out of the race. "You're uncommonly diligent!" I told her as the two Grady Davis Corvettes and Gendebien in Count Giovanni's Ferrari Belinetta went howling by in a cluster.

"Force of habit!" she sighed as she marked the times down on her chart. The track in front of us went empty for a moment and she looked over at me and smiled. "I was brought here to do a job for this team, and by God I'm going to do it."

"Even though things have gone to shit?"

She gave me a sour look. "Haven't you ever read Lord Tennyson's *Charge of the Light Brigade?*"

"Sure. I had to read it in school. *'Half a league, half a league, half a league on-ward, all in the valley of Death rode the six hundred....'*"

"I know the words," she cut me off as she clicked her watch on Freddie Fritter's #22 and wrote the time down. "But it's all about duty, isn't it? We British are big on that sort of thing. Famous for it, in fact."

"So I've heard."

I looked down at the lap chart in front of her. Each car number had its own row of lap boxes, and she had carefully noted each lap completed and written in the appropriate lap time in neat, rounded characters. Or an "M" for a missed lap (which happens now and then, even for the best timers and scorers) or a circled "P" for "Pit" when a car came in for refueling or repairs. It was important for a team to keep good lap charts, as the official timing and scoring systems have been known to get out of whack—even at major events like Sebring and Le Mans—and sometimes the teams have to produce their own charts to help settle things. But of course that all becomes pretty academic when your team suffers a problem and drops out of contention. Even so, Audrey was hard at it, clicking off the laps of two GT Ferraris, the Cunningham E-Type and another Corvette as they went past and writing their times in the proper rows and boxes.

"Doesn't it ever get boring?"

"Sometimes," she allowed. "But it's usually so hectic you can't find the time to be bored."

"Do you always do it alone? It seems like a pretty difficult job for just one person."

"Oh, I'll have help for the longer races. There'll be two or even three of us. But this is only three hours, so we thought we'd keep things lean."

"What happens when you have to pee?"

She glared at me. "One tries to not think about it."

"But what happens if you *really* have to pee."

She glared at me some more. "Above all else, we *certainly* don't talk about it."

We shared a laugh off of that.

"Well, I don't envy you. At least I get to move around. Shoot some pictures if the light and the angles are right. Drop by the press room to have a fresh cup of coffee and pick up the hourly results. Do a few interviews with drivers and team managers down here in the pits. You're pretty much welded to the stand here, aren't you?"

"I'm just part of the furniture."

"It must get terribly dull sometimes."

"Oh, times like this it does. I mean, in a 12- or a 24-hour race, there's always the chance that you can come back. Not *race* your way back necessarily, but have the fates deal a little hard luck to someone else for a change. It's terribly exciting when it looks like you're out of it at 7pm and then find yourself back in the thick of it at 10 in the morning...."

"That ever happen to you?"

"Not yet. Not at the races I've attended. But my father's told me a thousand times about that one year at Le Mans when he was with Aston."

"Oh?"

"The driver got the car stuck on a sandbank on the very first lap of the race. Said he got pushed off, of course," she gave off a little snort of a laugh "but they always say they got pushed off, don't they?"

"Mostly they do."

"It took him the better part of an hour to dig it free." She paused for dramatic effect. "And then things got even worse."

"Oh?"

She nodded. "There was some sort of electrical gremlin and the headlamps would switch themselves off. The driver would be flailing merrily along, doing every bit of a hundred-sixty on the straightaways, and then—just like *that!*—the lights would cut out. Pitch black in an instant!" She shook her head. "I can't even imagine it."

I could. And it sent a shiver through me. "So what happened?"

"Oh, it cost them at least another half-hour in the pits before they tracked it down. Bloody switch, wouldn't you know?"

"They must've been pretty far back by then."

"Oh, it was hopeless!" she laughed. "Absolutely hopeless. My father was so disgusted he left for a bite to eat and then went to get some sleep in the caravan." Her face went serious for an instant: "He'd been up for two days."

"I know how that goes."

Her face brightened. "But when he woke up a few hours later—it was just coming up dawn, I think—the car was running like absolute clockwork. In fact, it was bloody well *screaming!* It'd rained during the wee hours and Tommy'd done an absolutely brilliant stint through the worst of it. Made up two laps on the leaders and never put a wheel wrong. Not once." You could tell she thought a lot of Tommy Edwards. "And some of the other cars had troubles of their own as well." You could hear the excitement building in her voice. "By 11:00 in the morning, they were back on the same lap as the second-place car and only three laps down on the leader. And there were still five hours to go!" A big, self-satisfied grin spread across her face.

"So what happened?"

The grin faded. "Oh, the head gasket failed. Started steaming like a bloody teakettle at straight-up noon and they were out of it by 12:15. Cooked, you might say." She shrugged her shoulders. "But that's the game, isn't it?"

"Indeed it is."

"Yes, indeed it is." She agreed. Then looked out at the racetrack again. "Did I miss Tommy?"

"I don't think so."

She glanced down at her watches again and then back at the racetrack. "Are you *sure?* He should have been by 12 seconds ago."

I shook my head. "I didn't see him. But I was listening to your story. We might both have missed him...."

She didn't look convinced, and made a little circled "M" with a question mark next to it in the appropriate box on her chart.

And that's when Tommy and the Aston went by. We looked at each other. The engine sounded perfect. But then we heard it cut completely as he got on the brakes for Turn 1. You could see the back end rise up on tiptoes and go all squirrely with no engine braking to stabilize it, and then we heard the engine switch abruptly back on as Tommy coasted towards the end of Turn One. It wailed up through second gear, cut completely for a moment, switched back on, wailed up through most of third and then cut out again as Tommy approached the braking zone for the International Horseshoe. It didn't take a mechanical genius to figure out what the hell was going on: the damn throttle was stuck wide open and he was driving it on the key! It turned out Tommy'd gone straight off at the fast, daunting left-hander after the hairpin the first time it happened—under race conditions you normally kept off the brakes through there and just gave it a judicious lift—and he wound up going for one hell of a ride through the grass. But then it seemed to fix itself. Or at least it did until he lifted off for Turn One half a lap later. At least he was ready for it the second time.

Tommy pulled in with the engine switched off at the end of the lap. *"It's stuck wide open!"* he screamed at Geoff Britten. *"It stuck once and I fooled with the pedal and it came free, but then it stuck wide open again and stayed that way."*

Peter and Georgie had the hood up in an instant, fiddled with the linkage until it popped free, jiggled it back and forth a few times, shrugged at each other, dropped the hood and sent him off again. But he was in the very next lap with the throttles jammed wide open again. *"If I keep on like this, I'm going to bloody well wad it up!"*

After some searching around and head-scratching, Peter Bryant finally figured it out. A motor mount had broken, and that was allowing the engine to shift on its moorings and bind up the linkage. And there wasn't much they could do to fix it.

"You're just going to have to soldier on with it," they told Tommy.

"Why don't you put Ian back in?"

"Because we want to make the bloody finish."

So, with something like a half-hour to go, they sent Tommy back out with in- structions to do his best, be careful, drive it on the key when necessary and just try to make the finish. After all, the Cunningam E-Type of Walt Hansgen and the painfully off-the-pace 4-cylinder Tempest of Rodger Ward were the only cars still running in class, and while the Jag was well ahead (and running a semi-respectable 17th overall), the 4-cylinder Pontiac was bog slow and had suffered countless teething problems so it was many laps behind. And a second-in-class finish at a major international race—even a lucky, weak-field, attrition-aided and mired-well- back-in-the-final-results second-in-class finish—was just the sort of thing a chap like Clive Stanley could get puffed-up about in front of his motorsports-ignorant friends and family. But the prospect of trying to do the last half-hour with the throttles locking open didn't sound like much fun for my friend Tommy Edwards. Not much fun at all.

And then the brake pedal started going long.

You have to use the brakes harder and longer when you don't have downshifting and engine braking to help slow things down, and the inevitable result is that the brakes start getting hotter and hotter and don't tend to work as well. It was just a little problem at first, but then the pedal started going deeper and longer and getting spongier and spongier until Tommy had to pump the shit out of it to get any pres- sure at all. That's never a good feeling. It turned out that there was a hairline crack in the left front brake-line fitting that Georgie had supposedly "fixed" two nights before. But he'd only re-tightened it to stop the weeping, and it finally split wide open heading into Turn One just a few laps from the finish. Tommy was already committed to the corner when he felt the pedal drop helplessly to the floor and, as he rather entertainingly described it afterwards, "I was confronted with a choice between spinning it, knocking over a few rubber cones winding up who knows where or continuing on my original trajectory and motoring headlong into the guardrail. After due consideration, I decided to spin it and hope for the best...."

And that's how my friend Tommy Edwards wound up depositing Clive Stanley's Imperial Crown Tea Aston Martin DB4GT Zagato in the shallow ditch on the inside edge of Turn One with less than 10 minutes left to run. He had the engine switched off, of course, and had to take a long, slow think about just how he could get it fired up, out of the ditch, turned around and back onto the racetrack and the rest of the way to the finish with no brakes to speak of and the throttles jammed wide open. But it turned out to be a moot point. When Tommy licked his lips, took a deep breath, rolled his eyes up to the heavens and hit the starter, the only noise was a faint, fading *"gnnn...gnnn...gnnnnnn"* followed by a staccato clicking noise.

Dead battery.

Done.

Finished.

DAMN!

But what could you do?

At least the car was still in one piece.

But that's what makes endurance racing so damn fascinating. It's the drama. The suspense. The heartbreak. The lurking irony. The inevitable gallows humor. The weird, wacky, spooky, silly and utterly unpredictable things that always seem to happen....

After Tommy's car dropped out I headed up to the press room to watch the last few laps, and it turned out to be as incredible as it was unlikely. Thanks to other people's misfortune as well as his own, well-judged speed, Dan Gurney had stretched out an unassailable lead in Ernesto Julio's Lotus 19. Jim Hall was running a few laps back in second in his Chaparral, but his mirrors were filling alarmingly with hard-charging Ricardo Rodriguez in the 246SP Dino he was sharing with Phil Hill. Rodriguez was closing visibly on Hall through the infield—absolutely flying!— but then Hall would put his foot into that big Chevy V8 and the distance would stabilize and even stretch out a bit as they swept around the bankings. As so often happens after a long, droning endurance grind, we suddenly had a real *race* to watch right at the end. And then, with less than fifteen minutes to go, Gurney's Lotus started puffing out little wisps of smoke. Followed by bigger wisps. You could hear the engine was running rough as it passed under the press box, and at the same time Rodriguez had caught right up with Jim Hall's Chaparral and started hunting, poking and feinting for a way by. We watched Gurney slow markedly—just trying to make the finish since he was two full laps ahead—but, with barely five minutes left, the Lotus belched out a huge cloud of steam and smoke as a connecting rod exited through the side of the crankcase. *BANG!*

But it happened just as Dan was clawing his way around the Turn 3 and 4 bankings for the penultimate time! And Dan knew what to do. He coasted the Lotus way up to the very top of the banking and slowed it to a halt—just *parked* it!—about two feet shy of the start/finish stripe! And then he just *sat* there, foot on the brake to keep it from rolling and surrounded by a cloud of steam and oil mist, just waiting for the 3-hour time limit to expire....

And meanwhile, out on the track, Rodriguez' Ferrari was having one hell of a race for second (or might it be first?) with Jim Hall's Chaparral. The brave and fiery young Mexican was trying to sneak his way by almost everywhere through the infield, but Jim was covering his moves and then using the Chaparral's power to pull away by a car length or two down the backstraight and around the bankings. And meanwhile Gurney couldn't do anything but just sit there by the upper guardrail and watch them go by. As you can imagine, the scribes in the press room were going absolutely apeshit, and it was a hell of a show for the small handful of spectators who'd hung around for the finish.

In the end, the aggressive Rodriguez and the light, nimble 246 Dino finally managed to squeeze past Hall's Chaparral under braking in the infield. And quickly pulled out enough distance so the Chaparral couldn't attempt a re-pass on the bankings. Now the question was: could Rodriguez (and Hall, right in his wake and with his foot planted) make it around to the stripe before the three-hour time limit expired to steal first and second? It was a real nail-biter, right down to the last few seconds. But the clock ran out just as Rodriguez and Hall swept into the Turn 3/4 banking for the very last time. The checker waved in the air and Gurney nodded, released the brake pedal, hit the starter button so the officials would at least think the car was moving under its own power and let the Lotus coast silently down the banking. It rolled across the start/finish line at barely a walking pace just as Rodriguez' Ferrari and Hall's Chapparal thundered over the stripe to take second and third!

Wow!

What a finish!

I don't know exactly what it is with the Daytona International Speedway and dramatic finishes, but that was just the first of so many they've managed to keep serving up, race after race and year after year....

And we had even more drama in the smallbore GT classes. As expected, Porsche's factory-entered Abarth Carrera with Joakim Bonnier at the helm had been leading the 1600cc class and easily running away with the under 2-liter GT category. But the 4-cam Porsche uncharacteristically dropped a valve almost in sight of the checkered flag. Bonnier had no choice but to park it, and since the F.I.A. rules stipulate that a car must cross the finish line under its own power, the factory Porsche wouldn't even be classified as a finisher. That left the 1600cc GT class to a very nice guy named Pat Corrigan, who'd come home a distant 25th overall in an ordinary, pushrod Porsche 356B sponsored by a local dealer out of nearby Jacksonville called Brundage Motors. Or "Brumos," for short. And the whole team was pretty damn happy about winning their class and picking up some of those valuable Category 2 World Manufacturers' Championship points for the Porsche factory back in Stuttgart. Or at least they were until the reporter from *Competition Press* asked how they felt about finishing behind (and second in the points- and money-paying Under-2 Liter GT category to) lanky Floridian Charlie Kolb in a little 1300cc Alfa Romeo Giulietta SZ?

Ever see a great, big bunch of smiles fade into frowns?

As expected, Stirling Moss had run away with the over 2-liter GT category in Carlo Sebastian's Le Mans Speciale Aerodinamico Ferrari Berlinetta (in fact, he came in a rather astonishing 4th overall in the final standings) but Freddie Fritter also put in a great drive. Although he almost saw it crumble to nothing right there at the end. Like Stirling, Freddie had elected to run the whole three hours by himself, and things had been going swimmingly once he got around Ian Snell just before the first round of pit stops. Freddie was running quickly but carefully, making smart decisions in traffic, taking perfect care of the equipment and generally doing what you'd want and expect from a top class racing driver. But it damn near went to shit on the final fuel stop with less than an hour to go. That's when the hood catch got bent because one of Carlo Sebastian's mechanics accidentally slammed it down with a wrench still under it. They tried to get it to latch again, but the damn thing kept popping open. But it was hinged at the front, so Freddie went out for a lap to see how bad it was. And it was plenty bad. The air pressure underneath made the hood lift up so high on the straightaways and around the bankings that Freddie could barely see over it. And he was sure to get black-flagged even if he could somehow figure out how to drive it by looking out the side windows. So Freddie charged into the pits and hollered: *"RIP THE DAMN THING OFF, WILLYA??!!"* The two Italian mechanics looked at each other for a heartbeat, grabbed a pair of open-end wrenches each and had the damn thing unbolted and off in less than 30 seconds. And they were still standing there, holding it up in the air, when Freddie dropped the hammer and took off from underneath it, screaming back onto the racetrack with nothing above the carburetor throats but warm, rushing air and bright Florida sunshine! And that's the way he drove it the rest of the way, coming home a solid 2nd behind Moss in the big-bore GT category and a highly respectable 12th overall at the checker.

It was a pretty damn impressive performance, no two ways about it.

So I made a point of stopping by #22's garage area right after the race. *"I'll get the hang of this here road racing stuff,"* a smiling Freddie assured all the scribes, fans and hangers-on who'd gathered around. And nobody who knew him—particularly that rube sports writer from the next stool over in the press room—doubted it one bit. And by then I didn't, either. Freddie Fritter had beaten a lot of *very* good road racers that day.

Chapter 5: View from the Top of The Tower

There are moments in life when things change for you. And most times you don't see them coming or recognize it when they happen. It's only later, after you discover yourself heading off in a new and different direction that you think back and see how it happened. And this all started as I was gathering up my notes, result sheets and camera bag in the Daytona press room. The driver interviews were long over and most everybody was gone by then except an old guy emptying waste baskets—all the other scribes were probably on their way to a couple noisy, wasted hours in the airport bar—but I've always enjoyed that lonesome, hollow, bittersweet sort of melancholy that descends over a racetrack after everything's gone quiet and all the crowds have leaked away. Go ahead, call me a sap. But I like watching the few, remaining race crews loading up their cars and equipment, rolling up their tents and awnings, folding their tables and lawn chairs and packing everything away into their station wagons, pickup trucks and transporters for the long drive home. The amateurs inevitably take longer than the pros, even though they have far less to pack. But you can't blame them for wanting to savor their weekend in the Big Time, and I knew several of them would still be there, long after sunset—poking around at this and that with the last, lukewarm beer from the cooler in hand—until the scrawny old security guard with no bullets in his gun and his teeth in his shirt pocket came around to shoo them off the property....

I screwed on my longest telephoto lens and pointed it out towards where Clive Stanley's team had paddocked to see if Audrey or Tommy might still be around. But, like most teams with nothing to celebrate, they'd packed up quickly and were long gone. All they'd left behind was an empty patch of pavement with some oil stains on it, a couple dead tire carcasses and a trash can piled high with the residue of great human effort. The sun was just starting to droop low over the grandstands, and that sort of light can make for really neat pictures sometimes. Even if the magazines are rarely interested in that kind of stuff. So I set about mounting a mild, 85mm telephoto on my color-film Pentax and screwing a nice 35mm f1.9 wide-angle on my black-and-white camera body in hopes of being ready should I find anything worth shooting. Only then I got this strange, creepy feeling that I wasn't alone. That someone was watching me....

"Ex-excuse me? Mr. Lyons? Mr. Henry Lyons?" an unsteady voice from behind me asked.

I wheeled around and found myself face-to-face with an eager but apprehensive looking young man in a white dress shirt, narrow black tie and a crew cut. He was maybe in his early thirties but looked much younger—kind of baby-faced, really—and was wearing dark dress slacks with a razor-edged crease in them, polished wingtip oxfords and a gleaming little gold tie clip holding his tie to his shirt.

"You're Henry Lyons, aren't you?" he asked again. But it wasn't really a question.

"You can call me 'Hank,'" I offered, still fooling with my lens.

"I read your stuff all the time," he almost gushed. "I really like the way you write."

I had to say "thanks" to that. Hey, everybody enjoys a little ego fluff now and then. And writers moreso than most.

I kind of expected him to go away after that. Either that or start asking me how a person gets started writing for car magazines. Or telling me about some *great* story he knows that I really ought to write. It's usually about some relative, friend or neighbor who is destined to be the greatest racing driver since Nuvolari if he can only get a decent break. Or maybe that relative, friend or neighbor has a rare and absolutely *fascinating* automobile that I really need to do a feature about. Or, worst of all, he'll start filling me in about some wonderful book he's written (or is planning to write) and how do you go about getting published anyway? You get wary of those kinds of conversations once you've had a few. If you're not careful, they'll end with the person in question shoving a five-inch-thick, double-sided, single-spaced typed manuscript under your nose and asking you to read it. Which, if you have any brains at all, is something you just never, ever want to do. Trust me.

But this guy just stood there, staring at me, looking eager and apprehensive and maybe even a little bit expectant. He stuck out his hand. "I'm Danny Beagle," he said with terrific confidence. "I work for Bob Wright up at Fairway Motors in Detroit..."

That's when I noticed his tie clip had a little, rectangular Fairway Motors logo etched on it.

"...I'm his second assistant, actually," Danny Beagle continued with obvious pride. But you could see he'd embarrassed himself because a bright pink halo started glowing around the edges of his ears.

"Is that so?" I mumbled as I finished up with the lens.

His head bobbed up and down. Through the window, I could see the sky was starting to turn. It was time to get out there if I was going to catch the light. "Look, I gotta go," I said as cordially as I could. "Gotta try and catch the good light."

I started for the door but he stepped in front of me so quickly that our noses almost collided. *"Here!"* he said like it was a very big deal, and extended a crisp Fairway Motors business card between his fingers. "Take my card."

I looked at it. "Sure," I shrugged, "why not?"

"That's my home number there at the bottom."

"Uh...thanks."

He licked his lips expectantly. "Have you got a card?"

I fumbled around for one in my camera bag and handed it over. It had what looked like ketchup or gravy stains on it.

"This a good place to get hold of you?" he asked as he read through my London address. The one for the crappy little upstairs apartment where the hot cross bun and crumpet bakers got me up to write by banging their pans and mixing bowls around at fucking four in the morning.

"Yeah, that's the best place, I guess."

"Good," he nodded. "That's real good." He shook my hand again. "I know Bob Wright really wants to meet you."

I looked around to see if anyone was behind me. But we were alone in the room. "He wants to meet *me?*" I had to ask.

Danny Beagle's head bobbed up and down again. "Yep," he grinned. "In fact, he told me to make sure I found you while I was down here at Daytona."

"He did?"

Danny nodded again. "He made a point of it. I mean, he *really* wants to meet you."

I didn't get it, but I told him "sure" and started for the door again. But Danny Beagle grabbed my arm to stop me.

"I-I don't think you understand," he explained with a rush of desperation. "Bob Wright wants me to set up a meeting with you."

I looked at him kind of sideways. "Sure," I finally told him. "No problem. Why the heck not?"

I smile of radiant accomplishment blossomed across his face.

"Just tell me when and where," I nodded. And then I thought about it a little more. "At the races is probably best, you know, because the magazine helps out with the travel money and...."

"No," Danny interrupted. "He wants you up at headquarters. Up at Fairway Tower in Detroit." He could see the questions starting to swim around in my eyes and quickly added: "We'll take care of all the travel expenses, of course."

"Oh, of course."

"You won't have to worry about a thing."

"What would I have to be worried about?"

"Nothing," he beamed. "That's just it." I swear, his smile stretched halfway out to his ears. "Now all we need to do is set up a time."

"Sure thing," I shrugged, still trying to wrap my brain around it. "Just tell me what you have in mind."

"Well, he'd really like to see you this week."

"This week?"

Danny nodded. "Tomorrow, in fact..." he obviously saw the look of utter dismay flash across my face "...but Tuesday would be OK if tomorrow's no good for you."

I could feel the earth starting to shift a little under my feet. "Look," I tried to explain, "I have to be at Maserati's press launch in Modena on Tuesday. I'm leaving in a couple hours to fly up to Atlanta and then on to New York to make my connection for Milan..."

"But you'll be done that evening?"

I gave him a blank look.

"Tuesday, I mean. You'll be done in Modena by Tuesday evening."

"Well," I allowed evenly, "there's usually a dinner. And it's usually pretty good." My head was spinning. "But, yeah, I'll be done at Maserati sometime late Tuesday evening."

"That's fine," Danny nodded enthusiastically. "Just fine. We'll fly you back from Italy on Wednesday and set up your meeting with Bob for Thursday morning. Would that work for you?"

"Whoa! Hold up a second!" I whinnied at him. "I've got another press deal I've got to get back to at Ferrari on February 24th...." I also started thinking about that luxury yacht cruise down the Florida coastline Cal told me about on young Count Volpi's fancy new Benetti "...and I've got an, umm, road test and some, umm, Cunningham driver and team interviews I've got to take care of down here in Florida in between. They're all on deadline, too...."

"No problem," Danny assured me. "We'll just fly you back for those, too." He bent down and wrote something on the back of his card. "Just call this number from the airport tonight before you take off for Italy. It's usually good 24 hours a day."

"24 hours a day?"

"Absolutely," he nodded. "24 hours a day, seven days a week."

"Seven days a week?"

"Usually."

"Whose number is it?"

"You'll most likely be talking to Karen Sabelle. Or her answering service. But she usually likes to take care of things herself."

"Who the hell is she?"

"She's Bob Wright's personal secretary," he explained solemnly. Then added a knowing, insider nod. "She's *very* efficient."

"She is?"

Danny nodded again. "She'll take care of everything. Believe me...."

I wasn't really sure what "everything" meant at that point, but no question my curiosity was piqued. Even if there were a whole chorus of alarm bells going off in my head. "Look, what's this all about?" I asked him point-blank.

"I'd better let Bob Wright tell you that."

"You want me to go airport-hopping all over the whole fucking globe and you can't even tell me what it's about?"

"You'll find out soon enough," Danny assured me with total confidence. "And believe me, it'll be more than worth your while...."

And so here I was, just a few days and a breakneck round-trip to Italy later, waiting for those special, polished brass-and-nickel elevator doors to slide open and reveal the hallowed, high-ceilinged opulence of the top floor of Fairway Tower. I frankly couldn't believe I was really there, and wished again that I'd had a chance to shave....

The reception area on the uppermost floor of Fairway Tower was all high, cathedral-like walls of rose-colored marble on one side and angled, amber-tinted, floor-to-ceiling plate glass windows on the other. It was the kind of place that made you walk on soft, tentative footsteps and talk in low whispers, and even the tiniest sound seemed to have its own, hushed echo. Even though it was gray, cold and rainy outside, the amber-tinted windows bathed everything in a strange, rich, coppery-gold light.

A pleasant, pert and perky blonde receptionist with equally pert and perky breasts welcomed me from behind her marble-topped counter. "You must be Mr. Lyons," she said through an orthodontist-perfect smile. "We've been expecting you." She glanced down at the large, leather-bound appointment book that was the only thing in front of her. "Let's see now: Mr. Wright has you scheduled for 11, but you have a pre-meeting with Mr. Beagle first." She glanced over at the little brass clock on the corner of the counter. "He'll be out to get you in a few minutes." She flashed me another beauty pageant smile. "Would you like a cup of coffee while you're waiting? It's freshly made."

So I half-sat, half-slumped myself down in one of the low-slung, Mies van der Rohe Barcelona chairs across from her, sipped fresh, strong coffee from a blue-and-gray Fairway Motors ceramic mug and waited. It was strangely cool, cavernous and quiet there in the reception area—like a museum after closing time—and there was nothing on the low table in front of me except for the morning edition of *The Wall Street Journal* and a thick copy of Fairway Motors' latest annual report. I tried thumbing through *The Journal,* but of course it didn't have any funnies or movie reviews or even a sports section, and the business and financial news didn't really appeal (or apply) to a borderline-poverty-case motoring scribe like myself. I mean, who really *cared* if economic growth was flat while consumer prices remained steady (hell, that qualified for a banner headline in *The Wall Street Journal!*) or if G.E.'s overseas sales had reached record levels or if Kelsey Hampton was stepping down from his board chairmanship at Keller Fielding Randall following "several disappointing quarterly earnings reports." And it was hard to get too excited about Kraft Foods' efforts to "make additional inroads" on the domestic oleomargarine market with "fresh, new packaging and a revitalized advertising campaign for their already popular Parkay brand." The only two items that interested me at all were a management-slanted report on the deadlocked contract talks between the United Steelworkers' Union and the big American steel companies and a short, perfunctory blurb about eleven defunct New Jersey DeSoto dealers who were taking Chrysler to court over the way they axed the entire DeSoto line just 47 days after the new models came out in November of 1960. Not that it wasn't probably a necessary move. Chrysler had originally launched DeSoto to give them an entry into the mid-price market opposite Pontiac, Studebaker and the rest. That was back in 1929. Only then Chrysler bought out the Dodge brothers, which gave them an already established make in the same price range. But DeSoto continued on (hey, once an idea gains some fat-salaried top executives, office space and departmental staff and moreover a bit of history and momentum in Detroit, it's harder to get rid of than Bubonic Plague!) and enjoyed several strong sales years in the mid-to-late 1950s when DeSotos had the most outrageous tailfins and flashiest chrome trim of all the Chrysler lines. And that was really saying something if you're familiar with that era's Chrysler models. But therein also lay the problem. Too many of Chrysler's various lines and models were clustered around the same exact price points and appealed to the same sort of buyers. If you're a big, multi-line car company, you really need to think those things through in advance. And way up at the very top of your corporate hierarchy. Which naturally made me think about where I was and what most assuredly went on there every fucking day of the week.

I set down *The Wall Street Journal* and picked up the copy of the Fairway Motors annual report. It was about the size of a suburban metro phone book and bound in a handsome, pebblegrain leather cover with a big, embossed Fairway logo on the front. And it was absolutely chock-full of useful information, including all sorts of tables, graphs, balance sheets and numbers I either couldn't understand or didn't much give a shit about. But there were also a few pictures. Some of them showed happy, smiling, deliriously contented native workers at some of Fairway's far-flung factories and facilities all over the globe—I had absolutely no idea they operated a seat-stuffing plant in Nepal or molded dash radio buttons and window-crank bezels in Taiwan. And inside the front cover was a beautiful, full-color, fold-out insert on heavy, gloss-enamel stock featuring all the current Fairway models in typically stretched, lowered, widened, perfectly lit and magnificently idealized advertising layouts. They were none-too-subtly ranked by value (or retail price, anyway) and of course on the next-to-last page was a Fairway Flyer like the one I'd driven in from the airport. Only this one was a Flyer "Esquire Estate" station wagon the color of melted French Vanilla ice cream with a wide flash of wood-look vinyl trim down the side. It was parked in front of a street-corner ice cream stand where a lean, healthy, athletic-looking young den-mother type with a huge, friendly smile and a French Vanilla-colored bow in her hair was happily buying ice cream cones (also French Vanilla, of course) for more damn cub scouts than you could ever hope to fit into a car the size of a Fairway Flyer Esquire Estate station wagon. Underneath was the tag line: *"The modern, on-the-go car for the modern, on-the-go mom,"* and I recalled seeing that ad a few times in issues of *Life* or *Look* or *Good Housekeeping* that got left around waiting areas at assorted stateside airports.

The only page underneath the Fairway Flyer was devoted to Fairway's popular and highly successful line of light-duty commercial workhorses: the Fairway Fleetline panel van and the Fairway Fleetload pickup truck. The picture had them both parked in front of a rustic-looking hardware store (of course!) and painted in matching coats of Fairway Motors' magnificently bland "Quartermaster Khaki." The panel van was complete with a fanciful "Fairway Flowers" logo on the side while lengths of fresh 2x4s, a bundle of shiny, galvanized pipe, several gleaming porcelain commodes and a tail-wagging Labrador retriever filled the bed of the pickup.

I flipped a few pages forward to a "Bedouin Beige" edition of Fairway Motors's biggest seller: the bread-and-butter Fairway Freeway 4-door that had been a car-pool-to-cop-car staple of Middle America for generations. This particular example was parked in front of the all-glass main entrance of an impressive-looking downtown office building (where it would be sure to get a ticket in real life) and getting out of it and looking simultaneously down at his wristwatch and forward to a life of certain financial success was a self-assured, determined young man in a conservative, off-the-rack JC Penny suit, freshly shined shoes and a color-coordinated "Bedouin Beige" necktie. He was carrying a trim, black briefcase and looking like he was ready to take on the world. Or maybe sell you some life insurance?

One page further forward was an incredibly stretched-out, lowered, widened and air-brushed rendering of a Fairway Motors' top-of-the-line Freeway Frigate "Brougham Custom Coachman" luxury edition in glistening "Othello Black" with the optional, vinyl-clad "flying buttress opera roof" with "side landau irons" and riding on optional "Tornado Turbine" chrome wheel covers that gleamed like puddles of pure, liquid mercury. The Brougham Custom Coachman luxury edition was naturally parked by a marvelous, glistening fountain in the circular drive of some incredibly fashionable society hotel—complete with a glittering crystal chandelier over the entranceway—and a smiling, uniformed doorman with epaulets on his shoulders and gold-braid trim on his cap was just opening the door so a stunningly stylish, sexy and self-assured young woman who would have surely looked more at home in a Cadillac or Chrysler Imperial ad could step elegantly inside....

"Mr. Lyons? Henry?"

I looked up and there was Danny Beagle's earnest, open, eager young face peering at me from between his crew cut and the small, tight knot in his tie. I struggled to get up out of Mr. Mies van der Rohe's famously low-slung Barcelona chair. It's not as easy as you might think.

"Follow me," Danny instructed, and led me down the high-ceilinged, glass-and-marble hallway to a small meeting room with a tall black door and floor-to-ceiling glass windows looking out over the rain-slicked factory buildings and distant worker parking lots of the Fairway Motors plant. Danny closed the door behind him and made sure that it latched. There were just two black chairs inside with a plain black table between them, and the only things on that table were a telephone and a thin manila folder with my name—last name first—typed on the little adhesive label on the filing tab.

Danny stared at me for a moment or two like he couldn't decide quite where to begin. "Well, here we are," I offered, just trying to break the silence. You could hear the patter of the rain against the window.

Danny looked at me some more. And then he gave me that big, eager, boy-scout smile of his again. "You have no idea what this is all about, do you?"

I shook my head. "Not a clue."

His smile grew even bigger. "Well, it's pretty big," he said evenly. Then he drew in a little closer, looked me right in the eye and whispered: "*Really* big, in fact."

I could see he was waiting for some kind of reaction. "I'm sure it is," I told him.

"You *bet* it is!" he agreed, and slammed his palm down on the table for emphasis. Then his eyes lowered to the manila folder on the desk and he gently nudged it over to me. "But there's a little business formality to attend to first."

"Business formality?"

Danny nodded.

"What kind of business formality?"

"Oh, just the usual," he said matter-of-factly. "Legal stuff. Papers to sign. That kind of thing."

"Papers? What kind of papers?"

"Oh, the usual. Keep-quiet stuff. Non-disclosure agreements. It's all pretty standard." He gave me that big, boy-scout grin again. "Especially when we're dealing with members of the press."

"Members of the press?"

"Sure. Like yourself." He looked over both shoulders like someone might be listening, then leaned in close and whispered: "*If you want the truth of it, H.R. Fairway doesn't much care for press people. Doesn't trust them.*" He looked over both shoulders again, then drew in even closer and added even lower: "*Most people think he got it from his father, H.R. Senior. He didn't much care for press people, either....*"

"So I've heard," I said out loud, starting to feel a little insulted.

Danny whipped his finger nervously to his lips. I learned later in the day that some of the executive officers and staff managers on the uppermost floor of Fairway Tower suspected that the meeting rooms might be bugged.

The rest were absolutely sure of it.

But I'd already heard a lot of stories about Harold Richard Fairway—Senior *and* Junior—and it was easy to believe. Oh, the old man was a true American colossus—no question about it—who had earned a well-documented and well-deserved reputation for being a sharp, shrewd, tight, cunning, clever, decisive, innovative, guarded, evasive, unyielding, cold, ruthless, devious, imperious, paranoid and more than occasionally vindictive old bird who nurtured slights, grudges and vendettas the way some folks take care of prize begonias. And people said much the same about Harold Fairway Junior. Except for the sharp, shrewd, cunning, clever, decisive and innovative parts, anyway.

Old H.R. Senior started life as a bright, industrious and enterprising young farm lad whose parents worked the land raising rabbits, rhubarb, radishes, rye, roses, rutabagas and Swiss chard on the low, rolling plains near what is now Ypsilanti, Michigan. He was born on May 13th, 1865, which, by coincidence, was the day the very last cannon blasts and rifle shots were fired in the last, fitful battle of our nation's great Civil War. It happened at a generally unremembered place called Palmito Ranch on the Rio Grande River in Texas, and it went down as a sad, ironic footnote in the few history books that cared to mention it because it was generally considered a Confederate victory and took place more than five full weeks after General Lee surrendered to Ulysses S. Grant at Appomattox. That irony was never lost on old H.R. Senior, who regularly noted to newspaper and magazine interviewers who'd done their research and brought it up: *"War over or not, SOMEBODY made money on the rifle balls, bandages, boots and gunpowder they went through that day...."*

H.R. Senior turned out to be a natural-born tinkerer, and he was both captivated and motivated by the fast-emerging notion of a self-propelled, motorized personal vehicle that could eventually take the greater American populace wherever the hell it wanted to go and whenever the hell it wanted to go there. He saw that such a machine was destined to change the world. And the world of the man who built and sold a lot of them even more. So he started screwing one together out of some old hay wagon parts and a crude but clever single-cylinder engine that was largely the work of the local blacksmith. Many grade-school American history textbooks erroneously credit H.R. Senior with actually inventing the automobile. There was even a minor outcry—particularly in left-wing, fringe publications like *The Daily Worker*—when it came to light many years later that old H.R. Senior owned a substantial holding in the publishing company that produced and distributed those particular textbooks. Although it never came to anything after the chief investigative reporter involved had a previously unknown rich uncle die, leaving him a considerable yearly stipend and a plush oceanfront home in the Canary Islands.

But the real story was never about Harold Richard Fairway the inventor, but rather about Harold Richard Fairway the industrialist, entrepreneur, businessman, organizer, empire-builder and ardent, free-market capitalist. Like him or hate him (and there was never a lot of middle ground on that score) it was old H.R. Senior who reduced the complex, highly skilled process of building an automobile down to a large but finite number of simple, individual, repetitive tasks you could about train a monkey to do. But unfortunately the monkeys proved messy, noisy, undisciplined and hard to keep on task. And even harder to toilet train. Not to mention the way they left banana peels laying around just about everywhere. So H.R. Senior reluctantly switched to human laborers. His personal preference would have been slaves, of course, but that idea ran afoul of even some of his most faithful supporters in Washington. H.R. Senior complained bitterly in his later years that the industrial north had *"very likely backed the wrong damn horse"* during the Civil War. And he felt much the same about F.D.R. and the Democrats' stupidly sentimental, short-sighted decision to ally our country with England and communist Russia rather than Germany in World War Two.

But regardless of politics or his stands on social issues, there was no denying that H.R. Fairway was an industrial genius. He created the world's first-ever moving assembly line and, in the process, almost single-handedly pointed many long-established crafts and trades towards oblivion while simultaneously putting a working automobile within the outstretched reach of John Q. Public, Fred Average and every other able-bodied American with a dollar per day in disposable income. *"The fat part of the bell-shaped curve is right there in the middle!"* he often told little H.R. Junior as the young man was growing up. *"And those are the people you want to build cars for, son. The rich are picky, fickle, fussy and difficult to please. And they're also subject to the whims and passing fancies of trends and fashion. Plus they have money and power and are likely to know lawyers, so they can make a lot of trouble for you if you piss them off. And there aren't really enough of them, either. As for the poor and needy, they have no assets, no prospects and no disposable income, so they make exceedingly poor prospects as customers."* At that point he'd most usually shake his head and mutter: *"It's a wonder to me why they all just don't go die someplace and stop being such a damn drain on society. It's downright unconscionable."* But then his eyes would brighten and even mist up a little. *"Ah, but the man in the middle is the world's finest customer, son. He works hard, fears the Lord, believes in fair play and is an absolute sap for all the good things he sees rich people enjoying. In fact, he's willing to mortgage his soul and live way beyond his means in order to get just a crumb of it...Even though such a course will very likely lead him into the depths of ruin and despair."* There'd usually be a warm, gentle chuckle after that. *"God must have truly loved the common man,"* he'd advise little H.R. Junior knowingly, *"because he made so many of the damn assholes."*

Sage words, to be sure.

Although one doubts little H.R. Junior was actually paying attention....

And that, of course, was the second and more current part of the story. Seems old H.R. Senior married himself a sweet, thin, pale, loyal, quiet and hard-working Michigan farm girl from just a few miles up the road, and she gave him five fine daughters that he didn't give much of a shit about and ultimately died of influenza after spending her 41st birthday chopping cord wood for their Franklin stove in a snowstorm in sub-freezing temperatures. By that time, Fairway Motors had become a successful business venture and whispers were already going around that old H.R. Fairway had a little something going on the side. Those rumors were pretty much confirmed when H.R. Senior showed up with a date at his wife's funeral. She was a dazzling, doe-eyed, dumb-as-a-proverbial-fence-post photographers' model/aspiring actress/one-time Sutcliffe County Sweet Potato Queen named Rita Swain (although some said that was just her stage name, and that her real name was Gardenia Wosniak back home in Sutcliffe County) and they were married shortly thereafter. Six-and-a-half months later, she presented Harold Richard Fairway with what he thought and believed he had always wanted: a son to carry on his name and enterprise. But, thanks to yet another ironic and perhaps unfortunate twist of fate, little Harold Richard Fairway Junior wound up with his father's looks and his mother's brains. Or lack thereof, in either case. Oh, the old man did his best to try and teach his only son the ways of the world (at least on the rare days when he was home, anyway) and bring him up to speed on the murderously complex, gargantuan, diverse and hydra-headed business empire he would someday inherit. But, as Fairway vice-president in charge of manufacturing operations Ben Abernathy confided to me one noisy night over far too many drinks and cigarettes at the Black Mamba Lounge a few months later, *"the fucking kid just doesn't have it."*

But that's the eternal risk of running a country, a business or damn near any other type of human enterprise you'd care to mention according to the laws of primogeniture. The smarts and savvy don't necessarily follow along in the wake of the sperm spatter, and although I've never done any kind of deep, Mendelian study on it, I've got my own, personal suspicions that marrying yourself a doe-eyed, trophy-wife Sweet Potato Queen like Rita Swain (a.k.a. Gardenia Wosniak) can raise absolute hell with the old gene pool. And it can get even worse when the kid grows up burdened with way too much money, way too much privilege, a father who's either always away or busy to the point of distraction with other things, a fawning, doting, doe-eyed mother who doesn't have the brains or common sense of a stalk of celery, a succession of high priced, gold-digger nannies, tutors and private instructors, five older sisters who hate and envy the shit out of him and, most important of all, no one to give him a good crack across the backside or call "bullshit" on him when he sorely, sorely needs it. And that's precisely how Harold Richard Fairway Junior evolved into a loud, spoiled, loutish, tempestuous, unpredictable, slovenly, dim and unruly child who quickly discovered he could get anything he wanted—even a damn Shetland pony!—by simply throwing an appropriate fit or tantrum and holding his breath until his face turned the color of raw calves' liver. His mother would always cave in.

Harold Richard Fairway Junior was born on September 16th, 1920, right at the dawn of the Roaring Twenties and the very day, in fact, when suspected anarchists set off a time bomb hidden inside a one-horse wagon parked in New York's bustling Wall Street financial district. The blast killed 30 people and injured 300 more, and the papers saw it as a terrible, cowardly and thoroughly incomprehensible act with no seeming rhyme, reason or possible tactical value. But it had little effect on Harold Fairway Senior's booming car business in Detroit. To be honest, he didn't much care for bankers, lawyers and Wall Street types anyway. Or New

Yorkers in general, for that matter. Especially the Jews. H.R. Senior never much cared for the way the Jews went around reading books, discussing issues, believing in reason, talking like they were smarter than everybody else and eating cold fish. They were cliquish and kept among themselves, too, and that's why even the very richest ones were never allowed to move into the neighborhoods where H.R. Senior chose to live or join the clubs where H.R. Senior chose to be a member.

After all, they wouldn't have felt comfortable.

Meanwhile the Roaring Twenties were in full swing, and America's noble experiment with prohibition seemed to have produced the precise opposite effect the temperance-minded do-gooders had anticipated. Forbidden fruit, don't you know? Bootlegging and bathtub gin flourished, gangsters took control of the cities, governmental greed, kickbacks and corruption went epidemic and all the Volstead Act seemed to have accomplished was to drive an even bigger, wilder and bawdier party ever-so-slightly underground. The newspapers were full of outraged, front-page stories about gun battles in the streets and the Teapot Dome oil lease scandal along with worrisome op-ed columns about Mussolini's rise to power in Italy, the million-member Ku Klux Klan gaining momentum in the south (and fiercely opposing President Warren G. Harding's proposal for a World Court) and Adolph Hitler's disturbing *putsch* in the working-class beer halls of a disgraced and near bankrupt Germany. But even more worrisome—at least as far as old H.R. Fairway Senior was concerned—were the communist Reds in Russia and their dangerous, fellow-traveler egghead sympathizers and share-the-wealth union organizers over here. No question they wanted to take from the hard-working, inspired, intelligent, industrious and well-born few and give to the lazy, fat, foolish, dumb and indolent many.

What a preposterous idea!

Then came Black Thursday and the shattering stock market crash of 1929. Although the depression never really touched the Fairway household or troubled young Harold Richard Fairway Junior. Even though multiple thousands of his fathers' factory workers lost their jobs and sank into debt, despair and destitution when business slowed. *"Business is sometimes a ship without lifeboats,"* H.R. Senior explained sadly, and helped himself to another braised veal chop and a second serving of candied sweet potatoes.

In spite of and perhaps even oblivious to the Great Depression and the horrific world war that followed, H.R. Junior motored merrily along through life, attending a whole series of exclusive, respected, ivy-clad private boarding schools with the absolute finest in credentials and clientele. But none of them could do much of anything with H.R. Junior. He hit puberty like a runaway locomotive during his first year at a Botham's, a stately, restricted and quietly renowned (not to mention astronomically expensive) college preparatory school in Connecticut. In sex, young H.R. Junior finally found something he could do as well as just about anyone (excepting

Negroes, of course), and he committed himself to doing it as often and repeatedly as possible. He soon became notorious for his escapades with girls and women. Although never particularly favored when it came to looks, wit, charm or *savoir faire,* H.R. Junior soon discovered that wealth, privilege, an overactive libido (even by teen-age standards) and his wild, fuck-everybody, bad-boy recklessness could occasionally prove irresistible. Particularly since he wasn't overly picky about who the girls were or where they came from. What followed were a series of all-too-public girlie scandals, a few minor scrapes with the law and countless uncomfortable meetings with outraged and reproving school officials. Not to mention other types of scrapes carried out in assorted, after-hours doctors' offices and the back rooms of certain genuinely full-service street-corner pharmacies. But there were positive sides to the story as well. H.R. Junior's rambunctious, often irrepressible school years are the precise reason why you'll find a "Fairway Hall," a "Fairway Library" or a "Fairway Gymnasium" at many of the finest private prep schools and upper-bracket small colleges in New England.

As anyone who can count to 21 could tell you, H.R. Junior was at the prime age for military service the day the Japs bombed Pearl Harbor and sucker-punched America into World War II. He'd been out of school as much as in at that point and so was running a wee bit short of convenient draft deferments. That's when H.R. Senior (at the insistence of H.R. Junior's still doe-eyed and nicely endowed mother) brought him into the company and installed him as a top-security-clearance Military Procurement Advisor and Defense Department Liaison—a title that was actually about a half-sentence longer than his actual list of duties. To be honest about it, H.R. Senior thought it would've done the young man good to enter the army or navy like any other patriotic young American and serve his country proudly with the rest of his generation. Preferably on the front lines. Or maybe with one of the bomb-disposal crews taking care of unexploded incendiaries in sensitive locations. Like fuel depots, for example....

But the responsibilities of fatherhood (along with incessant pleading, whimpering and threats of cutting off certain bedtime favors on the part of his wife) eventually won out, and so H.R. Junior was placed in a mahogany-paneled office at the far end of the executive corridor on the uppermost floor of Fairway Tower and entrusted with the highly responsible task of showing middle-echelon members of the military procurement staff around the various and sundry Fairway plants that were hard at work three shifts a day building trucks, tanks, airplanes, armored cars and half-tracks for the war effort. And then he had to get them drunk and laid afterwards. Or laid and drunk, if that was their preference.

And it was in that exact capacity, during an extended-weekend, alcohol-fueled dog-and-pony-show tour of the Fairway Motors South Chicago Assembly Plant that H.R. Junior came to meet a gushy, bosomy, sparkly, peppy, generally empty-headed but inordinately enthusiastic and excitable ex-high school cheerleader named Amanda Cassandra Grayson Terryton-Fitch from Greenwich, Connecticut. She was attending Northwestern University at the time thanks to a small endowment of medical cadavers from one of her rich uncles (who happened to be in the mortuary business, strangely enough) which immediately gave them something in common, and it was pure, kind fate that put their parties at adjacent tables at a Saturday night Tommy Dorsey dance band show on the roof garden of Chicago's posh, place-to-be Edgewater Beach Hotel. Thanks to the enormous number of drinks already consumed, they hit it off immediately, and wound up necking and petting furiously behind a potted palm in a far, darkened corner of the roof garden a few hours later. Or leaned up against it, more accurately, since neither one of them could really stand by that point in the evening.

Amanda Cassandra Grayson Terryton-Fitch was known to all of her friends and sorority sisters (and just about anybody else she met after a few drinks) as "AC" or "Acey" or "Acey-cakes," and she was bright and shiny as a newly-minted silver dollar and as much fun as a basket of puppies. So long as you didn't have to clean up after them. She came from a respected old Connecticut family that had unfortunately lost the bulk of their fortune when her grandfather invested heavily—and perhaps unwisely—in a revolutionary new steam/electric automobile that sadly malfunctioned during its first public unveiling at Rockefeller Center in the late spring of 1917 and electrocuted everybody on board. Including Amanda Cassandra's grandfather. It made all the papers, of course, although only William Randolph Hearst's yellow-press tabloids were crass and insensitive enough to run the photos.

In an effort to reverse the family's downward financial spiral, four-year-old Amanda Cassandra's father invested heavily in the runaway Wall Street stock market during the middle- and late-1920s—on margin, of course—and lost the great majority of whatever was left when the market crashed with a thud heard 'round the world in October of 1929. Faced with financial ruin, he was but one of many who chose to take the coward's way out, leaping from the window ledge of his downtown Manhattan office building just four days after the market tanked. But his office was only on the fourth floor and the canvas awning on the Tiffany's jewelry store on the sidewalk level—ironically the same exact store where he'd bought his wife's engagement and wedding rings and where he'd also had little Amanda Cassandra's baby shoes silver-plated and mounted on a cigar-sized ashtray for the corner of his desk—broke his fall. So he survived with little more than two broken legs, a shattered pelvis, a cracked spine, a fractured skull, two dislocated shoulders, assorted cuts and lacerations and an outrageously large bill for the canvas awning from the Tiffany people four stories below.

Wealthy relatives thankfully saw to it that bright, lovable and ebullient little Amanda Cassandra had nice clothes, summer vacations on Cape Cod or out in the Hamptons and attended fine schools, but the immense and still-burgeoning size of H.R. Junior's family fortune led to no little familial pressure on young Amanda Cassandra to further the relationship. And she was only too happy to oblige. After all, H.R. Junior wasn't such a bad egg as far as spoiled, temperamental, given to tantrums, fits and grudges idiot sons of autocratic, egomaniac, skinflint industrial robber barons went. He enjoyed a good time, liked to have fun, had a nice car (lots of nice cars, in fact) and always had plenty of ready cash in his pockets. Plus she was genuinely attracted to the wild, impetuous, self-indulgent, fuck-the-consequences Bad Boy streak that smoldered inside of him like the business end of a five-cent cigar. In fact, it (and the money, of course) made him ever-so-slightly irresistible.

Besides, she liked to get drunk and fuck.

All things considered, you'd have to say it was a pretty good match. Or at least an equal one. As far as Amanda Cassandra was concerned, deep conversations generally revolved around the proper color-coordination of clothes, hats, shoes, makeup and accessories, the layout of crepe paper decorations on homecoming floats and sorority-house lawn displays and most especially furniture styles, drapery and upholstery fabrics and decorating hints. Amanda Cassandra was, as she said herself, "nutty as a fruitcake about decorating." And it should come as no particular surprise to anyone who has been following this story that she managed to get herself pregnant, and so she and young H.R. Junior were subsequently married (further yet establishing his draft status) on Saturday, April 3rd, 1943. Just two days, in fact, after the United States government announced wartime rationing of fats, cheeses and meats. Although this had no observable effect on their sumptuous wedding banquet—*"have you tried the lobster-claw appetizers or the hummingbird tongues on toast?"*—at an exclusive private club in Greenwich. Or the stocking of the pantry, refrigerator and larder at the palatial, fortress-like stone mansion in the most exclusive section of Grosse Pointe that H.R. Junior's family gave the young couple as a "starter house" as soon as they returned from their honeymoon. A house that, by the way, the new Mrs. Amanda Cassandra Fairway began redecorating the day she moved in and would never be finished with until the day, nine long years later, when she finally moved her family into the new, even bigger and even more palatial 47-room mansion that she'd built for them—from the ground up!—at the end of winding, private McElligot Lane overlooking Lake St. Clair in the very richest, ritziest section of Grosse Pointe Farms. A house that she would likewise never be finished decorating and re-decorating so long as life and breath were in her.

Several months later (although well short of nine), Amanda Cassandra Fairway presented H.R. Junior with a fine young son who looked and acted nothing like him, and there were faint, behind-the-hand whispers among her old high school gang in Connecticut and her sorority sisters at Northwestern that the child might actually have something to do with a slight, sad-eyed, freckle-faced New York Jew chess champion and honors-philosophy-student-cum-naval-intelligence-officer named Isador Weinshenker. The young man sadly lost both of his legs when a flaming Jap dive bomber came streaking out of the sky and exploded itself into the flight deck of the U.S.S. Enterprise during the Battle of Midway, and she met him briefly—and felt an immediate, sloe gin fizz-swelled wave of compassion for him—at a February War Bond benefit party in Lake Forest where he was more or less on display in his wheelchair as a returned war hero. H.R. Junior was passed out on the men's room floor by that point in the evening, and giggly, whispered rumors soon followed that young Lieutenant Weinshenker had only been injured from the lower thighs down and just may have done more than simply drum up War Bond sales and recuperate in his wheelchair that particular evening (although that was just scurrilous speculation, of course). In any case, Harold Richard Fairway the Third turned out to be—against all likely odds—a remarkably intelligent, studious, well disciplined, thoughtful, self-sufficient and compassionate child, and perhaps it was more than mere coincidence that he was pale, slight and sad-eyed with reddish-tinged hair, a nose like a Pontiac hood ornament and even had a few scattered freckles on his cheeks while his father was more the general shape and coloration of a fleshy pink fireplug.

H.R. The Third was born on Halloween Day, 1943, and quickly became the apple of his grandfather's eye. But H.R. Senior was somewhat less taken with the little sister born two years later on April 12, 1945. It should have been a memorable and uncommonly satisfying day for H.R. Senior, because it was also, by coincidence, the day Franklin Delano Roosevelt died. And H.R. Senior absolutely *hated* F.D.R. *"Serves the sonofabitch right. He sold us down the river to the God-damn communists!"* he whooped gleefully until snot ran down his chin. *"The bastard never really believed in free-market capitalism. Always wanted the government to fuss and meddle with things. And don't even get me started about that God-damn fellow-traveler Bolshevik wife of his...."* But the joy H.R. Senior felt on the day of little Amelia Camellia Fairway's birth (her mother picked the name, as should be obvious) faded quickly, as she turned out to be very much her father's child. She was cranky, demanding, mean-spirited, loud, argumentative, obstinate, tempestuous, rude, ruddy, hard to toilet train and given to tantrums, fits and outbursts at the slightest provocation. Whenever H.R. Senior saw her, she brought back memories of H.R. Junior as a wee tyke. And mostly unpleasant memories, at that.

But family is family, and so the H.R.s Junior and Senior worked side-by-side for many years in Fairway Tower. Or perhaps "from opposite ends of the hall" would be more accurate. Oh, they started off with their offices side-by-side at the far end of the executive corridor behind a set of massive, impenetrable, double-hung mahogany doors. But it wasn't long before both of them realized that they couldn't really stand one another. And it was amazing to all the vice presidents and department heads who worked with them that the two could be so diametrically different in terms of brains, talent, drive and savvy and yet so very much the same in terms of obstinacy, temper and vindictiveness. They were officially referred to around the plant and offices and all the way up to the uppermost floor of Fairway Tower as "HR Senior" and "HR Junior," but everyone from upper management down to the lowliest rear axle nut-torquer on the assembly line called them "Big Harry Dick" and "Little Harry Dick" when they were safely out of earshot.

Only now Big Harry Dick was gone and Little Harry Dick had inherited the helm of the largest privately controlled (if publicly held) industrial/manufacturing empire on the face of God's green earth. And I could see a whole, huge expanse of it spread out below me—as far as the eye could see!—underneath those rain-slicked factory roofs and beneath the columns of blackened smoke and foul-smelling steam issuing from dozens of smokestacks as I looked past Danny Beagle and out through those coppery-gold, floor-to-ceiling plate-glass windows of our little private meeting room on the 13th floor of Fairway Tower....

"Henry?"

"Huh?"

He nodded to the folder on the desk in front of me. "Go ahead. Open it."

So I did. Inside were several carbon-triplicate-with-color-coded-copies documents covered with paragraph after paragraph of single-spaced, fine print, thoroughly impenetrable legalese. I gave a shot at reading one of them (I mean, I *am* supposed to have a better than average grasp of the English language) but the only thing I could make heads-or-tails of were the blank lines at the bottom awaiting my signature. And Danny's co-signature as witness, of course. The notary seal, notary's signature and date were already on them.

"Don't bother reading it," Danny yawned. "It's just the usual crap about keeping your mouth shut and not writing anything about what you're going to see and hear today." I must have looked a little uncertain, because he quickly added: "You've got to sign them before I can take you to Bob Wright's office. Randall Perrune insists."

"Randall Perrune?"

"He's our head of legal. You don't want to mess with him."

"I'm sure I don't."

Danny gave me that cheery, boy-scout smile again. "You'll like Bob Wright. Everybody does."

"But what's this all about?" I wanted to know.

"Bob'll tell you." Danny took a ball point pen out of his shirt pocket and handed it over to me. "But you've got to sign these first." He leaned in close again and whispered: "There's a nice offer in it for you, too. A very *generous* offer...."

The word *"generous"* seemed to hang in the air like a party balloon. So I clicked the point out of the pen and signed the papers, one after the other.

I mean, why the hell not? Besides, the curiosity was eating me alive.

"VERY good!" Danny enthused, gathering up the signed sheets and peeling one carbon each off for me. For some reason I got the light blue copies. "Now let's get hustling!" he urged, glancing at his wristwatch. "We're a few minutes late already, and Bob's a real stickler when it comes to punctuality."

I can't tell you how strange and out of place I felt as Danny Beagle led me back down that long, cool marble hallway with its floor-to-ceiling copper-gold windows, past the pert, perky blond at the reception desk, around a corner and through a set of dark-tinted, double-thick glass doors on our right. We were in a carpeted interior corridor with no windows to the outside, and passed by several large, empty, glass-walled meeting rooms—one with theater-type seating, a big screen at the front and a projection booth in back. "We'd normally go around the outside," Danny explained, "but we're running late and this is shorter."

We went through another set of heavy glass doors and we were out in the outer corridor again. Danny was hustling us along at a pretty good clip, but paused for an instant to run his fingers over his crew cut and check the knot in his tie before we went around the next corner to face a set of truly massive mahogany doors. Danny cleared his throat and squared his shoulders a bit before opening them up and ushering us in. And now we were in the inner sanctum: Fairway Motors' long, softly lit Executive Corridor, with thick wool carpeting under our feet and a row of plush, mahogany-paneled offices on our left with heavy mahogany doors, floor-to-ceiling windows looking out over the factory landscape and personal secretaries' desks out front. Each office had a heavy brass plaque outside with engraved Roman letters identifying the particular vice-president inside. The personal secretaries' desks in front were all matching dark mahogany with brass-and-dark-brown-leather desk accessories and matching brass-and-dark-brown-leather Barcelona chairs and low, dark marble-topped coffee tables lined up against the wall across from them. You couldn't miss how the secretaries poring over paperwork at those desks came in a relatively narrow spectrum of types, shapes and ages, and there wasn't a fat, old, ugly, slovenly or poorly groomed one in the bunch. Several of them were genuine double-take material, in fact.

"You'll meet all the guys in time," Danny explained as he hustled me down the hallway. He nodded towards the first mahogany office door on our left. "That one is Manny Street's office. He's hardly ever in."

I could see the trim but weary-looking secretary in front of Manny Street's office trying desperately hard to remain cordial to whomever the heck she had on the phone. I noticed her other five lines were all lit up and blinking impatiently.

"Manny's our V.P. in charge of Dealer Relations," Danny continued airily. "It's the second-worst job in the world."

"Oh?"

"No question about it. He's almost always out on the road putting out fires."

"What kind of fires?"

Danny paused for just a moment to explain: "Oh, he'll have some dealer complaining that he can't get enough cars. Or that we're making him take too many cars. Or that the zone rep is giving all the hot models with all the hot colors and options to another dealer in the next town over because the zone rep is screwing around with the other dealership's receptionist. Or maybe a dealer starts handing all the money over to his bookie when he sells a car instead of paying off the bank that holds the paper. Or maybe the dealer's got a pissed-off customer threatening to blow his head off with a shotgun just because the front fenders are rusting off his year-old Fairway Flyer. Or maybe a rep from Chevy or Dodge has dropped by and asked him about switching brands? All you really know for certain is that, whatever it is, it's going to be hard as hell to fix because you're dealing with a guy who runs a car dealership for a living. And that means he's an angle-shooter and a horse trader ten times out of ten and that he's already heard every line of bullshit there is." Danny offered up half a shrug and started us walking again, "Like I said, it's the second-worst job in the world."

"So what's the worst job in the world?" I had to ask.

"That would be Ben Abernathy's job," Danny answered without hesitation. "We'll get to him a little further on down the corridor." Danny nodded towards the next mahogany door on our left. "That's Randall Perrune's office. I told you about him. He's vice-president in charge of legal. The papers you just signed came from him. Or his people, really. He's got plenty of bigger fish to fry...." Danny leaned in a little closer and whispered: "Nobody likes him much. But it's his job to be a sonofabitch. That's really what you want in a lawyer anyway...." Danny pointed to the next mahogany door as we went by. "That's Clifton Toole's spot. He's vice-president in charge of accounting and financial. He can make a column of figures jump through hoops when he wants to. Or roll over and play dead when he wants it, too." Danny shot me a mischievous grin and added in a whisper: "Nobody likes him much, either. Dick Flick calls him The Party Pooper."

"Dick Flick?"

Danny pointed ahead to the second office from the end. The one with the empty secretary's desk in front of it. "Dick's our V.P. of Marketing and Advertising. Sharp guy. Sharp dresser, too. Really looks the part. I bet his haircut costs more than your best pair of shoes."

"These are my best pair of shoes," I grumbled, but it didn't really register. Danny was already pointing to the next two sets of mahogany doorways ahead of us. The first one was closed. "That's Hugo Becker's office," Danny said respectfully. "He's our V.P. of engineering. But I'm pretty sure he's out at the proving grounds today. And Daryl Starling's in the next one." That door was open, and you couldn't miss the bright fuchsia desk top or the famous Man Ray print of bright ruby lips floating against the sky hanging behind the desk. "Daryl's our vice president in charge of styling," Danny continued in an arched whisper, "only he always insists on calling it 'design.' And then Hugo always corrects him." Danny switched to an even lower whisper. "Hugo's German, you know—I mean besides being a really top engineer— so he always wants things precise and correct. And Daryl's, well, you know, a *stylist...*" Danny kind of rolled his eyes "...Those two don't really get along very well."

"They don't?"

Danny raised a cautioning finger to his lips. "You've really got to learn to keep it down in here."

"But I *was* whispering," I whispered.

He looked at me kind of sideways, but didn't say anything.

The next office belonged to V.P. of Operations Ben Abernathy, who was right out front talking to his secretary, one Mabel Wozniak. Pushing 60 already and looking even older, Ben was a big, rumpled, chain-smoking, beleaguered looking heart-attack candidate with thinning hair, thick bifocals, sagging bloodhound jowls and a perpetually exasperated expression on his face. I learned later that he was actually an ex-union man who'd ascended through the ranks (after really cranking the shit out of Fairway Motors' convoy truck, personnel carrier and halftrack production as a shift steward and then plant manager during the war years) to become a salaried tower executive after the war and, eventually, Fairway Motors' overall head of production in 1956. He wasn't a particularly showy, aggressive or ambitious-looking guy for an executive-corridor V.P., but he was a proven survivor and an exemplary specimen of the weary, plodding, grunt-level "get it done" types who actually carry the bulk of the work load in any successful manufacturing operation. Big or small. Company scuttlebutt had it that Ben Abernathy was the only person on the entire 13th floor who actually knew how to build a fucking automobile, and in his own eternally discouraged and quietly disappointed way, Ben had become pretty much the trusted sage and elder statesman of Fairway Tower's executive corridor. The trust part was easy to understand because he was near retirement and had already had enough—more than enough, you could see it in his eyes—of life on the 13th floor. And so none of the other V.P.s had to be looking over their shoulders at Ben Abernathy or worry about him as competition for a possible promotion. Not that there was much of anywhere to go from department V.P. unless you had eyes on Bob Wright's job as President and chief executive officer.

Dick Flick's office came next. The brass nameplate on the empty secretary's desk said "Wanda Peters," but she was obviously either off to the powder room or taking dictation inside. The door was open a crack, and through it I could see this lean, handsome, leading-man type with perfect teeth, tanned skin, a Cary Grant dimple creasing his chin and razor-cut black hair with distinguished little silver dashes at the temples. He was leaned well back in his chair, staring out through the huge, plate-glass window and talking on two telephones at once. I couldn't see much more through the narrow doorway opening, but I did notice the business ends of a pair of high heels poking out from underneath his desk....

There was only one office left, and that of course belonged to Bob Wright. His secretary was a neat, trim, serious-looking woman in her late thirties, and you didn't have to watch for very long to see that she was industrious, purposeful, well-organized and terrifyingly efficient. The plaque on the desk identified her as Karen Sabelle, and she obviously knew who I was. "Welcome, Mr. Lyons," she said through a tight, perfunctory smile. "We've been expecting you." I recognized her voice immediately as the one on the other end of the line when I called to set up my travel arrangements between the Maserati press conference in Modena and Detroit. There was a stiff, almost military sense of discipline and precision about her. "I'm afraid Mr. Wright is on an unexpected long-distance conference call at the moment. Won't you have a seat?" She pointed me over to her set of Barcelona chairs. "Would you like a cup of coffee?"

"No, I'm fine."

"Can I get you anything else?"

I shook my head, and she immediately went back to poring through the stack of paperwork in front of her, comparing notes and columns of numbers and making little check marks and notations in the margins with a pencil that was red on one end and blue on the other. I watched her flip it around expertly from red to blue at regular intervals.

I looked up at Danny Beagle and whispered: "So now what?"

"Just stay put. It won't take long." And then turned as if he were leaving.

"Aren't you staying?" I asked with a thin edge of panic in my voice. I didn't much like the idea of being there all by myself.

"Nah," he shook his head, "I've got work to do. Bob Wright's got to handle things from here." He stuck out his hand and I shook it. "Besides," he added, looking just a wee bit hurt and embarrassed, "I'm only a Level 4 clearance on this project...."

"Oh? Only Level 4?"

He nodded sullenly.

"Gee, that's too bad," I commiserated as he walked away. But I don't think he heard me.

After that I pretty much just sat there in the deep leather sweep of that brass-and-dark-brown-leather Barcelona chair, looking around at the row of secretaries working busily away at those handsome mahogany desks in front of those impressive mahogany office doors. To my right, at the very end of the hallway, stood another, truly massive set of double-hung mahogany doors with yet another matching desk in front of them. I could see the name and title:

HAROLD RICHARD FAIRWAY, JR.
CHAIRMAN OF THE BOARD

etched into a polished brass plaque on the left-hand door and a much smaller brass plaque that read "Francine Niblitz" on the secretary's desk in front of it. As if on cue, the right-hand door flew open and I could hear muffled hollering coming from somewhere deep within as perhaps the single most luscious, striking and voluptuous young woman I had ever seen in my life came bursting out behind a sheer silk blouse housing a truly monumental pair of breasts. They were outstanding in every sense of the word—classic hood ornament material, if you know what I mean—and it took a major disciplinary effort on my part to work my gaze down to the tight woolen skirt that covered her perfectly rounded bottom, curvaceous thighs and on to the tasty dollops of calf muscle that stood out above her perfectly sculpted ankles and arched high heels. At which point my eyes made an involuntary U-turn and headed back north again, pausing at the ankles, the calves, the thighs, the perfect butt, the narrow waist, lingering again on the incredible bustline that seemed ready to burst right out of her ivory silk blouse, up past her perfect clavicles and on to the graceful arc of a creamy white throat that served as pedestal for a mane of gorgeous blonde hair and a terminally cute, heavily made up, kewpie-doll face that had obviously been crying....

And right about then is when I felt another pair of eyeballs glaring at me. Sure enough, Karen Sabelle was watching me take inventory of Miss Francine Niblitz' various assets, and her eyes were cold, steely and disapproving. I gave her a helpless shrug—I mean, how could you ignore anything like that—and that's when the intercom on her desk buzzed. "Mr. Wright will see you now," she said icily, and went back to making notes on the thick stack of reports in front of her with her red- and blue-tipped pencil.

My first and everlasting impression of Bob Wright was that he looked like a grown-up, spruced-up, improved, seasoned and matured edition of Danny Beagle. He had the same crew-cut hair—only graying at bit around the edges—and the same open, eager, boy-scout look in his eyes. Although you could see where disillusion with other people and disappointment at the way things sometimes turned out—in spite of your very best efforts—had left a nascent hint of caution and wariness on him. There was an infectious sense of energy, ambition and "we'll get it done together" team-spirit enthusiasm about Bob Wright, but you could see it was tempered with unusual calm, stick-to-itiveness and dedication. He reminded me a little of the nice young preacher we once had as our scout master during my single, fitful scout-camp summer out in California. The one who suddenly had to leave town to go save primitive souls over in Africa but (at least according to my mother's then-church group's grapevine) ultimately wound up as a set designer for small, off-Broadway musical tragedies in New York.

Looking around, it was apparent that Bob Wright's office was meticulously, almost painfully well organized. And I soon got the feeling that a lot of it (along with many, many other things I came to observe on the executive corridor of Fairway Tower) was thanks to Karen Sabelle's insatiable appetite for neatness and order. The walls around us, for example, were covered with built-in mahogany bookcases filled from top to bottom and door to window with all sorts of reference books, each one neatly sorted and cataloged according to the Dewey Decimal System. Plus one full wall case of oxblood leather-bound company records and reports, each one neatly filed according to subject or date or both. Bob's desk was even more unsettling. Especially as seen through the eyes of a career slob-bachelor writer who generally worked out of a cramped, paper-and-coffee-cup-strewn rats' nest of opened books, scattered magazines folded to articles I no longer cared about, cryptic notes and long-forgotten phone numbers scrawled on the backs of old envelopes and out-of-date newspapers carrying stories I never got around to finishing that should have been thrown out long ago. By contrast, Bob Wright's aircraft carrier-sized desk was stunningly bare except for his telephone/intercom unit, a picture of his family, a little mounted brass plaque on a mahogany base with that famous Davy Crockett quote *"BE SURE YOU'RE RIGHT, THEN GO AHEAD"* from the popular Disney television series engraved on it, that slender manila folder with my name on it front-and-center on the desk blotter in front of him, a few recent issues of *Car and Track* folded open to stories or race reports I'd done and a virgin yellow legal pad with a bright gold Schaeffer ball-point pen sitting next to it—the kind that well-meaning aunts and uncles are forever giving to graduating seniors.

There was one other thing on that desk. And I couldn't take my eyes off of it. Over on the far corner across from me—what looked like about a half-kilometer away—stood something roughly the size and shape of an average shoebox covered with a mysterious velvet cover. The material was cool slate gray, and you couldn't miss the familiar, rectangular Fairway corporate logo stitched on the velvet in iridescent blue thread. Bob Wright rose from behind his desk and smiled warmly. But his eyes weren't smiling. They were calculating my intentions and sizing me up. I could feel it.

"Good to finally meet you," he said with what sounded like genuine enthusiasm. "I've been a big fan of your writing for quite some time."

"Y-you have?"

"You bet I have," he assured me, and extended his hand.

"That's very flattering," I told him as he pumped my hand up and down.

"That's quite a job you have," he continued excitedly, "running all over the world covering all the great cars and all the big races. It must be thrilling."

"It has its moments."

"I bet it does."

"But it's like anything else: Everything looks better from the outside than it does from inside the trenches."

"The grass is always greener, eh?" he agreed through a smooth, self-deprecating smile. "I'm sure you could say the same about any job,"

"Even yours?"

"Oh, *especially* mine!" he laughed. And this time it was a genuine laugh. "But you know the grand old story about the farmer and his wife."

I tried to place it. "Most of the stories I've heard involve farmers' daughters more than farmers' wives..."

A fleeting scowl darkened his face. "No, this is the one about the farmer husband who toils out in the fields all day and farmer's wife who has to take care of the house and cook the meals and do all the laundry and so forth. Like all married couples, they each think that their chores are more difficult, and they of course start complaining to each other because each one thinks that *their* jobs are the hardest..."

I picked it up from there: "...and so they switch jobs for a day and, by the time supper rolls around, neither one can wait to have their old jobs back."

"That's the one!" he laughed. Only this time it wasn't a real one. Bob nodded for me to sit down and sat down behind his desk across from me. I could feel him looking me over again—sizing me up—and all around us the room had turned as quiet, dark and dense as the inside of a pincushion. When I swallowed, I actually thought I heard my own Adam's apple bobbing up and down. "You get all the weasel work done?" he finally asked me.

"The weasel work?"

"The legal papers. The ones Danny Beagle had for you."

"Yeah," I nodded. "I signed 'em all."

"Good!" he smiled. "Very good." And then the smile faded as he rubbed his chin and looked at me some more. "You have no idea what this is about, do you?" he asked, drawing his words out like taffy.

"Not a clue."

He leaned in a little closer. "You ever hear of the AMA racing ban?"

"Sure. I wouldn't be much of a motorsports reporter if I hadn't. Happened back in June of 1957. All the big American car companies got together and agreed to abandon their motorsports programs and never use racing or high performance in their advertising or marketing campaigns again."

"That's pretty much it," Bob nodded. And then he asked point-blank: "Do you think it's still working?"

"That's hard to say," I told him, not wanting to give the wrong answer. True, you didn't see any racing- or performance-oriented ads from the car companies themselves. But you saw plenty of race reports and pictures in the nutball car magazines and newspaper sports sections that couldn't help but heap a little reflected glory on the manufacturers of the winning cars. And there were lots of racing- and performance-oriented ads from the spark plug companies and the oil companies and the gasoline companies and the tire companies and the fan belt companies and the accessory companies (many of whom sold a *lot* of product to the big Detroit car manufacturers) that featured the winning cars. Plus it was an open secret that virtually all the big American car companies—including Fairway Motors—were providing freebie cars, "special duty" parts, encouragement and financial assistance to their favored race teams. It was rampant in stock car racing and drag racing, but you were also starting to see it in top-level road racing with well-funded, toe-in-the-water efforts like the Pontiac Tempests and Grady Davis Corvettes down at Daytona. "I've noticed a little under-the-table manufacturer involvement here and there for quite awhile," I said cautiously. "Hell, you can't miss it."

"People are cheating like crazy!" Bob almost shouted, and pounded his fist on the desk for emphasis. And then his face opened up in a big, just-between-you-and-me smile. "I know *we* are...."

"You *are?*"

"Sure we are!" he grinned triumphantly. "Why, I can walk you a few hundred yards from this very tower and take you to a dyno room where our new NASCAR V8s are being tested right now. If they work out, they'll be on all the Fairway cars at Darlington next month. And right next door, they're working on some pretty special hardware we're getting ready for next year. I can't show it to you right now, but mark my words: next year is going to be *our* year in stock car racing." Then his eyes narrowed. "You do understand that this is *NOT* for publication."

"I know what I signed," I told him, "and I'm the kind of guy who keeps his word."

"That's good," he nodded. "Very good. We don't want this leaking out just yet."

"What do you mean, *'just yet?'"*

A guilty, little-boy smile crept across his face. "Well, to tell the truth," he leaned across the desk and his voice dropped to a whisper, "we think the AMA racing ban is a crock. And we're planning to do something about it." He rocked back upright and all of a sudden he was delivering a motivational speech. You could tell he'd given it before. "We think the people who are going to be shopping for the kinds of cars that we here at Fairway Motors need to be building and selling are interested in *performance!* They want a car that will get up and *GO!* when that stoplight on Main Street turns green. They want driving to be *FUN* again! And they sure as heck want to know that the car they're driving can deliver the goods where it really counts...out on the racetrack and taking on all comers. They want to be *proud* when they park that shiny new car in their driveway for all the neighborhood to see! They want their neighbors to *envy* them!" He leaned forward across his desk again and almost snarled: "And that's precisely what we at Fairway Motors plan to give them!"

I let out a low whistle. "That's sure going to shake up a lot of people."

"You're darn tootin' it is!" he beamed. "Fairway Motors is going flat-out, full-tilt and wide-open for A.P. next year!"

"A.P.?"

"Absolute Performance!" he crowed. "Every car, every line, every kind of competition—across the board and around the whole blessed world!—Fairway Motors is going to be *there!*"

"Wow."

"And I'll tell you something else," he said fiercely, his eyes damn near blazing. "What's that?"

"We're not just going to be racing. No, sir. Fairway Motors is going to be *winning!"* You could see he was pretty worked up about it, and it was hard not to catch the heat off his radiated zeal. But I knew you had to be careful about racing. No matter who you are and what kind of resources you have, you've still got to slug it out with the people who are already there. All the way up to the very top. And over in Europe, that meant Ferrari.

"That's a pretty tall order," I allowed cautiously. "I don't know too awfully much about oval track racing or drag racing here in the states, but you've got some pretty good cars and teams to beat over in Europe. They've been at it kind of a long time...."

"And that's exactly where you come in!" he informed me enthusiastically. And then he paused and settled back expansively into his chair. You could hear the creak of the leather behind his shoulder blades. "Tell me," he said evenly. "What do you think of me?"

The question caught me completely off guard. "I, um, I only just met you, and..."

"You really don't know what to make of me, do you?"

I shook my head in agreement.

He led my eyes around his office with his hand. "It's obvious that I have a pretty important job here at Fairway Motors, and this is obviously a very big and successful company..."

I nodded, not sure exactly where he was going.

"...so I must be doing some things right or I wouldn't be here, would I?"

I nodded again.

"But you don't know what to make of me because you don't really know me. You don't know what I'm like. You don't know what I'm after. You don't know what pleases and excites me. You don't know if you can trust me. And you especially don't know what I want from you." He looked me right in the eyes. "Do you?"

I felt my head shake 'no.'

"Well, that's the same way it is with me and racing. Especially that European racing that you're such an expert on." He leaned forward and dropped his voice again. "I know in my heart what this company needs to do, but I don't know nearly enough about how to make it happen. And that's why I had Danny Beagle bring you here today. Because Fairway Motors needs *YOU!*" he pointed at me like an Uncle Sam recruiting poster. "We need you to educate us. To be our source of inside information. To help us understand what we're up against and what we need to do to be successful. To help us get the lay of the land over there...."

It was starting to make sense. Pretty good sense, in fact.

"....but it's all got to be on the Q.T. until at least this coming fall. You understand?"

I nodded.

"Nobody can know you're working for us until the cat is out of the bag." He gave me a strange, inscrutable smile. "Or should I say: *'the Ferret!'*"

"The what??"

His smile was beaming now. "All business deals are based on trust, Henry. And so, as a show of good faith, I'm going to trust you with something not even all the people on this floor know about yet."

"You are?"

He nodded and reached out for that strange, shoe box-shaped thing on the far corner of his desk. The one with the mysterious, cool gray velvet cover with the Fairway Motors logo stitched across it in iridescent blue thread. He took the velvet gently between his thumb and forefinger and whisked it away. And that's when I found myself staring into a handsome glass display case with a glistening model of Fairway's hush-hush, top-secret new Fairway Ferret "personal sporty car" on a pedestal inside. It was bright orange-red with a white convertible top and an all-white interior, and it had a long front hood, a short rear deck, aggressive wheel arches, razor-edged fender lines and, even in 1/16th model scale, obviously not much at all in the way of trunk space or rear-seat leg room. But it looked sporty as hell!

"Do you like it?" Bob asked nervously.

"It's pretty sharp," I allowed. But you could see he was disappointed with my lack of enthusiasm, so I quickly added: "In fact, I think it's really, *really* sharp!"

"Really?"

I nodded up-and-down.

"Do you like the color?"

To be honest, it looked a bit garish to me. Maybe even more than a bit. But no question the kids would love it. And the older guys trying to act like kids again, too.

"Daryl thinks we ought to call the color 'Persimmon' and Dick likes 'Sunset Tangerine,' but H.R. Junior is stuck on 'Harlem Orange.'"

"Either way, the kids will love it," I assured him.

"And the older guys trying to act like kids again, too."

I'd never seen a car like the new Fairway Ferret before. And nobody else in Detroit had, either.

"And you know what the real beauty part is?" Bob continued in a confident whisper.

I shook my head.

"It's going to be *affordable!*"

"Affordable?"

He nodded decisively. "We're going to price it so just about every route driver, dairy farmer, school teacher, appliance salesman, middle manager and typing-pool secretary in America can actually aspire to owning one," he beamed. Then quickly added: "But only the base model, of course. The 6-cylinder, 3-speed notchback hardtop with the houndstooth cloth seat inserts." And then his face brightened again. "But even the base 3-speed will have bucket seats and a floor shift—standard!—and the dealers won't be ordering many of those anyway. Just one to set out on the front corner of the lot with a big "$2368" price tag sign over it."

"$2368? That sounds awfully cheap..."

"This car *is* awfully cheap!" he bragged. "But you'll be able to option it up to almost double that if you and the dealer's salesman really put your minds to it. You can have air conditioning and styled custom wheel covers and a luxurious, leather-look Vinylite interior with faux fuzzy ferret fur seat inserts if you want!"

"Faux fuzzy ferret fur?"

Bob Wright nodded enthusiastically. "And you'll be able to make this little baby *fast,* too! We've got some driveline hardware coming on line that's really going to make people sit up and take notice!"

I let out another low whistle. Bob Wright's confidence and enthusiasm were infectious. Then again, that's why he was where he was and did what he did for a living. But then I watched his face turn stern and solemn. "Remember," he cautioned, raising a finger to his lips, "not a word about this to anyone. Not even your wife."

"I'm not married," I told him.

"OK, then not even your girlfriend." He looked at me kind of sideways. "Do you have one of those?"

I had to think about that one for a moment. And the truth is, I really didn't have an answer for him.

Chapter 6: The Wright Way and the Fairway

I spent the rest of that morning and well on into the afternoon in Bob Wright's office, and it turned out that Danny Beagle was right. I *did* like him. Everybody did. At first. It wasn't until later that his enthusiastic, dedicated, optimistic, straightforward, relentless, hard-working, nose-to-the-grindstone, gee-whiz/Jiminy Cricket/honest-Injun/eager-beaver/"*shouldn't we try it THIS way?*" approach started to drive you ever so slightly crazy. Don't get me wrong: Bob Wright was precisely the kind of bright boy you wanted up there at the front of a Fourth of July parade—nickel-plated whistle in his mouth and gleaming, ceremonial saber raised high—ready to lead the march down the middle of Main Street, USA, for God, country and the executives, management staff, stockholders and grunt-level employees of Fairway Motors. Then again who, given any real choice, wants to march in a fucking Fourth-of-July parade every day of the week? Not the rest of the brass on the uppermost floor of Fairway Tower, that's for sure. After all, most of them only reached their lofty positions by ducking swiftly out the back door whenever responsibility or accountability reared their ugly heads. To a man, they avoided either one (or, perish forbid, grabbing some bold or risky idea by the scruff of the neck and taking it on). Survival has always been the name of the game in any major corporation, and that means covering your ass, always leaving yourself an "out" and staying the hell out of the line of fire whenever possible. And even moreso when a spoiled, stupid, unpredictable, irascible, hair-trigger, impetuous and imperious second-generation asshole like "Little Harry Dick" Fairway is running the show.

Or at least wielding the power to hire and fire....

To be brutally honest about it, H.R. Junior wasn't very bright. But he was just sharp enough to know that he wasn't very bright, and that he needed a guy like Bob Wright around who had the vision, savvy, smarts, dedication, organization and drive it took to run the damn company. And take the fall in front of the stockholders if everything went to shit. Don't get me wrong: H.R. Junior understood that guys like Bob were one in a million. Which meant, at least according to the unique brand of math Little Harry Dick Fairway learned at his father's knee, that there were something like two hundred other guys out there—give or take a few—who could step in and take over if push came to shove. And Fairway Motors was big enough, rich enough, powerful enough and successful enough to muddle along on pure inertia until the right sort of replacement turned up. And he could always stick Dick Flick or Clifton Toole or Randall Perrune or even Ben Abernathy or Manny Streets in there temporarily (although he'd surely have to get rid of them when the new hire was made). Promotions were always a double-edged sword on the uppermost floor of Fairway Tower. There was never any "can I get my old job back?" if things didn't work out. Nope, old H.R. Senior had taught Little Harry Dick well: "*There are only two ways to go in the world of top management, son: UP or OUT!*"

Not that H.R. Junior particularly wanted to fire Bob Wright. Far from it! But his father had also taught him that a Chairman of the Board had to keep his motives under wraps and his options wide open. Just to keep everybody on their toes, you know? Even so, H.R. Junior valued Bob Wright's ideas and work ethic and respected his opinions highly. Rumor on the executive corridor had it that H.R. Junior even took Bob into his confidence occasionally during the one-on-one, face-to-face, behind-closed-door meetings they had every single Monday morning at the crack of 10 (or later, if H.R. Junior happened to sleep in) where Bob did his best to bring Little Harry Dick up to speed on all the things that were going on, going right, going wrong, being considered or likely to come unglued at Fairway Motors.

"That's not such a great thing," Ben Abernathy observed over drinks at The Steel Shed later that evening.

"It's not?" I asked him.

Ben shook his jowly head from side-to-side and lit up another Marlboro. "Nah," he exhaled thoughtfully, "the last thing you want is to be in that pudgy little fuck's confidence."

"Oh?"

"Sure. Once you've seen inside that spoiled mush head and dirt-black heart of his, you know too much and he can't trust you anymore."

I was beginning to understand.

Ben Abernathy took another swill of beer and added: "That's why I like to keep the little sonofabitch hating me."

"*Hating* you?"

"Oh, absolutely," he nodded. "It's the only way for a tired old fuck like me to survive." He swiveled his reddened, blood-hound eyes around to meet mine. "I'm less than two years from retirement after a whole fucking lifetime at that company. Forty-three fucking years! I put up with his asshole father and I can put up with that little fuck, too." He flashed me a grin that looked like the entrance to an abandoned mine. "In two years, I'm planning to walk off that 13th floor with a solid gold watch, both my legs still under me and a big, fat retirement package tucked under my arm." He looked up at a TV screen where a Michigan/Michigan State basketball game was fighting to be heard over the din at the bar. "Yep, and the only way I'm going to make it is if I can keep that fat little prick hating me. Not hating me a *lot,* of course. Not like he hates Dick Flick or Daryl Starling or Randall Perrune. Just a little bit. Just enough...."

I mulled it over and I was pretty sure Bob Wright understood all of that, too. Understood it maybe even better than old Fairway Motors warhorse Ben Abernathy. But he'd obviously come to the conclusion that he really *wanted* that President and Chief Executive Officer job. Wanted it desperately. And that's why he'd been there, waiting in the wings, ready to sweep into that office at the far end of the executive corridor, take the reins and run that company the way *he* thought it ought to be run as soon as the opportunity arrived. He had his organizational chart ready and his fresh, new ideas lined up like trained seals, and he didn't even blink while stepping over the recently deceased career of his previous boss, longtime personal friend and immediate predecessor in the President/CEO slot, Gordon Stritch. But Gordon had sealed his fate when he championed the upscale new Fairway Fantasia line that never really managed to find its niche in the marketplace. Not that the Fantasia was necessarily a bad idea. But it was unlucky and ill-timed. A mild recession had dampened America's appetite for upper-middle-price, "aspiring-to-luxury-level" car brands, and it cost the company a lot of money. Not to mention prestige. And somebody had to take the fall for it. When that kind of thing happened (and particularly when it happened on a fairly grand scale), the Search For Those Responsible rarely went any further than the big executive office at the far end of the hall. The one right next to the usually closed, double-hung mahogany doors of H.R. Junior's own corner suite....

Job security could be a precarious thing on the uppermost floor of Fairway Motors, and the higher you ascended, the more precarious it could become. But that didn't seem to faze Bob Wright. Or at least not so you could see it. Bob figured he had a divining finger on the pulse of the American consumer, and knew what kind of cars they wanted to buy just as surely as he knew that America was the greatest, noblest nation that had ever existed (or would ever exist) on the face of God's green earth. Bob had his crosshairs fixed on the robust and expanding American economy and all those bright-eyed, wholesome, baby-boomer kids (and their prosperous, modern-thinking, two-car-garage parents) just coming into the marketplace. As he saw it, Americans were generally good, proud, moral, loyal, hard-working, family-oriented and patriotic to the core. And that's why they were more than ready for some forward-thinking American car company to build something that had all-American youth, strength, spirit, pep and style written all over it. A new line of sporty, all-American performance cars built by a sporty, all-American performance car company. A company with the grit and guts to raise its collective middle finger and say *"fuck you!"* to that stupid AMA racing ban and go kick some ass. In fact, go kick *everybody's* ass. Here *and* overseas! Hey, fuck the Europeans with their snooty, nose-in-the-air attitudes and fruity little sit-down-to-pee performance cars. In fact, fuck them especially! Bob thought a move like that would turn Fairway Motors into the greatest King Kong/100-megaton/Holy-Father-in-Rome/beat-you-to-the-next-fucking-stoplight high performance automobile manufacturer in the world.

In fact, he was sure of it.

And this wasn't going to be just another wagonload of the usual, yawn-generating ad-copy bullshit. There were going to be striking new cars and muscular new engines and entire new model lines to back it up. And Fairway's hush-hush new Ferret was going to be the star and corporate spearhead of the whole fucking show. Better yet, the new Ferret was going to be *affordable*. It was going to be something John

Q. and Fred Average could actually think about fitting into the old family budget (after all, it was basically just a shortened, low-slung version of the Fairway Flyer economy compact underneath its dramatic, razor-edged, long hood/short deck exterior!) so long as they picked one with the standard, single-barrel carburetor 6, the standard 3-speed stick that virtually nobody wanted and the cheesy, base houndstooth Vinylite trim, which included Saran Wrap-weight seat upholstery and no less than five ashtrays...including four disguised as hubcaps. In time, of course (and in carefully orchestrated steps and stages after the first hyped-up sales rush was over) more and more engine choices and trim options and style and performance packages would become available so you could make any damn kind of sporty personal car you wanted out of a Fairway Ferret. And simultaneously run the suggested list price up to damn near double the original, introductory, sucker-you-in/stripped-to-the-bone $2368 base sticker price. Bob Wright was absolutely convinced they'd sell a lot of them. And I mean a *LOT* of them.

But, as he explained to me at length during that first afternoon at Fairway Tower, this was going to be far more than just a routine new model line introduction. The new Ferret was going to be the centerpiece of an entire, performance-oriented corporate makeover of the entire Fairway Motors product line and image. "Absolute Performance" was going to be the new company motto, credo, slogan, watchword, tag line and mission statement, and the way Bob saw it, the whole damn thing hinged on Fairway products racing—and moreover *winning!*—everywhere from stoplight sprints on Woodward Avenue to Saturday night hometown drag strips and dirt ovals to record runs across the Bonneville salt flats to the biggest of the big leagues (and the breathless, salivating media coverage that went with it) on the NASCAR stock car circuit, at the Indy 500 and even in European-style road racing and rallying. And of course that's where I came in. Bob wanted to know what series Fairway Motors ought to look at and what races they needed to win over in Europe.

And to my way of thinking, there was only one possible answer to that question: the 24 Hours of Le Mans! Hell, it was the biggest damn sports car race on the planet! "That's the one you really want to win," I told him. "Sure, there's Formula One. And you should really be there, too, if you want to do it up right. But Formula One always focuses more on the *drivers* than the *cars*. You want to go where the focus is more on the machines themselves and the manufacturers who build them."

Bob's head bobbed up and down enthusiastically. "I like it. I like the challenge and teamwork aspects of it, too."

"Then Le Mans is where you want to go. No question about it. That's the one with the crowd and the history and the cachet and all the media attention. And the magic. The one that really makes people stand up and take notice."

Bob rubbed his chin. "So what would it take?"

"Well, that depends on what you want to win."

"Winning is winning, isn't it?"

So I explained to him about the F.I.A. and their stupid new rules that awarded all the World Manufacturers' Championship points to the GT categories.

"But what do people really pay attention to?" he wanted to know. "What do the magazine writers write about? Who gets the newspaper headlines on Monday morning?" He looked me right in the eyes. "Who are the *real* winners, Hank?"

I didn't even have to think about it: "First across the finish line and no bullshit excuses. Most people don't care about anything but that. And a race win at Le Mans is worth a hell of a lot more than any dumb, you-have-to-explain-it-to-everybody end-of-season points championship that nobody really cares about."

I could tell he liked what I was saying. But he wanted more. I also think he wanted to press me a little. Just to see what I'd say. "You sound pretty sure about that," he said like he was cross-examining me.

"I am," I answered back without a flutter. Sure, season-long championships were important to guys like me who work in the sport (and also to that fringe group of diehard, nutball road-racing fans s who made my job possible), but I was realistic enough to know that we were a tiny, micro-minority. If you wanted to make an impression on the rank-and-file-rube John Q./Fred Average types, you had to do something important, indisputable, instantly recognizable, simple to wrap your imagination around and terrifically impressive. Like an overall win at the 24 Hours of Le Mans. *"Oh, yeah. My brudder was stationed someplace over near dere after the war. He was wit' the Quartermaster Corps. Great duty. Chocolate. Steaks. Booze. Nylons. Got himself a whole lot of French pussy. Nasty dose of clap, too. Anyhow, he an' his buddies went t'see that big race over there one time. Went on for 24 fucking hours! Without stopping, can you believe? An' I heard about that big wreck they had over dere in '55. 80-some people got killed. Even made the hometown paper here in Dubuque...."* Yeah, people had to know what you were talking about before you even started if you wanted to impress them. As Big Ed Baumstein always used to say when he was trying to break in a rookie car salesmen: *"Y'can't go buildin' somebody a fucking clock just t'tell 'em the time of day....."*

Bob Wright looked out his window and thought it all over. And then his eyes came back to me. "So," he continued slowly and deliberately, "who would we have to beat?"

"Well, Ferrari for starters. They've had things pretty much their own way ever since Mercedes-Benz, Jaguar and Aston Martin folded their factory teams. Sure, Maserati and Porsche are still out there, but Maserati's been struggling lately and Porsche doesn't build any big cars."

"So the only one we really have to worry about is Ferrari?"

"I'm not sure 'only' is the right word," I cautioned. "Ferrari's been doing this a long, long time, and they know what the hell they're doing. Enzo Ferrari is as shrewd, sharp and cagey as they come. And he knows how to play the game better than anybody. Knows how to finagle and finesse the politics as well as how to build the best damn endurance cars in the world. And he always gets the best talent to drive them."

"How does he do that? Does he pay them more?"

"No," I tried to explain. "He pays them less."

"*Less?*" You could see Bob's curiosity was aroused.

"Sure," I almost laughed. "All the top drivers want to drive for Ferrari because it gives them the best chance of winning. Simple as that. But remember that Ferrari didn't get to be the best in the world overnight. He fought and clawed his way up there, and I guarantee you he won't give up without one hell of a fight."

There was a soft knock at the door. "Mr. Wright?" Karen Sabelle's voice inquired from the other side.

"Yes?"

"H.R. is ready to see you now."

Bob Wright flashed me a big, fake grin. But you couldn't miss the look of apprehension that flickered across his eyes. "OK, Henry," he said evenly. "It's show time...*Into the lion's mouth!*" You could tell he'd watched Kirk Douglas, Gilbert Roland, Cesar Romero, Lee J. Cobb and Bella Darvi (say, what ever happened to Bella Darvi?) in 20th Century Fox's *The Racers* a few too many times while preparing for our meeting. And that's what I was thinking as Karen Sabelle led us out of Bob's office, past her desk, past the delectable Miss Francine Niblitz and her incredible set of chests and through the thick, double-hung mahogany doors leading into Harold Richard Fairway Junior's private office suite. The layout had obviously been designed to both impress and intimidate, starting with a solemnly lit grand hallway where the carpeting was a deep, rich navy blue and felt like cushioned velvet under the soles of your shoes. The walls were glowing polished mahogany, and there were paintings I thought I recognized by artists I should have known by name hanging along either side. We passed by three separate, mahogany-and-leather meeting rooms—two small, intimate ones on one side and a single, larger one across from it—and then onward to the regal and magnificent corner office where Harold Richard Fairway Junior spent at least two or three hours every single day of the week when he wasn't out of town, on vacation or busy doing something more important. Like sleeping late or golfing, for example.

H.R. Junior's impressive corner office was the same one he had boldly and perhaps even brazenly seized from his demanding and autocratic father mere hours after the headstone was laid firmly in place over H.R. Senior's grave. There was a huge mahogany desk in the corner where the two coppery-gold glass walls came together offering a wide-screen panorama of the southern and western vistas of Fairway Motors' sprawling Detroit assembly plant. It had almost stopped raining, and off to the west you could make out a thin seam of Titian-esque, antique-gold sunlight peeking out from under the edges of the gunpowder-gray cloud cover. It was pretty damn spectacular, if you want the truth of it.

I ran my eyes around the rest of the room. If you looked closely (and moreover knew what to look for) you could see how the floor had been cleverly, almost imperceptibly angled upwards towards the shrine-like corner where H.R. Junior's massive, altar-sized desk looked down disdainfully on the rest of the room. That desk had been hand-carved out of what I later came to learn was the largest chunk of pure, raw mahogany ever cut, and it had to be kept in a carefully regulated, temperature- and humidity-controlled environment to keep it from warping or cracking.

Behind that desk was a throne-like swivel chair with butter-soft, dark blue leather upholstery. But it was turned away from us, and all I could make out of the man inside was a spiral of phone cord dangling over one armrest, the top half-inch of a very expensive and natural-looking but slightly askew chestnut-brown hairpiece peeking over the top and the elbow of a custom-tailored Italian suit poking out the opposite side. An abrupt, agitated voice was coming from the other side: *"No, I don't GIVE a flying fuck if you go with the baby antelope, the lizard skin or the water buffalo hide...."*

Pause.

"But that's what you HIRED the sonofabitch for, dammit! That's why I'm paying the goddam queer three fucking thousand dollars a week...."

Pause.

"...of COURSE gold goes with veined rose marble. Gold has ALWAYS gone with veined rose marble. Ever since the fucking Romans, I think."

Pause.

"Okay, so maybe it WAS the fucking Greeks..."

Long pause as the chair rotated slowly around to face us. Sitting in a petulant slump inside a devouring cushion of supple blue leather was a soft, fleshy, thoroughly unremarkable-looking guy of about 40 wearing an Italian silk suit that probably cost more than a base Fairway Flyer and a dazzling, perfectly waved-and-sculptured chestnut-brown hairpiece with shimmering, coppery-gold highlights. Only it was cocked slightly back and to one side. A quick, harsh glance from Bob Wright made it clear that I had better not crack a smirk if I knew what was good for me. I also had to ignore how H.R. Junior's eyebrows didn't quite match his hairpiece. Or that he had a blunt, puffy nose, blunt, saggy ears and blunt, stubby fingers with most of the fingernails chewed off. H.R. Junior had one of those complexions that start out as stark white with pale pink highlights, but quickly flush to bright red whenever he exercised heavily (which was virtually never except when he was having sex) or when he got angry or upset. Which was virtually all the time.

H.R. Junior stared at me like I was a suspect side of beef. *"Look, Hon,"* he growled into the phone, *"I got some people here. We'll talk about the fucking water buffalos later."*

Pause.

"Sure. Me, too. Bye."

Harold Fairway Junior clicked the phone down on its cradle and shifted around in his chair. You could hear the leather squeak under him. "So this is the guy?" he asked like I wasn't even in the room.

"Hi. I'm Hank Lyons," I blurted out and extended my hand. But he just let it hang there. I could tell he was messing with me—just to show me how things were, you know?—but there wasn't anything I could do about it. I eased my hand awkwardly back to my side and resolved to keep my fucking mouth shut until somebody asked me a direct question.

H.R. Junior switched his attention back to Bob. "So what's this all about?" he demanded gruffly. As if he had hundreds—maybe even thousands?—of far more important things to attend to that day.

"What I told you," Bob answered patiently. "Hank's quite an expert on what goes on in the motorsports world over in Europe. He writes about it for *Car and Track* magazine."

H.R. Junior's eyes narrowed. "Those bastards hate us," he snarled. "All they ever do is write bad shit about us and complain about our cars..." he glared at me again, his cheeks and forehead starting to glow "...And I say *fuck 'em!"* He waited for me to say something. To give him an argument or make some lame sort of excuse. But I knew enough already to keep my mouth shut.

After it became apparent that I wasn't going to respond, the corners of H.R. Junior's mouth curled up into a cruel, self-satisfied little smile. And then he started right in again: "You guys from the magazines make me sick. You hate America."

Bob Wright saw that I was about to say something, so he quickly interceded. "Hank here doesn't hate America," he explained in a calm, soothing voice.

H.R. Junior's eyes flashed angrily. "Oh, yeah? Then why do they go all apeshit over those fucking foreign cars? Huh?" He glared back at me again, his eyes full of vitriol. "What izzit with you guys? You wanna drive a fucking Jag-wire so everybody at your fucking middle-rich country club thinks you make a lotta money and get a lotta hot broads? Huh? Izzat what you want? *HUH? IZZIT?? HUH???"*

"I-I don't do the road tests," I answered lamely. But there was no stopping H.R. Junior once he got rolling:

"...JAG-WIRES!!!" he spat out angrily. *"Buy one of those fuckers and next thing you know, you're sittin' by the side of the road, waiting for a fucking towtruck!"* The corners of his mouth curled into a withering sneer. *"Those fuckers break down all the time. ALL THE FUCKING TIME! AND EVERYBODY KNOWS IT!!!"*

I didn't say a thing.

"...*And the damn air conditioning is totally horse shit. HORSE SHIT!! I wouldn't put it on a fucking Flyer. And just wait till you trade that fucker in!*" he snorted triumphantly. "*You wanna talk Jag-wires? HUH??!! Izzat what you want? You just wait'll you see the fucking depreciation on that piece of crap as soon as you drive one off the showroom floor....*"

"He's not really here as a representative of the magazine," Bob interrupted.

H.R. Junior glared at him. "He isn't?"

Bob shook his head.

"And I don't particularly like Jaguars," I heard myself lying. But it seemed like the right thing to say.

"You *don't?*"

I shook my head while silently promising to write something really nice about Jaguars the very next chance I got.

Then Bob went on to explain to Little Harry Dick Fairway (for what was obviously not the first time) the plans he had for me regarding Fairway Motors: "I want to hire Hank on as a sort of an, umm, 'consultant' for our new European racing program."

Little Harry Dick's face screwed up into a questioning grimace. "Consultant?"

Bob Wright nodded. "I think he's just what we need. I had Karen and Danny Beagle do some background checks on him, and he looks really promising. He knows the lay of the land over there and he's got inside access just about everywhere."

It was beginning to occur to me that what Bob Wright really wanted was a spy. And I didn't much like the way it sounded or made me feel. But it looked like it might be a moot point anyway, since H.R. Junior didn't appear at all convinced. He ran his eyes up and down me again. "He dresses like shit."

"That could be," Bob countered. "But I think he could be a real asset to us over there. He could be a tremendous source of contacts and inside information."

H.R. Junior eyeballed me suspiciously. "Whaddaya mean by '*consultant?*'" Not too surprisingly, the same exact question was rolling through my own head.

"Oh, he'd be on the payroll, like anyone else," Bob explained. "But I want to keep it quiet and under wraps until the Ferret and the new racing program break cover. Want to keep him writing for the magazine like nothing is going on. It's better for all of us that way."

H.R. Junior's eyes narrowed again. "I don't much like part-timers and moonlighters, Bob. You know that." And that part was true. H.R. Junior didn't like part-time workers (although he liked time-and-a-half and double-time workers even less) because it didn't mean nearly as much when you threatened to fire them.

Bob Wright held his ground. "I think this is really the way we need to go on this," he insisted gently. "We need what's in his head and we need his connections, and I think he can be a lot more useful to us in an undercover role right now."

H.R. Junior still didn't look convinced, but Bob seemed confident he could bring him around. "I've been talking to Hank in my office, and he thinks what we need to do is win the 24 Hours of Le Mans."

"That's over in France someplace, isn't it?"

"Yes it is!" I congratulated him. "It sure is in France."

H.R. Junior glared at me again, then swiveled his eyes back to Bob. "So," he grumbled, "how much d'ya think it'll take?"

Bob nodded the question over to me.

I looked back at him blankly.

"In fucking DOLLARS!" H.R. Junior demanded, slamming his palm on the corner of his desk for emphasis. *"How much will it fucking COST??!!"*

"W-well," I more-or-less stammered. "You'll have to beat Ferrari."

"FERRARI??!!" H.R. Junior bull-snorted. I could see the heat building up again. *"I had one of those fuckers once. Worst fucking excuse for an automobile I ever owned. Worse even than a fucking Jag-wire, even. And fucking EX-PEN-SIVE...."*

"Which one did you have?" I asked, genuinely curious.

"Who the fuck knows?" he snapped at me. *"It was fucking red and it cost more than a fucking airplane and it was hotter'n hell inside in the damn summertime."* He stared at me, his face the color of raw liver. *"I burned up two fucking clutches in a fucking month!"* He held up two fingers to make sure I understood what "two" meant. "Fucking thing was always fouling plugs, too. Every other day," he muttered disgustedly. "You're telling me that's all we gotta beat? Fucking *Ferrari?*"

"It won't be easy," I cautioned.

H.R. Junior regarded me with withering contempt. "Tell me," he said with a dangerous new calm in his voice, "how many fucking cars does Ferrari sell in a year?"

"I-I don't have any exact figures on me," I stammered, "but I'd guess a couple hundred. Maybe a few more. In a good year, anyway...."

H.R. Junior glared at me like I'd just dropped four pounds of dog shit on his desk. "Hell, I got dealers in Hoboken who sell more cars'n that. A couple of 'em, in fact." He flipped his glare back to Bob. "So this is the brilliant fucking advice you bring me? That it's gonna be tough to beat some two-bit, horseshit little Dago outfit that only builds two hundred fucking cars a year?"

"Hank's right," Bob said evenly, looking him right back in the eyes. "Ferrari's well established and they're good at what they do. They build for a select, cost-no-object, performance- and style-oriented clientele. And they don't need to advertise..."

"No advertising??!!" H.R. Junior recoiled, his eyebrows shooting up behind the leading edge of his hairpiece.

Bob calmly shook his head.

"That's right," I nodded evenly, backing Bob up. "Their name and racing success is all they need to sell cars. And they sell everything they can build. In fact, there's usually a six-month waiting list..."

Bob sneaked me a quick wink of appreciation. Then added: "And they've got a huge head start on us, too."

H.R. Junior settled back thoughtfully into the sumptuous leather of his chair. Which in turn pushed his hairpiece even further forward. I had to stifle a laugh. "Well then," he mused, rolling his eyes upwards, "why don't we just *BUY* the fuckers?"

"B-Buy *FERRARI*??!!" I choked.

I mean, the idea was absolutely preposterous.

Wasn't it?

We stopped by Karen Sabelle's desk on the way out and Bob had her set me up for two more meetings the next day plus a room for the night at the Fairview Inn, a moderately priced, easy-to-find local motel with clean sheets, hard mattresses, reasonably new furniture and a dimly lit piano bar where many of Fairway Motors' top executives and upper-management types stopped off for a quick one on their way home from work. "We'll talk money and specifics tomorrow," Bob assured me. "In the meantime, have dinner on us and get yourself a good night's sleep..." he glanced down at the frayed cuffs of my corduroy jacket "...and do you have anything, umm, *different* to wear? I saw the way H.R. Junior was looking at your clothes."

I was already wearing the best—hell, the only—decent jacket and pair of slacks I owned. Well, semi-decent, anyway. "You're looking at it," I answered sheepishly.

Bob exchanged knowing glances with Karen Sabelle. Before I'd left her desk, she'd run through my jacket, pants, shirt and shoe sizes and whether I preferred button-down or collar stays and lace-ups or loafers.

Before I left, Bob took me for a whirlwind, stick-your-nose-in-and-say-hello tour of the other offices on the executive corridor. Dick Flick made by far the biggest impression simply because he looked like Cary Grant, dressed suavely and impeccably and had the kind of radiant self-assurance that you just can't get out of a bottle of cologne. Or any other kind of bottle, come to that. Daryl Starling was also a sharp dresser, but more colorful and flamboyant—as you might expect from a lead stylist. Daryl was a small, darty, tightly-wound little man with quick moves, an edgy smile, a nervous tic to go along with it and an outsized pompadour of orangey-blond hair that made him look like a game show host. He was wearing a Cerulean-blue blazer with mirror-finish gold buttons over an off-white silk dress shirt with a dashing blue, gold and peach paisley ascot wrapped elegantly around his neck. He was surely one of what Buddy Palumbo's old designer/engineer friend Brooks Stevens always called "those handkerchief-up-the-sleeve guys." But no question he was an accomplished designer—you could see that from all the drawings and awards around his office— and serious as a heart attack about his work. Daryl was on the phone when we stuck our noses in, berating some poor, hapless underling in the interior trim section about his "dreary interpretation" of the pattern of hydrangea blooms and honeysuckle blossoms H.R. Junior (or, to be more precise, Mrs. H.R. Junior) wanted for the green-and-gold brocade embroidered upholstery on the new Fairway Freeway Frigate Fragonard Special Edition. Daryl paused in mid-rant to flash us a perfunctory smile before lacing into the poor sap at the other end of the line again.

The door to the next office was closed because Hugo Becker was out at the proving grounds wringing out the latest test mule for the new Ferret project. *"Hugo's a real hands-on engineer and always wants to be there himself to oversee his pet projects,"* Bob whispered as if someone might be listening. *"But he can get lost in the details and minutiae sometimes and lose sight of the bigger picture."* Bob looked around like he hoped no one had overheard him and quickly added: *"But that's really what you want in a top engineer, isn't it?"*

Ben Abernathy's office was next and, except for the serene little gold-framed desk portrait of himself, his smiling, overweight but pleasant-looking wife, his four overweight but wholesome-looking daughters and their obviously ecstatic but also seriously overweight Golden Retriever, Gus, the whole place was an inconceivable mess. Ben was a big, saggy, disheveled-looking guy who always seemed harried, beleaguered and depressed. Then again, he had an awful lot to be harried, beleaguered and depressed about. His days were spent fixing things that went wrong, putting out fires, addressing dire emergencies, avoiding H.R. Junior and poring through endless reams of memos, directives, distress calls, reports and figures that were stacked in piles all around him—on the desk, on the floor, on the credenza, on the chairs across from him—while chain-smoking Marlboros one right after the other and talking two, three and sometimes even four at a time through his speaker phone to the grunt-level employees who held the present and immediate future of Fairway Motors in their hands. This particular Thursday afternoon the spotlight was on some poor, mid-level transportation manager at a big warehouse re-distribution center somewhere outside of Oxnard, California. Apparently forty-two cartons of Fairway Freeway driver's-side door handles had been mis-labeled and mis-shipped from a sub-assembly plant in Ohio, and now the entire, 10 block-long Fairway Freeway final assembly line was in danger of shutting down at precisely 9:43 the next morning if the shipment couldn't be located and re-directed in time. Normally, something like that would never have climbed as high as the desk of Fairway Motors' overall, world-wide head of manufacturing. But it was always different when the big, twenty-eight-football-field sized final assembly line building in the shadow of Fairway Tower threatened to go silent. Like his father before him, H.R. Fairway Junior always parked in a special, private spot at the end of a special, private entrance drive and walked through that building from one end to the other on his way to work every morning (which, totally unlike H.R. Senior, generally occurred sometime between 10:30am and noon). Heads would surely roll if that line wasn't up and running full steam when he came strutting through the following morning. Maybe even Ben Abernathy's.

"Ya gotta go look in all the fucking trucks," Ben growled wearily at the transportation manager on the other end of the line. *"Open 'em up with your own two hands and take a look inside. Reading the bill of lading's no fucking good. I'm pretty sure the shit's labeled wrong."*

"Every one?" crackled the voice in his speaker phone.

"Until you find 'em!" Ben nodded. He crushed another Marlboro butt into his overflowing ashtray and reached for the pack on his desk. *"And y'gotta call all the other managers at all the other centers out there and have them do the same. Until you find the fucking shit, unnerstand?"*

"ALL the depots?"

"All the depots! Y'gotta keep looking until we find the damn things."

"Then what?"

"You FIND the damn things first! Unnerstand? Then we'll have to, let's see..." he put down the cigarette he hadn't fired up yet and ran some numbers through the big, clattering calculator on his desk. His face fell when he saw the total. *"SHIT! Then we'll have to ship at least 1200 of the damn things by air and messenger and get them here by, let's see..."* you could see the calculations going on behind his eyelids as he worked out how long it would take to get the shipment in through receiving, re-directed to the main assembly line building, unpacked and properly staged so there wouldn't even be a hiccup in the production flow down that 10-block-long final assembly line *"...gotta be by 7:30 tomorrow morning."*

"1200 of those things?" the voice crackled incredulously. *"By 7:30 tomorrow morning?? Air freight? Do you know what that's gonna WEIGH? Do you know what that's gonna COST?"*

A dark cloud passed over Ben Abernathy's face. *"Of course I do. Clifton Toole over in accounting's gonna have my ass on a platter. He's gonna enjoy every fucking minute of it, too."* Ben lit up his new Marlboro and took a slow, steady draw. *"But I'll tell you one thing this deal's NOT gonna cost."*

"What's that?"

"Your job..." He exhaled slowly and watched the smoke curl upwards. *"...Or mine."*

There was a long, weighty silence at the other end. Then: *"Okay, Mr. Abernathy. Whatever you say. I'll get right on it."*

"Get back to me as soon as you have anything."

"Will do."

The line clicked dead and Ben Abernathy leaned back in his chair and fumbled for the cigarette that was already in his hand. That's when he noticed the two heads poking in through his doorway.

"Hi, Ben," Bob Wright grinned cheerily.

"Hi, Bob," Ben nodded back with a weak, defeated smile.

"Looks like you've got your hands full."

Ben replied with a near-imperceptible shrug. "Just the usual shit," he sighed, "running around at 200 miles-an-hour with my hair on fire and not getting much of anything accomplished." His face brightened up a few watts. "I don't know what I'd do without all this fucking aggravation. It's what keeps me young...."

"I can see that," Bob nodded. "Anyone could." He nudged me a little further into the doorway. "This is Hank Lyons, Ben. He writes for *Car and Track* magazine."

Ben smiled approvingly. It was a nice, genuine kind of smile. "I read your stuff now and then when I have the time. I guess you could say I'm kind of a fan, actually."

I thanked him.

"Anyhow," Bob continued as he glanced at his watch, "Hank's going to be helping us out on the European motorsports thing."

Ben Abernathy's eyebrows arched up. "So that's a done deal?"

"Looks like it."

The eyebrows came down again. "You think it's a good idea?"

"I think it's a *great* idea!" Bob enthused. "But it doesn't matter what I think, does it?" He rolled his eyes towards the double-hung mahogany doors at the far end of the corridor. "H.R. Junior thinks it's a good idea. In fact, he thinks it's a *great* idea..." he shot Ben a wink "...because he thinks it's *his* idea." A mischievous little grin flickered across Bob's face. "Or that's what he thinks, anyway."

Ben snorted out a laugh that turned into a wet, hacking cough. It went on for what seemed like ten or fifteen seconds.

Bob glared at the pack of Marlboros on Ben's desk. "Don't you think you ought to cut down on those things?"

"Can't," Ben gasped, dabbing at his eyes. "They keep me young...."

It felt strange walking out between those two massive, mostly-Corinthian marble columns flanking the main entrance of Fairway Tower, and even stranger wandering over to the visitor's lot where my Fairway Flyer Fiesta Flair Coupé courtesy car was parked. The rain had slacked off and the remains of a pretty spectacular sunset—at least by Detroit standards, anyway—was glowing across the western horizon. The cacophonous noise and overpowering stench of the Fairway Motors plant were swirling all around me. But I couldn't sense them. It was like walking in a dream. I thought I heard harpsichord music and smelled spring lilacs, actually.

To be honest, I didn't know what to do with myself. My room at the Fairview Inn was all set and I had directions to get there in my jacket pocket. But I felt way too revved-up and excited to face an empty motel room. Sure, I was dog-tired and badly in need of a bath or a shower (or, better yet, a bath *and* a shower) followed by a bed with clean, fresh sheets and lots of warm, fuzzy blankets to curl up under. But the prospect of heading over to the Fairview Inn and just checking in didn't sound particularly appealing. So I drove around the bleak outer perimeter of the enormous Fairway plant for awhile, trying to make sense of what had happened that day. I could hear the factory sounds coming from the other side of the walls and fences, and then, over all of them, a loud, off-key chorus of buzzers and alarm bells and air whistle blasts. About two-thirds of the clatter and pounding ceased instantly. Like some giant, invisible hand had reached down from the heavens and flipped a switch.

6 o'clock.

Quitting time.

Shift changeover.

I could see the sneaky early-leavers already sprinting for their cars in the employee lots, followed a few moments later by the vast lemming tide of union workers behind them. Traffic around the entire plant facility was going to become a complete mess in about one minute flat. I didn't really feel like sitting in traffic—that's the last thing you want when you just feel like driving around—so almost without thinking I wheeled into the near-empty parking lot of a dilapidated, barn-like bar across the road from the #4 plant entrance. It was a grimy, worn-down, industrial-looking place made out of concrete blocks, fire brick, old plank wood and a corrugated metal roof, and it was the only thing on the block except for a couple windowless storage warehouses and a city-owned bus garage. But the uneven gravel parking lot around it was big enough to hold a hundred cars. Maybe more. An illuminated plastic Stroh's Beer sign hung out front with "THE STEEL SHED" spelled out along the bottom in simple, block letters, and a steady stream of cars fresh out of the employee lots came wheeling in right behind me, splashing through puddles, showering off mud and stones and coming to a crunching halt on the wet gravel, one right after another. They were mostly battered, used-up examples of older Fairway Freeway coupes, hardtops and 4-doors, heavily abused Fairway Fleetline pickups and a smattering of clean, plain-Jane, base-level Flyer compacts bought on the Employee Discount plan. There were also a few rusting examples of once-top-of-the-line Freeway Frigate models with snaggle-tooth bumpers, burned-out opera lights, dead shocks and sagging springs. The men (and even a few women) getting out of all those vehicles were about what you'd expect for grimy, worn-down union workers at the end of yet another long, numbing, 8-hour shift on the second-to-the-last day of the work week.

They were all looking forward to their first beer of the evening.

And their second.

And their third....

Now when it comes to alcohol, I'm pretty much your typical writer in that I can take it or leave it. But mostly I take it. Particularly when other people are picking up the tab. And that tends to happen quite often in the writing game since there are inevitably a lot of car manufacturer PR flacks, race promoters, drivers looking for better rides (or rides, period), sponsors, team owners, etc. eager to see certain news, views and opinions expressed in print. To be honest, indulging in their self-serving largess is one of the core benefits of being an automotive journalist. It fact, it may be the only one, since the pay isn't anything to write home about. I generally try to be a little more subtle and appreciative about it than, say, Eric Gibbon, but I'm always ready to fill my face and gullet at someone else's expense. On the other hand (and, again, like most motoring journalists) I tend to be a bit more parsimonious when I'm paying for my own drinks. But The Steel Shed certainly seemed quite a bit cheaper and livelier than what I imagined the lounge at the Fairview Inn might be like at 6:30 pm on a Thursday evening. So I locked up my courtesy car, dropped the key in my pocket and meandered inside.

The Steel Shed was a big, high, dimly lit sort of place that smelled from decades of spilt beer, split lips, dried piss and sweat and regularly plungered toilets. There was a big, slightly lopsided old Wurlitzer jukebox sitting next to the front door, and it featured exclusively country music (except for *"Happy Birthday," "The Anniversary Waltz," "Frosty the Snowman"* and *"Auld Lang Sine,"* of course) and a row of pinball machines and a pool table with a low-hanging light over it in the back. The place was filling up fast with loud, thirsty plant workers, and I had to shoulder my way through a few of them to make my way to the bar. I ordered a bottle of Stroh's because that's what most everyone else seemed to be drinking (along with the occasional Miller or Budweiser) and nobody seemed to mind that I was the only guy in the place wearing a jacket and tie. Then again, it wasn't much of a jacket and tie.

I found an empty space along the wall next to a yellowed *Detroit Free Press* front page from August 15th, 1945—the day the Japanese surrendered at the end of World War II—flanked by an autographed picture of one of the many slow and forgettable Detroit Lions quarterbacks who never came close to making the Hall of Fame, a rusty tin Stroh's sign with a cluster of buckshot holes through it and a faded poster announcing an important union meeting that had taken place four years before. And all the while more and more Fairway shift workers were flooding in through the front and side doors and filling the place up until you could barely make your way to the bathroom. Not that you'd much want to go there if you had any other sort of option.

There were an awful lot of people crowded inside The Steel Shed, and I kind of wondered how the two bartenders were going to keep up. Or the old, black cook in back, who already had a grill full of burgers sizzling and two baskets of hand-cut fries working in the fryer.

"DOUBLE WITH CHEESE AND A SAUSAGE COMBO!" one of the bartenders hollered over the din of drink orders, jokes, guffaws, sports news, beefing about this or that on the assembly line and edgy, all-purpose grousing about how the hell the damn Rooskis managed to beat us into space or why the hell American

U-2 spy pilot Francis Gary Powers (who'd just been swapped on a prisoner-exchange deal for top Russian spy Rudolph Abel) let himself be taken alive. There was also a lot of muttered mutual concern about how those black folks, Negroes, coloreds, darkies, jigaboos, *mullenjons,* porch monkeys, jungle bunnies, burr heads, spades, splibs, coons or niggers (depending, of course, on who was doing the talking) were trying to weasel their way into all the white schools, decent jobs and good neighborhoods.

But the hottest topic of all that particular Thursday evening had to be the deadlocked United Steelworkers' contract negotiations and how any kind of extended strike would surely lead to a ripple-effect shutdown at the Fairway Motors plant across the street. An eventuality that would put every single person in the bar except myself, the bartenders and the old, black cook out of work until it was settled.

"ANOTHER DOUBLE! GRILLED ONIONS! NO CHEESE! RINGS INSTEAD OF FRIES!" the other bartender hollered, and the old black cook moved things around with his spatula and slapped two more fat patties on the grill. It had already occurred to me that the entire crowd inside The Steel Shed was white (excepting the cook, of course), even though I'd seen quite a few black union types working side-by-side with them on the assembly line. I learned later that most of the black employees who felt like blowing off a little steam after work tended to congregate at the Black Mamba Lounge on the opposite side of the Fairway plant, about half-a-mile and a whole world away.

It's the way things were.

Just then who should come ambling through the door—collar open, tie loosened, jowls and shirt-tail sagging and bent-up Marlboro dangling—but a slump-shouldered Ben Abernathy. But even in that posture, he towered a solid half-head over most of the crowd. It was apparent immediately that most of The Steel Shed regulars knew him. And liked him. *"Big Ben!"* one of them shouted.

"Hey, Ben! How's life up in the fucking clouds?" another added from the far end of the bar.

"Who has any time up there for fucking?" Ben shouted right back. *"All I get to do is work my ass off...Same as you!"*

That brought a ragged, bottles-hoisted cheer from the bar.

"Got any insider stuff on the steel strike?" another voice queried.

"You probably know more about it than I do."

"Hey!" the first voice shouted. *"Izzit true what everybody's saying about Little Harry Dick's secretary?"*

"You mean Miss Niblitz?"

A whole chorus of wolf whistles and *"YEAHs!"* erupted along the bar.

"What about her?"

"That she can't type?"

"*THAT'S COMPLETE BULLSHIT!*" hollered a new voice from the far end of the bar. "*I got it from a guy who knows that she can type five words a minute.*"

"*Five words per minute?*" the first voice barked back incredulously. "*That's not much of a machine rate.*"

"*Yeah, it's not,*" the second voice cackled, "*but she does it with her nipples.*"

The whole place roared.

Right on cue somebody dropped a series of quarters into the jukebox and moments later Patsy Cline was wailing "*I Fall to Pieces*" right out of the damn walls. It was awfully loud, and it didn't get any quieter when the next record dropped and I was surrounded by Faron Young's plaintive, soulful "*Hello, Walls.*" I was right under the damn speaker, so I headed over to where Ben Abernathy was standing to say "hello." I mean, why not? He was surrounded by grimy-looking union types in wool plaid lumberjack jackets, baggy jeans or coveralls and steel-toed work boots, but he seemed to fit right in anyway. I figured it was pretty unusual for a top management executive to blend in with that kind of company, but everybody seemed to know that he'd worked his way up from the factory floor, and you could see he'd never lost his feel for it.

I tapped Ben on the shoulder and he turned and gave me a blank look at first—like he couldn't quite remember where he knew me from—and I had to shout over the first few lines of George Jones' "*Oh, Lonesome Me.*"

"*I just met you up in The Tower,*" I hollered over the noise. "*Bob Wright brought me by your office....*"

I watched the light come on in his eyes. "*You're the magazine writer, aren't 'cha?*"

I nodded.

"*How'd'ja find this place?*"

I offered up a shrug. "*It kinda found me.*"

"*Buy you a drink?*"

"*Sure. Why not?*"

"*Whadd'r ya having?*"

"*Beer is fine.*"

"*Right. Beer it is. Any special brand?*"

"*I'm not choosy.*"

He only had to raise two fingers a quarter-inch up off the bar and, busy as both bartenders were, there were two frosty Stroh's in front of us in a heartbeat.

"*So you're going to be working with us?*"

Word obviously traveled fast along the executive corridor of Fairway Tower.

"*Yeah, I guess,*" I kind of shrugged. "*Bob wants me to do a little snooping around for him over in Europe. But it's really supposed to be under wraps until...*"

Ben flashed me a look that cut me off in mid-sentence. Then it dawned on me: the racing program and the new Fairway Ferret were still hush-hush Top Secret—even among Fairway Motors' rank-and-file employees. In fact, maybe *especially* around Fairway Motors' rank-and-file employees.

"Sorry," I said sheepishly. *"I'm kinda new at this executive cloak-and-dagger stuff."*

Ben gave me a sad-eyed smile. *"That's okay, son,"* he sighed. *"You'll get the hang of it."* He took a long, slow drag off his latest Marlboro and exhaled. *"Either that or you won't be around very long."*

"Sorry."

"Hey, don't worry about it. Just pay attention to the eyes and ears around you, that's all. Loose lips sink ships."

"Sorry," I repeated.

He gave me a reassuring wink. *"Hey, no sweat. Case closed as far as I'm concerned."*

I thanked him and took a pull off my beer. *"Y'know, I really can't figure out what they want ME for?"*

"Don't sell yourself short, son. If Bob Wright thinks he wants you, he's already done the research on it. Or he's had Karen and Danny do it. So take my advice."

"What's that?"

"Take as much as they'll give for as long as they'll give it, 'cause it ain't no way gonna last forever."

"I pretty much figured that already."

"And never, ever take their first offer!" He moved to clink our bottles together. *"Keep that in mind and you'll do fine."*

It was hard to talk in there with all the noise, but I enjoyed being around Ben Abernathy. I had the feeling I could trust him, you know? And that we were both more-or-less outsiders on the 13th floor, even though he worked there every single day of the week. So we talked about this and that and shared another couple rounds—I even went for my wallet a few times, but he wouldn't let me pay—and then somebody turned the jukebox up even higher in honor of Johnny Cash's *"I Walk the Line."*

"You like country music?" Ben bellowed over the twanging guitar intro.

"I can take it or leave it. I don't get to hear it much in Europe."

"It's pretty good if you give it a chance," Ben advised. *"And each song is like its own little story."* He took a long, thoughtful drag off his latest Marlboro. *"That's why all the truckers listen to it."*

"Oh?"

"Hell, yes! You'd fall asleep halfway between Denver and Des Moines listening to goddam Bach or Beethoven."

"I suppose."

"But I like all kinds of music," he explained, and punctuated with an affirming swig off his beer.

"Oh?" I was actually somewhat curious, since big Ben Abernathy didn't exactly strike you as the musical type. But you never really know about people, do you?

"Hell, yes," Ben grinned at me. *"I like most all kinds of music."* He looked me in the eye. *"You like Blues?"*

I nodded.

"Some Friday night I'll take you over to The Black Mamba Lounge and show you how the other half lives."

"The Black Mamba Lounge?"

Ben just smiled, drained the last of his beer and raised two fingers to order us a couple more. *"So how d'ya like Detroit?"* Ben asked as the bartender pushed two more icy bottles of Stroh's in front of us.

"This is my first time here. I haven't seen much of it."

"There's not much to see," he assured me, and we shared a pretty good laugh.

"And what did'ja think of Little Harry Dick Fairway?" he asked after the laugh died down.

I answered with an uneasy shrug. *"I never really met him before today."*

"Oh?" Ben's eyebrows arched up. *"So whad'ja think?"*

"Hard to say," I answered carefully. *"Really hard to say. He seems like he could be a little, um..."* I caught myself searching for the exact right word *"...difficult."*

A mischievous smile blossomed across the bottom of Ben Abernathy's saggy, worn-down old face. *"DIFFICULT?"* he snorted. *"Let me assure you, Little Harry Dick Fairway can be absolutely IMPOSSIBLE! He's a first-class prick, and don't you forget it. Hell, he's BETTER than first class!"* Ben took a long, thoughtful pull off his beer. *"But if you learn to keep your head down, your mouth shut and cover your ass,"* he clinked the bottoms of our bottles together again, *"you'll do just fine."*

"You think?"

Ben nodded. *"Just remember this, son: the secret to success is low expectations."*

"Low expectations?"

"Yep." He raised two fingers a quarter-inch off the bar to order us another round. *"Low expectations are the absolute key."*

"Why's that?"

He looked at me like I was thick in the skull. *"It keeps you from disappointing people, son,"* he explained like it was the central, cornerstone truth of the entire universe. He laid a hand the size of a catcher's mitt on my shoulder and gently repeated: *"It keeps you from disappointing people...."*

Chapter 7: The Ferret's Tale

Ben Abernathy and I stayed a lot later than we should have at The Steel Shed, but it was a good time and I enjoyed his company. But I had one hell of a headache when a rude, jangling wake-up call blasted me out of bed at 6:30 the following morning. I stumbled into the Fairview Inn's generically antiseptic tile bathroom, downed a large glass of Alka Seltzer and a handful of Anacin, got the coffee maker gurgling and was somewhat befuddled to find a brand new, Fairway Blue blazer and a pair of never-need-ironing Fairway Gray polyester dress slacks—just my size—hanging on the hook behind the bathroom door in a plastic cleaning bag. Not to mention a new, neatly folded white dress shirt with the tags still on it and a conservatively matching, diagonally-striped, Fairway Gray and Fairway Blue with gold and burgundy highlights polyester tie on the dresser. And a pair of brand new, black leather wingtips on the floor with a black leather belt coiled up inside one of them and a pair of new, dark navy socks rolled up in the other. Whoever dropped them off must've sneaked in pretty quietly. Then again, I was sleeping rather soundly (or "sucking the paint off the walls," as Big Ed Baumstein always used to say) following the press unveiling at the Maserati race shop in Modena what seemed like weeks ago, my generally sleepless, spanning far too many time zones trip across the Atlantic, my late morning through late afternoon meeting and tour on the 13th floor of Fairway Tower and my far too many rounds of drinks at The Steel Shed with Ben Abernathy and his union-buddy friends. They were a pretty damn friendly bunch as best I could remember.

It seemed strange getting showered and shaved and dressed in all the crisp new polyester that some unseen Fairway elf had left behind my door in the middle of the night. I almost couldn't recognize myself in the mirror. I looked like a damn car salesman. Except for the hair, of course, which was still more or less your standard British length because I hadn't really paid any attention to it since three or four weeks before Daytona. It seemed odd that they'd want me in this getup since Bob Wright had made it clear he wanted me working under cover. I found out later that this particular outfit was intended for meetings at The Tower only (plus any other official and/or semi-official company functions I might be invited to attend), and Karen Sabelle had explicit orders from Bob Wright that my new Fairway blazer outfit was to be left behind at the Fairview Inn and that I would be reunited with it whenever I was in town again and the situation required. As you can imagine, I was still feeling a little groggy when I ventured out into the parking lot and a blast of raw, icy, early-February-morning Detroit air hit me in the face like a frozen fence post. It woke me right up. Even if it didn't make me feel especially better.

It was an ugly, cold and gloomy sort of day, with a sky the color of old fish skin and not enough sun to cast a shadow. At least it wasn't raining, sleeting or snowing. On my way to The Tower, I did my best to clear my head, run through everything Bob Wright and Little Harry Dick had said the day before and tried to prepare myself a little for what might be in store. But my meetings that day were mostly a breeze. Danny Beagle took me under his wing as soon as I arrived, got me another couple much-needed cups of coffee and took me on a whirlwind tour of the plant. And it was pretty damned impressive, even if the noise and stink made my head hurt. The size and scale of it were absolutely staggering, and it gave you a new and even a bit frightening appreciation for Harold Richard Fairway Senior's original idea that you could take an incredibly large number of random, borderline average, semi-attentive but often preoccupied human beings of widely varying physical, mental, emotional and motivational aptitudes (all the while knowing that the great majority of them didn't really want to be there, didn't give much of a shit, might well be drunk, sleep-deprived or hung-over and weren't really paying a lot of attention to what the hell they were doing even when they were well-rested and sober) and perform incredibly complex and inter-connected mechanical and manufacturing processes so long as you:

a) Reduced each individual line worker's job to a single, simple, repetitive task that a well-trained monkey could do

b) Kept the line running at a pace that had everybody pretty much scrambling like mad to keep up

c) Kept a keen, watchful eye on everybody with a sophisticated organizational pyramid that included task managers, group coordinators, section chiefs, shift captains, union reps, roaming (and universally hated) corporate overseers, floor managers, line managers, production directors and a surreptitious legion of undercover snitches who reported directly to Scully Mungo in a little, hidden-away office on the 4th floor of Fairway Tower right next to the back stairway that went all the way down to the open-secret, sub-basement "electrical tunnel" between Fairway Tower and the main assembly line building

d) Came down like a ton of bricks on screw-ups, horseplay and fucking off

"The bare fact is this," Danny yelled as we clattered along the dizzying, expanded-metal catwalk high above Fairway Motors' pounding, twitching, grinding and ratcheting final assembly line, *"Bob says the very best we can expect out of our union workers is a 35% effort. Maybe 40% tops on a really good day. And it's our job to make the very best use of that 35 or 40% that we can. In fact,"* he turned to me with a rush of Home Team pride, *"we'll put our 35 or 40% effort up against any other car company's 35 or 40% effort—and I mean anywhere in the whole damn world!"*

He made it sound like something you could believe in.

Below us, a crew of expressionless, slow-moving union drones in Fairway Gray coveralls were fitting (and occasionally forcing, jamming and pounding) assorted carpet sections, trim strips, dashboards and occasional optional center consoles into glistening, door-less new Fairway Freeways and Fairway Freeway Frigates. And just beyond them was the crew that installed the seats, headliner, sun visors and steering wheels. And just beyond that, a set of overhead trolley tracks delivered shiny, fresh-out-of-the-paint-shop doors for the crew at the next work station to hang on the bodies. And, if everything worked as it should, a bright, shiny pair of Bedouin Beige doors showed up every time a door-less Bedouin Beige Fairway Freeway coupe went through and four glistening Everest White doors appeared as if by magic whenever an Everest White Freeway Frigate 4-door sedan came down the line. But of course the logistics broke down every now and then. And that's when some poor fish had to make the snap decision whether to simply bolt the Cornsilk Yellow doors on the Meridian Blue Freeway Frigate and sort it out later in the Rehash Barn, try setting the doors aside for whenever the damn Corn-silk Yellow Freeway Frigate finally showed up or—God Forbid!—reach for one of the big, ominous-looking red emergency buttons that were spaced out at regular intervals along the assembly line. The ones that brought the entire process to a sudden, clanking halt and set off alarms and air horns all through the plant like a damn prison break was in progress. At which point section leaders and task managers and union shop stewards and shift captains would go scurrying every which way to find out just what the fuck had happened and who the fuck was responsible. And the poor drool had better have a damn good reason when one of Scully Mungo's men came around and asked him why the hell he did it. Plus you need to understand that it's Standard Operating Procedure in any union plant for the lifer old-timers to indulge in a bit of rookie hazing and play a few pranks any time they had a new guy on the job. And particularly if the New Guy happened to be some open-faced, hardly-even-shaving-yet little summer-off-from-college twirp from Birmingham or St. Clair Shores whose daddy worked in Fairway Motors' purchasing department or whose family lived next door to one of the executives from Fairway Tower. Or one of those monstrous, muscular, V-shaped black kids who played football for Michigan State and always seemed to land cushy, union-wage jobs over the summer months (or at least until fall practice started up again) because one of the top U.A.W. union honchos was an M.S.U. alumnus and a rabid fan of the Spartan football program. In any case, the whole idea was to get the New Guy to panic and push one of those ominous-looking red buttons. One way to do that was to hook up a water line to the air gun he was using to tighten down all five left-front and left-rear lug nuts so the car could roll off the end of the assembly line on its own. I mean, here the poor fish is with his air gun spewing water all over the place and making sounds like a motorboat stuck in mud, and he knows that if the fucking car rolls off the end of the fucking line and its fucking wheels fall off because the lug nuts aren't even finger tight—and that would be the lug nuts *HE* was supposed to have tightened!—well, there'd be an even bigger mess because the cars coming right behind it are not about to stop and they'll run right into it. And meanwhile all the lifer old-timers are splitting their guts, peeing in their pants and biting into the back of their hands to keep from laughing out loud. Hell, the kid will probably get away with it. After all, he's new on the job. And his daddy (or his coach) has connections upstairs....

After our tour I had another meeting with Bob Wright, and this time he spelled out in greater detail what he had in mind for me, what he expected of me and what the amorphous thing he referred to as 'Our Future Together' might actually be.

"What we mostly need from you is to know where we need to go, how we need to get there and what kind of opposition we'll be up against."

"That's a pretty tall order."

"That's why we picked you for the job," he answered right back. "We're pretty confident you're the right man for it."

He had a knack for volleying the ball right back at you.

"We already know you think we need to win Le Mans," he continued like it was simply an item on a shopping list, "so we'll need all the details on the track and the cars we'll have to run against." He looked me in the eye. "Particularly Ferrari. Those are the guys we really need to know about."

"What sort of information do you need?"

"We need to know the specifications and capabilities of their current cars and also what sort of new models they have in the pipeline..."

My sad-eyed little Italian racing-scribe friend Vinci Pittacora came instantly to mind. But I didn't say anything.

"...Hugo and his engineering people will want to know all the technical details."

And that made me wonder if an engineering team that spent most of their time designing rocker panels that rusted out and shock absorbers that jiggled and wallowed over anything other than a sheet of plate glass were really up to taking on Ferrari at Le Mans. No matter how many engineering-school PhD's they had on the payroll or how much money they had in the budget. And I told Bob as much.

"I know what you're saying," Bob agreed. "And I truly appreciate your forthrightness in saying it." He leaned back in his chair. "You're going down to the 12 Hours of Sebring, right?"

"Sure I am."

"I want you to drop by and introduce yourself to Harlon Lee and his people."

"Harlon Lee the stock car guy?" Harlon was a genuine legend in stock car circles. He'd raced jalopies himself back in the old days, and earned quite a reputation as both a clever car-builder and a tough, savvy racer. But he'd retired from the driving to concentrate on his car-building and racing team businesses, and by that point ran a well-known and even better-respected race shop near Charlotte that fielded most all of Freddie Fritter's stock cars. Not to mention building the majority of chassis and engines for most of the front-running Fairway Freeways on the NASCAR circuit fielded by other teams. "He runs all the Fairway cars for Freddie Fritter, doesn't he?" I asked rhetorically.

"He's one of our guys," Bob allowed ambiguously. But then his face went solid. "But of course that's off the record and not for publication. Or at least not yet."

"But everybody knows about it already, don't they?"

"Of course everybody knows it already," he said like everybody knew it already. "We're not stupid. But there's a big difference between 'knowing' something and having it confirmed in print. And particularly that it's part of Fairway Motors' official policy and corporate budget."

I personally couldn't see much difference, but apparently it was some sort of major distinction on the uppermost floors of Fairway Tower.

"That time will come," Bob assured me. "But you have to understand that it's not here yet." He held his hands up like he was holding an imaginary Holy Grail. "You have to understand that these things become incredibly complicated when you've got a big company and stockholders and a board of directors to answer to and all sorts of legal implications and corporate image ramifications anytime you want to try something new. Try something..." he lifted his imaginary Holy Grail up so we could both get a better look at it "...something really *special!*"

I watched as the cup evaporated off the ends of his fingertips.

"In any case," he started in again, "Harlon's going to be down there with some-thing a little bit new for us. But you have to understand it's completely on the Q.T. and just for testing and evaluation."

"At Sebring?"

He nodded. "It looks more or less like a Flyer on the outside, but underneath it's a test mule for our Ferret racing program." He looked down at his fingernails. "Mind you, we don't want anybody getting too inquisitive or taking it too seriously. We want people to think Harlon's just doing it on his own."

"Like Ray and Frank Nichels did with the Pontiac Tempests at Daytona?"

Bob frowned. "I'm hoping we can do a little better than that."

"They led the first lap," I reminded him.

He gave off a muffled snort. "And who remembers that?"

I decided to skip the story about T.J. Huston and the ten bucks I still owed him.

"We don't expect much right away, of course. And we're purposely keeping a low profile on this. Almost invisible, in fact." He paused and made a quick note to himself on the legal pad in front of him. "But I have to tell you," he continued without looking up, "we've got one huge, long-term advantage over Pontiac."

"Oh? What's that?"

I watched a big, self-satisfied grin spread across his face. "We don't have to fight tooth-and-nail with Chevrolet for what we want inside our own blessed company!"

I could see where that might be a problem.

Bob glanced at his wristwatch and quickly wrapped things up. "Now I want you to keep a low profile on all of this, too. Nobody needs to know you're working for us. Or at least not yet, anyway." He looked me straight in the eye: "It's simply none of their business."

"Sure," I told him. But he kept staring at me like he wasn't really satisfied with my answer. So I repeated it. Only more gravely this time, like I'd taken time to think about it.

"Good," he nodded. "We understand each other." He stuck out his hand. Bob Wright had an amazingly solid grip for a guy his size. And you could really feel the energy coming through it.

"I'm going to have you meet with Dick Flick next," he added quickly. "All the copy and press information has to funnel through him. He's been working on the Absolute Performance program and the new Ferret launch for the better part of a year now." He looked up with a hand-in-the-cookie-jar gleam in his eye: *Even before we got the green light on it from H.R. Junior!* He shot me a conspiratorial wink. "I've been looking over his shoulder, of course, and I can't tell you how excited I am about what his team has on the drawing board for us. It's fantastic! You'll see. But the main thing is I don't want you free-lancing any of this or disturbing his plans or doing anything to compromise our security or upset our schedule. Do you understand?"

I nodded one more time. And then watched his face turn to solid granite as he repeated, one more time and very slowly: *"Do...you...un...der...stand?"*

"Yes," I assured him like I was addressing the next-of-kin at a funeral. "Yes, I do."

He seemed satisfied. And then he paused to make another quick note to himself on his legal pad. It wasn't even 9 am and the page was already half-full. "And after Sebring," he continued, still concentrating on his legal pad, "we want you to write that report about what it's going to take to beat Ferrari at Le Mans."

I felt a small, drafty hole opening up in the pit of my gut. "I-I'm not really sure I know how to do that...."

"Of course you don't," he went right on like it didn't make any difference. "It's never been done before." Then he gave me one of his famous, go-get-'em smiles. "I'm sure you'll do a bang-up job for us," he said with infectious conviction. "I have a lot of faith in you, Hank. I think you're the right man for the job. And I'm rarely if ever mistaken about those kinds of things."

To be honest, I wasn't entirely comfortable with what Bob Wright was telling me. Like I was a soldier being singled out for a dangerous mission behind enemy lines. Although part of it was probably that I wasn't real sure I could pull it off. Writers tend to be independent, free-spirited, poorly organized Lone Wolf types who don't much like taking orders, don't play well with others, don't enjoy being part of large, communal social groups or corporate hierarchies, don't acclimate well to long-term goals or prescribed modes of behavior and don't feel especially comfortable in polyester sport coats, regimental-striped ties or black leather wingtips that make their feet hurt.

But then Bob offered me roughly twice the pittance I made every year as a motorsports correspondent—*plus* an expense account!—and I started to feel a little more comfortable in those tight new shoes. Only then I remembered what Ben Abernathy had told me in the bar the night before. You know, about not taking the first deal offered. "I don't know," I allowed like I was genuinely thinking it over. "I have no idea how long this job with you might last, and I might lose my spot with the magazine if they ever find out about it...."

I had no idea whether that was true or not, but I thought it sounded pretty good.

That's when Bob pulled out the two-year, no-cut consulting contract he already had tucked away in my folder. The one that included the expense account, a company car wherever and whenever I needed one, health benefits, two weeks' paid vacation every year and a share in Fairway Motors' lower middle-management profit sharing and retirement plan as well.

You can bet your ass I signed it!

I was out of Bob Wright's office before the ink was even dry on the paper, and Karen Sabelle immediately escorted me down the corridor to Dick Flick's office. She gave an ugly little snort of disapproval when she saw that the door was closed and Wanda Peters' desk was vacant. "She's probably inside taking dictation," she observed with frigid distaste. "Have a seat until she comes out." And with that she turned and headed back to her desk. Karen Sabelle had an unusually stiff, almost military cadence to her walk, and it was amazing how she could almost seem to make her heels click, even on thick carpeting....

It was almost a half hour until Dick Flick's office door finally swung open and Wanda Peters came striding out, looking ever-so-slightly mussed but with really good color in her cheeks. "You can go right in," she said as she hurried past me towards the Ladies' Room down the hall. She had a hell of a walk, even when she was in a hurry.

Dick Flick's office was stylish, cool and modern, with just a small family picture on the edge of his desk featuring his tall, lean, dark-eyed and attractive ex-model wife standing next to him—smiling desperately—and two handsome, dark-haired boys in front of them with eyes full of charm and mischief. Although you couldn't miss that Dick wasn't wearing a wedding band. I heard later that he kept it in the ashtray of his company Freeway Frigate Fabergé special edition (the one with the faux gold-gilded instrument bezels and semiprecious stone key fob insert) and put it on every night like clockwork just before he pulled into his driveway in Grosse Pointe Shores. The walls of Dick's office were covered with framed advertising awards, Madison Avenue commendations and full-color blowups of some of the great and near-great ad campaigns he'd spearheaded for Fairway Motors. I recognized the one behind his desk immediately. It was the famous shot from the 1955 Freeway Frigate ad campaign (his very first as Director of Advertising when he was still working down on the 11th floor) and it featured a beautiful, tall, slender and elegant young woman—high cheekbones, dark hair piled on top of her head, dripping with jewelry and wearing a black evening gown cut so low in back it damn near revealed a second cleavage—standing next to a Formal Black "Tuxedo Edition" Fairway Freeway Frigate in front of the Plaza Hotel in New York. An approving and obsequious black doorman (just so everything matched, you know?) was just opening the door for her. That shot appeared on major-route billboards and in double-truck ads in all the popular magazines in 1955, accompanied by a simple, eloquent tag line in wedding-invitation script: *"When it comes to luxury, those on-the-go and in-the-know simply say 'Frigate.'"*

"I like that one, too," Dick Flick allowed through an impossible-to-read smile. "It's one of my favorites. But of course the car was a total piece of crap." He heaved out an elaborate, 'why me?' sigh. "Believe me, it's not easy trying to convince people that they can pass off a tarted-up Fairway Freeway with a vinyl roof and landau bars as a damn Cadillac." He nodded me into the chair across from him. "But that's where the advertising and marketing comes in, isn't it?"

"You do quite a job of it," I told him, mostly because I couldn't think of anything else to say. I could feel him watching me as I ran my eyes over all the ads, awards and citations on his walls. "Very impressive."

He looked at me like I was a total suck-up. Which I guess I was. But it was hard to get comfortable around a guy like Dick Flick. He was disgustingly handsome, effortlessly elegant and maddeningly self-assured. You just *knew* he did well with the ladies. But you also got the sense that Dick Flick was cat-quick, tiger wary, devious as the devil himself and never let anybody know what he was thinking. His eyes reminded me of the South American *fer-de-lance* pit viper I once saw devouring a not-quite-deceased white rat in the reptile house of the Los Angeles zoo. Those eyes were all business, and there was nothing the least bit sentimental behind them.

"Looks like we're going to be working together," I said, trying to break the ice.

The ends of his mouth curled down. "We're not exactly going to be working together," he corrected me with a steely edge to his voice. *"You're* going to be writing copy and *I'm* going to be approving it..." he locked eyes with me *"...Before* it goes out. Is that clear?"

I nodded.

He leaned back in his chair and eyeballed me for what seemed like an awfully long time. "You think I'm a prick, don't you?"

I recoiled visibly. "Why, I...I don't even know you."

"Of course you don't. But trust me on this," the ends of his mouth curled slowly upwards, "I am a prick. A complete prick. You can ask anybody."

I couldn't think of anything to say.

"But you have to be a prick to survive in this business," he continued matter-of-factly. "And if there's one thing I always intend to do, it's survive..." he swiveled around so I could better appreciate his tanned and chiseled profile "...and advance, if possible." It registered immediately that the only position above his own was Bob Wright's job at the far end of the corridor. And it occurred to me a half-heartbeat later that the only reason he'd said it was to see how I'd react. He swiveled around and looked me in the eye again. "Do I make myself clear?"

It was obvious he expected a reply. "Uh, sure," I told him. "Absolutely."

"Good!" He flashed me a hollow smile. "It's important that we understand each other." Then his eyes moved back to the coppery gold-tinted windows looking out over the factory buildings below. "Tell me," he said in a faraway voice, "do you know the difference between advertising and marketing?"

I thought it over. "No, I guess I don't. Not really."

"Well, let me enlighten you." He cleared his throat, and you could tell he'd delivered this particular speech before. "Advertising is trying to show people the features, benefits and advantages of your product so they'll hopefully make the choice you want them to make when they're in the market and ready to buy."

That made sense.

"But marketing is the art of convincing people that your product, whatever it may be, will improve their lives. Make them happier, healthier, smarter, younger, more successful, more loved, more self-assured and more sexually attractive—and *active!*—than they ever dreamed possible. Even in their wildest fantasies."

"That's a pretty tall order for a four-door sedan with a vinyl roof and landau bars."

"Yes it is," he agreed. "But, fortunately for us, most people are dull, stupid, vain, petty, easily misled and unbelievably gullible. That's the real magic of this business..." a Cheshire Cat smile spread out across his face "...people really *want* to believe." He looked at me quizzically. "Do you think that's terrible?"

I thought it over. "I-I guess not."

"Well, you're wrong," he corrected me. "It's absolutely, positively despicable." And then he laughed. But it wasn't a funny laugh or a belly laugh or even a nasty little chortle. It was more one of your snide, sarcastic, you-get-what-the-hell's-coming-to-you-in-this-world sort of snickers. There was no humor in it at all, and it left a faint, icy chill in the room. Dick Flick stared at me again through those uncaring, *fer-de-lance* eyes. "Do you have any idea why Bob Wright picked you for this job?"

I felt my shoulders shrug. "Not really. I guess mostly because I'm an American and a writer and I know my way around most of the people, teams and racetracks over in Europe."

"That's part of it," Dick agreed, teasing me along. "But you must realize that you have one additional, almost irresistible attribute."

"Oh? What's that?"

He looked at me like he was surprised I hadn't figured it out already. "Why, deniability, of course. If things don't work out, he can just sweep you under the rug and walk away like nothing ever happened." He gave me a knowing smile. "Reputation, saving face, covering your ass and keeping up appearances are every bit as important as selling product and making money in this business...."

I started feeling like one of John Wayne's crew members in *They Were Expendable.*

"...In any case," Dick continued, "we're committed to making our new 'Absolute Performance' program the biggest damn thing that ever hit this town. Or this industry. And the new Ferret is going to be right up at the sharp end of the spear when we launch it next spring."

"You're launching a new model in the *spring?*" I asked incredulously. No Detroit manufacturer had ever launched a new model in the spring. Hell, nobody had.

Dick's eyes fairly glistened. "We'll have the whole damn stage to ourselves!" he crowed. "Not to mention the hottest, sharpest, sexiest new car in history to go along with it!" He slammed his fist into his palm. "And a lot of the white-collar, working-stiff slobs in this very tower and even some of the lifer assembly-line drools out there on the factory floor will actually be able to afford one! Or at least they will if they're willing to take a base stripper with nothing on it and go into hock up to their eyebrows at their banks and credit unions." His nostrils flared in predatory anticipation.

It was an impressive and innovative plan, no question about it.

"The point is this," he continued evenly. "We want to make damn sure we catch everybody all-at-once, dead-in-their-tracks stunned and flat-footed with this thing. Particularly the other manufacturers." He trained those pit viper eyes on me again. "So the last thing we want or need are unauthorized leaks in the press. We'll have plenty of *authorized* unauthorized leaks when the right time comes." He pointed his finger across the desk at me. Aimed it right between my eyes, in fact. "If I find out something like that has happened and you're the cause of it, I'll have your balls hanging from my rearview mirror like a pair of baby shoes. Do we understand each other?"

I told him we did.

"Good," he smiled. "That's the way it has to be." He looked out his window again and sighed. "You can go now."

"I can? Just like that? The meeting's over?"

Dick looked at me strangely. "Why wouldn't it be?"

He had me there.

"Just remember this," he cautioned as I headed towards the door. "You have two rules and only two rules to live by. Rule Number One is that you don't say or write *anything* until I say it's okay for you to say or write it. And Rule Number Two is that when the time comes for you to put something in print for us, I approve the copy. And that's *before* you put it out where the public can read it. Do I make myself clear?"

That actually pissed me off a little, and I could feel the color creeping up into my cheeks. But then I thought about the money and the expense account and the company car and the profit sharing and the health care and the paid vacations and more-or-less nodded in agreement as I went through the door.

After the meeting Dick's secretary escorted me back to the 13th-floor reception area and those polished nickel-and-brass elevator doors leading down to the lower twelve floors. Walking behind her, you couldn't miss that Wanda Peters had a springy, athletic ass and leg muscles like a damn racehorse. "We'll see you again, I'm sure," she said without enthusiasm as she put me on the elevator.

"I'm sure you will," I answered as the doors slid slowly closed. She wasn't bad from the front, either.

And who should I meet as I walked out on the 12th floor landing but my old pal Carroll Shelby. He was standing there in his usual tanned, leathery face, wild, curly hair and conspiratorial, just-between-you-and-me smile. Only he was wearing a damn business suit—of all things!—and obviously on his way up to the 13th floor. Of course Carroll was the one-time air force pilot, Texas chicken farmer and natural-born hustler/promoter who'd turned into one of the top American road racers of the mid-1950s. He'd raced and won damn near everywhere in high-flying California car owner John Edgar's Ferraris and Maseratis, then made a name for himself in Europe driving for Aston Martin. He'd shared the winning Aston DBR1 with Roy Salvadori at the 24 Hours of Le Mans and helped out again later that year when Aston unexpectedly managed to snatch the 1959 World Manufacturers' Championship away from Ferrari and Porsche at the last race of the season at Goodwood. Carroll and I had come to know each other pretty well over the years and no question we got along, and I think we were about equally surprised to run into each other in front of that exclusive, 12th-to-13th floor elevator in Fairway Tower. Not to mention both dressed up in jackets and ties. "What the hell are *you* doing here?" I asked.

"I could ask you the same thing," Carroll grinned back as he looked me up and down. "You clean up pretty good for a damn typewriter jockey."

"So do you," I snorted back. "For a damn Texas chicken farmer."

We shared a quick laugh, and then a soft chime rang and the elevator doors started to slide closed.

"Gotta run," Carroll said as he stepped inside.

"But what are you *doing* here?" I asked again as the doors eased fluidly towards each other.

"Looking for a little help an' a little horsepower," Carroll smiled as his face disappeared behind the polished nickel-and-brass panels.

It made me wonder, that's for sure.

It took me quite some time to piece it all together, but in the end you'd have to say that the new Fairway Ferret "personal sporty car" was mostly Bob Wright's idea. You could also say it was Dick Flick's idea. Or Daryl Starling's. You might even say, in a strange, obtuse sort of way, that it was the luscious Miss Francine Niblitz' of the slightly scattered brain but outstanding set of hogans idea. But the one thing you could never, ever say was that it was Harold Richard Fairway Junior's idea. Even though he was ready to take full credit if it turned out to be a success. Or, conversely, fire the shit out of anybody and everybody who had anything to do with it if it flopped. After all, the stockholders expected it. And Harold Richard Fairway Junior expected it of himself, as well. It was part of the weighty, sometimes even troubling *noblesse oblige* that went along with being heir to the biggest damn family-directed manufacturing business on the face of the earth. H.R. Junior understood that you were *required* to do things like that because the Lord God in heaven, in His almighty and infinite wisdom, had put you in that position and given you that power in the first place. It was His will. And so it was *incumbent* on you, as His chosen representative and emissary, to acquiesce to His will and exercise the power He'd so obviously and intentionally granted. Keep it well exercised, in fact. After all, anything less would be blasphemy....

Best as I could figure, the entire Ferret project basically began thanks to new hire Hubert C. Bean and his fledgling computer data base. Hubert was a skinny, sniffly, nervous and bookish little twirp with a big, angular nose and a huge, elongated cranium that followed him around like a balding semi trailer. Hubert sported a nervous tic, a perpetually furrowed brow, thick glasses in heavy black frames and eyes like a lab rat in a high school biology class. But he was touted as some sort of Miracle Man Computer Genius when he came to Fairway Motors directly from IBM. Hubert C. Bean believed to the core of his two-dimensional soul in that binary, mathematically-driven modern religion that thinks you can identify, understand and even predict almost anything if you just have the right data—and plenty of it!—and can somehow sort and file and formulate and postulate and push it through a numeric meat grinder enough times that you can make sense of it and interpret it properly. Hubert was a direct hire by H.R. Junior himself after Little Harry Dick read one-half column of a three-column piece about computer-generated marketing models in a day-old edition of *The Wall Street Journal* that Clifton Toole had left behind—along with an extremely unpleasant odor—in one of the mahogany-lined stalls in the 13th floor Men's Room. That one-half column was enough to convince H.R. Junior that Fairway Motors really needed their own, in-house, up-to-the-minute, state-of-the-art, new-as-tomorrow computer-generated marketing model department. So he had his then-current company president, right-hand man, go-to guy, closest company friend and confidant Gordon Stritch do a little digging (which was actually done by his secretary Karen Sabelle, of course) to find out who at **IBM** was working on that kind of stuff and making about 5 grand less than $25,000 a year as a department head. His own personal secretary at the time, one Gloria S. Butz, was breathtaking to look at (particularly from behind) but not much good at anything that required more intelligence, common sense, organizational skill or stick-to-itiveness than you might expect from a colander of Brussels sprouts. In any case, H.R. Junior figured that $25,000 was a nice, round, impressive-sounding number and ought to be more than enough to secure the kind of technical expertise he was certain Fairway Motors needed. During his infamously rambunctious school days, H.R. Junior had often come to the blunt, unavoidable realization that virtually any problem, concern, desire or aspiration could be converted into a simple, finite, count-it-out-in-dollars figure that would either make what you wished for happen or, conversely, make it go away. In fact, all throughout his father's long and autocratic reign on the 13th floor, he'd never seen it fail. And H.R. Junior figured 25 grand (in 1960 dollars, remember) was an impressive enough bag of swag to get the job done.

Now as Bob Wright's immediate predecessor as President and C.E.O. at Fairway Motors, Gordon Stritch naturally had to handle the initial interview process. H.R. Junior generally preferred firing people to hiring them, and never much cared for face-to-face, one-on-one interviews involving people he suspected might be smarter or better educated than him. Which, when you get right down to it, covered an amazingly high percentage of the earth's entire adult population. Aborigines and Alzheimer's patients included. In any case, Karen Sabelle (who even then handled a lot of what actually got done up on the 13th floor) narrowed the field down to six potential candidates, and H.R. Junior narrowed that down to three just by looking at the snapshot pictures attached to their dossiers. *"Look at this guy's tie,"* he snorted as he tossed the file of an M.I.T. Phi Beta Kappa in the wastebasket. *"And this guy looks sneaky. Let's keep him in."*

Hubert C. Bean ultimately won the nod because he was easily bullied and intimidated and could lose almost anybody in 15 seconds whenever he started trying to explain the complex, intertwined, jargon-laced, inter-dependent and generally symbiotic topics of Computers, Hardware, Software, Computer Models, Sorting Functions and Raw Data. And yet he was enough of a wimp and milquetoast that he didn't represent a threat to anybody else's job! Particularly Karen's immediate boss, Gordon Stritch, who lived in mortal fear of losing his position from the time H.R. Junior promoted him to President and C.E.O. until the day H.R. Junior finally fired him (very loudly and angrily, and in front of almost the entire 13th floor staff) following the new Fairway Fantasia's embarrassing sales numbers and humiliating withdrawal from the market in late 1959. Of course, the new Fantasia was really H.R. Junior's idea (or, to be slightly more accurate, H.R. Junior's wife Amanda Cassandra Fairway's idea) and was *supposed* to be Fairway's new, modern, up-to-the-minute upper-middle-market car line strategically inserted between the Fairway Freeway and the Fairway Freeway Frigate and aimed smack-dab at traditional Buick, Oldsmobile and Chrysler buyers. But the combination of an iffy name choice (there were rumblings about a lawsuit from Disney), an instantly recognizable but not entirely attractive front-end treatment, an already overcrowded market segment, tough times in general and basically the same old Fairway Freeway chassis and driveline hardware hidden underneath the flashy new sheetmetal ultimately killed it off. Oh, there was a genuine spurt of interest, showroom traffic and sales success right there at first (sparked in no small measure by Dick Flick's massive—and *expensive!*—national advertising campaign that touted the new Fairway Fantasia as *"The car of tomorrow...today!"*). But then the jokes started about the front-end styling and how the bold new Fantasia grille treatment looked like an ass-crack with a hemorrhoid in it, and there was no salvaging the situation once the stand-up comics latched onto it on the television variety shows and sales dropped off a cliff.

Now H.R. Junior had personally loved the Fantasia project and even had a hand in the styling, color, feature and trim decisions (or at least his wife did, anyway) but he needed a fall guy when it all went to shit. Or at least someone to fire. And poor Gordon Stritch was right dead-center in the line of fire when the axe finally fell. Bob Wright felt absolutely terrible about it, of course, since Gordon had been his boss, his close personal friend and his longtime mentor, champion and colleague. But even so, Bob was more than ready to take the President/C.E.O. promotion in a heartbeat—even while the soft leather upholstery of the swivel chair in the office at the far end of the executive corridor was still slightly warm—as soon as H.R. Junior offered it to him.

Hubert C. Bean had already been hired at that point, and so there was a dangling decision to be made as to just where, exactly, he and his new Computer Marketing Model department would be positioned in the overall structure of Fairway Motors' corporate management. The fact is, nobody much wanted him. Hubert C. Bean looked like a crap-load of hard-to-answer questions and bothersome second-guessing ready to go off like a fragmentation bomb—with casualties—wherever he finally wound up. In the end, it was H.R. Junior himself who assigned Fairway's new computer marketing whiz to Dick Flick's staff. Even though Dick argued lamely that, since Hubert was really more of a numbers guy, he'd maybe be a better fit with Clifton Toole's accounting people or Ben Abernathy's production and logistics staff or maybe even Hugo Becker's engineers. But H.R. Junior cut Dick off at the knees: *"He's yours, asshole. And he sure as hell better produce results!"*

So Dick Flick dutifully set Hubert Bean up with a properly homely but not particularly bright or efficient young secretary and an office tucked away in a far corner of the 6th floor, and also gave him enough budget to buy some of the newest and latest techno-whizbang computers and hoped that they would keep him occupied and out of the way doing whatever it was that computer marketing model geniuses were supposed to do. And no doubt Dick Flick was hoping, in the coldest, darkest recesses of his icy heart, that it wouldn't be much and that he'd someday be able to fire the squeaky little bastard.

But he was wrong.

Because Hubert C. Bean didn't smoke, didn't drink, didn't gamble, didn't fool around with girls, didn't fool around with boys, didn't enjoy sports or hobbies, didn't involve himself with any particular church, temple, synagogue, fraternal order, cult or social club and also didn't get along very well with his henpecking wife, his surly and distant teenaged son, his wife's equally unpleasant extended family or, for that matter, anyone else. That didn't leave much for him to do except work, and he found that work uniquely satisfying because of his near-mystical belief in the dubious relationship between time spent, effort expended, quantity of data gathered, sifted, sorted and filed and any useful results or conclusions that might actually be achieved. But that was always the real beauty of a largely theoretical, numerical, empirical and statistical game: with any luck at all, you'd be long dead and buried before your work could be properly evaluated. Or even finished, come to that....

In any case, the whole Ferret thing started at one of Bob Wright's famous, brainstorming, management board meetings where all the department heads—and sometimes a few key underlings—got together in the big conference room on the 13th floor to drink coffee, eat doughnuts and talk over where the company was and where it needed to be going in both the immediate and long-range future. Now everyone involved (except Bob Wright, of course) both hated and feared these meetings. Hated because they were a huge waste of time, interfered with work that actually had to be done and rarely produced anything of value. Feared because H.R. Junior would occasionally drop in for lack of anything better to do, and that meant you could get your asshole reamed out to an entirely new aperture size—or even get fired—if you so much as twitched a nostril or an eyelid the wrong way or cleared your throat at an inopportune moment.

But Bob Wright loved his management board meetings, and was convinced they were of great value because they cemented in everyone's mind—and particularly H.R. Junior's—the idea that he, Bob Wright, was the Guy In Charge who made things happen, got things done and pressed important ideas forward. And the main thing on Bob's 12 Key Points of Discussion agenda this particular day turned out to be Future Product Planning. It being a cold and snowy Tuesday in December and not really fit for golf, H.R. Junior was in attendance, sitting in his father's old chair at the head of the conference table (the one with the seat cushion positioned three-quarters of an inch higher than any of the others) and looking typically bored, surly, agitated and ready to go off like a hair-trigger, buckshot-filled 12-gauge at anything that dared to stick its head out of its hole. In the meantime, he was doodling crude, lead-pencil images of World War Two Corsairs and P-51 Mustangs shooting Jap Zeroes and German Messerschmitts down with dotted-line tracer bullets.

Bob Wright was of course leading the proceedings from the chair on H.R.'s immediate right, and his Topic for the Day was "What kind of cars should Fairway Motors build in the future?" And the response from the rest of the management board was a nervous, edgy silence. H.R. Junior knew and enjoyed that kind of silence, because he could almost smell the fear in it. It also presented him with a key opportunity to step in, take charge like a genuine leader and really make everyone sweat. He rolled his eyes up from a rendering of a Corsair shooting the wings off a Zero and ran and swept them around the table. They landed hard on Daryl Starling. *"You! Starling!"* he grunted ominously. *"Tell me. Tell us all. What're people gonna wanna buy in five years?"*

A fleeting look of terror flashed through Daryl Starling's eyes. He shifted uneasily in his chair. It was *fun* picking on Daryl Starling.

But Daryl Starling hadn't gotten this far up the corporate ladder without knowing how to rear up on his spindly little haunches and fight back. He cleared his throat, flashed his trademark nervous smile, licked his lips one time and started in. His voice was high, shrill and pissy: "I only know things from the designer's perspective, of course..."

Hugo Becker rolled his eyes.

"...but I would think, given the new, young music that's coming out now and the new trends in clothes and fabrics and the postwar babies reaching driving age and all the social and political, umm, *uncertainties,* well..." he licked his lips again, searching for a worthy punch line, "...I think we'll have to be thinking *younger* and more *up to date* in five years' time." He looked furtively around the room, searching for support.

H.R. Junior grunted at him. "Izzat the best you got? We gotta think *younger?!?"* He glared at Daryl Starling like there was a fresh, stinking turd on the polished mahogany in front of him. H.R. Junior glared at him some more, just for good measure, then reloaded his eyes and swiveled them over to Dick Flick. "How 'bout you, Dick? You can't sell shit to a sewer this year. And you're always sayin' that the problem is the damn product, not your fucking, overpriced advertising..."

There was a tiny hint of a wince from Dick's face, but only if you were watching very closely.

"...So tell me. Tell us all. You got any great ideas about what people are gonna wanna buy five years? Huh? Have you?"

Dick Flick didn't bat an eye. "I think Daryl's on the right track..." he began calmly (and you could see a wave of thanks and relief go through Daryl Starling) "...Our demographic is going to be younger, trendier, sexier and more sophisticated. Everyone goes to the movies. Everyone watches TV. Some people even keep up with the news. As far as I'm concerned, that's going to be the key, emerging customer demographic that needs to lead the entire product line..."

"As far as I'm concerned," H.R. Junior mimicked poorly, "that's a big old crock of horse shit." He sneered at Dick Flick, but it reflected right off of him. "You're always one for the flowery words that don't mean much of anything. I need to know *specifics!*" He slammed his fist on the table, startling everyone. "I need to know fucking *nuts and bolts!*" His face drooped into a sour, dejected expression. But then it brightened. "Whaddabout that new guy?"

"New guy?"

"That computer guy!"

"Hubert Bean?" Dick answered uneasily.

"*Yeah!* That's the one! Why not ask his fucking computers what kind of cars people are gonna wanna buy in five years?" A big, powerful grin opened up below the blunt, rosy end of H.R. Junior's nose. "You *DO* that," he ordered Dick Flick. "You do that *right away,* unnerstand?"

Dick knew better than to argue or, worse yet, try to get any specifics or clarification. "I'm on it, H.R.!" he yelped with believable enthusiasm. "We'll get him started on it *today!*"

But of course knowing what people in the market for new cars might want (and moreover might be willing to pay for!) in five years' time was a complicated and involved sort of question. And, like all the other departmental Vice Presidents with offices on the 13th floor of Fairway Tower, Dick Flick had a great belief in and sympathy for the scientifically unsupportable (but generally correct) collection of hunches, notions, bright ideas, off-the-wall impulses and inner, gut feelings that drove most creative people to do whatever it was they were destined to do. Cynical and pragmatic as he was, Dick Flick railed at the notion of turning what he knew to be an art into something he firmly believed could never be a science. On the other hand, that's what H.R. Junior wanted, and setting fundamental principles aside was never, ever a problem for Dick Flick. Or at least not so long as he could see a little job security or a significant career benefit as part of the sacrifice.

Hubert C. Bean, on the other hand, didn't much believe in hunches, notions, bright ideas, off-the-wall impulses or inner, gut feelings because he rarely—if ever—had any. Probably the most impulsive thing he ever did was ask his wife to marry him. And that was really her idea, anyway. So he approached his newly assigned task with all the dedication and relentlessness of a Buddhist monk prayer-wheel spinner with only a million and a half spins to go (give or take a few) before reaching the next cosmic plane. Hubert set up programs and studies and behavior models and sly, surreptitious "consumer questionnaires" (written with the assistance of a whole legion of expensive Outside Consultant psychologists, psychiatrists, sociologists and anthropologists) intended to delve beneath the surface of the human psyche and reveal the true nature of the car-buying creature that dwelled within.

Unfortunately, the basic problem with asking the great, unwashed, rank-and-file masses of humanity what they really want is that most poor slobs have no idea whatsoever. Oh, they know it when they see it, all right. When some company offers up that right, exact, perfect, just-what-I've-always-been-looking-for gimcrack, gimmick or gizmo, old John Q. and Fred Average (and their wives) start taking out second mortgages and lining up on the showroom floor. But ask them what they really, truly *want* from a product, service or appliance and all you get back is the sound of feet shuffling around on polished linoleum and Juicy Fruit smacking around between gold-filled molars.

And most likely not the wisdom teeth, either....

Or that was Dick Flick's take on it, anyway.

And Daryl Starling's.

And Ben Abernathy's.

And even, deep down in his heart of hearts, Bob Wright's.

And even my own, come to think of it.

But not old Hubert C. Bean. He had his assignment, and he was hell-bent on digging deep and discovering The Truth about what the base, mean, norm, average, thick-part-of-the-bell-shaped-curve, all-American car-buying consumer might actually have in mind for himself. Or herself. And the results (which began pouring in a scant 17 months after the project first began) indicated that John Q. and Fred Average—and their wives, of course—were truly eager to buy a flashy, sharp, svelte, sexy and peppy little 2-seater sports coupe or convertible that would be fun to drive, great to be seen in, attract envy and/or attention in any supermarket parking lot or at any class or family reunion, leave steaming black streaks for at least 20 yards away from any stoplight in America, zoom from zero-to-sixty in less than ten seconds and hit 120 on a flat, level stretch of highway, handle like a sports car, get better than average gas mileage, hold both themselves and their 2.286 children (average age 7.643 years) as well as the family dog or cat (average count 0.895 per household, average weight 16.647 lbs.), have a superb heating, ventilating and air conditioning system as well as a great pushbutton radio with optional rear-seat speaker and carry roughly the same amount of cargo and/or luggage as a Fairway Fleetline panel van. Oh, and it had to be priced right around $2,000-$2,500 all up with taxes, license fees and transportation costs included. Or maybe a wee bit more for the convertible....

Following a Management Board update meeting several months later that H.R. Junior failed to attend because he was out playing golf, Dick Flick leaned over the desk of H.R. Junior's brand new personal secretary, Miss Francine Niblitz, far enough to get a mesmerizing view down the front of her blouse. "Tell me," he asked, still gazing into the deep, creamy white valley between her outstanding breasts, "what kind of car would you buy if you could have anything you wanted?"

"Oh, I wouldn't want to buy anything," she answered earnestly. The effort made her chest heave up and down.

"You wouldn't?"

"Oh, no," she repeated in a singsong voice. "I'd much rather if someone else bought it for me...." She gave him a wise and dazzling smile.

"Okay. Fair enough. Then let's say someone else is buying it for you."

"Like who?"

"Oh, say, like your father."

"My father's dead."

Dick Flick's leading-man lips bent down into a caring frown. "I'm so sorry."

"Oh, that's okay. He died when I was little. I don't even remember him too good." She gave him another brilliant smile. "You'll have to pick somebody else."

"How about your mother?"

Now it was Francine Niblitz's turn to frown. "We don't get along so good. She married a door-to-door bible salesman..."

"A bible salesman?"

"...and then she married a commercial plumber. But at least he worked steady. He wasn't door-to-door..."

"A plumber?"

"...Yes, sir. And then there was the veterinarian from Royal Oak..." she leaned in a little closer, vastly improving the view, and whispered: *"...but they didn't really get married. Not in a church or anything. I think he was still married to someone else...."*

"I see."

"...and then there was the guy who owned the butcher shop and the guy who laid carpeting in office buildings and..."

"I think we're getting a little off-subject here."

"You don't want to hear about the pig farmer?"

"Of *course* I do. Just not right now."

"He's the last one."

"That's good to know."

She leaned in close again. *"I didn't like him much, either,"* she added softly.

"Your mother seems to have had quite a career."

"She looks like me," Francine said proudly. "Only older."

"I see." Dick knew he had to think of something more to say, because there was no way he could gracefully stand up at that point. "Well, would any of those, uh, *men* have bought you a car?"

"Oh, I'm sure they all would have. But none of them had any money." She leaned in close again and whispered: *"My mother has terrible taste in men. Not one rich one in the bunch."*

Dick Flick curled his lip under. "Well, let's just imagine there was someone who would buy you a car."

"Oh!" she exclaimed breathlessly. "Do you know who he is?"

"We're just imagining here."

"But who do you *imagine* it is?"

Dick rolled his eyes, but quickly brought them back to Francine's blouse. "Let's just imagine it's anybody."

"Like who?"

"Oh, say..." he looked at Harold Fairway Junior's name spelled out in important etched letter on the impressive-looking brass plaque on his mahogany office doors. "...let's say your boss, for example."

"He's your boss, too."

"I know he is."

"Do you think he might?" she asked excitedly.

"I really have no idea."

"I don't think his wife would like it. She might think there was something going on..."

"We're getting a little off the subject again...."

"...But that's the right way to do it. Have him buy me a car. They already gave me a company car when I signed on. A brand new Fairway Flyer. But it rattles. And I bet I'd have to give it back if I leave to get married or I get fired or..."

"I'm sure you would."

"See? That's why owning's better!"

"No pulling any wool over your eyes."

"Yep! My mother always said you had to get up pretty early in the morning to put one over on a Niblitz."

"I'm sure you do."

A short, welcome silence followed. During which Daryl Starling fluttered by.

"So what are you two talking about?" he cooed as he followed Dick's gaze down the front of Francine Niblitz's blouse.

"You know, I forgot," Francine laughed. "What was it you asked me?"

Dick shared an unflattering smile with Daryl Starling. "I asked her what kind of car she might want..." Dick explained as his eyes returned to her cleavage "...if someone was willing to buy it for her."

"Sounds like Market Research to me," Daryl observed.

"Would they buy me any kind of car I wanted?" Miss Niblitz inquired breathlessly, her breasts heaving up and down. "Anything at all?"

"Oh, absolutely," Dick assured her as he stared down her front. Daryl was staring, too. But while Dick's eyes were filled with predatory lust and forbidden-fruit longing, Daryl's were green with envy.

"You're not moonlighting for Hubert Bean, are you?" Daryl asked without moving his eyes.

"It's important work," Dick observed, also without moving his eyes. "That's why we on the executive level need to know what type of car someone as sharp and savvy and typical of mainstream America as Miss Francine Niblitz here might want. Assuming someone else was buying it for her, of course."

"Oh, of course," Daryl agreed.

"Well," Miss Niblitz mused, thinking it over, "I'd like it to look like one of those Jaguar sports cars. You know, the ones with a real long front end and a short, tight back end..." she offered up a tittering blush, "...a little like *me...*"

"I see," Dick nodded.

Daryl Starling thought for a moment, then leaned over and started sketching something on the back of an envelope that was sitting on the edge of Miss Niblitz's desk.

"...But it has to have seats in back for my two little nieces for when we go out to play miniature golf. Not just two like a sports car..."

"I see."

Daryl Starling's drawing got slightly longer. Francine looked down at it and frowned. "...And not all soft and rounded like a Jaguar, either."

"Not all rounded?"

She shook her head. "No, not rounded at all. I'd like it, you know, *crisper.* Like the crease in a pair of nice pants." She smiled approvingly at Dick Flick. "Like the ones you've got on." She ran her eyes down the crease in his pants and observed the way the fine Italian silk draped from the knee and broke in a single neat, elegant fold across the gleaming crown of his Italian leather shoe. "You dress really nice, Mr. Flick. Anybody ever tell you that?"

"I hear it from time to time."

"Well, you do. It makes you really look like somebody."

"That's very flattering."

"It's not flattering at all. It's just true." She made a face. "But I don't want you to think I'm sucking up to you up or anything."

"Heaven forbid," Daryl observed, still engrossed in his sketch.

"After all, why would I suck up to the guy from the third office down when I'm already sucking up to the guy in the big office at the end of the hall? It wouldn't make any sense."

"Maybe you're just a hopeless flirt and can't help yourself?" Daryl offered without looking up.

"You think?" she cooed, fluttering her eyelashes.

"It's a distinct possibility," Dick agreed, double-teaming her.

"But if I can't help it," she pouted through a moist, glistening mouth, "then it's not really my fault, is it?"

Neither of them could argue with that.

Daryl Starling looked down at his work with pursed, critical lips, then rotated the drawing around so Dick and Francine Niblitz could see it. "Is that more or less what you have in mind?" he asked.

Francine looked at it and her eyes grew wide. "That's *it!*" she yelped excitedly. "That's *exactly* the kind of car I want!"

And that, in a nutshell, is how the new Fairway Ferret was born.

Chapter 8: Deadlines, Down Time and Double Time

Everybody in the racing business has a lot of down time to kill, and sometimes it's just empty motel rooms, cheap restaurants, unremarkable bars, crappy daytime television and a lot of lonely, aimless ennui mixed with idle speculation about what it must be like to have a real job. But of course the rest of the time it's up at the crack of dawn and until all hours at the racetrack followed by umpteen-cups-of-coffee three ayems hammering away at the old typewriter keys, scrambling to meet deadlines. Not to mention an utterly relentless travel schedule that has you living out of a suitcase, braving heat and bad weather, attending parties, manufacturer announcements and press functions you really don't care about and generally running around in circles with your hair on fire. That's just the way it is. And most of us on the inside (or at least those who've come to love and understand it) much prefer the busy, frantic double-times to the aimless, meandering down times. Staying busy helps keep the old juices flowing and the interest level up. It kills off a lot of the boredom, too....

But sometimes you get lucky with down time, too. That happens on a fairly regular basis when you rub elbows with the rich, well-born and mighty. Like Cal Carrington's bank-shot invite to join him on young Count Giovanni Volpi's yacht cruise down the Florida coastline aboard the count's amazing new *L'Albatro d'Oro* Benetti. Cal picked me up a precise and oh-so-typical 45 minutes late at the Jacksonville airport, and had to hustle like crazy because *L'Albatro d'Oro* was scheduled to set sail in time to catch the sunset over the Jacksonville skyline and he still needed to pick up his travel bag from the beachfront apartment he'd been "sharing with a friend" since Daytona. And it didn't help that he was driving a shiny new, 34 horsepower, turquoise-blue-with-off-white-interior Volkswagen convertible that he'd somehow managed to finagle out of the local VW zone rep thanks to dropping a few names (including our ex-VW dealer pals Big Ed Baumstein and Buddy Palumbo) and a rather large line of bullshit. "I told him you were going to do a road test on it," Cal grinned as he popped the clutch and launched us forward with a feeble chirp off the tires.

"I don't do the road tests," I growled at him. "You know that." To be honest, I was mostly just mad he was late. Getting the use of free cars now and then was all part of the game.

"Couldn't you maybe make an exception?" he winked as he up-shifted to 2nd without the clutch. Just for fun. You could do that in a VW Beetle if you had the right feel for it.

"The magazine's got a regular staff for that. And special tools and instruments, too. They want acceleration graphs and curb and test weights and interior room and trunk capacity and miles-per-gallon figures for both city and highway driving. And that's not even counting Tapley meter readings and calculated data like piston travel and cubic feet-per-ton mile."

"What the hell is cubic feet-per-ton mile?"

"How the hell should I know? I don't do the damn road tests." By that point Cal had deftly upshifted to 4th—again without the clutch—and we were burbling along at a giddy, foot-to-the-floor 55 or 60mph. In a 35mph residential zone! "You're going to get us a ticket," I warned him.

"No, I'm not," he grinned as the speedometer needle strained towards 70.

I must admit I had a genuine soft spot for VW Beetles. And it wasn't just because of my friendship with Buddy and Big Ed. I loved that VeeDubs were simple, affordable, rugged, practical, nicely finished and unbelievably well screwed together and reliable for a cheap economy car. Even if they didn't have much at all in the way of trunk room, had crappy heaters and even crappier defrosters, wandered all over the highway in a crosswind, handled like drunken jackrabbits when pushed hard and sounded like a fart in a bathtub. But, as Cal was proving once again before my very eyes, you could drive one of the little turds essentially flat-out all the time and no one seemed to notice!

"I've seen stuff you've written about new cars in the magazine," Cal continued as he concentrated on the street signs flashing by. "Couldn't you do something like that?"

"Oh, sometimes the magazine has me cover new-car introductions in Europe," I allowed as Cal went for a near-nonexistent hole between a taxicab with its door opening and a garbage truck pulling out of an alley. He made it with just fractions of an inch to spare on either side. "But that's just because I'm their only guy over there. And those are usually just 'driving impressions,' not full-blown road tests."

"What's the difference between a 'road test' and a 'driving impression?'" Cal asked as he threw the VW full-lock sideways into a beachfront apartment complex. And let me pause to explain that it's indeed possible to get a brand new, press-demo VW convertible up on two wheels and frighteningly close to the point of toppling over if you use the curbs to try and widen up your line through corners.

"A 'driving impression' is much more informal," I told him as my fingernails dug into the little vinyl-covered grab bar over the glove box that the VW designers had thoughtfully installed for these sorts of occasions.

"Well, couldn't you do one of those?" he continued like it was nothing at all to feel the earth tilt on its ear and see the grain of the pavement streaking past beneath your elbow. "I mean, it was awfully nice of the guy to let us have the car." Cal braked hard, blipped the throttle for another clutchless downshift and hurled our VW sideways into a driveway. "We've got it all the way until Sebring." The VW shuddered to a halt and I could smell hot metal and brake linings when he switched it off. "Think it over," he advised airily as he hopped out to get his luggage. "It'd be a nice thing to do."

A pretty brunette that I didn't recognize met him at the door and let him inside. And he was in there for what seemed like an awfully long time. In fact, I started to worry that we were going to miss our boat. But Cal eventually emerged with his leather travel bag at his side and his shirt half unbuttoned, and he drove like there were prize money and championship points at stake all the way to the Jacksonville marina. We made it with entire minutes to spare....

There's always an impressive sense of occasion when a ship sets out to sea, and especially when it's the newest, biggest, most elegant and extravagant private yacht on the entire Eastern Seaboard. The sun was well into the western horizon by the time we reached the harbor, and Count Giovanni's stunning new Benetti looked three stories high and four blocks long as we approached it on a dead run from the far end of the pier. *L'Alberto d'Oro* was gleaming, ivory-white enamel from stem to stern with dark wood and polished brass trim, and smart-looking caterers in starched white shirts and silk bowties were just finishing up serving cocktails and appetizers from bars and tables set up both on deck and at dockside. Count Giovanni was there himself in a fine white linen jacket and a big, gracious smile, and Cal was right about me being welcome so long as I was riding along in his slipstream. Most of the guests were Ferrari people I recognized from the paddock at Daytona, but there were also several older, tanned and bejeweled local types in genuine yacht-club attire whom I took to be family friends and well-to-do boat-slip neighbors just there to see us off. Even though he was young and somewhat callow, Count Giovanni had the kind of style and grace that only comes from many generations of *noblesse oblige.* He was an eager, charming host, and terrifically enthusiastic about motorsports, and he seemed to know just about everybody and made a point of introducing everyone to everyone else as he ushered his guests aboard. You had to love the rich, glorious roll of his Italianized English, and I was genuinely surprised to discover that he knew me by name and was "terribly awfully glad" that I had been able to make it. *"We mus' be careful 'ow we behave now,"* he announced grandly to the crowd gathered around us. *"Thees one will write it all down for everyone to see..."*

I recognized Clive Stanley and Ian Snell standing at the railing—they looked like they belonged in such a setting—and Tommy Edwards told us he would have never made the cut except for the other two. I really wanted to wander around and check out the boat—after all, I'd missed that nighttime cruise on *L'Albatro d'Oro*—and Tommy was happy to show me around. There was a sumptuous master bedroom suite in the bow with a movie screen, a bed roughly the size of a baseball diamond (but just the infield), carpet like young Irish Setter fur and high windows so you could sit up in bed and see out but no-one could really see in. The galley was all stainless steel and butcher block, and just beyond was a softly lit, wood-paneled inside bar and dining area with French doors opening onto a large, open-to-the-stars party deck strung with tiny, golden lights. The next level up had a sun deck, an open-air bar with a white canvas canopy over it plus eight "preferred guest" upper-level staterooms. One level further up was the impressive, state-of-the-art command bridge. Down below decks were eight tiny but well-appointed "not-so-preferred-guest" staterooms where I'd be staying plus quarters for the permanent crew of six. Although there were only five on board for this trip—including a *very* good Russian cook named Sascha—because they needed one room for the full-time bartender. Tommy introduced me to the captain, who was a lean, rugged-looking Aussie with blue eyes, quartz-colored hair, a ready laugh and a saddle-leather tan. He was retired navy and spoke in the usual, expletive-laden Aussie style, and I liked him right away. He allowed that Benettis were about the most stylish, luxurious, well-built and beautiful yachts you could buy if you were, as he put it: "in the genuinely *LARGE* asshole bracket."

We pulled out in time to catch the last of the sunset and motored south along the Florida coastline as sky turned dark and the stars and moon became visible. It was an intoxicating feeling being out there on the Atlantic on Count Giovanni's incredibly handsome and expensive new Benetti. Although that may also have had something to do with the bartender, who was apparently trying to conserve both steps and glassware by pouring some *really* stiff drinks.

Count Giovanni made a point of working his way around the ship to have little private conversations with every guest on board. It was part of being a proper host, don't you know? And he looked you right, square in the eye and showed tremendous interest in whatever you were saying, no matter who you were, how you got there or what the subject of discussion might be. But mostly it was about racing. We spent some time discussing the Ferrari team and drivers—he knew I was a good friend of Cal's—and the Rodriguez brothers in particular. Although he was careful and diplomatic about it, the count was obviously worried that Pedro and Ricardo's father was pushing them too hard and bringing them along too fast. After all, Pedro was only 22 and his younger brother Ricardo was barely 20. They'd both started out racing bicycles and motorcycles in thir early teens and had been racing cars for a half-dozen years, and no question they could run heads-up with the best drivers out there. But they were terribly young and brave, and perhaps lacked seasoning. I saw it as a classic case of Little League Father syndrome, and the count confided in me—in a judicious whisper, of course, and certainly not to be repeated—that he had personally overheard the elder Rodriguez urging his sons to go faster and questioning each one privately as to why the other brother seemed to be quicker. That was a dangerous thing to do, even in jest. And particularly at a racetrack, where the consequences can be dire. The count also thought old man Ferrari was taking advantage of the situation—no surprise there—by happily allowing his *concessionaires* to take large fistfuls of the Rodriguez family cash in return for putting Pedro and Ricardo into top-line cars (whether entered by the factory team or Carlo Sebastian's quasi-factory effort) while the Old Man prevaricated and dragged his feet about hiring them on as full-fledged team drivers or offering either one a fulltime Formula One opportunity. And he could have easily done that during the 1961 season, when Ferrari had everybody else covered anyway. Enzo finally offered Ricardo an older-spec car for the fateful penultimate race of the season at Monza, and he qualified it a rather amazing 2nd on the grid in his first-ever Grand Prix! But he fell out after 13 laps with fuel system troubles, and his exact status with *Scuderia Ferrari* was still uncertain for the 1962 season. Then again, Ferrari always liked to keep his drivers worried about their position on the team. He thought it made them try harder. "They are such wonderful boys," the count said with great sadness in his voice. "Very fast and very serious about their racing, yet so young and full of fun." He looked me in the eyes. "Sometimes I worry about their futures...."

He excused himself to move on to other guests, and five minutes after that Count Giovanni was laughing and joking in Italian with Carlo Sebastian's Modenese team manager. But I didn't think any less of him for it. His passion for the sport summed up everything grand, awful, stunning, worrisome, selfish, noble, frivolous, privileged, stupid, fun-loving and deadly about it, and everyone on the inside knew and accepted those things as part of the game.

We all turned in late that night—so far out in the Atlantic that we couldn't even see the coastline—and the next morning found a lot of us looking pasty in spite of calm seas and plenty of bright Florida sunshine. But a breakfast buffet served with with Bloody Marys, Screwdrivers and plenty of coffee brought most of us around by the time we docked in St. Augustine. Count Giovanni had arranged for a tour bus to take us out for a little sightseeing, first at the old Spanish fort at the mouth of the Matanzas River and then stopping by at Marineland for a catered picnic lunch and a specially guided tour. That was pretty damn neat. And then it was back to *L'Albatro d'Oro* for cocktails and appetizers as we watched the sun drool down into the coastline. Count Giovanni had the captain pull in as close as possible to the shallows at Ormond Beach so everyone could see the barely visible strip of shoreline where Fred Marriott's Stanley Rocket streamliner raced across the sand to up the World Land Speed Record to 127.66mph—over two miles a minute!—on January 26th, 1906. Count Giovanni was pretty damned excited about it—he was passionate about motorsports history—but it looked like just another dark, scraggly stretch of north Florida beachfront to me.

After that we had dinner—anyone at that end of the table need another crab claw? Another lobster tail?—and afterwards Tommy and I just kind of wandered along the railing, sipping some awfully good brandy while watching the distant shore lights ooze slowly by.

"So what did you do after Daytona?" Tommy asked, just making conversation.

"Oh, I had to go over to Modena for the Maserati press introduction."

"How was it?"

"Like a funeral."

"Did you stay in Italy?"

"Nah. I had to come back to the states right after it was over."

"Down here to Florida?"

And that got me wondering if I should tell Tommy about my visit to Fairway Tower. But I realized I probably shouldn't. Not yet. It felt stupid having to make something up for a good friend like Tommy. "I had a meeting up in Detroit," I said like it was no big thing.

"Oh really?' he said like it made no difference to him, either. "Anything important?"

"Nah. Not really. I...I had some interviews to do for a story."

"Oh? About what?"

"Nothing much, really. A new engineering thing one of the big Detroit companies has been working on. Nothing to do with racing."

"It must be pretty bloody important if the magazine paid for the travel." Tommy understood a little about what magazines pay and their general policies about travel expenses. Which generally fall into the "you're on your own, Bub" category unless you're on some colossally important assignment that no local stringer can handle or the person, team, car owner or car company in question is picking up the tab. Which happens from time to time when someone really wants you to write something nice about them.

"Nah," I told him. "The car company paid. They've got some new thing they want me to wrap up in fancy words. It's no big thing, really."

Tommy nodded like he understood, and I was thankful for it. Oh, I'd tell him soon enough. But there's a thing you learn about secrets. Once you tell one person, it's not really a secret any more. And that tempts you to whisper it—in strictest confidence, of course!—to someone else and someone else after that and they inevitably do the same to more people and more people until you've accidentally done the exact opposite of keeping a secret. It's hard to keep a secret. Especially when you're dying to tell someone and you're with a friend you trust and you've both had a few drinks. But I figured I was better off leaving it alone. Besides, there was something else I wanted to ask Tommy about. Something that was gnawing at me a little. Only I didn't know quite how to get around to it. "It's too bad Audrey couldn't make it," I started in cautiously.

"Oh, she doesn't like to be away from her father much these days. Or at least she doesn't think she should." He looked at me. "She really could, you know. If she really wanted to. Walter'd be all right by himself. Or she could get someone to come in and see after him. But she won't have it."

"It probably makes her feel guilty."

"That's it," he nodded. "That's it exactly."

"It's a shame. She really would have enjoyed all this."

We looked out at the lights twinkling on the horizon. "Listen," I continued carefully, "I have something I'd like to ask you. Something kind of personal..."

"I can bloody well imagine what it is."

I struggled to keep going: "...did you ever...I mean, did you and Audrey ever... I mean, were you ever..."

"Were the two of us ever an item?"

"Yeah," I exhaled awkwardly. "That's kind of what I was wondering...."

"That's a bit personal, isn't it?"

I felt my face heating up. "I-I'm sorry. It's just..."

Tommy waved me off with a hollow laugh. "That's all right, sport. It's within your rights to ask. I know you feel something for her."

I looked down at the railing under my hands. "Yeah, I guess I do," I admitted softly. "Or at least I think I do, anyway...."

"You do," he assured me. "Or you do if you've got a brain in your thick writer's skull." He looked at me again. "She's a very special creature, Audrey is."

"Yeah," I nodded. "I think so, too."

"Of course you do." He stared back out over the ocean and repeated so softly you could barely hear it: "Of course you do."

There was nothing else coming, so I prodded him again. "So did you and she ever...I mean, were you and she ever..."

"No we weren't," he answered flatly. And then added, almost apologetically: "Not that there wasn't interest. Particularly on my end. But I could never seem to make it work out or amount to anything..." he swiveled his eyes over to mine "... and it wasn't for lack of trying on my part."

That was something I'd never expected. Sure, there was the age difference and the unsettled nature of his career and his future, but I always thought Tommy was the kind of guy women fell for. Not only was he handsome and dashing and a racing driver and an ex-war hero fighter pilot, but he also had personality and manners and character and humor and real, genuine depth to him. He was the kind of guy you could count on. Or at least I thought so, anyway. How could any right-minded female think otherwise? But then, what did I really know about women and what they think? Not much, I had to admit. And most of it came from books and movies....

"She's been around a few drivers in the past," Tommy explained slowly, addressing the question I hadn't yet asked. "And she's perhaps come to the conclusion—perhaps rightly so—that we're too bloody much trouble and should bloody well be avoided."

"Oh?"

Tommy snorted out a laugh. "She thinks we're all crazy, immature egomaniacs and not to be trusted."

"That's kind of a blanket condemnation, isn't it?"

Tommy pulled out a cigarette, cupped his hands around it and touched a match to the end. "She has her reasons," he said between puffs.

"Like what?"

Tommy stared at me like it was a terribly stupid question. But then the harshness melted out of his eyes. He took a long, thoughtful draw off his cigarette and exhaled. "Do you know anything about her father?"

"She told me a little about him on the plane ride to Daytona. Aircraft engineer for DeHavilland, right? Worked on the Mosquito project during the war."

A pilot's smile blossomed under Tommy's mustache. "That was a bloody clever airplane, the Mosquito was. The airframe was made..."

"I know,' I interrupted. "Made out of plywood. With layers of balsa for lightness."

Tommy's smile faded. He'd obviously wanted to tell the story himself. He took another drag off his cigarette.

"So what about her father?" I prodded.

"Walter?" Tommy shrugged. "Oh, Walter's quite a piece of work."

"How so?"

The smile flickered back. But it wasn't a particularly nice or kindly smile. "You'll find out," he told me.

"I will?"

Tommy nodded. "I think you will."

"But what's he like?"

Tommy thought it over for a moment. "Oh, he's a prickly old bastard: tough, stubborn, opinionated, never particularly pleasant..."

"You make him sound pretty nasty."

"Let's just say he's not overly preoccupied with the pleasantries of life. He considers them a nuisance."

"I see."

Tommy took a long, last pull off his cigarette and flicked the butt over the railing. We watched the glowing orange tip vanish as it hit the water. "Walter did a cracking good job for DeHavilland during the war," Tommy continued evenly. "Give him a project and it was good as done. But he rubbed a lot of people the wrong way and ruffled a few feathers. He wasn't much for authority or chains of command. And he never suffered fools gladly." Tommy leaked out a small, wry laugh. "He would have been bloody well court-marshaled in the service."

"You really think so?"

"Oh, no doubt about it!" Tommy laughed, his eyes twinkling. "None at all. He'd have been out in a bloody month or two and most likely up on charges. But they kept him on at DeHavilland because he was a brilliant fabricating engineer, knew what the hell he was doing and bloody well got things done."

"So what happened?"

Tommy shrugged. "I don't think they really knew what to do with him after the war ended. It was either get rid of him or let him run the whole company. And he wasn't really equipped for that. Nor nearly practical or political enough. Or high enough up the ladder...."

"So what happened?"

"Oh, the usual. They eased him out sideways. Gave him a bloody gold watch and a pension and sent him on his way."

"I bet that didn't sit well with him."

"I'm not sure he bloody well cared by that point. He missed the urgency and sense of mission of the war years," Tommy looked me in the eyes. "I know what that's like, Hank. It can make you want to crawl right out of your skin."

"So what did he wind up doing?"

"Oh, he was bitter at first because nobody likes to get kicked in the teeth. But I think all the joy had gone out of it by then. And besides, he'd discovered motorsport. Or re-discovered it, actually."

"Re-discovered it?"

"Turns out he'd done some work between the wars on the record cars Sir Malcolm Campbell ran on the Pendine Sands in Wales and later on here at Daytona and the Bonneville salt flats. Campbell's cars used aircraft engines, and Walter was already a crack aero mechanic and fabricator at DeHavilland. He liked the urgency and sense of purpose in racing—a lot like the war, really—and he acquired a taste and talent for it."

"And so he went back to it?"

Tommy nodded. "It turns out there were some race-shop offers waiting when he left DeHavilland. Fabricating and machine work, mostly. I think the company may have even helped arrange it just to ease him away."

"So where does Audrey come in?"

"Oh, she was just a girl then. Growing up mostly with her mum because Walter was always off working till all hours on a DeHavilland project or away someplace with a race crew later on. But she'd come to visit him in the race shops around London while she was in school. Just to keep an eye on him for her mother as much as anything else. He wouldn't stop to eat his lunch or have his tea unless someone was there to bother him about it."

"How old was she?"

"Oh, she must've been just shy of twenty then. And full of spirit underneath all the manners and schooling." He looked straight at me. "She's a very bright girl, you know."

"Yes, I know."

"But not very experienced. At least not then...." he let his voice trail off. And it seemed like a long time before he started in again. "Eventually there was a driver she came to care about. Quite a bit, in fact. His name was Neal Clifton. Really nice young chap with a bit of talent and quite a sizeable family fortune to back it up. They made wafer wrappers, I think. At any rate, he bought a Cooper 500 and then a Kieft, and he jumped on the bandwagon with Colin Chapman at Lotus when the Mark 8 came out. But then he got himself killed at Dundrod in '55."

"I remember hearing about that race. There was a terrible accident and a fire."

"She doesn't talk about it, but I believe she was there with him that weekend."

"Oh?"

Tommy nodded. "I was there that weekend myself. Didn't know her then, of course. And it was a frightful circuit: narrow country lanes lined with hay bales, actually. It was marvelous to drive but terribly dangerous. But of course it was right after the war and nobody cared much about it then...."

"Do you know what happened?"

Tommy let out a weary, labored sigh. "It was early on in the race when all the cars were topped full-up with petrol. An amateur driver lost it coming off the crest at Deer's Leap. It's flat-out through there but the car goes all up on tiptoes. He had to be doing every bit of a hundred-ten." I watched Tommy's jaw tighten "You have to learn not to do anything when it goes all light and airy like that. You have to just keep your hands soft and steady on the wheel and trust in the car's ability to take you through."

"But he didn't?"

Tommy shook his head. "He probably felt the panic rising in his gut and lifted off the throttle. That's the last thing you should do. Or maybe he gave it a bit of steering lock when the car was still up on tiptoes..." Tommy looked down at the water breaking along the hull. "That's all it takes, really."

"So what happened?"

Tommy offered up a shrug. "When the car hit the barrier it broke clear in two, and then the pieces flipped over and caught fire. The smoke and flames were bloody well impenetrable. And you couldn't see over that crest anyway when you were approaching from the other side...." I could see he was searching for words to finish it.

"And that's when Neal Clifton came along, isn't it?"

Tommy didn't say anything for a moment. And then he nodded. "It was the usual mess," he continued matter-of-factly. "I think she wound up having to help with some of the arrangements. I mean for the remains and all. And it must have been hard for her at home when her father and mother found out."

"That must have been terrible for her."

"I'm sure it was." Tommy reached into his pocket for another cigarette. "But that wasn't all of it."

"Oh?"

"It seems one of Neal's teammates caught her on the rebound. They went out for tea and a bit of sympathy after the services and he started calling and they began going around together. After a respectable amount of time had passed, of course."

"Oh?"

Tommy lit up his cigarette and inhaled. "Only this one wasn't quite such a nice chap. Not quite such a nice chap at all." Tommy shook his head. "A few months later he threw her over for some stupid society girl with family money who loved going to the races and parties. Audrey'd lost her taste for all that after Dundrod. I think it might have been her first race weekend." A thin smile creased its way across Tommy's face. "Of course she's absolutely right about us. Drivers, I mean. We *are* all crazy, immature and self-centered." Tommy's eyebrows arched upwards. "I mean, we bloody well couldn't do it otherwise...."

Now it was my turn to shrug.

"I don't know it as truth," Tommy continued, "but I like to believe Neal Clifton really cared for her. It would have been a lucky match for her, too. He was a decent enough bloke and had a bit of money..." he took a slow, thoughtful drag off his cigarette. "In any case, it appears she doesn't want anything further to do with racing drivers."

It was sad, but it made sense. Especially for a self-possessed girl like Audrey who liked to keep her life in order.

"But that's racing, isn't it?" Tommy continued. "It can turn ugly in an instant. And if you don't like it or haven't got the stomach for it, you shouldn't be around it, should you?"

There was no question about that. In fact, I'd caught myself echoing those same exact sentiments—both verbally and in print—so many, many times when things had gone horribly wrong at a racetrack. But it always sounded so damned lame, empty and foolish. Even inside your own ears. You said it anyway, though. In fact, you said it every time.

The next morning Tommy, Cal and I were on the upper sun deck enjoying a breakfast of fluffed eggs with bits of shrimp and black olive mixed in and entirely too many tall, slender glasses of freshly squeezed Florida orange juice spiked with Russian potato vodka, and we hardly noticed it when the captain started wheeling *L'Albatro d'Oro* into a big, lazy arc. Or at least not until he throttled back the engines. I looked over at Cal and Tommy and they looked back at me as the big boat gently sagged back into the water and you could hear the lapping sounds of our own wake catching up to us and breaking along the hull. Then the captain's raw,

Aussie accent came crackling over the loudspeakers: *"G'MORNING, GENTS 'N MATES. I THINK YOU'LL BE WANTING T'HAVE A WEE LOOK AT THE STARBOARD COASTLINE ABOUT NOW. THERE'S SOMETHING YOU'LL BLOODY WELL WANT TO SEE!"*

Right at that precise moment, at exactly 9:47am Eastern Standard Time on Tuesday, February 20th, 1962, the NASA crew at Cape Canaveral lit the candle on an enormous Atlas booster rocket and sent astronaut John H. Glenn Jr. hurtling up into space. And we had ringside seats for the whole fucking show! It was an awesome, even frightening thing to behold as we watched that thin, fragile-looking white tube hurtling into the sky on a column of smoke, steam and fire. You couldn't help thinking about the tiny human being strapped inside and the incredible faith he must have had in all the hundreds and even thousands of people who'd designed and built that launch vehicle. Not to mention all the science, engineering, research, logistics, organization, processes and systems backing it up. It was as if Lieutenant Colonel John H. Glenn Jr. was rising into the heavens on the distilled essence of their hopes, dreams and effort as surely as the thrust from the rockets. The three of us stood there watching with our mouths dangling open—thunderstruck!—squinting our eyes and tilting our heads back as the mighty Atlas climbed higher and higher and higher until it was nothing but a tiny speck against the vast, cyan-blue emptiness of the sky. And then it was gone, with just a dissipating contrail of smoke to mark where it had been. "If all goes well," the captain said from behind us, "he's going to orbit around the earth three times." He made three happy little finger-swirls in the air. "Can you imagine what a fucking thrill that must be?"

"Can you imagine what it must look like from up there?" Tommy half-whispered.

"I bet it looks like a long way down."

Of course everybody and his brother knew that the Russians had already beaten us into space. Or, more accurately, the Nazi rocket scientists the Russians captured and spirited away at the end of World War Two had beaten the Nazi rocket scientists we captured and spirited away at the end of World War Two. But no question all of America turned pale and queasy inside when the Russians launched Sputnik in October of 1957. They followed that up by putting a dog named Laika up there (although some stateside news reports said she didn't make it back alive) and then trumped that when cosmonaut Yuri Gagarin became the first man into space when he orbited around the earth on April 12th of 1961. Our side countered by rocketing astronaut Alan Shepard into space a little over a month later. But that was just a simple, straight up/straight-down shot, and the launch we witnessed that February morning in 1962 was America's first-ever try at an earth orbit. And all of us could feel the wonder, awe and magic of it. At the same time, we frankly couldn't imagine having the calm confidence to just sit up there at the pointy end of an Atlas rocket waiting for people you couldn't see to flip a switch and send you blasting into the unknown. Particularly when you knew it was a government project and, like virtually every government project, all the little rivets, bolts, nuts, screws, tubes, panels and lock washers holding everything together and moreover all the wiring looms, relays, gauges, levers, screens, instruments and toggle switches that controlled everything and made it all work had been contracted out to the lowest bidder....

It was a humbling, even haunting thing to watch, and made you appreciate all over again what people could do when they put their hearts and minds to it. In fact, it made me want to haul out my manuscript and start working on my novel again. And I mean *right now!* But of course first we had to make a few champagne toasts to the successful launch and pretty soon after that it was lunchtime and then, well, all of a sudden I woke up in a deck chair and it was getting dark and they were getting the tables around me ready for dinner. Damn.

But I promised myself I'd get around to it first thing tomorrow.

Yeah, tomorrow for sure....

I'd heard from Buddy about our friend Cal Carrington's penchant for pranks, and so I had some idea who was behind it when strange things started happening on *L'Albatro d'Oro*. First someone "borrowed" the master pass key and locked all the stateroom doors. And when Clive Stanley finally got his open, the room was filled up completely—and I mean completely!—with an inflatable survival raft. Then there was the bottle of lunchtime wine that was actually cider vinegar. And then Ian Snell woke up with a fairly large, thoroughly slimy and not long dead dogfish shark in bed next to him. It happened in the middle of the night, and his shriek and explosion of expletives could probably be heard all the way back in Jacksonville. Then the foghorn inexplicably sounded just about the time everyone got back to sleep at around 4:30 in the morning. And then there was the live and obviously upset blue land crab sitting on a bed of lettuce under the sterling silver service dome over what Clive thought were his breakfast eggs and bacon. It was all dumb and funny at the same time and pretty harmless stuff, and Cal deadpanned his way through it like he never had anything to do with any of it. And maybe he didn't. Maybe it was the captain or Count Giovanni himself. But Cal was the key suspect as far as I was concerned. And it was nice to see a little of the old fun, guile and flair out of him. Driving for Ferrari had hidden a lot of that away.

We'd turned back towards Jacksonville after witnessing the launch at Cape Canaveral, but the captain announced that there was some fairly heavy weather on the way and that we'd be heading in for the night to let it blow over. So Tommy and Cal and I took a few drinks out on the back deck to watch the storm rolling in. We could see the coal-colored sky and flashes of lightning over the shoreline and feel the building swells and harsh gusts of wind whipping across the deck.

Something ugly was brewing. The rain started with just a few spits and spatters, but then it came down like someone had slit open the sky. We ran into the inside party room and watched and listened to the rain pounding down on the decks and the crashing thunder and the lightning freezing everything in icy-white flashes. It was pretty damn spectacular. Even a little scary. None of us said a word until that first front passed and the rain eased off to drips and patters.

"Geez, that was really something, wasn't it?"

Tommy and Cal nodded. It was suddenly very quiet, with just the low, steady hum off the big diesels and the sound of the wind outside.

"You planning on staying with Ferrari?" Tommy asked Cal out of nowhere.

Cal swirled his drink around in his glass. "I don't really know," he shrugged. "That's really up to Ferrari, isn't it?"

"But so far so good?"

"Well, I'm signed for this year. But who knows? Ferrari uses you when and where he wants. And things can change. I know Ferrari likes the Rodriguez brothers because their poppa has always brought money. But I think he likes them more as paying customers than paid drivers."

"You have any idea where the money comes from?" Tommy asked. "I've heard rumors that the father's a bloody policeman in Mexico."

"It's true," I nodded. "Or that's what people in the know seem to think."

"It's hard to believe a bloody policeman can make that much," Tommy scoffed.

"He's a lot more than an ordinary policeman," Cal laughed. "He's really well-connected in Mexico. He's got some oil deal and a railroad supply deal and ways to import cars that no one else can seem to get into the country. And he owns a pretty famous nightclub across from the opera house in Mexico City. Some even say he runs the secret police in Mexico. He's way up there with the government, and he's got lots of influential friends and connections."

Tommy rolled it around in his head. "I suppose there's a lot of money to be made being the law in a country like Mexico."

"I suppose there are a lot favors that need to be done..." Cal swirled the ice around in his glass "...or undone...."

"And they're not so worried about what people in the press might think like you are over in England or we are here in the States," I observed.

"That's true. They don't really give much of a shit. But I've heard rumors that Poppa Rodriguez may be stretched a little thin these days."

"Oh?"

"He's bloody well spent enough!" Tommy snorted with an edge of envy in his voice.

"Yeah," I agreed. "But there's no such thing as a bottomless pit. You keep buying cars and rides and taking your eye off the ball so you can go flying all over the damn world to watch your sons race and you can make even a really big bag of gold disappear."

"They like the high life a little bit, too," Cal nodded. "The family likes to travel first class, stay together and keep up appearances. And I think both boys have a taste for expensive girlfriends."

We watched the second storm front starting to move in.

"How about Phil Hill?" I asked Cal.

"Oh, Phil's locked in. Hell, he deserves it. He won the damn Formula One championship for them last year, and that's what Ferrari really needed. An American driver winning the world championship in a Ferrari will help the old man sell more cars over here."

"But you were faster sometimes," I reminded him.

"Sometimes I was faster. Sometimes he was faster. Sometimes the other guy was faster. Not even the driver knows how all that works out..."

"It's not a bloody science," Tommy agreed.

"...but the point is that Phil's World Champ and Number One until proven otherwise, and I'm more or less the expendable member of the team right now." Cal poured himself another drink. "Maybe one American's enough now that the championship's been won. Especially when Dragoni's got those two young Italian guys coming up..."

"Baghetti and Bandini?"

Cal nodded. "...and he's partial to Willy Mairesse, even though he's Belgian. And a little nuts. Have you ever looked in his eyes?"

"Mairesse is bloody crazy sometimes," Tommy agreed.

Cal raised his eyebrows. "The Old Man is partial to crazy. Crazy makes you try harder. Try things sane men won't dare try." A wan smile spread across Cal's face. "He used to like that about me."

"And with good reason," Tommy laughed.

Cal laughed, too. But then his face went serious. "Things change in a hurry in this sport. Your opportunities can pass you by." He drained the last of his drink and headed to the bar to get another. "Besides, I'm not so sure Ferrari is the place to be in Formula One this year." He gave Tommy a little nod of respect. "I think the Brits may have caught us up and passed us."

Tommy raised his glass. "And not before time."

"But what about sports cars?" I asked. "And Grand Touring?"

"Oh," Cal sighed, "that's pretty much in the bag, isn't it? I mean, there really isn't anyone for us to race against. Not seriously, anyway. Not any more." He looked over at Tommy. "No offense, old man."

"None taken."

Cal looked out through the rain-specked window. It was really coming down again, and we could hear the distant rumble of thunder and see dull flashes of lightning over the shoreline. "Endurance sports car racing is all about teamwork and pacing and discipline," Cal observed absently. "Formula One is supposed to be all about the driving. Even in these dumb little cars." He let out a long, sad sigh. "I think the cars are way too much of it now..."

"You didn't think so last year!" Tommy laughed.

"Of course not!" Cal grinned back at him. "We had the best car!" He raised his glass. "And here's to it. It wasn't even close."

It was quiet then, and we could really hear the rain pelting down against the deck and feel the big boat rolling on the swells.

"How about you?" I asked Tommy.

Now it was Tommy's turn to shrug. "Well, I've got the Aston deal with Clive, and I suppose that's as much as I can ask for at this bloody stage of my career. And I have to say I rather prefer the endurance racing. It's a bloody good sport. I like how everything has to mesh together. How you have to plan and think about pace and strategize and yet be ready to react in an instant when a window of opportunity opens up...."

Cal allowed him a half-hearted nod. "The driving's a slog, though."

"*Sure* it's a slog!" Tommy shot back. "But not all of us can be the young speedy boys any more. We've got to concentrate on the other things."

"What other things?" Cal wanted to know.

"Consistency. Taking car of the bloody car. That sort of thing."

Cal regarded Tommy with an unpleasant, almost deprecating sneer. It made Tommy's spine stiffen.

"Look," he said evenly, "you may not see it or feel it now, but the time will come when it gets..." he fumbled for the right word "...*difficult...*"

"What do you mean by '*difficult?*'"

"I mean when you find yourself having to think about doing things you used to do without thinking." He leveled his eyes into Cal's. "It'll come, trust me. You may not think so now, but it'll come."

Cal didn't look convinced. "So is that when I'll start enjoying driving down to a pace?"

It was kind of a cruel thing to say, but Tommy took it in stride. "That's what makes endurance racing so bloody worthwhile," he insisted. "That's where the special feeling comes from when you're out in the car, carrying the ball for the rest of the team. For your co-driver and the mechanics and your team manager and your car owner and all the blokes who have worked so long and hard back in the shop or factory. It's a lot of bloody responsibility."

"I know that feeling," Cal needled. "It's the feeling you get when it's four-thirty in the fucking morning at Le Mans and you can't see out of the windshield because bugs are splattered all over it and the fog's rolling in like wet cotton and you're bat-to-shit exhausted and either soaked through to the skin and shivering in an open car or you're in a damn coupe that's full of engine heat and exhaust fumes and the defroster's not working worth a shit and neither are the fucking wipers and you're wondering what the hell you're doing out there and why the hell you didn't take another pee before you got in the damn car at the last pit stop and..."

"My point exactly!" Tommy grinned. "That's what makes it so bloody brilliant: the ache, pain, effort and agony of it all!"

"It doesn't feel so wonderful when things screw up," Cal reminded him.

"No, it doesn't," Tommy had to agree. "But it wouldn't feel so bloody good when you do a decent job if it didn't feel so bloody awful when you cock things up."

We clinked our glasses together one last time and Cal headed off to bed. Or maybe to pull another prank. But Tommy and I stayed for one more round.

"You think your deal with Clive Stanley will last?"

"That's the big question, isn't it?" Tommy allowed with a granite smile. "You know how it is with 'wealthy sportsmen.' They bloody well come and they bloody well go, don't they?"

"That they do," I agreed.

"They can be all gung-ho and 'let's go do Le Mans together' one minute and then get disgusted or distracted or disillusioned or have their bloody families clamp down on the money. Or change their minds and take up hot-air ballooning or deep-sea diving or antiquity collecting instead...."

"But Clive Stanley's been around for quite awhile now, hasn't he?"

"Five seasons, I think. Maybe six. Got the bug in Nassau in '55. Oh, he realized straight off that he'd never make it as a driver. Family never would have let him anyway, even if he'd wanted to. But he had the bug, all right." Tommy fished in his pocket for a cigarette. "He started out with some wild young Irish kid in an XK140 and then a D-Type. Poor bloke managed to kill himself off in the rain at Spa."

"But Clive stuck with it, didn't he?"

"Oh, he knocked off for a few months, but he couldn't stay away. Old Clive does enjoy his motor racing."

"That's good for you, isn't it?"

"Hard to say. It's not like with drivers. Team owners can have a change of heart any old time. Part of the game." He lit up his cigarette and blew out a cloud of smoke. "Can't say as I recommend privateering as far as gainful employment is concerned. Or at least not compared to a factory drive, at any rate." He curled his lip under. "And I'm probably past that now, aren't I?"

I didn't say anything.

"...But I've got a few things working back in England..."

"Oh?"

Tommy nodded. "James Britten got me hooked up with Eric Broadley's Lola shops over in Bromley. I'm doing a few things for them...."

"Oh? Like what?"

"Oh, a little testing and sorting out..." he looked up apologetically from under his eyelids "...and selling a few cars if I possibly can."

"There's nothing wrong with that."

"No, I suppose there isn't," he admitted sheepishly. "Or at least not if you actually manage to sell any."

We had a good laugh off of that.

"How about you, sport?" Tommy asked. "How's the glamorous life of the major motorsports writer progressing?"

I let my eyes sweep around the gleaming, off-white enamel with ebony and polished brass trim party room around us. "Well, it's not always like this."

"Do tell?"

And that brought to mind all the nights I'd slept by the side of a race track curled up against the cold in my clapped-out Fiat Multipla. "Motorsports writing doesn't actually pay very well," I said like I was telling him something he didn't already know. "I know that may be hard for you to believe. But it actually works out better as more of what you English would call 'an avocation' rather than 'a vocation.'"

"But you treat it as a sole livelihood, don't you?"

"I kid myself that I do."

"And how has that been working for you?"

I made a face. "Hey, I never claimed to be bright...."

And to tell the truth, I knew it was starting to grind on me. There was too much traveling and too much loneliness and too much aimlessness and way, way too much living on the cheap. Oh, I still loved the racing and the camaraderie and the urgency and drama of it all. And also the incredible machinery and the sounds and the speed and most especially the usually wonderful and occasionally terrible characters I'd come to know. Loved particularly that a lot of them—like Tommy and Cal—seemed to enjoy spending time with me and considered me a friend. But that made it all the more difficult when one of them got hurt or killed. And you couldn't sweep that sort of thing under the rug. It happened way too often to ignore.

"I don't know," I finally told Tommy, "in one way I figure I'm lucky in that I'm getting to do something I genuinely love to do. Not many people can say that."

Tommy nodded, so I went on.

"And I think I can honestly say I'm pretty good at it, too. Not the greatest, maybe, but decent enough to be proud of what I do. Not many people can say that, either...."

"You *are* good at it," Tommy assured me. "You take pains to get it right." He shook his head. "Most bloody writers don't bother."

"...but even then," I continued, not quite sure where I was going with it "...but even then I have this feeling that I'm not *there* yet. That I'm somehow falling short. That there has to be something—I don't know—something *more*...."

"Everyone feels like that," Tommy said flatly. "No matter what line of work they're in." And there was no denying he was right.

It was calm and bright the next morning, and I actually did pull out my portable Olivetti and the small sheaf of paper I always carried in case I suffered an imagination attack, found myself a quiet little spot up on the sun deck and tried to work. But it was awfully bright and windy up there, so I went back down to try my stateroom—it wasn't really much more than a very nice bunk with a port hole on one side and a little closet of a bathroom on the other—but it felt stuffy and claustrophobic and I could really feel the roll of the ocean and hear the deep hum of the engines coming through the metal bulkheads. So I didn't get much done. But at least everyone on board thought I was working, and that was worth a little something all by itself.

Three days later I found myself some 4907 air miles away in Maranello for Old Man Ferrari's yearly press conference and new racing model introduction. And it had been a pretty rough trip. Cal was flying Alitalia out of Miami and Karen Sabelle had me booked on United out of Atlanta, and naturally the plane was delayed several hours with some sort of mechanical problems—that's always a great way to put all the passengers on edge—and the flight was sold out so I wound up trapped in the window seat I'd asked for next to a large, jolly and amazingly hairy Italian guy and his equally large, jolly and even hairier Italian wife. And their adorable twin babies, who seemed to be either screaming until their dear little faces were ready to explode, throwing up slimy globs of greenish stuff on the shoulder of my corduroy jacket or pooping enthusiastically into their diapers the entire way. And meanwhile the mother and father talked about food and argued about relatives in rapid-fire Italian, ate cheese that smelled like toe jam and devoured slimy-looking scungilli swimming in garlic oil that the wife carried in her purse in a folded-up sheet of waxed paper. The yelling and screaming from the twins didn't seem to bother them at all—it was like they couldn't even hear it!—and they'd proudly explain that their babies were surely destined to sing at *La Scala* in Milan whenever too many heads turned around in the rows ahead of us.

So I spent most of the flight with my face pressed against the window, looking out over the tops of clouds and occasional glimpses of the ocean while my mind tried to wrap itself around everything that had happened in the last two weeks. Starting with my visit to the 13th floor of Fairway Tower. It all seemed like a dream now—so surreal, so strangely out of context—and I couldn't really get comfortable with the notion that I'd possibly come to a fork in the road as far as my life, my work and my future earning capacity were concerned. And I wondered what it would be like to have extra money in my pocket and being able to buy things when

I felt the urge and stay in hotels where the bathroom wasn't located at the end of the hall. To be honest, it felt a little strange. Even claustrophobic. No question in some stubborn, free-spirited, set-in-its-ways little corner of my brain, I was already dreading working as some sort of undercover motorsports spy for Bob Wright and Fairway Motors. Particularly with that eager, well-meaning little sycophant Danny Beagle as my handler. Not that I disliked Danny. I just disliked being handled. I even caught myself wishing I hadn't taken the deal and that things could be back the way they were. I may not have had much of a life, but at least I knew where everything was....

The rest of the time I spent thinking about Audrey. I just kept visualizing her sitting beside me on our plane ride down to Daytona. Or seeing her up on Clive Stanley's timing stand during the race with her nose buried in her lap chart. Or, most especially, how she seemed that night on the little dock down behind Epifiano's Crab Shack in Daytona Beach (although that one was maybe a little bit embellished, since there now seemed to be a string orchestra playing in the background and her face was lit with the kind of tender, inner-glow lighting you see in love scenes from old black-and-white romance movies). And then that would dissolve into the empty, lonely, aching feeling I had the night I wound up at the end of the Daytona fishing pier with those two dead-end shark fishermen, watching Audrey and Count Giovanni's fancy yacht disappear into the horizon and wondering when I'd get to see her again.

You can spend an awful lot of time and waste an awful lot of mental energy slogging through stuff like that. But I also had the damn Daytona story on deadline, and I really needed to get around to it. I'd planned to try working a little of it out longhand in my notebook on the plane, but I couldn't get much of anything done except to go over the results sheets and press notes I'd gotten from that pleasant and accommodating young girl in the Daytona press room and scrawl a few notes in the margins. So I had to stay up well into the wee hours of the next morning, hammering it out in my damn hotel room, in order to send it off air-mail on my way to the Ferrari press conference. Of course you always plan to write those race reports right after the event wraps up—when it's all fresh in your head, right?—but if you're writing for a monthly magazine, there's always that lazy temptation to let the process slide until the damn deadline is staring you right in the face. Then the panic sets in and you wind up beating it out in some clammy 3 ayem hotel room in Modena at the Last Fucking Minute, all the while cursing yourself for your shameful sloth and indolence and wondering why the hell your parents didn't raise you better.

Naturally the lack of sleep and all the time-zone changes caught up with me by the time I arrived at the Ferrari factory on Abetone Road. In fact, I was red-eyed, rasping and exhausted before I even got to the front gate. Not to mention coming down with a cold that had me sneezing and coughing loud enough to make people turn around and stare. Even so, a visit to the Ferrari factory was always mesmerizing, and I couldn't help but feel a little flutter in my gut as I showed my invitation to the guard and headed through the hallowed tunnel entranceway to the factory's inner sanctum. It was like entering the Vatican. Why, if you closed your eyes, you could almost hear the impatient growl and crackle of all the great racing cars that had echoed through that tunnel on their way to their first-ever test runs up the Abetone Road. Cars that ultimately went on to win famous victories at Le Mans and Sebring and the Mille Miglia and *La Carrera Panamericana* and The Nurburgring 1000Ks and the Targa Florio and everywhere else that counted, crushing the opposition with their incredible strength, toughness and stamina as well as their outright speed....

FERRARI!

The name was like fire on your tongue.

I met my happy but eternally sad-eyed little Italian racing-scribe friend Vinci Pittacora in the courtyard, and I made a mental note to find him after the presentation and do a little judicious inquiring as to what Ferrari had on the drawing board for next year. Whenever old man Ferrari got ready to show something to the press, you could be sure it was Old News already and that his design room and experimental race shop were already hard at work on the next project. No question Bob Wright and his guys would want to know a little something about it, too. But there was no time to talk, because the presentation was about to begin. So we went inside and found Cal just as *Il Commendatore* himself ascended to the podium to a solid round of applause. "You look like shit," Cal whispered.

"I feel like shit," I wheezed back at him.

"Well, at least you match." He looked me up and down. "When did you get the new pants? Or did the moths finally finish off your old ones?"

"Very funny."

"Why, your pants almost have a crease in them!" he marveled. "And those look like new shoes, too."

"A guy can buy himself some new clothes, can't he?" I whispered back defensively.

"Sure you can," Cal smirked, "but it kind of goes against type for a motorsports writer, doesn't it?"

I couldn't think of a plausible answer for that, but fortunately *Il Commendatore* Ferrari had arrived at the microphone. And that meant it was time for everybody to shut up, listen attentively and then applaud—politely, but profusely—when he got to the end. Even if you couldn't make heads or tails of his Italian. Ferrari new model introductions were very much a one-man show, and the Old Man relished his time in the limelight—hell, he wallowed and slopped in it!—and no way would he countenance anything that interrupted the stagecraft he'd planned.

To begin with, there was no mention whatsoever of the handful of key employees who'd defected (or been fired?) the previous November and set up shop across town as *Automobili Tourismo e Sport*. But the fruits of their previous labors for Ferrari were proudly on display, with or without them. Ferrari was on top of the world right then: they'd dominated the 1961 Formula One Championship with five wins out of seven races (Ferrari didn't even bother to send his team to the 8th and final race at Watkins Glen since both the drivers' and constructors' championships had already been secured) along with a second straight—and 3rd out of the last 4!—victory at Le Mans and runaway World Manufacturers' Championship titles in both the sports car *and* Category 1 GT classes. Followed by yet another steamroller act in both categories at the first race of the '62 Manufacturers' Championship at Daytona. Not to mention that past arch-rivals Mercedes and Jaguar were long gone, Aston Martin had pulled in its horns after winning their own title in '59 and bitter cross-town adversary Maserati was on the ropes financially and unable to fund a true factory team. So there were really only the little cars from Porsche and a few pesky privateers and amateurs to worry about. Sure, there were worries about the new generation of V8-powered grand prix cars from England and rumored but so far unseen new coupes from Maserati and Aston for Le Mans. Plus the generally unloved F.I.A. regulations that made Ferrari wary of potential GT-class threats from Jaguar's slick new XKE, Aston's Zagatos and Chevrolet's powerful but plodding Corvettes. Ferrari respected and even feared the enormous financial muscle of the big Detroit manufacturers, and knew that if any of them decided to say *"ba fangu"* to the unloved AMA racing ban, they would become formidable opponents. As old man Ferrari knew better than anyone, it wasn't so much what you started with but how much money, effort and brains you threw at it that separated promise and potential from ultimate success.

In light of the new rules, Ferrari's motorsports design team (originally led by Giotto Bizzarrini and Carlo Chiti, both of whom were now across town at A.T.S.) had created the new GTO, which was kind of a stretched, smoothed, lightened, lowered, slightly more powerful and surely far sexier evolution of Ferrari's already dominant Short Wheelbase Berlinetta. Although it was built essentially to the letter of the rules, Ferrari's new GTO didn't fool anybody. As the name implied (GTO stood for *Gran Tourismo Omologato),* it was nothing but a "homologation special" racing coupe intended to qualify—at least on paper—as a production road car. And to thoroughly flatten the opposition (as Stirling Moss proved so convincingly proved with Carlo Sebastian's GTO-prototype Berlinetta Le Mans Speciale Aerodinamico at Daytona). But while the prototype looked a bit soft and ungraceful, the finished GTO was absolutely stunning. Aerodynamic work in the University of Pisa wind tunnel had yielded up one of the most beautiful and elegant racing shapes anyone had ever seen. The wheelbase had been stretched 200mm for better stability on long straights and through fast sweepers, and the low, slinky snout and long, lean fenders tapered back to a gracefully contoured roof and a low, almost concave back end. Just looking at Ferrari's new GTO led you to the conclusion that there was no other GT car on the planet—regardless of engine capacity—that could keep up with it. Especially over 24 long, grueling hours at Le Mans. And you could see from the twinkle in his eye that old Enzo knew it, too. Even though he spoke about it in cautious, measured tones...as if he were filled with doubts and second thoughts. Then again, that's how Ferrari always acted at his press conferences, playing the overmatched, martyred victim in order to elicit sympathy and appear humble. You had to be impressed with the way he could work a crowd. Old man Ferrari was one hell of an actor and showman, and he could turn up a smile as bright as aircraft landing lights, charm the birds clear out of the trees or summon up a trembling lip and a hint of nascent tears as easily as he could change the color of his tie.

The only real question on the new GTO was whether Ferrari would actually get around to building (and, more importantly to him, selling!) the necessary "100 examples" the rulebook required for homologation. But Ferrari was a master at getting around the F.I.A. officials when he needed to, and he would surely have no problem convincing the worshipful and partisan representatives from the F.I.A.'s Italian affiliate that he'd built enough cars. Especially after he invited them over for "a production line inspection," showed them the cars he had in progress on the shop floor, additional frames stacked up along the wall, a fat handful of orders in a file drawer and shipping documents for even more, and then bluff them around with a lunch, a few glasses of wine and a tour of the race shops. No question he'd come away with the required stamp of approval. It was in the bag.

Also on hand was the not nearly so handsome—in fact, brutal-looking—4.0-liter Testa Rossa sports/racer Ferrari had built for the new *Challenge Mondiale de Vitesse et Endurance* "experimental" class Le Mans. It was officially titled the 330TR/LM, and the bodywork seemed awkward to me with its tall and bulbous wraparound windscreen, an oddly stretched-out front end and all sorts of unsightly scoops, vents, humps and bulges all over it. Although far from the prettiest sports/racer Ferrari had ever built, the 330TR/LM had the very latest independent rear suspension and its monstrous engine promised to pound down the long, 8-kilometer straightaway at Le Mans like the hammers of hell. Some racetracks require agility and handling more than power, but an awful lot of winning at Le Mans came down to flat-out top speed. And the ability to sustain it—regardless of heat, cold, rain, fog, darkness of night or pure human exhaustion—for 24 solid hours....

Also on display were examples of Ferrari's little-changed, shark-nosed Type 156 grand prix cars and no less than three versions of his light, quick, modern and nimble little Dino sports/racers. Ferrari had taken a typically "kitchen sink" approach to winning at handling circuits like The Nurburgring and the Targa Florio, with both a 2.8-liter V6 "286SP" and a 2.4-liter V8 "248SP," but Ferrari always felt that finding the right, winning combination was equal parts engineering and alchemy. There was also a third Dino on display, powered by a smaller, 1983cc V6 and aimed directly at Porsche. Not to mention perhaps stealing the coveted (and lucrative!) Index of Performance award away from those odd little French-blue tiddlers at Le Mans. Although that could prove even tougher than racing for the outright win, since the officials at Le Mans were famously patriotic and extremely partisan concerning their homegrown little French cars.

You could tell old man Ferrari was winding towards the conclusion of his speech because he was sounding even more worn-down, martyred and betrayed than before. To hear him tell it, he was surrounded on all sides by usurpers, devious enemies, back-stabbing conspirators and envious rivals. The politics of the sport were always turned against him. Money was tight and there was no help forthcoming from either the Italian government or manufacturing giant Fiat, in spite of what Ferrari, his marvelous cars, his magnificent racing team, his proud racing tradition and his many, many victories and championships had done for the stature of Italian cars, Italian culture, Italian spirit, Italian style, Italian passion and Italian technology all over the world. His eyes slowly closed at the prospect of inevitable defeat and the emptiness and desolation that would surely follow. You could have heard a pin drop. But then, after a long, dramatic pause, his eyes slowly reopened and a wafer-thin glimmer of hope appeared....

Against all odds, he'd found the strength to go on.

A wrenching sigh of relief went through the crowd.

It was a pretty damn amazing performance, no two ways about it.

Then again, he grew up on opera....

I made a point of finding Vinci Pittacora while the guests were looking over the cars and lining up for coffee and pastries. "So what did you think?" I asked.

"Fantastico! Bellissimo! Astounding!" he exclaimed like it would have been inconceivable to expect anything less.

"Absolutely," I agreed.

"But then..." he rolled up his hands the way Italians do "...it's *Ferrari!*"

I handed him a cup of espresso and a profiterole. I knew he liked those. "So any idea what Ferrari's working on now?" I said like I was just making conversation.

He looked at me suspiciously. "How do you mean?"

"I mean for next year. And even beyond. Ferrari's always got something new up his sleeve, and you've always got your ear to the ground at Maranello."

He eyeballed me some more. "The new season, she's a-barely started," he reminded me.

"I know. But Ferrari never sits still." I tossed in a wink. "That's how he got to be Ferrari."

Vinci smiled, leaned in and whispered: "There are rumors of a mid-engined V-12..." he formed his hands into an ominous V-shape "...*molto* power!" His eyes narrowed and his voice went down even lower: "But not until next year—*l'anno prossimo*—And not to write about, *naturalmente....*"

"Oh, *naturalmente.*"

It *was* the next logical step....

I ran into Cal again over by the pastry trays. "You going back to Florida after this?" he asked between bites of biscotti.

"I've got my tickets right here." I patted the pocket with my passport and Karen Sabelle's ticket folder inside.

"Then what?"

"I dunno. I thought I might hang out by the beach or something. Maybe do a little writing if I feel inspired."

"You ever have trouble getting inspired?"

"Not too often. I've got a bigger problem actually getting around to it."

"Maybe you're not really inspired?"

"That's always a possibility. But I think I'm just lazy."

"Hey, if the shoe fits...."

I polished off the last of my profiterole. "So how about you? Any big plans before Sebring?"

"Not really."

"You're not going back to the brunette in Jacksonville?"

Cal shook his head. "Nah. I don't think so. She says she's separated, but you know how that can go...."

"I wouldn't have any idea."

"You know. Complications. Husbands re-appearing. Women on the rebound in general. It's not a healthy situation."

"That didn't stop you before," I reminded him.

"I didn't think about it before."

You couldn't miss the aimless look in his eye. To be honest, I thought he was still carrying a torch for that actress he'd been with the year before. You know, Gina LaScala. But I didn't say anything. Hell, what could you say? Better to change the subject. "I don't really have any plans, either," I told him. "I'm flying into Jacksonville through Atlanta."

"If you could get it switched, we could maybe go somewhere. I've still got the VW parked at the Miami airport. I've got it till Sebring. And it's really kind of your car anyway."

"Where would we go?"

"I don't know," Cal shrugged. "Anywhere."

"Like where?"

"My folks still have their place in Palm Beach. But I think my sister and her current boyfriend are there. It might be awkward."

"I'm not real big on awkward."

"Me, either."

"Christ almighty," Cal groused, "everybody in creation comes to fucking Florida
for vacation. There must be something there we'd want to see or do."

I thought it over but couldn't think of a thing. And then it dawned on me. *"Key
West!"* I blurted out so suddenly that it startled me.

"Key West?"

"Yeah, Key West. Ernest Hemingway had a house down there. I always kind of
wanted to see it."

"You a big Hemingway fan?"

"Isn't everybody?"

"Didn't he just blow his brains out?"

"Yeah. Last July. At his place in Ketchum, Idaho. Put the barrels of a 12-gauge
shotgun up against his forehead and pulled the trigger."

"That's a hell of a way to go."

"He had a lot of bad shit going on with his health, I think. And his head." I
looked at Cal kind of sideways. "I've always figured there's only two ways out of
this life: sick or sudden. Maybe he didn't want to hang on and just waste away.
Maybe he wanted to check out through the express."

"By blowing his brains out with a shotgun?"

"At least he got to make his own choice."

Cal shook his head like he didn't get it. "And now you want to go visit his empty
house in Key West?"

I stared at him. "You got any better ideas?"

The drive down to Key West was long, hot, noisy and windy, and naturally Cal
insisted on keeping the top down for the entire 160 miles ("there's no point having
a convertible if you're not going to put the fucking top down") and I got a whopper
of a sunburn after my cap blew off not five miles from the Miami airport. Cal
laughed like hell over that. We continued south through the low, stucco-white
sprawl of Miami, past unattractive, trailer-park retirement communities, roadside
fruit stands and empty stretches of scrub land and finally onto that long, long bridge
that island-hops its way down the Florida Keys between the Atlantic and the Gulf
of Mexico. It seemed to me that the Gulf water on the right looked more turquoise
than the deeper blue Atlantic water off to our left, but you couldn't really look at
both sides at the same time. We yelled back and forth over the wind noise and engine drone about maybe trying some fishing or snorkeling while we were down in
the Keys—especially when we saw the signs for the John Pennekamp Reef State

Park—but Cal was a typical driver and hated to stop for anything until he got to the end of his run. So we continued on through Key Largo and naturally spent most of it yelling back and forth about Humphrey Bogart, Lauren Bacall, Lionel Barrymore, Claire Trevor, Edward G. Robinson and old *film noir* gangster movies in general. We stopped for gas and had lunch at a little tumbled-down wooden place called The Oyster Shack on Marathon Key (Cal actually picked up the tab, can you believe it?) and I could see in the restroom mirror that the combination of bright Florida sun, no hat and a pair of 5-and-dime sunglasses was giving me a bit of a raccoon look. So I made Cal stop at a bait-and-tackle shop and bought myself a deep-sea fishing cap with a big blue sailfish on it. The kind big, fat retired guys wear all the time down in Florida.

"You look like a native," Cal grinned.

"I look like a rube."

"Same thing!" he laughed, and popped the clutch to launch us away from the tackle shop.

"You know they've got my name on this car," I reminded him.

"Hey, it's probably okay if I brutalize it a little on takeoff. I'm not even using the damn clutch the rest of the time...."

And he wasn't.

We got into Key West a little after sunset, and it was a quiet, pleasant and scenic little place on the outside but a hopping-mad little port town with an amazingly cosmopolitan flavor down on the waterfront. You have to understand that relations between Washington and Castro's Cuba had gone straight to shit following the botched Bay of Pigs invasion (not that they were anything special before that) and so almost the entire Atlantic fleet was trolling around in the vicinity. Along with assorted ships from a lot of our NATO allies. And there was a big Navy station on Key West where all the ships put in so the crews could enjoy a little shore leave and blow off a little pent-up steam. Not to mention that Key West was already a popular tourist spot as well as a regular port of call for cruise ships working the Caribbean. So the lively part of town down near the docks had the feel and texture of an international seaport, what with all sorts of bars, dives, hangouts and tawdry strip clubs along with the most amazing variety of languages and uniforms passing you by on the street. There's always a ready-for-anything/desperate-for-fun energy on tap whenever cooped-up Navy men, regardless of what flag they sail under, get loose for a few days' leave before hustling back to their ships to head out to sea again. They were out to have a good time, by God and Neptune, and they were sure as hell determined to find it! But we were both pretty exhausted after the long flight over from Italy and our four-and-a-half hour drive down the keys, so Cal and I found a cheap, stucco-finish motel not too far from the waterfront, got a couple mugs of beer and some good conch fritters at a joint just across the street and turned in.

The next morning I was up early—Cal was still sleeping—and I decided I'd take a walk over to the old Hemingway house at 907 Whitehead Street by myself. I'd always been a big fan of Hemingway's writing when I was in school. *The Sun Also Rises* and short stories like "Hills Like White Elephants," "The Short Happy Life of Francis Macomber," and "A Clean Well-Lighted Place," in particular. His work was so deceptively plain, clean, straightforward, simple and direct. But of course it was also solid as granite, deep as a moonless sky and layered like an onion with meaning. Not that Ernest Hemingway was ever one to mix his metaphors....

Anyhow, the house at 907 Whitehead Street was where Hemingway lived with his second wife, Pauline, and he did some of his very best work there during the 1930s. It was a pretty damn nice house for a writer, and I started getting crazy ideas about what you could actually make as a successful novelist. Only I found out later that his second wife's rich uncle Gus actually bought it for them (along with a new Ford roadster, which were hard to come by in 1929) and that took a little of the luster off. In any case, it was a block-shaped, kind of Spanish-looking 2-story thing with tall windows, wrought-iron railings on the second-floor balconies and a big, lush garden in back. But Hemingway hadn't been around there for years, and of course never would again since he'd put that shotgun to his head in Ketchum, Idaho, seven months before. I had a hard time understanding that, but I've come to believe that the less you know about the private lives of your heroes, the better off you are. It just confuses things.

It didn't look like much of anyone was home except for a colony of cats—many with six toes—who'd obviously been squatting there for years. I leaned against the fence and peered in through the windows, but it just looked empty. So whatever mystical illumination or inspiration I hoped to find there never really materialized. But I did get a lot of good, solid, Hemingway-esque material I had a hard time remembering the next morning when Cal and I cruised the bars, clip joints and strip clubs on the waterfront that night. We must have hit fifteen or twenty of them from one end of the street to the other—places with intriguing, lead-you-on names like *The Diablo Club, Seamen's Paradise, Dew Come Inn* and *Myrtle's Stage and Tables*—and although we came to the conclusion that the drinks were mostly watered, we made up for it by consuming a lot of them. And the on-stage talent in a few of the smaller, darker, dingier spots could do some truly amazing things with various parts of their anatomy. "I've seen women who could pick up dollar bills like that before," Cal observed with genuine if drunken amazement, "but never any who could make actual change...." The last thing I recall, through a swirling alcoholic haze, was three more drinks I surely didn't need on the table in front of me and this older, high-mileage stripper working up a hell of a sweat and damn near falling off the stage once or twice doing a rambunctious routine to Chubby Checker's popular *The Twist.*

The next morning didn't arrive until well past ten, when I woke up sprawled, sick, sweaty and shivering on a folding chair out under the eaves of our motel room in my skivvies. And Cal was hovering right over me with a big, nasty grin on his face and a cup of hot coffee in his hands. "Here," he said, handing me the cup. "You look like you need this more than I do."

"How the hell did I get here?" I groaned.

"Apparently you walked. Or maybe you crawled. On your belly. Like a lizard." His cruel yet friendly smile beamed down at me. "I think you maybe got up to use the bathroom, went out the wrong door and couldn't find your way back in. Or maybe the chair just looked too inviting?" Something in his smile made me suspect that might not be the whole story. But I felt too lousy to care.

"Drink that and have a hot shower," he advised, still grinning. "That'll make you feel better."

"It sure couldn't make me feel any worse," I rose unsteadily and stumbled through the door in the general direction of the bathroom. "You got any aspirin?" I called back over my shoulder.

"I took the last ones. But we'll find you some."

So I showered up, drank Cal's coffee, took one look in the mirror at my blood-shot eyes and raccoon-mask sunburn and decided it would be useless to shave. I mean, you can't polish a turd....

Cal drove us over to a little drugstore/coffee shop not far from 907 Whitehead Street and I bought myself a small tin of Anacin along with some dry toast and two more cups of coffee at the lunch counter. On the way out, I happened to notice this cheaply printed little booklet on the magazine rack titled <u>*The Dangerous Life and Tragic Death of Ernest Hemingway*</u>. So naturally I bought it. And did my best to read through it that afternoon sitting in the same lawn chair I'd slept in the night before. The copyright page listed the date of publication as October, 1961. Or, in other words, barely three months after Hemingway's suicide. And it made me feel even sicker as I thumbed my way through grainy, black-and-white photographs of Hemingway in uniform and Hemingway on the docks in Cuba with four gigantic marlins strung up next to him and Hemingway on safari in Africa with his rifle and bush jacket and a picture of him gray, grim and out-of-shape at the house in Ketchum, Idaho, where he finally blew his brains out. But the worst part was the smirking, innuendo-laced paragraphs about his failed marriages and his father's suicide and his chronic alcoholism and his cataclysmic accidents—he went down twice in plane crashes!—and the debilitating physical problems and hellish bouts with depression later on that led to electric shock treatments at the Menninger Clinic in Topeka. According to the booklet, Hemingway told an interviewer those shock treatments "robbed me of my memory and put me out of business as a writer," and that made his suicide a little easier to understand. Or that's what I chose to believe, anyway. But the real point is that you don't want to know too much about your heroes. Artistic or otherwise. You experience the very best of them when you see them doing whatever it is that they're good at, and finding out more about them as ordinary, mortal, vain, weak, stupid, fearful, feet-of-clay human beings just diminishes it all for you.

I knew it could be the same with racing drivers, too.

Or pick any other occupation....

I didn't feel much like going back to the strip clubs that night—that stuff can get pretty old, and particularly if it makes you a little uncomfortable—so we walked over to a cheap little seafood joint that the owner of the motel recommended (I think his cousin ran it) and then stopped in at a quiet little bar for a couple beers and a few games on the pinball machines in back. There were six of them—three on each side plus one of those bowling machines along the back wall—and they were all popular Gottlieb models with typically seafaring, waterfront-oriented names and motifs like "Captain Kidd," "Flag Ship," "Harbor Lites," "Sea Belles," "Seven Seas" and "Tropic Isle." And Cal beat me at every single one of them. Not to mention the bowling machine. Which got to me a little, since I always fancied myself as a fairly decent pinball player. Or at least not terrible, anyway. So we came back again the next night (after I actually put in a few feeble hours on my novel in the afternoon) and the night after that and the night after that as well. And he beat me every time. I even got myself in trouble by making a frustrated quarter bet with him on the second game of the second night, and promptly made it worse in a hurry by going double-or-nothing on the next one. But there was no beating him. Oh, he'd laugh and make wisecracks out of the side of his mouth while he was playing, but his eyes stayed hard and deadly and he never seemed to blink. It was frankly amazing the kind of hand raps and hip shots and knee bumps he could put into those machines without tilting them. And they always seemed to give the ball a little extra english. Whenever I tried that, there'd be a deep, tinny "clunk" from somewhere inside the backboard, the lights would go out, the flippers would go dead and I'd watch in miserable agony as the ball I was working on rolled slowly down the middle and clanked out of sight. Damn! By the end of the third night, my tab was up to roughly the gross national product of French Guiana, and Cal finally let me off the hook by picking the player end of the "Captain Kidd" machine right up off the ground to tilt it on purpose. He did it while I was up at the bar getting us a round of beers, but I saw him do it in the mirror. It was actually a pretty nice thing to do.

By the end of the fifth night we'd both had about enough of Key West. We'd walked all over and sat on the beach and went swimming and played pinball until our fingers calloused over and even spent one afternoon fishing from a rented skiff with rented tackle. That was my idea. I wanted to try it because I knew how much Hemingway enjoyed it—I even insisted we split the cost—but it was hot and sticky out there and the shrimp we were using for bait smelled a little long out of the water. Not to mention a sickening little roll to the ocean and that the last thing I really needed was more sun. But we did manage to catch a bunch of yellowtail grunts and a couple fairly good-sized blue runners, and I figured by the end we'd spent roughly two dollars-per-pound for more 49-cents-per-pound fresh fish than we could ever possibly eat. We kept a couple for dinner and gave the rest away to an enterprising Cuban kid who had quite a little business going for himself taking unwanted fish off the tourists' hands and delivering them to the local trailer-park retirees at a very good price. All he had to do was clean 'em, scale 'em and gut 'em.

By the next morning Cal and I had decided it was time to make our way back up Highway 1 towards the mainland. Sure, I'd gotten inspired for a few days and put a little work in on my novel, but it was all crap and I knew it. You can tell it's crap when you write it. Especially the dialogue. But you've got to keep at it anyway. Or that's what all my creative-writing teachers in high school and college always told me. Then again, what great books had any of them ever written?

It was a nice, easy drive up the keys, just rolling along in kind of a warm, sunny stupor and in no particular hurry to get anywhere. We didn't have to be at Sebring for almost two weeks, and neither of us had any idea what we should do with ourselves. I liked spending time with Cal, but you couldn't really get close to him. He kept everything upbeat, fun and easy on the outside, but he was locked up like a damn bank vault beyond that. There was no way he was going to let anyone see into his heart. But he gave you the same kind of privacy, and so it never made you feel uncomfortable. I've noticed it's the same way with a lot of the racers I've met. Or the really good ones, anyway. It's just the way they are.

I talked Cal into stopping at one of the beach stores so we could buy some cheap masks and swim fins—I hadn't mentioned anything yet about my deal with Fairway Motors and so Cal assumed I was as broke as motoring journalists usually are—and we spent a couple lazy hours doing a little snorkeling over the rocks and coral at John Pennekamp Reef State Park off Key Largo. I naturally worried about maneating sharks and sting rays and moray eels that could tear your arm off and stinging sea urchins and poisonous jelly fish and giant squids with long, sucking tentacles and cruel, jagged beaks like the one James Mason had to fight in *20,000 Leagues Under the Sea*. But it was breathtaking, too, gliding along like a hawk hovering over the earth with the most amazing, bluish-green panorama of coral and sea fans and lobsters and schools of brightly-colored fish everywhere you looked. I was entranced, and had the sunburn on my back to prove it the next morningr!

We kept heading north once we got to the mainland and just kept driving and driving and driving until we made it all the way up to New Jersey to drop in unexpectedly on our old pal Buddy Palumbo. It actually started out as kind of a joke. You know: *"As long as we're headed north, why don't we drive up and see Buddy?"*

"That's all the way up in New Jersey!"

"So? You got anyplace better to go?"

Silence.

So we went. Of course I told Cal that we should really call ahead and tell Buddy we were coming, but he thought that would spoil it. And I must say Buddy looked pretty damned shocked when the two of us wandered into his shop out of nowhere on a cold, blustery New Jersey morning in early March. Especially since Cal and I were still sporting Florida Keys tans.

"WHAT THE HELL ARE YOU GUYS DOING HERE??!!" Buddy pretty much shrieked.

"Hank said we needed an oil change," Cal deadpanned.

"I thought you might give us a deal on it," I chimed in.

"Jesus, you should have called ahead!" Buddy whopped, slapping his arms around our shoulders.

"That's what I told you," I sneered over at Cal. "But *you* said it would've ruined the surprise."

"It would have," Cal insisted like that should be the end of it.

"Jesus, it's great to see you!" Buddy grinned at us. "Lemme call Julie and I'll have you over to dinner...."

"We don't want you to go to any fuss."

"Bullshit! How often do I get to see you guys?"

"Hey, that's not *our* problem," Cal needled. "You know where to find us."

"Most weekends, anyway," I added in.

So Buddy went into his office and called Julie, and we gathered from what we could overhear that she was less than thrilled to be getting roughly 45 minutes' notice to get her house, her kitchen and herself in shape for a two-extra-guests/special-occasion dinner. "Listen, we could all go out someplace," I called in to him. "I'll treat."

Cal and Buddy both stared at me like a hole had opened up in the earth's crust.

Even so, Buddy absolutely insisted that we come over to his house for dinner. And we did. But not until he gave us a tour of his shop. A very thorough tour, in fact. Which made me guess that Julie had given him instructions to keep us the hell away for at least an hour. But that was okay because we had a lot of catching-up to do, and Buddy had some really neat cars in his shop.

I was surprised to see a beautiful black Maserati 3500 GT in the very first stall. "So when did you start working on Maseratis?" I asked.

"When my brother-in-law bought one!" he laughed. I figured old Carson Flegley had to be making out pretty well for himself in the funeral parlor business.

"What's it in for?"

"Nothing, really. He just doesn't want my sister to see it."

"Why not?"

"Because she'll ask him what it cost!" And of course we understood.

"Is he racing any more?"

"That's his 3000 with the roll bar in it over in the corner," Buddy kind of sighed, and pointed to an unmistakable Big Healey shape hidden under an MG Mitten car cover and a light coating of dust. "He had me do a lot of work on it after Lime Rock last year, and now I'd bet it's as good as any Healey racecar in the country. Maybe even better. But he hasn't been taking a lot of interest in it lately."

"Family?" I asked.

"Yeah. That and business. His uncle died and now he's pretty much running things at the death house. You know how that goes."

"Why doesn't he just sell it?"

"*The funeral parlor?*" Buddy asked incredulously.

"No, the car."

Buddy looked at me like I should already know the answer. And of course I did. You can still think of the guy in the mirror as a racing driver so long as you still own a racecar. Even if you never quite find your way clear to running it. But once you sell it, the door slams shut and you're just another rank-and-file rube with Brando-esque, *"I coulda been a contendah"* stories to tell about the guy you used to be. Stories, by the way, that nobody much wants to hear. And there was also the part about all the work Buddy'd put in on that Healey. Hell, it's one thing to get beat when you've got a stock engine and stock gears and the car's still wearing half of its road equipment. It's another story entirely when some other guy's got that car and you're wheeling the one with the high-compression pistons and California-spec race cam and straight-through exhaust system and welded-up ring-and-pinion gears and everything possible pulled off to make the damn thing lighter. That changes things....

Next to Carson Flegley's Maserati was an old prewar Bentley the size of a steam locomotive with the engine out for a rebuild. And next to that—in the Bentley's shadow, actually—was a pretty little pale blue Lotus Elite with some with ugly-looking crash damage to the right-rear. "I haven't really figured out how we're going to deal with that one," Buddy allowed, scratching his head. "My guy Steve did that on a test drive. Swerved to miss a dog. Or that's what he says, anyway." Buddy let out a helpless little laugh. "It was just in for a damn radiator leak. And the owner's due in to pick it up tomorrow...."

"So what are you going to do?"

"Catch hell, most likely," he laughed. "But at least we know how to fix it."

There was another Lotus next to it: a tiny, fragile-looking, lima bean-colored Type 17 sports/racer. Lotus originally built the little 17 to run with a 750cc motor for a try at the Index of Performance money at Le Mans, but the unexpected success of Eric Broadley's new Lola over Chapman's previously dominant Lotus 11 prompted Lotus to press the 17 into service for the 1100cc and even 1500cc classes. And the results had been kind of a mixed bag. It was terrifically small and light and poked a very tiny hole in the air, and works driver Alan Stacey had put the prototype on the pole for its very first race. Only then he refused to drive it because the handling was so unpredictable! It turned out that the strut-type front suspension would occasionally bind up solid under load. In the end, Colin Chapman somewhat uncharacteristically offered 17 owners a free kit—emphasis on "free"—to upgrade the cars already delivered to a conventional, dual A-arm setup. But by then Formula Junior was establishing itself as the new "nursery class" for aspiring World Champions, smallbore sports/racers were falling out of favor and the move to mid-engined designs was the coming thing. "It's a tiny little thing, isn't it?" I said to no one in particular.

"A guy named Whiteside owns it," Buddy said matter-of-factly, "but I'm not sure he knows exactly what to do with it. It's actually a pretty neat little car. But it's got a busted rear end, and those things are hell to work on—getting the diff in and out is like one of those Chinese wood puzzles—and it's getting a little past its prime. Oh, it could have been an absolute killer car in '59 if Lotus had gotten it sorted out. But they didn't, and now it's just another neat old racecar that nobody much wants."

"So where does it go from here?"

"Oh, it'll sit until we get the parts in and then we'll fix it when we get around to it. And then it'll sit some more until he either decides to take it out again or gets tired of paying storage and tries to sell it. He's a pretty keen racer, and I know he's got his eye on one of those new Lotus 20 Formula Juniors. That's really the way to go if you've got the stomach for open-wheelers. I know he's been dickering around with the Lotus dealer up in Millerton, and he'll probably try to throw this in as a trade if he can make the deal." Buddy gave the 17 a sad little smile. "Eventually it'll wind up with some asshole who can't really afford to run it and sooner or later it'll get Regional Maintenanced into oblivion. He'll eventually crash it or put a rod through the block and then it'll sit around his garage gathering mouse nests and spider webs until the guy's widow or ex-wife puts the remains up for sale...."

"Sounds pretty grim," I observed.

"That's just the way it goes for old racecars. You get used to it."

Things were a bit more optimistic in the next stall, where an enormous and rakish Duesenberg SJ with the driveline and interior stripped out and all the brakes and suspension apart ("that one's gonna be here for awhile") towered over the forlorn little Lotus like a cliff. Next to the Duesey was an alloy-bodied, crackers-and-cream Morgan Plus 4 Super Sports with a tripod roll bar ("they ought to break the fingers of the idiot who welded up that piece of shit") with its hood folded up and the head off for a little judicious porting and a triple-angle valve job. Next to the Morgan sat a creamy gray Porsche 356 coupe with the back end up on stands and the engine sitting on a floor jack next to it. "I've come to love those things," Buddy mused wistfully. "You can do a clutch job in well under an hour if you know what you're doing. The only reason that one's not back together is that we had to send the flywheel out for resurfacing."

Across the way was a gorgeous maroon Lancia Aurelia Spyder with a terminally ill transaxle ("some people just shouldn't own stick shifts, no matter how much they think they like sports cars") a brand-new Jag E-Type in for an oil change ("the guy doesn't trust the dealer"), a very nice XK150 drophead the same owner had refused to trade in on the new E-Type after he heard what Colin St. John's used car manager thought it was worth and now desperately wanted to sell. Next to the nearly sale-proof 150 drophead was an ageing and bricklike but still handsome old Aston DB2 racer with number circles on the sides, a perfect, British Racing Green AC Bristol with the rear end apart and a still brutal-looking but patched, banged and dented Lister-Jaguar in a dirty and fairly hideous orange-and-yellow paint scheme. "That's one of the old Cunningham team cars, can you believe it?" Buddy explained sadly. "That was the best damn sports/racing car you could buy back at the beginning of the '58 season. Fastest thing on wheels!" He let out a long, slow sigh. "And now look at it."

"What's it in for?"

"Well, it needs just about everything. The guy's been talking about maybe putting a Chevy in it, but I think what it really needs is a decent burial."

"Time moves on."

"That it does."

Parked next to the Lister was a stunning white Ferrari 250GT Pininfarina Cabriolet with red leather interior. It was immaculate from end to end, and I knew without asking that it had to belong to Big Ed Baumstein. And sure enough it did. "He doesn't drive it very much," Buddy allowed. "And we have to change the plugs for him almost every time he does."

I noticed one other car, hidden under a dusty car cover way over in the back corner of the shop behind the air compressor. And I knew from the general shape and the unmistakable triangular grille pressing against the cloth that it had to be Buddy's own Alfa Romeo Giulietta Spider racecar. We walked over and Buddy pulled the cover gently back like he was removing a baby's blanket from its crib.

"You planning on running it again this year?" Cal asked.

"Oh, I'll try to take it up to Lime Rock once or twice. And I'm hoping to maybe try that new track over at Vineland. But you know how it is. I'm so damn busy with the shop and the family and all, and we've been talking about packing up everything and moving it all to Connecticut. Julie's pretty set on that." He looked over at Cal and sighed. "Besides, it's just not the same without the old crowd around any more." For just the flicker of an instant, I almost saw tears welling up in his eyes. Fact is, I think we were all feeling a little misty right then....

Buddy's two-story house in the suburbs was *very* nice, and you had to figure Julie had been running around like a crazy person and yelling at the kids something awful to get everything neat, clean and squared-away before we arrived. Plus she'd somehow managed to whip us up a pretty damn incredible dinner of chicken cacciatore, green beans, tossed salad, minestrone soup, sautéed mushrooms with butter and garlic and a little pasta with home-made marinara sauce on the side. She'd gotten herself prettied up for the occasion, too. Oh, sure, she'd put on a few pounds—maybe a few more than a few, in fact—but she was always kind of a big girl. She gave us each a big smile and a kiss on the cheek as soon as we came through the doorway, but you could feel the frosty edge right under the surface. No question she was pissed as hell at Cal and me for just dropping in out of the sky like that. And at Buddy for inviting us over on such short notice. But even so you could see that she and Buddy and the kids had a pretty decent life worked out for themselves. Even if they were nailed to it like you get to be when you have a family and a two-story house in the suburbs and a thriving shop business to take care of. During dinner Buddy asked us if we wanted to stay over, and Julie chimed right in ("we got plenty of room") but Cal insisted we had to be going. Even though we were dog tired, had no place to go and didn't have to be back down to Sebring for almost another whole week. But I think Buddy and Julie's house and the family life inside it made him a little uneasy.

So we took off around ten and wound up staying in a cheesy little mom-and-pop motel with noisy radiators and rust-colored water coming out of the faucets near Philadelphia, not even 100 miles further south. And then we took off right around dawn the next morning and drove straight-through like we had a damn plane to catch and arrived at Sebring three days early.

Chapter 9: The Fun Bus

I'd found out more about the rumored sale of the magazine by the time I got to Sebring, and I'd have to say it had me a little worried. After all, I'd been with Warren and Isabelle from almost the very beginning—damn near 10 years, in fact—and I'd watched them grow and build *Car and Track* from a little two-bit startup into quite a successful venture. Maybe even too successful, since that's what ultimately attracted a big, shrewd, highly diversified magazine conglomerate like Pletsch & Deering. I'd of course called Warren about it, and he told me in his typically stiff, bloodless way that Isabelle had been in the hospital right after Thanksgiving "to have something looked at." Thankfully it turned out to be nothing, but no question it got both of them thinking. They knew in their hearts—as I did—that there was no way Warren could run the magazine without Isabelle backing him up. That would have been a mess turning into a disaster wrapped up in a calamity. After all, she was the one who got things finished, knew where things were, kept everything organized and whip-cracked the magazine into shape every month. Even if she rarely got any credit for it.

I'd also found out a little more about the Pletsch & Deering publishing empire, and it was a real, all-American, Horatio Alger-style success story. The whole thing started with a simple, struggling, Brooklyn-based hobbyist magazine about woodworking that Theodore Deering Sr. started more or less for the heck of it. He'd inherited a reasonably successful insurance brokerage business from his father and uncle, but his heart wasn't really in it. What Theodore Sr. loved was fooling around in his basement wood shop making tables and chairs and dressers and headboards and kitchen and bathroom cabinets and also restoring great old pieces that age, neglect, rot or bugs had gotten to. And that's how, without any evidence to back it up or any notion how to go about it, he thought it might be fun to publish a magazine on the subject. Much as Orson Welles' Charlie Kane thought "it might be fun to run a newspaper" in the landmark movie *Citizen Kane*. Only the fringe-interest publishing business turned out to be a hundred times more work and a thousand times more difficult than Theodore Sr. ever anticipated. And meanwhile his insurance business shrunk, withered and began to founder for lack of attention. It didn't take Theodore Deering long to find himself skewered on the notorious, five-pronged fork of the magazine publishing business. To wit:

In order to build circulation, you need distribution.

In order to get distribution, you've got to put copies out there on the newsstands where people can see them and thumb through them and maybe, just maybe, decide to buy a copy. And then, if they really, really like it and don't wind up just dropping it in a corner someplace and forgetting about it, maybe, just maybe, they'll take the time to fill out the little form inside and write out a check and put them in an envelope and remember to put a stamp on it and mail it in to get a subscription.

In order to put those copies out on the newsstands where people can see and thumb through them, you've got to somehow assemble everything that needs to go into a magazine and pay for the layout work and the paper stock and the printing and shipping required to get them out to the distributors. And you have to offer big, fat discounts to those distributors to get them to carry your title and moreover agree to take back all the unsold copies—at full credit!—at the end of each issue run. As you can well imagine, that takes lots and lots of *M-O-N-E-Y.*

In order to make that money, you've got to sell advertising. Magazines make all their real money on advertising revenues. You're lucky if the dollars that trickle in from subscriptions and newsstand sales cover the cost of the paper stock and printing. As any publisher will tell you (behind his hand, of course) the only reason to have editorial content inside a magazine is to keep the ads from crashing into each other.

And this is where the whole thing comes full circle: in order to sell all that advertising, you've got to show potential advertisers the kind of impressive circulation numbers they want to see and brag like hell about all the fine, upstanding, money-in-hand citizens your publication reaches out to every month that really need to know about their products or services. But of course you can't do that unless you already have the circulation numbers....

It can drive a person ever so slightly nuts!

To make matters worse, old Theodore Sr. had chosen to ignore the single, core principle of the successful risk-management business his father and uncle had left to him. Which was, simply put: "don't take any." In the end, Theodore Sr. was forced into an unhappy partnership-of-necessity with a crusty and taciturn local printer named Helmut Pletsch, to whom he owed more than he could possibly pay for the issues already printed. Unsold copies of which were now cluttering up his garage and basement wood shop until he could barely get to his beloved Kidder triple-arbor table saw. But, over time, the edgy and often angry collaboration between Pletsch and Deering blossomed into an unlikely but amazingly successful and symbiotic business relationship. The one thing they had in common was an appreciation of good, stout, well-engineered and well-thought-out industrial machinery. Theodore adored the flexibility, precision and easy familiarity of his old, three-arbor Kidder table saw and Helmut likewise appreciated the solid trustworthiness and reliability of his number one Kidder printing press (which he kept running—two shifts a day, six days a week—whenever he had the business to fill it). And out of that shared admiration for well-designed, well-built Kidder machinery grew the respect that needs to be at the core of any successful relationship, business or otherwise. You don't necessarily have to like the other person, but you sure as hell have to respect what they bring to the table.

Theodore Sr. was the dreaming, distracted, occasionally absent-minded conceptual spark behind most of Pletsch & Deering's ventures, and tough, hard-as-nails old German printer Helmut had all the nuts-and-bolts monetary ends covered. Between them they discovered that putting out one special-interest magazine was pretty much the same as putting out any another. And that there were moreover potential niche advertisers eager to reach out to the focused, fringe-interest audiences those magazines addressed. So they added another small, bi-monthly magazine about the kiln-fired jewelry and ceramics that Theodore Deering's wife liked to fool around with in her spare time. And then another on knitting and crocheting since that's what Helmut Pletsch's wife liked to do. And then a magazine dedicated to the braided lanyard, laced leather and wood-burning handicrafts their sons brought home from Coach Burns' Day Camp every summer. After a shaky start, those titles also began to find their audience and did tolerably well. Then Pletsch and Deering picked up a hunting and fishing magazine that was in financial trouble thanks to an ugly, expensive divorce (are there any other kind?), and then they bought another one about guns and ammunition to go along with it. Which brought them to the important discovery that overlapping spheres of interest allowed you to package and pitch attractive "twofer" deals to potential advertisers. Then came another title on golf and another about purebred dogs and then they started one up on model airplanes after they failed to reach an acceptable financial agreement with the gentleman who owned *Wings in Scale* (he eventually went bankrupt after they stole, finagled or finessed away the bulk of his advertisers). Followed by another on model trains and yet another on inboard and outboard power boating. They were all what are universally referred to in the publishing trade as "nutball books" (magazines aimed at a certain specific hobby or interest) and by then Pletsch and Deering had made the happy discovery that you could land genuine, full-page, full-color, inside-front-cover/inside-back-cover/outside back-cover mainstream advertisers like cigarette companies and pain relievers and automobile manufacturers and breakfast cereals and brands of beer, scotch and toothpaste if you could just wave enough total circulation under the noses of the ad space buyers at the advertising agencies. And they were eager for it, since they got paid in direct proportion to how much money they spent on their clients' behalf. Think about that. Not to mention that Pletsch & Deering made a point of hiring eager, aggressive, fast-talking young ad salesmen who knew a lot of unlisted phone numbers, knew how to show clients a good time and regularly passed along under-the-table gifts like bottles of fine liquor, behind-the-dugout Yankees tickets, dinners at fancy restaurants, occasional envelopes of cash and overnights with high-class call girls at the Plaza Hotel in order to close and keep those accounts.

It was a brilliant strategy.

To be honest, none of the second-generation Deering brothers had any special love for woodworking, jewelry, crocheting, handicrafts, fishing, hunting, guns, dogs, model airplanes, model train sets or power boating (although Miles and Quentin both enjoyed golf), but they were all desperately fond of the ever-growing piles of money those interests were generating for them. And, if the mood struck, they could use their publishing business to indulge their own personal fancies and write it all off as a business expense! Middle brother Miles did exactly that when he created *Equitation* magazine for the horsey types, tack addicts and dressage buffs he knew so well. Although he was careful to keep his name off the masthead, preferring to ghost-write stories and columns under a series of fanciful *noms de plume* like "Gerald Stirrup," "Pauline Pommel" and "Warren Oats" and direct editorial focus, bias and occasional slander from behind a curtain of comfortable anonymity. And now youngest brother Quentin wanted to do much the same thing with a car magazine. I'd never met Quentin Deering at that point, but I'd heard about him here and there from people involved in the exotic road car and "collector car" ends of the motoring hobby. No question he'd always fancied fast, flashy cars—the fastest, flashiest and most expensive you could buy, in fact—and drove them with a fierce and even reckless enthusiasm (if not much skill or judgment) at virtually every opportunity. Much to the horror of everyone who rode with him. Quentin Deering was convinced he could have been a world-class racing driver if he'd only put his mind to it. Although finding racecars he could actually fit in might have posed a bit of a problem, since he was rumored to be several fingers of scotch over six feet and pushing hard in the general direction of 300 pounds. He also fancied himself something of an expert on automobile mechanics since he'd personally changed at least three flat tires without professional assistance of any kind and once even added water to his own battery. The way I got the story, Quentin had been thinking about buying up a car-nut magazine for quite some time—he'd had his eye on *Car and Track* in particular—and he and his brothers quickly moved in when they came upon some insider information (perhaps from Eric Gibbon?) about Isabelle Bertrand's cancer scare. I could tell from the hollow echo in Warren's voice over the phone that he and Isabelle were giving the Deering brothers' offer some serious consideration. "But of course you'll be part of the package," he told me in his usual cold, bloodless way, "and I'll make sure you're the first to know if anything more develops...."

Somehow I didn't find that entirely reassuring.

But you have to put all that stuff aside when you arrive at a major race to do a report for a magazine. And I have to admit it felt comfortable as an old bedroom slipper to be back on my regular beat as an underpaid motoring scribe. Sure, I was sharing a dismal little room with my old photographer pal Hal Crockett at the migrant-fruit-plucker motel he'd discovered behind a defunct used-car lot and a broken-down shed of a liquor store off of Highway 27, but cheap rooms are hard to come by on a race weekend, and particularly at an out-in-the-middle-of-nowhere event like Sebring. Our accommodations were in a low, ugly, flat-roofed little place with an aging stucco exterior the color of an abandoned wasps' nest and water that smelled like old mushrooms constantly drip-drip-dripping in the bathroom sink.

And the mirror over that sink was all spider-webbed with cracks so it was like trying to shave in a damn jigsaw puzzle. But the beds were comfortable if you were tired enough (or maybe ever-so-slightly drunk), and the general ambience made for a nice match with Hal's hoary and rusty old '51 Studebaker Land Cruiser parked out front. He'd driven that thing straight-through down from Atlanta, and even though he had to coax it to life every morning because the choke didn't really work anymore and then listen to it shudder, fart and run-on for several long, embarrassing seconds whenever he switched it off, he loved that car. Hal was a big, tall, gangly guy with a shaggy beard and a gimpy right leg, and he liked the way he could stretch out across the Studebaker's wide front seat with his bum leg kind of angled out over the driveshaft tunnel. Not to mention how he could lock all of his camera gear away—and Hal had a *lot* of camera gear—in the Land Cruiser's enormous trunk. "If I can just get the old girl to the highway," he'd purr through a snaggle-toothed smile, "she'll take me anywhere I need to go."

I have to admit that Hal's old Studebaker was the perfect sort of transportation for a track like Sebring, which was just as gritty, dusty, ragged, rough and dilapidated as I remembered it. Truth be told, Sebring was a hell of a strange place to host a World Manufacturers' Championship motor race. It was hard to get to, sat out in the middle of nowhere and there was nothing but dusty orange groves, rusty, weather-beaten hangars, cracked concrete runways ribboned with tar strips and a ghostly graveyard of derelict World War II bombers off in the distance for ambience. But I guess if something's different, difficult and unique enough, it somehow becomes *special,* and—like most of the teams and drivers—I always looked forward to Sebring with a combination of giddy anticipation and nagging dread. There was no other race place like it in the world. And it had grown in stature over the years because all the top European teams supported it. The Brits in particular loved bringing their pale, pasty-white faces down to Sebring after being cooped up in their race shops all winter.

It was warm, bright and sunny the Wednesday morning we headed over to registration in Hal's chuffing old Studebaker, and we could both feel the growing buzz of excitement as we hit the inevitable traffic jam of transporters, rental cars, motor homes, pick-ups, station wagons and racecar trailers of every possible size and description trying to jockey their way in through the competitors' gate entrance. The license plates came from damn near everywhere. Even Canada, California and Connecticut. But Sebring was a hell of an occasion. It heralded the beginning of the stateside racing season and had been the only World Manufacturers' Championship round in North America since the championship began in 1953. Or at least it had until the F.I.A. added that new race at Daytona just six weeks before! And no question that was going to have a lot of noses out of joint at Sebring. Which I was actually looking forward to in a perverse sort of way. After all, disagreements between promoters and sanctioning bodies are part of the fabric of the sport, and the controversies and confrontations they inevitably engender give you things to write about. Which can be particularly useful when the outcome of the race is a foregone conclusion. There wasn't really a lot of drama about who was going to win at Sebring in 1962. It was going to be Ferrari. Hands down and running away. The only real question to be answered was 'which one?' Even so, Sebring had attracted a typically large and eclectic field of entries eager to make a race of it, and that's always good news for a writer with pages to fill. Including Clive Stanley's Imperial Crown Tea Aston Martin DB4GT Zagato with Ian Snell and Tommy Edwards as drivers and, hopefully, Miss Audrey Denbeigh handling their timing and scoring....

I also have to admit I was really looking forward to seeing Audrey again. Really, *really* looking forward to it. I caught myself thinking about her all the time when I wasn't busy doing something else. Or sometimes even when I *was* busy doing something else. Which is how I damn near sliced the end of my index finger off attempting to quarter a nice, fresh, juicy Florida orange while we were waiting in traffic to get in through the gate. And I know that orange was fresh and juicy because I'd sneaked my way into a roadside orange grove and snatched it off a tree just a few minutes before. And that fresh citrus juice really stung like hell, too. Not to mention that I was using Hal's pocket knife at the time (which looked like it had been picked off a dead soldier at Gettysburg) so infection was a near certainty. Fortunately Hal had a first-aid kit on board—a pretty big one, in fact—but it was a World War II, Army-surplus battlefield unit intended more for compound fractures, third-degree burns and sucking chest wounds than cut fingers requiring a simple band-aid and maybe a drop or two of iodine. And if you think that's funny, *you* try taking notes or typing out 2500 words with a gashed, sore and swollen-red index finger wrapped up in a gauze square the size of a cocktail napkin and two-inch-wide adhesive tape!

To be honest, I hadn't quite figured out what I was going to say to Audrey when I saw her again. Or how the hell I could maneuver us around towards wherever the hell it was we seemed to be going. I mean, even if she was willing, I couldn't very well invite her back to our migrant-fruit-picker motel for a romantic evening of listening to Hal snore and the bathroom faucet drip. And there wasn't a room to be had for any kind of money within 50 miles. And who the hell knew if she wanted that anyway? Or if I did, come to that? I might not have had much of a life, but at least I knew where everything was, didn't want for much and my days were relatively free of unexpected shocks, disappointments and complications. I knew things like that could change in a hurry once you and some other fine soul start feeding off the same plate of angst. And yet I couldn't wait to see her again, and trusted in the gods of hormones, hope and happenstance to show me the way.

Hal found a parking spot as close as possible to the block-long registration line and switched off the old Studebaker. Or tried to, anyway. But the engine fought back, shuddering and rattling and running on for twenty or thirty whole seconds after he removed the key. "You really ought to have that looked at," I needled him.

"Aw, she's just saying 'good night,'" he groused. And right on cue the old Studebaker spit out one last, massive backfire and labored into silence. It was loud enough to make everybody in the registration line turn around. And that's when I saw Audrey, way up near the front in a pretty yellow sundress, standing just two or three people back from the credential window. Part of me wanted to just leap out and run right up to her. But I knew all about Registration Line Etiquette, and you really didn't want to look like you were trying to cut in ahead with friends. Unless you really *were* trying to cut in with friends, of course, in which case you really didn't give a shit about what other people think anyway. So Hal and I took our proper place at the tail end of the line and waited. But I waved at her like an idiot the instant she turned around, and she stopped by to say "hi" when she was finished at the credential window. It was great to see her and hear her voice again. And she looked genuinely happy to see me, too. But you can never be sure about things like that.

She noticed the bulging wad of gauze and adhesive tape on my finger almost immediately. "My God, what have you done to your hand?"

"Aw, I got it cutting up an orange. It's not as bad as it looks."

"I should hope not."

"When the blood came out, it was black," Hal deadpanned.

I gave him one of those "take a hike" looks that most males instinctively understand, and he kindly remembered that he'd left something terribly important in the Studebaker and hobbled off to retrieve it. It suddenly felt like we were very much alone.

"I understand you had quite the yachting excursion and road trip after Daytona," she offered up with a smile.

I gave her what I hoped appeared to be a manly shrug of indifference. "Yeah, it was all right."

"I heard the clubs in Key West were particularly entertaining."

I felt the heat coming up in my cheeks. And wondered how the hell she'd found out about the strip club in Key West? And that's about when Tommy pulled up in a tapioca-yellow Fairway Freeway convertible with none other than Cal Carrington in the passenger seat and a big bag of carry-out sandwiches and several six-packs of cold beer and soda pop between them. It was Clive Stanley's rental car for Sebring, and Tommy had the top down and the radio turned up with Mr. Acker Bilk's *Stranger on the Shore* leaking gently out of the speakers.

"Yeah," I admitted, "we had a pretty good time."

"So I heard," she laughed. "So I heard."

Boy, did she ever look great! She was wearing this bright, yellow-print sun dress with a kind of squared-off neckline and a pair of big, tortoiseshell sunglasses stuck up in her hair the way girls do.

"So," I asked her, just trying to make conversation, "what did *you* do between races?"

"I went back to London, took care of those three miserable children in Mayfair and watched it rain, mostly."

"Oh?"

"Once or twice, I even managed to watch it snow."

"Well, I'm sure that was just as much fun as we had."

"Oh, I'm certain it was," she yawned. "Yachting and road trips down the Florida Keys can be such frightful bores."

"Can't they, though."

"And what are you up to now?"

"Oh, it's back to the old grindstone, watching races and writing priceless prose for the poor souls who can't be here in person."

"Is your prose truly priceless?"

"Well, given what the magazine pays, I suppose you could say it is."

She gave me an encouraging smile, and I fumbled for something more to say. "Y-you've never been to Sebring before, have you?"

"Never. It's my first trip. You'll have to show me the sights."

"You're pretty much looking at them."

Her eyes scanned the flat, scraggly landscape around us and the rusting hangers off in the distance. "No garden parties or high afternoon teas here, are there?"

"Well, the infield's kind of fun. Especially after night practice on Thursday."

"I've heard it gets a bit wild in there."

"You don't dare go in without a guide," I cautioned, only half joking.

"Oh? Is that an offer?"

"Sure," I told her. "You'll be with one of the best."

"Are you sure it's safe?"

"What's 'safe'?" I asked, rolling my eyeballs like Donald O'Connor. "It's just a state of mind, isn't it?"

She looked at me kind of sideways. "You do talk an amazing amount of rubbish, don't you?"

"Hey, it's what I do. Why, I'm borderline famous for it."

Tommy tapped the horn ring impatiently. Clive, Ian and the two mechanics were already in the paddock getting things set up and waiting for their lunches to arrive. "I'd better be running along now..." she explained with a playful smile "... And it's a date for Thursday evening after night practice."

"It's a date," I called after her as she climbed into the back seat. Tommy regarded me with a strange, stony expression and put Clive's rental car in gear. It made me ache a little as I watched them pull away. But it was a nice, warm, pleasant kind of ache.

"You've really got a thing for her, don't you?" Hal observed as the tapioca-yellow Fairway convertible disappeared into the paddock.

I couldn't think of an appropriate response. But I could feel the color coming up in my cheeks again.

"I think she maybe likes you a little, too..." he continued as my cheeks got even redder "...Lord in heaven only knows why."

It took us the better part of an hour to get our press credentials and parking pass squared away—registration is always hectic and confused on the first morning of any big race weekend—and then we headed for the press trailer to say "Hi" to some of our photographer and motoring scribe friends, grab a free cup of coffee and a sweet roll or two and check in with our longtime pal Kenny Breslauer, the Sebring press relations guy, who as usual was ready with copies of the official weekend schedule and the latest (but still provisional) entry list. He also suggested I stop in at the medical shack and have my outsized and thoroughly amateurish finger bandage exchanged for an ordinary band-aid. Which I did. Then it was time to wander off into the paddock to see who'd actually showed up, what they'd brought and where they were bivouacked. Wednesday morning was a good time to make a few notes, take a few pictures, do some early driver and team manager interviews and maybe even attempt a little freestyle handicapping.

As I said, there really wasn't a lot of drama about who was going to win the 12 Hours of Sebring that year. It was going to be Ferrari in both the overall sports/prototype and the big-bore GT category. The overpowering favorites had to be the quasi-factory entries out of Carlo Sebastian's stable, which included a pair of the latest, mid-engined Dino sports/racers—the new 2.4-liter V8 shown for the first time at Ferrari's press introduction just a month before and one of last season's 2.4-liter V6s—along with one of the older style, front-engined Testa Rossa V12s. There were also a few "guest driver" (read: "rent-a-ride") Short Wheelbase Berlinettas for the 3-liter GT class along with the very first GTO anyone had ever seen outside the factory walls in Maranello. It was a beautiful thing to look at, and I could see that they'd already been tweaking and developing it, adding a neat little ducktail spoiler in back to help keep the rear end planted at high speeds. In response to the F.I.A.'s stupid new points system, Ferrari had assigned the new GTO to his most experienced and successful endurance-race pairing (not to mention last year's overall winners), Phil Hill and Olivier Gendebien. And that figured to be dead trouble for everyone else in the over 2-liter GT category. Carlo Sebastian also had Stirling Moss signed on to drive again, and this time they'd paired him up with quick Scot Innes Ireland in the brand new Dino V8, while the two Rodriguez brothers were relegated to the older, V6-powered example. I was very happy to see that Cal and Peter Ryan had drawn the old, war-horse Testa Rossa. Given the notoriously brutal nature of the Sebring racetrack, I figured the rugged, proven and reliable Testa Rossa might give them an excellent shot at the overall victory. Unfortunately, Moss and Ireland came to the same exact conclusion after first practice and asked to be switched from their nimble but potentially fragile Dino to the older, heavier but sturdier Testa Rossa. That put Cal and Pete Ryan into the V8 Dino, and I had never seen two drivers more disappointed at being assigned to the fastest car in the paddock!

That eventuality cemented Moss and Ireland in as everybody in the press room's odds-on favorite for the overall victory, and seeing Moss at the wheel of a Ferrari for the second race in a row added fuel to the rumors that Rob Walker had done a deal to buy and campaign a Scottish-blue-with-a-white-stripe-around-its-nose Rob Walker Racing Ferrari 156 for Stirling during the upcoming Formula One season. That was a stunning development considering the long-standing rift between Moss and Ferrari. Not to mention that Ferrari hadn't sold a Formula One car to a privateer team for many, many years (and, even then, it was always last year's "old nail"). You can bet there was plenty of chatter about it in the Sebring paddock and press room.

As always, there were several dark-horse challengers squared off against the favored Ferraris. Briggs Cunningham had brought his somewhat unloved Maserati Tipo 64 with a widened-up radiator opening for better cooling for drivers Walt Hansgen and Dr. Dick Thompson. Plus a Maserati 4-cylinder dropped into a Cooper Monaco with tailfin-style rear bodywork (imagine a shrunken-down '57 DeSoto) for Bruce McLaren and Roger Penske. In spite of the usual, excellent preparation by Alf Momo and the Cunningham team, neither car seemed likely to go the distance. Or at least not without problems along the way. Meanwhile our young yachting host Count Giovanni had a new-style Tipo 64 Maserati for Vacarella/Abate with gun-turret exhausts and a strange, shovel-nosed front end that supposedly improved the aerodynamics (the Scuderia Serenissima mechanics were cutting large holes in it and fashioning crude scoops by the end of first practice to help keep the engine temperatures down) plus a 250 SWB Berlinetta in the GT category for Colin Davis/Fernand Tavano. Count Giovanni had also bought the previous year's winning Testa Rossa from Ferrari before their falling out, and with dapper Swiss ace Joakim Bonnier and comingman Italian-by-way-of-Belgium Lucien Bianchi handling the driving for him at Sebring, it looked like a genuine threat if the factory Ferraris—and particularly the Moss/Ireland car—hit trouble.

Jim Hall had entered a pair of Chaparrals with supposedly reduced capacity, 4.0-liter Chevy engines in the "Challenge Mondial" experimental class that the organizers at Sebring, Le Mans and the Nurburgring had thrown in to give the crowd-pleasing, big-inch sports/prototypes a place to run. Also entered in the "experimental" class was the NASCAR-ized Fairway Flyer out of Harlon Lee's North Carolina stock car shop that Bob Wright had told me about in Fairway Tower. But although it was listed on the entry sheet, it hadn't arrived yet and visions of the chaotic and frankly embarrassing Pontiac showing at Daytona came immediately to mind. The Pontiac Tempests were also on the entry list at Sebring, but they never showed up. And probably wisely so.

Among the smallbore sports/racers we had a nicely-turned-out Porsche RS60 in the hands of American privateers Bruce Jennings, Frank Rand and Bill Wuesthoff—all smart, quick, solid drivers—two of Elva's incredibly low and pretty Mk. 6 sports/racers entered in the 1150cc Sports class (they looked like terrific cars for club racing, but I questioned whether they were stout enough for a race like Sebring) and one of Colin Chapman's brand-new Lotus 23s entered by New Jersey Lotus dealer Sy Kaback. The sleek, slippery 23 had just been introduced at the London racing car show in January, and everyone was anticipating great things from it. But it arrived too late to make the show. I was personally rooting for the svelte little O.S.C.A. that my friend/fellow-scribe Denise McCluggage was sharing with Allen Eager in the 1150cc Sports class. They'd come through to win the big-bore GT category outright and take 10th overall the previous year in Denise's own Ferrari Berlinetta, and I always considered her an exceptional—and exceptionally smart—racing driver. She could run even-up with most of the men (and I'm talking everybody south of Moss and Gurney here) plus she was a hell of a writer and always one of the best interviews in the paddock. She just had so many interests—not just sports car racing—along with a rare knack for putting things into words. And not a whole lot of words, either. I hated her for that....

Carlo Sebastian had sold off the Berlinetta Le Mans Speciale Aerodinamico to a privateer team after Daytona (I mean, who needed it now that the GTO was here?) and at Sebring it was entered by a low-key but obviously bucks-up bunch from Maryland that called itself "Scuderia Bear." Ed Hugus and George Reed were handling the car—still wearing the same, ice blue-with-white paint scheme as when Moss won with it at Daytona—and somebody had stuck a cute little stuffed teddy bear in a red racing suit and a helmet made out of a ping-pong ball on top of the dashboard. And right there you had the difference between the cheeky, fun-loving amateurs and the serious factory teams.

We had a fat handful of Corvettes entered in the "Over 4-liter" GT class at Sebring, and the best of them figured to be the supposedly-independent "factory" pair out of Grady Davis' stable. But they would probably have a fight on their hands with the well-prepared and garishly painted "Purple People Eater" Corvette out of ace wrench Ronnie Kaplan's Nickey Chevrolet shop in Chicago. They had Bob Johnson and Indy 500 star Rodger Ward sharing the driving, so it looked to be a pretty serious effort. Briggs Cunningham brought a nicely turned out but still-under-development Jaguar XKE for himself and the experienced and cagey John Fitch, and I picked them to still be around (and most likely well up the order) come the end of the 12 hours. And of course we had Ian Snell and Tommy Edwards in Clive Stanley's Imperial Tea-green Aston Zagato. But bigger motors or not, none of the Corvettes, Jag or Aston entries figured to so much as sniff the exhaust off the top Ferrari Berlinettas. Let alone Enzo's stunning new GTO.

The Porsche factory sent over a pair of dull silver Abarth Carreras aimed squarely at the Category 2 World Manufacturers' Championship points that were up for grabs at Sebring. They weren't taking any chances on driving talent, either, with Dan Gurney and American Porsche ace Bob Holbert in the #48 car. They were both fast, savvy drivers who knew what it took to win at a race like Sebring. Their so-called "opposition" included a factory-backed, three-car team of MGAs and a similarly official squadron of four Sunbeam Alpines entered by the Rootes Group, including one for well-known West Coast racers Ken Miles and Lew Spencer. There was also a semi-factory Elva Courier (I think Elva importer Carl Haas paid the entry fee, and that, at least to some folks, made it a "factory" car) and no less than three squat, stubby TVR Grantura coupes, which looked like chubby little hop-toads to me and were manufactured two or three at a time in a modest garage in Blackpool. As my ace race-mechanic friend Buddy Palumbo always used to say: anybody with a welder and a pile of scrap steel can go into the car manufacturing business in England. All you need to do is hang out a shingle. In any case, none of them looked like they had a ghost of a chance against the Porsche factory's Abarth Carreras, but I thought the #55 TVR looked pretty damn quick though the esses during first practice. I found out later that the driver was a young mechanical engineer from New Jersey named Mark Donohue. My friend Buddy had seen him in a couple club races and told me to keep an eye on him, and no question the kid was good. In fact, I thought he might actually have some kind of future in the business if he stuck with it and got a few breaks. And stopped trying to beat the blessed Porsche factory team with some off-brand, MG-powered English hybrid....

In the 1300cc GT class, we had another entertaining skirmish brewing again between Alfa Romeo's charming Giulietta SZs and Colin Chapman's lovely little Lotus Elites. The pretty little SZs had become real personal favorites of mine. And they made a wonderful noise! In fact, you could recognize an Alfa's crackling, snarling exhaust note over most of the other cars—even the Ferraris!—and you had to love the SZ's slippery, pumpkinseed silhouette. But I was also partial to Colin Chapman's intriguing little Elite, which was about as sweet and petite a GT coupe as anyone had ever seen. And typically Champmanesque, what with an all-fiberglass monocoque chassis instead of a conventional, welded-up metal frame. Most insiders figured that the twin-cam, 1290cc Alfas made more raw power than the single-stick, 1220cc Climax engines in the Elites, but the Lotus looked a bit lighter, poked a smaller hole in the air and was arguably more supple through fast, sweeping corners. Chapman was a certified genius when it came to chassis and suspension design, and everybody knew it. Even so, I liked the Alfas' chances at Sebring. The Elites looked typically a bit fragile for a long, punishing race. And the Alfas were just the opposite. In fact, they seemed to thrive when both the track and their own drivers beat the living piss out of them....

The rest of the paddock was littered with the usual Sebring confusion of tiddlers, no-hopers, middleweights, makeweights, spear carriers and class- or team-trophy hopefuls in their usual, odd-lot assortment of club-racer AC Bristols, Triumph TR4s, Healey Sprites and Morgan Super Sports plus a cute little "factory entry" Fiat Abarth 850S all the way from Italy.

Sebring is an entirely different place after dark, and everybody gets really charged up for night practice on Thursday evening. Particularly the drivers who've never been there before and the boisterous, animated and generally over-served crowd in the Sebring infield. Especially the ones swarming all over the teeming human anthill of Green Park near the hairpin. Plus there was a wild card this particular Thursday evening since heavy rain was in the forecast, although most of the local meteorological pundits figured it wouldn't hit until well after midnight. Or, in other words, when the great majority of the Green Park revelers would either be long passed out or well past caring. You only hoped none of them would drown, since they occasionally come to rest face-down and the puddles at Sebring can get deep in a hurry. Sure enough the western horizon looked thick, dark and threatening as the cars started lining up on the false grid a little before dusk.

Night practice at Sebring is an unbelievable show. The sunset fades quickly as you get down close to the equator, and the darkness that settles in behind it is alive with a noisy fireworks display of bright, sweeping headlight and driving light beams, streaming red tail lights, brake discs glowing molten orange inside the spinning wheels and crackling, flaming exhaust pyrotechnics as cars downshift for the corners. And it's all played out against an echoing cacophony of internal-combustion howls, roars, screams, blares, rasps, snorts, snarls, barks and hollow, V8 gut-rumbles that will become as familiar and identifying as car number and color scheme by the end of 12 hours. It's an amazing thing to witness, and quite a show for the spectators.

I usually try to watch night practice from the restricted, photographer-pass-only area next to the Turn One corner station a hundred yards or so past Pit Out and also from the far opposite end of the start/finish straightaway where you can catch the cars skittering their way over the uneven concrete expanse of Sunset Bend. A lot of drivers will tell you that it's a wrestling match through there because of the rough surface or gripe that "there's no right line through it" because there's so damn much pavement available. But both spots are great places to try some "arty" nighttime shots (if one in five hundred comes out, I consider myself lucky) and in between I can wander up and down pit lane and watch the crews flailing away at assorted mechanical disasters or fiddle with the headlight and driving light alignment after drivers who have never done Sebring before come in with eyes wide as fried eggs and complain—usually with a bit of urgency—that they can't see a damn thing! And of course that's the problem with Sebring at night. You can put all the blessed candlepower you want on the front of your racecar, but if there's nothing for it to reflect off of, it's like shining a flashlight up into an empty, pitch-black sky. Experienced teams learn to "cross" their driving lights to illuminate the edges of the track up ahead and point the regular hi-beams kind of halfway towards the horizon. But not too far, or the light will lose contact with the pavement and the drivers won't be able to see anything but a bottomless pit of darkness up ahead! Like Tommy and Cal both told me, you just have to get used to the idea that you can't see much of anything at night at Sebring—particularly if you find yourself running on your own out there—and drivers need to rely on a combination of feel, rhythm, paint lines, tar strips and old rubber streaks and pavement scars to keep themselves on line and going in the right direction. It's not an easy thing to do—especially for first-timers—and lots of drivers have gone off without realizing it and found themselves lost out there in the darkness. "You only know you've gone off because you can't see other cars any more and notice bloody weeds growing up through the pavement cracks and tar strips," I overheard Tommy telling Audrey, "and sometimes you have to simply wait for another car to come around so you can follow its bloody taillights back to the circuit!"

James Britten sent Ian out first so he could get his brain wrapped around the track while dusk was still fading rather than just pitch him out into full darkness and hope that he didn't collect anything while he was learning his way around at night. But of course he managed to loop it into Turn One on his second lap. Turn One at Sebring is a daunting, high-speed sweeper that funnels down from five or six lanes wide to just a single proper line, and it's totally blind even in broad daylight. It's also absolutely key to a respectable lap time as well as one of the prime overtaking opportunities at Sebring. It's a corner that intimidates many, but also punishes those who aren't smart enough to be intimidated.

Fortunately Ian didn't hit anything just spun around a few times but he brought the car in to have it checked over and to replace the tires he'd managed to flat spot. But James refused to give him another set. *"You were supposed to be bloody well scrubbing that set in for the race!"* he growled at Ian. *"Those were brand new tires!"*

Ian stared straight forward and didn't say a thing. As soon as James pulled his head out of the side window, Ian stuck the car in gear and pulled away. You could hear the flap-flap-flap of the flat spots as Clive Stanley's Aston headed down pit lane and accelerated back onto the circuit.

"He's a bloody impetuous little shit, isn't he," James Britten groused to no one in particular. I watched Clive Stanley stiffen a bit as his Imperial Crown Tea Aston Zagato disappeared around Turn One.

"He just doesn't have any bloody patience," Tommy muttered under his breath. "He'd be better off trying to kill himself with a bloody formula car. Probably kill a few other blokes off in the process...."

I climbed up on the timing stand Peter and Georgie had nailed together out of some old grandstand seating planks and a few 2x4s and sat down next to Audrey. She had a pillow underneath her and James had set her up with a pair of hooded instrument lights over her timing board, and she noticed the new, small band-aid on my index finger immediately. "I see your field injury seems to have healed up quite nicely since this morning."

"It's the same way with Christmas presents: it's not so much what's inside but the size of the package that impresses people."

"I think you were just looking for sympathy."

"And what if I was?"

"Then you're no different from any other man...just stupidly honest about it."

I could see she was concentrating pretty hard on trying to keep track of all the Category 1 GT entries in the fading light after sundown. And that meant all the various Ferrari Berlinettas, Carlo Sebastian's new GTO, all the Corvettes, the Cunningham E-Type and of course Clive Stanley's Aston. She was also trying to figure out from the helmets which drivers were at the wheel as the cars grumbled down pit lane and headed out into the advancing darkness.

"That's a lot to keep track of," I observed over her shoulder.

"Oh, it's not too bad," she answered without looking up. "It's only fourteen cars, and the laps are well over three minutes here."

"Are you having any trouble telling the cars apart?"

"It's a little hard to sort out some of the Corvettes and Ferrari Berlinettas because they all look and sound so much alike. But I should be on top of it by the time the session is over."

I had no doubt that she would. Some of the teams helped out by putting little amber or green or blue marker lights on the tops or fenders to distinguish them from similar cars. But other teams didn't bother, and it was easy to get confused.

"I had one of the Grady Davis Corvettes turning a 2:14 a moment ago," Audrey laughed. "But I'm fairly certain it was two separate cars."

"Either that or he just knocked over a minute off the track record!"

"He might have taken a bit of a shortcut," Tommy offered from behind us. "I know drivers who've done that on purpose."

"Oh?"

"Oh, absolutely," Tommy nodded. "It takes a bit of planning, but you can kill the lights and sneak off on the little access road after the end of Turn One if no other cars are around you."

"What on earth for?"

"Well, if you follow it around to the right for a bit, you can slip back on again just before the back straight."

"And why would anyone want to do that?"

A mischievous little grin spread across Tommy's face. "Because if you time it just right, you can have people thinking you're one hell of a lot quicker than you really are."

"But won't the corner workers call it in?"

"Of course they will!" Tommy laughed. "But the teams up and down pit row won't know about it." And that included your own team. And your own teammate, of course....

Tommy Edwards looked over Audrey's shoulder to see the time as Ian and the Aston sped by again, sounding absolutely glorious. Although you could hear the staccato patter off the flat-spotted tires underneath the hard, hollow blare of the Aston's exhaust. Audrey looked at Ian's lap time and frowned. "That's faster than he went this afternoon."

Tommy frowned, too. "He really shouldn't be trying so bloody hard."

"Hey," I reminded him, "racing drivers are supposed to go fast."

"Of course they are," Tommy growled, "but they don't have to be bloody stupid about it."

James Britten had his own stopwatch in hand, and immediately yelled for Georgie to hold out the "PIT" sign the next time Ian came around.

"Looks like it's time to go to work," Tommy sighed like it was all terribly boring. But there was still plenty of time. It would be another three-and-a-half minutes before Ian got the "PIT" sign and then, assuming he saw it in the jumbled, bright-lights-and-deep-shadows confusion of pit lane, it would be another three-and-a-half minutes before he came in. And a guy like Ian might well pretend to not see it for a lap or two.

"Why would he do that?" Audrey wanted to know.

"Sometimes a driver feels like he's really getting into a groove—like everything's really starting to come together—and they just want to keep it going for awhile longer."

She made a face. "They're like little boys who want to stay out and chase fireflies after their mother calls them in for dinner."

"Sometimes they just want to keep their bloody teammate out of the car," Tommy laughed as he pulled on his helmet.

A few minutes later Ian came storming down pit lane and brought the Aston to a panting, slithering halt right in front of us. He leaped out of the car and then waited, hair-trigger, for Tommy to jump inside. James had told them to practice their driver changes every time they switched over during practice, and Ian was obviously trying to impress James and Clive with his sense of urgency. But Tommy wasn't having any of it. He sauntered leisurely over to the Aston and paused right in front of Ian to give each of his driving gloves a fussy and exaggerated final tug and folding them fastidiously over the cuffs of his coveralls before easing himself elegantly inside. And meanwhile Ian stood there damn near electrified looking desperately eager and tremendously foolish all at the same time. Tommy settled himself back into the seat and waited like an emperor being dressed as Ian flailed away at the lap belts. That accomplished, Tommy casually checked the adjustment of the rear-view mirror, pulled the door gently closed, fired up the big Aston six, selected first gear, eased out the clutch and trundled off down pit lane.

It was priceless.

And you couldn't miss the smirk of approval on James Britten's face.

Clive Stanley, on the other hand, looked a bit ashen.

"They're like the best of grown men and the worst of little boys all wrapped into one, aren't they?" Audrey observed under her breath.

"I never really thought about it that way."

"Of course not," she needled. "You're one of them."

"I'm not a driver," I said like it was a major distinction.

"No, but you're in with them. You're part of the cult and culture of it."

"Not true," I argued. "Not true at all. Drivers are, well, *different.*" I looked her in the eye. "You should know that as well as anybody."

Her face hardened. But just as quickly it softened again. "You know about that then, don't you? About Neal and the rest of it, I mean."

I nodded.

She took a short, sharp breath and exhaled. "Well, it's not any deep, hidden secret." She clicked off the Cunningham E-Type and wrote the time down. "But I'd just as soon my father didn't know. I mean, not know for certain..." she looked at me "...it's one of those things he knows but then he doesn't know, and I think things are better off that way. Do you understand?"

I assured her that I did.

"You'll be meeting him," she said with an airy certainty that surprised me. "You'll see that it's important to keep him..." I could sense her searching for the appropriate word "...on balance." It seemed to me like she wanted to say more, but nothing more was forthcoming. "You'll see for yourself," she finally left it. "You'll see."

We watched Phil Hill howl past in the new GTO. He was already comfortably quickest among the Category 1 GT cars, and looking typically relaxed and businesslike behind the wheel. "So," I asked as Audrey wrote the time down, "am I to assume you've sworn off of racing drivers?"

She thought it over for a moment. "Let's just say I've discovered it's not terribly smart to let yourself get too close to them."

"But you still enjoy going to the races, don't you?"

"Oh, I *love* the races," she answered with unmistakable enthusiasm. "But only if I'm working them. I don't think I'd ever want to go again as a driver's girl. It's just too nerve-wracking. And I've no interest whatsoever in becoming a spectator."

"Being on the inside is important," I quickly agreed. "Once you know what that feels like, you could never stand life on the far side of the fences."

"I honestly don't know what spectators see in it."

"Oh, they love the cars and the heroes and the spectacle and competition," I argued. "It's thrilling and colorful and exciting to them."

"It's noisy, boring and dangerous is more like it."

"Then why do you go?"

"Well, to start with, it's a fantastic opportunity to get the bloody hell away from everything else! It's a chance to escape from all your dreary, everyday responsibilities and routines..." she curled her lip under as she thought about it "...a chance to get wound up in something—to be a *part* of something—that feels so terribly, stupidly, desperately important."

"I know exactly what you mean."

Audrey looked at me with her eyes all lit up. "It's marvelous to try something truly difficult, isn't it? Something brash and challenging and perhaps just a wee, small bit antisocial..." she offered up a conspiratorial smile "...The kind of thing most people never, ever get a chance to try."

"Yes, it is," I agreed. "In fact, it's a privilege."

"But you don't want to let it get too close," she added carefully. "You have to be wary of that part."

"How so?"

"Other people..." I could see she was searching for the right words again "... other people tend to *complicate* things...." She regarded me with a detached, almost clinical expression. "And it's not just drivers, Hank. It's all kinds of other people. They can make things difficult if you let them get too close."

"That's a pretty bleak outlook, isn't it?"

"I'm just being practical, Hank. Sure, every little girl daydreams about some gallant white knight who's going to appear out of nowhere and whisk her away. But you learn to set those fairytale notions aside as you grow older."

"You could be just shutting yourself off after a bad experience."

"Maybe I am, but I don't think so. You need to protect yourself, Hank. I work very hard at being self-sufficient, and the heart of that is learning to see things and be content with things as they are. You don't want to deceive yourself with silly romantic notions or impossible visions of the future."

"Isn't that what life's for?"

She shook her head. "It doesn't work like that. You let people inside and they go banging through your life slamming doors and leaving windows open and dropping their bloody socks all over the floor and...and..."

I waited for more, but nothing came. "So then what happens?"

Audrey looked down at the chart in front of her. "...And then they're gone, Hank. Just like that." She gave her shoulders a tiny, helpless shrug, straightened herself up and clicked a watch as Rodger Ward bellowed past in the Purple People Eater Corvette. You couldn't miss the iridescent-purple paint scheme—even at night—or that Ronnie Kaplan's engine sounded a bit healthier than most of the Chevy V8s at Sebring. And in its wake we had another of those eerie, hollow silences when no cars were passing on the pit straight and all we could hear were the clank of tools and two of the Scuderia Serenissima mechanics yelling back and forth at each other in Italian. And beyond that, the echoes, howls and screams of racing cars clawing their way around in the darkness.

"So tell me a little more about drivers," I asked like I was researching a story.

"Oh, you know how they are..."

"Not from a woman's perspective."

She looked at me kind of sideways.

"No, really," I insisted. "I ought to know these things..."

"You're not just being nosy?"

"Of course I'm being nosy. That's what writers do. Only we like to lie and call it 'research.'"

That earned me a smile. And an answer:

"I've met a few drivers over the years," she started in cautiously, "and it's terribly easy to be drawn in by them."

"Oh?"

"Of course it is. They're young and aggressive and confident and a lot of them are genuinely charming..."

"Rich, too," I reminded her.

"Rich, too," she agreed.

"And every girl harbors a secret desire for the bad boy, don't they?"

"We do?"

"Sure you do! It's always the lure of the outlaw hero. The renegade bandit. The swashbuckling pirate. The irresistible scoundrel...."

"You really ought to be writing romance novels," Audrey laughed. "You'd make a bloody fortune."

"You think?"

"Not a question about it!"

I felt myself blush.

But then her face turned serious again. "Reality is a long way from romance, Henry. Racing drivers can be particularly confounding that way."

"Oh?"

She nodded. "You see all their bravery and skill and self-possession out on a racetrack and you start believing it has something to do with character. But it doesn't. Many of them are selfish, tiresome and immature once you get them away from the racetrack."

I knew that part was true. A lot of racers were genuine heroes of mine and had the code and conduct to back it up. But even they could be self-centered, narcissistic, rude, childish, edgy and even downright flaky once you really got to know them. And still others were haunted, detached and tormented. Like until you could see death itself floating in their eyes. Many didn't sleep well and couldn't sit still when they were away from the racing. Others acted bored, dissatisfied and disdainful. They were almost all terribly impatient and not many knew how to relax. And a remarkably large number were just plain spoiled. You had to have money to go racing, and so a lot of drivers (although certainly not all) came from sizable family fortunes. Money and especially old, multi-generational money can give a person an unbecoming sense of privilege and entitlement. I'd seen it. And none of them let other people inside.

"You have to be especially careful of the funny, charming ones that are such good company," Audrey continued with a knowing smile.

"Why is that?"

"They'll bloody well suck you in," she sighed. "And that's when you discover that the fun ones aren't steady and the steady ones simply aren't fun." She clicked off Tommy's time and gave it a satisfied nod of approval. "Besides," she concluded as she wrote down his time, "I already have a life. I have my obligations and responsibilities and routines to attend to...."

"Do you like it?" I interrupted.

"Like what?"

"Your life? Do you like it the way it is, I mean?"

"Who can say they like their life just as it is?" she scoffed. "Can you?"

"I suppose I like it well enough."

"There's nothing you would change? Nothing you'd have better?"

I had to laugh. "Of course there is. Everybody has aspirations."

"And what difference does it make anyway? You are who you are and you do what you do and that's just the way things have worked out for you." You had to love the confusion of defiant determination and utter resignation mixed up in her voice. Or I did, anyway. "Tell me," she asked out of nowhere, "how well do we know one another?"

It took me a moment to answer. "I'm really not sure," I finally admitted. "It seems like—feels like—I know you better than I probably do."

"It feels that way to me, too," she agreed cautiously. "It seems, I don't know, *comfortable...*" I wanted to hear more, of course, but a whole gaggle of Category 1 cars including two of the slower Corvettes, Hill's GTO, the Cunningham E-Type and the Serenissima Berlinetta came pounding out of Sunset Bend all mixed up with the Morgan, one of the Carrera Abarths, the Elva Courier, a DB, an Alfa SZ, one of the Chaparrals hammering past all of them, Denise McCluggage in the little O.S.C.A. and one of the TVR Granturas. Audrey expertly clicked off the four Category 1 cars and wrote the times down on her chart. "If you're lucky," she continued without looking up, "you get to do some of the things you enjoy in life—some of the things that make you feel worthwhile—and you put up with the rest so you can look yourself in the eye in your mirror every morning." Her face turned up to mine. "Isn't that the way it is?"

"Yeah," I had to agree, "I suppose it is."

"That's why I'm better off keeping the team and the races as a place to run off to," she continued matter-of-factly, "as a bit of an escape hatch from the rest of my life. It works out better for me that way."

"So no more getting involved with racing people?" I asked like the question was completely hypothetical.

She gave me an unexpectedly dirty smile. "I often say 'no,' Hank..." she grinned, "...But I never say 'never'...."

Tommy came howling out of Sunset Bend in the Aston, and you couldn't miss the shocked expression on Audrey's face as she clicked off the time. "That's *very* bloody quick," she almost gasped. I looked over her shoulder and it *was* bloody quick.

Suspiciously bloody quick, in fact.

"Do you think he took that shortcut he was talking about?" Audrey whispered under her breath.

My eyes wandered out to where James, Clive and Ian were standing along the pit wall with the two mechanics. They were all staring down at the stopwatch in Peter Bryant's hand. Ian, in particular, looked visibly shaken. "If he did," I observed with a glow of satisfaction, "he made a damn good job of it...."

"He can do that sort of thing," she nodded approvingly.

I looked over at her. "So how about Tommy?"

"What about him?"

"Oh, come on. Anyone with eyes can see it."

Her expression stiffened. "That's a bit private, isn't it?"

"I'm not trying to pry..."

"Of course you are!" she snapped. But I couldn't tell if she was needling me or dead serious. I'm not sure if she really knew, either. "Look," she finally answered, "there are lots of things you want to do in this life that you bloody well shouldn't...."

"And Tommy was one of them?"

She didn't say anything. But I could feel her wrestling with it. "Tommy's a great bloke," she finally continued, "I find him tremendously attractive in many ways, and he can be terribly good company when he puts his mind to it." She took a quick breath and slowly exhaled. "But you've got to look on the sensible side, Hank. See if it could work out. I mean, look at the age difference. Look at my own life and responsibilities. Look at what would probably lay ahead for us...."

"That's awfully practical, isn't it?"

"You need to be practical, Hank. It keeps you from being disappointed."

I wanted to say *'and that's your goal in life: to not be disappointed?'* but I held my tongue. Sometimes knowing what not to say is more important than knowing what to say.

As if on cue, Tommy came trundling down pit lane, gave the crew a perfunctory thumbs-up and turned Clive Stanley's Aston into the paddock. He'd only done a handful of laps, but that last one was going to have Ian Snell muttering to himself long into the night. I watched as Audrey started gathering up her watches, pencils and lap chart.

"So are we heading into the infield tonight?"

"I wouldn't miss it!" she beamed. "I've got my safari hat ready."

That night I took Audrey on the Official Grand Tour of the Sebring infield from what I have always considered to be the best seat in the house. There's a narrow path that runs along the inner perimeter of the circuit between the pavement and the spectator fences, and official vehicles use it throughout the weekend to move track personnel, relief corner crews, safety vehicles, wreckers and shuttles full of credentialed photographers around the circuit. Most people don't even know it's there. You're supposed to need special clearance to use it, but I knew a few people from the local SCCA region who helped put the race on every year—particularly a big, funny Irishman named John Anderson, who was well known for the camp-stove spaghetti dinners he made for all comers every Friday night at the 12 Hours—and he arranged for Audrey and me to hitch a ride on the justly infamous "Fun Bus" that toured that perimeter path around the infield every year after Thursday's night practice. On highly official track business, of course!

Now the Fun Bus was one of the rare and unusual types of mongrel automotive machinery that you run into all the time at Sebring. Starting who knows when and for reasons no one will ever fully understand, the infield at Sebring has become magnet, Mecca and even elephant graveyard for a unique subspecies of stripped-down, cobbled-up, thrown-together and often garishly and/or crudely painted vehicles that exist in a half-life limbo somewhere between junkyard scrap and parade float. It's a better show than the race some years! Most are large, chuffing, graffiti-covered older-model Detroit convertibles with sagging springs and shot mufflers, and they're inevitably crammed full of wisecracking, beer-in-hand college kids with sunburned faces and terribly bloodshot eyes. They creep along at barely a walking pace, rusted-out rocker panels almost scraping the ground while bass-fuzzed, Top

40 radio hits blare through blown-out speakers. The tops are down, of course (or, if the car happened to start out as a sedan, the tops have simply—although not necessarily neatly—been cut off with a blow torch or saber saw) and many of the trunk lids have been removed so Salvation Army Store pillows, couches and love seats can be crammed inside like reversed rumble seats. There are always a lot of them at Sebring—some wearing latex house-paint flame jobs, scallops or zebra stripes, some with propellers or outboard motors on the back—and a few are left behind as little more than charred remains come Sunday morning.

You also see a few stripped-to-nothing old VW Beetles scooting around the Sebring infield beach-buggy style with all the fenders, doors and bumpers removed and all the window glass broken out. And there's always a couple open-air, wicker-seat Fiat Jollys, a fat handful of war-surplus Jeeps (some with ill-advised V8 conversions), a flatbed truck or two converted into an alfresco living room complete with overstuffed chairs, sofas, tables and floor lamps bolted to the bed. And it wouldn't be Sebring without a ghoulishly painted retired hearse or two.

But the "Fun Bus" was something special even among this august company. It started out as a locally owned 1948 International KB-2 pickup truck that had been pressed into service as a tow vehicle for the very first Sebring race on New Years' Eve of 1950. It had been rented for the weekend from a local citrus grower, and had already served heavy duty in the neighboring orange groves. Especially during harvest time. It was ultimately bought outright after the fruit farmer was driven out of business following a disastrous spring frost, and the aging International did regular maintenance duty at the track and worked every single race at Sebring right through the eleventh hour of Ferrari's very first victory there with Phil Hill and Peter Collins in 1958. But something inside the transmission case broke that night, leaving the International with nothing but 1st and Reverse gears. Which, given the ratios, limited its top speed in either direction to something like 8 or 10mph. And the grating, grinding noises coming from inside that poor transmission sounded very desperate indeed. But it still ran—gnashing sounds and all—and that made it plenty good enough for after-hours Infield Tour service. Somewhere along the line, a couple of the maintenance shop regulars unbolted the doors and cut off the top with a torch and a grinding wheel—watch that you don't cut your finger off there!—and then some self-styled Florida *carrozzeria* added on an additional section of pickup bed from another junked International so the tailgate extended nearly eight feet behind the rear wheels. If you put enough people back there, you could bring the front wheels right up off the ground! Or at least you could after they pulled the hood, windshield frame and front fenders off to make the nose a little lighter. A pair of longtime Sebring volunteer emergency workers named Roy and Steve borrowed some yellow safety paint and a well-used push broom from the maintenance shop the Sunday after the 1960 race and painted the Fun Bus a particularly streaked, splotchy and bug be-spotted shade of school-bus yellow. The weekend before the next race they threw a bunch of old mattresses in back to give potential passengers something cushy to sit on. Or lie on. Or pass out on. They finished it all off by bolting a couple aircraft landing lights and a rotating red Mars light in where the grille would have been if it had such a thing, and added a loud and extremely abrasive ah-ooh-gah horn on the front cowling. And that, dear friends, became the semi-official, known-only-to-track-insiders Fun Bus that toured the perimeter of the infield every year after night practice....

By the time Audrey and I caught up with it, the Fun Bus was already idling at the end of pit lane and loaded chock-full of laughing, chattering race officials, track volunteers, safety crews and corner workers in "worker whites," plus two enormous coolers of beer and several huge thermos jugs full of wicked rum-and-cokes with lime, wickeder yet Mai Tais and a strange, murky-green concoction known as "Okefenokee Swamp Water," which smelled a bit like mineral spirits but tasted more like kerosene mixed with linseed oil and pond scum. It was obvious that quite a bit had already been consumed, and an energetic group on the very back end of the Fun Bus was bouncing up and down in heaving, dysfunctional unison, trying to make the front wheels lift off the ground. But of course there were way too many people up ahead of the rear axle centerline to make it work. Although it was apparent that they were putting an impressive amount of flex into the frame....

To be honest, it didn't really look like there was any room left for Audrey and me. But a big, brassy-looking strawberry blonde wearing worker whites and an awful lot of makeup screamed for us to: *"CLIMB ABOARD!!! CLIMB ABOARD!!! WE'RE GETTIN' READY T'WEIGH ANCHOR!!!"*

Instantly hands and arms we'd never known before were pulling and dragging us in over the gunwales. We bumped and jostled over heads, shoulders, knees, torsos, laps and feet until we finally found ourselves scrunched together in a crowded elbow-, shoulder- and-gut-lined corner just behind the ragged, racer-tape-and-styrofoam-covered edges where the top had been cut off. There was laughing and shouting and even some singing going on all around us, and it was apparent that the beer cooler and the thermos jugs had already seen some fairly heavy service. Needless to say, the Fun Bus was a pretty damn entertaining place to be after night practice at Sebring! And it got even better as we lurched out of pit lane (almost losing the big, brassy blonde over the side) and began our tour around the track. We waved and shouted at all the tents, Airstream trailers, campers and motorhomes parked along the pit straight between Pit Out and Corner One, and the people there waved and hooted right back at us. After which a few good-natured moons were exchanged in both directions. Some right over our heads, in fact. Audrey did her best to ignore it, of course, but some things are difficult to ignore. And meanwhile, back on the tailgate, an exultant male falsetto backed up by an enthusiastic (if somewhat off-key) chorus of tenors, basses and baritones stumbled their way through an endlessly repeating version of Gene Chandler's popular Top 40 hit, *Duke of Earl.*

"This is quite a party!" Audrey shouted into my ear.

"You haven't seen anything yet," I told her as the guy behind us pushed two large paper cups of Okefenokee Swamp Water into our hands. I took a gulp and felt a flash of slimy, citrus sour in my mouth followed by an electrified burn all the way down. I gave Audrey a nod like I'd just had a pleasant swallow of holiday eggnog. So she took a sip. And her eyes grew instantly larger. "This is *terrible!*" she almost gasped.

"It gets better the more you have!" the guy behind us laughed.

And you know what?

He was right.

If they gave out awards for strange and unusual behavior, many of the top plaques and medals would surely be presented in the infield at Sebring every year. And particularly around Green Park, which sits on the far side of a narrow, rickety, damn-near-45 degree-angle up/damn-near-45 degree-angle down MG "Safety Fast" pedestrian bridge and extends all the way down to the hairpin and then all the way up to the hard, busy, right-left esses of the Webster chicane. It's a lot of acreage, and on race weekend it's packed chock-full of tents, campers and motorhomes and an awful lot of people looking to have a good time. And the seriously over-loaded, alcohol-fueled bed of the Fun Bus was a great place to see it from. Who-ever was driving kept the red Mars light rotating in the grille and the ah-ooh-gah horn blasting like a fog horn now and then, and strange hands and arms were con-stantly passing around refills of whatever you were drinking back on the mattresses in the pickup bed. The only things you had to worry about were the occasional nose, heel or elbow in your ear, spilled Okefenokee Swamp Water that might burn through light clothing like battery acid or your legs falling asleep from people you hardly knew sitting, kneeling or standing on them. Or banging your head off the metal sides of the pickup bed as the Fun Bus bounced, lurched and jostled its way along the occasionally rough path outside the spectator fences. There were shouts, guffaws, hollers, shrieks of laughter and plenty of loud music—some of it from ac-tual live bands with makeshift stages, huge speakers and amplifiers—and even oc-casional, semi-horrified screams coming out of the shadowy jumble of bodies, awnings, lanterns, flashlight beams, party lights and leaping, crackling bonfires in Green Park. The pulse and energy of it all throbbed right through you. And there was so much to see....

Audrey and I agreed that our favorite had to be the guy who'd towed a large sail-boat on a trailer into the Sebring infield parked it right along the spectator fencing just a little ways up from the hairpin. And I mean a full-sized sloop with a cabin and a big, tall spike of a mast and a deep, sweeping keel that put the boat's deck a good ten or twelve feet off the ground. And that's where he and his lady friend (if she was indeed a lady?) stayed for the entire weekend. They came out in the evening (and particularly on Thursday for night practice) to stand on the deck in full yachting attire—he in blue blazer, white pants, deck shoes, silk ascot and captain's cap, "she" in a flowing chiffon gown—to sip champagne from fluted glasses and marvel diffidently at all the people staring and gawking at them.

"You don't see *that* every day," I observed.

"I'm not sure I'm seeing it now," Audrey marveled, and we both had to laugh.

By this time the big, brassy blonde was up on the wheel well engaged in a desperate, groping, near-suffocating embrace with some equally huge, white-clad track worker with a scraggly beard and an orange rubber pylon on top of his head like a dunce cap. It looked like they had at least four sets of hands and arms working between them, and they were just about impossible to ignore. Especially after they melted into a sloppy-wet kiss that made him tilt his head a little to get a little better tongue angle and dumped his rubber-pylon dunce cap squarely into our laps. But neither of them seemed to notice. And meanwhile the off-key tenor, bass, falsetto and baritone chorus on the tailgate had surged into a repetitive, don't-really-know-all-the-words rendition of The Corsairs' nifty new doo-wop hit, *Smoky Places.*

Further on past the hairpin, some obvious Sebring regulars had set up a sort of outdoorsy country-western bar complete with a trucked-in bandstand, jukebox, colored lights, beer signs, bar, bar stools and even a full-size slate pool table. "That looks like quite an operation," Audrey observed.

"They're here every year," I told her. "We can go over later if you like. The band's usually pretty good if you like Country-Western music."

"I like it fine," Audrey smiled. "But I'm not sure I'd be up to it tonight." She nodded in the general direction of her paper cup. As if on cue, a thermos jug passed over our heads and tilted to fill us up again.

"Oh, it'll be fun," I needled. "There might even be a fight."

"I think this is probably close enough for me. I tend to be on the timid side."

"I don't believe that for an instant."

"You'd be very much surprised."

By this time we were well past the hairpin and heading into the right-left Webster chicane. The path was pretty rough through there, and the Fun Bus lurched and teetered and even scraped against the spectator fencing once or twice as the driver attempted to negotiate the ruts. The obvious conclusion was that he'd been sampling a little of the Okefenokee Swamp Water right along with the rest of us. And meanwhile the two people on the wheel well were still locked in a desperate, drunken kiss, oblivious to everything around them. Or maybe they just didn't care. "Don't they eventually have to come up for air?" Audrey asked clinically.

"Maybe they breathe through their ears?"

Just then the Fun Bus rocked through another, deeper ditch, and that sent the two of them sprawling all over us. The brassy blonde's head hit the side of the pickup bed with a hollow, resonating thud that you could hear over the laughter, shouts and music from the infield, the umpty-umpth chorus of *Smoky Places* coming from the tailgate and the omnipresent grinding, gnashing noises issuing from the Fun Bus' transmission.

"OW!" the big blonde yelped, looking drunkenly surprised and more than a little pissed off. She shook her fist in the general direction of the driver up ahead and hollered: *"HEY! TAKE IT EASY UP THERE, ASSHOLE!"* She rubbed the fresh bump on her head and added to no one in particular: "That's my fucking husband up there driving..." she looked at her hand to see if there was any blood "...the rat-bastard sonofabitch...."

Audrey and I fought to keep from laughing. But we couldn't help it. And after that we were just looking at each other. Like we were all alone, you know, even though there were people pressed in all around us. But it was like they weren't even there.

"Could I kiss you?" I heard myself ask.

"I don't know," she said like she wasn't really sure either. "Could you?"

It turned out that I could.

Chapter 10: A Dramatic Curtain-Raiser

I'm not exactly sure how I got back to the transient fruit-plucker motel after our Fun Bus tour on Thursday evening. Or how Audrey got back to her room at The Kenilworth, for that matter. I do know that Hal and his stuttering old Studebaker were long gone by that point in the evening. Like most folks in the journalism game, Hal was self-sufficient and pretty much a loner. And that meant he wasn't about to wait around for you on some kind of open-ended, worry-about-everybody-else's-damn-business basis. And he asked for and expected the same sort of treatment in return. To him (and to me, for that matter) the phrase "you're on your own" was the most basic, noble and welcome kind of social contract imaginable.

It turned out that Roy and Steve, the two emergency-crew guys, had a lot to do with getting us back to our respective hotel rooms. As did one of the track ambulances, which they pressed into service because it seemed less likely to get pulled over. Especially if they kept the lights and siren on. I foggily seemed to recall the warm, dreamy sensation of having Audrey cuddled up next to me on the gurney in back while an upside-down world wheeled past and the reflection of the rotating Mars light glistened through the rain droplets on the windows. It looked like Christmas.

Or maybe it was just a dream....

In any case, I awoke the following morning to an uncertain stomach, a splitting headache, the sour, acid taste of way too much Okefenokee Swamp Water on my tongue (imagine chewing on a lime rind) and the mellifluous tones of Hal yelling at me to get my ass the hell out of bed. "The bus for the track is leaving in ten minutes," he bellowed like a Marine sergeant, "and this ain't no Fun Bus, either."

"My head hurts."

"Of course your head hurts. That's what happens when amateurs go drinking."

"I don't feel so good."

"You don't smell so good, either. I'd take a shower if I was you."

"O-Okay," I nodded as I attempted to rock myself upright. I could feel my brain shudder and re-settle inside my cranium like a dish of jostled pudding. "What the hell time is it, anyway?"

"It's ten minutes before the fucking track bus leaves. That's all you need to know." But then he glanced at his wristwatch and corrected himself: "No, see, I'm lying again. It's down to nine minutes...."

It was clear Hal was taking a measure of sadistic pleasure from my condition.

I probed my temples with the tips of my fingers. "I think I need a couple aspirin and a Bromo Seltzer."

"You think that works?"

"Butch Bohunk used to swear by it."

"Who the hell is Butch Bohunk?"

"Oh, he's..." But there was no way I could go into it. Not the way I felt. So I just waved him off with a feeble: "...never mind."

I won't bore you with the sorry details of attempting to get myself showered, shaved in that oil slick-colored, jigsaw-puzzle of a mirror and more-or-less dressed. You know you're in trouble when you have a hard time getting your shirt buttoned properly or the laces on your tennis shoes tied. "Hey, my shoes are all wet," I grumbled to no one in particular.

"Of course your shoes are all wet," Hal said like it made perfect sense. Then he opened the front door to reveal a gray, dismal-looking morning with heavy rain pelting down into puddles like lakes in the parking lot.

"Jeez, did it rain last night?"

"It poured," Hal assured me. "Came down in fucking buckets a little after midnight." He shook his head. "Not that *you'd* know...."

I answered with a groan as I grabbed for my umbrella and track bag. But I hesitated at the doorway. The rain was really coming down, and I had to resist the urge to put my track bag and umbrella back down next to the door, untie my shoes, unbutton my shirt, take off my clothes and crawl back into bed with the covers pulled up over my eyebrows until sometime in mid-afternoon. But I knew I couldn't.

"You got your rain gear?" Hal asked.

I nodded.

"*Then let's go for it!*" he yelped, and bolted for the Studebaker. But of course I beat him there because of his bum leg, and then I had to wait while he struggled to unlock the door, folded his bad leg inside and only then reached over to unlock my side. By which time I was pretty well drenched. "I had a new set of keys made last summer," he explained triumphantly, "on account of I kept losing the old ones all the time." He held up a rabbit's foot keychain with two shiny new keys on it as proof. "But they never seemed to fit in and turn as good as the originals. You know how that is with keys and locks and mechanical things in general once the metal gets used to each other."

It wasn't great English, but I knew what he meant. "What happened to the originals?" I had to ask.

"Oh, I'm *savin'* those," he grinned expansively.

"What for?"

"Why, for if I ever lose these new ones!" He said like it made perfect sense. And I wasn't about to argue. Hal jammed his shiny new key in the ignition but had to jiggle it to get it to turn. Followed by the well-practiced ritual of coaxing his old Studebaker to life. Which was even tougher than usual on a cold, wet morning. It churned reluctantly against the starter before staggering to a coughing, stuttering semblance of life. Hal raced it gently to keep it running, and eventually it settled down to a steady, wheezing idle. Once satisfied that his old Studebaker was up to acceptable temperature, Hal stuck it in gear, got the wipers flapping, and sloshed us away. "You want any breakfast?" he asked as he swung the big old Land Cruiser out northbound on Highway 17.

I answered with a retching noise.

"Okay, then. We'll have something really greasy with butter and jelly and raw eggs and bacon all over it at the track..." he watched me wince with obvious satisfaction. "...then maybe top it off with a tall, refreshing glass of cold pork gravy..."

He kept it up like that all the way to the track, and as you can imagine I was feeling pretty rocky by the time we rolled into the paddock at a little past 7. Audrey was far luckier, since there were just two curtain-raiser races scheduled for Friday—a 3-hour enduro for under-1000cc production cars at 10am and a 25-lap Formula Junior race later on in the afternoon—and Clive and James decided not to even attend the final, 8am "emergency practice" for the 12 Hour because of the rain. All the local weathermen said the front would pass over by noon, and the balance of the weekend forecast looked clear, bright and sunny. So there was no point taking a chance and sending the Aston out in the wet just so the drivers could learn where the puddles and slick spots were. So Audrey got to sleep in. And I hated her for it. Although it sure would have been nice to be there with her....

I stopped by the press room for a few cups of coffee and a sticky sweet roll I probably would have been better off avoiding, and after that I put on my rain hat and poncho, grabbed my umbrella and went prowling around the paddock to see if I could walk off the rest of my hangover and maybe start feeling a little better. The sky was still drooling rain and the paddock looked gray, sad and empty that Friday morning, and everyone was huddled inside their trailers, holed up in their tow vehicles or standing around under sagging, waterlogged awnings waiting for the rain to pass. But even so I heard a few, scattered engines firing up for the 8am "emergency practice." Including a loud new voice that I knew I hadn't heard before. It was an American V8—no question about it—but no question it was a little leaner and harder-edged than the Chevy V8s in the Corvettes and Chaparrals. I figured it had to be that new Fairway Flyer "Challenger V8" out of Harlon Lee's stock car shop in Mooresville, a little ways north of Charlotte. The one Bob Wright had told me about on the 13th floor of Fairway Tower what seemed like a hundred years ago. I couldn't catch a glimpse of it as it headed for the false grid, but I could follow the sound with my ears, and decided to make my way over to the fences to watch it go by.

The rain had pretty much slacked off by then, but the track was still soaking with puddles of standing water everywhere. And the thing about standing water is that a driver never knows how deep it is without trying it. Sometimes it's not too deep and the tires squish right through to the pavement underneath and sometimes it's deep enough that the tires climb right up on top of it and the car goes skating merrily off like it's on greased ice. So not many cars ventured out on Friday morning.

Just those that had to because they had things to sort out plus a few late-arriving stragglers who'd never even seen the place before. And Harlon Lee's Fairway Flyer Challenger qualified on all counts. I saw from the entry list that they had Freddie Fritter and fellow stock-car ace Marvin Panch signed on to drive the thing (and Freddie had already showed what he could do in a sports car race at Daytona) but you had to wonder if the car was really ready. Every shop runs out of time now and then trying to get a new car to the racetrack (and particularly when you're running a full-tilt stock car program every other weekend out of the same damn garage) and you could see that they'd barely made it to Sebring at all. Harlon Lee's rig had apparently arrived during the wee hours of the morning, and the crew guys had to hustle like hell to get everything unloaded and get the car through tech inspection in time for that final, 8am practice session. Not to mention that a soaking wet track was hardly what you wanted for a first-attempt shakedown on a car with lots of power but lots of bulk and weight to go along with it. But they had no choice. They needed to get some laps in to make sure the damn thing ran and to see if anything was leaking or about to fall off. Plus neither of the drivers had ever seen the race-track at Sebring before....

So I was there on the sidelines, camera and stopwatch in hand, watching Harlon Lee's bulky, out-of-place new Fairway Flyer "Challenger V8" making its lonely, tentative maiden laps around a soaking wet Sebring International Raceway. They had the car painted up in an odd, two-tone, Fairway-blue-with-light-Fairway-gray side panels paint scheme with just big roundels on the doors with the number "9" inside and no other markings or lettering of any kind. But you could tell from the exhaust note and the imperceptibly bulged-out fenders (you weren't supposed to do that sort of thing, but making room for widened tracks, fatter tires and ridiculous camber angles had become a genuine art form on the NASCAR circuit) that this was a seriously professional effort. But the way the car skittered, skated and fishtailed its way around the circuit made it look foolish indeed, and you could see that the stiff, oval-style suspension was having a devil of a time getting a grip on the wet concrete. You really want a racecar set up soft for the rain, and Harlon Lee's new Fairway Flyer was anything but. It damn near understeered its way clear off the track once or twice at the hairpin, and no question it was just as bad—or worse—at other places around the racetrack. Plus the front tires were rubbing against the fenders at full lock (which the drivers were using on a pretty regular basis) and the windshield was fogging up something awful. Only the drivers couldn't swipe at it with a rag because they'd moved the damn seat back for better weight distribution. Not to mention that the car was in and out of the pits repeatedly for assorted troubles and adjustments. All things considered, it was an almost comically desperate situation.

Naturally I went looking for Harlon Lee and his guys as soon as the session was over. But it took me awhile to find them because they were paddocked about halfway to Fort Pierce. Then again, Bob Wright had told them to keep a low profile, so they'd tucked the car away in its trailer just as soon as it came in off the track. But then Freddie Fritter couldn't get out of the damn thing because he's six-foot-plus and a yard wide at the shoulders, and there was only about half that distance available between the Flyer's door and the inside wall of the trailer. He got pretty much stuck there, and the only way around the situation was for Freddie to wrestle his way back into the car, fire it up, ease it back down the ramps, get out and then try to muster up enough volunteers to push it back into the trailer. And I arrived at precisely the right moment to serve as one of the volunteer pushers. Believe me, it took a *lot* of muscle to get that Fairway Flyer "Challenger V8" back into its trailer. "Jesus," I grunted as we strained to get it up the ramps, "what the hell does this thing weigh?"

"Enough," a big, gray-haired guy on the opposite side panted.

"*More* than enough," Freddie Fritter laughed from behind me.

Eventually we got the Flyer inside and the tailgate closed, and then Freddie introduced me to the grey-haired gent from the other side of the car. "Hank, this here's Harlon Lee," he said with an obvious combination of admiration and respect. "Harlon," he continued with not quite so much of either, "This here is Hank Lyons. He writes about sportycar racin' for a livin'."

"You kin make a livin' doin' thet?" Harlon asked with mock astonishment.

"It's not much of a living," I assured him.

He shook my hand. You could feel from the scars and calluses that he'd spent his life working on racecars. "Well, thanks fr'the help, friend," he said sincerely. Then he pulled a clean shop rag out of his back pocket and dabbed at the mixture of sweat and rainwater on his forehead. Harlon Lee was a big, tall, sturdy-looking specimen with graying, neatly trimmed hair and white team coveralls with no name or company logo on them. He had a rugged, straightforward-looking face that most usually had a toothpick sticking out of it, and Freddie told me later that you could judge the way old Harlon was feeling about things simply by watching which way that toothpick was pointing. And right at that particular moment it was aiming straight at the grass. No question Harlon Lee was pretty damn disgusted about how things were going with his new racecar. He looked me square in the eye. "We didn't have no real time t'git this thing done," he explained apologetically.

"Yep," Freddie agreed. "The boys up in Dee-troit bit off a little more'n ole Harlon could chew this time." He shook his head, but the grin never left his face. "As enny fool kin see, we ain't quite ready with this'n yet."

"Not hardly," Harlon echoed through no grin at all. He cocked his head to one side and attempted to flesh it out for me: "Y'gotta understan' that we couldn't very well put the stock car work on hold in order t'do this here. Hell, we got two cars in a dang dirt race weekend after next, and another on banked asphalt two weeks after that. An' I got engines an' transmissions an' rear ends buildin' up fr' three other Fairway teams..." he folded his shop rag and put it back in his pocket "...an' that shit's jest gotta come first."

"'Course it does!" Freddie nodded. "That's yer bread an' butter."

"That it is," Harlon agreed, "that it is." His toothpick made a long, slow roll across his lower lip. "But you'd like t'have enough tahm t'do a little more professional job than this here." He took the toothpick out of his mouth long enough to spit, then put it back again. "Thass how we wound up with m'nephew—that'd be m' brother Cecil's boy—doin' most a'the dang seam weldin' on the body." He looked at me with just the faintest hint of a twinkle in his eyes. "As you'll see, th' boy he needed th' practice...."

"Hey," Freddie told him, "y'cain't have th' boy sweepin' up th' damn shop all his life."

"I s'pose not," Harlon allowed. "But it sure looks like hell." He let out a long, slow sigh. "Geez, I jest hate t'have my name on somethin' like this here."

"Yer name ain't on it," Freddie reminded him. "Nobody's is."

The toothpick in Harlon's mouth flipped up for just a moment, then drooped back down again. "Yeah, but ever'body an' his uncle knows it's ours." He looked over at me. "You know it's ours, don'cha?"

"Yeah," I admitted, "I guess I do."

"And ever'body else in the dang press room, too, right?"

"Yeah, I guess so."

"*See!*" he sneered at Freddie. Then, under his breath: "Dang. I tole Bob an' the rest a'those fellas in Detroit we wasn't gonna be anywheres near ready fr' this...."

Freddie rolled his palms up in a classic *'what can you do?'* shrug. Then he asked if I wanted a hot cup of coffee—*"it was bran' fresh about two hours ago"*—or a cold Nehi out of the cooler.

"Thanks," I told him, "but I had a kind of rough night of it last night. What I could really use is another couple aspirin or Anacin or something like that."

"I got me some Goody's up in the glove box," Harlon offered.

I gave him a blank look. "Goody's? What's that?"

Freddie and Harlon looked at each other like it was the stupidest thing they'd ever heard. "Aw, whaddaya expect from a damn Yankee?" Freddie snickered.

"Hey, I'm from California," I reminded him.

"Northern or Southern?" Harlon asked, his toothpick aiming straight at me.

"Southern," I told him, and watched a tight, thin smile creep across his face.

"You'll find it up there in the glove box, son."

So I ambled over to the passenger side of his pickup, but jumped back in a hurry when his enormous, black-and-tan coonhound bounded up against the window glass and started barking, snapping, snarling and drooling like he was getting ready to rip my arms off like chicken-wing appetizers. "Don't mind him," Freddie yelled, "Thass jus' ole Beauregard. He likes goin' along t'the races with me when he can."

I looked in at ole Beauregard and he stared right back at me with teeth bared and eyes full of worrying anticipation. But his tail was wagging like crazy.

"He won't mess with you unless'n he don't like you," Freddie advised as I watched ole Beauregard drool, lick his chops, and drool some more.

"Y-you sure it's okay?"

"Absolutely!" Freddie assured me.

"He only ever eats possum, fried chicken, pork loin, moon pies an' Yankees," Harlon offered. "An' you did say you was from *Southern* California, din'tcha...."

"G'wan," Freddie insisted. "Open 'er up. You'll be fine. Just don't act scairt."

I wasn't so sure. But I could feel both of their eyes on me, so I reached for the door handle. On the other side of the glass, ole Beauregard shivered, shook, drooled and licked his chops some more. His head was about the size of a prize Thanksgiving turkey.

"Y-you *sure* it's okay?" I asked again.

"Shit, *yes!*" Freddie nodded. "What are you, some kinda ole woman?"

Well, a man simply can't back away from an inference like that. Especially south of the Mason-Dixon line. So I reached out a trembling hand, grasped hold of the handle, shut my eyes and gave it a twist. I could imagine ole Beauregard trying to decide which portion of my ears, arms, face or torso might taste most like possum, fried chicken or pork loin....

I swung the door open.

Nothing.

I opened my eyes.

And that's about when Freddie hollered *"BEAUREGARD!"* and the old coon hound bolted past me like a slobbering fighting bull shot out of a cannon. I thought he was going to take off on a dead run for God-only-knows where, but he stopped in his tracks the instant Freddie yelled: *"HOLD!"* In fact, he froze up like an ice sculpture—ears up, tail rigid—and that's how he stayed while I opened the glove box, rummaged around for Harlon's packet of Goody's Headache Powder and closed it up again. The dog was still standing stock still, but keeping his eyes on Freddie and whimpering faintly from somewhere deep inside his chest, begging for release. "Now lissen here," Freddie told the dog through a big, affectionate grin, "you know you ain't allowed t'run free aroun' here!"

The dog cocked its head like it understood every word, then drooped its ears and inched tentatively back towards the pickup.

"Aw, OK," Freddie relented. "S'long as yer out already, c'mon over here for a li'l ole head scratch."

The big coonhound's ears perked up and its tail wagged eagerly.

"C'mon," Freddie repeated, and the dog bounded over to him in two gigantic leaps and cuddled its enormous head between his knees. "Ole Beauregard's about th' best damn black n'tan coon hound anybody ever had..." Freddie bragged as he scratched behind the dog's ears.

"That's a fact," Harlon nodded. "But you done made him too dang spoiled. An' he never did run well with the pack."

"Well, he's more a loner an' a lover, see," Freddie argued playfully. Then he looked up at me. "C'mon over an' say hello."

"You sure?"

Freddie looked at me like I was being ridiculous.

So I went over and scratched ole Beauregard behind the ears, and he recipro-cated by sniffing every fold, crease and crevice on my body while drooling a good half-pint of dog spit on my shoes.

"Beauregard," Freddie told the dog, "show ole Hank here how much y'like him." Beauregard looked up at me with a big, sloppy, hound-dog grin, jumped up on his hind legs, clasped his forelegs around my hips and started humping away at me like crazy. I tried pulling away, but ole Beauregard just grabbed on even tighter and humped even harder. "See, he *likes* you!" Freddie laughed.

I tried stepping away, but ole Beauregard was plenty strong and not about to be denied. Then Freddie said *"HOLD!"* and the dog stopped humping instantly, let go of my hips and sat down in front of me with another happy, friendly and oh-so-satisfied coonhound grin wrapped across his face.

"See," Freddie laughed, "I tole you he'd like you...."

To tell the truth, I was a little pissed off. "Do you let him do that to just any-body?" I growled.

"Only folks we like," Freddie laughed even harder.

"An' even some folks we don't like!" Harlon chimed in.

Pretty soon all three of us were laughing, and ole Beauregard was grinning away right along with us. "Y'all be sure an' come back in a couple hours fr' some lunch," Freddie grinned at me. "Ol' Harlon'll have some a'his Brunswick stew simmerin' on the camp stove by then...."

"What's Brunswick stew?"

Harlon and Freddie just looked back and forth at each other and shook their heads.

"Lissen, son," Freddie asked suspiciously, "you absolutely *sure* you're from Southern California?"

After Freddie put ole Beauregard back in the pickup, I asked Harlon to fill me in a little more about his new racecar.

"Aw, it ain't hardly done yet," he groused. "An' a lot of it's all-new hardware t'my guys at the shop."

"Oh?"

"Yep," Harlon nodded. "We ain't never messed with a l'il peanut motor like that 'un before." And that was true enough. The new, compact and relatively light-weight (for cast iron, anyway) Fairway V8 was ostensibly put into production as a step-up option from the leaden, hoary old straight six that came as standard equipment in base Fairway Flyers and stripper Fairway Freeways. But of course its real mission was to power the high-performance and racing versions of the still top-secret Fairway Ferret. And Harlon was quick to acknowledge that it had a lot of potential. "But down at th' shop, we're used t'piston holes big around as grapefruits, not oranges. An' engine blocks it takes two strong men t'carry."

"But it's still just an ordinary pushrod V8, isn't it."

Harlon looked at me like "ordinary" was a dirty word. But then a sly, fatherly little smile worked its way across his face. "Lemme 'splain somethin' to you, son. Ever' motor's different when it comes t'racin'. Y'gotta learn how t'massage it an' tickle its feet. An' y'gotta find out where it's weak an' needs a l'il help."

"Thass really why we're here," Freddie added with a shrug. "T'see what th'hell is gonna break."

"Y'mean t'see what th'hell is gonna break *first!*" Harlon corrected him through a weary but bemused smile. "Developin' new motors is like stickin' your hand down a bunch a'dang snake holes. You *know* yer gonna get bit, but there ain't no other way t'find the dang snakes...."

I asked Harlon if I could maybe get a little closer look at the car. He didn't look too pleased about it, but he eventually heaved out a heavy sigh and opened up the back end of the trailer for me. "I s'pose y'might s'well go in an' take a look at the dang thing," he grumbled. "It ain't about t'git no purtier."

So I climbed in and inched my way along the side of Harlon Lee's new Challenger V8 racecar. It was a Fairway Flyer, all right, but you could see someone had done an awful lot of fooling around with it. Like up close you could see that the two-tone paint scheme—a dull, gritty coat of Fairway's corporate navy blue with light, Fairway Gray bands down the sides between the beltline and rockers—was really there to hide how someone (like Harlon's nephew, perhaps?) had sectioned a good four inches out of the car's height. Including almost an inch out of the top pillars, windshield and backlight glass so the sectioning job wouldn't look too obvious. Only up close you could see that the sheetmetal work was really pretty crude and covered up with an awful lot of Bondo. In fact, it was damn near impossible to miss from a foot-and-a-half away. At least if you knew what you were looking at.

"My brother Cecil's boy don't understand some of th' subtleties of th' bidness jest yet," Harlon muttered. "Seems a dang shame to pull two hunnert pounds outta a dang racecar tryin' t'lighten it up an' git the weight t'sit a little lower in th'chassis an' then slather dang near half of it back on in body filler...."

"Aw, take it easy on th' kid," Freddie argued. "He'll learn."

Harlon Lee's toothpick flicked up and down like a light switch. "Tomorrow won't be too soon fr' me."

Freddie clapped his arm around Harlon Lee's shoulders. "Hell, Harlon, I've won damn races fr' you in cars at' looked a lot worse'n this."

"Yeah," Harlon groused, "but you hadda bounce 'em off a few walls first."

We had a good laugh off of that.

Freddie's eyes studied the horizon. "Looks like it's brightenin' up a bit. Y'all know the forecast?"

"Weatherman says it looks good for tomorrow," I offered.

"That's a good thing," Freddie yawned. "Lissen, if ol' Marvin wants t'take this thing out iffen it rains, thass fine by me. But I already know what it's like, and I got no big urge t'be tryin' it agin.'"

"That bad?"

"Hell," Freddie grinned, "it handles like an ole, sick sow on roller skates."

"So you won't drive it if it rains during the race?"

Freddie's eyes turned dead serious. "I didn't say that," he said evenly, picking his words. "I'm a racin' driver, son, and if things work out that I gotta drive a damn car off the rim a'the Grand Coulee Dam into a vat of flaming hog fat, by God, that's what I'm gonna do..." I watched the smile creep back across Freddie's face "...but my daddy always said th' world's divvied up between things a man's *gotta* do and things he might or might not *want* to do, and the trick to it is all in the divvyin'...."

"Amen to that," Harlon nodded.

"Sounds like he had it all figured out," I agreed.

"Not hardly," Freddie laughed. "But I'll tell you this: if it's pouring rain an' it's my turn t'drive, by God I'm gonna do it. But you can bet'cher granma's muffins I'm gonna try t'make ol' Marvin think I think I'm better'n him at it first."

I gave Freddie a blank look. "If you don't want to do it, why on earth would you try to make your co-driver think you're better at it?"

"I don't want him t'think I'm better at it," Freddie corrected me.

"Isn't that what you said?"

Freddie shook his head.

"I don't get it."

"You wasn't listenin,' son. What I said was: 'I want him t'*think* I think I'm better'n him at it.'" He regarded me with an exasperated grimace. "Don't be like all them other writer guys, willya?"

"What do you mean?"

"You know: big with th' words an' questions an' opinions but a l'il short in th' damn hearing an' understanding departments...."

I couldn't much argue with that.

Freddie let out a slow, fatherly sigh and explained: "Th' whole point is this, son: if ol' Marvin thinks that I think I'm better'n him at it, that'll make him wanna do it more, see? An' if he wants t'do it more, that'll mean I don't hafta." And right then is when I realized that I didn't understand the underlying subtleties, psychology and unspoken subtexts of southern stock car racing. Or southern folks in general, come to that. "Y'gotta unnerstan' how it is back up in the Franklin County hills where I come from..." Freddie continued with the same infectious, down-home, just-between-you-and-me smile that had made him so incredibly popular with stock car fans "...my momma an' daddy drowned all the dumb ones...."

Friday's 3-hour enduro for under-1000cc GT cars turned out to be about the best race of the weekend at Sebring that year. There were 31 cars entered—mostly Austin-Healey Sprites and Fiat-Abarth 1000 Bialberos—and it was really nice to see the little cars getting a chance at the limelight. Not to mention that the opportunity to play on a big stage with follow-up ink assured in all the nutball car magazines got a lot of the manufacturers involved. BMC sent over an entire squadron of factory-prepared, Mk. II Healey Sprites with fiberglass hardtops and plenty of tricks and tweaks underneath the sheetmetal. Plus none other than Donald Healey himself to oversee the operation. And, since they were down there anyway for the 12 hour, they'd lined up major racing stars Stirling Moss, Pedro Rodriguez and Innes Ireland to handle the cars along with popular Hollywood actor-cum-racer Steve McQueen. And they were all happy to do it since BMC had some money to throw around and the cars were unquestionably well prepared. Briggs Cunningham countered the factory Sprite effort with a team of four pumpkinseed-shaped Fiat-Abarth 1000 Bialberos for Bruce McLaren (who'd won the first and only Grand Prix ever held at Sebring back in 1959), regular Cunningham team leader Walt Hansgen, my friend Cal Carrington whom Briggs had always liked and fast-emerging Pennsylvania hotshoe Roger Penske. There were also four "factory" Fiat-Abarth Bialberos from Italy, two more from Jacques Swaters' Belgian team (one driven by previous 12-Hour winner Olivier Gendebien), a pair of well-prepared French DBs from California contesting the 850cc class and a horde of hopeful privateers in everything from more Sprites and Fiat-Abarths to a Saab 750GT and an Excelsior motorcycle-engined Berkeley 500. But everybody in the press room expected the race it to come down to a grudge-match battle between the BMC factory Sprites and the Cunningham Fiat-Abarths. And I was really glad to see that Cal was in one of them.

As far as anyone could tell from practice times and pre-race handicapping, the sleek little Italian coupes had maybe a few more horsepower and better aerodynamics than the boxy little Sprites (and also went further on a tank of fuel) but the Sprites looked lighter, whippier and handier through the twisty stuff. And that promised to make things interesting, since great races are almost always about contrast. Plus with cheap, low-powered, essentially throw-away racecars and genuine, international-level driving aces behind the wheel (and those types *always* have something to prove!) the stage was set for a highly entertaining show. Especially since the track was still soaking wet for the start but certain to dry out as the race wore on....

As a journalist, you really look forward to races like that—even if it's just a little "day-before curtain-raiser" that the editor will never give you more than a few measly paragraphs to cover. If that! And that can drive you ever-so-slightly nuts, because there's always so much drama and so many great, insider stories begging to be told. Like the situation revolving around a certain low-buck amateur racer named Lester P. Jackson, which was driving the promoters, organizers and officials at Sebring ever-so-slightly nuts. Lester P. Jackson had entered his own, Speedwell-modified Healey Sprite in Friday's 3-hour enduro, and the problem—which virtually no one saw coming—was that Lester P. and his crew just happened to be colored. Or Negro. Or black. Or African American. Or whatever the hell else you wanted to call them (and, take my word for it as a professional motorsports writer with access to both control tower and press room, there were a *lot* of alternative word choices available!). What you need to understand is that Sebring, Florida, for whatever else it might have been, was still a sleepy little town deep in the heart of the American southland. And that spelled trouble.

The situation caught everyone off guard—I mean, there was no little check box for race on the race entry forms—and so old Lester P. and his crew generated quite a stir. Which got even bigger thanks to the good, upstanding, God-fearing and moreover media-savvy folks over at the N.A.A.C.P., who saw an opportunity to drive a wedge into the long-standing "whites only" policies at Sebring-area hotels and eateries. This put the race organizers directly in the middle of a mess they wanted no part of, and they had to scramble like hell to get a few of the local innkeepers and restaurants to become a little more forward-thinking and set their long-standing segregationist policies aside. At least for the weekend, anyway. Integration was a huge, highly volatile issue from the buses, schools and lunch counters of Alabama, Arkansas and Mississippi to the back porches, coffee break rooms, union halls and tsk-tsking church socials of Passaic, Piscataway, Providence, Pittsburgh, Pocatello and Peoria. And all the mainstream newspapers, magazines, TV and radio stations and syndicated news services wanted as much of that controversy as they could get. After all, keeping the racial fires burning and even fanning the flames now and then generated headlines. And, as any newspaper publisher worth his salt could tell you (albeit behind his hand), headlines sell newspapers! And the more outrageous, controversial, scandalous and inflammatory, the better!

Now the organizers at Sebring tended to be pretty cosmopolitan on general principles, but they also understood where they were both socially and geographically. And they were painfully aware of the sort of adverse publicity it might generate if the wrong sort of incident or confrontation took place. Nobody wanted that. Only then they discovered they had an even bigger—and potentially far more danger-ous—kind of problem wrapped up inside the one they already knew about. And there was really no delicate way to put it. Back, white, yellow, green, purple or even see-through transparent, Lester P. Jackson was one piss-poor excuse for a racing driver. And it didn't have one single thing to do with his race, cultural background or the color of his skin. You could put it down to simple lack of experience if you wanted to be charitable, but the inescapable fact was that Lester P. Jackson was slow, erratic, unpredictable, rarely looked in his mirrors, regularly chopped people off and went sliding merrily off the pavement an inordinate number of times. And that was just first practice! In fact, a few of the major international stars (having ab-solutely no idea if he was black, white, purple, pink, heliotrope or chartreuse) went to race officials to complain about the rude, clueless and even dangerous driver in the #10 Austin-Healey Sprite. I happened to be standing in pit lane with one of the local Florida stick-and-ball writers when Innes Ireland's factory Sprite came storming into the pits a good fifteen minutes before the first practice session was over. *"He's a bloody menace!"* Innes fumed to one of the pit stewards as he scram-bled out of the car. *"The stupid fucking bastard had me off once and would have again if I hadn't locked up the bloody brakes. Had absolutely no bloody idea where I was or that I was coming around him."* He shook his fist angrily under the stew-ard's nose. *"I flat-spotted two brand new tires trying to avoid the stupid bastard."*

"Did you know he's a Negro?" the local scribe asked.

"What bloody difference does THAT make?" Innes snapped at him. *"Someday there may be a bloody world champion who's as black as the ace of spades. And if there is, you can bet I'll be first bloody man in line to shake his hand."*

The local scribe's eyes went wide as fried eggs. "D-do you think that could ever h-happen?" he sputtered.

"Why the bloody hell not?" Innes demanded.

The local scribe's jaw worked up and down a few times, but nothing came out.

A hint of a smile flickered up on Innes' face. "But believe me, mate," he added with a reassuring twist of irony, "this bloke *definitely* isn't him!"

But of course the fact that Lester P. Jackson was black *did* make a difference. Particularly if you were writing about it for publication. And so you felt obliged to kind of tiptoe around the situation and try to put some sort of enlightened, elevated, forward-thinking and socially conscious perspective on it. Only you couldn't, be-cause that was every bit as ugly, inappropriate, dumb and hypocritical as the stupid damn racial prejudice you were trying to be so damn enlightened, elevated, for-ward-thinking and socially conscious about in the first place. To tell the truth, all the resident cynics in the press room—and there are always a lot of them in *any* press room—were enjoying the fucking hell out of watching everybody squirm. Some of them were even placing side bets as to how it would all work out and how the poor race officials were going to handle it. And they really couldn't do much more than wring their hands, roll their eyes skyward and pray for some kind of divine intervention....

Believe it or not, that's precisely what they got!

I should explain at this point that, during the brief, four-month period when my mother decided to become an irritatingly devout Christian (she was seeing a lot of a renegade evangelical preacher from Oxnard at the time), she took pains to tell anybody and everybody who would listen about the miracle of faith, God's infinite love, His divine plan for all of us and the infinite, restorative and healing power of prayer. Although I must say I had my doubts, since the only thing I ever prayed for was that she would stop being such an overbearing pain in the ass about it! And those prayers went largely unanswered until the night she caught that preacher with a pair of wayward schoolgirls from the choir he was supposedly supplying both musical direction and uplifting spiritual guidance to, and she stopped seeing him. And it was frankly amazing how she lost her faith with the same sort of speed, zeal certainty and intensity she'd found it with just a few months before. Ever since, I guess I've been a wee bit skeptical about the power and efficacy of prayer. Only now, so many years later, at a dusty, forlorn-looking racetrack stuck out in the middle of the orange groves of central Florida, I finally witnessed in person how prayers could indeed be answered. And here's how it happened:

The night after practice and maybe a few too many packing-up beers in the paddock, Lester P. Jackson was driving his noisy little Sprite down the vacant, unlit two-lane road between the Sebring racetrack and his newly (and most likely temporarily) integrated motel on the outskirts of town. And that's when a Mighty Hand apparently reached down out of the heavens and caused Lester P. to do the organizers, officials and everybody else involved an enormous favor by causing him to swerve unexpectedly (perhaps by sending some small, furry little suicide-mission Agent of the Almighty into his path) and sent Lester P.'s Speedwell Sprite careening off the road, bounding through a shallow sand ditch and running pretty much headlong into a row of orange trees. But the boughs were thankfully hanging low with sweet, juicy, ready-to-pick oranges, and they served to cushion the impact. Imagine the sound of an un-muffled Sprite engine at full song (Lester P. had pretty big feet, and he'd managed to catch the gas pedal as well when he slammed on the brakes in panic) along with branches scraping and snapping off against front end sheetmetal, fenders and hardtop. Interspersed with a barrage of soft, spluttering, squishy-squirty noises from the quietly exploding oranges. Thanks to them, old Lester P. came out pretty much unscathed except for a few bumps and bruises and a badly sprained left wrist from hanging onto the wheel when he really should have let go of it.

Everyone was genuinely thrilled that Lester P. escaped serious harm. And even more thrilled that his Speedwell Sprite was too badly damaged (not to mention too sticky!) to race the following day. And so it was apparent that prayer and faith (or fate, or destiny, or irony, or coincidence, or sheer, dumb luck...take your pick) had successfully de-fused a prickly and potentially explosive situation that was clearly beyond the scope of mere, mortal race promoters and track officials.

Hallelujah.

That problem solved, Friday's small-bore enduro turned into one of the highlights of the weekend. The track was still soaking as the cars and drivers lined up for the traditional, Le Mans-style start, but the rain had eased off to a light spit and the sky to the west was actually looking pretty clear as the flag dropped and the drivers scampered across the puddles to their waiting racecars. Stirling Moss made his usual lightning getaway (typically jumping the gun by a stride or two as I saw it) and immediately began pulling away. No question he was consensus pick as Best Damn Driver in the World ever since Fangio retired and Hawthorne managed to kill himself, and he proceeded to prove it all over again every time he buckled on a damn crash helmet. And particularly in wet weather, where he was inevitably brilliant. Moss had this uncanny ability to get it right from the get-go while most drivers required a lap or two to feel their way around, find out where the puddles were and check out the conditions. By that time, Stirling was generally long gone! He'd pulled out a thoroughly obscene *SEVEN SECOND* lead by the end of the first lap, and there was a long, heavy silence between Moss' Sprite and the jumbled, snarling, scrabbling pack of tiny racecars that followed. I was thrilled to see my friend Cal Carrington had his Cunningham Fiat-Abarth up into second place (just!) but there was all sorts of dicing, diving, feinting and bluffing going on all around him. It was mostly more Abarths, but you could see Pedro Rodriguez and Innes Ireland busily elbowing their factory Sprites through traffic and actor/racer Steve McQueen's Sprite wasn't very far behind, either.

Things sorted themselves out a bit over the next few laps, and so we had Moss' number 15 Sprite well clear of everybody, Cal in the Abarth trying desperately to keep him in sight (but losing the odd tenth or two here and there), and then a few car-lengths back to an utterly fierce—and absolutely hilarious!—side-by-side/nose-to-tail battle between the Cunningham Abarths of Walt Hansgen and Bruce McLaren. Now young New Zealander Bruce was already an established international star and a grand prix winner, but Walt was the regular lead driver on the Cunningham team and not about to take a back seat to anybody. Particularly in one of Briggs' own cars! And he was good enough to make it stick, too. But their back-and-forth scrapping was letting Cal ease ever-so-slightly away. And I have to admit I was happy to see it. Cal was long overdue for a good result, even if it was just a goofy little joke of a Friday curtain-raiser. Besides, there was no question as to the relative quality and equality of the cars or the caliber of the drivers he was up against.

Cal was trying everything he could to try and stabilize or perhaps even reduce the gap to Moss, and my observation from the end of the back straightaway was that his Abarth did seem to have superior top-end speed. But Moss' Sprite looked more stable under braking and far more nimble through the corners. By contrast, Cal's Abarth looked a bit skittish, particularly at the back end. Although how much of that was car and how much was simply the genius of Stirling Moss on a wet track was hard to tell. Surely none of the other Sprites seemed to be working quite so well. Or maybe Moss had done something a bit different with his tires? Who knows?

Cal was really trying, though, and he managed to stabilize the gap to Moss and maybe even pulled back a second or two as a single-car-width line began to slowly dry out on the track surface. That can be particularly difficult for a driver, since you can pick up all kinds of speed and time if you stay on it, but God only help you if you pull out onto the wet part again to attempt a pass. I was really getting excited as I watched the gap between Moss' Sprite and Cal's Fiat-Abarth continued to shrink, and I had it figured that he'd catch Stirling well before the end. Only then Cal's brake pedal started getting spongy. A driver doesn't necessarily know if he's simply overheated the brakes or if there's something going wrong mechanically, but all you can do is soldier on, pump the brakes to get the pressure up when you need them and maybe tap the pedal with your left foot down the straightaways to make sure there's someone still at home. And that seemed to work just fine until the pedal suddenly and unnervingly went all the way to the floor as Cal was heading into the hairpin. He tried pumping it, but the fluid had boiled and so the pedal just flopped up and down without any measurable effect. He was going off, and he knew it. He also knew that there's a big, solid sandbank on the outside of the hairpin at Sebring, and so he had no choice but to try and slow down a little before he went off. A driver doesn't really have time to think about what to do in situations like that. They just react and rely on instinct. And there was really nothing he could do at that point but try whipping the car into a spin to get rid of some of the speed and then brace for whatever might come next. Which he did. The problem is that you'd really rather go off straight if you're going to go off (particularly when the grass and dirt at trackside is wet) because that gives you the best chance of maintaining control and maybe gathering things back up again. Poor Cal wound up going off more-or-less sideways—still spinning like mad and showering off sloppy roostertails of mud—and then his tires hooked a rut all funny and tipped that poor little Cunningham Abarth right over on its roof. It was one of those stupid-looking, slow-motion roll-overs (my friend Hal was there to capture the entire sequence, frame by painful frame, with his trusty Nikon motor drive) and you could look through the pictures and see in perfect, precise detail how Cal's tires dug in and levered the car up on its side. And that's where it sat for a long, agonized moment, teetering back-and-forth against the sky, before it finally gave in to temptation and flopped over on its roof with a loud, muddy *"SMACK!"* Naturally the small gaggle of seriously hung-over Green Park spectators cheered the performance mightily, and you knew Cal had to be feeling pretty damn humiliated as he crawled out the side window into the trackside muck on his hands and knees. The car actually didn't look too bad—the windshield glass wasn't even broken!—but it was upside down in a bad spot and absolutely covered in sand slime with large, muddy clumps of grass caught in all the panel gaps and wheel wells. I felt bad for Cal, but it was kind of funny, too.

At least he was OK.

Meanwhile Moss was leading comfortably from McLaren and Hansgen, who were still going at it hammer-and-tongs in two of the other Cunningham Abarths. They were side by side as often as not—through the corners as well as down the straightaways!—and McLaren finally decided it might be wiser to just sit on Hansgen's tail and try to worry him into a mistake rather than risk an incident with his own teammate. Especially on a drying track where conditions were changing with every lap. The strategy ultimately worked, as Hansgen slid off after his brake pedal went long and bounced high over the curbing at the esses. He was back on in a hurry, but that was all McLaren needed to spring free and take off in pursuit of Moss. And you could see he was catching Stirling a little as the track continued to dry (which seemed to favor the Abarths more than the Sprites). Only then McLaren got a little greedy and slid off, too, and lost precious seconds gathering it back up again. Only then Moss spun trying to pull out an advantage on McLaren! It was pretty wild stuff, and you could tell that both drivers were really going at it! I was trying to do the math in my head, and best as I could figure McLaren was about a second a lap quicker at that point but really didn't have enough laps left to make up the difference to the Sprite. Plus catching someone and passing them are always highly distinct propositions, and particularly when the guy you're trying to pass is Stirling Moss! Although the long backstraight leading into Sunset Bend surely gave an advantage to the Abarth....

If McLaren could just get close enough!

But the smiling, relaxed-looking Cunningham crew and the dour-faced mechanics in the BMC pits all knew something that we didn't: none of the Sprites could make the distance without a splash of fuel, but the Abarths could. Sure enough, Rodriguez and Ireland both had to pit for quick fuel stops with just two laps left to run, and Moss' car started sputtering and cutting out through the corners on the very same lap. Considering that a lap at Sebring runs a full 5.2 miles and moreover that it's flat as an ironing board so there's no place to coast downhill to save gas, Moss had no option but to pull in for a half-gallon himself with just one lap to go. And that was all the Cunningham Abarths needed, as McLaren and Hansgen crossed under the checker ten seconds apart for a dramatic and well-deserved one-two finish. Moss did manage a distant 3rd, but it was all Abarths around him as the little Italian cars copped four of the first five places, chased by Rodriguez and Ireland in 6th and 7th in the other two factory Sprites. And actor/racer Steve McQueen did a pretty workmanlike job bringing his Sprite home in a respectable 9th place at the checker. So it was a really good show, what with star drivers, munchkin cars, some great racing in difficult conditions and a pinch of drama, surprise and heart-break thrown in right at the end for good measure. As we always say in the press room after a really good one: *"the story writes itself."*

We could only hope Saturday's 12 Hours would be half as good....

Friday night I shared a nice, quiet spaghetti dinner with my friend Cal Carrington courtesy of the Italian cooks from Brooklyn who always traveled with Carlo Sebastian's team. We were sitting in the open doorway of the team trailer while everyone else was gathered around a big table with a big, Ferrari-red tablecloth underneath a big, Ferrari-red awning with flags at both ends. They had citronella candles and yard lanterns burning, and there were bottles of Lambrusco and everybody looked like they were having a lot of fun. But it was mostly just the team mechanics talking in rapid-fire Italian. Moss had disappeared with some young lovely he'd met, the Rodriguez brothers were off with their parents and "official" girlfriends and Ireland was surely in a bar somewhere. In any case, I don't think Cal felt like being around a bunch of people after his mishap with the Cunningham Fiat-Abarth earlier in the day.

"It's a shame," I commiserated as I twirled some spaghetti around the end of my fork.

"It happens," Cal shrugged in a bored, disgusted sort of way.

"You had a great start," I reminded him.

He didn't say anything.

"And you were hanging right there with Moss...."

Cal glared at me. I could feel it without looking up. "Look, Hank," he snarled at me, "I fucked up today, okay? Simple as that. Someone gave me a car that could've won the damn race and I put it on its lid before the first hour was up!" He stabbed at a meatball with his fork.

"Look, it happens..." I told him.

Cal took a long, slow breath and let it out. To be honest, I'd never really seen him like this.

"You race cars and you're going to wreck one every now and then," I offered encouragingly. "It's just the way things are...."

"But it was just so fucking *stupid!*" he insisted angrily. You could see he was pretty damn furious with himself.

"You'll get over it."

"Of course I will," he growled, and took a large, angry bite out of his meatball. He chewed for a few moments and then—just like *that!*—he flashed me a big, idiot grin with a few pieces of ground beef stuck in it and added: "Only not tonight, Hank. Not tonight..."

Chapter 11: Of Ferraris, Flyers and Futures

I was in the paddock press room early the next morning to pick up the official results from Friday's smallbore enduro along with pit assignments for the 12 Hour. But the pit assignment sheets weren't done yet—there'd been some last-minute changes—and they asked me to stop back in half an hour. Which was fine with me, since I really wanted to find Audrey before everything started getting crazy. On my way out of the press room, whom should I see hunched over his little Olivetti portable, pounding out mellifluous prose (in flowing Italian, of course!) but my favorite little Italian motorsports journo Vinci Pittacora. "How goes it?" I asked.

He held up a cautioning forefinger while he finished off the final punctuation on a sentence with his other hand. Then he looked up and smiled broadly. *"Bene!"* he beamed. "Is a beautiful day for a race, no? The sun, she's a-shining—*bella giornata!*—and the fastest cars are all a-painted *rossa!"* You had to love the way Vinci rolled the "r" whenever he pronounced "rossa."

"The Chaparral's white," I reminded him.

"Is good car," Vinci allowed earnestly, "but..." He let his voice trail off and rolled his palms up in the classic Italian gesture of helplessness.

"So who are you picking?"

"Ferrari! Naturalmente!" he trumpeted, pumping his fist in the air.

"Yeah, but which one?"

Vinci pretended to think it over. But everybody in the press room except the local stick-and-ball guys who didn't know any better were picking Moss and Ireland in the factory Testa Rossa for the overall, Hill and Gendebien in the new GTO for Category 1 GT and the Gurney/Holbert factory Abarth Carrera for under 2-liter Category 2 championship points. In fact, all three were prohibitive favorites.

"What about Carrington and Ryan and the Rodriguez brothers in the two Dinos?"

"They will be fast on the track—*velocissima!*—but is a long race, my friend. *Molto difficile!"* He nodded knowingly. "They have the speed..." he flexed his bicep and pointed to it "...But not the muscle."

"How about the Maseratis?"

Vinci's eyebrows rose up like the stage curtains at an opera. *"Sono ripertitivo—* I repeat myself: it's a very long race."

"And the Serenissima Testa Rossa? It won here last year...."

You could see Vinci appreciated the potential irony if out-of-favor young Count Giovanni somehow managed to defeat the factory team with their own last-year's car. But he allowed himself only a brief moment to savor the idea because he was, above all else, a loyal and even devout Ferrari man. And that made me think I might try a little digging for Bob Wright. Like how much faster that secret, mid-engined V12 prototype he'd told me about at the Ferrari press conference might be than this year's cars. And you really needed to ask somebody in the know, since everyone who attended Ferrari's press conferences knew that the numbers and specifications he handed out to the media could be either ridiculously optimistic or intentionally conservative.

"You know," I said in an offhand, conversational tone, "one of the Grady Davis mechanics asked me how much horsepower a good, strong 3-liter, Ferrari V12 makes? I've heard well over 300."

Vinci shook his head. "Maybe 275. Maybe 290," he allowed with an insider wink. "And it all depends on the size of the horses, no?"

"But it's still a lot more than the V6s and V8s in the Dinos?"

"Not only more..." he held up an index finger "...*better!*"

And that was surely true. Like my old ace race-mechanic pal Buddy Palumbo always said: *"There's really only three ways to make more power: build it bigger, pack it tighter or wind it higher!"* The beauty of Ferrari's V12 was its marvelous flexibility and ability to both rev and last. Not to mention the way drivers could dial up the power like a damn rheostat, which made the cars much easier to drive. The downside of course was their size, weight and worrisome complexity compared to an inline 4, inline 6, V6 or V8. But Ferrari knew more about engine configurations than anybody because he'd tried them all. And won with virtually all of them. But there was no question—at least for endurance racing—that the V12 was king.

After my chat with Vinci, I picked up my notebook and camera bag and headed into the paddock in search of Audrey. I hadn't seen her since our highly inebriated Fun Bus tour and barely-remembered ambulance ride to our hotels two nights before, and I was a little uneasy about how things might feel between us. You never really know about those things, and it was genuinely unnerving how unnerved it was making me (if that makes any sense). In fact, I was having some seriously mixed feelings about what getting close to her was doing to my equilibrium. But all of that vanished when I finally located her, setting up her charts, pencils, lights, snacks, sun umbrella and a small thermos of tea on the timing stand Peter and Georgie had built in Clive Stanley's pit stall. She greeted me with the kind of bright, reassuring smile I'd hoped she would and seemed genuinely enthusiastic about seeing me. And that made me feel very fine indeed. "I see you've recovered," I grinned at her.

"Barely," she laughed. "I had a pretty rocky time of it yesterday morning."

"So did I."

"And so you should."

"Hey, if you wanna dance, you gotta pay the piper."

"Just desserts for bad behavior is more like it!" She snickered. "Tell me, do you do that every year?"

I looked at her sheepishly. "I think I must."

"You're not sure?"

"Well, I know I swear it off every year, so I guess that means I probably do."

She shook her head. "You have astoundingly little character."

"Yeah, but I've always tried to treat it as an asset."

"Oh? And how does that seem to work for you?"

"I get by."

And then it went quiet for a moment and we were just kind of looking at each other. "That was a really nice time, though," I said softly. "With you, I mean...."

She actually blushed a little. And I could feel the heat coming up in my cheeks, too. Without even thinking about it, I leaned forward and gave her a nice, soft little kiss on the forehead.

"What was that for?"

"Does it have to be for anything?"

"I think it should be."

"Then it's for being a good sport."

"You're a pretty good sport yourself."

And then the moment just kind of hung there, with neither one of us having any idea where to go with it. I felt my ears burning red. "L-Look," I finally stammered, "I've kinda gotta get back to the press room before the start..."

"Don't let me stop you," she agreed awkwardly, avoiding my eyes. "I know you've got work to do."

We stood there for a moment like a pair of naked plastic mannequins in a store window, waiting to be dressed. And then she did the nicest thing. She put her hand on my forearm, smiled up at me and said: "But do stop back from time to time during the race, won't you?" I swear, her voice rose up through me like a helium balloon, and I was damn near floating as I made my way back to the press room.

Wow.

But my sense of euphoria didn't last very long, since who should come strutting through the press-room door right behind me but that squeaky little English weasel Eric Gibbon. And right in his wake was this large, beefy, red-faced, come-in-like-you-own-the-place gent in a Ramar-of-the-Jungle bush jacket topped off with a copper-colored silk ascot, a matching pith helmet and a scraggly mutton-chop mustache and smelled a little from old whiskey and pipe smoke. A lot like Eric, actually. He looked vaguely familiar, although I couldn't really place him. Still, it was hard to miss the way Eric was leading him around like a prize St. Bernard. And it was only a matter of time before the two of them got around to me. "I'm certain you two have met before," Eric said obliquely as the two of us stared at each other.

"Can't say as I've had the pleasure," the ruddy face inside the mutton chops grumbled.

"I'm Hank Lyons," I told him. But he just looked down his nose at me, like he was sizing me up. I asked him if he was a friend of Eric's.

"I'm not sure 'friend' is the appropriate word," he sniffed obliquely.

"Hey, that's OK," I needled. "Any friend of Eric's is probably a lousy judge of character anyway...."

The big guy in the pith helmet didn't even crack a smile. In fact, he pretty much scowled at me. He was about two-thirds of the way to a classic, prickly-pear drunkard's nose, and the piercing, pale blue eyes on either side of that nose were seriously bloodshot. I looked him up and down again, trying to figure out who the hell he was and trying even harder to make some sense of his outfit. I wanted to say *"Is there some costume party no one told me about?"* but decided it would be bad manners. So I asked him instead if this was his first trip to Sebring?

"Never been here before," he said like he was proud of it. "But I know Florida. I've done a lot of deep sea fishing down in the Keys and off the coasts."

"Oh?" I said, trying to sound interested. "Atlantic side or Gulf side?"

"Both."

"You do any good?"

"I've got a pretty good sized tarpon and a nice sailfish on the walls of my den at home," he more or less harrumphed, "and a black marlin and a wahoo in my office." He elevated his chin and puffed out his chest a little: "I once held the U.S. record for hammerhead shark."

I was obviously supposed to be impressed.

"Well," I said, "you know what Ed Zern always used to say about big game fishermen..."

"Who the hell is Ed Zern?"

"He writes a column on the back page of *Field & Stream* every month."

"Oh?"

"He's *very* funny."

The guy in the pith helmet didn't look convinced. But he favored me with a half-raised eyebrow's worth of interest anyway. "Do you hunt or fish?" he wanted to know.

"Nah, not really," I told him. "A little fishing now and then when I was a kid. You know: party boats off Seal Beach where you're elbow-to-elbow and they rent you all the tackle and park you on the edge of a kelp bed to catch sheepshead and rockfish and calico bass. And some freshwater stuff once or twice on a farm pond with a bamboo pole and a bobber. But nothing serious. Not really."

He appeared to be genuinely curious now. But not in a particularly nice sort of way. "Then why do you buy the magazine?" he pretty much demanded.

"I don't."

"But you said you read it."

"Sometimes I pick it up when I'm waiting in a dentist's office or something. Or I thumb through it on the newsstand just to read Ed Zern's column."

His bloodshot eyes glared at me. "Why in hell would you pick up a magazine about something you don't really care about?"

"Hey," I shrugged. "Like I said, he's a really good writer. He writes some awfully funny stuff sometimes."

"Funny stuff about *fishing?*"

"Sure!" I told him. "Like what he said about the difference between big game salt water fishermen and weight lifters..."

This time both eyebrows went up. "The difference between big game salt water fishermen and weight lifters?" he repeated.

"...Yup," I nodded. "Ed Zern said the only real difference between big game salt water fishermen and weight lifters is that weight lifters don't clutter up their living room walls with stuffed barbells..."

Not even a hint of a smile. In fact, more like a frown. His eyes swept disdainfully around the Sebring press room. "I suppose you think *this* makes more sense?"

"Hey, I'm not here to be an apologist for racing. It's like any other nutball sport or special interest. If you love it and follow it and understand it, it means a whole lot to you. But you're wasting your time if you try to make somebody who doesn't love it see it and feel it the way you do."

"You're quite the expert, aren't you?" he observed icily.

"Henry Lyons," Eric Gibbon broke in, obviously delighted, "I'd like you to meet Quentin Deering."

"I prefer 'Q.E.,'" he corrected Eric in an aloof, impatient voice.

"N-nice to meet you," I said uncertainly, and extended my hand.

"I'm sure it is," Q.E. snorted, and slowly, hesitantly, reluctantly put his hand out. It felt like a dead roasting chicken ready to be put in a pot.

"He's read your stuff, Hank," Eric continued through a wide, crocodile smile, "but he may just keep you on at the magazine anyway...."

I felt a cold wind blow through my stomach. Could it be that this pompous, overstuffed bozo was the actual new owner of *Car and Track* magazine? But Quentin E. Deering didn't say a thing. He just continued looking down his nose at me and sizing me up. It made me feel pretty damn uncomfortable, if you want the truth of it.

"I, uhh, I hadn't heard anything about a sale of the magazine from Warren or Isabelle..." I more-or-less stammered.

"There was nothing to hear," Quentin explained tersely. "It's not out there yet."

"Oh?"

But he'd obviously grown bored with answering questions. *"ERIC!"* he commanded over his shoulder, *"let's be on our way. I want to view the cars before the start!"* With that he turned on his heel and headed for the door. I had a sinking feeling in the pit of my gut as I watched them head for the door, Q.E. striding ahead like an overstuffed little kid playing Teddy Roosevelt and Eric Gibbon following eagerly along in his wake like a new beagle puppy. I suspected I hadn't seen the last of either one.

Meanwhile, out in the paddock, the sense of excitement, anticipation, confusion, frenzy and downright panic was building to a fever pitch. Drivers, workers, mechanics, team managers, hangers-on and people who had somehow managed to score race-day paddock passes were milling and swarming everywhere. Lines of service trucks and rental cars crept through the teeming swarm of bodies at barely a walking pace, searching in vain for a place to park. Through it all, nervous-looking crew members in fresh team coveralls rolled tool cabinets and floor jacks and mounted tires and drink coolers and boxes of spare parts into pit lane.

There was less than an hour to go....

I made one final tour of the pits, eyeballing all the teams and wishing all my friends good luck, and I ran into Cal just a few moments before he had to head across the front straight to take his place in the little circles they paint on the concrete directly across from the cars. Cal had a big smile on his face and looked pretty damn relaxed for a guy who was about to scamper across the track, jump into a very fast racecar and hurl his way into the worst damn traffic jam in the universe. "I thought drivers were supposed to look nervous before a big race," I teased him.

"We think it's better if we let Phil handle that," Cal grinned cheekily. "We figure he worries enough for the entire team." And that was true enough. Phil Hill always looked like a bundle of nerves before a big race. He was as nice and approachable a guy as you could ever hope to meet—a real gentleman—but he took his job seriously, understood the risks and never pretended to have the kind of carefree, fuck-it-all attitude that some of the other drivers pretended to have. And his apparent, wrought-up nervousness never seemed to affect his performance in the car. When the green flag went down, Phil Hill put his foot down as hard as anybody. And he kept it there until either the car broke or the checker came down. That's how he came to win the '61 World Driving Championship in Formula One along with 2 sports car wins at Le Mans and 3 at Sebring for Scuderia Ferrari. But he always looked nervous as hell before a race. Any race. By contrast, Cal's expression was upbeat and almost serene.

"So you're not worried?" I needled again.

"Why should I be? I've probably got the fastest fucking car in the race and it's probably not going to last the distance anyway." He shrugged his shoulders. "Hell, all I've gotta do is get in the damn thing and drive...."

"So there are no ill effects from the wreck yesterday?"

"What wreck?" Cal deadpanned. And then flashed me an easy smile, gathered up his helmet and gloves and headed across the track to his little painted circle on the far side of the start/finish straightaway. There were only minutes to go, and the murmuring and chatter from the crowd and the co-drivers and the car owners and team managers and mechanics and timing and scoring people and white-clad stewards and officials in pit lane hushed down to a breathless, expectant silence.

In just a few short moments, all hell was going to break loose....

To be perfectly honest, the 1962 12 Hours of Sebring wasn't nearly as exciting, entertaining or dramatic as the three-hour curtain-raiser for the little tiddler production cars on Friday. Oh, it was thrilling enough at first. Hell, every race is. We had beautiful weather and a big crowd on hand and the usual mélange of high school marching bands and parade laps by celebrities and dignitaries (including John Fitch in one of the magnificent 300SL coupes he'd raced for Mercedes 10 years before, although never at Sebring) followed by a mercifully short welcoming speech by a Florida state senator. And meanwhile 65 racecars glistened in the sunlight along the start/finish straightaway as their soon-to-be drivers took positions in the little painted circles across from them and fidgeted with their gloves and helmet straps as the time drew near. The cars were once again lined up by engine displacement rather than qualifying times, and that put the seven all-American Corvettes right up at the front of the queue. Even if everybody knew they wouldn't stay there for long! And neither would Harlon Lee's Fairway Flyer "Challenger V8" right behind them or the Ian Snell/Tommy Edwards Aston Martin GT or the John Fitch/Briggs Cunningham Jaguar E-Type. Or the two Chevy-powered Chaparrals, which figured to run at a smooth, conservative pace in hopes of making the finish. No, the real race was going to be between the phalanx of blood-red Ferraris that came next. And sure enough it was the favored Moss/Ireland Testa Rossa in the lead and holding a couple seconds margin by the end of the first lap. Ireland had uncharacteristically taken the initial stint since Le Mans-start-expert Moss had somehow managed to twist his ankle the night before—supposedly while dancing—and Innes was determined to show what he could do in Moss' absence. So he added to his advantage every lap, and there was little doubt that Moss would pile on more of the same once his turn came. Barring unexpected troubles, the race for the lead looked over in the first ten minutes.

But we had some interesting back-and-forth battles going on behind the flying #26 Testa Rossa. The 246SP Dino of the Rodriguez brothers was having a hell of a scrap for second with the 248SP Dino that Cal was sharing with Peter Ryan, Jim Hall was hustling along nicely in his quick but prudently driven Chaparral, Walt Hansgen was typically going like hell and carving his way up the field in Cunningham's ugly but undeniably fast Maserati Tipo 64 after an uncharacteristically poor start, and behind him came a far more circumspect Bruce McLaren in Cunningham's Cooper-Maserati. And not far behind at all and running at a carefully measured pace was the Bonnier/Bianchi Testa Rossa out of young Count Giovanni's

Scuderia Serenissima stable. In the GT ranks, the Corvettes had slipped inexorably backwards, Harlon Lee's Challenger V8 had already made two pit stops to address teething problems and the Hill/Gendebien duo were already running away from the rest of the Category 1 GT entries in Ferrari's new GTO. It was almost like they were in a different class. And maybe they were.

Things settled down to a rhythm pretty quickly, and the only real changes came as teams cycled through their pit-stop schedules. The V6 and V8 Dinos could go a couple laps further between fuel stops than the bigger-engined, slightly heavier Testa Rossas, and Cal actually had the lead for a few laps with the Rodriguez Dino not far behind. Only then they had to pit and the Moss/Ireland Testa Rossa assumed a commanding lead once again. Still, you never know at a race like Sebring, and it wasn't long before the track and the fates started claiming their victims....

After running as high as second at one point, the tubby-looking Walt Hansgen/Dick Thompson Tipo 64 started handling funny and it wasn't many more laps before something at the back end broke and the rear suspension collapsed. The front end had done much the same thing during practice, and it made you wonder about the sturdiness of all those tiny little welded-together tubes at a punishing, pounding track like Sebring. That left Cal dicing it up with Ricardo Rodriguez in Carlo Sebastian's other Dino for second—they both claimed later that they were "taking it easy and just playing around," but it looked pretty damn serious from my side of the fences!—and they were swapping positions every few laps. Ricardo had just gotten in front again after Cal got balked trying to follow a side-by-side Corvette and Jaguar E-Type into Sunset Bend, and it all ended in tears just a few corners later when Cal had to do a "phenomenal avoidance" to keep from collecting a club racer in a Sunbeam Alpine who'd been startled clear off the damn pavement when Rodriguez went under him like a missile shot (with two wheels in the grass!) heading into the long, fast sweeper under the MG pedestrian bridge! As any driver will tell you, when a car goes off directly in front of you at something approaching 100mph, gets it all sideways on the grass and comes scything merrily back across the track again, there are only two basic options:

      a) Try to steer around the stupid bastard and hope he doesn't come snapping back the other way and wind up in your lap.

      b) Aim for where he is now in hopes that he won't be there any more by the time you get there.

There's no time to think at moments like that. All you can do is act. Or react. And whatever the hell you're going to do, you sure as hell better do it *NOW!* Keeping in mind, however, that you need to stay calm and focused and remember not to do anything too sudden or too much or too stupid or too late or (heaven forbid!) go into Full Panic Mode and hammer on the damn brakes. Because then the front wheels lock up and you can't steer! If you allow that to happen, about all you can do is hang on, close your eyes and brace for impact....

In any case, Cal wound up trying the avoidance maneuver, and he almost got away with it. He swerved onto the grass at something like 120 to try and get around the spinning car. And the whole idea at that point is just to try and keep it straight and get it whoa'd down enough to rejoin the pavement a little further down. But the grass was still pretty slick from Friday's rain and Cal went into a hellacious slide and couldn't avoid nicking the left-side guardrail. It wasn't much of a hit, but it was enough to spin him around and send him pinwheeling down the grass verge between the track surface and the guardrail. But his trajectory ran pretty much parallel to the fences and he somehow—to his utter amazement—didn't hit anything. Although it was more pure, dumb luck than driving skill, as he was quick to point out later: *"I went off in a big way, and I was just cleaning my shorts out and congratulating myself on my unbelievable good fortune when all of a sudden, right there at the end, the right-front hit something buried in the grass—a piece of concrete or a metal pipe or something?—and there was this almighty 'CLUNK!' that damn near ripped the fucking steering wheel out of my hands. I could tell right away that something was bent because the car wouldn't track worth a shit and the steering wheel was cocked at a whole new angle."* Cal got the Dino back to the pits so Carlo Sebastian's mechanics could take a look at it, and sure enough the tie rod was bent like a pretzel and the lower A-arm mount was tweaked enough that you could see it with the naked eye. There wasn't much the mechanics could do but shake all the pieces to see if anything was fractured or about to fall off, try their best to straighten out the tie rod, eyeball the toe-in back in line and send the car back out again. Neither Cal nor Peter Ryan were particularly enthusiastic about the way the car wandered down the straightaways and handled differently through right- and left-hand corners after that. "It's the shits when you've lost confidence in the car," Cal groused after his next stint, and both drivers were relieved when the engine started losing power and then oil pressure a little before dusk and team manager Dragoni elected to park it rather than risk having it blow up in front of everybody. Ferraris hardly ever retired due to engine problems—the Old Man prided himself on that—but Cal confided that you could help things along a little if you stretched the redline a bit out on the back side of the circuit where nobody could hear it. Although you had to remember to reach behind the dash and punch the little button that re-set the telltale a lap or two before you came in....

I stopped by Clive Stanley's pit around sunset to see how things were going for Tommy and Ian in the Aston, and also of course to check in on Audrey. I climbed up on the timing stand next to her. "Everything going well?" I asked.

"So far so good."

"No problems to report?"

"Not for us. But not for the Cunningham Jaguar or any of the GT Ferraris, either, unfortunately."

"It's a long race."

"It's *already* a long race," she sighed, "and I badly need a visit to the loo."

"I could cover for you."

"Georgie or Peter can cover for me. I know you're busy."

"No, really. I'd be happy to."

"Are you sure?"

"Absolutely."

So Audrey showed me how she wanted me to stop and re-set the watches and write all the times down on her chart and keep track of who came in and out of the pits and so forth. I mean, can you believe that *she* was trying to show *me* how to time and score a fucking sports car race?

Needless to say, by the time she returned (and she was gone a long time, since the lines at the so-called "ladies' rooms" in the Sebring paddock are deservedly legendary) I had somehow managed to zero her Total Race Time stopwatch, miss laps on two of the GT Ferraris, get the near-identical Grady Davis Corvettes mixed up and fail to clock the Cunningham Jaguar in and out of the pits on a routine fuel stop and driver change. I didn't even realize the damn car was in for service until it came screaming past on its way back onto the racetrack. But of course the worst of it was when Audrey came back and I had to tell her what I'd done. And immediately witnessed a thunderhead of anger building up behind her eyes.

"YOU'VE MADE AN INCREDIBLE MESS OF THINGS!!!" she all but screamed. *"HOW IN BLOODY HELL COULD YOU DO SUCH A THING???!!!"* You could tell she was *really* mad. Why, you could almost see flames shooting out of her eyes.

"I-I didn't mean to...."

"Good Lord," she wailed in helpless, furious desperation, *"I could have had Georgie or Peter do this! I could have had James do this! I could have even had bloody Clive do this..."*

"I, umm, I haven't done timing and scoring for a long time," I protested lamely. "And I haven't really been paying a lot of attention to the Category One GT cars. Or not specifically, anyway...."

"THEN WHY IN BLOODY HELL DID YOU OFFER??!!"

The Bob Johnson/Rodger Ward Purple People Eater Corvette thundered past and Audrey scrambled to get the time and mark it down.

"I...I'm sorry," I kind of mumbled. But she was ignoring me. Like I wasn't even there, in fact. And so there was nothing more to do but apologize my face off a few dozen times and then slink off down pit lane with my tail between my legs. I'd never really seen Audrey angry before and, to be honest, it was actually a little frightening. More than a little frightening, in fact. And I knew it wasn't the kind of thing I ever wanted to see again. The only good news was that Tommy and Ian were running dead on schedule and right on pace in Clive Stanley's Aston, and I hoped that might melt away some of Audrey's anger as the evening and the race wore on. I certainly hoped it would.

But if things were going uncharacteristically well for Clive Stanley's Imperial Crown Tea Aston Martin, they were a tangle of snakes for Harlon Lee's crew and their Fairway Flyer Challenger V8. Both Freddie and Marvin Panch had been in and out of the pits innumerable times with all sorts of problems: fading brakes, grabbing brakes, a stripped hose clamp that let most of the water out before they caught and fixed it, heavy steering that they couldn't do much of anything about, a balky shifter that stuck in gear from time to time, a leaking axle seal that was oiling the left-rear brake and enough heat coming up through the floor and in through the firewall to roast a Thanksgiving turkey. And then, about five hours in, the engine started running real hot and sucking up all the coolant. Freddie and Harlon both figured it was related to the earlier hose clamp problem, and at first they tried coming in and adding water every time the temperature gauge started creeping into the red zone. But the trips to the pits grew more and more frequent until they could only make a lap or two between stops. And the power was fading now, too. They couldn't find any external leaks around the radiator, hoses or water pump and there appeared to be a little steam in the exhaust and water in the oil, so the inescapable diagnosis was a blown head gasket. But it turned out to be even worse: a cracked cylinder head. Or make that *two* cracked cylinder heads—one on either side! I happened to be there as Harlon and his guys huddled over the engine bay right around sunset, trying to figure it out. And the meaning was hardly lost on me when all three of them unbent in unison and stared back and forth at each other. You could tell from the glum silence and the way they shuffled around like a surgical team who'd just lost a patient that things had gone straight to hell. There was no sense of urgency any more....

"We got another pair a'them things in th' trailer, don't we?" Harlon finally asked.

The mechanic next to him nodded.

"Well then let's go get the dang things an' put 'em on."

"I'm not sure that's ezzactly legal," the mechanic said.

"We're gonna change 'em *here?*" the second mechanic asked.

Harlon glared at him. "Well, we got 'em, don't we?"

"But what *for?*" the second mechanic wanted to know. It probably wasn't legal to change a major engine component like a cylinder head during the race, and they were so far behind already that there was no way they'd be classified as finishers, even if they made it to the end of the 12 Hours.

"*WHAT FOR??!*" Harlon snarled at him. "Why, so's we kin find out what the hell *else* is gonna break...."

Freddie looked over the pit counter at me and winked. "Y'gotta hand it t'ole Harlon. He don't give up easy."

"It sure looks that way."

"Yep," Freddie allowed through an appreciative smile, "y'gotta respect a man who's that damn stubborn."

I understood what he meant.

The final outcome of the 1962 12 Hours of Sebring ultimately hinged on a stupid pit incident around the four-hour mark that nobody even much noticed at the time. At that point, the Moss/Ireland Ferrari V12 was well out front, running like a freight train, sitting on an utterly commanding lead and continuing to pull away from its pursuers. Plus you could see that both Moss and Ireland were driving well within their limits, taking it easy on the car and being extra careful through traffic. And meanwhile the cars chasing after them were having all sorts of problems, falling completely by the wayside or spending lots of extra time in the pits. So the race at the front was pretty much over: Stirling Moss, Innes Ireland and Carlo Sebastian's "factory" Testa Rossa had everybody covered, and that's all there was to it!

Only right around 2 in the afternoon—with barely a third of the race run—Ireland brought the Ferrari in to have it checked over after he: *ran over some big, hard chunk of metal that came flying out from under that bloody monstrous Fairway thing. It made a hell of a bang when I went over it!*" And that's when everything went to straight to shit, even though the Testa Rossa turned out to be fine! You need to understand here that the F.I.A. endurance racing rules at Sebring specified a minimum of 20 laps (or just a bit over 100 miles) between refueling stops. And to make sure that rule was properly followed, there were white-suited refueling marshals stationed all up and down pit lane. Their responsibilities pretty much boiled down to placing a strip of special tape over each car's gas cap before the start and when the crews were done filling them up during pit stops, and peeling that same strip off each time the cars came in to refuel. In fact, the teams themselves were expressly prohibited from touching that tape or adding any fuel until their assigned refueling marshal had personally removed it (at the prescribed 20-lap minimum, of course) and replaced it again when the refueling was completed. Now this all sounds pretty simple and straightforward (and not a little stupid, if you ask me) but rules are rules, and if there's one thing the F.I.A. is terrifically strict about, it's their precious fucking rulebook.

But things can get a little complicated and confused as a race wears on, what with all the different cars running at different speeds, fuel mileage and strategies, and moreover having their own assorted emergencies, mechanical problems and delays along the way. This puts them on vastly different pit stop schedules, and even experienced hands need to consult a good lap chart now and then to keep up with just what the hell is going on. And particularly after the second or third round of stops.

Car AND Track

The enthusiat magazine for insufferable bores and strokes

MAY 1962

FIFTY CENTS
STOP COMPLAINING!

We track test the Jim Hall/Troutman & Barnes Chevy V8 Chaparral!

(eat your hearts out!)

Racing Season Hits Full Swing!

MOSS vs. GURNEY
Take yer pick!

INDY 500 PREVIEW: *The greatest spectacle in racing or a dung heap for dinosaurs?*

RAZY LOTUS JUNIOR
ICE IN SAVANNAH!

BRRRRR!
We Drive Four
Classic British Roadsters from Boston to Buffalo in a Freaking Blizzard!

COLD WAR ISSUE!
RUSSIAN RACECARS: SHOULD ENZO WORRY?
EXCLUSIVE SPY PHOTOS!

OUR WONDERFUL FRIENDS, SPONSORS & SUPPORTERS

Warren, Sandra & Melissa Alpin

Archer Racing

Roy Armstrong & Lelane Lemond

Jim Arthurs

Bill Babcock (Friends of Triumph)

John A. Balzer (thanks to Jacki King)

Scott Barr (Friends of Triumph)

Ross Bremer & Karen Perrin
(a little O.F.F. racing)

Jagnutz Danny & Sandi Burnstein

Serial Ride-Mooch Victim Dave Burton

Peter Cheplick

Patrick & Margaret Clark
(owners of Minihaha)

Ed Conway (who says nice things
about Burt's books on the PA)

Kerry & Lisa Cowart

Joe Curto (who knows both *why*
and *how* S.U. caraburetors suck!)

Rich Cwik (Lotus Corpse)

Dennis Delap (Friends of Triumph)

Bill & Shirley Dentinger (Beady Eye
Racing/Friends of Triumph)

Ben & Nancy DeWitt (annuder wurdsmith)

Karen Lavery Dickinson
(The Old Ladies' Race Club)

Tony Drews (Friends of Triumph)

John Fippin (who says nice stuff about
Burt's books over the PA at Mid Ohio)

Rick & Karen Fiske (Elva owners
who should know better by now!)

Paul Flowers (Lee Chapman Racing)

Pat Froehlke (thanks to
Jason Kavmeyer & Missy Froehkle)

Gary Fuqua (Age & Treachery Racing)

Ken Gano (specialist in speeding
tickets & racing team bankruptcies)

Robert Gault

Geneva Concours d'Elegance
(thanks to John Barrett)

Jim Godfrey (thanks to Rich Grudens)

Les Gonda (Battle of Britain Racing)

Christopher Guido (Sporting Motorcar
Association of Somerset Hills)

Les Halls

Jim Hassall (Friends of Triumph)

John L. Heffron (Austin Healey
Sports & Touring Club)

Tom Hnatiw (the mouth that roared!)

Bill Hollingsworth III

John Hubbard (thanks to Edie Hubbard)

John Hurabiell (Age & Treachery Racing)

James Keith (thanks to Amanda Keith)

Chris & Judy Kellner (7/10ths Racing)

Blaise A. Kern (Jag wrench extraordinaire)

The Jag Lovers #pub Crew (Jeffrey Kern)

Dan Kirby (Hammer & Tongs MG Registry)

Michael Kluck (Fat City Flyers)

Jim, Jamie, Jeff & Lynn Knupp

Ed & Pat Kovalchick (Manic MG Manglers)

Diane & Ron Kramer

Jeff Laird

Neil Lefley

Richard T. Liebhaber (Ferrari Flailer)

Richard Lim

Marty & Bill Luken (The Lotus Position)

Larry & Jeff Luser (Alfanatics)

R. John Lye (Friends of Triumph)

Douglas Mancini

Kevin J. McCormick (Bruisers' Cruisers)

Gordon Medenica (Lee Chapman Racing)

MG Car Club of Long Island Centre
(thanks to Steve Becker)

David Miller (Lost Cause Corvairs)

Tim & Sally Murphy (Friends of Triumph)

Graham and Martin Nance

J. Wally Nesbitt

David & Yvonne Oliver

David T. N. Patton (Age & Treachery Racing)

Linda & Mike Querio

John & Terry Reed (Friends of Triumph)

Andy Reid (master motoring scribe)

Splinter Group Racing

The Squeelers

Stephen Ross

Schlomo Rabinowitz (Rabinowitz Racing)

Steve & Elaine Shell

Tony, Janet, Lian & Maya Shoviak

Mark & Sharon Simpson

Jeff Snook (Friends of Triumph)

Rich Sorenson
(Odyspeed Minivan Hot Rods)

Steve & Sally Steyers

In memory of Joe Stimola

Lee & Marty Talbot

John Targett (in worn-out & broken
MG parts if not actual cash)

VIR Flag Crew (thanks to Lee Brantley)

Ambassador Henry & Helen Wang
(thanks to Jerry Wang)

Richard Waltman

Bill & Jane Warner
(Amelia Island Concours)

John & Lisa Weinberger

Trevor Welowszky

Gary H. Wiezorek (Friends of Triumph)

Tod & Wendy Wilson

Bob Woodman (repeat offender)

Mark A. York (Friends of Triumph)

Photographers represented in this section (and probably without their permission): Hugo Becker, Hal Crocker, Art Eastman, Bob Harrington, Carol Levy, Bill Lyman, Ron Nelson, Scott Paceley, Walter & LouAnn Pietrowicz, John Reed

TESTY · MOANY · EELS

"Burt's co-driven with me lots of times, and he's never come back to the pits on foot with just one of these in his hands!" **MARK SIMPSON**

"I love it when Burt co-drives with one of our customers. Not only is he reasonably fast, terribly competitive and a lot of fun to be around, he's also **INCREDIBLY** hard on equipment! That adds up to a lot more parts sales, machine shop work and billable labour hours for my company."
LEE CHAPMAN

"Burt's co-driven my Causey P6 many times, and except for brutaliaing a few CV joints, pumping out so much oil at Road America that it took a record 50 bags of Oil-Dri to clean up the mess and breaking the entire frame in half at Gingerman, it's been smooth sailing all the way. I look forward to co-driving with him again some day if he ever buys his own car!"
Mike Kaske

"We love having Burt race with us! Sure, he blew a big hole through our best motor at Mid Ohio, tried to set our car on fire at Road Atlanta and parked it in the gravel trap trying to beat a couple whaletail Porsches, but we can't wait to have him back!"
Kevin, Jamie, Mike & Sean
YESTERYEAR MOTORSPORTS

"Okay, so maybe he did go flying off the road trying to pass that 510, but Burt fixed most of what he broke on my car and didn't hit the tire wall very hard at all" **RICK FISKE**

3

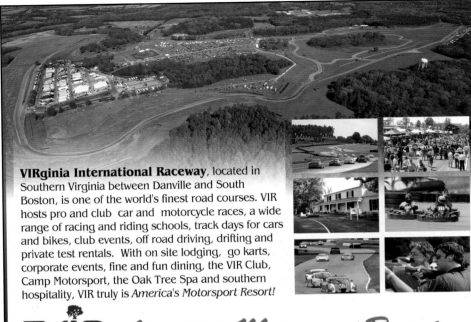

VIRginia International Raceway, located in Southern Virginia between Danville and South Boston, is one of the world's finest road courses. VIR hosts pro and club car and motorcycle races, a wide range of racing and riding schools, track days for cars and bikes, club events, off road driving, drifting and private test rentals. With on site lodging, go karts, corporate events, fine and fun dining, the VIR Club, Camp Motorsport, the Oak Tree Spa and southern hospitality, VIR truly is *America's Motorsport Resort!*

VIRginia International Raceway • Danville, Virginia 24520 • 434.822.7700 • www.VIRnow.com

BS in Al Lewis' Chevron B27 at Road America

SPORTSCAR VINTAGE RACING ASSOCIATION

Racing the Past into the Future

Since its founding in 1980, SVRA has run quality, professionally run events at some of America's most prestigous tracks. Watkins Glen, Sebring, Mid-Ohio, Road Atlanta, Road America, Lime Rock, Mosport, and Virginia International Raceway have all hosted SVRA events.

Keeping history alive at these historic venues, SVRA has hosted reunions of all the great series; Can-Am; TransAm; Formula One; Formula 5000; and I.M.S.A have all been part of a SVRA weekend.

It has been said that the "Cars are the Stars" in Vintage Racing and that is especially true in SVRA. Ferrari, Porsche, Aston Martin, Ford GT40, Cobra, Corvette, Lotus, McLaren, the list goes on and on. All have added to the excitement of a SVRA Race Weekend. Of course, not to be forgotten, are the cars that attracted so many of us to Sports Cars. The MGs, Triumphs and Austin Healeys, come out in large numbers, not only to compete but to spectate and dream.

Reading this book shows you have a keen interest in MotorSport History. Take that interest to the next level! Go to a SVRA event. The paddock is always open, talk to the drivers, drool over the cars, and then get involved. The dream of driving your own Vintage racecar may not be as far off as you thought!

For further information go to http://www.svra.com

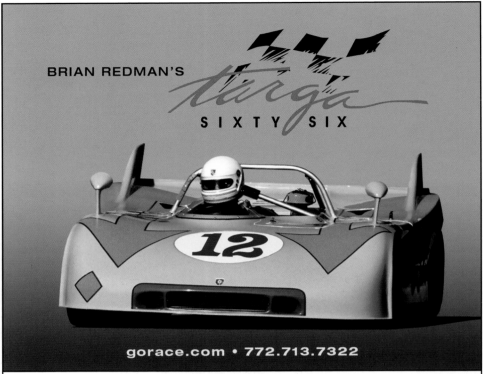
BS in the original 003 Reventlow Scarab

Sometimes things don't go
exactly as planned

Robert H. Fergus
1924 - 1999

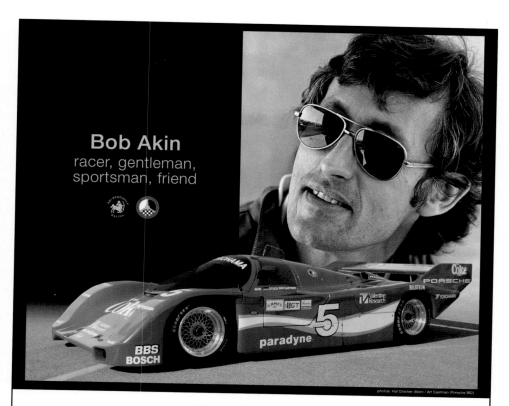

BS in Joe Marchetti's Ferrari
250LM at Road America

BS in a Bill Thomas
Cheetah at Road America

BS in his Alfa AUSCA
Spider at Mid Ohio

In Memory of Gary Dewey # 05

Sheree Dewey and Rusty Nuts Racing

Eleven battle at Summit Point BS in white car

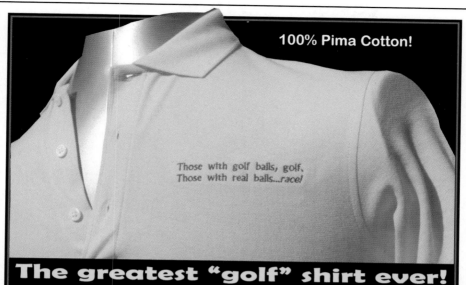

Natalie Fenaroli with Lynn St. James

14

MOSPORT ONTARIO CANADA

The VARAC Vintage Racing Festival features all classes of Vintage, Historic and G70+ cars. Held annually the 3rd. weekend of June

WWW.VARAC.CA

BS in a Kurtis 500G Indycar at the Milwaukee Mile

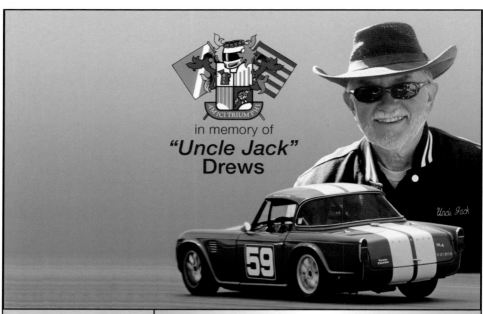

in memory of
"Uncle Jack" Drews

BS signs books at the Milwaukee Masterpiece concours

Mike Amalfitano
resto nella pace

BS in Dave Burton's Porsche 356 getting ready to knock the infamous Team Thicko Red Rat off the road at Grattan

17

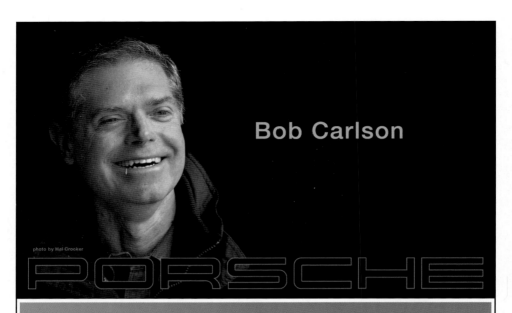

Bob Carlson

photo by Hal Crocker

PORSCHE

BS racing a Caterham at VIR

www.monticellomotorclub.com
Info@monticellomotorclub.com

It takes a brave man to let BS drive his car, but an even braver one to let BS WORK on his car

BS in Steve Simpson's Elva Mk 7

Co-driving with Stacey Bondon and the stalwarts of Splinter Group Racing at Road Atlanta.

23

BSin356

Motorsports Photograph y

Denise McCluggage in her Ferrari at Meadowdale

24

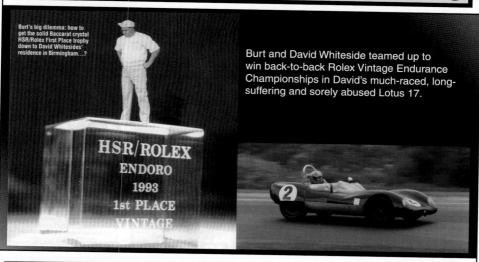

Burt's big dilemma: how to get the solid Baccarat crystal HSR/Rolex First Place trophy down to David Whitesides' residence in Birmingham...?

HSR/ROLEX
ENDORO
1993
1st PLACE
VINTAGE

Burt and David Whiteside teamed up to win back-to-back Rolex Vintage Endurance Championships in David's much-raced, long-suffering and sorely abused Lotus 17.

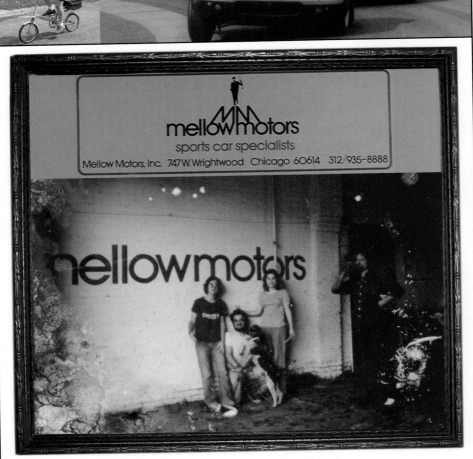

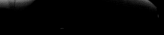

31

POWER IS OUR BUSINESS

KOHLER. POWER
ENGINES • GENERATORS • RENTAL SERVICES

In any case, what happened was that the Moss/Ireland Ferrari—which had been running to absolute perfection!—ran over whatever the hell fell off the bottom of Harlon Lee's lumbering Fairway Flyer Challenger V8 and came in for a quick look-see at the end of lap 73 to see if there was any damage. It turned out to be nothing serious—just a couple dented exhaust pipes—but the car was still a couple laps shy of its required "20 lap-minimum" refueling window. Only the white-suited refueling marshal apparently hadn't been counting his laps properly, and he removed the special tape over the Testa Rossa's flip-up filler cap and indicated that it would be OK for the crew to refuel. So they did. And then Moss motored off to resume the lead again just as the 2nd-place Rodriguez Dino began having transmission problems that ultimately put it out less than two hours later. Which left the Moss/Ireland car with an even more enormous lead and, with the Hill/Gendebien GTO likewise steamrollering all the Category 1 GT entries and the Gurney/Holbert Porsche doing the same to the Category 2 cars, there really wasn't much drama left except among the disappointed collection of unfortunates licking their wounds along pit row.

Speaking of which, I went over to check in with Harlon Lee's bunch to see what the heck had fallen off the bottom off their car. "Th' whole damn shifter linkage broke off," Harlon told me with a rare combination of disgust and amazement. "I never seen a track that pounds the shit outta a car like this here place!" And then Harlon proceeded to list the Challenger V8's near-endless litany of mechanical woes: "Th' dang transmission's stuck in 4th, th' shocks an' brakes is pretty much gone, the front end got bashed in some thanks t'the brakes, the clutch is slippin' if y'git on it too hard an' the engine's startin' to lose water agin', too." But it was still running and Freddie and Marvin were still soldiering on with it, even if there was no way they could complete enough laps to be qualified as finishers. I believe I was the one who christened the car "Rasputin" at that point, because the damn thing just flat refused to die. And of course the name stuck.

Meanwhile things were also turning rapidly to shit in the Imperial Crown Tea pits just a few stalls down. An amazingly solid and trouble-free first six hours had them first in class ahead of the Cunningham/Fitch E-type and a promising 4th among the Category 1 GTs behind the Hill/Gendebien GTO, the Scuderia Bear Berlinetta Le Mans Speciale Aerodinamico and one of the other Short Wheelbase Berlinettas. But a split oil line cost them the better part of a half-hour in the pits and then Ian stuffed it into the barriers trying to make up time. He went in backwards and it initially looked like the damage was mostly cosmetic. But the car wouldn't track straight after that. It quickly became apparent that the rear axle had been knocked ever-so-slightly askew. And that's why they started running through rear tires at a truly alarming rate. For about an hour and a half they had a real circus act going on, what with the car coming in for new tires and either Georgie or Peter having to hustle the take-offs over to the Dunlop trailer to have new skins put on and make it back in time for the next pit stop. It was becoming clear that they were going to run out of tires unless some of the other cars that ran that size dropped out. But then the bearings on the bent end of the axle started howling and pretty soon it was loud enough that you could hear it over the exhaust blare as the car pounded down the start/finish straight. A couple laps later it finally broke and the wheel came off and that was the end of it. It happened with Tommy at the wheel going into the big, wide U-turn through Sunset Bend, and I was right there to see it as the wheel snapped off and went bounding across the concrete and sent the car went into a truly vicious spin. But fortunately there was plenty of room there so at least Clive Stanley's Aston didn't hit anything. Tommy did his best to claw the car the rest of the way around to the pit entrance, but the left-rear was dragging on the ground, showering off sparks and making horrible noises, and he finally just switched it off and waited for a tow truck. I mean, what else could he do?

I made my way back to Clive Stanley's pit to let them know what had happened, and I was hoping that Audrey would be settled down a bit by the time I got there. I'd been avoiding her ever since I'd screwed up her chart, but I really wanted to see her again before she left Sebring and headed back to London. After all, I didn't even have her phone number or address or know when or where I'd ever get to see her again.

James Britten was still standing at the pit wall, stopwatch in hand, but you could see from his expression that he knew it was pretty much over. I told him what had happened, and a few moments later one of the pit stewards came up and told him that the car was coming in on a hook with the RR wheel missing and wondered if he wanted it here in the pits or towed back into the paddock. "You'd best take it back to the paddock," James told him. "We're packing it in..."

I looked over at the timing stand and I could see Audrey was already gathering up her lap chart, timing board and watches. "So this is the way the world ends..." I called over to her, "...not with a bang but a whimper."

"You like T.S. Eliot?" she asked without looking up. Her voice was cool and distant, but at least it wasn't angry.

"I can take him or leave him," I answered, happy to have something to talk about. "How about you?"

"Not all that much. He's got an awfully grim view of things, doesn't he?"

"He's famous for it."

"If it absolutely has to be poetry," she continued absently as she stepped down from her timing stand and stretched, "I suppose I'm more the John Keats/Elizabeth Barrett Browning type."

"You're a hopeless romantic."

She looked up at me with a thin, exasperated smile. "If you're going to be hopeless, Henry, that's not the most horrible way to do it."

Things were still pretty strained between us. I could feel it. "Look," I finally told her, "I'm really sorry about screwing up your charts...."

"That's all right. It turns out it didn't really matter much anyway, did it?"

"No, I guess not."

She looked up at me with something complicated and unsettled in her eyes. "I'm really sorry I got so angry with you. There's no excuse for behavior like that."

"Sure there is! You'd worked really hard and conscientiously on something and I came along and screwed it all up."

"And with the most cavalier attitude, I might add!"

I looked down at my shoes. "Yeah," I kind of mumbled. "I'm sorry for that, too."

"It's all right. Men are just like that. No harm done."

We looked out at the racing cars sailing past, their headlights starting to come on against the advancing darkness, while Georgie and Peter began packing up all the tools, spares and pit equipment. They moved like their shoes were filled with lead.

"So when are you heading back?"

"I'm sure Clive and James will want to pack everything up as quickly as possible and beat the rush out of here." She looked up at me. "There's not much point in hanging about, is there?"

"I dunno," I shrugged. "Sometimes the race gets interesting right at the end."

"I'm not really all that interested, Hank," she said through a yawn. "Besides, I'm traveling with the team, so I've really got to leave when they do."

I rolled it over in my mind, trying to come up with something—anything!—to keep our conversation going. "Do you have any ideas about when we'll see each other again?" I finally asked.

"That's usually up to the man involved, isn't it?"

"Yeah," I kind of shrugged. "Traditionally...."

"Well, why don't we just say that I'm a bit of an old-fashioned girl?"

"Okay," I hemmed and hawed, feeling terrifically uncomfortable, "let's just say I'm asking."

She gave me a schoolteacher scowl. "Is that the best you can do?"

"I haven't had a lot of practice..." I apologized, and looked down at my knuckles "...or not lately, anyway."

"I'm afraid it shows."

I felt my ears starting to burn. "But I'd really like to see you again," I muttered into the top button of my shirt.

She reached out her hand so the tips of her fingers touched against the sleeve of my shirt. "I think I'd like that, too," she said softly.

"You *would?*"

"Don't sound so surprised!" she smirked. "It could give a girl doubts."

Everything north of my shirt collar seemed to be on fire.

"When are you going back to London?" she continued airily. "You could look me up there if you like."

"I-I'd like that a lot," I stammered. And then I asked for her phone number. She started to give it to me, but seemed to think better of it.

"Why don't you ring me up over at the Lola shops? Or just drop by if you like. I'll be there late afternoons for the next week or so doing travel arrangements for Le Mans."

"That sounds really good," I told her. "Really, *really* good. Maybe I can buy you dinner or something."

"Maybe you can," she smiled, "but let's not get too far ahead of ourselves." And with that she gave me an ambiguous little peck on the cheek and headed back into the paddock. I watched her until she disappeared into the darkness, and wondered for a moment why she wouldn't give me her number. It seemed curious, but not in any devious or sinister sort of way. I assumed it had something to do with her father. And then the tow truck carrying Clive Stanley's Aston Martin came chuffing and squeaking by. The car was back-to-front with the damaged rear end dangling in a sling and the front wheels following behind. Tommy was in the cab, looking absolutely spent as he gave the driver directions back to Clive Stanley's spot in the paddock. He offered up a weak smile and an even weaker thumbs-up as he went by. I watched as the tow truck turned to the right and, just like Audrey, disappeared into the gathering darkness of the paddock.

There was nothing much to do at that point but head over to Harlon Lee's pit to see how things were going with Rasputin. Marvin was still out there somewhere in the darkness, nursing the crippled car around the racetrack while Freddie and Harlon sat in the pits hunched over bowls of Harlon's infamous Brunswick stew. I must admit it smelled pretty good. "Have summa this," Harlon offered, and spooned a big, steaming glop of the stuff into another paper bowl. "It'll put lead in yer pencil."

"What's in it?"

"You don' really wanna know," Freddie advised. "But it's critter parts, mostly."

"Them l'il things what look like sausages ain't really sausages," Harlon cackled. He seemed pretty happy in spite of all the terrible things that had gone on with the car. The latest was a crack clear through the front crossmember that they'd patch-welded during their last stop. Harlon and Freddie apparently had some kind of bet going as to how long it would last.

At least the Brunswick stew was good.

"You guys have had a pretty tough race," I commiserated.

"Nah, it's okay," Harlon allowed as he loaded up another spoonful of stew. "This here's jest turned inta kind of a test session fr' us." He ushered the stew into his mouth and chewed on it thoughtfully. "As long as we's here," he continued philosophically, "we might as ought try t'figger out how this stuff is done."

"Yep," Freddie agreed. "Iff'n we make it all th' way to th' end, we're gonna let ole Beauregard come out an' pee on th' tahrs...."

"But only if we make it all th' way," Harlon cautioned.

It was nice that they could see it that way. But, as Freddie put it: *"Y'cain't learn how t' win lessen y'already know how t'lose...."*

Meanwhile, out on the racetrack, the Moss/Ireland Testa Rossa had pulled out to an insurmountable, three-lap lead—more than fifteen miles!—and was continuing to motor serenely along with no worries at all and no competition in sight. And that's about when the stewards (who were possibly put wise by the manager of Count Volpi's Scuderia Serenissima team just a few spaces down pit row) came over to inform Carlo Sebastian's crew that the Moss/Ireland car was being disqualified because of their "refueling infraction" almost four hours before. As you can imagine, that didn't go over especially well. In fact, there was yelling and arguing and shaking fists and bared teeth and a whole collection of rude Italian hand gestures. Not to mention a bit of top-of-your-lungs screaming in American English, English English, Scottish English and Modenese-dialect Italian. Stirling Moss, in particular, was absolutely livid. Not only had the refueling steward removed the special tape and essentially *invited* the team to refuel, but the race officials had allowed the car to run for more than three additional hours before bothering to come around and tell the team they were out of it. But none of the arguing or posturing or threats of boycotting future races did any good. The Moss/Ireland car had unquestionably (if inadvertently) taken fuel on just 18 laps after its previous stop when it came in for damage evaluation after running over the Challenger V8's wayward shift linkage back on lap 73. And, as far as the race officials and on-site F.I.A. representatives were concerned, there was no arguing the point. Rules, after all, were rules. Eventually, after the officials turned their backs on all the pleading and arguing and walked away, the fury and anger in Carlo Sebastian's pit slowly melted down into anguish, despair and disappointment. In the end, the mechanics had no choice but to push the Moss/Ireland Testa Rossa back into the paddock and load it into the transporter. Their race was over....

This turn of events left the privateer Testa Rossa of the anxious but deliriously happy Scuderia Serenissima team with a dominating lead and less than four hours yet to run, and Bonnier and Bianchi duly cut their pace back and tiptoed gently through traffic on their way to a dull, droning victory with ten full laps in hand over the 2nd place car. Which turned out to be the Category 1-winning Ferrari GTO of Phil Hill and Olivier Gendebien, which gave Carlo Sebastian's crew at least something to cheer about. Not to mention gaining old man Enzo the World Manufacturers' Championship points he wanted and earning his new GTO a thoroughly decisive win on its very first outing. It was a pretty damn impressive showing, even if the race was generally a bore.

At least the weather was nice.

Chapter 12: Lola

It was a long, wearing return trip from Florida—three different flights plus entirely too many lonely, empty, can't-get-comfortable-here hours waiting at airport gates in between—and I was happy to be back in my cheesy little flat over a commercial bakery in a worn-down industrial section southwest of London. It was a dim, cruddy little place overlooking a workshop roof and the narrow brick alleyway where my forlorn Fiat Multipla sat waiting for me with a flat battery and at least one flat tire. It was one of those deals where I had to add air every week or so, and whenever I was out of town for an extended period, as I was between Daytona and Sebring, it would most certainly go flat. And there was really no excuse for not fixing it properly, but it was one of those things I just never seemed to get around to. Besides, the bakery downstairs had a compressed air line, and they were happy to let me pump it up. Although there was one early Sunday morning when I had to go somewhere and the place was locked up and I wound up trying to inflate it with a bicycle pump. That's not something you really want to make a habit of.

Even so, it felt great to be back to what passed for home in my shabby little life—such as it was—and to the solid little table pressed up tight against the window where I did my writing for the magazine. The window faced north so it never let much sunshine inside, but the view included a nice line of trees beyond the buildings, a thick carpeting of ivy over the brickwork on the electric motor rewinding shop across the alleyway and a mossy old stone fence that surely dated back to before our beloved United States was even a country. England was always good for a little dose of historical perspective when you needed it.

The spry old Irish lady who took care of the johns and sinks downstairs and occasionally smelled faintly of whiskey looked after the place for me, and thanks to the bakery downstairs, it always smelled homey, warm and wonderful first thing in the morning—especially after a long race weekend—even if you got sick to death of that smell by the middle of the week. I didn't need an alarm clock because the clamor of muffin tins, loaf pans and baking sheets banging around downstairs and the crotchety old owner snapping at the hired help got me up at a little past four every morning except Sunday. An hour or two later, the aroma of freshly baked muffins, buns and breakfast cakes would begin wafting up through the floorboards. But it was good for my writing, what with the noise below quieting down once all the batters were mixed, stirred, poured into appropriate tins and loaded safely into the ovens. After that it was pretty quiet, and the early morning street outside would be dark and deathly silent except for the occasional whine of electric milk floats and rumble of newspaper trucks making their rounds and the birds chirping back and forth to each other in the ivy. It was nice to look up from whatever I was working on and see the fresh promise of an awakening world outside. Far better than turning my head to the left or right to take in the piles of opened books and magazines, scribbled-on envelopes and note pads, early drafts of stories long sent off to the magazine and old newspapers folded open to circled passages that had once been—at least momentarily—critically important to some story idea or other that I'd either abandoned, forgotten about entirely or still hoped to get around to someday.

To be honest, my table and surrounding work space looked like a quarter-sized, low-rent version of Ben Abernathy's train-wreck of an office in Fairway Tower. Except for the décor, of course. And the view. And the fine film of powdery-white flour dust that was forever finding its way up through the flooring and ventilation ducts and settling over everything in the apartment. The disapproving old Irish lady did her best to keep everything reasonably in order, but she'd learned better than to touch anything around my writing desk unless it was a half-empty coffee mug or odd scraps of bakery goods that were threatening to grow mold. She chided me now and then about my chronic taste for disorder but, being Irish, she considered writing a noble profession and did her best to keep the place clean. She even picked up my clothes from wherever I'd dropped them—particularly after a night at the pub—did my laundry once a week and folded everything neatly away in the resale-shop, printed-veneer Chippendale reproduction dresser with a brick for one leg and drawer runners that would wedge solid if you weren't careful opening and closing them. She also took care of any pots, pans or dishes I'd inadvertently left in the sink on the rare occasions when I actually cooked something for myself. But that didn't happen very often. It was just so much easier to buy something ready-to-eat from the chips and sandwich shop around the corner or, better yet, go out someplace cheap and enjoy a bit of what the world looked like outside. My favorite haunt was the pub a few blocks down where some of the guys from the Cooper garage habitually dropped by for a pint or two after work.

Humble as it was, my flat was also, by far, the best place I'd ever found to write. I could never make much headway writing things out longhand—I really needed the neat, orderly appearance of typewritten pages—and I had trouble writing anything worthwhile in airports or on airplanes. Some writers are good at that sort of thing, but it just never worked very well for me. So it was always reassuring to get back to my flat, have the bakery downstairs wake me up while it was still dark outside, make myself a nice mug of American instant coffee with way too much sugar in it or a cup of Imperial Crown English Breakfast Tea with honey (I always like to support a racing sponsor, especially since Clive Stanley once gave me a whole bloody case of it!) and get to work. And I could always get plenty of warm, tasty muffins, buns or breakfast cakes right downstairs—fresh out of the oven and for practically nothing!—so long as I didn't mind if they were broken or a bit burned around the edges.

My writing usually went pretty well in that apartment. Or better than it ever did on the road, anyway (although I could write just about anywhere if I was on deadline and really had to, so long as I could find someplace either terribly quiet or incomprehensibly noisy to work). But I always felt like the things I wrote in the solitude and familiarity of my flat were generally the best. I'd sit there with my steaming hot cup of tea or coffee and stare for what seemed like hours at the empty page in front of me and wonder just how the hell I was going to bring it to life. And then I'd give it a few, hesitant pecks on the keys. And then a few more. Some days, that was the best you could do, because it would all come out dumb, stiff and awkward and you knew it was crap even while you were writing it. And sometimes you had no choice but to send that crap off to the magazine because you were on deadline and either you or the subject matter (or both) were sadly lacking. But other times—oh, those other times!—you'd make those first, few pecks on the keys and then a few more and before you knew it the stuff would come vomiting out of you in torrents. It wasn't the sort of thing you could understand or control, but it would flat sweep you away when it happened. I have absolutely no idea where that stuff comes from—I don't think any writer does—but at that point you're nothing more than the tube it flows through. So you let it. And then you look up and it's four hours later and your tea has gone cold and there's just one solitary bite out of the corner of your muffin and you've got three or four (or sometimes even five or six!) good pages done and your head is throbbing and you've got to pee something awful.

That can be a pretty damn wonderful feeling!

During the winter months I always promised myself to make some serious headway on the forever-unfinished racing novel that I'd started back in California more than five years before. But it seemed the best I could manage each winter was to keep re-writing the first 200 pages over and over and over again. I'd pick and peck away at it from the end of one racing season to the beginning of the next, but of course I'd have to set it aside to take care of my magazine commitments once the new cars started appearing and the momentum started building for another season. I'd always promise to get back to it, of course, but it was pretty much impossible once the racing started. My assignments had me traveling to all the Formula One races to cover those and to all the World Manufacturers' Championship endurance rounds to do those reports as well, and even though the races had the same basic story line and featured a lot of the same exact characters, they were two entirely different disciplines. And you had to try to capture that difference and explain it to people who might not know. Or care. Formula One was essentially a driver's championship that depended on the cars and the World Manufacturers' Championship was for the cars and manufacturers, but depended very much on the drivers. Like anything else in life, the more you knew about it the more layered, nuanced, complex, intricate and fascinating it became, and a genuine motorsports nutcase like myself could lose an ordinary person completely in just a few short sentences of conversation.

This is called being an expert.

Or, conversely, an insufferable, droning bore.

Take your pick.

But the point is that I'd never get back to my novel until the next season ended and the last race report went off in the mail. That's when I'd invariably decide that I really needed to go back to the beginning of my story—just to refresh my memory and "bring myself up to speed," you know?—and of course then I'd see things I wanted to change or things that didn't make sense or sounded forced, stupid or awkward and, well, that's how I wound up re-writing the first 200 pages five fucking times! It hadn't yet dawned on me that you really need to get to the end at least once, and *then* go back and make yourself miserable with all the clumsy, dull, dreary, uncoordinated, unlikely or flat-out impossible things you'd managed to set down. In the end, it finally occurred to me—just like Freddie Fritter said about Harlon Lee at Sebring—that a writer's greatest asset was probably a hefty oversupply of sheer stubbornness. You eventually come to realize—in any field—that talent is relatively plentiful, success is both fleeting and elusive and true inspiration comes and goes. But sheer, bull-headed stick-to-itiveness—the kind that keeps you plodding through the muck even when you can't see back to where you've come from or as far ahead as where you're going—is what gets you to the end of any major project. And that's if you're lucky....

As you can imagine, I was eager to visit the modest little Lola shop in Bromley and reconnect with Audrey Denbeigh. And I had a thoroughly plausible reason for dropping by, since Lola was hard at work on a new grand prix car commissioned by Reg Parnell's Bowmaker Finance-sponsored Formula One team. They'd had a reasonably good season in 1961 running customer Coopers for multiple World Motorcycle Champion John Surtees and journeyman ace Roy Salvadori, but had come to the unavoidable conclusion that a customer car was never going to be the equal of a full works entry. James Britten worked with the team quite a bit when he wasn't busy running Clive Stanley's operation, and he's the one who recommended having Lola build them a new car. But they'd hedged their bets by ordering one of Colin Chapman's promising Lotus 24s to back up the new Lola. No question bike man Surtees had already proved that he was one of the quickest, most dedicated, most determined drivers out there—on two wheels or four—and deserved first-class equipment.

Even so, the selection of Lola to do the new car was stunning news, since the company had only been in business for a handful of years and had only built three previous models: a small-displacement sports/racer, a front-engined formula junior and a rear-engined formula junior. Sure, the cars had all been smart, neat and quick and had achieved quite a lot of success on the club and national levels. But that still didn't amount to much of a résumé for an assault on Formula One! In fact, some thought it was downright presumptuous....

So on the dull Thursday morning after I finished up my Sebring report, I got a jump from one of the bakery trucks, put some air in that flat LR tire and aimed my rusty, musty, clattery Fiat Multipla east towards Bromley and an interview with the man, drive and talent behind Lola, Eric Broadley. Along the way I thought over the prospects for the upcoming Formula One season 1961 champ Ferrari had pretty much stood pat following the much-discussed "defection of the brains," while the new crop of chassis and V8 engines from England looked more than merely promising and I also wondered if the feelings I seemed to have for Audrey Denbeigh were genuine or just a passing, will-o'-the-wisp illusion. And I worried, somewhere in the deep, anxious pit of my gut, if she wondered the same about me? I also had to concentrate on shifting slowly and deliberately and getting on the gas as smoothly and gently as possible since I could sense the clutch starting to slip again. Especially on the up-shift to top. I'd already adjusted the damn thing twice with the help of some of my race-mechanic friends, but no question it was teetering on the brink of a major repair. But I didn't care. For the first time since I could recall, I actually had a little money in the bank to cover unexpected emergencies. It wasn't a tremendous sum, but enough that I didn't have to constantly be on the lookout for manufacturer PR flacks or race team owners who might put me onto a good meal in return for a few lines of ink. And that was a refreshing situation, to say the least. But I also knew that my amorphous and lucrative new relationship with the uppermost floor of Fairway Tower could easily turn out to be a flash-in-the-pan windfall, and there was no point deluding myself about how long it might last or where it might be going. All I could do was ride it as far as it would go and hope that I could bring something they considered valuable back to Bob Wright and Danny Beagle. And then I'd catch myself thinking about Audrey again. Oh, maybe she wasn't the type to make heads whip around in pit lane, but she was neat and trim and had great, warm eyes and a wonderful smile and one of those perfect British mixtures of fine manners, self-reliance and good humor spiked with a keen edge of sarcasm. I liked that a lot. Along with how easy it felt to be around her. And then of course I started wondering and worrying if it would still be there when I saw her again....

Eric Broadley was the engineering talent and entrepreneurial force behind Lola Racing Cars, Ltd., and he was undoubtedly some kind of genius. Even if he wasn't a particularly imposing character or an especially scintillating press interview. But that's the way it often is with brilliant designers. They tend to be preoccupied and out in the ozone a bit, and it's usually because there's really something else (or maybe a hundred things else!) they'd rather be doing or thinking about rather than talking to some bothersome magazine reporter who's going to take up a lot of time, ask a lot of stupid questions and then get it all wrong anyway.

Like a lot of racecar constructors, Eric started out with dreams of being a racing driver. It was the usual, post-adolescent strain of motorsports addiction, but the passion ran unusually deep beneath his reserved and serious exterior. Eric's family ran a successful tailoring business in Bromley and he'd been trained as an architect, but he and his cousin Graham finally got around to scratching their motorsports itch with a miniscule-budget and well-used 750cc club racer in 1954. For reasons that probably had more to do with finance than inspiration, they decided to build their own car next, and the obvious choice was the thriving 1172cc class, which was based around a thoroughly uninspiring but terrifically cheap and readily available four-cylinder engine out of a staid British economy sedan. Eric did the design and engineering work on the "Broadley Special," and it turned out to be a fast, well-thought-out, well-built and effective track weapon. To the point that other racers started inquiring about copies.

By that time, Coventry Climax had introduced their wonderful little light-alloy, overhead-cam racing engine (which was actually developed out of a portable fire pump motor, but that's another story), and the Coventry Climax quickly established itself as the racing motor-of-choice for the competitive and well-supported small-bore sports/racing classes. Which had become the Place to Race for keen, well-to-do amateur racers as well as the accepted "nursery class" for aspiring world champions. And since all the top cars were using the same exact Coventry Climax engines (and moreover since Climax did their best to keep the engines equal and refused to play favorites with "special" motors), any performance advantage had to come from the chassis. Which naturally motivated sales-hungry designer/constructors like John and Charlie Cooper, Frank Nichols at Elva, John Tojeiro and of course Colin Chapman at Lotus to extend themselves and push one another in the process. Chapman's cars had already earned a reputation for innovative thinking and clever, lightweight design by the time his Lotus Eleven burst on the scene in early 1956, and pretty soon Elevens were winning everywhere from minor club meetings on both sides of the Atlantic to class and Index-of-Performance victories at Le Mans. Colin Chapman sold a *lot* of them. In fact, it seemed incredible—impossible, even—that some young architectural surveyor with but one amateur home-built to his credit would attempt to challenge the Lotus Eleven's supremacy. But that's precisely what Eric Broadley did. He called his new car "Lola" and unveiled it at Brands Hatch in August of 1958, and everyone agreed it was tiny, lovely, light, low and beautifully proportioned. And even in Eric's own hands, it looked bloody quick. But it turned out that Eric Broadley was a bit less than a stellar driving talent. Not that he didn't try. But he was wild and even hairy behind the wheel, and never seemed to have that smooth, patient "something extra" that all the great ones have. That rare ability to *flow* a car around a racetrack rather than fighting it every inch of the way. But the car was impressive nonetheless, and things really came to a head the day he let young comingman Peter Ashdown try it out at Brands Hatch. Ashdown blistered the lap record with it, and keen racers quickly started lining up with money in hand to buy copies. Eric Broadley's time as an aspiring racing driver may have been over, but his new career as owner, manager, designer and driving force behind Lola Racing Cars, Ltd., had just begun....

The Formula One assignment was both a great compliment and a tremendous challenge for Broadley and Lola, and I was extremely curious to see how the little firm was progressing with it. The Lola "works" in Bromley were really just a rented portion of a larger garage/machine shop business that you accessed through a dark, narrow brick hallway behind an unimpressive set of painted wooden doors. There was a small open-air courtyard behind filled with a few garage-customer cars awaiting repair or pickup plus the occasional racecar frame set out for painting. A quiet little office/drafting studio with curtains on the windows sat in front, facing the street, and that's where I found Eric Broadley, sitting at his desk and more-or-less staring off into space while he rolled a drafting pencil slowly around in his fingers. I looked around for Audrey, but she obviously wasn't there. Eric offered up ten percent of a smile and nodded for me to sit down on the drafting-table stool across from him. I took out my notebook and pen. "So," I asked him right off the bat, "are you nervous at all about building a Formula One car?"

"Should I be?" came his distracted reply. You could tell there were other things on his mind.

"Well, it's the pinnacle, isn't it?" I asked rhetorically, trying to prompt some sort of decent response for the magazine. "It's what every little racing car constructor dreams of, isn't it?"

An ironic smile blossomed across his face. "What every little racing car constructor dreams of doing," he corrected me, "is to sell enough cars so it can continue to be a little racing car constructor!"

"Touché," I grinned, and scribbled what he'd said down on my pad. But it turned out to be about the only decent quote of the entire interview. That tends to happen when you interview designers. They can't help it. But afterwards Eric took me through the courtyard for a tour around the shop, and that was absolutely fascinating. It made for quite a contrast with the imposing Ferrari factory in Maranello! Hell, you could have put the entire Lola operation into the space where Ferrari gave his new-car introduction press conferences every year! The Lola shop was stained and worn but kept very tidy, and there were several of the older, Mk. 1 sports/racers in for service and repair, two of the Mk. 3 Formula Juniors under construction and three of the new Formula One Mk. 4s in various states of assembly—one almost completed, one naked chassis with a dummy Climax V8 in back and one frame being brazed together on a heavy, I-section frame jig. You could see that a lot of work was getting done without a lot of fuss, noise or bother. "We're nothing like Ferrari, Porsche or Lotus," Eric explained apologetically, "but we do get on with things."

I saw James Britten in the back by the lathe and drill press, and he was involved in a deep, heated conversation with a rough, rumpled little Englishman with a mausoleum complexion and wild, wiry tufts of gray hair over his ears. I knew in an instant it had to be Audrey's father. I excused myself from Eric—he seemed genuinely relieved to be rid of me—and made my way over to say "hello." But you just don't barge in when two racing men are having a serious difference of opinion about how a hub should be machined. It just isn't done. Eric was busy with the mechanic working on the new F1 car, so I wandered back through the courtyard to the drawing office and did a little quiet nosing around. Most of it was semi-incomprehensible plan and cross-sectional views of various uprights, links, hub carriers, mounting brackets and such that wouldn't mean much to anyone except the draftsman who drew them up and the machinists and fabricators who actually had to bring them to life. Although the design process is the most finite, precise and scientific part of any racing car's development, it often seems the most obscure, mystical and abstracted to an outside observer. But there was one small pencil sketch tacked up on the wall behind the drawing board that really caught my eye. It looked like it had been done on a cocktail napkin, and amounted to a more-or-less ¾-view cutaway rendering of a low, wide, broad-shouldered racing coupe with a big, fat tires and a big, sketchy lump of a V8 sitting behind the cockpit bulkhead. It was the only drawing in the entire office that actually looked like a car.

"And what are *you* up to?" Audrey's voice snapped from behind me. "Stealing secrets?" She'd pretty much ambushed me, sneaking up so quietly that I didn't even know she was there.

"I'm a spy," I told her. "I'm here stealing secrets for Lotus."

"I should have guessed you were with the other side." She clapped her hand on my shoulder, police fashion. "Come along quietly, now."

Her fingers sent a shiver up my neck. "C-can't we work out some sort of deal here?"

"I really ought to turn you in," she mused, staying in character. "But I suppose I might be better off trying to turn you around to our side. That is what they do with spies, isn't it?"

"It is in the movies."

She turned me around to face her. "The movies are better than real life anyway, aren't they?" You couldn't miss that her eyes seemed very tired—maybe even a little sad—but she still looked pretty damn great to me.

"It's good to see you again."

"I have an idea," she continued like she hadn't heard me at all. "Why don't you switch it around and steal a couple of Lotus' secrets for us?"

"I suppose I could do that," I agreed like I was weighing it carefully, "but what are you offering?"

"What sort of motivation would you require?"

"Well, that all depends. Are you looking for specific things like springs, damper rates and camber angles or do you want me to just roll up a set of drawings or two and bring them on over."

"I think that would be best. Just bring the whole bloody lot over." She wagged a finger at me. "But just the prime material, please. Leave all the rubbish and the bits that break and fall off there."

"Oh? And how will I tell which is which?"

She flashed me a sly grin. "Isn't that always the problem at Lotus?"

We both laughed. Audrey really looked grand when she laughed.

"I-it's really good to see you," I gushed again like a school kid. And immediately felt the color creeping up into my cheeks.

"It's good to see you, too," she said encouragingly. "You look lovely in red."

"Thanks," I told her, and turned even redder. "Are...uhh...are things are going well for you?"

"I suppose so."

"Your father's okay?"

"Have you met him yet?"

I shook my head. "I saw him in back with James, but I haven't met him yet."

"Oh, you'll enjoy him. Particularly if you fancy mean, short-tempered, opinionated old men who don't bloody listen and won't take their medicine."

"He sounds like a real charmer."

"Oh, he's a dear, of course," she assured me without much conviction, "but he can be a bit, er, *difficult* now and then."

"I just saw him arguing about a hub or something with James Britten."

"Oh, that's an easy one!" she laughed. "James will ultimately turn a lovely shade of crimson, pull rank and tell him what to do. After which Walter will grumble off and do exactly as he pleases. He's a bit obstinate when he thinks he's right."

"And that happens often?"

"Only all the time...."

I caught myself staring at her. But I couldn't help it. And damn if I could think of another thing to say. My cheeks started heating up again. "I-I don't know what to say," I finally admitted.

"I've always believed that when you haven't anything worthwhile to say, you probably shouldn't say it..."

"That makes sense."

"...but if you feel a desperate need to prattle on anyway, it's probably best to stick to small talk."

"I-I'm not very good at small talk. It makes me impatient."

"Nonsense. I've heard you do it at the races all the time."

"But that's different. That's about racing."

"Exactly! All you really need is another subject."

"I'm afraid I don't have another subject."

"Oh, it's easy," she assured me. "You know how to discuss the weather, don't you?"

"I think I could manage that."

"Well then, why don't you give it a go?"

"Okay." I straightened up and gave her an ad-campaign smile. "Lovely weather we're having, isn't it?"

"Isn't it?"

"I bet it'll be even nicer in a few weeks."

"Oh, undoubtedly. That's what generally happens when spring rolls into summer."

"Even here in damp, foggy old England?"

"Even here."

I looked at her sideways. "I think this is the dumbest conversation I've ever had."

"I'll wager it isn't."

"You'll lose."

"No, I won't. I believe in you, Hank, and have boundless faith in your talent and expertise when it comes to inane conversations."

"It *is* one of my strong points, isn't it?"

"Yes, it does seem to be. You could become famous for it."

And that was the thing about Audrey. We could talk about absolutely nothing—*nothing!*—and it still came out fun. She had this knack for volleying back just the exact right thing with just the exact right edge to it. I ran my tongue nervously across the back of my teeth. "D-do you think you might want to have another inane conversation sometime?"

"Did you have some particular time or place in mind?"

My mouth was suddenly very dry. "I-I was thinking maybe over a meal or drinks or something...."

She arched one eyebrow up and held it like an open drawbridge. "Does this mean you're asking me on a date?"

I thought she might be making me squirm just for the fun of it, but I couldn't be sure. "Ehh, it sure sounds that way, doesn't it?"

"It does indeed."

"W-well then, I suppose I am."

"W-well then," she mimicked, "I suppose I'm accepting."

"You *are?*"

"Of course I am. It sounds lovely."

"It does?"

"Don't sound so amazed. It could change a girl's mind."

"I-I'm sorry."

"And don't say you're sorry. That could spoil things as well."

I looked down at the floor. "I'm not very good at this, am I?"

"Oh, you did quite well, Hank. Honestly you did. I think you may just be a wee bit out of practice."

"Since the summer after high school," I admitted, and we both laughed.

And that's when the drawing office door banged open and Audrey's father came hobbling in on two stiff legs and a cane. I guess he'd been watching us through the window. Walter Denbeigh was a short, flinty, unkempt-looking old man with tiny, piercing eyes, sunken cheeks and wild clumps of steel-wool hair around his ears. He was wearing rumpled gray shop coveralls with machine-oil stains down the front and a ripped back pocket, and he glared at us like we'd been overheard plotting a bomb attack on Parliament as he advanced towards us on a series of abrupt, awkward steps, his shoulders jerking with every movement and the rubber tip on the end of his cane chirping off the floor. I couldn't help noticing that his cane was made out of a length of aluminum tubing with a rubber table-leg cover on the bottom end and a beautifully machined, knurled aluminum knob attached to the top with a short, threaded coupling and two anodized jam nuts so it could be adjusted for length. Audrey's father pulled up to a halt right in front of us and stared at me through two angry, suspicious eyes. But he didn't say a word.

"Hank," Audrey said evenly, "this is Walter."

Walter kept staring at me, his eyes like rifle sights.

"Father," Audrey continued, "this is Hank..."

His eyes didn't change.

"...I've mentioned him to you several times...."

I waited for something to happen—for *anything* to happen!—but the moment just sort of hung there, suspended. I finally extended my hand. "Audrey's told me an awful lot about you..." I began.

"There's nothing to tell," he snapped, ignoring my hand. And then he turned to Audrey and growled: "Did you get my pills?"

"I've got them right here," she nodded, and pulled a little paper bag out of her purse and handed it over.

He opened it up with jittery, blackened fingers that were covered with cuts, scrapes and scar tissue and held the little brown pill bottle directly in front of his nose. "What're these damn things for?" he demanded.

"Those are for your heart, father," she answered patiently. "You've had them before. You just couldn't find the bottle."

"These are the ones I put under my tongue?"

"When you need to," she cautioned. "When you...when you feel something."

"They taste terrible," he scowled. "It's like eating metal."

"I can't help that. You need to take them when you need them."

"For my heart, right?"

"Yes," she nodded. "But they ought to be for your disposition."

"There's nothing wrong with my bloody disposition!" he snapped. And then his eyes swiveled around like he was noticing me for the very first time. I watched with amazement as, out of nowhere, his scowl melted away and his eyes softened. "There's nothing wrong with my disposition, is there?" he asked me in a perfectly pleasant, reasonable voice. "You must be the young book author Audrey's been telling me about."

I blinked a few times. "I-I haven't actually written any books," I told him. "I mean, I haven't actually *finished* any..." I licked my lips "...sure, I'm *working* on one. But it isn't quite done yet...."

"Oh?" he said, sounding genuinely disappointed.

"It takes a long time," I tried to explain. "And you can get lost in it sometimes..."

He looked at me like he was waiting for more.

"...In the meantime, I'm writing for a magazine..."

"Oh, really? What about?"

"He writes about car racing, father," Audrey interrupted with a mild fizz of irritation. "I've told you that. That's how I met him. At the Daytona and Sebring races. With Clive's team..."

He looked at her like it was all news to him. And then he looked back at me and his eyes hardened down to gun slits again. "I don't much care for magazine writers," he sneered venomously. "They always get things wrong..."

"You're absolutely right!" I quickly agreed.

"...and then they bloody well brag about it!" he continued like he hadn't even heard me. He waved his hand dismissively through the air. "I've got to get back to work," he grumbled at the floor. "I've got bloody hubs to finish." And with that he turned on his heels and shuffled out of the drawing office, the rubber tip on his cane chirping against the floor.

Audrey closed the door behind him, then looked at me: "You see how it is."

I gave her half a shrug. "I'm surprised he can still work."

"It's a bit amazing, isn't it?" she exhaled. "But he's still fine with the blueprints and machinery and all. He can still make anything out of anything if you just leave him alone and give him a proper bit of metal to work with."

"Doesn't he get..." I found myself searching for the right words "...*difficult?*"

"He's all right when you leave him to his work. And when I'm not around, James knows how to deal with him. He's the one who brought him over from Aston, and he's known him a very long time. You've already seen about the worst of it." She let out a long, sad sigh and looked up at me. "You're new and different, Hank, and Walter doesn't react very well to anything that threatens to upset his world."

"You think *I'm* going to upset his world?"

"I'm actually rather hoping you will," she said evenly. "But we'll have to see how that goes, won't we?"

"Uh, yeah," I mumbled as a nervous mixture of fear and anticipation swirled around inside of me. "I guess we will."

"He'll get used to you."

"You think?"

Audrey nodded.

"But what about the future?" I had to ask.

"What about it?" she shrugged. "All you can do is keep taking care of today, isn't it? You keep doing that every day and tomorrow never comes...."

Everybody except the racecar constructors had a lot of down time going on after Sebring, what with five weeks before the next World Manufacturers' Championship round in Sicily and another two weeks before the first Grand Prix of the year at Zandvoort on May 20th. Sure, we had the usual, non-championship Formula One rounds coming up in April to give the British teams and fans a good look at each other, but those weren't far away and didn't require extended travel. So I made use of the opportunity and asked Audrey out. Several times, in fact. Although it felt awfully strange to be calling a girl up for a date again! I hadn't really done that sort of thing since high school (or maybe it was junior college?) and not with particularly inspiring results at the time. But Audrey helped things along by casually mentioning that there was a movie she really wanted to see, so we wound up going to *"A Taste of Honey"* together. Now you have to understand that all the lah-de-dah movie critics had been absolutely swooning over this particular show because *"A Taste of Honey"* was filmed in gritty black-and-white and touched on a lot of the hot-button current social issues like interracial dating, unwanted pregnancies and homosexuality. Not to mention that it had a catchy theme song that became a pop-chart hit several times over. *"A Taste of Honey"* starred a frumpy-looking Rita Tushingham as a poor, lonely, not-particularly-attractive working-class girl living in a small, crappy apartment with her promiscuous, alcoholic, loudmouth mother, and she winds up getting more-or-less squeezed out of the flat one night by her mother's crude, crass and thoroughly dislikable new boyfriend. So the Rita Tushingham character wanders around town looking all forlorn and lost and lonely and out-of-place and winds up shacking up with this sympathetic but ultimately characterless young sailor (who just naturally happens to be black) and of course not long after that he disappears off to sea and she discovers—you guessed it!—that she's pregnant. How about that! But the real meat of the story is how she faces all this adversity and manages to get a crappy little job for herself in a crappy little shoe store and moves into her very own, even smaller and crappier little apartment. How inspiring! And the manager of the shoe store turns out to be this equally lonely, lost and miserable homosexual guy named Geoffrey (but with a heart of gold, of course), and they wind up sharing that tiny, crappy little flat together and he (heart of gold, remember) tries to help her come to terms with having this illegitimate, probably-won't-be-exactly-white new baby. He even offers to marry her so the baby will have a father, even though both of them know it will be an awkward, loveless, sexless compromise that may well cut them off from any hope of finding something better for themselves in the future. And if that's not depressing enough, the terrifically nasty and unpleasant (and still alcoholic, promiscuous and loud-mouthed) mother reappears again right at the end, moves herself in and Geoffrey out, and you just know, as the final credits start rolling, that the lead character you've spent the last hundred minutes or so identifying with and empathizing with is set prime for a thoroughly awful, miserable and unsatisfying life....

Now all the simpering reviewers were over the moon about *"A Taste of Honey"* because they said it represented *"a new wave of realistic, 'slice-of-life' British films"* that everybody should go see and then discuss afterwards *ad nauseum* over way too many cigarettes and strong cups of espresso. Or perhaps even a brandy or two. But I thought it was dreary, dull, deadening and depressing. As I told Audrey, I generally prefer actual entertainment over shared misery when I go out to see a show, and therefore favored old Errol Flynn swashbucklers like *"Robin Hood"* and *"Captain Blood"* or Ronald Coleman in *"The Prisoner of Zenda,"* where you at least have some kind of inspiring (albeit mythical) hero to root for and admire. And you always knew who he was because the heroes in those movies were inevitably handsome, clean-cut, self-effacing, devil-may-care, believed in Hard Work and Fair Play and wore billowy dueling shirts open halfway down to their navels. And the bad guys always looked properly mean, sneaky, snaky, slimy and untrustworthy, which made them easy to spot. Plus the leading-man hero was not only taller, leaner and handsomer than any other male character in the movie, he was also invariably smarter, braver, stronger, cleverer, a better sword fighter and more honest, noble, upright, funny, humble, fair-minded and self-deprecating to boot. And that's what you really want in a hero figure, isn't it? Plus you always knew he'd win out in the end and get the girl (Olivia DeHavilland, as often as not) and you walked out of that movie feeling that there really *were* such things as honor and loyalty and gallantry in this world. And that goodness and justice—albeit never, ever before halfway through the third reel—would ultimately prevail. Those were pretty nice feelings to have, even if they never lasted much further than the soda fountain at the end of the block.

"But that's not what reality's all about," Audrey protested over tea and cake at a little corner pastry shop.

"You don't go to movies to see reality," I tried to explain. "You go to movies to *get away* from reality. That's the whole idea."

"So you just like macho, swashbuckling sword fantasies where the hero overcomes impossible odds, wins a great victory and rides off into the bloody sunset?"

"With the girl," I reminded her. "He's got to get the girl at the end, too. It's part of the standard deal."

Audrey snorted at me. But it was a relatively genteel sort of snort. "So tell me," she asked, "are there any other kinds of movies that you like?"

"Oh, of course there are!" I assured her enthusiastically. "Almost anything with racecars. Even crap melodramas like *'The Big Wheel'* with Mickey Rooney and *'To Please a Lady'* with Clark Gable and Barbara Stanwyck—even if the ending was crap—and of course Kirk Douglas, Gilbert Roland, Cesar Romero and Lee J. Cobb in *'The Racers.'* Hell, I know just about every line from that one by heart."

"And that's it? Adolescent swordplay and adolescent speed fantasies?"

"Not at all," I insisted. "Even though it wasn't a racing movie and even though it was British..." I watched Audrey stiffen a little "...I really liked *'School for Scoundrels'* with Terry-Thomas. He drives an Aston DB3S in it, you know."

"Yes. I know."

"But I like lots of movies. All different kinds, in fact."

Her eyebrows arched playfully. "Oh? Like what?"

And so I started rattling off what I hoped would be viewed as a pretty damn impressive list of titles, directors, writers, stars and genres that included Hitchcock suspense dramas like *"The Man Who Knew Too Much"* (the color version with Jimmy Stewart and Doris Day, of course) and those brilliant Charlie Chaplin silents like *"City Lights,"* *"Modern Times"* and *"The Gold Rush"* and Bob Hope comedies like *"The Ghost Breakers"* and *"My Favorite Brunette."* Not to mention all those great old black-and-white gangster epics from the 1930s and 40s like *"The Big Sleep"* and of course the entire William Powell/Myrna Loy *"Thin Man"* series of smart, classy whodunits. And I really had a thing for those creepy old horror movies like *"Frankenstein"* and *"Dracula"* and *"The Invisible Man"* and *"The Wolf Man"* that Universal Studios cranked out one-right-after-the-other back in the thirties. I enjoyed a good war movie, western or adventure flick as much as anybody and I could even muddle my way through dark, obscure, hard-to-fathom intellectual fare like Ingmar Bergman's *"Wild Strawberries"* or *"The Seventh Seal."* But to my way of thinking, what was the damn point of spending an hour and a half in a movie theater watching an anything-but-uplifting story about unfortunate, unhandsome, awkward, depressed, plain, poor, hopelessly ordinary characters and their sorry little lives? I mean, didn't you get enough of that just looking out your fucking window? Or back at yourself in your shaving mirror every morning?

Who needed it?

But Audrey liked *"A Taste of Honey"* a lot. She even got a little bit sniffly once or twice. And I did have to admit that the acting was pretty good, even if the characters and story line were depressing as hell. But I guess that was the point. You look in on a life that's even worse than your own and I suppose it can be uplifting in a stupid, perverse, reverse-angle-idiotic sort of way. Make you feel a bit better about things, you know? Or at least that's how I summed it up for Audrey over the last of our coffee and dessert. And that's when she called me "a Neanderthal." Or maybe it was "a Visigoth." Or maybe it was both. But she did it in a way that made us both laugh.

We finished up our coffees and the last flakes of our pastries and I paid the bill, but to be honest, I didn't really want to take her home. I didn't want our first evening together to end, and I got the impression that she didn't, either. So we just drove around for awhile in my crappy old Fiat. And that's when I noticed that, besides the irritating rattle from the loose window in the driver's-side door and the *clunk!* over bumps from something in the front suspension and the clatter from the valves that I'd pretty much gotten used to and the way you had to gingerly caress every shift into second to avoid a *graunch!* from the synchros, the clutch slip was reaching truly epic proportions. Especially on the up-shift to top. So I explained that it would really be best if we headed back to her place before we got stranded somewhere with no appreciable drive to the rear wheels. But I still didn't want the night to end—I could tell she didn't, either—so we dropped into a pub around the corner from the row house she shared with her father and had ourselves a nightcap or two. And wound up staying until closing time. We didn't really talk about anything in particular—even though we talked the whole time—and I had this feeling like we were really getting along. Even if I had no idea where it was heading or how it was going to get there. And I was beginning to believe that, underneath all her intelligence, organization, good manners, sly wit, sense of responsibility and astonishing self-reliance, Audrey was just as lost and uncertain about it as I was. But even so, it felt kind of nice to be stumbling around in the dark together....

We went out together several more times over the next few weeks, and the awkward part always came when I tried to say good-night to her at her father's front door. Walter was always up when we got there—no matter what time it was— waiting in his favorite chair in the front room with the curtains slightly parted, reading the paper or watching his telly or just sitting there with a book across his lap, half-dozed off but waiting for the sound of her key in the lock. And you always knew he had one eye peeled over the top of his television set or around the corner of his newspaper, watching us under the entirely-too-bright light that he made sure was burning over the front stoop. I'd thought about asking Audrey over to my apartment (I even half-believed that she might go) but the place was such a rancid little shit-hole that I couldn't bring myself to do it. I even spent a whole day trying to straighten it up—tidying up my writing area and putting things away and washing all the dishes in the sink and hiding all my renegade socks and underwear in the bottom drawer of my resale-shop reproduction Chippendale dresser—but it still looked like a rancid little shit hole. Plus it was terribly awkward about her father. She couldn't be somewhere with me without being absent from him, and that was always hanging over us wherever we went. We tried going out to dinner with him one night—all three of us—and I was fortunate to have a brand-new Series III Humber Super Snipe sedan for the occasion thanks to the Rootes Group press relations people, who hoped I would write something nice about it. And I was glad to have it, since my old Fiat didn't make a very good impression and the latest adjustment hadn't made much of an improvement on what was now a terminal case of clutch slip. But Walter Denbeigh didn't so much as flicker an eye at the shiny new Humber, and our dinner together was an exercise in stilted bits of conversation and long, awkward silences. And when Audrey excused herself to go to the ladies' room, Walter glared at me the entire time and never said a word. It made me uneasy as hell, and I kept looking towards the back of the restaurant, waiting helplessly for Audrey to come out of the loo. And then, without any warning at all, Walter spoke:

"Yer lookin' t'give m'little Audrey a bloody good rogering, aren't y'now?" he hissed through clenched teeth. But it came out so suddenly and unexpectedly that I couldn't believe I'd heard him right.

"I beg your pardon?"

But Walter didn't say another word. He just glared at me even harder and meaner than before. And he didn't bother to thank me for picking up the tab for dinner. When we got back to their row house, Audrey lingered for a moment under that too-bright front porch light after Walter shuffled his way inside. "I'm sorry," she whispered as he disappeared through the hallway.

"It's not your fault," I whispered back.

"But now you see how things are." She looked up at me. "It's not that he doesn't like you."

"You could've fooled me."

"No, it's change he doesn't like, Hank. Anything that upsets his sense of order or set routines..."

"Well," I whispered just a little louder (like maybe even loud enough for Walter to hear), "where the hell does that leave things with us?"

She didn't seem to have an answer. "Look, I've got to go inside now," she told me, and planted a resigned little peck on my cheek. I watched the door close behind her with a hollow click.

Chapter 13: The Mansion on McElligot Lane

The British open-wheeler racing season always kicked off with a series of early, non-championship races for Formula One and Formula Two cars, and they generally drew large crowds and solid entry lists (in spite of the occasionally dank and soggy English spring weather) because the Brits are just plain over-the-moon nuts about their motor racing. Plus they also offered decent starting money, so most of the top English teams turned out to pocket some of the cash, test out their new cars and perhaps try to get one last, good run out of the previous season's "old nail" so they could hopefully sell the bugger off to some wide-eyed privateer. The first race was the Lombank Trophy at Snetterton on Saturday, April 14th, followed just over a week later by the Glover Trophy at Goodwood on Easter Monday followed by the Aintree 200 on April 28 and the International Trophy at Silverstone two weeks later on May 12th (giving the contracted drivers a chance to scamper off to Sicily for the Targa Florio in between). I always looked forward to those races— even if the magazine rarely gave me more than a paragraph or two to cover them— because they allowed fans and scribes alike to get a preview peek at the new crop of British grand prix cars and see what sort of form the drivers were showing. And it was hardly lost on me that Audrey might well be helping out with the timing and scoring for Reg Parnell, James Britten and the Bowmaker team. By then I'd come to the realization that Audrey was an altogether more relaxed, carefree, less encumbered and easier going person on race weekends than she was looking after her cantankerous father, making foreign-language travel arrangements for racing teams and tutoring spoiled children back in London.

I thought the finished Lola grand prix car looked really terrific (I'd made a habit of more-or-less "just dropping by" the Lola shop in Bromley on the days I knew Audrey would be there) although you never really know about a new racecar until it's on the track in anger. But to my way of thinking both Surtees and the Climax V8 looked like potential winners if the chassis was up to the job. And it surely looked the part, all slender and elegant in blue paint so dark it almost seemed black and with a handsome red band around its nose. To be honest, I was getting a little bit of a rah-rah, home-team feeling for the Bowmaker bunch. Although a lot of that was probably down to the connection with Audrey. But no matter how good it looked on a shop floor, the new Lola was up against some stiff, well-entrenched opposition. Lotus and Cooper were always to be reckoned with—albeit for different reasons—and BRM's new V8-powered car looked trim, poised and powerful, and their driving lineup was solid with the determined Graham Hill as team leader and ex-Ferrari man/ace test driver Richie Ginther in the second car. Twice world champ Jack Brabham had left Cooper to build his own cars with designer Ron Tauranac, but their new chassis wouldn't be ready for several months and so he was starting out the season in a customer Lotus 24. Which you can bet Colin Chapman was only too pleased to sell him, since constructor points accrued to the manufacturer regardless of which team entered the car. Neither Porsche nor Ferrari were expected to make the pre-season rounds in England, Porsche preferring to test on their own at home and Ferrari turning up his nose at the appearance money offered. Besides, Ferrari's cars were little changed from the ones that dominated the '61 season, so everyone pretty much knew what they could do. I'd seen a few pictures of the new Porsche flat 8, and it was altogether sleeker and more purposeful-looking than their tubby-looking 4-cylinder cars from the previous season. Plus they had Dan Gurney and Jo Bonnier as drivers, and even that xenophobic English jerk Eric Gibbon had to admit that Dan was really something special. And of course the wild card for the upcoming grand prix season had to be Stirling Moss in Rob Walker's much-talked-about privateer Ferrari. Although it was common knowledge that the car hadn't shown up yet, which came as no big surprise to anyone who knew anything about Ferrari's past record when it came to delivering customer cars on time to privateer teams. For the pre-season races, Moss was being re-united with the same Lotus 18/24 that he'd driven for Rob the previous year, only now wearing the signature pale green of the UDT-Laystall team. It was still a good car and no question Stirling knew it intimately, so it figured to be the yardstick against which all the new cars would be measured.

As you can imagine, I was really looking forward to that first round at Snetterton on April 14th to see how things were shaping up. Only then I got a four ayem long-distance phone call from Danny Beagle, insisting that I drop everything and head back to Detroit immediately for another urgent meeting with Bob Wright. I hated the idea of missing the Snetterton race—and seeing Audrey at a racetrack again, of course—but it was Fairway's money that allowed me to take her out in the first place (and would no doubt be paying for the much-needed clutch job my decrepit old Fiat) and so when Bob Wright wanted a meeting, I had sure as hell better be there. Although I was starting to wonder how this was going to sort itself out once the new season got rolling and we had sports car and Formula One races scattered all over Europe damn near every weekend.

I arrived in Detroit late Wednesday morning looking typically rumpled, sleep-deprived and disheveled, but Danny Beagle was adamant that we had to hustle over to Fairway Tower immediately to have lunch with Bob Wright. He met us in front of the 12th floor executive cafeteria and ushered us quickly inside after a few perfunctory handshakes and hellos. You always got the feeling that Bob Wright was a man in a terrific hurry and had literally dozens of other places he desperately needed to be. But even so he insisted on buying us lunch. The 12th-floor executive cafeteria was all warm, polished walnut and gleaming marble flooring, and one whole wall was a huge, panoramic picture window overlooking the dreary smoke-stacks and factory buildings below. But the food was pretty damn amazing. They had ½-pound steakburgers with all the trimmings and pot roast with buttered noodles and chicken cacciatore over rice pilaf and three different kinds of steak—your choice of rib eye, T-bone or New York strip—plus spaghetti with ground sirloin meatballs, club sandwiches as thick as the Detroit metro phone book and deep-fried fresh lake perch with macaroni and cheese. And your choice of baked, mashed, country fried, French fried or au gratin potatoes and green beans, peas, candied carrots, beets or succotash as side dishes. Plus soup and salad if you wanted. Don't even get me started on the desserts.

But none of it looked very good to me. My internal clock was all twisted around from the flight over and I had that queasy, up-all-night/maybe-a-few-too-many-drinks-on-the-plane feeling in the pit of my stomach. So Bob asked the smiling old lady behind the counter to make me some plain scrambled eggs with dry toast—that's what he said his mother always made for him when his stomach was a little off—and at least I could look at it without turning the same approximate green as Stirling Moss' UDT-Laystall Lotus. Danny had no such problem, and ordered himself an extra-large portion of the pot roast and noodles with a big scoopful of au gratin potatoes and about a half-pound of succotash on the side. You wouldn't think a guy his size could eat that much, but he could.

Bob Wright kept the conversation light for about the first ten seconds or so, asking how my flight over was plus a few polite questions about the upcoming season and what I thought about the new crop of cars. But you could tell he had something else on his mind. And it didn't take long for him to come to the point: "So what's it going to take to beat Ferrari at Le Mans?" he asked out of nowhere. He made it sound like a simple sort of question that probably deserved to have a simple sort of answer.

But of course it wasn't. And it didn't.

"That's an awfully complicated question," I tried to explain.

"Of course it is!" he agreed energetically. And then added, just as energetically: "But does it really have to be?"

I looked over at Danny Beagle for help, but he was working his way through his pot roast and noodles and didn't seem much interested. It was obvious I was flying solo on this. So I gave Bob Wright about two-thirds of an equivocal shrug and started in: "If you had, say, 500 horsepower in a car that weighed, oh, say, 2200 pounds and handled and stopped really well and was rock-solid reliable and didn't lift its damn front end off the ground when you got it up around 200 or so where the aerodynamics start getting iffy, and if nothing ever broke or fell off and you had two top drivers who simply never made mistakes and the right tires from the right tire company and a crew who could change all four wheels, fill it up with gas and swap out the brake pads in less than two minutes, and moreover had driving lights and fog lights that were worth a shit and wipers that could actually clear the rain off the windscreen at 190-plus and then, on top of all that, if you had all the fucking luck in the world..." I paused to clear my throat "...well, if you had all that going for you, you wouldn't even have to show up. They could pretty much just mail you out the trophy and the prize money...."

A strange, even eerie smile spread across Bob's face. "Good," he nodded. "Now we're getting somewhere."

"We are?"

He nodded emphatically. "We're getting down to what it'll take. And that's what our people are going to need to know!" He rapped his knuckles on the table for emphasis. "Brass tacks, Hank! That's what we need!" He looked me squarely in the eyes. "That's why we wanted you on the team, Hank: to help us get down to brass tacks..."

I didn't say anything.

"...and that's why we need you here in The Tower this week."

"It is?"

He nodded gravely. "We need to get our people up to speed and fired up about this Le Mans thing over in Europe. Need them to get their brains and hearts wrapped around it. And that's why I want you to sit in on a few preliminary group meetings with Danny here..."

"Preliminary group meetings?"

He nodded again. "We've got a lot of engineering groups here in The Tower, and I've had Danny put together a little presentation that he's going to make to each and every one of them. We've got an engine and driveline group and a chassis and suspension group and a controls and instruments group and of course our body, trim and styling group. We're even looking at adding a full-time aerodynamic team—we've got some pretty good guys on loan from McDonnell-Douglas right now—and we'll need our logistics and procurement and supply people on board...."

"How many people do you plan to have working on this?" I interrupted.

He looked at me like it was a silly sort of question. "Why, as many as it takes, of course." He leaned in closer and chided: "After all, Hank, we *do* have the resources...."

And that's when I tried to explain to him that big committees and sheer force of numbers aren't always the right answer, and that the very best racing cars come from a single, gifted human brain with a ruthless edge of genius in it. Oh, a lot of people inevitably get involved and throw their two-cents'-worth in on any racecar project, but you really needed a Colin Chapman or a Ferdinand Porsche or a Vittorio Jano or even an Eric Broadley at the head of the snake to make sure you stayed focused on a single, integrated design concept rather than a Frankenstein-monster collection of mismatched bits and pieces.

Bob Wright didn't look convinced. "We've been building cars by committee for an awfully long time," he explained somewhat testily, "and we've always found that two heads are better than one. And that four are usually better than two."

"It depends on whose heads they are," I argued right back.

Bob's eyes went icy hard for just an instant, but they softened up again just as quickly. "Look, I know Danny and I brought you in here as our field expert—and we did that because we really think you're the best man for the job—but you're going to have to get used to the way we do things around here."

I didn't say a thing.

"Now I'm going to have you sit in on these preliminary group meetings for us, and I want you to listen and I want you to answer questions when you're asked and I want you to speak up when you've got something worthwhile to say..."

"That sounds fair enough."

"...but I want you to speak up to *me*, not to the committees and working groups..."

For just a moment, I thought I heard the sound of The Other Shoe Dropping.

"...or to Danny here, if I'm not available." Bob's face opened up into a broad, encouraging smile. "And I expect you to be every bit as honest, candid and forthcoming as you have been here today."

And with that, our luncheon meeting was over. Even though Bob had barely touched the club sandwich and ginger ale in front of him. And I can't say I was particularly happy about where we'd left things.

"Well then, it's all set!" Bob concluded as he got up to excuse himself. "Karen will have your meeting list ready upstairs. I think she's got you scheduled for four of them. Or maybe it's five." And with that he turned to leave.

"Uh...I, um, kind of wanted to know something else..." I stammered at his back.

He wheeled around and regarded me with an irritated, puzzled expression. As if to ask *'what more could there possibly be?'*

"...Uh, I kind of wanted to know when I can go back to England?"

Bob Wright stared at me for a moment, thinking it over. And then his eyes lit up: "Tell you what!" he answered decisively, "H.R. Junior's having a big party at his house in Grosse Pointe Farms Friday night. It's for his daughter's 17th birthday..." Bob and Danny exchanged knowing grimaces "...She might even be there...."

Danny stifled a laugh.

"We'll get your meetings done during the week and then I think it'd be a great idea if you dropped by at the party. Got to know the guys on my team a little better in a relaxed, social sort of setting. It'll be *good* for you."

"Uh...I've, uh, got this race I'm supposed to be covering for the magazine back in England this weekend..."

Bob Wright thought it over for two whole seconds. "I think this is more important for you," he decreed like there was no room for argument. "I'm sure you can afford to miss that race in England."

"Uh...I...well..."

"Is it a *major* race?"

"Well, not really. It's just that..."

"Can't you get the information you need for your report from someone else? One of the other writers perhaps? Or one of your associates?"

"I don't have any associates."

"*Everyone* has associates," Bob insisted. "I'm sure you can get one of them to help you out on this..." he flashed me his most unassailable Commanding Officer smile "...at least if you try."

And that was the end of it. Case closed. Over and out. Bob shook hands with both of us—he had one hell of a grip—and hurried off towards those special elevators to the 13th floor on long, purposeful strides.

I don't want to bore you with the details of my various and sundry closed-door preliminary group meetings on the lower floors of Fairway Tower over the next few days, but suffice to say I was fascinated by just how many sub-groups and fragmented responsibilities you could break the design of a car down into and still have no overall concept of what the hell it was going to look like when you were done. Inside or out. Vice President of Engineering Hugo Becker had taken time off from wringing out the latest Ferret prototypes at the proving grounds so he could sit in on most of the meetings, and I was pleased to see that he at least seemed to have some sort of inkling as to the size, scope and technical challenge of Le Mans and how it differed from figuring out the proper roll-under on a Ferret rocker panel or getting the price down on a dashboard and instrument cluster or fixing a faulty heater fan design so the plastic blades wouldn't flex up against the housing duct on "HI" and make a noise like a moth the size of a blue jay was trying to escape from behind the dashboard.

Hugo Becker was a stern-faced, no-nonsense engineer with a second-generation hint of a German accent, and he always wore white lab coats over his suit pants, white dress shirts and ties because it made him look efficient, scientific and professional. But he was definitely a good guy under that severe, habitually dissatisfied Germanic exterior. You rarely heard Hugo laugh, but he had this sly, thin, somewhat mean-spirited smile that would creep across his face whenever he saw anything that proved, yet once again, that he was surrounded by mostly fools, morons, yes-men, milquetoasts, cover-your-ass paycheck collectors and outright idiots. And I saw that smile crease its way across his face a lot over the next few days as we listened to the body-and-styling group's afternoon-long discussion about whether a potential Le Mans winner ought to be a coupe or an open car—a few of the Fairway stylists referred to them as "hardtops" and "convertibles"—and that took us from lunch right through afternoon break. At which point the conversation veered off in the direction of if it were to be a coupe, should it have conventional or gullwing doors? Which took us right on through to nearly six o'clock. Now these were honest, serious questions that every racecar designer needs to ask. And answer. After all, a coupe should cheat the wind better and be sleeker aerodynamically—yielding higher top speed from the same available power—but it's also inevitably heavier and carries its weight higher up off the ground. Which raises the center of gravity, and raising the center of gravity is something you just never, ever willingly want to do with a racing car. Then again, Le Mans is a very special sort of race in that so much of every lap boils down to balls-out top speed. So that made the coupe the better choice, right? Only then Hugo asked me what I thought and I had to remind them all that a coupe can be harder on the driver because of all the heat, fumes and engine noise that get trapped inside the cockpit. Then again, an open car is going to put the driver out where the weather can get at him. And that's always a real concern at Le Mans, where rain and fog are more of likelihood than a possibility. Only most drivers will tell you that they can actually see *better* out of an open car in foul weather. That's because they can peer out over the top edge of the windscreen—even in terrible, driving rain—while the poor fish in a coupe will most likely be cursing the cozy, protective windshield that the wipers have just spread the goo of a thousand squashed insects and a half-quart of engine oil across like a coating of suet. Not to mention the defroster vents that nine times out of ten can't keep the damn thing from fogging up on the inside....

As to the late afternoon session, the Fairway designers spent several confusing hours debating the relative merits of gullwing versus conventional doors on a coupe. Sure, the drivers can hop in and out more easily during pit stops with gullwing doors—and particularly if the car is built really low to the ground—but you lose the strength and structural integrity that comes with a full roof section. But that was really a question to pass on to the chassis and frame group, wasn't it? And then Hugo had me remind everyone that some drivers aren't especially fond of gullwing doors.

"Why is that?" a bright-looking young door-hinge engineer inquired.

"Because if the car flips over and winds up on its roof..." I watched the young door-hinge engineer lean forward expectantly in his chair "...the poor fish inside can't get out! That's terribly inconvenient," I explained. "Particularly if there's a fire...."

It was apparent that hadn't occurred to him.

By Friday afternoon, I'd come to the unavoidable conclusion that there were quite a few sharp, earnest, committed, straight-thinking people on staff in the various engineering departments at Fairway Motors. On the other hand, it was equally clear that they didn't know their asses from a hole in the ground when it came to racing car design. And it looked like Hugo Becker and I (and maybe Danny Beagle) were the only ones who appreciated that fact.

"Look, this is just never going to work out the way you're trying to do it," I told Bob Wright at our final de-briefing on Friday afternoon. It was Friday the 13th, wouldn't you know it?

"What do you mean, 'it's never going to work out?'"

"You've got way too many people involved. And they're doing way too much supposing and postulating and theoretical thinking. Racing happens *fast*. The technology happens *fast*. None of your people have the right sort of background for this."

I thought that observation might make Bob angry. And I surely didn't want to lose my new job with Fairway Motors (or those fat company checks that were showing up like clockwork every other week at my cruddy little flat in London!) but I felt I had no option except to call it the way I saw it. Bob looked threatening at first, but that passed in an instant and I could see he was actually considering what I'd said. "So what would *you* do?" he finally asked.

"Well, you're going to have to start with a smaller, more specialized group. Some racing people. Guys who've been there already and know what it takes."

He rubbed his chin between his thumb and forefinger. "We've got Harlon Lee," he mused, "and we've been talking to this Carroll Shelby fellow...."

"That's a start! That's a start!" I nodded enthusiastically. "I like both of those choices. And Shelby's actually won at Le Mans, so he's got some idea what it takes."

"So he's told us."

"That's the kind of talent and experience you need to get working on this," I told him. "Sure, your people here in The Tower will be working with them and backing them up—like you said, you have tremendous engineering resources here..."

"We've got the best in the world!" he interjected with a patriotic surge of pride. But then a worried look flashed across his face. "We don't want this to leak out, though..."

I took a deep breath. "Look, you're just not going to get where you need to be any other way. You're going to need more talent and more experience. More than even Shelby or Harlon Lee have."

"What do you mean?"

And of course I was thinking already of guys like Colin Chapman and Eric Broadley over in England. And of that little cocktail-napkin sketch of a low, broad-shouldered GT coupe with a big lump of a V8 engine in back that I'd seen in Eric Broadley's drafting office. But I didn't say anything about it. Not yet, anyway. Besides, I was beginning to get an idea. "The kind of talent and experience you need is all over in Europe right now," I said flatly. "And the very best of it these days is not very far from where I live back in London."

Bob didn't need an anvil to fall on him, and he had Karen Sabelle book me a Saturday morning flight back to Heathrow before we left Fairway Tower that evening.

That night—Friday the 13th, remember—I found myself waiting for Danny Beagle to pick me up and take me out to the most exclusive section of Grosse Pointe Farms to join the teeming multitude of middle-aged-and-older Fairway Tower guests and employees at dear little Amelia Camellia Fairway's seventeenth birthday party. Danny showed up around quarter past seven, and after he'd checked to make sure I was wearing my Fairway-blue blazer and that my tie was properly knotted, my shoes were properly shined and that I'd actually gotten the haircut he'd made me promise to get, he handed me a package wrapped in bright pink gift paper with a shiny, pink satin bow on top. I stared at it blankly. "What the hell is this?"

"It's your gift."

"My gift?"

"Not *your* gift, dummy. It's the gift you're going to give Little Harry Dick's spoiled little shithead of a daughter. For her birthday..."

"But what the hell *is* it?"

"How the hell should I know? Karen Sabelle picked it out. I've got one, too. We all got one."

"And you have no idea what they are?"

"Who the hell cares? The stinking little brat is probably gonna throw them out anyway. Unless she can figure out how to smash 'em to pieces or set fire to them... " He shook his head. "She's a wild, hateful little bitch..." he muttered under his breath "...You'll see."

"Sounds like a real fun evening."

"Oh, it'll be fine," he assured me. "Hell, you probably won't even see her. She's just the excuse for the party. What it's *really* all about is parked outside."

"Parked outside?"

Danny led me out into the Fairway Inn parking lot. And there, bathed in the lavender-white glow of the Fairview Inn's illuminated marquee (which, that particular evening, was welcoming the "SAINT IGNATIUS HI-LO BINGO BADGERS") sat a gleaming, oddly two-toned example of Fairway Motors' enormous Freeway Frigate Custom Coachman Coupé—a car that made you wonder why anyone would put only two doors on a vehicle that large, since each of those doors was the approximate size and shape of a railroad car! And this particular Fairway Freeway Frigate Custom Coachman Coupé looked even longer than usual since it was fitted with low, rocker panel-extending fender skirts in back and one of Fairway's stylish, convenient, optional-at-plenty-of-extra-cost "flip down" continental kits that put the spare tire (at least according to the sales brochure) "within easy, fingertip reach" and provided quite a bit of extra luggage space in the bargain. Unfortunately, it also made the trunk lid damn near impossible to open—or get at the jack and lug wrench stowed inside—without breaking off a few of those fingertips or getting help from a beefy passerby. A copy of the owners' manual helped.

But not much.

The real story, however, was the way this particular Freeway Frigate Custom Coachman Coupé was painted, trimmed, and detailed. As Danny took pains to explain while we wheeled smoothly and silently east-northeast up Jefferson Avenue towards Grosse Pointe Farms—the bloated coupe floating over pavement irregularities like its springs were filled with marshmallows—the car we were riding in was the just-finished prototype for the exciting new "Fragonard Special Edition" package that had been championed, herded and ram-rodded through the executive line review process by none other than chairman of the board Little Harry Dick Fairway himself. And that's because the original idea for the "Fragonard Special Edition" had been suggested by (and ultimately color-coordinated, trimmed and detailed according to the whims, wishes and wiles of) none other than his pretty, willful, somewhat scatter-brained and occasionally devoted wife, Amanda Cassandra Fairway!

It seems Amanda Fairway fancied herself as not only a patron of the arts, but also as a genuinely gifted artistic designer in her own right. She loved working with colors, patterns, fabrics, hues, textures and finishes, and absolutely adored the grand European and Russian art and architectural styles of the eighteenth and nineteenth centuries that she studied in college. As she was always quick to point out, that's when so many poor, downtrodden peasants found meaningful work (not to mention sustenance for their poor, miserable families) building fabulous churches, glorious palaces and sumptuous summer estates for the clergy and aristocracy. The gifted hands of those sad-eyed, arm-weary artisans crafted everything from stained glass windows and flying buttresses with masonry gargoyles on top to spouting garden fountains and statues of famous conquerors on horseback to goose down comforters and solid gold pee pots for the bedrooms. "And what a marvelous time it must have been for them!" she'd gush excitedly. "Why, they didn't need labor unions or government intervention or welfare programs, either. Back then, people knew how to starve when they had to...."

Amanda Cassandra Fairway was quite sure she knew what she was talking about, since she'd studied it all at length (when she bothered to go to class, anyway) during the time when art history and architecture emerged as two of her all-time favorites among the many different majors she tried and soon tired of in college. She'd done very well at them, too. Even if rumors persisted that she'd paid an effete, Boston-born grad student to shave his mustache and put on a dress to take the finals for her (supposedly under the condition that he got to pick out and keep the dresses). But the point is that she loved it all passionately, and most especially the filigreed opulence, ornate detail and runaway excess of the Baroque and Rococo periods. Which, in a nutshell, is how Fairway Motors wound up building the new special edition Danny was driving: as a celebration of the Baroque and Rococo styles and moreover as an *homage* to Amanda Cassandra Fairway's very favorite artist, Jean-Honoré Frangonard. Now you may not recognize him by name, but Jean-Honoré Frangonard was a very, very famous French painter who lived from 1732 to 1806, and his pictures hang in many of the world's most prominent galleries today. Taken as a group, his paintings ooze the same sort of syrupy sweetness and swooning, breathless sensuality you generally might associate with the covers of bosomy romance novels aimed at preteen girls who have yet to experience their first period. His most famous painting, by far, is titled *"The Swing"* (you've surely seen it) and, depending on your point of view, it is either:

a) A soaring, sumptuous and romantic visualization of a beautiful young maiden on a flower-encrusted garden swing being demurely adored by an attentive young swain stretched out on the ground below. Or:

b) A picture of a guy looking up a girl's skirt.

Take your pick.

But the point is that Amanda Cassandra Fairway felt the American car-buying public would just *love* a car that captured the grand elegance of the rococo style and that moreover commemorated the life and work of her favorite painter. Even if most Americans had no idea who the hell Jean-Honoré Fragonard was. In any case, that's why this particular Fairway Freeway Frigate Custom Coachman Coupé had shimmering green satin brocade upholstery with gold highlight stitching, a matching, padded, roll-top dashboard featuring creamy, porcelain-look instrument faces with gilded roman numerals on the dials—*"Slow down, Harry! You're doing LXXXVII miles an hour! You're gonna get us a ticket!"*—along with etched crystal bud vases on the "B" pillars, a matching brocade vinyl top and continental kit cover, antique gold-anodized wheel covers and, to top it all off and bring it all together, a retch-worthy, spoiled-cream-over-seasick-green paint scheme (with antique gold pinstriping, of course) that the guys in the Fairway paint shop quietly referred to as "pus over puke."

"This thing is hideous," I observed as our Fairway Freeway Frigate Custom Coachman Coupé Fragonard Special Edition floated gently northeast along the Lake St. Clair shoreline.

"You'd better keep that to yourself," Danny advised. "Mrs. H.R. Junior is pretty damn serious about her decorating."

That turned out to be something of an understatement.

In person, Amanda Cassandra Grayson Terryton-Fitch Fairway turned out to be a beaming, sparkly, happy-eyed (at least so long as the liquor cabinet remained well-stocked and her prescriptions were kept up to date), immaculately dressed, groomed and accessorized, socially active, charitable-to-a-fault, occasionally obtuse, oftentimes silly and generally shallow as the six-inch-deep reflecting pool in her beloved formal garden example of what money and family connections could get you in an upper-bracket wife. And she'd been a good wife to H.R. Junior as best she could remember. After all, she'd given him two bright, beautiful and possibly even exceptional children. Even if she rarely had any idea where they were or what they might be doing. But it was easy to lose people in a 47-room mansion with so many hallways, doorways and places to hide. And they generally turned up before they actually seemed to be missing. Besides, the kitchen staff made sure they had plenty to eat, vitamins to take and lots of nourishing milk to drink if they wanted any.

But life could be difficult at the top. As Amanda Cassandra Fairway and her glossy, socialite Grosse Pointe friends constantly agreed over luncheons or cocktails (or both), unending leisure could be a heavy burden, and life could become lonely, isolated and lacking in meaning for the overly rich and privileged. And so Amanda Cassandra and her upper-bracket girlfriends (who all called her "A.C." or "Acey" or "Acey-Cakes" just like her sorority sisters back in college) held long, serious lunchtime meetings at all the latest, trendiest restaurants and country clubs so they could dedicate and re-dedicate themselves—sometimes several times in the same afternoon if the drinks were especially strong—to all the many causes, community service projects, philanthropic enterprises and patron-of-the-arts fundraising campaigns that so desperately demanded their attention. Which generally amounted to signing a few checks. Or having their accountants do it. Some of those meetings dragged well on into the late afternoon or early evening, and they were the only thing that Amanda Fairway ever let interfere with her one real, true love....

Decorating!

Or perhaps re-decorating would be a more accurate description, since Amanda Cassandra Fairway was constantly, relentlessly and unstoppably in the throes of renovating, refurbishing, re-inventing, knocking down, adding on, altering, re-configuring, re-accessorizing, changing the look, theme and ambience of and in every other conceivable way altering, improving, augmenting and "enhancing the value of" her palatial 47-room mansion overlooking Lake St. Clair. The one at the far end of McElligot Lane that she shared with her husband, the two children she hardly ever saw and a staff that usually numbered around eleven. Depending on whom she or Little Harry Dick Fairway had fired lately. Plus an endlessly rotating retinue of architects, contractors, interior designers, carpenters, plumbers, electricians, plasterers, painters, landscapers, decorators, upholsterers and the inevitable trash collectors who came to haul away all the cast-offs, refuse and residue on Tuesday mornings and Friday afternoons.

Getting her house "right" was the single, burning passion in Amanda Cassandra Fairway's life. But that goal was regularly compromised by the fact that her vision of "right" was in a constant, ever-evolving state of flux. It changed like the weather with every new issue of *Home Beautiful, Elysian Estate, Architectural Digest,* or *Town and Country* that arrived in her mailbox, each new "professional expert" she hired or talked to, almost every costume-drama movie she ever saw and each and every visit she made to any of her rich friends' houses to see what they had going on. As a result, the long, tree-lined driveway at the far end of McElligot Lane was forever jammed with tradesmen's trucks and panel vans, contractors' pickups, interior decorators' Mercedes-Benz

190SLs, Facellias and Volkswagen convertibles, tile, trim and carpet salesmen's station wagons, landscapers' equipment trailers and the dumpsters that filled up regularly with the inevitable trash. As you can imagine, the interior rooms and hallways were likewise littered with ladders, scaffolding, buckets, tools, brushes, nails, screws, piles of 2x4s, crates of Italian marble floor tile, sheets of imported hardwood paneling, lengths of walnut, maple or mahogany trim molding, rolls of colored wire, bundles of conduit tubing and boxes of junction boxes, cartons of plumbing tees and elbow bends, dusty or muddy footprints and the dusty or muddy tradesmen who made them and swishy designers, color coordinators and interior decorators tiptoeing delicately around it all brandishing paint chips, fabric swatches and catalog pictures of furniture, lamps, draperies and accessories. And that's not even mentioning the commando teams of uniformed delivery men who were forever arriving with new paintings and mirrors and taking out old paintings and mirrors, replacing old furniture, sculptures and grand pianos with new furniture, sculptures and grand pianos and swapping new bathroom fixtures and kitchen appliances out for old bathroom fixtures and kitchen appliances. Some of which still had the tags on them. According to what Danny heard from the second butler (who had a fine, cultured British accent and whom he'd caught sneaking a few snorts of Little Harry Dick's hundred-bucks-a-bottle cognac at a party on New years' Eve), Amanda Fairway would actually lose track of where the hell she was and start in on the first or second room all over again before she'd even finished up on the 47th! He said it was a bona fide miracle that the staff ever managed to get the house ready for a party, since there was usually so much decorating and renovating going on and so much crap lying around everywhere that it wasn't a fit place to live. In fact, she and H.R. Junior had quite a row about it once after the fourth or fifth complete make-over. Or maybe it was the sixth? That's when Little Harry Dick Fairway, in a rare home showing of the vicious, bullying manner he displayed with such relish and regularity at Fairway Tower, rose up in a mighty rage and demanded that she: *"KEEP IT DOWN TO TWO OR THREE GOD-FUCKING-DAMMIT ROOMS AT A TIME, AMY, SO WE CAN HAVE SOME FUCKING PLACE TO LIVE!!!"*

According to the second butler, Little Harry Dick's voice boomed through the vast Main Ballroom, reverberated around in the dome of the Grand Entrance Hall and echoed all the way down the stairwell to the servants' quarters on the lower level. And it was easy to understand his frustration. At the time, the main kitchen was being re-done (again!) with avocado appliances this time and both the football field-sized formal dining room and the glass-enclosed, twenty-foot-by-forty-foot, conservatory-style "breakfast nook" off the kitchen were in the process of being thoroughly renovated. Meanwhile, outside in the Fairway Mansion's 22-acre back yard, trees, flower beds and rose bushes were being uprooted and either moved to new locations or hauled away and replaced by new and different trees, flower beds and rose bushes. But the worst of it by far was the Grand Entrance Hall, which was in yet another cataclysmic state of transformation. Amanda Fairway had grown weary of the dramatic but somewhat Disneyland-esque African Veldt theme she'd settled on with her then-favorite interior designer, Elliott Mansard. She'd come up with the idea right after she and H.R. Junior returned from a somewhat uncomfortable but nonetheless eye-opening safari to Kenya. "Oh, it was *very* interesting," she told her friends at a charity arts luncheon benefitting the I.I.L.A.B. (Indigenous Itinerant Loom Artisans of Borneo), "but they really need to do something about the bugs. And the snakes. And the plumbing. And the air conditioning in the tents." She leaned in close and whispered: "The heat and humidity are just *terrible!*" But even so, Amanda Fairway was greatly moved by her trip to Africa. In fact, she started a campaign shortly after her return to send factory-second Converse children's sneakers to the pygmies, fiberglass porta-potties and cases of cushy, two-ply toilet paper to the safari outfitters and refurbished window fans and air conditioners to all the native villages she'd visited. They will surely be appreciated whenever electric service ultimately arrives.

But Amanda Fairway was deeply affected by Africa—at least for a few months, anyway—and in the wake of that trip joined at least eight new charities and commissioned Elliott Mansard to re-do her Grand Entrance Hall with a thatched straw ceiling, native artwork and artifacts such as spears, jungle drums, zebra-skin shields, grinning fertility gods with oversized genitalia, rough jute mats and colorful African fabrics draped dramatically here and there among the various mounted lion, panther, leopard, antelope, impala, gazelle, zebra, giraffe, water buffalo, hyena, warthog, hippopotamus and wildebeest heads that Little Harry Dick had personally bagged (sometimes with less than six shots and with no help whatsoever from the guide!) shooting down at a steep, difficult angle from a what looked like a small canvas hut perched on top of a very large elephant.

The *piece de resistance* of Amanda Fairway's African-theme Grand Entrance Hall was undoubtedly the central reflecting pool, which featured a huge stuffed elephant (which bore a remarkable resemblance to the one H.R. Junior rode on when he shot all those other animals) reared up on its hind legs and towering over an obviously overmatched but nonetheless game and scrappy-looking stuffed rhinoceros. Giving credit where credit was due, Amanda had to admit that her reflecting-pool scene was actually inspired by the life-size statues of a Tyrannosaurus Rex squared off against a Triceratops that she'd seen in the main entrance hall of the Chicago Natural History Museum once on an anthropology class field trip. And she also had to admit (at least to her closest friends) that Elliott Mansard had to go out and find the stuffed rhino, since the only time H.R. Junior ever saw one within range was while riding in the back of a Land Rover, and Little Harry Dick never felt comfortable drawing a bead on anything he wasn't looking down on. In any case, it was her own idea to put the two of them in the middle of the reflecting pool together (which was presented as an African veldt watering hole, of course, complete with stuffed birds, baboons, hyenas, appropriate sound effects and a half-submerged crocodile) with a huge arc of water spouting gracefully out of the elephant's trunk and a smaller stream spurting up from a copper pipe hidden inside the rhinoceros' horn. She'd actually been quite happy with the way it all came out, and her brand new favorite interior designer, Dempsey Devine (who hadn't worked on the project himself and wore what appeared to be a trout fly in his left earlobe) said he absolutely *adored* it! But then came a big charity dinner for the N.V.V.S. (the New Vermeer Vision Society, which was hard at work bringing an enhanced appreciation of Flemish Renaissance painting to the blind) where some goatee-wearing, textbook-writing, know-it-all Art History Professor from the University of Michigan happened to ask why she had an African elephant—as just *everybody* knew, they were the ones with the big ears—squared off against an *Asian* rhinoceros (which, as absolutely everybody also knew, had but one horn while African rhinos had two). Besides, elephants and rhinos, be they African *or* Asian, were not known to be natural enemies or on each other's menu list.

"Well," Amanda Fairway argued on the strength of two Miltowns and a few tall Grasshopper Frappes, "maybe one of them stepped on the other one's eggs."

But the awkward encounter made an impression, and Amanda Cassandra Fairway had her favorite demolition crew over before noon the following Monday to start tearing it all down. With the aid of Dempsey Devine, the "African Veldt" Grand Entrance Hall was quickly transformed into a freely-interpreted "Knights of the Round Table/Camelot" theme in honor of President Kennedy (even though she hadn't voted for him) complete with high stone cupola, stained glass windows, period-correct arrow slits in the walls, suits of armor, plumed helmets, assorted maces, broadswords and battle axes set off by brightly painted jousting shields and gold-fringed pennants featuring colorful and authentic heraldic coats-of-arms. Dempsey even located an actual antique torture rack (although, in all honesty, he was pretty certain it was of Spanish Inquisition rather than British Medieval ancestry) and had it wired up with flickering yellow lights as a conversation-piece novelty chandelier. But the focal point of the whole room was a dead-on accurate reproduction (or at least that's what the mysterious little antique dealer from New York told her) of the Holy Grail! Better yet, it was mounted on top of an impressively large and handsome chunk of stone and surrounded by a burbling ring of fountain jets in the center of her now round table-shaped reflecting pool. And that stone was worthy of mention as well, since Dempsey had it on very good authority that it likewise came from the early middle ages and might actually *be* the storied, world-famous chunk of rock from which Arthur Pendragon himself allegedly pulled the sword Excalibur from on the day he ascended to the throne of England. Or at least that's what the black-market antiquities dealer in Coventry had told the mysterious little antique dealer in New York, anyway, and they were both highly respected in the trade....

In time, the magic of the Camelot theme grew tiresome as well, and that's when Amanda Fairway and her new favorite designer, Sean Shawn, decided to return to the classic opulence, ornamentation and elegance of the Baroque and Rococo styles she loved so well. Which was more or less what she'd started with when the house was originally built. I was beginning to understand why H.R. Junior insisted on going to work at The Tower every day and liked getting out of town whenever he could.

As Danny and I continued eastward, Jefferson Avenue expanded into a divided boulevard with lush, green medians and changed its name to Lakeshore Drive. It ran along the shoreline of Lake St. Clair with the docks, beaches and yacht clubs on one side and huge, beautifully landscaped homes on the other. I was actually feeling a little on edge about attending a party in such a fancy, upscale sort of neighborhood. And especially a non-racing party where I probably wouldn't have much to talk about or anything in common with most of the other guests. "Boy, these homes are really something," I muttered nervously.

"These are *nothing!*" Danny snorted. "Just wait'll you see the Fairways' place..."

I reached out and switched on the radio. But of course the guys in the detail shop had the radio set to the local black station, so we had Solomon Burke's pleading, soulful rendition of *"Cry to Me"* pouring out of the speakers.

"I hate that stuff," Danny snapped, and punched the next button. That turned out to be the popular mainstream (read: white) Top 40 station, and the cranked-up, mile-a-minute, machine gun-voiced DJ was just introducing *"The absolute, make-no-mistake-about-it, you-heard-it-here-first NUMBER ONE HIT RECORD in the country today! And here it is: on the SMASH label, Bruce Channel's fantastic, foot-tapping chart-topper....'HEYYYYYY BABY!'"*

I hit the next button.

"Hey! That's a good song!" Danny protested.

"Sorry," I said, and punched it back. "But that DJ's just way too far past the redline for me."

Danny looked over at me. "You nervous?"

"Nah," I lied. Then quickly added: "Yeah. Maybe. A little bit."

"You should be," Danny laughed as he turned through a high, dark, somber-looking wrought iron gate marked with an etched brass plaque that read:

McElligot Lane
- PRIVATE -

NO TRESSPASSING – NO COMMERCIAL VEHICLES
ALL DELIVERIES VIA SERVICE DRIVE

We headed up a gently meandering ribbon of perfect black asphalt under a canopy of towering oaks, elms and maples interspersed here and there with decorative ferns, lilacs, blossoming fruit trees, slender shafts of handsome silver birch, cedars imported directly from the Holy Land, manicured stands of pine, fir and evergreen and tall, dense, perfectly clipped hedges that hid whatever was behind them completely from view. You could almost smell the wealth, power and privilege wafting in along with the scent of the cedars, lilacs, apple blossoms and pine needles. But even so, I wasn't really prepared for the over-the-top grandeur and outright presumption of the Fairway family's palatial, 47-room mansion at the far end of McElligot Lane. It sat on its own cul-de-sac on a gentle, sculptured rise overlooking Lake St. Clair, and it was surrounded by a virtual formal orchestra of trees, flower beds and shrubbery. It was all at once massive and elegant and regal and magnificent and heroic and gaudy and stupid and decadent and ostentatious and terribly, terribly overdone. I vaguely recognized some of the conflicting shapes, details and architectural features from pictures I must have seen in schoolbooks and encyclopedias. As Amanda Cassandra Grayson Terryton-Fitch Fairway personally and somewhat tipsily explained when she greeted us at the doorway—drink in hand, of course—the original design was adapted from three of her very favorite buildings: Andrea Palladio's Villa Badoer in northern Italy, Germain Boffrand's *Hotel de Soubise* in Paris and court-architect-to-the-czars Bartolomeo Francesco Rastelli's opulent and colorful (if somewhat outrageous) Catherine Palace at Tsarskoye Selo near St. Petersburg. With maybe just a tiny little hint of mad King Ludwig's Neuschwanstein Castle in Bavaria thrown in just for the hell of it. "At first I wanted to do it as sort of a toy-poodle version of *Versailles,*" she explained airily. "But just everyone does that nowadays, don't they?"

I allowed that they probably did.

"Those czars and czarinas really knew how to live, too!" she added with genuine gusto. "And so did old King Ludwig, even if he *was* a little crazy..." she took a hefty swig of her drink "...and fruitier than a nutcake!" You could tell she thought that was a devastatingly clever turn of phrase.

"Old Louis the Fourteenth didn't do so badly, either," I tossed in, just to be polite.

"Ah, yes," Amanda sighed, and leaned back against one of her fluted marble columns for support. She was wearing a revealing-yet-concealing silver-sequined cocktail dress that showed off the best parts of her figure—both of them—and set off by a whole, dazzling fireworks display of diamonds sparkling around her neck and ears. She was a good-looking woman in an aging-high-school-cheerleader sort of way, and you could tell she really enjoyed being sociable. "They built so many grand, grand things back then, didn't they?" she continued dreamily, followed by another long, thoughtful pull on her drink. "It's a pity they all got their heads chopped off by the little people."

"If I remember it right," I said without thinking, "the last czar and czarina were shot. And King Ludwig got himself drowned in Lake Starnberg (even if everyone pretty much agrees it was murder). And didn't Louis the Fourteenth live to a ripe old age and die peacefully in bed? Just short of his 77th birthday, if I'm not mistaken..."

Amanda Cassandra Fairway eyeballed me suspiciously. "I know Danny," she said through a frigid smile. "But who might you be?"

"Uh...I'm Henry Lyons," I admitted sheepishly. "I'm kind of a writer."

Her eyes narrowed. "You're not one of those damn gossip columnists, are you?"

"Oh, no," Danny jumped in. "He's not that kind of writer at all. He writes about cars. He's helping us out on a project we've got working back in The Tower."

She didn't look convinced.

"I write about car racing," I explained. "It's what I do for a living."

She looked at me kind of sideways. But then she smiled and leaned in close enough that I could smell the liquor on her breath. "Those Goddam gossip columnists!" she hissed. "They're always snooping and sneaking around about my daughter, you know. Going through our garbage. Peeking in through the trees." She leaned in even closer. "The low-life bastards."

"Well, he's sure not one of *those* guys!" Danny assured her. "Hank just writes about cars and racing over in Europe."

Her face lit up instantly. "Oh, that's wonderful!" she beamed. "We don't care what the hell they write about us over in Europe." And that's when she noticed the just-finished prototype of the new Fairway Freeway Frigate Fragonard Special Edition parked behind us in the cul-de-sac. "That's *IT,* isn't it?" she almost gasped.

"Yes it is!" Danny agreed excitedly. "I just picked it up from the trim shop less than an hour ago. H.R. Junior couldn't wait for you to see it!"

She ran her eyes critically down from the antique gold-anodized front headlight bezels to the padded, gold-and-green brocade continental kit cover in back.

"We'll be leaving it here so you and Lit—I mean, you and H.R. Junior—can look it over and drive it around a bit!" Danny continued excitedly. "So you can give us your reaction and any thoughts or ideas you might have...."

Amanda Fairway tilted her head to one side and then the other as she looked at it, doing her best to take it all in. "It really is grand, isn't it?" she sighed to no one in particular.

"Yes it is!" Danny agreed.

"No question about it!" I tossed in.

Suddenly, out of nowhere, the ends of her smile bent down. "But weren't they supposed to continue the gilded porcelain theme on the wheel covers?"

"Ahh, umm, yes," Danny admitted. "Yes they were." He licked his lips nervously. "But I'm afraid they weren't ready. Something about the porcelain enamel cracking. So we went with the antique gold anodized wheel covers for now..." he swallowed hard "...and you can't hardly see them in back because of the fender skirts..."

Amanda Fairway didn't say a thing.

"...It's just temporary until the real ones are ready."

She looked at it for a few seconds more, still frowning. Then she told one of the colored parking attendants in starched white uniforms to take it away. "But put in by the side court, not in the garage," she commanded icily. "I need Danny to take it back again to have the correct, porcelin wheel covers put on." She turned to me with weary, put-upon eyes. "It just doesn't look *done* without them, does it?"

"No, it doesn't," I agreed, and that earned me a big smile and an invitation to follow her inside. She didn't even look at Danny. After all, he'd disappointed her.

Amanda Fairway led us through the massive and imposing double doors into her even more massive and imposing Grand Entrance Hall, and along the way she went through a well-rehearsed apology that she'd obviously repeated many, many times already that evening: "The east wing on the water side is just a *mess!*" she fretted. "I'd hoped to have it all done and cleaned up by now, but you know how those contractors and tradesmen are..."

I told her I understood completely.

She escorted us across the gold-veined marble floor of her domed Grand Entrance Hall so she could show us its then-current focal point: an authentic gurgling, swirling and spouting, quarter-scale replica of the famous Trevi Fountain in Rome. "Do you like it?" she asked.

"Oh, it's *very* impressive!" I assured her.

"Isn't it!" she gushed excitedly. Then she flashed me an appreciative, self-satisfied smile, spun around on her heels and headed back to her doorway to greet more guests. By way of one of the bars, of course, for a quick refill. Danny and I looked at each other.

"She's really something, isn't she?" Danny whispered.

I tried to think of something complimentary to say. But "she's sure got a lot of pep" was about all I could come up with.

Beyond Amanda Cassandra Fairway's domed grand entrance hall with its accurate and authentic quarter-scale replica of the Trevi Fountain was a cathedral-like archway leading into her glittering and immense grand ballroom. It was a haughty and trying-hard-to-look-refined sort of place with lots of famous renaissance paintings (including a few originals by Jean-Honoré Fragonard, of course), a serious oversupply of mirrors, sconces and waist-high vases filled with irises, magnolia blossoms and calla lilies and rich-looking, gold-fringed Fairway Blue velvet draperies on all the windows and on the multiple French doors leading out onto the terrace overlooking Amanda Fairway's expansive formal gardens. The place was chockfull of noise and people—many of whom I recognized from my visits to Fairway Tower—but not a single teenager anywhere. Which seemed a bit odd for what was supposed to be a 17-year-old's birthday party.

Danny led me to one of the seven or eight bars they had scattered around the room and I got myself a beer (I didn't think it would be too smart to start in with hard liquor in these particular surroundings) and then he took off to chat up one of the girls from Clifton Toole's accounting staff. I thought she looked kind of plain in the face department, but she had a nice, big smile for him when he walked up to her. Not to mention a very nice shape. That left me pretty much alone in a crowd with a beer in my hand like some blue-collar, out-of-town cousin at a big, upscale wedding, and I began scanning the room furtively for somebody I could talk to. That's when I saw Ben Abernathy standing over by the food tables with the agreeable-looking woman I recognized from the picture he kept on the corner of his desk. Only she looked about 20 or 30 pounds heavier than she did in the picture. Then again, so did he. The two of them were hovering over a big copper chafing dish filled with crabmeat crepes, and they were being industrious indeed in their efforts to empty it so another one could be brought out. Hugo Becker was standing on the other side of the chafing dish, and I hardly recognized him in his gray business suit instead of his usual white lab coat. But his expression was the same, and Hugo looked just as humorless, serious and dissatisfied as ever.

I decided to mosey over and join them (and try out a few of those crabmeat crepes!) and as I drew closer, I could hear them discussing President Kennedy's threatened and highly controversial anti-trust action against the big steel companies. U.S. Steel had announced a six-dollar-a-ton price hike on April 10th, and Bethlehem Steel and five other steel-industry heavyweights had followed suit within days. A lot of people were plenty upset about it. Including President John F. Kennedy and virtually anybody who manufactured anything made out of steel in North America. Which of course included everyone who worked in the American automobile industry in any capacity and, by extension, everybody in the room.

"It's just damn greed!" old union man Ben Abernathy insisted. "They're going to cut their own damn throats if they're not careful. It's not like it was after the war. We've got ourselves some genuine competition from overseas nowadays."

"Und not chust in cars," Hugo agreed. But he was pretty much from the other side of the political spectrum from Ben Abernathy and didn't like Kennedy's populism or liberalism at all. Hugo was more of your classic upper-management type—he was a solid Barry Goldwater supporter—and didn't like to see the government pushing big business around or meddling in the markets. "He hass threatened to pull ze defenzse contracts from zeez companies and give zem to ze steel companies who do not raise zer prices," Hugo said like it was something to get outraged about. *"Zsigned* contracts!"

"Good for him!" Ben hooted between bites of crepe. You could see he enjoyed needling Hugo. And also that they more-or-less liked, understood and respected each other in spite of their political differences. "Lissen, Hugo, *somebody's* gotta stand up to those greedy sonofabitch bastards! I understand he's even got the F.B.I. on their case."

You could tell that Ben was an old union man.

And also that his wife didn't like him swearing.

Typical of political arguments, it sounded like the kind of discussion that would go 'round and 'round for hours without actually getting anywhere. In fact, it might well go on all night. So I said my "good-byes" not long after my "hellos," shook hands all around, filled up an appetizer plate with more of those scrumptious crab-meat crepes, grabbed another beer from one of the bars and moved on. I saw Karen Sabelle and another woman with close-cropped hair and not much makeup sitting next to the piano—Amanda Fairway had some slick, mustachioed young lounge lizard in a tux playing everything from show tunes to Rachmaninoff—but the two of them looked to be in pretty serious conversation, so I continued circulating. But I didn't see anybody I much wanted to talk to, so I ventured down one of the high-ceilinged hallways off the grand ballroom and wandered into the west wing. That's where I found the library.

The Fairway mansion library was like something out of a movie. It reminded me of some fine old English men's club, what with studded leather chairs and dark maple end tables bathed in soft, warm pools of reading light, a large, dark maple desk with a leather-trimmed blotter, marble-based gold pen-and-pencil set and matching reading light and dark maple shelves, stacks and railings all around the room filled from floor to ceiling with an incredible number of books. There had to be literally thousands of them! I wandered over for a closer look, and saw that they were mostly important-looking, leather-bound sets with gold-embossed titles on the spines, and I felt fairly certain that neither H.R. Junior nor his wife ever opened any of them. Particularly the original first edition of John Milton's *"Paradise Lost"* that I noticed just to the right of a full, four-volume, first-edition set of A.A. Milne's Winnie-the-Pooh books. And that was just two or three shelves over from an authentic-looking first edition (in German, of course) of Hitler's

Mein Kampf and what appeared to be an actual Gutenberg Bible. On the wall be-hind the reading desk was a large, ominous portrait of old H.R. Senior holding an ostrich-quill pen in one hand and a half-inch combination wrench in the other. He had a dark, menacing scowl on his face, and his eyes seemed to follow me as I wandered around the room. *"Probably just making sure I don't walk off with anything!"* I muttered into the silence.

"I beg your pardon?" a polite young voice asked from behind one of the stacks. I walked over and peered around the set of bookshelves to find a pale, slender young man with a Pontiac-hood-ornament nose, reddish-brown hair and a few freckles curled up in an oxblood leather chair with a copy of Jean-Paul Sartre's *Being and Nothingness* up close in front of his eyes and an opened copy of Friedrich Nietzsche's *Beyond Good and Evil* sitting on the small table next to him. A pair of intelligent brown eyes stared up at me from behind the binding.

"Sorry," I said. "I didn't mean to disturb you."

"Oh, that's okay," the eyes said. "This is all bullshit anyway."

"Oh?"

The young man nodded disappointedly. "Yeah, I'm afraid it is."

"Then why do you read it?"

"Oh, I've got a paper to write for this stupid honors course. It's due next month, and I want to get a good grade on it."

"It's not due till next month?" I asked incredulously. I happened to know a little bit about deadlines, and most writers figure "next month" is almost as good as five or six years away. "You've got an admirable approach to your studies," I told him.

"Not really. I just want to get into a good school, that's all."

"Do you usually get good grades?"

The eyes looked down, embarrassed. "Yeah, I suppose so," he mumbled. "A's mostly." He nodded towards the Sartre in front of him and the copy of Nietzsche on the table. "But this stuff is *such* bullshit." He shook his head. "These guys think *way* too much."

I surveyed the bookshelves around us. "So what do you *like* to read?"

He looked at me suspiciously. "Why would you want to know that?" And then his eyes narrowed. "You're not one of those damn shrinks my mom hires, are you?"

"Not hardly," I laughed. "I'm just a writer."

"A *writer?*"

I nodded.

"Then what the heck are you doing here?"

"I write for a car magazine," I told him. "About car racing over in Europe."

They eyes looked mildly interested. *"Really?"*

"Hell, I might even turn out to be a mediocre novelist someday."

"Really?" he repeated.

I nodded again.

"A novelist, huh? I bet that's hard to do."

"I bet it is, too," I laughed. "In fact, that's probably why I'm not one yet."

The binding of the Sartre book came down far enough so I could see a pleasant, friendly smile.

"You must be H.R. Junior's son."

"Yeah, I guess I am." He stuck out a small, limp hand. "H.R. the Third. Same as him."

"You don't seem to be the same as him at all."

The smile broadened. "Thanks for noticing."

My eyes swept around the library again. "So tell me, H.R. the Third: what do you *like* to read?"

His bony shoulders jerked up in a noncommittal shrug. "History mostly. And sometimes stuff about politics."

"You read any novels?"

He shook his head. "Nah, not too much. They're mostly bullshit, too..." he caught himself and blushed. "Sorry. No offense."

"None taken." I laughed. "And, like I said, I'm not a novelist yet."

"Oh, sometimes I'll read a little science fiction. Short stories, mostly. I like Heinlein and Asimov and Arthur C. Clarke okay. But that's just for fun."

A platter of glassware crashed to the floor somewhere down the hallway outside. "Here it comes," H.R. the Third warned.

"Here what comes?"

"Once everybody gets drunk enough, they'll all start singing around the piano."

"Oh?"

H.R. the Third nodded. "My mom instigates it. She loves all that ancient big band stuff. You know: *Stardust, Moonglow, The Chattanooga Choo-Choo.* It's pretty hard to take unless you're hard of hearing."

"I don't know," I shrugged. "It sounds like it might be fun."

"Trust me..." he shot me a wink "...It's not."

Within seconds, the unkempt sound of a few mismatched, untrained adult voices that obviously didn't know all the words attempting to follow the professional piano player's flourishes through Cole Porter's *"Embraceable You"* echoed down the hallway.

"You see what I mean?"

"How about your sister?" I asked, just making conversation "Will she be there at the piano? I mean, this *is* supposed to be her party."

"She wouldn't be caught dead with that crowd. She thinks they should all be shot."

"Shot?"

H.R. the Third nodded gravely.

325

"Really? For what?"

"Oh, for having too much money. For keeping minorities down. For raping the world's natural resources. For ignoring the underprivileged. For oppressing all the oppressed peoples of the world. For voting Republican. That sort of thing."

"So she has causes."

He rolled his eyes. "Oh, does she ever! Or at least she thinks she does. But I think it's just a new way she's found to be a brat." He let out a long, weary sigh. "She likes pissing our mom and dad off. Sometimes it seems like it's the best thing she knows how to do...."

Eventually I left H.R. the Third to his reading and headed back towards the grand ballroom to get myself a refill. On the strength of two beers, I'd decided it was probably time for a good glass of scotch. Or better than I'd ever buy for myself, anyway. Along the way, I saw Dick Flick chatting up his secretary, Wanda Peters, in the hallway just outside the ballroom. He was doing it right in front of his wife Linda, too. And you could tell she didn't think too much of Wanda Peters. Not too much at all. But she was far too stylish and classy to do anything but just stand there like a dumb cardboard cutout, smiling and nodding from time to time like everything was just fine. Then again, she was a fashion model by trade when Dick met her, so she knew how to do that sort of thing. But you could tell it was eating her up a little inside, since Wanda Peters had defiantly flirty and adventurous eyes, big, moist, red lips and some pretty outstanding curves on her. And she liked to show them off, too. Particularly to Dick Flick and even more particularly in front of his wife. Wanda was wearing a tight little black cocktail dress with a deeply scooped neckline and doing her level best to keep the crease of her cleavage directly under the Cary Grant cleft in the middle of Dick Flick's chin. Which was making Dick's wife very uncomfortable indeed. Linda Flick was a trim, slender, immaculately groomed woman who wore beautiful clothes beautifully and one of those frozen, near-desperate smiles women seem to acquire when they worry too much about their husbands, their age and their appearance and try way too hard to stay thin. I found out later that she was the second Mrs. Flick, and that Dick had used her as the featured model on one of the very first ad campaigns he ever did as Director of Print Media Advertising for Fairway Motors. That was several years before he rose to his elevated position as V.P. of Advertising and Marketing and his paneled office on the 13th floor executive corridor. In fact, I recognized Linda Flick as the striking, elegant young woman in the back-less gown I'd seen standing next to that mirror-finish Freeway Frigate "Tuxedo Edition" 4-door in the framed ad layout hanging behind Dick Flick's desk. The same ad that appeared on thousands of highway billboards and in double-truck magazine layouts in *Life, Look, Colliers* and the *Saturday Evening Post* in the early spring of 1955. But that was seven long years and two large, broad-shouldered male children ago. Which is probably why the only things on Linda Flick's appetizer plate were a couple carrot sticks, two radishes and one sad, lonely stalk of celery. With no cream cheese on it, either. In any case, it looked like a pretty awkward situation, so I eased back into the shadows and headed in the opposite direction. And that's what led me to the Fairway mansion kitchen....

As you can imagine, the kitchen was a bustling hive of activity that particular evening, what with the regular cooking and wait staff bumping heads, backs and elbows with a virtual legion of hired-for-the-night caterers, servers, bartenders, ice carriers and busboys, all of them stumbling all over each other trying to get their various jobs done and stay out of each others' way. They were under strict, right-from-the-top orders from Mrs. Little Harry Dick herself to keep the food tables filled, the appetizer trays circulating and to make sure all the guests had full, fresh drinks in their hands at all times. Amanda Fairway was a real stickler about that last one. "Liquor is the lubricant that greases a successful party along!" she told them all cheerily at her late-afternoon staff briefing. Right before threatening to fire each and every last one of them if she noticed many people with empty glassware in their hands.

I ventured up the two wide, imported volcanic slate steps from Amanda Cassandra Fairway's kitchen to her high, cool and airy "conservatory-style" breakfast nook. Which was hardly a nook at all, since it was roughly the size of your average formal dining room and surrounded on all sides by heavily leaded glass with smart, Frank Lloyd Wright-style stained-glass accents. The hanging, stained glass lighting fixtures were also by Frank Lloyd Wright, as were the table and chairs...which is to say handsome in a simple, austere, Calvinist sort of way, but only comfortable for thin, bony people with absurdly good posture. Like Amanda Fairway's current favorite interior designer Sean Shawn and Fairway Motors' VP of Design Daryl Starling, who were sitting in a pair of them engaged in deep discussion at the far end of the table. To be honest, Amanda Fairway's "breakfast nook" didn't strike me as a particularly cozy or inviting place to enjoy breakfast—an omelet would go cold there in about 30 seconds flat in the wintertime—but then, cozy wasn't really the point, was it? After all (as I overheard Mrs. Little Harry Dick's favorite current designer explaining to Daryl Starling) this particular breakfast nook had been the subject of an approving, four-page feature on the coveted and prestigious pages of *Architectural Digest* magazine. And Daryl was listening intently, following every little dramatic pause, pout and fingertip flourish with rapt attention. You could see that he and Sean Shawn spoke the same language.

With nothing better to do, I poured myself a hefty tumbler of scotch right there at the kitchen counter where nobody that mattered could see me and sat myself down on the lowest of Amanda Cassandra Fairway's volcanic slate stairs to eavesdrop on Sean and Daryl's conversation. By that point it was Daryl's turn, and he was fretting dramatically about what he was going to do and where on earth he was going to go with the new "Great Art and Artists" series of Special Editions that Mrs. H.R. Junior wanted so badly. It wasn't going to be easy. After all, you couldn't expect Joe Putz from Peoria (or his overweight wife and kids who bought all their clothing at Sears Roebuck) to appreciate the subtle differences between genuine Hellenic and Neo-classic, could you? And although the Turner, Rembrandt and Monet Special Editions were coming along nicely, the upholstery and interior trim on the Jackson Pollack, Joan Miró and Mondrian versions was threatening to look a trifle busy. And Daryl was getting all sorts of crap from Hugo Becker and Ben Abernathy—already—about the proposed dripping dash clock on the Salvador Dali edition....

Eventually I got bored with their conversation, grabbed a refill of scotch and went wandering around a little more—you could get lost in that place easily—and eventually found my way down to the Billiard Room on the lower level of the East Wing where Little Harry Dick Fairway had gone to get away from his family and guests. The door was open just a crack and I could just barely make him out sitting in a big, frog-green leather chair with his back towards me and a good bottle of Napoleon brandy for company. But I knew it was him because I could see the fine, silky flop of his chestnut-colored toupee peeking up over the top of the chair back. It looked like he was leafing through some sort of big blue folder filled with photographs, and I could tell he didn't know I was there. As I watched, he would take a photo out, look at it, tilt his head to one side and then the other, flip to the next photograph and do the same. I was kind of curious to know what they were. But the last thing I wanted was an impromptu one-on-one with Little Harry Dick Fairway. And particularly when he so obviously thought he was alone. And even more particularly when it became obvious that he was doing something with himself in his lap while he looked at those pictures! In fact, he was becoming very animated indeed. I swallowed hard and backed quietly, stealthily away. I mean, I didn't even breathe! And immediately headed back to the main ballroom, stopped at the very first bar I came to and ordered myself a double scotch.

Just as H.R. the Third had predicted, a noisy, red-faced and somewhat unsteady crowd had gathered around the grand piano—led by a loud, boozy, arm-waving, *"HEY, C'MON OVA HERE!!!"* Amanda Cassandra Fairway—and it frankly didn't look like the sort of thing I'd enjoy. So I pretended not to hear her, grabbed yet another double scotch for my other hand and wandered out the double French doors onto the terrace. It was dark and a little chilly out there—as you might expect for the middle of April in Detroit—but at least it was relatively quiet. To be honest, it was kind of nice to be away from the crowd and the noise and the music and the chatter and the occasionally strange and unusual behavior going on inside. There was a pretty good three-quarter moon dangling over Lake St. Clair—for some reason it reminded me of Diogenes' lantern, but that was probably the scotch—and I decided to do a little exploring.

Amanda Cassandra Fairway's massive and immaculately landscaped back yard began with a mirror-image spiral stone stairway that led down to the ornate formal garden below. The centerpiece was a big, rectangular reflecting pool with a copy of that famous-but-kind-of-hideous Greek sculpture of Laocoon and his sons battling a giant sea serpent on a slowly-rotating island in the middle and little prancing, water-spouting cherubim and seraphim from the much-later High Renaissance period dancing all around it. I noticed a few fat goldfish swimming around in the water, and I wondered if they ever got cold in the wintertime when the pool iced over? Or did uniformed butlers in rubber gloves and wading boots transfer them to indoor holding tanks every November? Or were they simply thrown out in the trash or donated to the lion house at the Detroit zoo and replaced with new, even bigger and fatter goldfish the following spring?

The reflecting pool was surrounded by beginning-to-bloom flower gardens laid out in ornate geometric patterns, and beyond them were great, graceful expanses of smoothly rolling grass interspersed with plantings of lilacs, rose bushes, honeysuckle and magnolia. And beyond them all, I could make out the tall, shadowy walls of one of those intriguing, labyrinthine garden mazes that became so popular at castles, parks and royal country estates—particularly in France and England—during the seventeenth and eighteenth centuries. I wandered over and was impressed to discover, at least according to the etched plaque that one of Mrs. Little Harry Dick's landscape architects had thoughtfully mounted by the entrance, that it was *"an exact, 8/10ths-scale reproduction of the well-known garden maze at Charleval, France, designed by famous landscape architect and acknowledged garden maze genius Androuet du Cerceau."* My, my, my. And as I stood there, sipping my right-hand double scotch and reading that plaque in the moonlight, I became aware of muffled voices coming from somewhere inside the maze. And soft music, too. Along with a somewhat familiar, acrid smell. With nothing much better to do, I drained the rest of my right-hand scotch and wandered on in.

Now the core idea behind garden mazes is to find the little bench or statue or fountain or birdbath or whatever hidden away in the secret little inner sanctum in the middle, and it's a maze designer's job to make that task just as difficult, entertaining and frustrating as possible. After all, they didn't have TV back then, and you could only listen to so many fugues or violin concertos. And I have to say this du Cerceau guy certainly earned his paycheck. I found myself inside a narrow, shadowy, tightly-wound hedge corridor full of curves and turns and sudden, abrupt dead-ends, and the foliage walls were tall, dense and seemingly impenetrable. I couldn't hear the voices anymore, but I'd seem to get closer to that acrid smell and the music (I could recognize it now as Sam Cooke's *"Twistin' the Night Away")* but then I'd hit a dead end or the corridor I was in would bend around and send me off in the opposite direction again. And I had to pee something awful. I wanted to go back inside the house to do it, of course, but I'd finished the other double scotch and, to be perfectly honest, I was kind of using the hedges for support now and then and had no fucking idea how the hell to get out! Not to mention that I was just sober enough to realize that I was really, *really* drunk, and probably didn't want to demonstrate that fact to some of the Fairway Tower people inside. But I still had to pee, so I finally gave up, unzipped, leaned my forehead against the hedge, and...

"HEY!!!" a young female voice shrieked from somewhere beyond the end of my stream.

"WHATTHEFUCK???!!!" a much deeper, darker voice boomed right behind it.

"WHO THE FUCK IS THERE??!!" the shrill female voice demanded.

"I GOTS A FUCKIN' GUN HERE, MAN!" the other voice warned ominously. It sounded like he was probably colored. I mean, it wasn't the sort of thing you could miss.

"Sorry! Sorry! Sorry!" I pleaded into the hedge wall greenery. *"I didn't mean..."*

"But who the fuck ARE you?" the shrill voice wanted to know.

"I'm Henry Lyons!" I shouted back desperately. *"I'm nobody!"*

"If you're nobody, what the fuck are you doing here??!!"

"We ain't messin' with you, man," the black voice warned.

"I'm just a damn writer," I almost whimpered. *"I was just passing by! I came here with Danny Beagle..."*

Suddenly there was silence. Except for the final few strains of Sam Cooke's *"Twistin' the Night Away"* coming from the other side of the hedge wall and the unmistakable rustle of bodies wrestling their way into clothing. And then the shrill voice started in again. Only not quite so shrill this time. "A fucking *writer? Are you sure?"*

"Yeah, I'm sure," I nodded like somebody could actually see me. "I write for car magazines. About the racing scene over in Europe."

More silence. Followed by a suspicious: *"Then what the fuck are you doing HERE?"*

"Yeah," the dark voice echoed, *"whut th'fuck you doin' here, man?"*

"Bob Wright invited me," I tried to explain. "I'm doing some stuff on a project over in The Tower." I tried to think of something else to say. "I...I brought a present."

"You work for my father?" the female voice asked as if working for Little Harry Dick Fairway was a truly despicable thing.

"Uh...No. Not really. They just brought me in for this one, um, *project...*"
More silence.

"...I'm, um, like kind of like a consultant."

"Whut th'fuck is a 'consultant?'" the dark voice wanted to know.

"It's, aah, sort of like a part-time job with no hourly wage, not much of a future and no fringe benefits..."

There was a sudden, heavy click from an unseen latch and then the hedge wall in front of me swung slowly aside like it was on greased rollers. On the opposite side, a petite, pretty, defiantly snotty young white girl with tousled blond hair and no makeup was sitting cross-legged on the ground wearing an oversized, mostly un-zipped car-hiker jacket on top and with her bottom half wrapped in a blanket. Kneeling next to her was this huge, statuesque young black guy in an unbuttoned white dress shirt and red silk boxer shorts. His white car-hiker pants were folded neatly on the ground next to them. Right beside her jeans, shoes, panties and tran-sistor radio, in fact. "You must be Amelia Camellia Fairway," I ventured.

"You're a real fucking Sherlock Holmes, aren't you?"

"And who's this?"

"I'm the guy you never saw here, man," the big, good-looking black guy answered nervously. "An' I wuz just shittin' you about the gun..."

"Hey, I don't care," I told them both. "What you two do is your own damn business."

They looked back and forth at each other.

"You mean that?" she asked warily.

"Sure I mean that," I said as earnestly and expansively as I could. "Why the hell wouldn't I?"

"Because you work for my asshole father."

"Like I already told you: I don't really work for him. They just hired me on tem-porarily. For just this one project. I live over on the other side of the ocean."

"Really?"

"Yeah, really," I assured them both. "I live in London."

"You don't sound like you're from fucking England!" Amelia Fairway growled suspiciously.

"Yeah! You don't sound like you's from fuckin' England," the black guy echoed.

"I'm not. I'm from southern California. I grew up around L.A." I wanted to take another slug of scotch, but my glass was empty. I looked for the other glass in my other hand, but it was gone entirely. That happens when you drink too much.

"L.A., huh?" she said like there was something vaguely fascinating about it. And then a wicked little smile crinkled its way across her face. "You like weed?"

"Weed?"

"You know: pot, boo, grass, hemp, reefer, Mary Jane, wacky tobaccy..."

"I know what the hell it is."

"But do you *like* it?"

I shrugged like I knew all about it. I mean, after all, I *was* from California. "I like it well enough," I told her.

"Then try some of this." She pulled a half-smoked joint out of a fold in her blanket, fired it up with a fancy little enameled box of matches from her parents' country club and took a long, deep drag. *"Here,"* she gasped, fighting to keep the smoke in. *"Take a hit. This shit is fucking DYNAMITE!"*

So I took it, eyeballed it for a moment and tried a quick, tentative drag.

"No, y'gotta go *deep* man," the good-looking black guy instructed. "An' then y'-gotta *hold* it, see...."

So I tried that. In fact, I tried it several times.

"I just don't need any shit from her people, man," the big black guy explained while Amelia Fairway took another long, deep hit. "I'm on full scholarship at State so long as I can stay first string..."

"Oh? What do you play?"

"Running back, man," he grinned proudly. Amelia Fairway seemed pretty pleased about that as well. She gave the handsome black guy an approving kiss on the cheek and then, watching me out of the corner of her eye to see how I'd react, she ran her tongue up the side of his face, buried it deep inside his ear, waggled it around a little and then more or less lost interest when I didn't appear properly horrified. But of course I was too drunk and stoned to look properly horrified. Amelia Camellia Fairway appeared vaguely disappointed about it, but then she lost interest in being vaguely disappointed, sighed heavily and slid languidly down the black guy's shoulders and torso until she was nothing but a curled-up heap next to his thigh. Her eyes were a million miles away. The big, handsome black guy glanced down at her and shook his head. "She's really something,' isn't she?" he whispered with genuine awe. But then a worried look passed across his face. "But she's trouble waitin' t'happen for me, man. Trouble waitin' t'happen. Her old man could really fuck me up if he ever found out about this."

"I don't *care* if they find out about us!" Amelia Fairway damn near shouted, startling the crap out of both of us. "In fact, I wish they *would!"*

The black guy's eyes went wide. "You'd just love that shit, wouldn't you?" he snarled at her. "You don't give half a fuck about me. You just want to jam it up your folks' ass, thass all. And I'm just the poor dumb black fool who can do it."

And of course that was it exactly. Even if newly 17-year-old Amelia Camellia Fairway would never admit it. Not even to herself. Sure, she liked the big, handsome halfback from Michigan State. Just like she liked the whiny, pasty-faced senior she'd met when she was just a freshman. The one who played shitty guitar and knew all Bob Dylan's songs and wore work shirts and Dingos before anybody else and claimed he was going to be a poet or a marine biologist someday. Or the high school English teacher who drank espresso coffee, wore corduroy jackets with leather patches on the elbows, spoke through his nose about great modern literature, assigned racy novels by James Joyce, Lawrence Durrell and Henry Miller to all of his "most promising" female students and held his cigarettes upside down between his thumb and forefinger in the European style. Then came the black running back from Detroit who worked on the line at the Fairway plant during the summer months (it wasn't unheard of for enthusiastic, well-connected Michigan State alumni to pull a few strings in order to put promising football and basketball prospects into high-paying summer jobs) and moonlighted part-time—weekends, mostly—for the hire-out car-parking business the Fairways always used for their parties. And soon enough there'd be the nasal, strident and chronically outraged Jewish community organizer from Brooklyn who'd been everywhere and done everything and still found the world terribly wanting. And the bitter, inner-city Malcolm X disciple who hated rich white people but wasn't above screwing a few of their daughters. And the fugitive underground newspaper publisher from Washington, DC, who claimed he had to hide in cellars and attics because he'd gotten his hands on a top-secret C.I.A. file that implicated just about everybody on Capitol Hill in all sorts of illegal things. And the tragically earnest coffee-house folk singer from Menomonee Falls and the Mexican-American migrant-worker organizer from California with the sad eyes, gold tooth and snakeskin boots and the Jazz saxophone player from Memphis who wore sunglasses even at night and was high all the time. And the 28-year-old, self-styled American Indian holy man who seemed to know and understood virtually everything about the great cosmic oneness but still maintained a fondness for earthly things like pot, pussy and peyote. And the Indian Indian exchange student/sitar player from New Dehli who couldn't play sitar for shit but did quite well for himself smuggling hashish into the country in his instrument case. Not to mention the twin Peruvian gardeners her mother hired to do the lawn or the furniture delivery guy from Jamaica or the sad, wrinkled little Chinese widower from St. Clair Shores who did the family laundry.

It turned out that Amelia Camellia Fairway's greatest ambition was to be caught by her properly horrified parents having hot, lurid, slippery, sloppy, sweaty, panting-and-pulsating sex with an oh-so-deserving member of a different disenfranchised minority group in every fucking room of her father and mother's endlessly re-decorated mansion at the end of McElligot Lane. Including the kitchen, the pantry, on top of the Frank Lloyd Wright table in the conservatory breakfast nook, across the green felt playing field of her father's beloved slate pool table in the downstairs billiard room and in every single one of the bathrooms! And each time, she wanted to be caught red-handed—*in flagrante delicto!*—wrapped up tight and pumping like mad against whatever representative example of the poor, the downtrodden, the underprivileged, the socially, culturally or monetarily disadvantaged, depressed, repressed or oppressed dregs of humanity she'd managed to find and bring home with her.

Just to see the fucking look on their faces!

"That's quite an aspiration," I allowed with what sounded, even to my own ears, like genuine admiration. And then I laughed out loud because it was also the funniest damn thing I'd ever heard. Honest it was.

"My parents are fucking assholes!" Amelia Fairway proclaimed with self-righteous fervor. And then went on to explain that she *hated* them for all the unwanted wealth and privilege they'd so unfairly forced upon her. By this time, all three of us were all laying on our backs, looking up through the tall hedge walls towering over us like we were at the bottom of some surrealistic jungle canyon. And high above them, my Diogenes' lantern of a moon hung in the vast, endless suction of the nighttime sky. The whole fucking universe was up there, and it seemed like we were part of it. At the very center of it, in fact! And for just one wild, crazy moment, I actually felt like I was floating up into it. Like the Goodyear blimp getting ready to glide over the Rose Bowl or the Hindenburg on its tether lines just before it blew up in a slow-motion explosion of flame—*"Oh! The Humanity!"*—or maybe one of those huge, helium-filled Disney characters from the Macy's Thanksgiving Day Parade. Goofy, most likely. Or maybe Felix the Cat. Only he wasn't Disney, was he? And he wasn't really around much anymore anyway. Not like when I was a kid. "Felix the Cat isn't around anymore, is he?" I said to no one in particular. And it made perfect sense, too. And we all laughed like it was the funniest damn thing we'd ever heard. And then I started wondering out loud about what happens to old cartoon characters when nobody wants them or watches them anymore. It seemed so terribly sad. And I decided for all three of us that there really needed to be some kind of Retirement Home for Out-of-Print Cartoon Characters—I could see Betty Boop and Felix the Cat up on the front porch with poor, bald Henry in his red T-shirt and black shorts who never spoke because he didn't have a mouth and the fucking Katzenjammer Kids chasing each other around the front lawn with saws and hammers and....

Somebody switched on the radio again, and I was amazed that I'd never really *listened* to the deep, deep longing and hidden, sociologically aspirational meanings in Gene Chandler's magnificent *"Duke of Earl"* before. "I'm kinda thirsty," I heard myself say. And was I ever! Why, it was like I'd been licking the damn Bonneville Salt Flats.

Somewhere, far away, I heard Amelia Camellia Fairway giggle.

"We got nuthin' here, man," the handsome black guy commiserated. *"But they gots plenty t'drink inside."* He shuffled his shoulders across the ground so his head was closer to mine and whispered: *"An' we'd really kinda like t'be alone again, y'dig?"*

I dug. But the notion of getting up sounded roughly equivalent to trying to raise the *Andrea Doria* from the depths of the Atlantic with a roll of dental floss. And I said as much.

"You kin do it, man," the big black guy laughed. *"You'll see."*

So I gave it a try. And that's when I actually became that inflatable Macy's Thanksgiving Day Parade cartoon character, rising up on the strength of all the helium in my arms, legs, hands, head and torso and kind of hovering there in space instead of actually standing. And that was funny, too. In the background, I could hear the strangely haunting echo of Shelley Fabares singing *"Johnny Angel,"* and it seemed like her voice was breathing right through the hedge walls all around me. Why, I could almost feel it through my skin....

But then a sudden wave of panic shuddered through me. *"How the hell do I get outta here?"* I heard myself ask from what sounded like several feet away.

"It's easy," Amelia Camellia's voice floated up and told me. *"But you gotta open your eyes."*

"Oh," I kind of mumbled. And you know what? She was right.

We laughed like hell about that, too.

"Just keep turning left every time you can until you hit a dead end. Then back up to the next opening and start alternating—right-left-right-left—until you hit another dead end. It's only a couple turns. Then back up to the next opening and it's just three more rights and you're outta here."

Right.

"Have a good night, man," the big, handsome black guy called after me as I disappeared into the maze. And promptly got myself completely, totally lost. Not to mention disoriented. But that was funny, too. Lord only knows how long I bumped and wandered and staggered around in there, but it felt like I was in some dumb jungle movie—*"King Solomon's Mines,"* maybe—just about dying of thirst and trying to hack my way through the bush (angry cannibals with glinting spears and razor-sharp machetes were probably after me, too) and I was just starting to feel a little bit panicky when I heard this familiar voice calling to me from the other side of the hedge wall. *"HANK? HANK? YOU IN THERE, HANK?"*

It was Danny Beagle! He'd come to rescue me! Probably had Stanley and Livingstone and Frank Buck and Sir Edmund Fucking Hillary with him, too.

"I'M IN HERE!" I called back hoarsely. My mouth felt like I'd been chewing on a mummy. It tasted faintly Egyptian. I tried spitting the mummy dust out, but I was too parched to do it.

"What the hell are you doing in there?" Danny asked from the outside.

"Looking for something to drink!" I answered desperately.

"Then why the hell don't you come out? There's nothing to drink in there."

It sounded like he was right on the other side of the hedge. *Right on the other side of the fucking wall!* Without even thinking, I hauled myself back, lowered my shoulders and flat-out *charged* at that hedge wall. And damn if I didn't crash right through it!

More or less....

"*JESUS!*" Danny yelped. "*What the hell did'ja do THAT for?*"

It was pretty hard to come up with a coherent answer. Especially considering that I was not only dead drunk and terrifically high, but also sprawled across Danny's feet with telltale shreds, chunks and pieces of Mrs. Little Harry Dick's beloved Androuet du Cerceau garden maze all over me. Not to mention the big, fresh gash over my left eyebrow, a large new rip in my pants and the huge, jagged hole I'd made in the hedge wall just a few feet behind me.

It was the funniest place I'd ever been!

"*The entrance is just around the damn corner!*" Danny just about screamed at me. "*And what's so damn funny?*"

"*Shorry,*" I apologized.

"*Jesus! You look like hell!*"

"*Yesh!*" I said like I'd just discovered Newton's third law of motion, "*I sh'pose that I do....*"

"*Jesus, what the hell happened to you?*"

From somewhere inside the maze, I thought I heard The Drifters starting in on "*When My Little Girl is Smiling.*" I always liked that song.

"Uhh," I kind of mumbled, "I shorta ran into the birtshday girl in there...."

"Oh, *great!*" Danny moaned.

"*Ishn't it?*" I happily agreed.

"Jesus, you're *plastered!*" And then a panicked expression streaked across his face. "You didn't, you know, *do* anything with her..."

"Of coursh not!" I shot back with as much indignation as I could muster while laying flat on my ass with the universe spinning around me like a damn special-effects whirlpool while the pleasant, distant echo of the Drifters floated through my ears.

"We gotta get you the hell outta here before anyone sees you!" Danny said urgently. "We'll go around the side."

"*What?!!*" I countered incredulously. "*Aren't we even going to shay good-bye?*"

"I don't think that's such a good idea," Danny grunted as he helped me to my feet. But I had to hang onto him to keep from falling down again. "You're fucking stinko, Hank," he said disgustedly. "And you've got branches and shit all over you. In your hair, too..." he shook his head "...And you're bleeding. Here." He handed me the napkin from under his drink and moved my hand up to my forehead when it became apparent that I had no idea what to do with it. His eyes scanned me over, top-to-bottom and then bottom-to-top. "Trust me on this, Hank. You really don't want anybody from The Tower to see you like this."

"*I'm fine! Jesh fine!*" I argued. And promptly staggered back into Amanda Cassandra Fairway's Androuet du Cerceau hedge wall and damn near punched another hole in it. "*Then again,*" I conceded as I grabbed two fistfuls of privet to keep from falling right over, "*perhapsh you hab a point.*"

Danny looked in horror at the large, ragged hole I'd left in the wall of our hostess' beloved garden maze. Then he looked back at me again, his eyes brimming with disapproval. "You look like hell, man," he repeated under his breath.

"Shorry."

He shook his head. "We gotta get you outta here."

"But I'm *thirshty!*" I protested. "And I could really use shome more of thosh crabmeat crepsh. And the Swedissssshh meat ballsh. And the shcallopsh wrapped in bacon. And the Napoleon shlices I shaw on the dessshhert table. And...."

"We can stop for a burger or something on Jefferson Avenue on the way home," Danny insisted as he started helping and herding me towards the shrubbery that ran along the side of the house. But I dug my heels in when we got to the reflecting pool.

"Jusht a shec," I told him. "I *gotta* get shomething to drink!" And with that I more or less stepped right into Amanda Cassandra Fairway's magnificent garden reflecting pool—boy, that water felt cold around my ankles!—and watched those fat goldfish scatter as I sloshed my way over to one of the mincing bronze seraphim with water spurting out of its penis and took a nice, long drink.

"JESUS CHRIST, HANK!" Danny yelped. And he was right, of course. But that water was just so damn cool, sweet and refreshing! Even if it did taste a little of goldfish....

On our way to the airport the next morning, I did my foggy, mumbling best to thank Danny Beagle for hustling me out of the party at the Fairway mansion the previous evening. And particularly for doing it by way of the shrubbery along the dark side of the house. "You were pretty well blitzed," Danny scolded with a rare mixture of scorn and admiration.

"Yeah, I guess I was kinda messed up."

"You should've seen your eyes."

"I did. I was looking out of them."

"And you couldn't stop laughing! What the hell was so damn funny?"

"Everything, I guess."

"And then you ate *two* Double King cheeseburgers, two orders of fries and a *pair* of banana splits at the Burger Barn." He shook his head. "It looked like you'd never seen food before."

"It just all tasted so good."

"You had butterscotch sauce and hot fudge drooling down your chin."

What could I say?

"And then you found the end of an old submarine sandwich that one of the detail shop guys must've left under the front seat. You would've eaten that, too, if I hadn't taken it away from you."

"I was just hungry, that's all."

Danny shook his head and sighed. "It was frankly disgusting."

"It was probably only a couple days old," I protested feebly.

Danny eyeballed me in the rearview mirror. "You weren't smoking any of that funny stuff, were you?"

"Are you *kidding?*" I scoffed with what I hoped sounded like genuine indignation. "Where the hell would I get it?" I figured the less said about the newly 17-year-old Amelia Camellia Fairway, her bag of potent weed and her big, handsome black running back from Michigan State, the better off everyone was going to be. Me included. So I just kept my mouth shut and concentrated on looking as hungover, headachy and miserable as possible. Which wasn't too hard to pull off, given the circumstances.

"So how do you feel this morning?" Danny sneered.

"Like a dried-up piece of dog shit."

"Well, trust me on this," he advised with a glow of satisfaction. "You look worse."

And I'm sure I did.

Plus I was heartsick about missing the Lombank Trophy race at Snetterton which, as best as I could figure, was going on *at that very moment* at the Norfolk circuit. And the lovely Audrey Denbeigh was probably there, too. And meanwhile here I was, feeling like a dried-up piece of dogshit on the green velvet brocade upholstery of Amanda Cassandra Fairway's frankly hideous new Freeway Frigate Fragonard Special Edition prototype that Danny was using to take me to the Detroit Metro Airport. Damn!

Then the fucking plane was delayed for more than an hour thanks to some problem with the latching mechanism on the luggage compartment door (you really don't want the damn thing popping open somewhere over the Atlantic...particularly if your luggage is inside!) and so all I could do was sit around the gate area drinking paper cups of vending-machine coffee and feeling generally, all-purpose shitty from the very top of my hair follicles clear down to the calluses on the bottom of my feet. I picked up a wrinkled copy of *The Detroit News* that some other traveler had left behind, and the big news of the day was that the steel companies had knuckled under after President Kennedy threatened to get the F.B.I. on their case and rolled back their price increases. Which I'm sure had everybody in Detroit breathing a big sigh of relief. Meanwhile the Shah of Iran and his wife were visiting Washington, where Jackie Kennedy showed Empress Fatah around the White House grounds while the Shah made his case for continued foreign aid so he could keep the godless communists from taking over his freedom-loving country. And its freedom-loving oil fields. The Western-educated Shah was quoted as saying: "this king business has given me personally nothing but headaches."

Speaking of communists, Castro's Cuba had convicted the 1,179 captured "Cuban exiles" they'd put on trial after the abortive and disastrous Bay of Pigs invasion. And there was a lot of ill feeling about that in certain quarters, since the expected American air and naval support never showed up. That left the invasion force pretty much stranded, and now Castro wanted $62 million in ransom to return them stateside or he was going to send them all off to prison for 30 years. He'd originally asked for 500 tractors, but of course our fine diplomatic types in Washington had to kind of look at the ceiling and explain that they had no idea what the Cubans were talking about, since the United States of America would never, *ever* attack its neighbors—regardless of their totally unacceptable political leanings—and therefore had nothing whatever to do with the Bay of Pigs invasion. So there. But they did allow that they would "put the word out" in case some patriotic, sympathetic, totally private U.S. citizens who of course had nothing to do with it either might be willing to pass the hat. It was a pretty shitty deal for the poor Cuban ex-pat foot-soldier types who got left on the beach no matter how you looked at it. On another front in the ongoing Cold War, two East Berliners were getting a nickel-skyrocket burst of fame for escaping to the west by essentially driving a dump truck right through the Berlin wall! That had to take a lot of balls, no matter whose side you were on. Oh, and old Nikita Khrushchev surprised absolutely no one by rebuffing a "final" U.S./British proposal for a nuclear test ban treaty. That was all pretty unnerving stuff, so I flipped to the Sports section. But, it being *The Detroit News,* there was nothing but five solid pages of unseemly crowing about the Tigers' 5-to-3 Opening Day home win over the hated New York Yankees. To be honest, I didn't really feel much like reading about it. Hell, I didn't feel much like being inside my own skin that particular Saturday morning.

But all of that melted into a numb, sledge-hammered stupor by the time we finally landed at Heathrow. It was well past midnight by the time I got back my shitty little flat over that commercial bakery near Surbiton, took a long, hot shower followed by an even longer, even hotter bath and fell into a deep, dreamless sleep in my own, lumpy bed. Only my time zones were all twisted around so I woke up at about three in the afternoon feeling terribly groggy and thirsty—and terrible in general, in fact—and tried calling Audrey. But there was no answer. So I sat down at my trusty little Olivetti Lettera 22 and tried to do some work on that novel I was probably never going to finish. But mostly all I did was think about Audrey and wonder how she would have reacted to Amelia Camellia Fairway's birthday party in the 47-room mansion at the end of McElligot Lane....

Chapter 14: The Unthinkable Happens

I called Audrey early Monday morning and hoped to drop by and see her at the Lola shop. But she was in a rush because she had to get her father hustled off to some therapy appointment or other and then she had the whole rest of the week tied up with a fill-in governess/tutoring job at some toney address in Mayfair. It would be all she could do to get Walter ready and where he needed to be and get to Mayfair on time.

"Did you *have* to take it?" I more or less whined.

"I'm afraid some of us aren't independently wealthy, Henry," she replied icily. "The opportunity came up because another girl decided to elope or something, and the agency was kind enough to remember my name and rang me up. And I felt damn lucky to get it!" But then her voice softened. "We can really use the money, Hank," she almost apologized. "The pay is awfully good."

I couldn't think of anything to say except: "I'm sorry."

"It's a lot of bother, really," she sighed into the receiver. "I mean, I've got to make sure Walter gets to his therapy appointment and to the shop and all."

"I could help with the shuttling around."

"That's very kind of you," she laughed. "But as I recall, the clutch in your Fiat is slipping so badly it can barely get down the street. And I don't think I want to be riding up to an address in Mayfair in it anyway. Besides, they've offered to send a car for me—I think it's a bloody Rolls Royce!—and I'm hoping we can drop Walter off along the way or I'll have to send him by taxi." She paused for a moment. "I don't really think you want to be dealing with him on your own just yet, in any case."

"You're probably right," I agreed. "But we're going to have to get around to that sooner or later, aren't we?"

"Of course we are. But I think later is probably better than sooner right now."

"I'm not so sure it's going to get any easier."

"Of course it isn't. But you'll have to just trust me on this, Hank. I know what I'm doing." She said it with the sort of finality you don't need to question.

"OK," I told her. "Whatever you think is best..."

To be honest, I was actually kind of relieved. I wasn't sure I was ready for a one-on-one with Walter just yet. I decided to switch topics: "So are you going to be at Goodwood on Easter Monday?"

"That's the plan. John Britten said the Bowmaker team wants times on all the new chassis—every car, every lap—so they've asked me to tag along. Will I see you there?"

"You couldn't keep me away."

There was a long pause at the other end.

"I've missed you," she whispered into the phone.

"I've missed you, too," I whispered back.

Another long pause.

"Well!" she exhaled suddenly (I could visualize her straightening up at the other end of the line), "don't we sound like a couple of dizzy schoolchildren?"

"And what's wrong with that?"

"Don't go all soft and squishy on me now, Henry," she replied playfully. And then she said she had to run and hung up. Click. And I sat there for the longest time just staring at the receiver in my hand.

It was hard making the week go by without her, and about all I could do was visit the Cooper, Lotus, BRM and Lola shops to get a look at the cars and catch up on the news and gossip from the Snetterton race the previous Saturday. I was particularly impressed by the new Type 23 sports/racers I saw coming together over at Lotus. To be honest, it wasn't much more than one of Chapman's highly successful Type 22 Formula Juniors widened up enough to carry two seats and a slick little full-width fiberglass body. It made one of Ferrari's 246 Dinos look absolutely huge by comparison, and it was an open secret that Lotus was hard at work on a new, in-house 1500cc twincam engine for Chapman's soon-to-be-introduced Elan sports car. If the motor was any good at all, it was going to put quite a serious sting in the 23's tail. Oh, it would never threaten the Ferraris or any of the other big-bore sports/racers on a long, fast course like Le Mans and it didn't really look sturdy enough for 12 Hours at Sebring or the Targa Florio. But it was probably going to be fast as stink on tight, twisty circuits like the Nurburgring. And with a small, light, powerful and reliable engine in back, it was surely going to be a threat for Index of Performance honors at Le Mans. Which wasn't going to sit well at all with the odd little French cars (or their rabidly xenophobic supporters) that were in the habit of copping the Index of Performance prize at Le Mans *pour la glorie de France.* It was sure to be interesting. I was also impressed by what I *wasn't* allowed to see at Lotus, which appeared to be some sort of small, taut little formula car chassis hidden away under a tarp. When I asked what it was, all I got back from Colin Chapman was a cool, stony silence....

Speaking of Lotus, it was common knowledge that the much-discussed Formula One Ferrari 156 *still* hadn't shown up at Rob Walker's garage, and Rob had covered his bets by ordering one of Colin Chapman's new Lotus 24s as a backup. Which Colin of course promised would arrive on time and be "absolutely identical in every respect" to the cars Team Lotus themselves would be running that year. Right. But the 24 wasn't ready yet, either, so Stirling had taken a drive for the pre-season British rounds in his old, ex-Rob Walker Lotus 18/21 that had been sold off to the British Racing Partnership and repainted in sponsor UDT/Laystall's pale shade of pea-soup green. The car had originally been delivered as an 18 with one of the aging but generally reliable Climax FPF inline 4s in back, but mechanic Alf Francis had made some major modifications to it (replacing Chapman's brilliant-on-paper but gremlin-prone "queerbox" transmission with a more conventional

Colotti transaxle, strengthening the halfshafts and switching to outboard rear brakes, among other things) and the car had generally proven—at least in Moss' hands—to be faster and more reliable than Chapman's own Team Lotus entries throughout the '61 season. Which can't have set particularly well with old Colin! The car was updated to 21 specs during the season (revised rear suspension and sleeker body-work, mostly) and the British Racing Partnership boys had installed one of the new Climax V8s that all the top British teams were going to be running for 1962 (except for **BRM**, of course, who tended to do everything in-house even when it made more sense not to).

Now the British Racing Partnership mechanics had to do quite a bit of cutting, hacking and welding to make the Climax V8 fit, but Stirling seemed to get along quite well with his old car, and he turned heads once again when he put it on the pole at Snetterton (ahead of—ahem!—Jimmy Clark in the very latest factory Lotus, Graham Hill in BRM's handsome new P57 V8 and surprising dark horse John Surtees in the sharp new Bowmaker Lola!). But things fell apart a bit during the race. First the Lola overheated and Surtees went out, and then the throttle started sticking on Moss' British Racing Partnership Lotus. He had to stop at the pits a few times to get the linkage freed up, and that was enough to let Clark through to win. Followed by Graham Hill in the new **BRM**. But Stirling still managed to grab fastest lap, cobbled-up, two-year-old racecar or not! He was famous for that sort of thing. Sometimes, when his car was delayed by problems or unscheduled pit stops shuffled him well back in the order, Stirling would head back out anyway—full steam and flat out as usual—to try and set fastest lap. Or, better yet, a new lap record. Just to show he could do it. And more often than not, he could. Grand Prix races offered a single, bonus point for fastest lap, and it was hardly lost on Stirling that Mike Hawthorn had beaten him to the 1958 World Championship by exactly that margin. Although he was cool, polite and thoughtful in person, Stirling was incredibly skillful, precise and competitive on a racetrack. That's why just about everyone ranked him as the best damn racing driver on the planet. Me included.

So it was great to be heading out to watch him drive again at Goodwood. Not to mention that I'd be seeing Audrey there. Although the drive out was pretty dodgy because I'd had to return the Humber press car (and the Singer Gazelle that followed) and the clutch in my Fiat had pretty much had it. I'd tried having it adjusted again, but the adjuster was about out of threads and I had to be *very* careful about the shift into top gear and treading gingerly on the gas pedal. And when you've got to be judicious with the power delivery from a 6-year-old, 22 horsepower-when-brand-spanking-new Fiat, you know you have a fairly serious problem. Not to mention that I was running a bit short on ready cash—in spite of the extra money from Fairway Motors—because I'd been traveling so much and buying food and snacks and too many drinks in airport bars and also taking Audrey out for shows and meals that were well beyond my usual, bare subsistence-level budget. Oh, I had that promised corporate expense account from Fairway, but I hadn't been especially good about saving receipts or filling out the required forms (if you don't do it on a daily basis, it's easy to get hopelessly behind) and it didn't cover drinks or nights out on the town with Audrey in any case.

Goodwood is an unusual sort of racetrack with a very colorful history, and I always considered it one of the real treasures of English motor racing. It's located near the coast in West Sussex—not far at all from central London—and Goodwood has been the gracious home estate of the noble Dukes of Richmond for more than three centuries. But it was willingly pressed into service as an impromptu airfield during World War II, and Freddie March—the reigning earl at the time—was an avid motorsports fan and even an occasional participant. After the war's end, he was easily convinced that turning the access and service roads around the airfield into some sort of motor racing track would be a jolly good idea. After all, they'd had horse racing at Goodwood as far back as 1802, and adding a little exhaust noise, tire squeal, valve clatter and a few wisps of burned oil seemed like a natural evolution into the modern era. Not to mention that the roadways were already there. Goodwood opened up for motor racing in 1948, and although the track wasn't very long by continental standards—just a little over 2 miles—and looked to be a comparatively simple layout, it was terrifically fast, challenging and deceptive. A great portion of every lap was spent in extended, glorious drifts around long, graceful corners, and the subtle, car-unsettling bumps and heaves here and there made it very much a drivers' track. So it was no surprise that Stirling Moss loved it! He'd won his very first true circuit race at Goodwood in September of 1948 at the wheel of a sputtering and thumping little 500cc Cooper/J.A.P. Formula Three car—just one day short of his 19th birthday!—and he'd excelled there ever since. Including an incredible succession of wins, pole positions and fastest laps and a genuinely stunning performance for Aston Martin at the season-ending R.A.C. Tourist Trophy in 1959. The World Manufacturers' Championship had come down to a straight, mano-a-mano fight between Aston Martin and Ferrari (with Porsche also in the hunt with a mathematical, underdog's shot at the title) but the odds favored Moss and Aston Martin on the strength of their win, pole position and new lap record at the Tourist Trophy the year before. Plus Aston brought along a bit of a Secret Weapon to help ensure a victory. The abrasive surface and long, sweeping corners at Goodwood were notoriously hard on tires (heavier cars often had to pit for new rubber long before they needed to refuel) and Aston had cleverly added air jacks underneath the team cars. It made jaws drop all up and down the pit lane during practice—and particularly in the Ferrari and Porsche pits!—when the Aston DBR1s whooshed in, a mechanic snapped an air line onto a fitting and the car obligingly leaped up into the air to have its tires changed! To be honest, I thought the psychological advantage was probably greater than the actual time saved, but it made for a lot of anxious faces and Modenese muttering in the Ferrari camp.

It all started out true to form, with Moss setting the fastest qualifying time and sprinting away immediately from the start with teammate Carroll Shelby not far behind in the second factory Aston. Plus Phil Hill's usually bulletproof Ferrari fell out with a dropped valve on the very first lap! So it looked like Moss and co-driver Roy Salvadori were home free. But then Salvadori came in for a routine refueling stop and all hell broke loose. He screeched to a halt and when he switched off, a huge backfire blasted through the side pipes just as the crew began pouring the fuel the fuel jugs in! With a mighty, instantaneous *"WHUMPPPFFF,"* the entire Aston pit stall was engulfed in flames! It was a genuine inferno, and it was pure, dumb luck that no one was seriously injured (although poor Salvadori was painfully burned). By the time the fire marshals and crewmen got it extinguished, the car was done for and Aston's pit was a charred, soaking, unusable mess. Aston privateer Graham Whitehead gallantly withdrew his own entry so the factory team could use his pit stall, and team leader Moss was summarily inserted into the Shelby/Fairman Aston Martin and went on to win handily, sealing the 1959 World Manufacturers' Championship for Aston over highly-favored Ferrari. At which point the highly xenophobic English fans and motoring scribes went utterly and predictably berserk....

Stirling Moss truly enjoyed the challenge of Goodwood's fast, sweeping curves and subtle bumps and camber changes, and he was obviously happy to be kick-starting what all the Englishmen in the press room (and all of England, come to that) fully expected to be his long-overdue Formula One World Championship season at the wheel of the as-yet undelivered Rob Walker Ferrari. Typical of England in April, it was generally damp, misty and miserable throughout morning practice and qualifying. But it felt wonderful anyway, since I was standing underneath a big, bright red Cinzano umbrella with Audrey Denbeigh. She was hard at work getting times on all the F1 cars and marking them down on her clipboard (although I really wondered if the data was worth much of anything because of the weather), and I did my best to hold up the umbrella and a soggy copy of the morning *Times* to keep the rain off her charts. In the end, it was Stirling responding to the conditions in typical Moss style, putting the aging, somewhat cobbled-up looking UDT Laystall Lotus 18/21 on pole by over two full seconds! It was a pretty damn impressive performance! Next came dapper, mustachioed Graham Hill in the handsome new BRM and, on the outside, young New Zealander Bruce McLaren in the team-leading factory Cooper. Chapman's Lotus bunch were off racing on the streets of Pau in southwestern France that weekend, preferring the climate and starting money there along with a pre-season opportunity to square off against Ferrari. And the news murmuring through the paddock was that young Jim Clark had put his

Lotus 24 on pole by nearly two full seconds over Ricardo Rodriguez in the latest-spec Ferrari. In the dry! That couldn't have been received very well down in Maranello! Or for Rob Walker's deal to run a privateer Ferrari for Moss during the regular season. I was disappointed to hear that the second Ferrari at Pau had been assigned to Lorenzo Bandini, as I'd kind of hoped Cal would get the seat. Then again, if Ferrari was in for an off year in Formula One, maybe he was better off with the sports cars. But it was terribly easy to get on the outs at Ferrari and find yourself fired off the team. Or to get fed up with the way the Old Man mistreated and manipulated his drivers—as both Ginther and Gurney ultimately did—and try to find a competitive ride someplace else. But there really weren't any decent seats left open in Formula One, and if you were going to race sports cars, Ferrari was still the team you wanted to drive for. And everybody and his brother knew it.

Audrey and I were both pleased to see John Surtees qualify fifth on the grid in the new Bowmaker Lola, and I thought that was pretty damn good for a guy who was still mostly known as a motorcycle racer (albeit a multiple champion) and a car that was fresh out of the box. We celebrated by having soggy sandwiches with the team at lunchtime and happily watched the weather start to clear up a bit. While the mechanics did a final once-over on the car, I asked Audrey how her tutoring-cum-governess job had gone in Mayfair.

"They were proper little monsters," she snorted. "I put the boy down as squandering the entire family fortune by the time he's twenty."

"How old is he now?"

"Six. But you can see the tendencies."

"Spoiled?"

"Rotten!" She laughed, rolling her eyes. "They have two little girls, too."

"Were they nice?"

"The fat one or the disgusting one?"

"Take your pick."

"The fat one was not quite so horrid as the other two. Although she did like to whinge and carry on." Audrey gave me one of those 'let's not talk about it' grimaces. "So how was your trip to America?"

"Okay, I guess. I went to a party you would not have believed."

"Really?"

"It was at Harold Richard Fairway's house. A mansion, really. Damn near a castle."

"Was it ostentatious?"

"It defined the word."

She gave me an odd look. "Did you meet any girls there?"

"Oh, of course," I shrugged. "You know me. I wound up with a very over-sexed lady lion tamer from the Barnum & Bailey Circus. You know how those things go...."

"Oh? Did you fancy her whip?"

"I'll show you the scar tissue some day."

"I can hardly wait to see it."

"It's in a very private area."

"So much the better."

It was all utter nonsense, of course. But I was really flattered that she'd asked.

By then the engines were firing up and Audrey had to scramble over to her timing stand for the race. I wanted to join her, but there was more to see and far better photo opportunities out on the corners. Although it was still overcast, the track had dried out nicely, and Bruce McLaren got it dead perfect with the clutch and gas and blasted his Cooper away from the outside of the front row like he'd been shot out of a gun. But he was overhauled a lap later by Graham Hill's BRM with Moss lurking right behind, and the general feeling was that it would only be a matter of time before Stirling asserted himself, swept past them both and left them to squabble for second place. Only then it all began to unravel for Stirling as the shift linkage started playing up and he had no choice but to stop in the pits for an adjustment. Meanwhile Hill pulled out a useful distance on McLaren while Surtees pulled into the Bowmaker pits to retire with engine trouble. Still, both he and the brand-new Lola had shown promising speed—setting fastest lap up to that point in the race—even if "Big John" wasn't exactly thrilled with the way the car felt under him. Then again, teething problems and sorting things out were always part of the game with a new racecar.

It took more than two laps for the BRP mechanics to get the linkage freed up on Stirling's Lotus, and perhaps the wise thing would have been to pack it in and call it a day. But Moss loved his racing and moreover felt a keen responsibility to all the fans who'd turned out to see him run. Although the race was hopelessly out of reach, he once again told his mechanics: *"Well, there's always the lap record to go for,"* and stormed back out onto the circuit. And immediately started cranking off fast laps, one right after the other. Until he was actually closing in on leader Graham Hill's BRM (which was two laps ahead and just stroking along, well clear of McLaren's Cooper) and that's when Easter Monday, April 23rd, 1962, turned into one of the darkest days in motor racing history....

There was no general consensus afterwards, and some eyewitnesses said Moss had an engine blow while others suspected a halfshaft might have snapped and still others thought the shifter might have jumped out of gear again. But most seemed to think he got chopped pretty rudely by Graham Hill (who might not have even known he was there because the flagman at Fordwater didn't wave the blue "passing" flag aggressively enough—or maybe he didn't wave it at all?—to let Graham know that Moss was coming up in his mirrors). Of course Eric Gibbon claimed that he was *right there* when it happened (even though he had no mud on his shoes!) and told everyone that Moss came up on Hill heading into the ultra-fast righthand sweeper leading into the difficult and unsettling change of direction/braking zone for the far slower left at St. Mary's. Moss had it lined up as if he was going to try to go around Hill on the outside (which was a pretty damn audacious move by any standards!) as that would put him on the favored inside line as the track swept back the other way into St. Mary's. But Hill either didn't see him or didn't expect anyone—not even Stirling Moss!—to attempt such a pass, and several witnesses thought he moved slightly left just as Moss' front wheels were pulling even with the BRM's rears. That (at least according to Eric) left Moss no choice but to jink left to avoid an immediate collision. It was an instinctive move at very high speed, and it sent the pale green Lotus flying off the track and bounding across the rough, uneven field between the pavement and the crash barriers. Everyone agreed it was an unusual place to go off—the end of the corner would have been much more likely—and the uneven ground launched the car into a terrifying series of leaps, flips and barrel rolls. It finally hurtled to rest with a hard, sickening crunch, and corner marshals were already on their way towards it on a dead run. When they arrived, they found Moss bloody and unconscious inside a twisted heap of broken tubing and shattered fiberglass—wheels pointed every which way—and it took them the better part of an hour to cut Stirling out of the wreck and send him off in an ambulance to Chichester Hospital. Rumors spread quickly through the paddock that he was dead. They fortunately turned out to be false, but he was very gravely injured and had lapsed into a deep coma.

Everyone was stunned.

As you can imagine, Stirling's crash became front-page news all over England and Europe. The best damn racing driver on earth had been grievously hurt and his life hung in the balance, and all from an accident that never should have happened in a race that didn't really matter and while trying for the questionable consolation of a new lap record in a contest that was already lost. And there was nothing anybody—not his father or his manager or his loyal British fans or even the medical crew that did their best to patch him back together—could do except hope and pray and wait on the daily news reports to see if his condition had improved. Moss' wreck had a deep, lingering effect on all the top drivers, too, because they knew that if it could happen to Stirling, it could happen to any of them....

Moss was ultimately transferred to Atkinson Morely Hospital near Wimbledon, still in a coma, and stayed that way for over a month. But, just as in wartime or show business, the racing had to go on. And that's both the shame and the salvation of it. No matter what terrible thing has happened or what great hero has fallen, the upcoming schedule is always there to catch you like some grim sort of safety net. And all the fear, worry, outrage and uncertainty get silently swept under the mat as the next race looms and all the drivers, teams and fans start gathering themselves together to be ready for it. Racing's losses and tragedies are never forgotton—in fact, they seem over time to become almost cherished—but it's amazing how easily they're set aside in the rush to make the next event. I tried to explain all that to Audrey on our way home from Goodwood. Or maybe I was just trying to explain it again to myself. About how uncomfortable and even guilty it made me feel when I tried to dress it up in fine words and make it sound like there was something noble and gallant and valuable and worthwhile underneath all the pain, blood, burns and broken bones. And I felt guiltier still that, somewhere deep inside, I felt a strange, giddy little shiver of awe and even admiration when the worst happened. That's when the stakes of the game became crystal clear in an instant and when you realized all over again what the drivers had to either face or ignore each time they strapped on a helmet. But of course Audrey'd been around it herself and knew exactly what I was thinking and feeling. She put her arm around my shoulders. "Maybe it's best to not try and put everything into words, Hank."

"But that's what I do, Audrey. Or that's what I'm supposed to do, anyway."

She looked at me like mothers look at hurt children. "Do you like what you do?"

"You know I do."

"Well, then, I think you're going to have to try and come to terms with this." She leaned her head gently against my shoulder. "It's just the way things are, Hank, and it's not about to change...."

Chapter 15: Big Plans in Detroit

I found myself back on the 13th floor of Fairway Tower again the following week after yet another surprise phone call from Danny Beagle. But I didn't mind. Audrey was back with the three little "Monsters from Mayfair" all week and all the people I knew in the motorsports world were walking around in a daze like zombies because of what had happened to Stirling Moss. He was still in a deep coma at Atkinson Morley Hospital with the right side of his brain partially detached from his skull, a crushed left eye socket and cheekbone, internal injuries, a fractured left arm and multiple fractures to his left leg. But the head injury was the main thing. Everyone was waiting for some kind of news, but nothing was forthcoming, so everything seemed uncomfortably unsettled and hanging in the balance, and I was honestly relieved to get away.

I couldn't really imagine why Bob Wright wanted me back in Detroit again so quickly—I hadn't really heard or seen anything that might matter to Fairway Motors since the previous week—but it turned out that this was about something entirely different. Bob's grand plan was to attack in force and everywhere possible when he launched Fairway Motors' still-secret "Absolute Performance" program, and he wanted to pick my brain and get my opinion on some of the things that he'd been considering. Harlon Lee's shop down in North Carolina was already hard at work on the next generation of Fairway stock cars, and Bob was also making a few inquiries as to how Fairway Motors might best make a name for itself at the Indy 500. After all, it *was* the biggest damn race in the world....

"Well, it is for Americans," I cautioned. And then I went on to say that I thought the mid-engined, independently-sprung single-seaters they were running on road courses in Europe were a lot more sophisticated and advanced than the solid-axle, front-engined Offy roadsters that the Indianapolis teams traditionally ran. Wealthy American sportsman and road-racing enthusiast Jim Kimberly (who was also an accomplished amateur racer and not incidentally heir to the more-than-sizeable Kimberly-Clark Kleenex and bathroom-tissue fortune!) managed to arrange a midweek test day at Indy for newly-crowned World Champion Jack Brabham and his Formula One Cooper the week after the 1960 United States Grand Prix at Watkins Glen. And Brabham stunned a lot of the Indy regulars with how quickly he adapted to the daunting Indianapolis oval and how incredibly quick and nimble the little Cooper seemed through the corners. Even if its gasoline-fed, 2.5-liter Climax FPF was no match power-wise for the alcohol-fueled, 4.2-liter Offenhausers that had powered virtually the entire, 33-car field at the 500 that year. In fact, the results of the test were so encouraging (and the Indy purse was so enormous!) that Kimberly persuaded John and Charlie Cooper to adapt one of their Formula One chassis for a try at Indy. They once again brought Brabham as their driver, and even got Climax to build a special, 2.7-liter version of their FPF engine specifically for Indianapolis. It was still way down on power compared to the Offies, but it was fast as stink through the corners, nimble through traffic and got far better gas mileage than the big, alcohol-burning Indy roadsters. But the Cooper had problems with its tires wearing out too quickly during the race, which played hell with their "we'll make fewer pit stops" strategy. In the end, Brabham and the Cooper came home an encouraging but nonetheless lackluster 9th overall at the checker, and the know-nothing railbirds scoffed down their noses at what the so-called "World Champions" had done against their homegrown American heroes and beloved Offy roadsters. But those who knew what the hell they were looking at—including a lot of the top drivers and car builders—realized the Indianapolis 500 they knew and loved was about to change forever.

"Then why the hell don't they just come over here and win it?" Bob asked with an unmistakable crackle of challenge in his voice. Like most Americans, Bob considered the Indy 500 a genuine, red-white-and-blue institution, and he didn't much fancy the idea that a bunch of foreigners might be able to come over and steal it away.

"Well, it's not so simple," I did my best to explain. "Indy is a very unique sort of race on a very specialized kind of racetrack, and the cars that run there have been evolving and developing for a very long time. I may think they're big, crude and antiquated, but there's no question that they're pretty damn good at what they do. Besides, the English constructors are all busy with their own racing programs over in Europe. It would require a lot of money and a big commitment to build a whole new car just to run one single race. Even if it is the biggest damn race in the world. Plus they'd have to find something to use for an engine."

"If their chassis are so superior, why don't they just bolt in the same kind of motor the Americans are using?"

"Well, to start with, a good Offy would rattle a Lotus to pieces in about half an hour. And it's a big, tall motor so it wouldn't really fit too well. And you'd need bigger fuel tanks and oil tanks to keep it fed. And I don't think there's a transaxle on earth that could handle the torque."

"But you could *build* an engine, couldn't you?"

I shook my head. "You've got to understand that none of them are really big companies. Ferrari's surely the biggest and best equipped, but he's sent cars over to Indy a couple times and got his ears pinned back every time."

"And why was that, if his cars are supposed to be so good?"

"To be honest, I don't think he took it seriously enough. You really need a dedicated, specialized, purpose-built car and engine package for Indy. That's just the nature of the place."

Bob nodded absently, mulling it over. And then he leaned in and asked: "So how would you go about it? If you really wanted to win it, I mean."

That was a question I'd already spent a lot of pub time discussing with racing friends over in England, so I was ready with an answer: "Well, I think you'd want to get one of the top constructors in England to do you a chassis. But bigger, tougher and stronger than one of their Formula One cars, and built to just turn left. And then you'd either have to buy yourself an Offy—and, like I said, they're tall and they're thirsty and they vibrate like hell—or figure out something else for a motor."

He rubbed his chin. "So tell me: who are the top guys over there?"

"Well, Colin Chapman at Lotus is usually considered to be the most creative and cleverest. But he can be stubborn, willful and difficult sometimes, and his plate is really, really full right now. Plus not all of his brilliant ideas turn out to be quite so brilliant in the long run. But that's what you generally get with geniuses, isn't it?"

"I suspect it is."

"He's a terrifically driven and competitive guy. Ambitious, too. And maybe even a little bit ruthless when he needs to be."

"That's not necessarily a bad thing."

"I suppose. But Colin's also got a bit of a reputation as a horse trader and an angle shooter, and he can turn Machiavellian on you in a heartbeat if the situation demands."

"Oh, really?" Bob said with an ill-disguised glow of admiration.

"A few team owners have told me you need to count your fingers after you shake hands on a deal with Colin Chapman."

Bob looked out his window at the smoke and fumes fumes rising from the battery of smokestacks below. "But you think he's the best, right?"

"He thinks he is, that's for sure. And I suppose, if I'm really honest about it, I probably do, too."

"Hm. I see," Bob allowed, thinking it over. "Whom else do you rate?"

"Oh, John and Charlie Cooper are good, straight, solid guys who build good, straight, solid racecars. Hell, Jack Brabham won back-to-back World Championships for them in '59 and '60. And, like I said, they brought one to Indy last year and finished 9th overall with shit tires and 150 less horsepower than the Offies."

"I'm not really interested in finishing ninth...."

"Oh, the car could do it for sure with equal power and decent tires. But at the same time, I'd have to say that Cooper's stock is slipping just a bit as the sport gets more technical and scientific. They've always been more thumb-and-eyeball 'builders' rather than theoretical 'designers' or 'engineers.' But a lot of drivers think their cars are safer, solider and friendlier to drive because of it. Colin Chapman's cars are probably more advanced and more elegant, but they're also built lighter—maybe even *too* light—and they've gotten kind of a reputation for falling apart at inopportune moments."

You could see Bob absorbing and processing the information as he listened. "Anybody else worth knowing about?"

And that's when I told him about Eric Broadley. "He's the new kid on the block, of course, and not all that experienced. But everyone's been impressed with everything he's done so far, and his cars have run at the front pretty much everywhere they've raced. He's one to watch for sure."

I could almost hear the wheels turning and gears meshing behind Bob Wright's eyes. And then he thoroughly surprised me by asking: "So which one would you link up with if you wanted to race Formula One over in Europe?"

I thought that one over for quite awhile before I gave Bob my answer: "I wouldn't go with any of them."

I watched his eyebrows arch up. *"None* of them?"

I shook my head. "No, I think I'd be better off doing what Coventry Climax has done: build a really good engine and sell it to all of them. Then you don't care which one builds the best chassis or which one wins. And that way you've got them *all* working for you instead of just one constructor..."

I could tell Bob was intrigued.

"...Only I wouldn't do it just yet."

His eyebrows arched up even higher. "Oh?"

I gave him a sly, insider smile. "Not yet," I cautioned, drawing the words out like taffy.

"And why not yet?"

I let that one simmer for just a heartbeat or two. And I've got to say it felt pretty good. But I made sure to start explaining before he got impatient with me: "Look, a lot of people—and particularly the scribes, fans and race promoters— aren't real happy with the current formula. They don't think the little 1.5-liter cars are powerful enough or impressive enough for Formula One. Hell, most of us think they look like pumped-up Formula Juniors."

"So?"

"So instead of doing a motor for a formula that a lot of people don't like and that's very likely to be changed in a few years, I'd keep my powder dry until I know for sure what the new formula is going to be. And then I'd get a jump on everybody and build a really, *really* great new engine for it."

For the very first time, Bob looked at me like I was actually worth the Fairway Motors checks I'd been getting. "That's a good thing to know," he allowed, rolling it over in his mind, "a good thing to know indeed." Bob looked down at his watch and realized he was running late for a meeting with Dick Flick and his top advertising guys about advance planning for the new Ferret's launch in the spring of 1964. But before he left, he wanted me to fill him in a little regarding Ferrari the *man* and Ferrari the *company,* as opposed to Ferrari the racing team and the specs and performance of the road and racing machines that came out of the famous red brick factory in Maranello.

"I don't really know too much about that," I had to admit. "I don't think anybody does."

"But there must be rumors. Scuttlebutt. He must have bankers or backers and a board of directors like any other company."

"Old Enzo plays it pretty close to the vest. He only tells you what he wants you to know. And then only at a press conference."

"Could you get a one-on-one interview with him?"

"I don't know, really. To be honest, I've never tried." In the back of my mind, I was thinking that the only scribe I knew who might be able to pull that sort of thing off would be my sad-eyed little Italian friend and colleague Vinci Pittacora. But I didn't say anything. As Danny had advised me on my very first trip to The Tower, when you're dealing with top management in a big corporation, you never want to supply your answers too quickly, because it makes your job look too easy. "I could do some checking around for you," I said with decisively open-ended vagueness.

Bob gave my professionalism a little nod of approval. "I think we'd like that," he allowed. "Do a little digging for us. See if you can find out a little something about where Ferrari's money comes from? How much he's worth? Who he owes? If he's making money or not?"

"He's always crying poor, I know that much. And it's pretty much common knowledge that he's trying to get Fiat or the Italian Government to come up with some money to help support his racing teams."

"But you don't know the details, do you?"

"No, not for sure. I couldn't say as I know any of the specifics."

"Well," Bob continued through a thin, reptilian smile, "why don't you see if you can find some of that out for us?"

"I don't know if I can," I said honestly.

"But you can give it a try for us, can't you?"

"I suppose I can."

You could see that my answer didn't hit quite the right note for him. Bob's eyes narrowed and stared deep into mine. "Make it a real *good* try, won't you?"

It didn't exactly sound like a question.

Bob Wright had me back in his office the very next day to pick my brain about Carroll Shelby. It seems Carroll had approached him about dropping one of Fairway's new, small-block Flyer V8s into an English A.C. chassis to make some sort of Anglo-American hot rod of a sports car, and he wanted to know what I thought of the idea. And I had mixed feelings, to be honest. Carroll was one hell of a guy and a truly top driver. Back in the early- and mid-1950s when I was covering races out on the west coast for the magazine before I went to Europe, Carroll was pretty much considered to be either the best or the second-best road-racing driver in America (alongside Phil Hill), and he'd gone on to do one hell of a job for Aston Martin, sharing the winning car at Le Mans and also at the title-clinching Goodwood Tourist Trophy in 1959. But Carroll had a pretty checkered history as a jack-of-all-trades hustler, promoter and snake-oil salesman when he was away from the race-track, and you tended to wonder sometimes if he could really deliver the goods outside of a racecar as well as he could in one. He'd led a pretty amazing life, serving as a fighter pilot and flight instructor in Texas during World War II, and then kind of bouncing around afterwards with a dump truck business, a chicken ranch that went broke when all the chickens came down with limberneck disease, a sports car dealership with Jim and Chuck Hall in Dallas and a then a Goodyear racing tire distributorship and a High Performance Driving School out in California. Carroll was a great guy to spend time with and had an incredible line of bullshit when he was trying to sell you something (along with an admirable entrepreneurial streak and a whole fucking boatload of chutzpah) but, to be honest, he didn't have a particularly stellar track record when it came to finishing things he'd started. It was pretty common knowledge that he'd retired from racing because of heart problems—I'd personally seen him sneak little nitroglycerin pills under his tongue before he went out to race—but I think he was also getting tired of it by the time he quit and genuinely wanted to move on to other things. There's nothing like a health problem to get you thinking about your own mortality, and that's not really the kind of thing you can afford to have floating through your head when you're racing at places like Spa, Le Mans and Monza. Plus Carroll had seen a lot of his friends and teammates get themselves killed, and there comes a point for almost every professional driver when you start thinking it's just a big game of Russian Roulette and that you've already spun the chambers around maybe a few too many times. You need to understand that I liked Carroll a lot and admired the hell out of his guts, drive and gumption, and I really *liked* the idea of his idea for an English chassis/American V8-powered hybrid sports car. But I had serious questions as to whether he could pull it off.

On the other hand, it sounded like it actually might work. A.C. was a shopworn little English car company that started building higher-end, performance-oriented motorcars way back in 1901. They'd been through the usual gauntlet of flush times, hard times, financial disasters, receiverships and changes of ownership that you come to expect from a small British automobile company. But they'd somehow staggered along and managed to survive, and wound up in the hands of the well-to-do Hurlock family through the war years and on into the fifties. And their lean, handsome new A.C. "Ace" sports roadster introduced at the Earl's Court show in

October of 1953 was an immediate hit. The car was really just a production-ized version of the Bristol-engined racing special that John Tojeiro built for London car dealer/club racer Cliff Davis, which had been tremendously successful, winning six events outright during the 1953 British club season. It transpired that the Hurlock brothers were invited to a test day, and were impressed enough with Davis' car to want to put a road-worthy version into production. The resulting car looked absolutely stunning (as it should, since the bodywork was really nothing but a shameless knockoff of a Ferrari *Barchetta!*) and the company made them available with A.C.'s own, long-in-the-tooth straight six and also, starting in 1957, with the almost-as-antique but far more potent and promising Bristol straight six. Which was really just a BMW 328 motor from the 1930s that had been brought back to England (along with its designer, Fritz Fiedler) as essentially spoils of war after Germany's surrender. But that's another story.

As you might expect from a sports car that started out as a successful racing special, the A.C. Ace turned out to be a damn good track weapon. Particularly in amateur events, where A.C. Bristols pretty much dominated 2-liter "production class" races on both sides of the Atlantic through the late 1950s. A factory-supported Ace with Ken Rudd and Peter Bolton up even managed to finish 10th overall at Le Mans in 1957 (although it was seven full laps behind the class-winning 2-liter Ferrari!). The inescapable conclusion was that the A.C. Ace was a pretty damn good sports car. For the middle fifties, anyway....

But now it was the late spring of 1962 and the Hurlock brothers' Ace hadn't really changed very much. And their supply of Bristol engines was in the process of drying up because Bristol was getting itself out of the automobile engine manufacturing business. This left A.C. desperately in need of something new, modern, and hopefully reasonably affordable to stick under the hood of their sports cars. Ken Rudd had championed the Zephyr six, but it was Shelby who wrote to the Hurlock brothers about shoe-horning a big, rumbleguts American V8 between the frame rails. And they wrote back and said: "see what you can put together, old boy," and that's how the whole thing started coming together. I heard later that Carroll went to Chevy first (just about everybody considered Chevy's 265/283/327 cubic-inch "smallblock" an extraordinarily good motor) but of course Chevy already had the Corvette in their lineup and weren't really interested. But then Shelby heard about the new, small V8 that Fairway had in the works for the Flyer (and upcoming—but still top-secret—Ferret), and in short order he was knocking on the door at Fairway Tower. Which is obviously why I'd seen him getting into those special, polished brass elevators that led up to the 13th floor on my first-ever trip to Fairway Tower. But while I really liked Carroll (and genuinely *loved* his idea!) I had to be honest and share the concerns I had with Bob Wright. After all, that's what he was paying me for.

"Have you ever driven an A.C.?"

Bob shook his head.

"Well, it's one of your classic 1950s British roadsters. Which means it hasn't got much in the way of weather protection. And the seatbacks are damn near bolt upright. And the top takes absolutely forever to put up. Especially in a rainstorm. And even then it's probably going to leak a little, because it doesn't have roll-up windows or..."

"So what are you saying?"

"Well, Chevy didn't do very well with their Corvette back when it had side curtains instead of roll-up windows. I just wonder if your typical American car buyer is going to be willing to put up with that sort of thing?"

"They put up with MGs and Triumphs, don't they?"

He had me there.

"And we wouldn't be looking for your typical American car buyer, anyway. This would be a strictly low-volume, hair-on-its-chest, image-building, high-performance sports car."

And that's when I mentioned quality and reliability (and their corporate near-homonym, "liability"), since it would take a bit of doing to get an antiquated, single-plane, ladder-frame British chassis with transverse leaf springs at both ends and the approximate torsional rigidity of a damp pizza crust to cope with the heft, weight and muscle of a hot-rodded American V8. After all, that chassis had originally been designed to handle something on the near side of 150 horsepower. Although I had to admit that I'd seen guys in back-alley shops in L.A. shove just about anything into anything and make it work. At least for a quarter mile or so....

"Carroll says it'll blow the doors off a Corvette," Bob continued evenly, watching my eyes.

I didn't take long to think it over. Sure, everybody who was anybody in the car business had heard about the long-promised, "all-new" Corvette that Chevrolet was planning to introduce in the fall as a '63 model. And that it was furthermore going to have independent rear suspension—like a Jaguar XKE—along with a *very* sexy, beamed-down-from-outer-space new shape based on the "Sting Ray" racing special that GM Head of Styling Bill Mitchell had been campaigning with Corvette ace Dick Thompson at the wheel. The car started out as the test mule for the futuristic Corvette SS that created such a stir at Sebring back in 1957. Both Stirling Moss and Juan Manuel Fangio drove the car in practice (and praised its torque and power, if not its weight, brakes or handling) but it never ran in the actual race. My good friend John Fitch was spearheading the whole program for Chevrolet at the time, and the "real" SS broke its suspension and dropped out of the race after a little more than 100 miles. But the production Corvette they'd brought along to run in the GT class soldiered on and managed to finish 12th overall and first in class, which was pretty damn good for a first try. Of course GM's involvement was very much under the table (the cars were entered by John Fitch and longtime Indianapolis team owner Lindsey Hopkins) but of course everybody and his brother knew what was really going on. And that apparently got some noses out of joint at GM, and they pulled the plug on the entire project in deference to the stupid AMA racing ban. Still, there was nothing to prevent an individual, private GM employee (like Bill Mitchell, for instance) from building and entering a car on his own. And so, with a lot of help from the same guys who built GM's dream cars for the auto show circuit, Bill had the SS test hack covered with a strikingly handsome (if somewhat Buck Rogers) fiberglass body shell and started entering it in some SCCA races. And they'd done pretty well at that level, including a couple solid class wins (albeit against marginal opposition). Mitchell even drove the damn thing to work now and then on sunny days, and no question it really looked like something out of a science fiction movie.

But independent rear suspension and futuristic new bodywork aside, the "all new" '63 Corvette was still going to have a stamped steel frame and stamped steel suspension arms and drum brakes all around and it was still going to come in awfully big and heavy for a 2-seater sports car. And that was the real crux of the whole thing. It was simple math, really. Assuming Shelby's new Anglo-American hybrid came in somewhere between 500 and 900 pounds lighter than the new Corvette (not to mention with fully independent suspension and 4-wheel disc brakes), if the two cars had anywhere near the same horsepower and tires, the results would be a foregone conclusion. Hell, you might even be able to blow off a few of old Enzo's Ferraris with something like that!

If you could keep it in one piece....

And that was a pretty big "if."

"So do you think it could beat a Corvette?" Bob repeated.

"It sounds like an interesting idea," I allowed like I wasn't nearly as pumped up about the idea as I was. "I think it most likely could."

A big grin formed under Bob's nose. "It's not a whole lot of money, either," he added with a conspiratorial wink.

"Where would you build it?"

"Oh, Shelby's found someplace out in California. Venice, I think."

That was perfect. If you wanted to tap into a ready-made workforce/talent pool that already knew all there was to know about building fast cars, you only had three real choices: London, Modena or Southern California.

"So you'd do it?" Bob asked.

There was only one possible answer: "You bet your ass I would!!!"

"Good!" he grinned, slapping his desk. And then he looked up at me with this sheepish, little-boy-caught-with-his-hand-in-the-cookie-jar expression on his face and added: "Because I've already done it."

"You *have?*"

He nodded. "We'll have the prototype on our stand at the New York Auto Show next weekend, and the car magazines are going to start road-testing it next week."

That was pretty big news, all right.

"Aren't you worried about, you know, lawsuits and liability and that sort of stuff?"

Bob straightened in his chair. "As far as we're concerned, the car is a Shelby, not a Fairway. And we're going to make damn sure we keep it that way. Arm's length and separate tables from start to finish. According to Randall Perrune's legal people, all we're doing is selling Shelby some engines and transmissions and renting him a little piece of carpet at the auto shows so he can show his cars off and try to drum up a few sales."

I could see the intelligence of putting a set of shallow pockets between a big, rich company like Fairway Motors and anybody who might somehow manage to hurt themselves (or a few unfortunate, innocent bystanders) with a lightweight, high horse-power, hair-trigger new sports car that could very likely leap from stoplight to stoplight faster than anything on the street. It was a pretty sly plan adapted to a really audacious idea, and my opinion of Bob Wright went up several notches on the spot.

"Oh, we did have him hire away a couple of our guys," Bob continued expansively. "A production-line guy that Ben Abernathy picked out personally and a Harvard business school type from Clifton Toole's staff for his front office. Just to keep an eye on things for us...."

I was beginning to get the picture.

"But this is just a little side deal," Bob cautioned. "Something that just came up out of nowhere and may never go anywhere. But it didn't cost us much and we've got it positioned so if it falls on its face it won't affect us too much. And if it does turn out to be a thorn in the Corvette's hide," he flashed me a mean, predatory smile, "that'd be worth it just to watch the Chevy guys squirm." The smile faded as quickly as it had appeared. "In any case, we don't want to let it distract us from our real mission here."

"And that would be?"

Bob Wright stared at me for a few moments. I could almost hear the gears turning behind his eyes. "You know," he said slowly, drawing out his words, "I've got a big pre-launch meeting with our second tier managers coming up in about fifteen minutes." He looked me over thoughtfully. "How would you like to sit in on it?"

"*Me?*"

Bob Wright nodded. "We're embarking on some pretty important things here right now, and there's a chance somebody may want to put it all down on paper one day..." he eyeballed me kind of sideways "...Who knows, you might be just the guy to do it."

And that, in a nutshell, is how I wound up sitting in the third row of Fairway Tower's 12th floor "presentation room" (which was really more like a small auditorium) less than a half-hour later, looking forward over neat, orderly rows of pale, clean-cut, clean-shaven guys wearing crew cuts, white dress shirts—some with their sleeves rolled up a few turns—shined dress shoes and dark, skinny ties. Plus a few women in "please take me seriously" tailored wool business outfits scattered around the room. The whole place smelled of coffee, after shave and cigarettes (mostly Winstons, Tereytons, Benson & Hedges and Marlboros as far as I could tell) and every single person in the room—me, included—was wondering just what the hell they were doing there. Up in front was a low, carpeted stage with podium on it, a big, white projection screen behind it and a row of folding chairs for all the top brass from the 13th floor. Except for Little Harry Dick Fairway, of course, who didn't much like speaking in front of audiences he actually had to prepare for. He much preferred the impromptu verbal assaults, blindside sniping, situational ambushes and off-the-cuff character assassinations of his regular staff meetings. Besides, he was probably either off playing golf or hard at work "giving dictation" to the impressively endowed Miss Francine Niblitz anyway....

You could hear the "wonder what's up?" hubbub murmuring its way through the room as the house lights dimmed, and everyone hushed as Bob Wright led his staff in from the side of the stage: Bob in a smart, Fairway Blue blazer and a matching, regimental silk tie, Ben Abernathy in his shirtsleeves rolled up and looking typically rumpled, worn out and like he had an awful lot of things to get back to, Dick Flick in his slick, razor-cut hair, perpetual tan, hard, confident smile with its signature Cary Grant dimple underneath and a Savile Row suit that probably cost more than most of the cars in the employee parking lot. Hugo Becker followed in his white lab coat, looking mildly annoyed that he had to be there at all and even more annoyed that he had to sit next to Daryl Starling, Daryl in a stand-out-from-the-crowd, salmon-colored jacket with a peach silk ascot around his neck and clearly enjoying the chance to be onstage, Randall Perrune from legal and Clifton Toole from accounting both looking cheerful as fresh corpses and obviously wondering why the hell they had to be there in the first place and then, bringing up the rear but getting to sit right next to Dick Flick on the left side of the lectern, an obviously nervous, fidgety and rodent-like Hubert C. Bean from Computer Modeling. Manny Street from Dealer Relations was typically out of town, working out some differences of opinion on who was getting the good cars, color combinations and financing deals and who was getting the shit and the shaft down in Louisiana. But Manny liked Cajun food and he liked Bourbon Street even more, so he didn't mind.

The house lights dimmed and you could hear a hush settle over the room as a single spotlight followed Bob Wright up to the podium. He looked out over the crowd, leaned in close to the mike, and in a sly, inspired stage whisper said: *"I bet a lot of you are wondering just what the heck we're doing here today?"* He let that hang for a moment, and you could hear a wave of murmuring roll through the crowd. He waited for it to die down. *"Well, let me tell you,"* he continued, straightening up and gaining volume, *"this company is about to embark on the most exciting product and marketing campaign in automotive history!"* His eyes swept around the room. *"You and I—together!—are about to knock the rest of Detroit—the rest of the world!— right back on its heels!"*

"ALL RIGHT!" somebody shouted from the back row. But I recognized Danny Beagle's voice immediately. And I'm sure a lot of other people did, too.

Bob squared his shoulders above the podium. *"Friends and fellow workers, let me make it clear to you: Fairway Motors is about to do something that no car company on earth has ever done before!"* He waited for a moment to let the idea settle in, and then cut loose with explosive, holy-roller fervor: *"AND THE TIME HAS COME FOR YOU TO KNOW ABOUT IT!"*

A feeble sputter of applause echoed from the back of the room.

Bob leaned in close to the mike again and went back down to a whisper. *"Always in the past, as far back as cars have been built,"* he began earnestly, *"the engineers and designers put their heads and hearts together, did what they thought was right and built the very best darn automobiles they knew how to build..."* he paused dramatically, then reared his shoulders back and damn near shouted to the heavens: *"...BUT THOSE DAYS ARE OVER AS OF RIGHT NOW!"*

A collective gasp sucked half of the air out of the room.

At which point Bob's face melted into a friendly, just-between-you-and-me smile. *"You're probably wondering just what the heck I'm talking about?"*

Mumbled agreement.

"Well, let me let you in on a little secret, my friends and fellow workers," his eyes narrowed and his voice turned hard and fierce, *"you and I and everybody up on this stage,"* he swept his arms inclusively around the room, *"are about to do something that no car company on earth has ever done before!"* He leaned in close to the mike again and stage whispered: *"And it's still top secret, so I don't want any of you telling anybody about it—not even your wives, friends and families—until we're ready to go public. And that's not going to be for another two years."* He turned to Dick Flick. *"That's right, isn't it, Dick?"*

Dick Flick nodded knowingly.

Bob leaned back into the mike again. *"And that means I don't want any of you getting fired after you know about this..."* he threw in a crocodile smile *"...because then we'd have to shoot you..."*

An uneasy titter flickered through the crowd.

Bob pulled himself up straight again and his voice went upbeat, confident and matter-of-fact. "What we've done is simply harness the incredible calculating, tabulating and information-gathering capabilities of the modern supercomputer and applied the tools and models of modern, up-to-the-minute market research and let..." he paused for emphasis *"...AND – LET – OUR – CUSTOMERS – TELL – US – WHAT – KIND – OF – AUTOMOBILES – THEY – WANT – US – TO – BUILD!!!"*

Stunned silence.

"And you know what?" he whispered into the mike.

More numb silence.

"WE'RE – GOING – TO – BUILD – THEM!!!!!!"

A sudden, ominous drum roll came building and crescendoing through the sound system as a dazzling image of the new Fairway Ferret "personal sporty car" exploded on the screen behind him in a fireworks display of colored lights. When the noise faded, you could've heard a pin drop. And then, starting at the back again, Danny Beagle's two-hands-clapping caught momentum and thundered raucously through the room. With a few cheers, hoots and whistles thrown in! And you couldn't blame them. That car looked *neat!* It was cool. It was hot. It was fresh. It was young. It was impossibly sexy, sporty and irresistible. And it wasn't like anything else on the road, either. I recognized it immediately as the glass-case model I'd seen in Bob Wright's office on my very first trip to Fairway Tower. The one he kept hidden away under that gray velvet cover and locked up in his credenza at night so the cleaning people wouldn't see it. Only Dick Flick's ad guys had done their usual magic with an airbrush and distortion so it looked even longer, lower, wider and more rakish than the final production versions would ever be. The panel fit was probably better, too. But that was all part of the game.

Bob waited for the hubbub to die down. "This is the new Fairway Ferret," he said simply, "and I think it's safe to say that it's the first car in the history of Detroit—heck, the first car in the history of this whole, amazing, God-fearing world—where our marketing people went out and asked people what they wanted. Asked people what kind of car they wanted to drive! Asked them what kind of car they wanted to be seen in! Asked them how much they could afford to spend! Asked them what they cared about and looked for in an automobile! Asked them what they liked and disliked about the cars that they're driving today! Asked them what kind of car would turn their neighbors bright green with envy when they brought it home and parked it in their driveway!" He paused to let it all sink in. "And then we took all that information and handed it to this man right here..." he nodded in Hubert C. Bean's direction, and I watched Hubert flinch like an jolt of electricity had been sent through his testicles "...and he took all those answers—all that information, all that data—and he added it up and sifted through it and boiled it down and stirred it around until he could hand it over to our marketing people..." he nodded towards Dick Flick, who immediately flashed his dazzling, Cary Grant smile with the dimple underneath "...and they turned it into some real, concrete concepts and ideas and parameters, and then they took those concepts and ideas and parameters over to our wonderful design and engineering departments..." Daryl Starling absolutely beamed, while Hugo Becker more-or-less winced "...and they drew it up and sculpted it and styled it until it was exactly, precisely and decisively what we already *knew* the public wanted..." he paused one more time so he could nod appreciatively in Hugo Becker and Ben Abernathy's general direction "...and handed the whole project over to Hugo and Ben here from Engineering and Manufacturing, so they could figure out how to build it the way we knew it had to be built and moreover bring it in at the price point where we knew it had to be." He offered them a curt bow of appreciation. "Thank you, gentlemen!"

Hugo and Ben responded with the forced, helpless smiles of condemned prisoners.

Bob's eyes swept down the entire row of executive corridor faces behind him. "Thank you all, in fact. You've given us what I think, I hope and I truly, fervently believe..." his voice rose to a fever pitch again "...*will be THE — BIGGEST — SUCCESS — STORY — IN — AUTOMOTIVE — HISTORY!!!*"

Thunderous applause exploded all around me—hell, I was clapping like mad, too— as yet another tympani roll crescendoed through the sound system and more and more images of the new Ferret flashed on the screen like fireworks going off. And then, after a sustained period of near-ecstatic intensity, the images faded to black, the tympani roll diminished, both screen and room went dark and the crowd hushed into an awed silence. There was just one tiny, baby spotlight trained on Bob Wright's face and torso as he leaned into the mike one last time. "But you know," he started in evenly, "I'm afraid I lied to you a little while back..."

The crowd looked back and forth at each other as the first picture of the new Ferret reappeared silently on the screen behind him.

"...I said that 'we were going to build it'..." he indicated the executive-corridor group on stage behind him and the image of the new Fairway Ferret hovering over his shoulder "...but that's not true..."

More questioning looks.

"...No, the truth is, my friends, that *YOU...*" he pointed to the rows of Fairway employees leaning eagerly forward in front of him as his voice rose dramatically *"...YOU ARE GOING TO BUILD IT! YOU'RE THE PEOPLE AND THE TALENT AND THE DRIVE AND THE DEDICATION THAT'S GOING TO GET THIS JOB DONE!!!"* He lifted his arms to the heavens. *"AND I CONGRATULATE YOU FOR IT!!!"*

And with that there was a blinding flash of light and a boom that surely blew out every speaker in the room and everything went totally, thoroughly and completely black. It was just an old magician's trick, really. A profusion of flashbulbs and flashpowder triggered off all at once (and just when your pupils were opened up to about f1.9 from the darkness!) along with a huge, echoing *BANG!* through the sound system. But it made everybody jump right out of their seats. Me included.

And when the house lights slowly, almost painfully came up, Bob Wright and all the brass from the 13th floor were long gone and the only thing left on stage was a fading cloud of flash-powder smoke with a veritable sea of dazed, bewildered faces, stunned looks, dropped jaws and fried-egg eyes standing in front of it.

You had to give Bob Wright credit. He sure as hell knew how to run a meeting....

Chapter 16: Things Change

I had to head back up to the 13th floor after Bob Wright's Ferret presentation to pick up my tickets and travel arrangements from Karen Sabelle and get my final marching orders, and of course I waited patiently at the 12th floor elevator landing for all the top brass to go up ahead of me. I'd already gotten the message from Danny Beagle that it was a good idea to let those guys go up first—even for that short, one-floor trip—because, just as in England, the unmanaged mingling of the classes often made everyone involved uncomfortable. While I was waiting for the empty elevator to return, I took a moment to mull over what I'd just witnessed at Bob Wright's meeting. And in spite of how true and pure and straightforward and honest the words sounded when they were coming out of his mouth, I came to the somewhat embarrassing conclusion that I didn't really believe in a lot of what he was saying. As far as I was concerned—and I'm talking from deep inside my own head and heart here—you couldn't come up with much more than dogshit, design-wise, by handing out questionnaires and holding consumer clinics and doing extensive market research studies and organizing shirtsleeve symposiums so that John Q. Public and Fred Average and their wives, friends and families could tell you just what the hell they wanted in an automobile. The plain, unvarnished truth—at least as I saw it—was that great cars were inevitably the products of great designers, thinkers and entrepreneurs with grand ideas (and moreover great faith in those grand ideas) plus enough ambition, drive, savvy, resources, luck and hard-core gumption to see them through. And I was equally certain that John Q. and Fred A. and their wives and friends and families had no fucking clue as to what they really wanted. In an automobile or any other type of product. All they knew is that they sure as hell recognized it when they saw it on a store shelf or a showroom floor. And that's why it was the job of all the department heads and designers and engineers and stylists and conceptual thinkers and bean counters and marketing guys clear down to the poor schnook in the far corner desk of the drafting office who spent eight dreary weeks drawing nothing but chrome fucking instrument bezels so they could put something out there that would knock John Q. and Fred Average and their friends' and families' socks off when they saw it. And I had to chuckle a little, as those polished brass-and-nickel doors slid open once again, about how Daryl Starling sketched out the basic look, style and layout of the new Fairway Ferret on the back of an empty envelope on the edge of Miss Francine Niblitz' desk while Dick Flick was hovering over her like a gargoyle and damn near drooling down her cleavage.

I was also mulling over the various humps, twists and hurdles of my upcoming schedule and trying to figure out just how the hell I was going to get everything done. Things were about to get *very* hectic over on the European motorsports scene, and I knew I had to make it clear in no uncertain terms that I couldn't be flying back and forth to Detroit every time Bob Wright got a bug up his ass about something. And that's pretty much what I told him (but not in those exact words, of course) after Karen Sabelle led me into his office. Or at least after I congratulated him on the bang-up, holy-roller, fire-and-brimstone presentation he'd given downstairs, anyway.

"Thanks," he said earnestly. "But it's easy when you believe in what you're talking about." The evangelical look in his eyes was just a little bit scary. And then he looked down at his wristwatch, just to let me know he was in his usual, overcommitted hurry and that I was on the clock. "So where are you off to next?" he asked without looking up.

"I'm off to cover the Targa Florio in Sicily for *Car and Track* next weekend. Karen's got me booked out of Detroit Metro on Sunday morning and that'll give me a couple days to get my things packed and make my way down to Sicily."

"Do you think you might be able to get an interview with Mr. Ferrari while you're there?"

I looked at Bob like I didn't know what he was getting at.

"Tell him you want to do a piece on *'Ferrari, The Company'* or something like that," he continued. "See if you can get us some of the information we want."

At which point I had to explain that Enzo Ferrari simply didn't go to the races any more. Except to nearby Monza now and then for the Italian Grand Prix. And only when it looked like a Ferrari was going to win, of course. Other than that, Old Man Ferrari had made a habit of staying away from the racetrack and sending his harpy of a wife Laura to keep an eye on things for him. Which didn't sit very well with his racing-team managers, who found her troublesome, irksome, meddlesome and unpleasant. Especially the key group who walked out on him (or got fired?) *en masse* the previous November. But Ferrari figured he needed an insider spy on the scene because he always believed that loyalty was easier to enforce than to engender or enjoin.

Some—like my Italian scribe friend and devout Ferrari stooge Vinci Pittacora— claimed that Old Man Ferrari didn't come to the races anymore because he couldn't bear to see his brave, gallant drivers getting themselves hurt, maimed or perhaps even killed in his automobiles. After all, they were like sons to him! And (as Vinci would continue dramatically, wringing his hands), Enzo Ferrari knew better than anyone what it meant to lose a beloved son. And then Vinci would wipe away a heartfelt Italian tear with just a hint of garlic and basil in it. Which is precisely why Vinci Pittacora always got the best seat in the house at Ferrari's press conferences and first preview peek at whatever new project was taking shape in the Maranello race shops. But other people—like my good friends Cal Carrington, Richie Ginther and Denise McCluggage, for instance—painted a somewhat darker, less flattering picture of Old Man Ferrari. They said he didn't go to the races because he couldn't bear to see those brave, gallant drivers that he hired, fired, agitated, denigrated, manipulated and occasionally left twisting in the wind beating the living crap out of his magnificent and beloved Ferrari racecars. Couldn't stand to hear them over-revving his marvelous engines or missing shifts in his miraculous gearboxes with their clumsy, ham-fisted hands and feet. Or, worse yet, smashing their fierce, elegant beauty into twisted, steaming, oil- and blood-streaked hulks against assorted, unyielding chunks of trackside scenery. Besides, the Old Man had bigger fish to fry back in Maranello, keeping his eye on the factory workers and the race shop mechanics and all the suppliers, special customers and *concessionaires* who were undoubtedly trying to cheat him. And that's not even mentioning all the nearby and distant competitors, untrustworthy newspaper and magazine scribes and disloyal, traitorous defectors who were trying to challenge his supremacy, undermine his power, eat away at his accomplishments and diminish his empire. Like the Pope in the Vatican, Ferrari felt he had things under greatest control when he stayed in the seat of power and had his lieutenants, spies and confidants watching over things for him in the field. Plus staying away from the racetrack protected old Enzo from the personal agony, humiliation and loss of prestige on those rare occasions when the red cars from Maranello actually lost.

And then I had to explain to Bob Wright that, in any case, you didn't just "take Old Man Ferrari aside." Not in Sicily, not at Monza, and certainly not in Maranello. But Bob was adamant that the way you did business was to be there in person—face to face—and "let them see your eyes." And I knew Old Man Ferrari would have agreed with that, since he was famous for doing all of his important deals—including driver signings—in person, in his office, one-on-one and face-to-face.

Hearing that, Bob decided it would be best if I just "dropped in" at the Ferrari plant in Maranello on my way down to Sicily and tried to get an interview. He called Karen Sabelle in to set me up a travel schedule that had me flying from Detroit back to London for a few days, then down to Milan or Bologna—my choice—where a Fairway courtesy car would be waiting, take a day or so to get my interview with Ferrari, and then fly on down to Palermo, where another Fairway courtesy car would be waiting for me at the airport. At which point I had to remind him that we were still trying to keep a low profile on my connection with The Tower, and that people were going to get suspicious when a poor American motoring scribe started flying all over Europe and showing up here and there in shiny new English Fairway company cars.

"I see your point," Bob nodded, "and we certainly would like to keep you under wraps for now." Behind my shoulder, I heard Karen Sabelle tearing up my new itinerary and dropping it into the wastebasket. "We'll give you a car in England and have you drive it down to Sicily. We'll call it a 'Press Car.' You can say you're doing an extended road test or something. But I still want you to stop in and see Ferrari along the way."

"That might be a problem."

"How so?"

"I'm supposed to be riding down there with Hal Crockett. He's a photographer friend that I work with from time to time."

"So?"

"Like I said, it might be a problem."

"Is he trustworthy?"

"That's a complicated question," I answered carefully. "I mean, he's *honest.* Hell, I'd trust him with my life..."

"But?"

"Well, he's a photographer, see. And photographers are just like writers. They're nosy, curious and suspicious by nature. And neither one can resist the smell of a hot story. He might think something was up if I wind up driving one of your courtesy cars all the way down to Sicily and back. They normally don't trust us with press cars like that. And it'd be pretty hard to just 'drop in' at Maranello and not have him get suspicious."

"Then you'll just have to use your own car and make a separate trip to Maranello as soon as you get back."

I was about to argue with him. Only then I had a pretty damn great idea. "I'm, umm, probably going to need an interpreter...."

"An interpreter?"

I nodded gravely. "Ferrari always pretends that he doesn't speak any English."

"Does he?"

"I don't know. Maybe he does, maybe he doesn't. But I know I don't have anything more than get-by-in-a-restaurant-or-hotel Italian, and you need better than that to do an interview with Ferrari. At least if you want to pick up on the nuances."

"So how does Ferrari conduct business with his English-speaking customers and associates?"

"He's got this English woman who handles things like that for him..." I glanced respectfully over at Karen Sabelle "...she's very organized, protective of Ferrari's interests and she's very, *very* efficient."

"So?"

"So I don't think you want the conversation funneling through her. She controls it that way."

I could see Bob understood what I was getting at. "OK, I'll have Karen find you an interpreter. We can do it through the American embassy in Rome. We know people who know people there."

"That's not going to look very believable for a shoestring American motoring scribe," I quickly countered. "Besides, I've got a better idea."

"Oh?"

I cleared my throat. "See, I know this girl...er, woman...er, lady...er..."

"We get the idea."

And that's when I told Bob Wright and Karen Sabelle about Audrey Denbeigh. Not *all* about her, of course, but enough so they understood she was pleasant and efficient and intelligent and sharp and aware and a whiz with all sorts of languages and knew the subject because she worked part time setting up over-the-Channel travel arrangements for English racing teams and....

"She sounds perfect," Bob agreed before I rambled on any more. And then he gave me a sly, insinuating look out of the corner of his eye. "There's not any other reason why you want to take this particular female to Italy, is there?"

I could feel my ears starting to burn. Like hot coals, in fact. "Uhh, no," I protested lamely. "I just think she'd be perfect for the job, that's all." I could feel my face heating up like and electric burner.

Bob Wright and Karen Sabelle exchanged glances. "Tell me," Bob asked evenly, "are you, umm, 'friends' with her?"

I wriggled around uncomfortably in my chair. "Uhh...yeah. I guess you could say that. We know each other..." my cheeks were probably the color of a neon sign "...but that's not why I want to use her. I really feel like she's perfect for the job. Really I do. First of all, she's smart. And she's pretty good looking, too. And everybody knows Ferrari's got a weakness for pretty girls...."

Bob nodded for me to go on.

"...And we could make it look casual, too. Like we were down there on holiday together and decided to just 'drop in' after I had the story idea...."

I could see Bob wrapping his brain around it. I could also feel a disapproving chill coming from the general direction of Karen Sabelle. But Bob waved it off with no more than a tiny sweep of his forefinger. The temperature in the room came back to normal immediately.

"I could pretend like the idea just came to me, see," I continued enthusiastically, "and that I just dropped by to see if it might be possible to set up an appointment to do the interview at Ferrari's convenience. He's a well-known egomaniac when it comes to press coverage. Or at least flattering press coverage, anyway. If Audrey wears that yellow sun dress she had on at Sebring and he sees her, he might even agree to give us the interview on the spot. Why...."

Bob raised his hand abruptly to cut me off. "Okay," he said decisively. "You've sold me. Let Karen know what we'll have to pay her and if she thinks it's in line, she'll start setting up the travel arrangements."

"With separate rooms," Karen Sabelle added icily, just to make sure I understood the company's position on things like that.

Bob glanced at his watch and rose instantly from his chair to let me know our meeting was over. "I'll want you back here with a report as soon as possible after you've seen Mr. Ferrari."

"Uh, the season gets pretty hectic now," I tried to explain. "I mean, I've got the Targa in Italy on May 6th and then the Dutch Grand Prix at Zandvoort a week later and then the Nurburgring in Germany two weeks after that and then..."

"You'll just have to make time," he interrupted like there was no room for argument. And then he nodded for Karen Sabelle to lead me out of his office so he could get back to all the infinitely more pressing and important things on his agenda. We stopped at her desk outside to get my travel arrangements sorted out.

"Uhh, there's one more thing...." I ventured nervously.

"Yes?" she replied without looking up.

"My clutch."

"Your *what?*"

"My clutch. Or the clutch on my Fiat, actually. It's shot." I looked at her sheepishly. "I've already had it adjusted twice, but..."

"How much?"

"Huh?"

"How much will it cost?'

"I dunno," I shrugged. "Maybe a hundred. Maybe more...."

Karen Sabelle glared at me.

"...maybe less."

She exhaled sharply, opened a drawer in her desk, fiddled out of sight for a moment and handed me a Fairway Motors corporate envelope with four twenty-dollar bills, a ten and two fives in it.

"I'll need a receipt for the petty cash account," she said succinctly, then handed me my tickets and itinerary and sent me on my way.

To be honest, nothing on earth prepared me for what happened next. I was riding that polished brass-and-nickel elevator down from the 13th to the 12th floor, thinking about my upcoming trip to Sicily and wondering if I could somehow sneak in another date with Audrey before I left London. I'd initially hoped that she'd also be going to the Targa but, like a lot of the British privateer teams (and especially those with bigger, heavier cars), Clive Stanley's Imperial Crown Tea bunch was taking a pass on both the Targa and the Nurburgring 1000 Ks in Germany three weeks later so they could concentrate on their preparations for Le Mans. I mean, Clive had no ambitions about contesting the entire World Manufacturers' Championship season on Aston Martin's behalf, and the one race that really counted—the one every privateer English GT and sports car team focused on—was Le Mans. It didn't make sense to risk the car (or the expense) of contesting a lesser pair events on notoriously long, twisty, difficult, demanding and moreover unforgiving circuits that didn't really suit the DB4GT Zagato's strengths anyway. Not to mention the perils of sharing the road with all sorts of wide-eyed, over-stimulated local amateurs and second-tier pros in nimble, small-bore Alfas, Lancias, Fiat-Abarths, Porsche 356s and what-have-you who would love nothing better than to harass and possibly get around a far more powerful and expensive Aston Martin. Add in that Ian Snell had never even seen the mountainous, 45-mile *Piccolo Madione* circuit around Sicily and had only done a lap and a half of the Nurburgring in practice before depositing Clive Stanley's aging Aston DBR1 in a hedgerow the year before. So the prospects for a trouble-free run or a promising outcome at either race were definitely dim. Which meant I would be heading off to Sicily with Hal Crockett (and a brand-new clutch in my Fiat!) while Audrey would be staying back home in London taking care of Walter and putting in more well-paid days with the Monsters of Mayfair.

I had an impulse to find a phone in some empty office and call her immediately. I couldn't wait to tell her about the swell interpreter job I'd lined up for her with Fairway Motors (strictly under cover, of course!) and our upcoming, all-expenses-paid trip to Italy! If she agreed to go, that is. And if she could get away from tending to the Monsters of Mayfair and moreover if she could live with the idea of leaving Walter on his own for a few days. That was going to be a tough one. And that's when I decided not to call her, because this was the sort of thing you really needed to present in person. So you could do a little selling, you know? Dangle the money in front of her nose! And then use your utmost powers of persuasion (along with your very best selection of orphaned puppy dog facial expressions) to make it impossible for her to say "no." And that's what was running through my mind when the brass-and-nickel elevator doors slid silently open and I found myself staring up into a pair of vaguely familiar, bloodshot, piercing blue eyes. Below those eyes were a matched set of puffy, ruddy cheeks and an overdone, mutton-chop mustache, and above them sat the snappy, aggressive brim of a Tyrolean hat with a whisk broom-sized brush on the side.

"*Henry Lyons?*" the eyes asked menacingly.

"*Quentin Deering?*" I asked right back.

We stood there staring at each other for so long that the door started to slide closed again. Quentin shot out a large, heavy hand to stop it. And meanwhile, his eyes narrowed. Almost in unison we asked: "*What the hell are YOU doing here?*"

And then we stared at each other some more.

The door tried to close again, and Quentin motioned for me to come out of the elevator. But he didn't get in. I felt a cold whoosh of air on the back of my neck as the doors slid closed behind me. "Go ahead," he continued, still staring at me. "I'm curious to know just what the hell you're doing here."

"I'm curious to know what you're doing here, too," I answered like we were having a polite conversation. But there was no mistaking the seriousness of his scowl or the disdainful look in his eyes.

I had no idea what to say.

"Fair enough," he continued icily, and moved in close enough that I could smell the traces of single-malt scotch and blended Turkish tobacco on his breath. I was standing pretty much in his shadow now, looking steeply uphill into his pale blue eyes. "I'm here to take Dick Flick to lunch," he began slowly and evenly, "and I plan to buy him several drinks and then tell him that Pletsch and Deering has completed its buyout of *Car and Track* magazine..."

"Y-you *have???*"

"...and that we can now offer him a comprehensive and attractive package of ad space in the entire collection of Pletsch and Deering publications. Ad space that will allow him to reach out to an impressive cross-section of his demographic targets, regardless of their hobbies, tastes or interests." He allowed himself a pompous, self-satisfied flicker of a smile. But then the scowl returned immediately and his voice went dangerously low and cold: "And now I believe it's your turn."

I felt an empty hole opening up in the pit of my gut as I tried to think of something plausible to say. I knew I wasn't supposed to mention anything about Fairway Motors getting ready to thumb its nose at the AMA racing ban and jump into motorsports with both feet, and for sure I wasn't supposed to say anything about the new Ferret project. "Uh, I'm, umm, working on a story about the new Shelby sports car," I finally answered. "Have you heard about it?"

"Of course I've heard about it. It's called the 'Cobra.' They've already built one or two and there'll be a bright yellow prototype on the Fairway stand at the New York Auto Show this coming weekend." His eyes narrowed down even further. "But Warren's got Randy Riggs on that story already. Your name isn't even on the assignment board for it." He leaned in so close our noses were almost touching. "Besides, that's a California story. You're supposed to be covering things for us over in Europe, aren't you?"

I swallowed hard. "Y-yeah. I-I know. But I got this, um..."

"And who *paid* for this trip?" he wanted to know. I could see he was adding two-and-two together. "I know what we pay you, and that means I also know you sure as hell can't afford to be traipsing back and forth across the Atlantic just for the fucking hell of it..."

I couldn't think of a single thing to say.

"...And what the hell would *you* be doing up on the 13th floor of Fairway Tower, anyway?" He ran his pudgy fingers down the buttons of his green plaid vest. Every single one of them looked like it was about ready to pop. And then, without a word, he turned back towards those polished brass-and-nickel doors and reached out to press the call button. "You know what?" he said without looking back at me.

I shook my head.

He turned to me with cold, rattlesnake eyes. And then, very calmly, quietly and precisely, he said: "You're *fired,* Lyons."

It took a moment to sink in. "I-I'm *what?*"

"You heard me," he repeated patiently. "You're fired."

I could feel my jaw hanging open, but no words were coming out.

"And don't look so surprised. You either work for my magazine or you work for one of our advertisers. But you can't do both..." his voice turned all self-right-eous and sanctimonious "...not at a Pletsch and Deering publication..."

I felt like a truck had run over me.

"...And just so you know," he continued as the doors slid open, "I was planning to terminate you anyway."

"Y-you *were?*" I barely mumbled.

"Yes, I was," he continued like he was proud of it. "I've already inked a deal with Eric Gibbon to be our new European correspondent. It's just going to happen a little sooner than I expected."

The doors started to slide closed.

"But I'm leaving for the Targa Florio in a few days," I almost whimpered. "I'm on assignment for the magazine. All my travel arrangements are already made..."

"Enjoy your trip," he smiled as the doors slid closed, "but don't bother filing a story when you get back. We won't use it...."

Ben Abernathy found me sitting on the front steps of Fairway Tower something like a half-hour later. I think I had my head in my hands. "You okay?" he asked.

"Not really."

"What happened?"

So I told him.

"Is that so bad?" he asked, trying to sound encouraging. "You can't have been making much money writing for a damn car magazine."

"That's for sure."

"I wouldn't be at all surprised if I could get Bob Wright to put you on full time. He likes you."

"He does?"

"Sure he does. He doesn't let just anybody wander into his office. He thinks you have something to offer us or you wouldn't be there."

"That's nice to hear," I told him. But I still felt like shit.

"Why, he could have you writing ad copy for Dick Flick next week."

That didn't sound particularly appealing. But I looked up at him anyway. "Could I do that from London?" I asked miserably.

Ben slowly shook his head. "Nah, he'd probably want you to relocate over here so you could work in The Tower and sit in on meetings. Even guys like Manny who are on the road all the time have to call Detroit home base. That's just the way it is." He forced out an encouraging smile. "But Detroit's not such a bad place. Really it isn't. Except for the Lions and the Tigers, anyway...."

Instead of being funny, Ben's words made me go all weak and queasy inside. He could see right away that he'd made me feel worse instead of better.

"What's so damn special about living in some shitass apartment in London and writing for a fucking car magazine?" he asked rhetorically. "Traipsing all over everywhere on the cheap just so you can watch some spoiled kids who never grew up trying to kill themselves with racing cars."

"There's more to it than that," I argued instinctively. And then this cold wave of realization and emptiness went through me—right through my gut—and I felt like I was going to cry. "The thing is I love it," I choked out hoarsely. I could hear the unseemly waver in my voice when I said it.

Ben let out a long, slow sigh. "I know you do, Hank. I'm sorry. Really I am. I was just trying to help."

"I know you were. Thanks."

Ben heaved himself down onto the marble step next to me. "You know," he said in a fatherly sort of way, "this isn't a very good place for moping around and feeling sorry for yourself. It's too bright. Too noisy. Too public. Too much foot traffic going by. Too many nosy people and prying eyes."

"I just kind of sat down here when I came out of the building," I explained miserably. "I didn't mean to. I just didn't have anything to do or anyplace to go...."

"I know how it is when you get fired. Even from a shitty job." He fished around in his pocket for his latest pack of Marlboros and offered me one. "It knocks the crap out of you, doesn't it?"

"Yeah, it sure does," I nodded. "And my fucking plane doesn't leave until early Sunday morning."

Ben Abernathy took out his stainless steel Zippo and lit us up. "So you've got no place to go and nothing to do, right?" he asked between puffs.

I shook my head. "Nah, not really. Just back to the Fairview Inn to go drink myself into a stupor in the lounge."

"All by yourself?"

I nodded.

"That's pretty damn miserable, isn't it?"

I nodded again.

And that's when Ben's face suddenly brightened. "Lissen," he said, "I got an idea. This is Friday night, right?"

I slid my eyes over in his direction, trying to figure out what he was getting at.

"You're pissed off and you're angry and you've got the blues so damn bad you're feeling lower than a snake fart?"

I nodded weakly.

Ben glanced at his wristwatch. "Hm. First shift should be getting off in less than an hour now..."

"So?"

He snaked a big, friendly arm around my shoulders. "I think I got just the place for us to go, son...."

"Oh?"

And that's how I wound up, not a half-hour later, sitting next to Ben at the end of a long, empty bar and about three drinks into what would turn out to be a very noisy and eventful Friday evening at the Black Mamba Lounge. The place was a long, low, nondescript-looking cinderblock building on the other side of the Fairway plant from The Steel Shed, and it was painted dull black inside and out and smelled like an old maintenance garage that had been filled up with smoke, beer, hot grease, cheap perfume, sweat, piss and spilled whiskey a half a million times or more. The "BLACK MAMBA LOUNGE" sign over the front door was just crude, bile-green paint right over the black cinderblocks and the window in the side door was boarded over, and even when the place was damn near empty—like it was when Ben and I got there—a haze of mostly mentholated cigarette smoke laced with occasional whiffs of reefer hung in the air like the early morning fog at Le Mans.

When Ben and I first wandered in, there were just the two of us, a coal-black bartender with a Bahamian accent, a big, fake smile and slicked-back hair covered in Dixie Peach pomade and an old black guy in an apron sweeping off the small dance floor and the even smaller, one-riser stage in front of it. The bartender seemed to know Ben and got us our first round of drinks. Then the side door opened and this huge colored guy with a shaved head, wraparound sunglasses and a build like a beer keg came in like he owned the place. And it turned out he did. He also filled in as bouncer on the weekends, and there was no question he looked up to the job. His arms were as big around as your average guy's thighs, and he wore a bright yellow Banlon knit shirt about two sizes too small for him just to show them off. I'd guess it was an XXL.

But The Black Mamba didn't stay empty for long on Friday nights. Not thirty seconds after the day shift whistle blew across the street, a steady stream of black, brown and tan Fairway factory workers started streaming in though both the front and side doors. And every single pair of dark, luminous eyes that came through those doors noticed Ben and me sitting at the bar—we were the only white people in the place—and I'd have to say it made me feel pretty damn uncomfortable. And maybe a little nervous, too. I mean, you couldn't miss how all those eyes filing through the doorways and taking up positions along the bar and against the wall or sitting down at the few scattered tables in between seemed to be staring at us. Or maybe glaring at us would be more like it. I felt like I'd been sprayed with a coating of luminous, reflective white paint—like a damn highway sign, you know?—and had a spotlight trained on me from somewhere up in the ceiling. It made me pretty damn uncomfortable, if you want to know the truth of it. So I had another drink. And another one after that. To be honest, I think the drinks at the Black Mamba Lounge may have been watered down ever so slightly. And the well liquor wasn't anything to write home about, either. But they made up for it by being cheap, so you could order lots of them. And I did.

It became obvious pretty quickly that most of the Black Mamba's patrons knew and accepted Ben Abernathy (although with a cool, wary edge to it) just like the white shift workers who were surely filling up The Steel Shed on the other side of the Fairway plant complex at exactly the same time. And I was surprised to discover that Ben Abernathy was a huge fan of rhythm-and-blues music. He'd wandered over to the jukebox right after we walked in and dumped the better part of five bucks into it, punching in a whole slew of popular and familiar pop hits from groups like The Drifters, The Miracles, The Coasters, The Contours, The Marvelettes, The Crystals, The Shirelles and The Ronettes along with records by single artists like Ray Charles, Jackie Wilson, Bo Diddly, Mary Wells and Etta James. And that was some damn good music! But he also punched in some 45s I'd never heard of that never got played on the mainstream Top 40 radio airwaves. Songs from recording artists and record labels I didn't even know existed; hardcore, gut-level blues from people like Muddy Waters, Howlin' Wolf, B.B. King, Buddy Guy, Sonnyboy Williamson, Big Bill Broonzy, Sonny Terry and Brownie McGhee and an up-and-coming bluesman out of Chicago who was actually going to be playing there live that night, Junior Wells. In fact, some of the members of Junior's band were already starting to set up their instruments on the little elevated stage across from the far end of the bar.

I must admit that the music and the drinks really got to me—went right through me and took me over, in fact—until I was bobbing my head up and down and tapping my feet right along with the beat. And it didn't even bother me anymore that all the eyes along the bar and back wall and sitting around the tables were still sneaking suspicious, sideways glances at me all the time. Besides Ben and one of his shift managers from the paint shop and occasional musicians, the only white people who ever came into the Black Mamba Lounge were scraggly, pasty-faced college kids who occasionally came in on Friday and Saturday nights to listen to the music and try to look cool. And maybe try to score a little weed in the bargain. But not too many white folks ever ventured through the front or side doors of the Black

Mamba Lounge. And you got the impression that the regular patrons liked it that way just fine. Although it did make me think, over in a little side corner of my brain, what it must feel like to be black as a fucking bowling ball and wander into a busy, bustling bar where everyone is white.

Like at The Steel Shed on the other side of the Fairway plant, for example....

And then, much to my surprise, I saw a face I recognized! Standing at the bar, not ten feet away from me, was that tall, handsome, chiseled-looking black running back from Michigan State that I'd run into when he was supposed to be parking cars at the Fairway mansion but was actually doing a little free-form screwing and reefer smoking with the Birthday Girl herself. *"HEY!"* I shouted without even thinking about it, and immediately started blundering my way towards him. I have to admit I was a little unsteady on my feet by that point in the evening, but the place was so jam-packed hip-to-hip, butt-to-butt and shoulder-to-shoulder with people talking and drinking and laughing and arguing and dancing at close quarters with moves I'd never seen before that there was no way I could fall down. There simply wasn't room for it.

"Hey!" I yelled again when I got up next to him.

His eyes flashed up at me like he was seeing me for the first time. But I'd caught him glancing over my way several times already, so I didn't really know what to make of it. But before I could do or say anything, the woman standing between us wheeled herself around and glared at me. And just about sucked my eyes right out of their sockets! She was a big, striking, even regal-looking amazon of a black woman with glistening, flawless skin and a truly jaw-dropping body. And you could see damn near all of it, since she was wearing a tight-fitting, bright red knit halter top about three sizes too small for her with nothing but a monumental set of breasts and an hourglass of a waist underneath it plus a pair of bright red satin short-shorts— they couldn't have been more than ten inches high from top to bottom—over a butt like a pair of perfectly rounded, aggressively protruding basketballs. It looked like she probably had to grease those shorts up on the inside just to get them on! I couldn't help staring. But when my eyes got up to her face, I could see she was one of those proud, tough, above-it-all/angry-at-everything black women with high, haughty cheekbones and 'don't-you-fuck-with-me' eyes. She had phenomenal skin—real dark, with shimmering, almost purplish highlights—and she didn't look happy to see me at all. In fact, she looked pretty damn angry that I'd made my way over to them. Not to mention suspicious as hell as to how I might have come to know the chiseled young halfback from Michigan State. No question she looked a few years older than he did—maybe even more than a few years—and she was glaring at me with a decidedly unfriendly 'who-the-fuck-are-*you?*' sort of stare. Which quickly turned into a 'who-the-fuck-is-*he?*" sort of stare when she swiveled it over in the halfback's direction. You couldn't miss the look of panic that flashed through his eyes, even though he was trying his best to hide it.

"Hey," he said uneasily.

"Hey," I answered back.

He smiled apologetically at the smoldering pair of eyes between us. "I met him at the party at the Fairway place..." he started to explain, "...when I was parking cars on that Friday night...I don't even know his name..." Her eyes flashed accusingly over at me. And while that was going on, he shot me one of those 'keep your fucking mouth shut or I'm a dead man' glances that all men seem to know and understand.

"Thass right," I drunkenly agreed. "We were truly, truly never introduced." I stuck out my hand. "Hi!" I said expansively. "I'm Hank Lyons."

"What the fuck you doin' here, man?" the statuesque black woman demanded. Her body may have been magnificent, but her eyes were cold and hard as tempered steel.

"You're the writer guy, right?" the halfback ventured tentatively.

"Thass right!" I nodded energetically, and stuck my hand out even further. He looked at it like it was the head of a snake. But then I flashed him a wink—from the side away from her—and he managed an uneasy smile, took my hand in a soul-brother forearm grip and shook it. "Otis Jenkins," he said politely. And then his eyes shifted over to the angry looking but incredibly built black woman between us. "And this is my fiancée, Zenobia Smith."

"Your fiancée?" I asked incredulously. And that was of course a mistake.

Her eyes flashed angrily.

So did his, in fact.

"Zenobia," I continued as grandly as I could. "That's quite an unusual name."

"Zenobia was the great black warrior queen of Palmyra," Otis quickly explained, eager to change the subject.

She struck a proud, regal pose and told me all about it. "Zenobia conquered all of Egypt and threw the sorry-ass Romans out on their butts!" she snarled defiantly towards the ceiling. "And when they tried to come back, she kicked their sorry white asses again and cut their motherfucking heads off!" And with that she folded her arms over her incredible black breasts and stuck her chin out nearly as far. She looked like the damn hood ornament on a great, classic car.

"We've been going together for over a year," Otis explained quickly, just to make sure I understood the finer points of the situation. "And believe me," he added with a laugh that had nothing to do with anything funny, "you don't want to go messin' with my Zenobia here."

Of that I had no doubt.

"So what the fuck you doin' here, white boy?" she asked again. Only this time not quite so much like she wanted to cut my head off and stomp on it.

"My fren' Ben Abernathy brought me," I explained somewhat drunkenly. And then felt a profound wave of sadness shudder through me as I recalled what prompted Ben to bring me to the Black Mamba Lounge that evening. Or maybe it was just Solomon Burke's soulful rendition of *"Cry to Me"* wailing out of the jukebox in the background. But whatever it was, I suddenly felt miserable all over— inside and out—and I missed the shit out of Audrey and I was heartsick about losing my writing job for *Car and Track* and it was all I could do to keep from crying. *"I got fired today, man,"* I damn near blubbered into my drink.

They both looked at me. And for the very first time, there was something besides dislike, anger and mistrust in Zenobia Smith's eyes.

Then the huge owner/bouncer in the skin-tight yellow golf shirt pulled the plug on the jukebox and stepped up on stage to introduce Junior Wells and his band from Chicago. *"YOU ALL KNOW WHO WE GOTS HERE!"* he trumpeted grandly to the crowd. And then quickly, rhythmically, rolling back-and-forth on his heels in machine-gun rapid fire: *"THIS HERE IS WITHOUT A DOUBT THE GREAT-EST, GRANDEST, MOST BODACIOUS, NEEDS-ABSOLUTELY-NO-IN-TRODUCTION BLUES BAND WE EVAH HAD HERE AT THE WORL' FAMOUS BLACK MAMBA LOUNGE!"* He paused for a dramatic moment and then, like a holy roller preacher and a ring announcer at a prize fight all rolled into one: *"FROM CHICAGO, THE HEART AN' SOUL A' THE BLUES, THE BLACK MAMBA LOUNGE PROUDLY PRESENTS FO' YOU LISTENIN' AND DANCIN' PLEASURE, THE ONE, THE ONLY, RIGHT-HERE-LIVE-ON-OUR-STAGE/MAKE-NO-MISTAKE-ABOUT-IT...JUNIOR WELLS!"*

And with that the band rocked right into its amped up, pounding rendition of *"Messin' with the Kid,"* and within seconds bodies started stepping out onto the dance floor and into the narrow aisle between the bar and the tables, bumping, bopping, swaying, slinking, writhing, twisting, shimmying, jiving, hip-grinding and nodding along with the music. Otis flashed me a big, proud smile as he took Zeno-bia's arm and led her wordlessly out onto the crowded dance floor. He obviously thought I was going to see something special. And did I ever! Otis had smooth, fluid moves and an unruffled, graceful style, and you just knew that no white kid could ever dance like that. But she was the one I couldn't take my eyes off. In fact, I had to remind myself repeatedly to keep it cool and watch out of the corner of my eye in order to keep from staring at her and the way she moved with my eyeballs bugged out on stalks....

Only then I saw a fleeting look of horror flash across Otis Jenkins' face. I turned around and followed his eyes towards the front door. And who should be sauntering through that front door but Amelia Camellia Fairway and a few of her scraggly-looking Grosse Pointe friends! I flat couldn't believe it! They looked way too young, pale white and scruffy to be there, and everyone in the place stopped in the middle of what they were doing for an instant to stare at them. Even some of the band members. While most of the regulars at the Black Mamba Lounge tried to dress up and look a little sharp on a weekend night, Amelia Camellia Fairway and her friends were the exact opposite, proudly wearing old, torn blue jeans and rumpled college sweatshirts with their shirttails hanging out. As if it was some sort of badge of honor to be stinking rich but look dirty, unkempt and disheveled.

In any case, a shudder of recognition went through Otis as soon as he saw her, and Zenobia Smith picked up in an instant that something was wrong. She had senses like a damn cat, Zenobia did. *"Y'know any a'dem ofay kids?"* she asked suspiciously as she kept on dancing.

"I, uh, jus' thought they looked a li'l some underage t'me..." Otis answered lamely. He maneuvered himself around with a not-very-casual turn move so his back was towards the door.

Hell, *I* didn't even buy it.

Zenobia stopped dancing and walked off the floor. Otis followed right behind her, looking down at the floor and trying to keep his head hidden behind hers. Zenobia turned and faced him as soon as they got back to the bar. She didn't look happy. *"Since when would you give two shits about some young, rich white kids bein' underage?"* she demanded with a nasty, agitated edge to her voice.

"He's right," I chimed in. "I bet that girl with the long hair isn't much over seventeen." I pretended to lean forward for a closer look. *"Jesus!"* I spit out in a stage whisper. *"Do you have any idea who that is??!!"*

Zenobia looked at me suspiciously.

"That's Little Harry Dick Fairway's kid!" I pretended to gasp. *"I saw her at a company party once!"*

Otis leaned in a little closer (although I knew he was really trying to hide his head behind mine) and stage whispered back: *"You really ought to try to get her out of here, man!"* He made sure he said it loud enough for Zenobia to hear. *"She could close this fuckin' place down if the cops or her family ever find out."*

I nodded in solemn agreement. Then Otis motioned the bartender over (still keeping his face pointed away from Amelia Fairway) and whispered something urgently into his ear. The bartender nodded and headed over to where the big, black owner/bouncer in the tight yellow golf shirt was standing at the end of the bar.

"She's probably in here looking for grass," I muttered disgustedly.

Zenobia's eyes widened up a millimeter or two, and it was just possible her opinion of me had gone up by the same amount.

Otis put his hand on my forearm. *"Come into the john with me, man,"* he said like it was desperately important. You couldn't miss the urgent, pleading look on his face.

So I followed Otis into the dank, smelly men's room of the Black Mamba Lounge and into the one stall with a door still on it. Otis closed the door and latched it behind us. There really wasn't room for two full-sized, adult human beings in there, and especially not when one of them was a hot prospect running back at Michigan State. So we were pretty much nose-to-nose in there. Or nose-to-Adam's-apple would be more like it. Otis checked again to make sure the latch was secure, peered out through the crack to make sure the room was empty and looked over both of his shoulders before reaching down into the front of his pants and pulling a little folded plastic baggie out of his underwear. *"You got anything to put some of this in?"* he whispered urgently.

I shook my head.

So he took a few sheets of toilet paper, gently opened the bag, shook a little mound of grass into them and carefully folded them up. *"This is really good shit, man,"* he assured me hoarsely. *"This oughta be plenty fo' alls of you."*

That straightened me right up. *"Hey, man,"* I told him, *"I don't need this kind of trouble. No, sir. Do you have any idea what'll happen to me if somebody finds out I'm supplying fucking drugs to the underage fucking daughter of the fucking chairman of the board of fucking Fairway Motors?"*

"I know! I know!" Otis whispered back desperately. And then he looked up at me with the panicky, helpless eyes of a man on his way to the gas chamber. *"But y'gotta do this fr' me, man,"* he pleaded. *"This is my life here..."*

He pressed the little wad of toilet paper into my palm.

"...and it's not like you're selling it or anything. Just give her th' shit an' git her th' fuck outta here!"

I still didn't like it. Not one bit. But for reasons I will probably never understand, I took that little wadded-up packet of weed and stuffed it in my back pocket.

"You got any papers, man?"

"Papers?"

"Ssshh!"

He reached down into his sock and pulled out a half-empty pack of Zig-Zags. *"Here. Give 'em this, too."* And then he looked up at me with those wide, pleading eyes again. *"Just get 'em the fuck outta here, man! PLEASE...."*

Maybe it was the drinks, but it seemed like the right thing to do. So I went back out into the lounge, swallowed hard a couple times and pushed my way through the crowd and noise until I was standing right in front of the ragged, out-of-place little squadron of teenagers from Grosse Pointe, Grosse Pointe Woods, Grosse Pointe Park, Grosse Point Shores and Grosse Pointe Farms. There were five of them: three boys, Amelia Camellia Fairway and a skinny, pasty-faced girl with long black hair, an awkward slouch and a permanent frown. You could see that one of the boys looked pretty high already. He was a little sawed-off kid with way too much hair and a bad case of acne, and you could see he was struggling to grow the sketchy shadow of a mustache over his upper lip. He had his eyes three-quarters closed and his head and shoulders were swaying, bopping and jiving along with the music. He didn't look old enough to drive. Neither did the boy next to him, who was glancing around nervously from underneath a shaggy flop of blonde hair and looking very uncomfortable indeed. The third boy looked like he was going to be sick. But Amelia Camellia Fairway didn't look nervous at all. In fact, she looked like she owned the damn place.

By that time the big black owner/bouncer had made his way over to have a little Father Duffy chat with the contingent from Grosse Point. He stood at least six-four and a yard wide at the shoulders, with a chest like an oak barrel, a twenty-two-inch neck and a pair of cold, dangerous eyes. You could tell by the way people moved aside when he came across the floor that he could handle just about anything. Of course the first thing he wanted to see was their IDs. But they were rich, wiseass white kids from the suburbs so they had some really good (if thoroughly unbelievable) fakes to show him. And meanwhile Junior Wells swung into his signature *"Good Mawnin' Little Schoolgirl,"* which seemed particularly appropriate to the moment.

The big, black bouncer stared at the ID cards in his hand and then at the faces that supposedly belonged to them. *"YOU KIDS IS TOO YOUNG T'BE IN HERE!"* he boomed over the music.

"But my ID right there in your hand says I'm 21!" Amelia Fairway insisted defiantly.

The big black bouncer rolled his eyes in her direction. *"You wants me t'call the fuckin' cops in here t'let them have a look at these here IDs?"*

She was about to answer, but he held the fistful of fake IDs up like a winning poker hand and you could see all the air kind of go out of her. *"Try these here somewheres else, little white girl,"* he advised as he handed back the fake IDs.

You could see the frustration and spoiled-rotten fury building up inside Amelia Fairway. She gathered herself up and shouted *"FUCK YOU!"* right into his face at the very top of her lungs. It was so loud you could hear it over the music! But it didn't seem to faze him. And so then she gave him the finger. Right in front of his nose, in fact. But the big, black bouncer just smiled at her benignly and pointed to the door. By that point everybody in the place was staring at the five scruffy-looking white kids in blue jeans and sweatshirts. Not to mention the older, slightly better groomed and marginally better dressed white guy standing right next to them. The one who looked an awful lot like me. And that's about when Amelia

Camellia Fairway noticed me, too. Just as all six of us were being herded out the door. She couldn't place me at first, but then a confused look of recognition floated up in her eyes.

"Hi!" I shouted over the music as we passed through the doorway. *"Fancy meeting you here."*

"What the fuck are you doing here?" she wanted to know.

"I like blues music," I explained as we stepped into the parking lot. It was a lot quieter out there, even though you could still hear the strains of *"Good Mawnin' Little Schoolgirl"* pounding out through the doorway. "I stop by and listen now and then when I'm in town," I lied. "And I just got back in town tonight. From L.A." I lied some more.

She looked at me uncertainly. "You're the writer guy, right?"

"Yeah, that's right. I suppose you could say I am..."

"Fuck!" the kid with the scraggly flop of blonde hair spat out. *"What the fuck're we gonna do now?"*

"I thought you said we could get some weed in there," the girl with the awkward slouch and the permanent frown whined.

"Well if your brother didn't get us such shitty fucking IDs," the flop of blonde hair sniped right back at her.

"Those are great IDs!" she argued back angrily. *"We drank all weekend in Saugatuck on those!"*

"Everybody drinks all weekend in Saugatuck!"

"Why don't you shut the fuck up?"

"Why don't you?"

Suddenly the kid who was already way too high spoke up: "We could just wait here and ask people as they come out," he opined dreamily. "I'm sure somebody's gotta have some weed in there."

"You want to just hang around the fucking parking lot of a boo-boo bar all night?" the kid with the flop of blonde hair demanded.

"You got a better idea, asshole?" the girl with the permanent frown snorted back.

And right away I was having visions of what would happen if Otis Jenkins and Zenobia Smith came out of the bar and Amelia Camellia Fairway and her friends were there to meet them. I had no doubt it would get ugly in a hurry. *"Look,"* I whispered to Amelia Fairway as I pulled her gently aside. *"I think I may have something for you."*

She stared at me like I wasn't making sense. "What the fuck do you mean, 'you may have something for me?'"

"Ssshhh!" I hissed, putting my finger over her lips. *"I think I have some, you know, some of what you're looking for...."* I made like I was holding a joint between my thumb and forefinger and sucking in the smoke.

"Where the fuck would *you* get any stuff?"

For some reason, I felt a little bit insulted. I mean, I was from L.A., for gosh sake! And I always figured I was as cool as the next guy, even out there. Or almost as cool, anyway. And no question I was as cool (or cooler) than the snotty, pasty-faced, know-nothing-but-think-they-know-everything high school seniors or possibly soon-to-flunk-out college freshmen she was running around with. "I get around," I assured her in my coolest, most cosmopolitan voice. "And I told you I just got back from L.A...."

She still didn't look impressed. So I took the little folded-up packet of toilet paper and the half-empty pack of Zig-Zags out of my back pocket. *"Here."* I whispered, and pushed them into her hand.

She looked at them suspiciously. "How much?"

"Hey, I'm not trying to *sell* you anything!" I explained somewhat desperately.

"But why the fuck would you just want to *give* it to me?" she asked like I was trying to get away with something.

"Uh, well, see," I more or less stammered, "You shared some with me the other night at the party, see, and I just thought I might, you know, reciprocate...."

She looked at me and the stuff in her hand and then back at her friends, who were busy climbing into the white Morrokide interior of a gleaming, Bamboo Cream 1962 Pontiac Grand Prix with 8-lug aluminum wheels. The Grand Prix was the hot new "performance model" from Pontiac that year, and was basically their lightest Catalina 2-door hardtop with their biggest, hottest 389 V8 under the hood, front bucket seats with a floor-shift console in between and surprisingly tasteful, understated trim. Based on the color combination, I figured it had to be one of their mothers' cars. Although the engine made one hell of a deep-register rumble when the kid with the flop of blonde hair fired it up. No question it had a cam in it and a set of glass-packs.

Amelia Camellia Fairway looked up at me with a devilish new smile. "So do you wanna come get high with us?"

I immediately heard a crash-dive alarm going off in my head. "Uhh, I, uh...I really shouldn't. I gotta finish up something I'm working on back in my room, see. Something I'm writing..."

"You really oughta come with us," she urged playfully. You couldn't miss the strange, artless mixture of taunt, dare and tease in her voice. And I could feel some stupid thing inside of me straining up to take the bait. But I quashed it immediately.

"Look, I really have to finish up this thing that I'm working on..." I repeated lamely. "...It's on deadline...."

Her eyes narrowed down to suspicious slits. "And that's why you're out having drinks at a fucking blues bar?"

I scrambled for an answer. "Uhh, see, the piece I'm working on is about blues music, see..." I lied through my teeth "...I was just looking for a little inspiration." "I thought you wrote about car shit?"

"I do. I do," I agreed reflexively. "Only I thought I'd like to try something a little different for a change. Do something hip. Expand my horizons..." she didn't look like she was buying any of it "...Freelance, you know?"

She didn't look convinced at all. But she didn't look like she really gave a shit, either. "Like I said, you're welcome to come with us," she repeated with a bored, impatient roll of her eyes. "We're probably going back to my folks' house. I think they're out tonight. But it doesn't matter. There's plenty of places we can go to get high even if they're home."

"Well, that's awfully kind of you," I assured her, "but I really shouldn't. Not tonight. Besides, I've got my car here and you've already got five in that one and..."

She gave me an abrupt, 'who cares' shrug and turned to go back to her friends. But then she stopped and turned around again. "Thanks," she said simply. And then she leaned up and kissed me. But it wasn't just your average, friendly, 'thank-you' sort of a teenage kiss. All of a sudden, out of nowhere and completely without warning, she opened up her mouth and this hot, wet, eager young tongue came snaking out of it, darted into mine and started probing around like it was looking for something. It startled the living shit out of me! And it did something else to me, too, if you know what I mean. Even though alarm bells, fog horns, referee whistles, overtime buzzers, banging trash-can lids and the chimes of old Big Ben itself were going off in my brain like fucking Times Square on New Year's Eve. And then she stopped just as suddenly and abruptly as she'd started and looked up at me with eyes full of vicious mischief. "We ought to get high and ball some time," she said like she was talking about the weather. "I've never fucked anybody who works for my father before." And then she spun around on her promiscuous little 17-year-old heels and skipped lightly across the parking lot to where that shiny new Pontiac Grand Prix with the cast aluminum, 8-lug wheels was waiting, its hopped-up 389 grumbling a deep, lopey idle through the glass-packs. Amelia Camellia jumped into the right-front seat and before her door was even closed, the blonde kid behind the wheel mashed the gas to the floor mat and sent the car in a wild, fishtailing slide across the parking-lot gravel before launching out onto the highway in a showering roostertail of stones. I listened to the Pontiac's deep, V8 warble fade and watched its taillights shrink and disappear into the darkness like a pair of glowing red eyes being sucked away in a vacuum.

Chapter 17: Audrey

I called Audrey as soon as I got back to London and told her what had happened. Well, not all of what happened. I left out the part about Amelia Camellia Fairway in the parking lot of the Black Mamba Lounge. But I did tell her about getting fired off the magazine and how lousy it made me feel and also that there was an equally revolting outside possibility that I might be going to work in Detroit writing shitty ad copy for Dick Flick. At least if I wanted to continue eating on a regular basis. Audrey could tell I was pretty damned upset, and she agreed to let me come over and pick her up right away. I got the impression from the noises in the background that Walter wasn't especially thrilled about that. I mean, it was already pretty late. But we went out for a drink at that pub we'd stayed at until closing time the first night we went out, and that's when I told her, face to face over a couple of strong mixed drinks, about my "undercover" work for Bob Wright up in Fairway Tower (she was the only person I dared tell, because I trusted her completely and knew she'd keep her mouth shut) and about the casually clandestine interpreter gig I'd lined up for her in Maranello and the money they'd pay her and the swell, all-expenses-paid trip to Italy we had in the offing after I got back from Sicily if she only agreed she could go. The news seemed to shock her a little, and she looked genuinely excited and worried as hell about it all at the same time.

"This is getting pretty serious, isn't it?" she asked without expecting an answer.

I gave her half a shrug. "I don't know...Is it?"

She took a long, slow sip of her drink. In fact, it was more than a sip. She was down to the ice by the time she put her glass down. "You know it's strange, Hank," she said in a bemused, detached sort of voice. "It's as if one half of me wants to go ahead and one half of me wants to hold back."

I told her I understood. And I actually did, because I felt more or less the same way. Only I was at about 90% "go ahead" and 10% "hold back." I really liked Audrey—she was really special to me in a way that no one had ever been special to me before—and yet I worried about how things would work out as we got to know each other better and also about all the complications that inevitably land in your lap when you get your life all twisted and tangled up with someone else's. And I worried most of all about what it would be like if and when we ever had sex and how it would be and if I would be any good and how the hell I was going to get up the nerve and the guile and the planning and the sincerity and the salesmanship and the sheer, look-it-right-straight-in-the-eye gumption to try to maneuver us around to that in the first place.

"When you're done with your drink," she said out of nowhere and with no special emphasis whatsoever, "why don't we go back to your flat?"

I didn't think I heard her properly at first. But then I looked at her like I didn't get it and she looked right back at me like I was a world-class idiot and I pounded down the rest of my drink, threw five bucks American on the table to cover the drinks and an unusually generous tip (at least for me, anyway) and damn near burned right through the little bit of remaining clutch lining on my Fiat hustling to get us back to my apartment before she could change her mind. And she stayed damn near the whole night, too! Just like that. She even did a good job of hiding the look of abject horror on her face when she saw where I lived and what the place looked like inside. We were both pretty nervous about the whole thing beforehand, but I had two-thirds of a bottle of fairly decent white wine in the fridge and some leftover French brandy in a commemorative ceramic bottle the shape of the Eifel Tower from a Peugeot press unveiling, and things didn't turn out nearly as stupid, clumsy, awkward or apologetic as I'd feared. In fact, it all went rather well. You could even say wonderful. And I'm quite sure I did. Several times over. And I got the distinct impression that Audrey felt much the same way. Not that it's any of your damn business, in any case. Some writers like going into all the kissing, stroking, groping, grappling, panting, grunting, gasping details of this sort of thing, but I'm not one of them. Although I can surely recommend some people to you if that's the sort of thing you fancy....

Audrey made it clear in her typically straightforward, let's-get-things-understood-beforehand way that she'd have to be up and out early so she could get herself home before Walter got up. Even if he knew she'd been gone most of the night. "It's just something I need to do," she explained as she started to wind my alarm clock.

"You won't need that," I assured her.

She gave me a funny look. Much funnier, in fact, than the groggy, startled expression I saw on the other side of the pillow when the muffin tins, loaf pans and baking sheets started banging around downstairs at just shy of 4 in the morning.

"You know," she told me as she brushed out her hair and gathered up her things, "civilized people don't live like this."

"Writers don't consider themselves civilized people," I yawned expansively as I put a sauce pan of water on my hot plate, grabbed two fresh Imperial Crown Tea bags out of the box and rummaged around on my sink for two semi-presentable cups to put our tea into. I'd used the best of the lot for our brandy the night before. "Besides," I reminded her, "I'm not here all that often except in the wintertime."

"That's no excuse for being messy."

"I'm not messy," I corrected her playfully. "I'm simply disorganized. There's a difference."

That earned me a wonderfully contemptuous snort, and I must admit it felt really grand to be with her like that early in the morning. Sure, everything in my life was tumbling upside-down and I'd lost the job I loved and lived for and I was very possibly teetering on the precipice of economic free-fall if I failed to come through as expected for Bob Wright back up on the executive corridor of Fairway Tower, but being around Audrey somehow made it all seem a million miles away. "It was really nice of you to come over like this," I told her, the words kind of clogging up a little in my throat.

"Well, don't get too used to it," she cautioned sternly. "I mean, I can't be coming over here like this on any sort of regular basis..." her eyes swept around the room "...and this is a rotten sort of a place to take a girl anyway."

I had to agree with that. "I'm sorry," I told her. And I meant it.

"Don't be sorry..." she scolded "...Be *better.*"

"My God," I had to laugh, "we've barely gotten involved with each other and you're already trying to change me."

"Only the things that need changing, my dear," she laughed in neat, precise tones. "It wouldn't be very worthwhile to leave you as you are."

And there was no point arguing with that. Not even in fun.

I could barely get my old Fiat out of its parking place because the clutch was slipping so badly, and on our way over to her place I had to drive like there was an egg under the gas pedal. Make that a Fabergé egg. But I didn't mind, because Audrey had her head leaned over against my shoulder with her eyes closed, and that plus the quiet, empty London streets with the first purplish-gray light of dawn just starting to creep over them filled me with the most glowing, satiated and delicious sense of romantic melancholy that I'd ever experienced. It was the kind of feeling you wanted to savor and wallow in and never let end.

"So what are you going to do now?" she asked dreamily without opening her eyes.

"I haven't really thought about it," I lied.

"You mean you haven't come up with anything yet, don't you?"

We hadn't known each other very long, but already I thought Audrey knew more about what was going on inside my head than I did.

After I dropped Audrey off, I nursed the Fiat over to the Lola shop in Bromley where Peter Bryant had agreed to take it on as a side job and fix the clutch for me. On the cheap, of course. He worked at Broadley's Lola shop almost all the time now since Clive Stanley's Aston was in a long, slow building-up process for Le Mans in June and he'd been added on as one of the race mechanics for the Bow-maker team's Lola Formula One car. And I was frankly glad to see him moving up in the world. Peter was an excellent wrench, a keen diagnostician and a sharp, straight thinker when it came to mechanical problems (as he put it, "I have a mar-velous grasp of the obvious") plus he was a hell of a lot of fun to hang around with both at the races and after the racing was over. Although the latter occasionally kept him out rather late.

In any case, I got to the shop well before it opened—well before anything opened, really—and so I had to wait around while the town more or less woke up around me. And that was kind of nice, actually. I got a cup of tea from the place across the street as soon as the manager pulled the shades up and, wouldn't you know it, a few minutes later this big, dark-blue-over-even-darker-blue Rolls pulls up in front of Broadley's shop and who else but Walter Denbeigh comes creaking, cursing and ratcheting his way out of the back seat. He looked angry as hell. But then, he always looked angry as hell. I could see Audrey in the back seat, too, wishing him good-bye, handing him his lunch pail and reminding him to take his cane and his medicine. She gave me a helpless little wave as the door swung closed, and it bothered me to see how tired and worn-out she looked. But it made me a little proud, too, if you know what I mean.

I watched the Rolls whisk smoothly and silently away, leaving Walter and me standing on opposite sides of the street, he in front of the Lola shop and I in front of the tea and pastry shop across from it. He was looking at me like a gardener might look at an infestation of slugs. "Good morning," I called over to him.

He favored me with a good-morning wince.

"Would you like a cup of tea and a pastry? I could get one for you."

Nothing.

"Looks like it's going to be a fine day," I tried again.

He cocked his head like the hammer on a revolver. *"Late night last night, wasn't it?"* he sneered loud enough that you could hear it from the far end of the street.

I tried to think of something to say, but there just wasn't anything there. And he seemed perfectly happy to just stand there, glaring at me, doing his level best to make me as uncomfortable as possible. It was pretty damn awkward, if you want the truth of it, and it seemed to go on for an awfully long time. I finally crossed the street and walked right up to him. "Look," I said in my very best 'let's-be-reasonable-about-this' voice, "you and I are going to be seeing a lot of each other if I have anything to say about it, and it's going to make it a hell of a lot easier for everyone involved if we try to get along."

"Who says YOU have anything to say about it??!!" he snarled right back at me, his pupils damn near vibrating. And that was more than enough to get my back up, too.

"Look!" I snapped at him, moving in nose-to-nose and eyeball-to-eyeball, *"I like Audrey a lot and I know she likes me a lot, too. I plan to see a lot of her, and that's going to happen whether you like it or not! So it'd be better off for everyone if you just got used to the idea and accepted it!"* But then I caught myself, and did my best to come up with some sort of conciliatory smile. "Look," I told him sheepishly, "I'm not such a bad guy."

"You don't even have a bloody job!" he snorted.

"That's not true!" I growled back at him.

"Sod off!"

Fortunately Eric Broadley arrived at that precise moment and, in typical Eric Broadley fashion, he took one look at the two of us glaring and glowering at each other—nose-to-nose with steam damn near rising out of our ears—and he did a miraculous job of simply ignoring the whole thing. "Come inside, Walter," he said like nothing at all was going on. "I have the new hub drawings for you to look over." And just that quickly it was over. Just like that.

I had another cup of tea while I waited for Peter Bryant to show up, and in the meantime I wandered aimlessly around Eric's little front office and tried to imagine what it might be like to relocate to Detroit and go to work writing fucking ad copy for Dick Flick in a stupid fucking suit and tie every day and wondering if there was any way I could get back in with *Car and Track*. I'd thought about seeing if I could catch on with any of the other magazines, but *Car and Track* was the only American magazine that really covered the European scene (or at least in any depth or detail) and none of the English magazines were ever going to hire on an American. Hell, they didn't even think we knew how to speak the language! Let alone write it. Not to mention that the English have never really forgiven us for the American Revolution (or the War of 1812, for that matter) or the way we swaggered around like we singlehandedly came over and saved their sorry asses after Hitler had them cornered and up against oblivion in World War Two. Even if we did. I sighed hard and sat down heavily at Eric's drawing table. And that's where I noticed a more detailed but still sketchy rendering of the mid-engined coupe idea I'd seen there the first time I visited Eric's shop. It was still more of a rough idea than a full engineering schematic, but there were some measurements and detail notes on it now. Although the engine in back was still just a big, crudely drawn, empty V-shaped block and there was a "*???!!!*" notation over the similarly sketchy transaxle.

"What's this going to be?" I asked when Eric came into the front office.

"Oh, it's just something I'm fooling around with. Just an idea, really." He looked almost embarrassed about it. "It's for Le Mans, actually."

My ears perked up. "Oh, really?"

He nodded. "But, as I said, it's just the germ of an idea at the moment. We don't really have the funding to pursue it any further right now, even if I knew where I wanted to go with it."

I looked at the big, sketchy block of a V8 behind the cockpit. "What sort of motor do you have in mind?"

"Well, GTs are the thing this year, aren't they? And they've opened up the regs to allow 4-liter prototypes at Le Mans this year. It wouldn't surprise me if they continued in that direction to attract some of the American manufacturers." He looked up at me earnestly. "I think the organizers would really like to have them involved, you know. It gets a bit boring watching the bloody Ferraris parade around, doesn't it?"

"It'd make a lot of sense," I allowed, being careful what I let slip. "But all the American manufacturers agreed to that AMA 'no racing' ban back in 1957. Do you think any of them would break ranks?"

He shot me a calculated smile. "Everything changes eventually, doesn't it?"

I had to admit that it did. "So you're planning on using an American V8?"

"If we ever actually built the thing, yes, I think so. Oh, they're great, crude, heavy lumps, but they offer an awful lot of power for not much money at all. And there's been a lot of useful development work done on them already over in the States."

"Indeed there has," I readily agreed. It was great to be talking nuts-and-bolts racing again with someone who really knew and understood it. In fact, it struck me how much I'd missed that sort of conversation. I pointed to the *"???!!!"* notation over the transaxle. "So what have you got in mind for a gearbox?"

An inquisitive, almost little-boy smile blossomed on Eric's face. "Ah, that's the rub, isn't it?" he grinned. "The bloody transaxle! If I had the answer to that, we might be further along with the project." He let out a short, weary sigh. "There's not much out there that could handle the torque of an American V8, is there? Especially over 24 hours."

"Valerio Colotti did that 'box for Alf Francis that they put in all of Rob Walker's Formula One cars," I reminded him.

"I thought about that, too," Eric nodded. He seemed mildly impressed that I'd paid that much attention to the mechanical details. "But a two-point-five Climax FPF is a far cry from a five-liter American V8. Even if it is a real racing motor and the V8 is a big, cast-iron, pushrod lump. And we're not looking at a two-hour Grand Prix here, either...."

I had to agree with that. But it was still awfully intriguing. "If you could find a transaxle, which engine would you choose?"

"Well, it's got to be the Chevrolet, doesn't it? That's the one everyone seems to go with. It's reasonably light and compact—comparatively speaking, of course—and they've been running them for quite awhile now so you'd hope they've worried their way through most of the weak spots."

I ran my tongue across the roof of my mouth. "You know," I started in carefully, "Fairway's got a new, smallblock V8 that looks like it could be pretty good, too."

"Oh?"

I nodded. "I know some of the tuners and hot rodders have already started fooling around with it, and I understand it looks fairly promising. And Fairway started with a clean sheet of paper and used a new, thinwall casting process, so I believe it's a little lighter than the Chevy. And it should be almost as good on power once they've done some dyno time and testing miles on it and come up with a few parts."

Eric seemed more than mildly interested. "How much do you think one might be?" he asked bluntly.

"I don't really know," I told him. "After all, it's brand new." And then I shot him just the hint of an insider wink. "But I have a feeling you might be able to get a really, really good deal on one...."

Eric looked keen to hear more. "We haven't gone any further than rough sketches yet because we really don't have a budget..." he more or less apologized. Then quickly added: "What makes you think we could get some sort of deal?"

"Let's just say I know some people," I explained cautiously. "If you like, I could ask around for you."

"I'd appreciate that," he said simply. And then he looked down at his drawing again. "It would be a pretty interesting project, wouldn't it?" he mused in a distant, abstracted voice.

"It sure would," I had to agree. "If it was any good, Old Man Ferrari wouldn't like it much at all...."

I went for a little tour of the workshop in back after that, and I saw Peter Bryant had set up a stationary frame jig to do some deflection and torsional stiffness testing on the new Lola Formula One chassis because Surtees had complained it was "too lively" after the initial, pre-season races at Snetterton and Goodwood. Although Eric wasn't entirely convinced because Surtees was still thought of as more of a 'bike man' than a 'car man' and the new Lola had been extraordinarily quick between mechanical gremlins. There was no question that in Surtees' hands it had been right up there with the BRM V8, the T55 Cooper and the Lotus Type 24, and only a series of new-car gremlins and mechanical glitches had kept it from finishing well in the races. But Peter Bryant believed in his driver, and if John Surtees felt it was "too lively," he was sure as hell going to look into it. Peter put it into perspective for me over a cup of tea after he arrived a few minutes later: "Speed and feel are two entirely different things in a racing car, Hank, and the difficult part is finding the proper balance between the two. Everyone's seen cars that are incredibly fast but difficult as hell to drive. And also chassis that seem sweet to the drivers but just can't seem to muster up competitive speed." He lit up a cigarette and took a long, slow draw. "The key to the whole bloody thing is driver confidence, don't you see? Give a driver something that feels good, safe and honest under his bum and that will allow him to take it closer to the limit and hold it there more easily." He took another thoughtful drag and blew out a round, perfect smoke ring. "The sorry bit is that great feel isn't enough to make up the difference when a car's further away from the leading edge than the opposition." His face opened up in a big, ironic grin. "That's what makes it all so bloody fascinating, isn't it?"

I wound up hanging around the Lola shop most of the day while Peter put a new clutch in my Fiat, and it was very nice of Eric to let him do it there instead of making him take it outside or off to some back-alley shed to work on it after hours like mechanics usually have to do with side jobs. I did my best to help out by handing Peter tools as he needed them and running up the jack and holding the hoist chain and steadying the engine so it didn't crush his fingers while he was taking off the pressure plate bolts. And then I ran off to the parts store in Peter's old Austin to pick up one of everything—clutch disc, rebuilt pressure plate, rear main seal and throwout bearing—while he had Walter resurface the flywheel. And Walter did it without comment or complaint. In fact, I thought my stock might have gone up with him just a tiny bit from watching me do something useful and mechanical. But I couldn't be sure.

In any case, I was glad to get it fixed and happy to have something to keep myself occupied, since I'd been waiting pretty impatiently for 9am California time to roll around so I could call Warren and Isabelle and see if there was any possibility of resurrecting my job with the magazine. And of course that wouldn't be until 5pm London time. So I drove my still sorry and rattling but happy once again in the clutch department little Fiat back to my apartment to pack for my trip to Sicily and wait for the hours to grind by. I caught myself often looking longingly at the bed where Audrey and I had been sleeping together (and, yes, doing other things with each other) barely a half-day before. But it seemed so far away—so frankly unbelievable—that I couldn't really wrap my brain around it. I even wondered if it had been real?

But I knew that it was.

Eventually 5pm London time rolled around and I put a call in to Orange County. But it transpired that Pletsch and Deering had installed a receptionist—I think she might have been just an answering service and not even on location at the *Car and Track* offices—and she kept telling me that Warren and Isabelle weren't available because they were either out of the office chasing stories or in meetings so important that they couldn't be disturbed. Which wasn't like Warren and Isabelle at all, and it got to where I wondered if she was even giving them my messages. When I finally did get through—on their home phone at something like 6am the next morning London time—it was a pretty damn uncomfortable conversation. Warren kind of hemmed and hawed without saying much of anything and then handed the phone over to Isabelle, and I could tell that she was trying hard to keep from crying. "There's not much we can do about it, Hank," she said in a voice that broke your heart. "Warren and I could threaten to walk out over it, of course, but that would just void our contract and Pletsch and Deering would have the magazine without paying us off." She sounded so twisted-up and miserable about it that I actually started feeling worse for her than I did for myself. "We might still be able to use you for travel pieces and auto show coverage and new car reviews now and then," she added hopefully, trying to sound positive, "and I'm sure we could find things for you to do here if you ever wanted to come back to California."

"You could?"

"I think so. Maybe. After a little time goes by." I heard her swallow hard at the other end of the line. "But it would all have to be freelance...."

I thanked her, of course. And I even congratulated her and Warren on the sale of the magazine. I mean, they'd worked hard to get where they were—her, especially—and I was genuinely happy for the way they'd been able to cash in on their efforts. Even if I flat couldn't stand Quentin E. Deering and was pretty damn sure that he and the Pletsch and Deering publishing team were going to fuck up the magazine. Even if they did manage to double the circulation, triple the subscription base and quadruple the damn advertising revenues. They were still going to fuck it up. Not to mention that I didn't much fancy doing fluff travel pieces, breathless, hyped-up auto show coverage or gratuitous new-car reviews on the latest hot new Renault, Austin, Simca, Vauxhall or Fiat "economy sedan" shitboxes that would soon be gracing the showroom floors of crappy, fly-by-night "little furrin' car" dealerships all across America (and, not all that many years later, find themselves rusting sullenly and silently away in nearby junkyards). I mean, I never wrote that sort of stuff except to fill in the downtime and make a few extra column-inch bucks between racing seasons, and it never did much for me. Worse yet, it would all have to be freelance, and freelance was just another way of saying that the work isn't steady, the money is shit and there are no fringe benefits of any kind. Or travel expense allowances. Period. It's not really enough to live on, even if you're willing to starve. Plus I didn't much fancy the idea of moving back to the states. Sure, I missed the near-eternal summertime of southern California, but now everything that truly mattered to me—everything I really loved and lived for—was anchored right here in England. And that included Audrey. And Formula One. And the World Manufacturers' Championship. That's the stuff that got my interest up and my blood pumping. I'd worked long and hard to become a genuine insider in that world, and I knew in my heart it was where I *belonged!* Even though I knew it was a difficult, fickle and often frivolous, thankless and senseless sort of business, and that it could—and would!—turn horrible in a heartbeat. As it had for Stirling Moss, who was still in a deep coma in Atkinson Morley Hospital near Wimbledon.

But that dark side was part of the magic, too....

Chapter 18: A Sojourn to Sicily

I got a long-distance phone call from Danny Beagle late the next evening while I was packing for my trip to Sicily. He'd called to tell me that Ban Abernathy had told Bob Wright about what had happened with me and the magazine, and although he wasn't thrilled about it, he understood the situation and moreover knew that Quentin Deering was a pompous, arrogant, capricious and belligerent sonofabitch asshole. Not that Bob Wright would have put it in those exact words. But Danny was cautiously optimistic that we could get things worked out, and that Bob wanted me to keep my situation with Fairway Motors under wraps—at least for now—and he wanted me back in Detroit just as quickly as possible after my hoped-for, face-to-face interview with Enzo Ferrari. I started to argue that I had the first Grand Prix of the season coming up at Zandvoort in Holland the weekend after the Targa Florio, but caught myself. I really had no reason to be at that first Grand Prix of the season. At least not professionally, anyway. And that made me a little sick inside all over again.

It was probably silly, but since my travel arrangements had already been made and moreover since I didn't want to screw up my photographer friend Hal Crockett's plans, I'd decided to go down to the Targa Florio anyway, magazine assignment or no magazine assignment. I maybe even held out a dim half-hope that Eric Gibbon would somehow slide off the edge of the earth—a tumble off a nice, steep Sicilian cliff would do—so I could reclaim my position with *Car and Track*. Besides, the rich young husband-and-wife who owned the blue-over-blue Rolls Royce and the fancy house in Mayfair were going on private holiday and they'd asked Audrey to stay on with their dear little monsters all week and clear on through the weekend. So she might as well have been on the dark side of the moon as far as seeing her was concerned. And Warren and Isabelle were nice enough to offer to pick up my travel expenses—at my usual, bare-subsistence level, of course—because the plans and commitments had already been made before that asshole Quentin Deering had a chance to fire me. Isabelle even suggested that I might think about doing some sort of travel piece about touring in Sicily—maybe for them under a different name or maybe for some travel magazine—even though I only ever went to Sicily for the Targa and most other tourists come there to visit the places their families came from and meet and argue with their relatives there. Families are everything in Sicily. It's a charming, ancient, scenic, friendly and terrifically romantic sort of place, but also somewhat backward, set in its ways, suspicious of outsiders and absolutely seething with dark, ominous superstitions, mafia turf wars and vicious, brooding, generations-old blood vendettas that dated back to when people had to stab, beat, slash, strangle, garrote or bludgeon each other to death because there was no such thing as gunpowder. There were still bandit gangs roaming around in the Sicilian hill country, and it was taken for granted that the government law in

Palermo and the ancient, dirt-level justice of the mafia chieftains out in the countryside were just two sides of the same coin. But of course you couldn't write that in a magazine travel piece. Or even if you could, you wouldn't.

But Sicily had an unbridled passion for motor racing, and absolutely lived for speed, noise, color, glamour, money, danger, delicious confusion, drama and inevitable emotional excess that the Targa Florio brought there every spring. The entire island threw its arms open to the racers, and that made it a uniquely incredible event. More importantly, it was the very last of the true, wild, open-road classics like the *Mille Miglia* and *La Carrera Panamericana*—both now gone and surely never to return—and as such held a singular stature, style and romance. But many worried that the cars were getting too fast, light and sophisticated for the rough, bumpy, poorly patched and regularly treacherous Sicilian roads. Not to mention the general lack of crowd control and the dangerously solid scenery that sat close by the roadside, waiting for the unwary. Some of the drivers loved it, more hated it and virtually everyone except the locals considered getting there a colossal pain in the ass. But it never failed to be an adventure! Hal and I were planning to drive pretty much straight-through to Naples—it was almost 24 hours under the best of circumstances in a Fiat 600—and then sleep it off on the 10-hour car ferry ride that got us into Palermo at 6:30 Thursday morning. There were always a lot of racing people on that boat, and it never failed to be a good time. And a good sleep after the long trip down and what would certainly turn out to be a lot of great racing stories and even more Lambrusco. It was important to get your head into the proper, Sicilian street-festival frame of mind when you were heading for the Targa Florio! At least if you wanted full value out of the experience. Besides, we'd have all day Friday to recuperate before the racing engines fired up for the only "official" practice sessions on Saturday.

The Targa was a genuine and and amazing anachronism in the modern world, and survived to a great degree because of the local passion for it, a typically Sicilian disdain for modern notions, fears and cautions and fantastic sense of the race's history and meaning. Originally the brainchild of a wealthy, prominent, motorsports-smitten Sicilian enthusiast named Vincenzo Florio way back in 1906, the Targa Florio was the last true open-road race on the World Manufacturers' Championship calendar. And what roads they were! The Targa's *Picolo Madonie* circuit snaked, climbed, dived, twisted, leaped and doubled back on itself for an astounding 72 kilometers (roughly 45 miles) through the scenic hills and mountains that rose up out of the Tyrrhenian Sea, and the only straight stretch worth mentioning was a short, flat-out, 4-kilometer blast along the coastline before heading back up into the hills again. The track climbs and claws its way from sea level up to 600 meters and then plunges back down, and takes the screaming racecars right through the heart of ancient towns and villages like Cerda, Caltavuturo, Collesano and Campofelice—arrowing like howling rockets between old stone walls and fading whitewashed buildings where the noise of the engines seems to double back on itself. Besides being narrow, blind and bumpy in many places, the *Piccolo Madonie* layout was bedeviled with pavement patches and humpbacked bridges that sent the cars flying or skittering and played hell with suspensions. Not to mention all manner of ditches, trees, walls, fences, bridge abutments, kilometer stones and sheer, terrifying dropoffs waiting for the incautious or impetuous. Drivers also needed to be on the lookout for stray farm animals wandering out into the roadway and not much at all in the way of crowd control. The Targa was like a time machine into racing's past—utterly unique and magnificent!—but even its staunchest supporters agreed it was *very* easy to use up a car there!

But the most daunting part for beginners was that a lap of the *Piccolo Madonie* circuit featured no less than 710 turns, bends and corners, and that was a *lot* to commit to memory. Which gave an enormous advantage to the one-race-a-year locals and experienced Targa veterans who knew the place well. There was just no way a driver could hope to pick up all of its tricks, subtleties and nuances—or even remember it all—during the scant few hours of "official practice" the day before the race! So newcomers had no choice but to do reconnaissance laps in rented Fiats or expendable team "recce" cars during the highly unofficial "familiarization days" that came before the race. And of course the roads weren't closed for them, so those rented Fiats and "recce" cars found themselves dodging through delivery trucks, donkey carts, motorbikes, slow-moving farm tractors pulling hay wagons, ancient, chuffing Fiat Topolinos, meandering farm animals, local priests on bicycles, peddlers with pushcarts and and craggy, black-clad old Sicilian women on their way to church. It got pretty damn hairy now and again. But both the racers and the locals seemed to love it for exactly that reason.

It felt good being on the road with Hal again, and I knew I could count on him to keep his mouth shut and not ask me what I was going to do next after I told him what had happened with the magazine. He was similarly circumspect when I somewhat proudly (and even more clumsily) started rambling on about what had happened between me and Audrey Denbeigh. I wanted to make it sound sweet, wholesome and uplifting rather than like locker-room bragging, and I'd give myself about a C-minus on that score. Which isn't too bad for a man. But, like I said, Hal knew how to keep his mouth shut. He just flared his eyeballs a little in surprise and nodded with what appeared to be approval. I also wanted to tell him about all the things that were swirling around me up in Fairway Tower. And about the big, blowout birthday party in the mansion on McElligot Lane and about the garden maze and the pot and the reflecting-pond water that tasted like goldfish. And The Steel Shed and the Black Mamba Lounge and how frankly terrifying—even if a little bit exciting—if felt when Amelia Camellia Fairway unexpectedly stuck her tongue down my throat in the Black Mamba Lounge's parking lot. I was dying to tell somebody—hell, *anybody*—about that just so I wouldn't have to keep it bottled up inside. I even thought half-seriously about dropping into a Catholic church in some little town where nobody knew me—I could dress up in a low, floppy hat and a fake mustache for the occasion—just so I could go into the confessional and unburden myself. I mean, I hadn't actually *done* anything (and had neither intentions nor inclinations in that direction) but I didn't much like the way it made me feel. It kept popping up in my head and making me shiver like one of those scary, falling moments in a bad dream. And I just couldn't shake it. But of course there was no way I could share any of that with Hal—at least not yet—because then the conversation would naturally follow its way around to just what the hell I was doing running around with the executive corridor gang from Fairway Tower, and I knew Bob Wright wanted me to keep that under wraps. At least for now.

Hal and I got delayed just south of the Swiss border when the damn left-rear tire on my Fiat that was always leaking air lost all of it in fairly dramatic fashion coming down out of the mountains. Hal was stretched out as best he could and dozing when there was this big *"BANG!"* and we were suddenly going sideways. He shook awake with a startled, sleepy *"whatth'fuck??!!"* just as the back end of the Fiat clipped off a well-placed railing (with an ugly dropoff on the other side!) and sent us spinning around the opposite way. But we came to a halt in the middle of the road without further damage, and I quickly stuck it in gear and limped out of the way before some overloaded truck or speeding Mercedes sedan could blast our poor little Fiat into smithereens. It was several more miles before I found a place where we could pull off, and by then the rim was pretty well chewed up. Then we had to unload all of our stuff to get at the jack and spare and naturally it was flat, too (wouldn't you know it) and so we were pretty much stranded until a Good Samaritan from Bologna in another Fiat 600 stopped to help out. He let us put his spare on (for a few thousand lira that he at first refused to accept and then looked at like it might not really be enough) and then he followed us to the next town where we gave it back to him after I bought us a new tire. Make that a new *used* tire. And then we had to wait for the guy at the station to beat out the bent rim and file down the edges so it would hold air and not cause another blowout. Hal insisted on chipping in, of course, and I ultimately had to take it just to keep from arousing suspicion.

In any case, the tire episode put us seriously behind schedule (and a weary, overloaded Fiat 600 Multipla is hardly the sort of vehicle you'd use to make up time, even in Italy) and so we missed the ferryboat to Palermo on Wednesday evening. The next morning's ferry was booked solid (as you might expect on the days leading up to the Targa), so we wound up wandering around Naples for a day and just barely squeaking onto the 8pm Thursday night ferry that would have us into Palermo at 6:30 Friday morning. They didn't have any of the cheaper, inside state-rooms left, so we wound up trying to sleep on the deck in deck chairs while happy Italian race fans partied all around us until two or three in the morning.

Needless to say, Hal and I were looking pretty ragged by the time we got un-loaded from the boat in Palermo, but it was way too early to head for our ram-shackle but clean little tourist room up the road from the start/finish line in Cefalu. We'd called the night before to let them know we wouldn't be arriving until the following day, but of course we were going to have to pay for the unused night any-way since it was Targa weekend and all rooms were booked far in advance. With nothing much to do and not nearly enough sleep under our hats, we decided to drop by the permanent pits and grandstand area at the start/finish line and do a little nosing around. And that's where I saw that sneaky little weasel Eric Gibbon again. He was standing over the engine compartment of Ferrari's latest, 8-cylinder Dino, sucking on his pipe and considering it like a discerning fellow trying to pick out a particularly fine piece of fruit. He noticed me out of the corner of his eye but pretended not to, and it was nice to see that the stinking little bastard was avoiding me. Oh, he saw me all right, but he'd make sure to immediately turn his back or look off the other way or amble off in some other direction on those bandy little legs of his. Maybe the guy did have a few nagging shreds of guilt, shame and de-cency inside his grubby, unctuous soul after all. But I was certain they were small, tiny shreds, if they were there at all. Hal made a point of backing up into him a few times so he could step on the little weasel's foot, but he always did it with one eye squinted through the viewfinder of his Nikon like he was trying to line up a shot so it looked like an accident. And you must remember that my friend Hal is a pretty big guy with really huge feet and towered a good, solid head-and-a-half over Eric Gibbon's stupid little deerstalker hat. Of course Hal always said "sorry" or "excuse me," but I think Eric got the message by the second or third time it happened. Es-pecially after Hal stepped on his toes really hard one time and then, with a perfectly benign and angelic look on his face, apologized by way of saying: "You know, Eric, I just didn't smell you there behind me."

By nature, the Targa Florio always favored nimble, handy, durable cars over fly-weight nickel rockets or the heavy, fast, powerful brutes that generally dominated at places like Sebring and Le Mans. Which is why Porsche damn near won it out-right in 1958 (the 1500cc Jean Behra/Giorgio Scarlatti RSK coming in an astounding 2nd overall to the 3-liter Testa Rossa of Musso and Gendebien and ahead of the two other factory Testa Rossas) and then won it fair and square over the red cars in 1959 with Edgar Barth and Wolfgang Seidel leading a 1-2-3-4 Porsche sweep—cop-ping both the sports and GT categories!—while all the factory Ferraris dropped out early. It was a stunning and humiliating loss for Old Man Ferrari (particularly in what everyone perceived to be his own back yard) and it got even worse the following year when Jo Bonnier and Hans Herrmann repeated with yet another Porsche victory over Ferrari's latest, shark-nosed, mid-engined Dino 246SPs. It was Ferrari's turn again—finally—in 1961, but it was a lucky win and everybody and his brother knew it. Porsche had hired Stirling Moss on for the occasion and paired him with Graham Hill in their latest-spec RS61, and Moss had worked his usual magic and had more than a minute in hand over the 2nd-place Ferrari Dino as he began the final, 45-mile lap. It looked like a sure Porsche victory—which would have made it three in a row over the red cars in Sicily!—but then the ring and pinion gears on the leading Porsche stripped with just 8 kilometers to go. It was a bitter loss for Moss and Porsche after a truly outstanding drive, and it must have been a somewhat empty victory for Ferrari. But no question they would take it.

For 1962, Porsche had sent down a pair of new, sleeker and more potent-looking flat-8 cars—one coupe and one spyder—that threatened to be quite a bit quicker than the old, 4-cylkinder RSKs and RS61s. Plus they'd made a one-off deal with our old yachting pal Count Giovanni Volpi di Misurata's Scuderia Serenissima team to run their factory cars in Sicily because the factory race shop in Stuttgart was working overtime trying to get their new Porsche Formula One machines ready for the first grand prix of the season the following weekend at Zandvoort. And you'd have to say it was a good choice, since Count Volpi's bunch were talented, well-funded and reasonably well-organized (at least for an Italian privateer team, anyway) and moreover highly motivated to beat the living crap out of both Signore Ferrari and his cars. Even though the guys on the Scuderia Ferrari and Scuderia Serenissima teams had known each other for a long time and got along fairly well at the races, there was a blood feud building between the rich young privateer team from Venice and the factory boys from Maranello. But, typical of Italian differences of opinion, the situation was layered like an onion and full of nuances and contradictions, since drivers and mechanics had been poached back-and-forth between the teams for years. Sure, young count Volpi had helped back the fired Ferrari employees (or defectors, if you preferred Enzo's version of the story) so they could set themselves up across town as blossoming rival A.T.S., but he'd also won Sebring for Ferrari after all the factory cars either stumbled or crapped out. And his money had always been good (not to mention plentiful) at Ferrari's customer race shop. But the grudge match had been building all the same, and with the promised new A.T.S. racecars still at least a full season away, young count Giovanni had no choice but to rely on Ferrari and Maserati customer cars throughout the balance of the '62 season. In fact, it was an open secret that he'd tried to buy himself another GTO for Le Mans (he'd already taken delivery of one) but Old Man Ferrari refused to sell him one. *Ba Fangu!* And yet I'd seen some of the young count's cars, engines and transmissions being worked on in the Ferrari customer race shop in Maranello when I was there for the Old Man's press conference. According to my friend Vinci Pittacora, one or two of them were still there.

Ahh, only in Italy....

In any case, Count Volpi's team had made a one-off deal with Porsche to run their factory cars and drivers at the Targa, and that meant fielding two of their promising new flat-8 cars in the 2-liter Prototype class: a typically dull silver spyder for Gurney/Bonnier and, in deference to Count Volpi's team and nationality, a bright red coupe for Graham Hill and local Palermo schoolteacher and acknowledged Targa expert Nino Vacarrella. Along with a pair of Carrera Abarths for the 1600cc GT class and those all-important Category 2 World Manufacturers' Championship points. Scuderia Serenissima also brought their somewhat unloved and untrustworthy Maserati Tipo 64 with a few mechanical tweaks and bodywork modifications, but it was still on the fat side of ugly as far as I was concerned and looked like a prime candidate for First Car Out once the race actually started. But the two Porsche prototypes looked absolutely terrific, and with Gurney, Bonnier, Graham Hill and Nino Vacarrella handling the driving, I thought they had a very solid shot at the overall win. Sure, the Ferrari Dinos would probably be faster, but the Porsches always seemed to run strong and reliably and no question local boy Nino Vacarrella knew the 45-mile *Piccolo Madonie* race circuit better than anyone else on the planet. And that counted for a *lot* at a race like the Targa Florio....

In response to the Porsche threat, Ferrari showed up loaded for bear, eager to not only win the race, but to put both Porsche and Scuderia Serenissima in their place in the bargain. So team manager Dragoni had three of the latest and fastest mid-engined Dinos at his disposal: a 2.4-liter 6-cylinder and a 2.6-liter 8-cylinder version for the 3-liter "sports" class plus a special, 1983cc "196SP" V6 version with new boys (and Dragoni favorites) Bandini and Baghetti up and aimed squarely at snatching the 2-liter honors away from Porsche as well.

While we were standing there looking at the cars, who should tootle by in a rented Fiat but Cal Carrington. He was about to go out on a recce lap with Phil Hill (who knew the Targa circuit well) and asked if we'd like to ride along.

Hal and I looked at each other. "Are you going to behave?" Hal asked.

"Of course he's going to behave," Phil Hill said with a perfectly straight face. "That's why I've got this," he held up a brass-head knockoff hammer. "If he starts getting too brave or racy, I just use this on his kneecaps. One shot on each is usually enough...."

So we clambered into the back of the Fiat sedan—Hal had to pretty much fold himself double to get inside, but he was eager to check out some shooting locations from a racing car's perspective—and we didn't even have the doors all the way closed before Cal popped the clutch and lurched us off towards the mountains. Mind you, the Fiat couldn't accelerate very hard with four people on board (and especially with one of them as big as Hal) but once he had it up to speed, Cal did his very best to keep it there. And Cal's very best was very good indeed. Plus it was fascinating to hear Phil giving a calm, running commentary while Cal squealed the Fiat around hairpins with its tires pretty much folded under and shot over blind crests and around blind, deceptive sweepers at as much over 100 km/h as the Fiat 4-door could muster.

"The thing here is not just remembering all the tight, ridiculous little bootlace corners where you have to slow way down to keep from barreling over a cliff or collecting a face-full of rock, but remembering all the places where it *looks* like you have to slow down but you really don't. That's where the real time is: keeping your foot down when your eyes and heart tell you the road looks iffy up ahead but when your brain and memory know it really isn't."

Cal went flying over a totally blind crest just to prove it. And naturally came on a dawdling poultry truck and an old man on a bicycle carrying long loaves of bread on the other side. He braked hard, getting the Fiat all up on tiptoes with the front and rear tires sliding, and released the brake just in time to sashay neatly between the end of the loaves of bread and crates of squawking chickens. The poultry truck driver and the old man on the bicycle apparently recognized Phil and Cal as racing drivers and cheered wildly as we went past. It was nuts.

"You've got to love the Targa," Cal grinned helplessly as the Fiat struggled to regain lost momentum.

"Yeah, but you've also got to survive it," Phil cautioned. "The speeds are generally low—I mean, it's not like Spa or Le Mans or anything—but the penalty for going off is still pretty high in a lot of places." His eyes looked up at Hal and me in the rear-view mirror. "There's a lot of stuff to hit out there," he said by way of explanation.

By the time we reached the uppermost point of the circuit at Caltavutura, Hal was about the same seasick green color as the BRP/UDT Laystall racing cars, and he asked to get out to "line up a few locations and angles."

"We can pick you up next time around," Cal offered.

"No sweat either way," Hal assured him, looking queasy as hell, "I can make it back on my own if I have to."

"I'll be driving on the next lap," Phil deadpanned.

Hal thought it over for a moment. "Howsabout if I just stick my thumb out if I'm still up here and need a ride."

"Suit yourself," Cal grinned, then revved the motor, popped the clutch and launched us off on the tricky downhill run to the shoreline. To be honest, I was kind of glad Hal got out. I mean, the brakes were *really* starting to fade by the time we got back down to sea level, and the last thing that poor Fiat needed was another 230 pounds of ballast and momentum throwing up in the back seat.

The 4-kilometer, pretty much arrow-straight run along the coast from Campofe-lice to the quick squiggle and hard left into the start/finish line gave Cal and Phil a few uninterrupted minutes to talk about their car and the team. And I was ab-solutely thrilled to be in the back seat listening. The first thing Phil pointed out was that they'd be up against the redline in top long before they got to the braking zone for the final complex of corners. "It's not like Le Mans," he almost scoffed. "The mechanics have no choice but to gear the cars tight for the climb through the moun-tains, so you'll have to feather it in top here if you don't want to blow it up.."

"Why don't they just give us another gear?" Cal asked.

"Why don't they give us another four cylinders and another half-liter?" Phil chided him. "Ferrari likes to use what he has. Particularly if he thinks it's good enough to win. I mean, you're not racing against perfection, just other cars...."

It became apparent that neither one of them seemed to think very much of Ferrari's new-for-1962 racing team manager, Eugenio Dragoni. Dragoni didn't re-ally need the Ferrari job, as he owned a profitable and successful perfume manu-facturing business in Milan. But he loved the thrill, command, stature and authority of beingh Ferrari's team manager, and he felt it suited him well because he was wealthy, well-connected and used to getting things his own way. I personally thought he was a bit headstrong to be a team manager, but apparently there was something in his driven, severe, autocratic and athoritarian manner that Ferrari liked. Or at least appreciated. And Dragoni knew how to keep his drivers off balance, and that, as Ferrari well knew, usually kept them in line. For the Targa, Dragoni teamed Cal and Phil in the supposedly fastest Dino (the new, 8-cylinder car) and put fearless wild men Willy Mairesse and Ricardo Rodriguez in the older but more proven V6. Phil personally would have preferred the older car, as he thought it wasn't quite as high revving or high strung and might well be more reliable and easier to drive. But Dragoni had been making something of a habit of giving his American drivers what-ever they didn't want. Just to keep them on edge and pushing....

I took a second lap in the Fiat with Phil driving, and it was interesting to see the differences between the styles of the two drivers. Cal was kind of what-the-fuck and devil-may-care—as if he could get himself out of damn near any situation he man-aged to get himself into—while Phil was more serious and cautiously, even shrewdly aware of the dangers that lurked just about everywhere at the Targa. But he was every bit as fast (and maybe even faster?) only in a calm, measured, more cerebral sort of way. Even Cal had to agree that Phil was really, really good, and I thought it was a real privilege riding with the reigning World Champion! Even if I almost threw up once or twice.

I got out after one more lap and not long afterward Hal showed up in a sedately driven Fiat with one of the local Sicilian race officials. "You may enjoy riding with racing drivers," he sighed, shaking his head, "but it seems the better they are, the closer I come to losing my lunch."

I told him I had no idea what he was talking about.

We meandered around the pits a little more after that, nosing around the legions of privateer, Italian-team Alfa Romeos, Lancias and Fiat-Abarths that showed up to contest the smallbore GT classes and have their moment of glory under the bright Sicilian sun contesting what was now, following the demise of the Mille Miglia, the biggest sports car race in all of Italy and the only remaining open-road sports car race on the World Manufacturers' Championship calendar. But a lot of those Alfa, Lancia and Fiat-Abarth pilots were casting uneasy glances in the direction of the pair of factory-team Porsche Abarth Carreras in the Scuderia Serenissima bivouac. And also, for completely different reasons, at the unlikely looking, tiny-wheeled little shoebox of an Austin Mini Cooper. It had been entered by well-to-do French racing photographer, raconteur and all-'round fascinating character Bernard Cahier, and his co-driver was his fellow enthusiast and aristocratic racing friend, Prince Paul Metternich. But the boxy, clown-car little Mini looked anything but regal.

In fact, if ever a car looked completely, almost comically unsuited to motor-sports, the Austin Mini had to be it. Its chief engineer, Alec Issigonis, surely had no design aspirations beyond building a cheap, well-thought-out little economy sedan that was terrifically small on the outside but surprisingly large on the inside. In fact, Issigonis' Mini was essentially little more than a reasonably roomy and comfortable box of an interior (for two people, a small child or two and their luggage, anyway) surrounded by as little as possible in the way of wheels, tires, driveline and running gear. Issigonis (who had a bit of racing in his background and had built a few racing cars himself) probably turned a bright, pasty white at the thought of anyone *racing* the damn things. After all, they were tall, boxy little bricks with an uncomfortably high center of gravity, front wheel drive with *lots* of torque steer, rubber suspension, tiny little wheels and tires (and therefore tiny little *brakes* inside those tiny little wheels and tires!) and the aerodynamics of your average garden shed. Not to mention a crude and uninspiring little 850cc pushrod motor that somewhat unfortunately shared its oil supply with a clever but equally crude and uninspiring little FWD transmission. Since every gearbox ever built is essentially a great, high-speed grinding machine, coupling it in-unit with the engine ensured that near-microscopic bits of ground-off gear teeth fragments, sheared-off shreds of copper synchro rings and assorted shards of high-strength steel bearing swarf were forever contaminating the oil supply. Over time, this did no good whatsoever for the engine's bottom end and con-rod bearings. But give an Englishman an interesting chunk of metal and he'll eventually do something foolish with it, and pretty soon John and Charlie Cooper started building a high-performance version and Austin Mini Coopers began taking to the racetracks and rallye trails all over Europe. They made good rallye cars—in spite of their tiny engines—because they were small and whippy and usually had crazy drivers, and the front-wheel-drive was a real asset when traction was at a premium. And they instantly became crowd favorites on the racetracks because they were entertaining as hell and frankly hilarious to watch. Mini drivers had to more-or-less sling, hurl and wrestle them around corners—often with wheels flailing and pawing at the air and occasional, munchkin-like puffs of rubbersmoke squeaking off the tires—and everyone loved seeing a Mini Cooper harassing (or, better yet, *passing!*) a more powerful, prestigious or presumptuous type of car. Which naturally included just about everything else on the track!

Hal had booked us into a third-floor, walk-up room in an old and creaky but relatively clean little pensione located well up the side of the Gibraltar-like rock formation that overlooked the quaint, scenic little seaside village of Cefalu. It was an ancient old place with masonry like a Civil War tombstone, but it was only a dozen kilometers up the coastline from the permanent pit area and start/finish line and a *lot* cheaper than the favored, far fancier hotels and albergos along the coastline. It was quite a climb to get there (followed by yet another tough climb up the steep, narrow wooden stairway to our room) but our tiny balcony offered a magnificent view of the Tyrrhenian Sea. At least if you looked over the alleyway behind the fish market and between the taller building in front of ours and the tower of the 12th-century granite church the town was famous for and across the scattered carpeting of terra cotta rooftops and the fishing docks screeching with seagulls that bordered on the pristine, cerulean blue of the Tyrrhenian Sea. The energetic, mustachioed little manager was profusely apologetic about having to charge us for the night we weren't there, and gave us a free drink at the narrow, varnished oak bar conveniently situated right next to the check-in desk. And that turned out to be a pretty good investment on his part, since we came back after dinner to have many more at our own expense. But I think he rather expected that.

We were up early and somewhat groggy but fairly well refreshed the next morning, and headed over to the pits before the roads were closed down for practice. Or that was our intention, anyway, but most of the barriers were already up. But Hal noticed one spot where all they had was a kind of three-legged sawhorse deal blocking a drive, so he hobbled over on his bum leg, looked both ways for police helmets and, seeing none, lifted the crossbar like a gate to let my old Fiat through. Naturally we had nearby race officials and volunteer workers screaming at us instantly to get off of the racetrack—Sicilians can get quite colorful with their language and gestures when they put their minds, lungs and passion to it—but we knew there was still almost an hour before practice was scheduled to start. So Hal dropped the wooden gate behind us with a *thunk!,* fairly leaped into the passenger side of the Fiat and we tore off in as much of a hurry as my tired old engine and brand new clutch would allow, waving our press passes out the windows, pretending not to understand Italian and doing our level best to look English. One particularly outraged official even made a move towards standing in our way. But I handled it the time-honored Sicilian way by keeping my foot flat to the floor, and he ultimately came to the equally time-honored conclusion that discretion was indeed the better part of valor and leaped out of the way with a flourish at the very last second—matador style—but he did give the Fiat's roof an angry fist thump as we flashed past. Judging from the size and depth of the dent, he probably cracked a few knuckles in the process. Figuring that other, even more outraged officials might well be waiting to have a chat with us if we came into the pit area, we moved another barrier after the hard left that led away from the coastline, sneaked our way into the paddock and hid the Fiat in a dark, narrow little space between the Ferrari transporter and a tire truck.

It was exciting and even intoxicating to find ourselves wandering around the early-morning pit area as the engines fired up and revved to warm up the oil, the bustle of activity rose to a fever pitch and then, finally, the cars began roaring, howling, wailing, screaming and occasionally sputtering out of the pits—one after another, but usually with gaps of five to twenty seconds in between—and disappeared up into the hills and out of sight. When the last of them had gone, a strange, nervous silence descended. You could hear the echoes of racing engines straining up the hills and downshifting for the corners off in the distance, but it grew fainter and fainter until you couldn't hear anything except the questioning murmur of the racing teams and officials and the occasional buzz of insects. Like all the other classic open road races, cars would start the Targa Florio at 30-second intervals—fastest cars first—because it would be utter mayhem otherwise as the entire, snaking pack tried to force, jerk, jostle and sort itself out up the narrow mountain roadways. But there was no such provision during practice, so caution and courtesy were an absolute must.

Even so, there were incidents.

Probably the most unnerving problem befell our friend Phil Hill, who came in after just one lap complaining of a sticking throttle. A sticking throttle was no fun anywhere, but it could easily prove lethal here at the Targa where there were so many things to hit and so few escape roads. Dragoni had his mechanics look it over and make a few perfunctory wrench-passes, and then sent Cal out to try the car. But Cal ran into the same exact problem while trying to set up for a sweeping and deceptive downhill right-hander. He allowed afterwards that he had one hell of a moment when he lifted off the gas and the pedal stayed down like it was bolted to the bulkhead! As he put it: "I didn't even get the *'OH'* of *'OH SHIT!'* out of my mouth before I was bouncing off a fucking wall!" The Dino slammed into the wall, ricocheted back across the roadway, catapulted over a ditch, bounced and bounded through a planted field and ultimately plowed to a shuddering halt just a foot or two shy of a very solid-looking stone farmhouse. Cal was lucky to suffer nothing worse than a sprained wrist, a cut lip and some painfully bruised ribs. But the car was pretty much finished as far as the balance of the Targa weekend was concerned, what with the front suspension badly deranged and the frame tweaked beyond any hope of field repair. Cal returned to the pits on the back of a motor scooter and in a *lot* of pain, and Dragoni only made it worse by yelling at him for wrecking the car and, worse yet, leaving it out in the countryside where the local bandits and souvenir seekers could pick it over. Cal wasn't happy about that at all—especially after the damn throttle linkage that they'd supposedly "fixed" had jammed wide-open again—and pretty soon he and Dragoni were at it nose-to-nose and eyeball-to-eyeball, screaming their lungs out at each other in two different languages. But you couldn't miss what was being communicated, even if you only spoke Chinese.

Within five minutes, my friend Cal had yelled, screamed, stomped, snarled and cursed his way right off the Ferrari team....

Chapter 19: A Night by the Sea

As you can imagine, Cal and I had a lot to commiserate about that evening as we headed off for dinner and entirely too many glasses of wine at the little fish joint where the major players from the Ferrari team had eaten the night before. But Cal knew they wouldn't be there again the Saturday night before the big race. No, they'd be having a quiet, private and subdued little supper in the leafy back courtyard of the old hotel they were staying at just a few streets away. Cal was sharing a room there with Phil Hill, but he didn't much want to go back there that evening. It was just going to be awkward and uncomfortable and Phil was going to feel upset and angry and apologetic and Cal was going to feel upset and angry and not apologetic at all, and what the hell were they going to talk about anyway? And what about breakfast the next morning? Showing up at the pre-dawn, race-day Ferrari team breakfast didn't sound appealing at all. Unless it was to smash a big, juicy half grapefruit into team manager Dragoni's face, Jimmy Cagney style....

I told Cal he was more than welcome to stay in the crappy but reasonably clean little tourist room at the far cheaper pensione up the hillside with Hal and me if he wanted to. Hal was apparently still up in the mountains somewhere—perhaps having dinner and wine with some of the local bandits and maybe shooting a few pictures?—and there was no way of knowing if or when he'd return. It wouldn't be unusual at all for him to just stay up in the hills all night so he'd be set to shoot the race first thing in the morning when the light was best. That was always part of the deal between Hal and me on race weekends: don't wonder, don't worry and for God's sake don't wait up. But of course with the understanding that you didn't leave for home or the airport without, as Hal put it, either having *a)* the other person in the front seat next to you, *b)* having visited him in the hospital to see if he needs anything or *c)* having seen both the death certificate and the body. But of course if Hal did make it back that night, one of us was going to have to sleep on the hard, narrow strip of floor between the equally narrow and only slightly softer beds. And be ready to get up—or at least roll out of the way—if one of the other two had to shuffle off down the hall to the bathroom.

"Thanks," Cal said without any measurable enthusiasm. "Something'll work out. It always does."

We were passing through the shadow of the fortress-like old Norman cathedral that was one of the primary tourist attractions in Cefalu any other weekend of the year. It was a massive-looking old thing made out of granite with two stout, square towers and parapets running along the top of the outer walls, and it reminded me more of a medieval castle than any kind of church. I'd read someplace that it dated all the way back to the twelfth century and was famous for its Byzantine mosaics. In fact, they were supposed to be the finest Byzantine mosaics anywhere outside of Constantinople. But it just looked empty, ancient and forgotten on the Saturday evening the Targa Florio was in town. I tried telling Cal what I knew about the church—just to make a little conversation, you know?—but it was like he wasn't even listening. We could hear our footsteps echoing off the granite walls.

"How about your stuff?" I asked to break the silence.

"My stuff?"

"You know, your clothes and toiletries and stuff."

"I hadn't really thought about it. I brought my helmet and race bag back to the room after...after..." I felt him searching for words, but all he could come up with was a tight, irritated little shrug.

"And it's all still there?

Cal nodded, looking as miserable and uncertain as I'd ever seen him look. Which wasn't very, if you want the truth of it, but still looked uncomfortable as hell on him. "I guess I'll call the desk and tell them I'll come around to collect it tomorrow morning after everyone's gone. I don't really think I want to see any of them tonight." He punctuated with a gruff little snort of a laugh. "They probably don't want to see me again, either. Except for maybe Phil. He's a real gentleman, Phil is."

"That he is."

Of course what neither of us knew at the time was that Dragoni had also demoted Phil off the team (at least for the balance of the weekend, anyway) for siding with Cal and arguing on his behalf. Insubordination, don't you know? And then he went a step further by re-assigning the smooth, experienced Gendebien to partner 20-year-old Ricardo Rodriguez and "Wild Willy" Mairesse in the remaining Dino V6. Just in case it somehow survived those two and looked set for a top finish. Dragoni knew he needed a nice, quiet, subdued and non-public place to break that particular news to the other two drivers. Although they both surely respected Gendebien, they weren't going to like it one bit.

Cal slid his eyes over towards mine. "I don't think Phil's very long for Ferrari, either."

"Oh?"

He nodded like he knew what he was talking about. "I think Dragoni's got it in for him. He thinks Phil thinks too much. Worries too much. He'd rather have guys like Ricardo and Willy who are either too young or too damn crazy to worry about things." Cal turned and looked at me. "Don't get me wrong, Hank. Ricardo's very, *very* good. But he's terribly young and terribly driven. You can just feel it burning inside of him."

"I know what you mean."

"He's just not afraid to stick his neck out. It doesn't even occur to him that something bad might happen." Cal let out a dry, uneasy snort of a laugh. "I used to be like that."

I didn't say anything.

"It's like Tommy Edwards said," Cal continued, sounding utterly contemptuous of himself: *"these days I've got to think about doing things I used to do without thinking...."*

"You're just getting smarter, that's all," I argued. "There's nothing wrong with wanting to stay on the right side of the grass."

Cal shook his head. "No, I'm starting to think too much, too. It gets in the way."

"You're just angry and pissed off and disgusted. We'll have a nice dinner and a few glasses of wine and you'll feel better. Really you will."

But Cal couldn't let go of it: "Have you ever looked into Willy's eyes? I mean *really* looked?"

I nodded.

"You can't see bottom, can you?"

I shook my head in agreement. "Nope, you really can't, can you?"

"Oh, he can be a charming guy," Cal acknowledged, "but he's way, way out there."

"Out where?"

"You know: on the edge."

I knew exactly what he meant.

"And of course Dragoni loves his two new Italian boys. So don't be surprised if Phil's the next one to go."

"He won them a fucking world championship last year."

"That was last year. Besides, Phil told me Ferrari knows about the conversations he's had with Chiti and the rest over at A.T.S."

"That can't have gone down very well. How the hell did they find out?"

"Ferrari's got a lot of eyes and ears out there. A *lot* of eyes and ears...."

We got to the little seafood joint by the harbor just before sunset, and the place was already jam-packed and bustling with race fans and even more standing in line to get in. Everybody was jabbering and gesturing back-and-forth in a confusion of languages (but mostly in various Italian dialects, of course) and naturally some of them recognized Cal and waved or wanted an autograph or a picture with the great American Ferrari *corridore* because they had no idea he'd been fired off the Ferrari factory team that very afternoon. Fortunately the agitated-looking little man with the plastered-over hair, cook's apron and waxed mustache who ran the place also recognized Cal. He'd apparently gotten wind of what took place at the end of practice that morning, and he smiled at Cal with sad, almost trembling emotion. And then put his finger to his lips and led us quickly and quietly up a small back stairway to a narrow rooftop balcony overlooking the harbor and the Tyrrhenian Sea. There was a brisk, salt-air wind blowing in and the view was fantastic, but the best thing was that there was only a single, small, wrought-iron table and two matching garden chairs, so we had a little peace and privacy. Cal reached in his pocket to give the little Sicilian guy a tip, but he shook his head vigorously. It was an honor to do something accommodating for one of the gallant *pilotas.* So we sat down and watched the glowing, orange-red ball of the sun melt down into the ocean as the stars slowly faded up from nothing to a million brilliant pinpricks of light scattered across a deep, vast, velvety-black sky. It was so beautiful it made you feel hollow inside.

The little man with the waxed mustache brought us steaming bowls of the house-specialty seafood pasta with shrimp, mussels, octopus, black and green olives and calamari rings, but we just picked at it while we worked our way through two full bottles of Lambrusco followed by entirely too many glasses of some particularly lethal local grappa. Cal was still in a tight, mean, vindictive sort of mood—he said he really should have thrown a sucker punch at Dragoni, just for the sheer pleasure it would have brought to his knuckles—but his anger slowly burned off as the alcohol started settling in, and that left him sullen and even a little morose.

"You're probably better off this way," I said to encourage him. "I mean, look at Gurney. Look at Ginther. Hell, look at Juan Manuel Fangio, for chrissakes! They were all better off after they left Ferrari."

"Yeah, sure," he agreed without meaning a word of it. "But where the hell am I gonna go?" And he had me there. No question he was plain and simple fucked as far as any sort of competitive, front-line Grand Prix ride was concerned. And no matter what I thought about Formula One and its relative merits compared to sports car racing, conventional wisdom throughout the sport—and especially here in Europe and even more especially among the drivers—held that Formula One was the pinnacle and everything else was second-best. Everybody seemed convinced of it. And now here Cal was with the first Grand Prix of the season just two weeks away and no drive. Worse yet, Dragoni had already been kind of fading him into the background at Ferrari—through no fault of Cal's, as far as I could see—and now he had that stupid Fiat-Abarth rollover at Sebring to live down as well as the practice wreck here at the Targa. Racing team managers tend to have keen memories when it comes to that sort of thing. The better ones know that raw talent and driving skill are almost always in ample supply and that, money issues aside, it's inevitably desire, determination, attitude, experience and most of all confidence that separate the ones you really want from the ones you don't want nearly so much. And once that attitude starts developing cracks or that confidence gets shaken, it's rare that any combination of talent, desire, experience and determination can put things right again. I wasn't going to say anything, of course, but I knew in my gut that most racing careers tend to follow a fairly predictable, parabolic arc...like a skyrocket shooting up into the nighttime sky. Some burst early, crackle or fizzle out, but others climb way up into the stratosphere, explode gloriously and, for a greater or lesser period of time, illuminate the heavens. But all of them ultimately fall back down to earth. One way or another. So smart team managers are justifiably wary of guys who may have passed their peak and are heading into the fading, slippery downslide of their careers. Cal understood without either of us saying it that he'd be facing exactly that sort of perception. And there wasn't much of anything he could do about it. Sure, he could start off an interview by telling whoever-the-hell-it-was about the stuck throttle on the 248SP Dino triggering his practice crash at the Targa. And no question Phil would back him up. But racing team managers don't really want to start off their interviews listening to excuses. They get quite enough of that from the drivers they've already hired....

Besides, all the contracts were long since signed and all the good seats already taken on all the top Formula One teams. Lotus were perfectly happy with Jimmy Clark and Trevor Taylor (Taylor had done a hell of a job for Lotus in Formula Junior and helped Colin Chapman sell a *lot* of Lotus 20 and 22 customer cars). BRM was set with Graham Hill and ex-Ferrari man Richie Ginther, and they were both not only proven quantities but also particularly keen when it came to car development and nuts-and-bolts mechanics. Which was precisely what BRM needed, as far as I could see. Two-time world champ Jack Brabham had left Cooper to form his own team with fellow-Aussie designer Ron Tauranac, but he'd wisely decided to keep it a one-car effort for the first year and, in any case, their own F1 car wasn't going to be ready until at least mid-season. He'd be campaigning a customer Lotus 24 until then. Back in Surbiton, Cooper seemed content with quick and savvy young New Zealander Bruce McLaren backed up by up-and-coming South African Tony Maggs (who'd won a share of the 1961 European Formula Junior title in Ken Tyrrell's Cooper and was rumored to be bringing some family money to the deal). The air-cooled Porsche flat-8 didn't appear quite as slick or neat as the new crop of British V8 cars, but it was a huge improvement over the tubby and inelegant 4-cylinder cars that came before, and you could always count on Porsches to be well-designed, well-built and finish races. And with Stirling Moss still in a coma at Atkinson Morely Hospital, Porsche had arguably the quickest driver out there in Dan Gurney with the fast, hard and experienced Jo Bonnier to back him up. Of course I mentioned how impressed I'd been with the new Bowmaker Lola, but Reg Parnell already had Surtees signed on as lead driver with seasoned, reliable Brit Roy Salvadori in the second car, and so there wasn't really an opportunity there, either. Besides, neither one of us thought taking a "second driver" seat would really be the best next step for Cal. Almost all Formula One teams are built around an acknowledged team leader (except for Ferrari, of course, who regularly dangled number-one status in front of all of his drivers in order to push them into trying harder), and the number one guy on any team usually got the best of everything while the number two either struggled with what the number one was through with or wound up saddled with all the untried, experimental hardware that the team didn't want to risk on the number one yet.

In any case, it was all academic, since all the top works teams were full-up and all the decent seats were already taken. There was always A.T.S., of course, but we both knew that although they had a lot in the way of promise, engineering talent, grand plans and lurking potential, they were still several months away from having an actual car. Plus their financing was more than a little suspect now that our yachting friend Count Giovanni was out of the picture.

Below those teams you had decent privateer efforts like Rob Walker and UDT Laystall. But UDT already had contracts inked with Innes Ireland and Masten Gregory to drive Lotus Type 24 customer cars, and Walker had elected to go with what he knew following Moss' horrific accident, and re-signed the likeable, experienced and reliable little Frenchman Maurice Trintignant. He was probably getting a bit past his prime, but Trintignant was a smooth, solid and dependable performer who was known to be easy on equipment. He'd won the Grand Prix of Monaco for Walker's team in 1958, and no question the team knew him and trusted him and everybody got along. Cal, on the other hand, would have come in as very much an outsider. And who knew if Walker's Ferrari gamble was going to pay off anyway? By that point Rob had hedged his bets by ordering a backup Lotus 24 from Colin Chapman just in case the Ferrari option didn't pan out. And Chapman had promised him on a handshake that it would be "absolutely identical" to the cars the factory team themselves would be running.

Right.

Beyond that, the quality, resources and competitiveness fell right off a cliff, and you were in the realm of either complete no-hopers or having to bring a sizeable wad of cash along to secure a seat. And even a guy like Cal, who had some family money to fall back on and was hungry as hell for another opportunity, knew he had to be careful about where he wound up. A bum car or a bad team could send his F1 career into an inexorable graveyard spin, and he knew it.

"What I need is for somebody to get killed," he said only half-jokingly, and poured us each an after-dinner glass of grappa.

"That's not funny."

"Okay, how about hurt?"

"How about get fired?"

"Sure," he nodded, clinking our glasses together. "That'd work, too."

I took a long, healthy slug of the grappa and felt it burn all the way down.

"It's not just the racing, either," Cal said out of nowhere.

"Oh?"

His shoulders rose up in a helpless shrug. "Nah, it's more than that. It's, I don't know, everything...."

"What do you mean?"

He didn't say anything. Just looked out over the ocean. And then, without any emotion and sounding like he was very far away: "Y'know, sometimes I wish I hadn't screwed things up with Gina."

"The actress?"

Cal nodded. "Sometimes I think I shouldn't have dropped that. Or it's more like we shouldn't have dropped each other...."

"But you both had your careers," I reminded him.

"Yeah," he agreed, "that's what did it. We just didn't have the time or the place for it. She was always off someplace shooting and I was always off someplace racing and that's just the way it had to be...."

"And so now you miss her?"

He swirled the grappa around in its glass. "Nah, probably not. Not really. I mean, we never really had whatever the hell it was we thought we were going to have. I... I really don't know how to explain it."

I told him that I understood. And maybe I did. "It's really nice when you have someone special," I ventured cautiously. "Somebody you really, you know, *care* about. Somebody who really *means* something to you...."

I watched Cal's eyes slowly turn to ice. "Yeah," he almost sneered, "but it makes you weak inside. You start thinking and worrying about things too much. You start caring too much." He tossed off the last of his grappa. "That's probably not very good for guys in my line of work."

I could tell that this particular line of conversation had come to an abrupt end. And, to be honest, it wasn't the sort of thing you normally heard out of a guy like Cal Carrington anyway. Then again, he was in one hell of a dark frame of mind. And who could blame him? So I tried to perk him up by pouring us each another grappa and telling him about my problems. Just to get his mind off his own, you know? Although I must admit I was dying to talk to somebody—hell, anybody— about what was going on in my life. I couldn't tell Hal because that would mean spilling the beans about what I'd been doing up on the executive corridor of Fairway Tower, and there was no way you could let just a little of that slip without letting the whole business rush out like air out of a ruptured balloon. I could talk to Audrey about it, of course—hell, I could talk to Audrey about damn near anything!— but since so much of what I wanted to talk about was really about her (and her jerk father), that simply wouldn't work.

And that's how I wound up pouring my guts out to Cal on that narrow little wrought-iron balcony overlooking the Tyrrhenian Sea. I told him everything. About how I'd been fired off the fucking magazine by fucking Quentin E. Deering himself and also about what had been going on between me and the suits and ties in Fairway Tower and about my side-job spying work for Bob Wright and Danny Beagle and my secret trips to Detroit and I even told him about the checks and expense account that came with it. And also how much I missed the magazine writing and why I still had to stay in that creaky (but clean) old fleabag of a pensione with Hal so as not to arouse suspicion. Thanks to the wine and the grappa, I also told him about how strange, temporary and uncertain my situation with Fairway Motors seemed and about the looming possibility of being asked to weigh anchor in London and move to fucking Detroit. And that of course led to Audrey and how much I really seemed to care about her and how much I wanted to be around her and how edgy and awkward things were with her mean-spirited, jealous prick asshole of a father and how very desperately I wanted to stay in England to see if I could make it work out. But then there was the little problem about just what the hell I was going to do for a living.

"So what are you going to do?" Cal asked me point-blank.

And of course I'd thought that one over. Too much, in fact. And without reaching any sort of worthwhile conclusion. "Oh, I suppose I could go try and peddle myself around to the other nutball car magazines. But *Car and Track* is the only one stateside that offers any kind of regular, in-depth coverage of the European scene. And no way are any of the English magazines going to hire anyone who's not a Brit. At least not for a regular staff position, anyway."

"You've got to go where the breaks and opportunities take you," Cal observed flatly. "That's just the way it is."

"I dunno," I mused. "I always thought that, too. But do you just let the winds and tides take you wherever the hell they're going?"

Cal thought it over for a moment. "That's what fucking Chris Columbus did, didn't he? And he discovered America." You could tell the grappa was starting to get to him.

"No, he didn't," I corrected him.

"Oh? Who says?"

"Lots of people. They say it was Leif Ericson."

"Never heard of him."

"That's because you didn't have a proper education."

"I had a very proper education," Cal insisted. "I just didn't pay any fucking attention..."

"I stand corrected."

"...And I bet a lot more people think it was Christopher Columbus than that Leaf whatever-his-name-was...."

"You don't get to vote on history!" I argued back with surprising conviction. The grappa was obviously starting to get to me, too.

"Sure you do! People do it all the time. They vote with what they think. That's how history's made." His eyes narrowed down to sly, twinkling slits. "All you really need is a couple sympathetic schoolbook writers and a hot-shit press agent."

There was no way to argue with anything as ridiculous as that. So I poured us each another glass of grappa that we didn't really need and we toasted Christopher Columbus for his fame, good fortune and hot-shit press agent.

By that point I think Cal was getting a little tired of listening to all the crap about what was going on in my life. I mean, *he* was the one who'd crashed into a fucking wall and gotten himself fired off the Ferrari factory team that day. And so I figured it was time to reciprocate the way drunks often do. "So how about you?" I asked like it was terribly, terribly important to me. "What are *you* going to do?"

Cal rolled his palms up and stared up into the sky.

"What about sports cars?"

"What about them?" he sighed dismissively. "There's really nobody out there but Ferrari and Porsche. You know that. And with Porsche, the only places you'd ever have a shot at anything but a fucking class win are here at the Targa and at the Nurburgring." He took another long, thoughtful swallow of grappa. "That's just the way it is and everybody knows it."

"How about Count Volpi's team?"

"What? That Tipo 64 monstrosity?"

"It's not so bad, is it?"

Cal answered with a dismissive snort.

"He's got Ferraris, too," I reminded him. "And he'd probably just love to hire an ex-Ferrari works driver just to put the old needle in back at Maranello." But you could see from Cal's eyes that he wasn't thrilled with the prospect of going from Ferrari's factory team to one of their privateer customers. "Hell," I added, trying to talk the notion up, "Scuderia Serenissima won the whole ball of wax at Sebring."

Cal's face softened a little. But then it went hard again. "The Count's on the outs with Ferrari now. Everybody knows that. Scuderia Serenissima won't get shit-on-a-stick from the factory anymore. You can count on it."

"But I've heard the guys at A.T.S. will be building their own cars pretty soon," I argued. "Formula One and sports cars from what I've heard. And they'll be de-signed and built by the same guys who used to do it at Ferrari...."

You could see the possibilities swirling around in Cal's head. But he had the same doubts about A.T.S. I did. Neither of us wanted to admit it, particularly under the current set of circumstances, but there was no escaping the sense that it was the singular, manipulative genius of old Enzo himself—all the behind-the-scenes juggling and maneuvering and wheedling and inveigling and instigating and cajoling and threatening and castigating and sweet-talking and constantly keeping everybody on edge and looking over their shoulders—that made things work at Ferrari. Old Enzo was a master at all of it, and even his detractors had to admit he had no peer when it came to spotting talent, throwing personalities together, stirring people up, and drawing more effort, talent and ideas out of his underlings than they ever thought they had. Sure, there were a lot of corpses scattered along the way—real and figurative—but that's because Old Man Ferrari understood the basic rules of command: they don't have to understand it and they sure as hell don't have to like it, but good soldiers need to fear failure more than either death or the enemy....

I watched a hard, competitive glint flicker up in Cal's eyes. I could tell he was savoring what it might feel like to put the screws to old man Ferrari in a car designed and built by the same guys who walked out on him (or were they fired?) just a few months before. It was almost too delicious. "You know," Cal mused, swirling the last quarter-inch of grappa around in his glass, "maybe I'll give young Count Giovanni a call. In fact..." he started to get up from the table "...maybe I'll give him a call at his hotel right this minute!" But you could see he was pretty unsteady. In fact, he had to grab his chair to keep from falling right over the railing.

"Better make it tomorrow!" I laughed as I filled up our glasses again. "I think you may be a little drunk right now."

Cal's chin jutted out as he swayed back and forth against his wrought-iron chair. *"Oh?"* he demanded defiantly. *"What makes you think so?"*

"Because I sure as hell am, and you've had more than me."

Cal glared at me. But then you could see his face kind of soften up and he was laughing as he flopped back down into his chair again. I poured us two more and we raised our glasses and clinked them together to toast the mutual uncertainty of our futures. By that point the liquor didn't even burn on the way down.

"You ever think about racing back in the states?" I wondered out loud.

"Oh, I suppose I'd like to do Indianapolis some time," he allowed. "But it's kind of a closed shop, isn't it? And I really don't know much of anything about those cars. Or racing on ovals, come to that. You really need a good car and a sharp crew chief if you don't want to look stupid." He took another slug of grappa. "If there's one thing you need at Indy, it's a good, solid ride."

"A lot of awfully good guys have gone there and looked like rank amateurs."

Cal shook his head. "My career couldn't really stand that right now, could it?"

"No," I had to agree. "It probably couldn't."

So we drank to that, too.

"How about Cunningham's team?" I asked him. "You know Briggs thinks a lot of you."

"Even after I wadded up his Abarth at Sebring?"

"No, really he does. I think he'd hire you in a minute if you let him know you're available."

I could see Cal rolling it around in his head. Sure, it would be a hell of a come-down from Scuderia Ferrari. But Briggs always had good cars, good people taking care of them and topnotch preparation. And that counted for a lot. But it was almost all endurance racing and mostly in production-based cars. "I dunno..." Cal mused absently.

"You know," I added in, "you might want to check out some other things that are brewing back in the states, too...."

"Oh? Like what?"

So I told him about how Fairway Motors was very probably going to want to win Le Mans sometime soon—even if they had no idea exactly when or how yet—and no question they had the muscle and money to make it happen if they really wanted to. And I said as much. Being a top American driver with an established international résumé would surely make Cal an attractive option. And particularly since he'd driven for Scuderia Ferrari and knew firsthand how the cars were and what went on inside the team. I watched Cal's ears perk up as he listened. "So when d'ya think thish might happen?" he asked. You could tell that the wine and grappa were really catching up with him now.

Me, too, for that matter.

"No way of telling for absholute shure..." I answered, aware of the slur in my words but unable to do much about it "...But you sure ash hell oughta get'cher hat in the fucking ring."

Cal's head bobbed up and down in solemn agreement.

"Y'oughta check out what'sh going on in Shelby's shop out in Venish, too," I advised. Drunks are always real big on giving advice. "I know guys who've tesht-driven hish new Cobrash, an' they all shay if Carroll can get a rope around itsh neck and tame it, it'sh gonna be one hell of a fucking car."

"Oh?"

I nodded vehemently. "I even shink it might even be able to take one of Old Man Ferrari'sh GTOsh."

Cal stared at me like I was an idiot. "Maybe from here to the nexsht shtoplight," he pretty much sneered at me.

"No, really," I insisted. "He'sh gonna have *money* t'play with! Fairway'sh gonna be jumping into thish with both feet pretty shoon." I stared him right, straight in the eyes. "You should be *in* there, buddy!" I damn near shouted at him. And then slammed my palm into the table for emphasis the way drunks often do when they have some great notion by the scruff of the neck. "And I mean right from the fucking *shtart!*"

"Well, at leasht it's shomething to think about," Cal yawned.

But I was full of alcoholic zeal and the amazing—if temporary—surge of energy that usually comes along with it. I looked out over the harbor and felt all over again how fucking angry and wronged and hurt and pissed off and even vengeful I was—that sort of thing really comes to a boil with too much liquor—and I could almost see the fucking snide, smug, arrogant, wouldn't-you-like-to-take-a-swing-at-me smirk on Quentin Deering's face when he fired me at point-blank range in front of those nickel-and-brass elevator doors on the 12th floor of Fairway Tower. And so I cursed the sonofabitch rat-bastard asshole a few dozen times—right out loud and with a commendable variety of anatomical and ancestral references—and took a fresh snort of grappa with every third or fourth one. And then I moved on to Eric Fucking Gibbon and did the same.

"Doesh that make you feel any better?" Cal asked like he might like to try it.

"It helpsh if you try to get a l'il creative with the language," I explained expansively. "Thash what makesh it speshial."

"You hash a rare gift for it," Cal nodded appreciatively.

"Thanksh. But I think it's becaush I drink too much."

"Well, we all require shome short of fuel...."

"Yesh, that we do," I agreed, and took one final snort just to prove it.

And that's when I looked down at the remains of the seafood pasta in front of me and got one of those grand, inebriated insights that seem so very important and mean so very much at the time. "Do you know what we're doing?" I demanded rhetorically.

Cal looked like he was only half listening. The wine and grappa had pretty much gotten to him. So I shook his arm to get his attention and repeated somewhat drunkenly: "Do you know what we're doing, you and me?"

He looked at me like I wasn't making sense. "I hash no fucking idea."

I pulled myself up semi-erect and crowed: "We're molting!" like it was sort of major cosmic revelation.

"Molting?"

"*Sure!*" I agreed with myself, and poured us each another glass of grappa that we surely didn't need.

"What the hell ish 'molting?'" Cal mumbled sleepily. To be honest, he sounded like he didn't much care one way or the other.

"It'sh when you shed your shkin," I tried to explain.

"Shed your shkin?"

"Sure! Like shnakes and reptilesh and crustacheans do!"

He stared at me blankly. "Shnakes and reptilesh and crustacheans?"

My head bobbed up and down. No question I was really on to something. "Our livesh are going through big changesh now, right?"

He just stared at me.

"Don't you shee it?" I insisted. "We're..." I waited like there maybe should have been a drum roll *"...shedding our shkins!"*

Cal mulled it over. And then he blew it up like a cheap Hong Kong firecracker. "But even if you shed your shkin," he mused absently, "whatever you are underneath shtays the shame, doeshn't it?"

He had me there.

So I looked out over the harbor and the Tyrrhenian Sea beyond, and found the opening line of my favorite Robert Frost poem wandering through my head:

"Two roads diverged in a yellow wood...."

When I looked back over at Cal, I saw his chin was lolled down against his chest and he was snoring loudly into his shirt collar.

So I swiveled myself around again and looked back out over the harbor and the sea and endless, slow suction of the starscape beyond, and I felt my brain soaring and plunging though a strange, alcohol-fueled rollercoaster ride that ranged from grandiose philosophy to the very smallest and pettiest of life's envies, hatreds and misgivings. And all with seamless, perfect and elliptical logic! And all the while the sea rolled in like I was hearing it inside a shell, and it filled me with alternating waves of worry, wonder, fear and reassurance. There was a timeless, endless, helpless inevitability about things. Some you could control or at least affect and some you couldn't do much of anything about. Like getting this fucking, stinking, can't-even-stand-up drunk, for example. I really needed to start trying to control my drinking a little more. The only problem was that it only seemed to occur to me after I'd already gotten myself drunk. Which was magnificently ironic, don't you think? And then I caught myself thinking about Audrey again, and missing her and trying to remember what her smile looked like and what her voice sounded like and what her skin felt like when I touched it.

Yeah, there were things you could control in this life and things you couldn't do much of anything about. But if there was one thing I knew—one thing I was absolutely fucking cock-sure positive about!—it was that I *had* to find a way to stay in England. Even if I had to take a fucking job working at the fucking crumpet and muffin bakery downstairs from my apartment.

Whatever the hell else happened, I just had to stay in London....

And the sea kept rolling in and rolling in like it was agreeing with me.

Cal and I awoke in great pain to the distant whisper of racing engines screaming through the Madonie hills and mountains and a brutal oversupply of brilliant Sicilian sunshine. Someone had come during the night—perhaps the little man with the cook's apron and waxed mustache—and covered us over with a couple of old army blankets. They smelled like they'd come out of a horse barn. Or maybe that was us. I looked over at Cal with the only eye I could open. "You awake?"

Cal's head nodded feebly up and down.

"You look like shit."

"You look even worse," he assured me. "That's why I'm not opening my eyes."

No question we were both in predictably terrible shape. We'd drunk way too much and spent the entire night slumped in wrought-iron garden chairs, and the cramps, aches and pain of it seemed to be growing like an off-key crescendo with every additional moment of consciousness.

"Why the hell did we do that to ourselves?" I asked the smell off my blanket. But the blanket didn't answer.

We eventually roused ourselves, stumbled weakly down the stairs—leaning on the railing for support—got paper cups of coffee from the old guy sweeping up the kitchen, paid our dinner, wine and grappa bill and headed back uphill to the pensione where Hal and I were staying. The town was damn near empty—everyone but a few mothers with bawling infants and the too aged or infirm to make it was off watching the race—and we didn't even have to wait in line in front of the bathroom at the end of the hall in order to get ourselves cleaned up. When I went downstairs to take care of the bill, the old grandmother tending the desk explained in a combination of hand gestures, hoarse, guttural Italian and some impromptu charades that "the other, tall, bearded one with the bad leg would meet us at the flag stand at the start/finish line after the race." I thanked her, and Cal and I headed out again into the piercing sunlight. Cal regarded my Fiat Multipla with ill-concealed derision. "You really know how to travel first class, don't you?" he observed sarcastically.

"Look, if you want a ride back to the fucking airport after the race, you'd better show some fucking respect."

Cal bowed obsequiously in the Fiat's direction. "So sorry. Didn't mean to offend the transport."

"Ahh, shut the fuck up," I told him. I wasn't really in the mood for snappy patter. Not hardly. Not at all.

We rode in silence to the Ferrari team's hotel, Cal picked up his bags and then we made our way westward along the coastline road. But of course we couldn't get very far, because just ten miles up the road was where the racecars came screaming down out of the mountains and turned hard left through Campofelice to make their run along the coastline. We got as close as we could before running out of places to park and then, with nothing better to do, we walked like a pair of mesmerized zombies towards the sound of the cars and the cheers of the crowd.

Campofelice was packed full of people. Teeming crowds lined the barriers along both sides of the roadway, and there were other, luckier or more adventurous spectators hanging off balconies or perched up on rooftops or hanging off the branches of trees virtually everywhere. We couldn't really get close to it. The best we could do was to pay a small fistful of lira to climb up on top of an egg van with a group of garlicky local fans and watch the cars go by. The people around us cheered mightily for the legion of Italian Alfas, Lancias, Oscas and older, privateer Maserati Birdcages (the more luridly driven, the louder the cheers!) that came hustling down out of the mountains. But the car that brought out the biggest and most boisterous reaction—louder even than the leading Ferrari!—was the unlikely little Austin Mini-Cooper driven by French journalist Bernard Cahier and his aristocratic enthusiast pal, Prince Paul Metternich. It looked like a shoebox on shopping-cart casters and handled about the same, and it was furthermore entered in the 2-liter prototype class where it had no chance at all. But it was entertaining as hell to watch as the drivers wrestled, flung, skittered and fought the damn thing around every corner, and the crowd absolutely loved it!

But it didn't take long for the fun to go out of it for Cal and me. Watching as spectators, there was just no overview or perspective or sense to it, just car after car wailing madly, mindlessly out of the mountains, getting hard on the brakes with the tires all scrabbling for traction on the uneven pavement, ripping off a downshift or two and then laying on the power again to rocket off on the flat-out, four-kilometer blast along the coastline towards the final few corners and the pits and start/finish line to complete another lap. It was a long race at 10 laps of the roughly 4.5-mile circuit with one or two pit stops thrown in, and by the time we got there it was impossible to understand who was where and what was going on. Someone near us had a crackling, fuzzy radio turned up as loud as it would go, but it was all in Italian and made no sense to either one of us. Oh, it was fun to watch for awhile for the sheer color, noise and spectacle of it, but Cal and I had seen it all before—and from the inside—and we eventually wandered off to sit under a tree above the shoreline with our backs turned towards the race. It was quieter there, and we could watch the waves rolling in and the seagulls arcing gracefully through the sky and nurse our hangovers.

We didn't find out until much later what actually happened in the race. Crazy, haunted-looking Willy Mairesse was leading on the time sheets at the end of the first lap in the Dino 246SP he was sharing with Ricardo Rodriguez and Oliver Gendebien. And he was running it right to the limit as usual. Gurney was chasing hard after him in the 8-cylinder Porsche coupe he was sharing with Bonnier, and Vaccarella was lurking not too far behind in the other Serenissima-entered Porsche prototype (the one they'd painted bright Italian red for the occasion). Then Gurney had a really tense moment when the rear brakes on his Porsche unexpectedly locked up and sent him *HARD!* into a stone bridge abutment. The car was smashed up pretty badly, but fortunately Dan was okay. If a little bewildered. Things like that didn't usually happen with Porsches, and you could pretty much bet they'd get the brake problem addressed before the next race. Count Volpi responded by re-assigning Bonnier to partner Vaccarella in the remaining red Porsche prototype, and then Scuderia Serenissima's other big threat ran into trouble as the rear bodywork on their Tipo 64 Maserati came loose! The poor driver had to hold it down with one hand while attempting to steer and shift with the other for the better part of an entire lap before he could get back to the pits for repairs. After a typically comic opera Italian pit stop with much screaming, arm-waving, wire, rivets and racer's tape, they sent the car back out again. Only to have a steering arm snap in the middle of a fast downhill section. Which must have been pretty exciting for the poor drool in the cockpit!

So much for Count Volpi's Maserati.

By mid-afternoon, the Mairesse/Rodriguez Dino was holding down an unassailable lead, and Rodriguez either by mistake or intentionally stayed out an extra lap—perhaps just to show Dragoni and the Old Man back in Maranello that he could handle it—before coming in to hand over to Gendebien for the final three laps. Baghetti and Bandini were similarly secure in second overall and on their way to a solid 2-liter class win in the smaller-engined 196SP Dino, and the lone GTO entered was running 4th overall and first by miles in the GT category. So Cal and I waited around aimlessly for the laps to run out and the traffic and our heads to clear so we could make our way over to the start/finish line to pick up Hal. Then it would be off to wherever the hell home was and whatever the hell our futures might hold. And meanwhile, behind us, the lean, loud and relentless red cars from Maranello pounded on to yet another dominating win.